ISBN 0-276-44111-7

www.readersdigest.co.uk

The Reader's Digest Association Limited, 11 Westferry Circus, Canary Wharf, London E14 4HE

# of love & life

Three novels selected and condensed
by **Reader's Digest**

The Reader's Digest Association Limited, London

CONTENTS

Iris & Ruby

ROSIE THOMAS

In her rambling, shadow-filled house in Cairo, eighty-two-year-old Iris lives in the past, remembering the wartime days when she lost her heart to her one true love—the enigmatic Captain Xan Molyneux. How can she capture these memories for ever? How can she ever describe to her granddaughter, Ruby, just how alive true love can make you feel?

chapter one

I REMEMBER.

And even as I say the words aloud in the silent room and hear the whisper dying away in the shadows of the house, I realise that it's not true. Because I don't, I can't remember.

I am old, and I am beginning to forget things.

Sometimes I'm aware that great tracts of memory have gone, slipping away out of my reach. When I try to recall a particular day, or an entire year, if I'm lucky there are the bare facts unadorned with colour. More often than otherwise there's nothing at all. A blank.

And when I can remember where I have lived, and who I was living with and why, if I try to conjure up what it was like to be there, the texture of my life and what impelled me to wake up every morning and pace out the journey of the day, I cannot do it. Familiar and even beloved faces have silently melted away, their names and events that once seemed momentous, all collapsed and buried beyond reach.

The disappearing is like the desert itself. Sand blows from the four corners of the earth and it builds up in slow drifts and dun ripples, and it blurs the proudest structures, and in the end obliterates them.

This is what's happening to me. The sands of time. (It is a no less accurate image for being a cliché.)

I am eighty-two. I am not afraid of death, which after all can't be far away. What does frighten me, though, is the halfway stage. I am afraid of reduction. After a lifetime's independence—yes, selfish independence as my daughter would rightly claim—I am terrified of being reduced to childhood once more, to helplessness, to seas of confusion from which the cruel lucid intervals poke up like rock shoals.

I don't want to sit in my chair and be fed by Mamdooh or by Auntie; much less do I want to be handed over to medical professionals. I know what that will be like. I am a doctor myself and as well as remembering too little, I have seen too much.

Now Mamdooh is coming. His leather slippers make a soft swish on the boards of the women's stairway. There is nothing wrong with my hearing. The door creaks open, heavy on its hinges.

'Good evening, Ma'am Iris,' Mamdooh softly says. The deferential form of address has become so elided, so rubbed with usage that it is a pet name now, Mum-reese. 'Have you been sleeping, perhaps?'

'No,' I tell him.

I have been thinking. Turning matters over in my mind.

Mamdooh puts down a tray. A glass of mint tea. A linen napkin, some triangles of sweet pastry that I do not want. I eat very little now.

He is holding out my glass of tea. I take it from him, poking my head forward to breathe in the sweet and fragrant scent.

'Auntie has made baklava,' he says, encouraging me by turning back the napkin on the plate.

'Later. Go on now, Mamdooh. You must have some food yourself.'

Mamdooh will not have eaten a mouthful or taken even a sip of water since before sunrise. It is Ramadan.

When I am alone again, I drink my tea and listen to the sounds of the city. The cobbled street outside my screened windows is narrow, barely wide enough for a single car to pass, and beyond the angle of wall that shelters my doorway there are only the steps of the great mosque. The traffic that submerges the modern city like a tidal wave is no more than a dull rumble here. Much closer at hand are shouts and laughter as families prepare their evening meal and gather to eat in the cool dusk. Hearing this, it might be the same Cairo of sixty years ago.

Some things I can never forget. I must not. Otherwise, what do I have left? I close my eyes. The glass tips in my fingers, spilling the last drops of liquid on the worn cushions.

Sixty years ago there were soldiers in these streets. Swarms of British officers and men, New Zealanders and Australians, French, Canadians, Indians and Greeks and South Africans and Poles, all in their dusty khaki. The city was a sunbaked magnet for the troops who flooded into it, whenever the war in the desert briefly released them, in search of bars and brothels. Turning their backs on the prospect of death in the sand, Cairo absorbed them with its own ancient indifference.

One of those soldiers from sixty years ago was my lover. The only man I have ever loved.

His name was Captain Alexander Napier Molyneux. Xan.

He wore the same khaki bush shirt and baggy shorts as all the others, distinguished only by badges of rank and regiment, but there was a further anonymity about Xan. You wouldn't have singled him out at the bar in Shepheard's Hotel, or at any of the raucous parties we all went to in Garden City or Zamalek, simply because he seemed so ordinary.

The absence of peculiar characteristics was intentional. Xan worked deep in the desert and it was one of his talents to blend into the scenery. He rode a horse like the cavalry officer he really was, but if you saw him on a camel with a white *kuffiyeh* swathed over his head and face, you would take him for an Arab. At the Gezira Club he played tennis and fooled around beside the pool like any other ornament of the Cairo cocktail circuit, but then he would disappear for days or a week at a time, and there would be no news about where he might have gone. He vanished into the desert like a lizard darting under a rock.

I loved him from the moment I first set eyes on him.

I remember.

In this evening's reverie every detail of it—and of that first evening—comes back to me. I have revisited it so many thousands of times, it seems more real than my eighty-two-year-old reality.

At least I haven't lost this, thank God, not yet.

It was an airless night thick with the scent of tuberoses.

There were two dozen little round tables set out in a lush garden, candle lanterns hanging in the branches of the mango and mimosa trees, and beyond tall windows a band playing in a panelled ballroom.

I was twenty-two years old, fresh from the wartime austerity of London, drunk on the glamour of Cairo as well as on champagne.

Giggling, my friend Faria led me over to a table and introduced me to a group of men in evening clothes.

'This is Iris Black. Stay right where you are, Jessie, please.'

But the young man with pale yellow hair was already on his feet, his head bent low as he lifted my hand to his mouth. His moustache tickled my fingers. 'I can't possibly sit still,' he murmured. 'She is too beautiful.'

Inside my head I was still the London typist, making do on a tiny wage in a basement flat in South Ken, but I had learned enough in my weeks in Cairo not to glance over my shoulder in search of whoever the beauty might be. Here, in this exotic garden with the band playing and the orchid presented by my evening's date pinned to the bodice of my evening dress, I knew that she was *me*.

'Frederick James. Captain, 11th Hussars,' he murmured. 'For some reason, everyone calls me Jessie James.'

'How do you do?' I said.

'Ah, she is nice, our Iris,' Faria gurgled. 'A good girl, from a diplomatic family. When she was twelve, you know, her daddy was Head of Chancery right here in Cairo. She is practically a native citizen.'

Faria was one of my two flatmates. Two years older than me, the elegant daughter of a prosperous Anglo-Egyptian family, and engaged to the son of one of her father's business associates, she had taken me under her wing almost as soon as I arrived.

We were drawn into the group. Chairs were brought over and placed at the table as the officers eagerly made room. I accepted a glass of whisky, at the same time looking around the glimmering garden for my escort. Sandy Allardyce was one of the young men from the British embassy. He insisted to anyone who would listen that he was desperate to get into uniform, but so far he was still chained to his office desk. I guessed that he felt uncomfortable in the company of so many men who were actually fighting, and that he dealt with this by drinking too much.

'So you lived here as a young girl?' one of the officers asked. The man next to him clicked his lighter to a cigarette and I glimpsed his face, briefly lit by the umber flare.

'Just in the holidays. I was at school in England most of the time.'

Jessie leaned forward to command my attention again. 'Are you looking for Sandy? I saw you dancing with him.' He had noticed my anxiety.

'Yes. He brought me to the party. I ought to go and find him. He . . .'

Then the man with the cigarette moved his chair so the light from one of the candle lanterns threw his face into relief. I looked at him and forgot whatever remark I had been on the point of uttering.

He was dark-haired, dark-skinned. He might have appeared saturnine if there hadn't been so much fun in his face. He leaned across the table. I saw the way his mouth formed a smile. 'Don't dance with Allardyce. And if it's a choice between Jessie and me—well, that's not really a choice at all, is it?' He drew back my chair and, as I stood up, put his hand under my arm.

'Xan Molyneux,' he said calmly. We walked across the lawn together, under the branches of the trees. The heat-withered grass smelt acrid, nothing like an English garden. I had never felt so far from home, yet so happily and entirely not homesick.

'I'm Iris.'

'I know. Faria did introduce you. Is she a friend of yours?'

'Yes. We share the same flat. Sarah Walker-Wilson lives there too. I suppose you know her?'

I can't bear it, I thought. Every man in Cairo adores Sarah. Since I had moved in, Sarah had not spent a single evening at home.

'The three flowers of Garden City,' he murmured. Garden City was the quarter of Cairo where we lived.

We reached the dance floor. Xan's expression was serene and he was humming the tune as he took me in his arms. He was a good dancer, but I had had other partners who were better. It was more that Xan gave the steps and the music and me all his attention. I felt energy beating like a pulse under the black weft of his jacket, transmitting itself through my hands and arms and singing between us, and an answering rhythm began to beat in me. We looked straight into one another's eyes, not talking but communicating in a language I had never used before.

That first dance seamlessly ran into the next, and the one after that.

I stopped being drunk on champagne and whisky, and grew intoxicated with Xan Molyneux's closeness instead. We had exchanged hardly more than a dozen words but I felt that I knew him already, better than anyone I had met in Cairo.

I also felt a clear, absolute certainty that from now on all things were and would be possible. Happiness became wound up with anticipation to a point of tension that was almost unbearable, and it made me suddenly giddy. As Xan swung us in an exuberant circle I tripped and overbalanced on my high heel. A hot skewer of pain stabbed from my ankle up my calf and I would have fallen if he hadn't wrapped his arm more tightly round my waist.

'Are you all right?'

I drew in a breath and blew it out hard to stop myself howling.

'Just . . . twisted it.' Some dancers formed a circle round us.

'Here, I'll carry you.' He slid his other arm beneath my thighs, ready to lift me off my feet. At that moment I saw Sandy. He came steaming through the dancers towards us, crimson in the face.

'Molyneux?' he shouted. 'What d'you think you're doing?'

'Helping Miss Black to a chair,' Xan drily replied, straightening up. 'She has twisted her ankle.'

I took a step away from his side and nearly fell over, Xan immediately lunged to my rescue, and we almost toppled in a heap. I laughed up at him, in spite of the pain in my ankle, and I heard a wounded bellow from Sandy. He came flailing at Xan and caught the collar of his evening coat. Xan let go of me and twisted round to face Sandy who planted a wild punch on his jaw.

'Leave my girl alone,' Sandy shouted, but having landed his awkward blow the belligerence was visibly draining out of him. I watched miserably, balancing on one foot, wanting to say that I wasn't Sandy's girl, and feeling ashamed of the impulse.

'You know, I really don't want to hit you back, Allardyce,' Xan drawled, not at all perturbed. 'It would make such a mess.'

'He's right, it would,' another voice chipped in. Jessie James had appeared, with Faria beside him. She held out her arm and I leaned on it as Sandy caught hold of me on the other side. He jerked his head at Xan and Jessie, but he was already in retreat.

'It's not funny.'

'Are we laughing?' Jessie innocently asked.

Sandy turned away from them and muttered to me, 'C'mon, s'get another drink. Be all right.'

Faria clicked her tongue. 'No it won't. I'm taking Iris home. Can't you see she's hurt?'

The next minute I was hobbling into the hallway, supported on one side by Faria and with Sandy weaving on the other. I felt, rather than saw, Xan and Jessie at the back of our ungainly procession as our hostess, Lady Gibson Pasha, came surging towards us.

'My dear, dear girl. You must put your foot up, we need an ice pack.'

She was clapping her hands, calling at a passing servant to bring ice.

'It's nothing, really. I'm so sorry, Lady Gibson. Just a silly sprain.'

'Daddy's car and driver are here,' Faria said. 'We'll go home. I'll make sure Iris is looked after.'

Sandy vehemently nodded his head. Another servant was at hand with Faria's bolero and my evening wrap. With Lady Gibson's instructions floating after us, we hobbled out. Amman Pasha's chauffeur was waiting at the steps with the big black car. He opened the door and I was handed into the expanse of cream-coloured leather. Sandy collapsed beside me, tugging at his tie to undo the bow. Faria slipped in on the other side.

The car began to roll over the gravel. I twisted round to see through the rear window and caught a last glimpse of Xan and Jessie standing side by side at the foot of the steps, black head and blond, watching us go. I couldn't really see Xan's face, but I thought he was still smiling.

'God,' Sandy groaned, letting his head fall against the seat cushions.

'We'll drop you at the embassy,' Faria said coolly and leaned forward to give the driver instructions in Arabic. Faria yawned. 'Oh dear. I completely forgot to tell the poet we were leaving. Whatever will he think?'

It wasn't a question that required an answer. Jeremy—known as the poet—was the most fervent of Faria's admirers, a mournful young man who worked for the British Council. Ali was away and Jeremy had been her escort for the evening.

Sandy had passed out. I could hear the breath catching thickly in the back of his throat. Whisky fumes and Faria's perfume mingled with the smell of leather and the uniquely Cairene stink of kerosene and incense and animal dung. The pain in my ankle was intense and the faint nausea it engendered made my senses keener. I let every turn of the route print itself in my mind, the black silhouette of each dome against the paler sky, the profile of a beggar sitting on a step. I wanted to absorb each tiny impression and keep it, because tonight was so important.

Later I lay in bed with the wooden shutters latched open and watched the sky. My bandaged ankle throbbed but I didn't mind that it kept me awake. All I could think of was Xan, who had left me stricken with desire from the moment I saw him. On that first sleepless night I never doubted that Xan and I would meet again. I would tell him I wasn't, and never had been, Sandy Allardyce's girl, and we would claim each other. That was exactly how it was meant to be.

How simple, how innocent it seems. And how joyful.

Garden City was set beside the Nile, an enclave of curving streets with tall cocoa-brown and dirty cream houses and apartment blocks deep in gardens of thick, dusty greenery. Our apartment belonged to Faria's parents who lived in a grand house nearby. There were wood-block floors and heavy furniture, and every room had a ceiling fan that lazily circulated the scalding air.

My room was a narrow, high-ceilinged box at the end of a corridor away from the main part of the flat. The furniture was on a humbler scale and there was a view from the window of a jacaranda tree in the next-door garden. I didn't know Faria and Sarah very well but they were lively company, and I was pleased to have a comfortable place to live. It was even conveniently close to where I worked, at British Army GHQ, just off Sharia Qasr el Aini. I was clerical and administrative assistant to a lieu-tenant-colonel in Intelligence called Roderick Boyce, known to everyone as Roddy Boy. Colonel Boyce and my father had hunted together before the war. A letter from my father had been enough to gain me the job.

The morning after Xan and I met I got up early to go to work, as I had done on every ordinary day since I had come back to Cairo.

In the stifling mid afternoons, the streets cowered under the hammer blow of the sun out of a white sky, but at 8 a.m. it was cool enough to walk between the flat and the office. That day, with my bandaged ankle, I had to take a taxi. Roddy Boy looked at me as I half hopped to my desk, supported by a walking stick belonging to Faria's father.

'Oh dear. Tennis? Camel racing? Or something more strenuous?'

'Dancing,' I replied.

'Ah. Of course. I hope your injury will not impede your typing?'

'Not at all,' I said. I rolled a sandwich of requisition forms and carbon paper into my machine and forced myself to concentrate.

When at last I came home again, Mamdooh, the *suffragi* who looked after us and the apartment, greeted me in his stately way: 'Good afternoon, Miss Iris. These were delivered for you an hour ago.'

'Oh, beautiful.'

There was a big bunch of white lilies, gardenias and tuberoses. I buried my face in the cool blooms.

I sat down awkwardly and opened the envelope that came with them. There was a plain white card with the words *I hope your ankle will mend soon*. It was signed simply *X*. That was all.

Mamdooh was still standing there in his white *galabiyeh*.

'Just from a friend,' I said.

'Of course, Miss. I will put in water for you.'

I admired my flowers and waited, but a week and then another went by. The whole month of June 1941 crawled past and I heard nothing more from Xan.

In my outer office at GHQ I typed reports and delivered signals for Roddy Boy, and chatted to the staff officers who hurried in and out to see him. As a civilian I was on the lowest level of clearance, but because of my family I was judged to be safe and many of the secret plans that flew in and out of Roddy Boy's office crossed my desk first.

The Allied troops, except for those besieged in Tobruk, had withdrawn into Egypt and the Germans were at the Libyan border. In an attempt to dislodge them, Operation Battleaxe was launched.

Almost one hundred of our armoured tanks were lost to German antitank guns, their smouldering wrecks lying abandoned in a thick pall of dust and smoke. Many of their crews were dead or wounded.

As July approached I began accepting every invitation that came my way. I went to cocktail parties and tennis tournaments, fancy-dress balls, and poetry readings at the British Council, scanning the crowds for a glimpse of Xan. I sat beside the pool at the Gezira Club every lunchtime, always in the hope of hearing news of him.

He had simply vanished, and Jessie James with him. My certainty about us ebbed away. Maybe he had been posted elsewhere. Maybe he was married. Maybe he was dead.

I kept my fears to myself. What I felt seemed too significant and also too equivocal, too fragile, to share with Faria and Sarah.

Then, at the end of the first week of July, on an evening when the heat made it an effort to dress to go out, even to move, the telephone rang in the hallway and I heard Mamdooh answer it. His big round head appeared in the doorway.

'For you, Miss.'

'Hello?' I said into the receiver.

'This is Xan,' he said. 'May I come and see you?'

I laid my head against the door frame, electric shocks of relief and delight chasing up my spine. I managed to answer, 'Yes. Now?'

'Right now.'

'Yes,' I said again. 'Yes, please come.'

That was how it was.

Shit and double shit, Ruby said to herself as she caught a glimpse of what lay beyond the doors. Is *this* what it's like?

It was dark outside. Beyond a barrier there was a heaving wall of waving arms and shouting faces. The airport was air-conditioned, but clammy, and she could feel the heat rolling towards her through the doors as they slid open and hissed shut again. The crowd of arriving passengers pushed her forward, catching her rucksack with their own baggage. The doors opened once more and hot, humid air rushed into her lungs. Sweat immediately prickled under her arms and in her hairline.

A chorus of yelling rose around her. Hands grabbed at her arms, tried to hoist the pack off her back.

'Lady! Taxi, very good, cheap.'

'Hotel, lady. Nice hotel.'

'Stop it,' Ruby shouted. 'Leave me alone.' She hadn't bargained for this onslaught. The noise and the heat were overwhelming. Ruby glared into the boiling sea of dark faces, moustaches, open mouths. At the back of the throng was a younger face, imploringly watching her.

She dragged an arm free, pointed at him. 'You. Taxi?'

Instantly he dived through the scrum of bodies, grabbed her wrist with one hand and snatched her rucksack with the other. Ruby kept her smaller nylon sack tightly pressed to her side. They scuttled through the mass together and emerged into a clearer space beyond.

The driver's taxi was parked under a palm tree. Two ragged children were sitting propped against it. The driver gave them a coin, threw her rucksack into the boot and opened the passenger door. With relief Ruby sank into the back seat. The springs had collapsed and foam padding bulged through a split in the brown plastic seat cover. The interior of the car smelt strongly of cigarettes and cheap air freshener.

The driver thrust the car into gear and they roared forward, then jerked to an almost immediate halt in a queue for the exit road. Even though it was dark, the heat was intense. Ruby had never encountered this phenomenon before. The driver flashed her a smile over his shoulder. His teeth were cartoon-white in his brown face.

'Where you go?'

She unfolded the sheet of paper that she had kept in her jeans pocket all through the flight and read out the address.

'Why you go there? I know nice hotel, very clean, cheap. I take you there instead.'

'We're going where I told you,' Ruby insisted. 'No arguing. Got that?'

He laughed and slapped his hands on the steering wheel.

The traffic began to move. There were roads everywhere, the sodium-lit elevated sections crazily perched over complex intersections, all hemmed in by drab concrete tower blocks and hung about with giant advertisement hoardings. Every foot of road was clogged with hooting cars and trucks and big blue buses.

Ruby lounged in the sagging seat and stared at it all. Now that she was actually here, she realised that she had hardly considered her destination. To get away, that was what she had fixed on. But now all kinds of other problems reared up, competing for her attention. She didn't know how to handle this place at all. And nobody knew where she was; no one was looking out for her arrival. She felt a long way from home.

'How much?' she demanded.

The driver swung the wheel to overtake a donkey cart that was plodding along the inner lane of the motorway. He shot the smile at her again.

'Ah, money, no broblem. Where you from?'

'London.'

'Very nice place. David Beckham.'

'Yeah. Or no. Whatever.' At least they were moving now, presumably towards the city centre.

'My name Nafouz.'

'Right.'

There was a pause. Nafouz reached under the dash and produced a pack of Marlboro, half turned to offer it to her. Ruby hesitated. She had run out and she was longing for one.

'Thanks.' She lit it with her own Bic, ignoring his.

'You have boyfriend in Cairo?'

Ruby gave a snort of derisive laughter. 'I've never been here before.'

'I be your boyfriend.'

She had hardly looked at him, except to notice his teeth, but now she saw his white shirt, his black leather jacket and his long black hair, combed back from his face. She lifted her head. This, at least, was familiar territory. 'In. Your. Dreams,' she said clearly.

Nafouz's delighted laughter filled the car.

'I dream always. Dreaming cheap. Cost nothing at all.'

'Just watch the road, all right?'

She huddled in her corner, smoking and looking out at the wilderness. She had been abroad before, of course, with Lesley and Andrew to places like Tuscany and Kos and the Loire valley, but she had never seen anything like this steaming mess of concrete and metal. As they got nearer to what must be the middle of the city the traffic jam got even worse. There were long stationary intervals during which she peered down the side streets. There were tiny open-fronted shops with men sitting smoking at tin tables. Shafts of light came out of open doorways, shining on women with black shawls over their heads who sat on stone steps with children squirming around them. Neon lights blinked everywhere and there was the endless honking of horns.

'Busy place,' she said at last, wanting to make it smaller and less threatening with a casual phrase.

Nafouz shrugged. 'Who your friends here?'

'Family,' she said discouragingly.

They were winding down smaller streets now, leaving the main thoroughfares behind. Ruby glanced upwards and saw onion domes and tall thin towers pasted against dark blue sky. The street was so narrow that there was only room for one car to pass. There was one great dome just ahead, cutting an arc of sky, and a trio of thin spires that rose beside it.

Nafouz stopped when he could go no further. The street had become a cobbled alley and it took a sharp-angled turn just in front of them. In the angle of a pale blank wall was a door with a small flight of stone steps leading up to it.

'Here is place,' Nafouz announced.

Ruby stared at the door. She could just see that it was painted blue, old paint that had bubbled to expose wood split by the sun. She hadn't at all worked out what to expect, but it wasn't this.

She summoned up her resolve. 'Yeah. How much money d'you want?' She opened up her nylon sack and her Discman and headphones and an apple and tubes of make-up rolled over the seat.

'Fifty bounds.'

'*Fifty?* D'you think I'm stupid or something? I'll give you twenty.' She opened her purse and fumbled with torn filthy notes.

'From airport, fifty.' Nafouz wasn't smiling any longer.

'Get lost.' Ruby gathered up her belongings and hopped out of the car but the driver was quicker. He ran round and held down the boot so she couldn't retrieve her rucksack. They squared up to each other.

'Twenty-five,' Ruby said.

'Fifty.'

'Give me my bloody *bag*.' She kicked his shin as hard as she could. Unfortunately she was only wearing flip-flops.

Nafouz yelped. 'Lady, lady. You are not behaving nicely.'

'Really? Now hand over my bag.'

'You pay first.' But Nafouz was relenting. This tourist's resistance earned a glimmer of his respect. Usually they just gave in and handed over the money. 'Thirty,' he conceded.

'Fuck's sake.' But she sighed and took another note out of her purse. Nafouz's smile was restored. Thirty Egyptian pounds was the going rate for a ride in from the airport.

Ruby took her rucksack, hoisted it over her shoulder and marched up the stone steps. She heard Nafouz reversing the car the way they had come, then a squeal of tyres as he raced away.

As soon as he was gone she regretted the loss of even this brief relationship. Maybe she should have asked him to wait. What if there was nobody here? What if the address was wrong? Then she lifted her head, straightened her shoulders and knocked on the blistered paint.

There was no sound from within.

Ruby clenched her fist and hammered even harder. Some poem that they had all been made to learn at school floated into her head and, without thinking, she yelled the words in time to the banging: '"*Is there anybody there?" said the Traveller.*'

The door suddenly creaked open, revealing a six-inch slice of dim light. Ruby could just see a big fat man in a white dress.

She said, 'I am Ruby Sawyer. I am here to see my grandmother. Let me in, please.'

Having taken one look at her, the man was trying to close the door again. Immediately Ruby put her shoulder to it and pushed hard. The door swung open and she fell inwards with a clatter of spilt belongings. The man's face was a dark purplish moon of disapproval. He frowned, but he did help her to her feet.

Ruby looked around. Her first impression was of the inside of a church. There was a stone floor, musty wood panelling, a pale, weak light suspended on chains inside a glass vessel. A smell of spicy cooking.

'Madam is resting,' the man said frigidly.

The best course was obviously to be conciliatory. 'I don't want to disturb her. I'm sorry if I made a noise. But, you know . . .' The man went on impassively staring at her. 'I have come all the way from London. My mother, you see . . . Um, my mother is Madam's daughter. You know?'

There was another silence. Whether he knew or not, the connection didn't seem to impress him. But at last he sighed heavily and said, 'Follow me, please. Leave this here.' He pointed to her bags. She relinquished them with pleasure.

He led the way beneath an arch and through a bare room. Behind a heavy door there was a flight of enclosed wooden stairs. The lights were dim, just single bulbs in the angles of walls, shaded with metal grilles. They went up the stairs and along a panelled corridor. It was a big house, Ruby thought, but it was dusty and bare, and all the stairs and corners and screens made it secretive. A place of shadow and whispers.

The man stopped at a closed door. He bent his head and listened. She noticed that his face had turned soft and concerned. There was no sound, so he lifted a latch and eased the door open. There was a light burning in a teardrop of crimson glass, a carved divan seat piled with cushions under a shuttered window. In a low cushioned chair with a padded footstool a very old woman was propped up with her eyes closed. A spilt glass lay on the kilim rug. Ruby took a step forward and she opened her eyes.

'**M**amdooh, who is this? What do you think you are doing? Don't let people walk in here as if it's a public library. Go away.'

The woman, apparition, whoever she is, doesn't move.

Mamdooh kneels down, picks up the glass. I can see the blotches on his old, bald skull. At once I feel sorry, and confused. I put my hand out to him and it's shaking. 'Forgive me. Who is she?'

The woman—very young, strange-looking—comes closer.

'I'm Ruby.'

'*Who?*'

'Your granddaughter. Lesley's daughter.'

Lesley's daughter? A memory disinters itself. A pale, rather podgy child, dressed in a wool kilt and hair-slides. Silent, yet somehow mutinous. Have I got that right?

'You are Granny Iris, my mother's mother, Cairo Granny. Last time I saw you I was ten. You came for a holiday.'

I am *tired*. The effort of recall is too much. Poor Lesley, I think.

'Does she know you are here?'

The child blinks. Now I look at her, I can see that she *is* hardly more than a child. She has made the effort to appear otherwise, with startling face paint and metal rings and bolts driven into nose and ears, and with a six-inch slice of pale abdomen revealed between the two halves of her costume, but I would put her age at eighteen or nineteen.

'Your *mother*. Does she know?'

'No, actually.'

Her answer is deadpan but, to my surprise, the way she delivers it makes me want to smile. Mamdooh has picked up the tea glass, tidied the tray. Now he stands over me, a protective mountain.

'Ma'am Iris, it is late,' he protests.

'I know that.' To the child I say, 'I don't know why you are here, Miss. You will go straight back where you came from. I'm tired now, but I will speak to you in the morning.'

'Shall I send Auntie to you?' Mamdooh asks me.

'No.' I don't want to be undressed and put to bed. I don't want to reveal to the child that sometimes this happens. 'Just get her to make up a bed for, for . . . what did you say your name is?'

'Ruby.'

'A bed and some food, if she wants it. Thank you, Mamdooh. Good night, Ruby.'

I make my way to my own room. When at last I am lying down with the white curtains drawn around the bed, the longing for sleep of course deserts me. I lie staring at the luminous folds of muslin, seeing faces and hearing voices.

Majestically disapproving, Mamdooh led Ruby downstairs again. A little old woman, about five foot tall, with a shawl wrapped round her head and neck, appeared in the hallway. They spoke rapidly to each other.

'You would like to eat some food?' Mamdooh asked stiffly.

'No, thanks very much. Had some on the plane.'

'Go with Auntie, then.'

Ruby hoisted her luggage once more and followed the old woman up the enclosed stairs and through the shadowy galleries to a small room with a divan under an arched window. Auntie, if that was the name she went by, showed her a bathroom across the way.

'Thank you,' Ruby said.

'*Ahlan wa sahlan*,' Auntie murmured.

When she had gone, Ruby peeled off her clothes and dropped them on the floor. She got under the thin starched sheet just as she was, and fell instantly into a dreamless sleep.

'**N**o, no, don't worry at all. I just wondered if she and Chloe might be together . . . Is she? In Chile? How marvellous. Give her my best wishes, won't you? Yes, that would be lovely. I'll give you a call. 'Bye.'

Lesley replaced the receiver. 'She's not there either.'

Her neat leather address book lay open on the side table, but there were no more numbers left to try. She had been through them all and none of Ruby's friends or their parents had seen her recently. None of Ruby's friends who were also known to her mother, at least.

Andrew was sitting in an armchair in a circle of lamplight, a pile of papers on his lap. A V of wrinkles formed in the centre of his forehead as he stared at her over his reading glasses.

'She's nineteen. It's really time she started taking responsibility for herself. You can't stand in the firing line for her for ever.'

'I don't think I do,' Lesley answered mildly. 'Do I?'

Andrew exhaled sharply through his nose, pulling down the corners of his mouth to indicate disagreement without bothering to disagree.

Looking away from him, at the pleasant room that was arranged just how she wanted it, with the duck-egg blue shade of the walls that was restful without being cold and the cushion and curtain borders exactly matching it, Lesley felt anxiety fogging the atmosphere. Concern about Ruby distorted the room's generous proportions and made it loom around her, sharp with threatening edges.

Where was Ruby? What was she doing, and who was she with?

She never experienced the same anxiety about Edward, Ruby's half-brother. Edward was always in the right place, doing the right thing.

Lesley closed her address book and secured it with a woven band.

Ruby had been gone since yesterday afternoon. She had slipped out of the house without a word to anyone.

Just to break the silence Lesley asked, 'Would you like a drink?'

'No, thanks.' Andrew didn't even look up.

'I'll go and . . . see if Ed's all right with his homework.'

Lesley went slowly up the stairs. At the top she hesitated, then tapped on her son's door: 'Hello?'

Ed was sitting at his table, an exercise book, coloured pencils and an encyclopedia open in front of him.

'How's it going?'

'OK'. His thick fair hair, the same colour as his father's, stuck up in a tuft at the front and made him look like a placid bird. He was the opposite of Ruby in every single respect.

'No word from Ruby,' she said. 'I thought she'd ring this evening.'

Ed nodded, looking thoughtful. 'You know, I don't think we should worry. She's probably staying in town with one of her mates. It's not like it's the first time she's just forgotten to come home, is it?'

For an eleven-year-old, Edward was remarkably well thought out.

'No,' Lesley agreed.

'Have you tried her mobile again?'

Only a dozen times. 'Still turned off.'

'Well, I think we should just tell ourselves that no news is good news. She'll probably ring you tomorrow.'

'Yes. All right, darling. I'll pop in later and say good night.'

'OK.' He had his nose in his book again before the door closed.

Lesley went along the landing to another door at the far end. She leaned against the handle for a moment, then walked into the room.

It was dark and stuffy, and the room's close smell had a distinctly brackish quality to it. Lesley had already looked in here two or three times during the day but the otherness of Ruby's bedroom, the way it seemed to rebuff her, never failed to take her by surprise. She felt cautiously along the wall for the light switch, then clicked it on.

The smell was from Ruby's collection of shells. She had lost interest in adding to it at least eight years ago but the cowries and spindles never quite gave up the traces of fish and salt locked in their pearly whorls. The wall cabinets that Lesley had had put up to display them contained a jumbled, teetering mass of sandy jars and broken conches.

Ruby had moved on to shells after her enthusiasm for collecting autographs had waned, and after shells lost their fascination she became obsessed with beetles. There were boxes and cases of preserved specimens on every flat surface.

Lesley crouched down beside a row of mahogany display cases and peered through the dusty glass fronts. Some of the beetles were two-inch monsters with stiff jointed legs, minutely articulated antennae and folded wings with an iridescent polish.

The beetle passion eventually faded like its precursors, but Ruby would never consider selling any of her acquisitions or even allowing them to be stored up in the loft. Almost everything, including the shoe-boxes full of autographs, was in this room.

There was hardly room to place her feet among the boxes and cartons, the scribbled drawings, discarded clothes and spilt tubes of make-up. It was impossible to tell what, if anything, Ruby had taken with her. Lesley stepped gingerly across the floor and sat down on the bed. She placed her hand in the hollow of the pillow, but no warmth lingered there.

Ruby had gone.

Lesley placed her feet together and rested her hands in her lap as if to offer up her own composure in response to the room's disorder.

Ruby hadn't gone like her contemporaries were going, on well-planned gap-year travels or amid clouds of A-level glory to good universities. Not mutinous, truanting, dyslexic and serially expelled Ruby. She hadn't passed any exams, or spent a summer raising money to fund a year's work with children in Nepal. Ruby had left the family house in Kent to lodge with Andrew's brother and his family in London, supposedly while she attended sixth-form college. But college hadn't lasted long and in Camden Town, Ruby had spent her days hanging out with new friends that none of the Ellises approved of. Then, just recently, she had abruptly moved back home again. She passed long hours closeted in her room and when she emerged spoke only when spoken to. Andrew chivvied her for decisions about a career. Making a contribution to the world, as he called it.

Ruby had lifted her black-painted eyes and stared at him as if he belonged to a species she didn't recognise.

And now, she had simply removed herself altogether.

'I love you,' her mother said to the motionless, smelly air.

Tenderness and longing sprang from the marrow in her bones. The feeling was turbulent, baffled, nothing like the calm, sturdy love she had for Edward, or her regularly thwarted affection for Andrew.

Her love for Ruby was the deepest passion in Lesley's life.

There was no ready explanation to be found, in this room or anywhere else, for what had gone wrong with her daughter. Or with me, Lesley added meticulously. It wasn't that she blamed Ruby for being difficult. She took all the responsibility for that on herself, which further irritated Andrew. In their late-night conversations she had asked the same questions over and over: *What have I done wrong? Have I been a bad mother?*

'You have lacked a role model,' Andrew tended to say.

Lesley bent her head. She examined her knees in their second skin of smooth nylon mesh. She picked at a loose thread in the grosgrain hem of her skirt and, to her shame even though there was no one to see, tears suddenly ran out of her eyes and dripped on the fabric.

Ruby opened her eyes.

White light poured in through the arched window, filling the bare room until the air seemed almost solid with floating particles of dust. It wasn't the sunshine that had woken her, however, but a burst of chanting. The words were incomprehensible, delivered in a rich singsong voice distorted by heavy amplification. She pushed back the sheet and scrambled to look outside. Her eyes widened in amazement.

In the street below, rows of men were kneeling on mats laid over the cobbles, with their foreheads pressed to the ground and the soles of their feet turned innocently upwards.

The city was stilled. Ruby rested her own forehead against the thick greenish glass and tried to hear the prayers. A few minutes later, the men knelt upright and stood up. The mats were casually whisked away and movement flowed back into the street again. Realising that she was hungry, Ruby reluctantly turned from the view.

The house was so quiet. She couldn't remember which way Auntie had brought her last night and the layout of interconnecting rooms was confusing. Here was a broader corridor with seats facing a carved screen with little hinged trap doors in it. She peered casually through one of the propped-up hatches and was surprised by the grand double-height space it overlooked. This big hall was almost unfurnished except for a long table and some high-backed chairs pushed against the walls. At the far end was a low dais backed by a wall painting of entwined flowers and fruit and exotic foliage. It would be a pretty good space for a party, she reflected.

She suddenly sensed that there was someone behind her. Whirling round, she came face to top of head with Auntie.

'Hello,' Ruby said brightly.

Auntie peered up at her. '*Sabah il-kheer*,' she murmured. Her face was like a walnut.

'I'm looking for my grandmother.'

'Mum-reese,' Auntie agreed, nodding. She indicated with a small hand movement that Ruby should follow her. The house wasn't really as big as it appeared. Just a few steps round a corner brought another surprise.

Ruby said, 'Oh. It's lovely.'

At the heart of the old house was a little open courtyard. It was enclosed by terracotta walls pierced by simple rounded arches faced with grass-green and turquoise glazed tiles. In the four corners were big square tubs of trailing greenery and to one side a waterspout splashed into a green glazed bowl. A lemon-sharp slice of sunlight obliquely bisected the courtyard and in the shady portion was a padded chair. Iris was sitting there watching her. Her thin grey hair was held up with a pair of combs and she was wearing an elegant silk robe. She looked displeased.

Ruby considered. She wanted to find a way to stay, not just because to come here at all had been a last resort and she had no intention of being sent back home, but because it was so intriguing. Therefore she must find a way to ingratiate herself. A shadow of a thought passed through her head—an acknowledgment that she was out of practice at making herself agreeable. She didn't even know what to call this disconcerting old lady. She was way too unfamiliar and beady for 'Granny', which was how Lesley referred to her at home. Not that Ruby's mother talked about her own mother very often.

'Hi,' she said in the end, shuffling her feet.

Mamdooh had to remind me when he brought my morning tea that we have a visitor. Now here is the girl. She wears peculiar, ugly clothes. A pair of dusty black trousers, safety-pinned in the front across her plump belly, so long that they drag on the ground. The hems are all dusty and torn. On the top half, or third because the garment is so shrunken that it exposes six inches of white midriff, is a little grey thing with some black motif on the front. She has so many silvery rings on her fingers that they reach up to her knuckles, more rings in her ears, one in her nose, and a silver stud pierces her top lip. She hasn't washed this morning, there is black stuff smudged round her eyes. Her face is round, pale as the moon, and innocent.

Why is she here? Lesley's daughter.

'Don't you have any proper clothes?'

She sticks her chin out at me.

'These are proper.'

'They are not decent.'

Her eyes meet mine. She scowls, then thinks better of it. Her metal-cased fingers pluck at the bottom of the vest garment.

'Too short?'

I am already tired of this exchange. There is a white shawl across the arm of my chair and I hold it out to her. She shakes out the folds and twirls it like a matador's cape, and I am struck by the grace of the sudden movement and, yes, the happy exuberance of it. It's pretty to see. Then she seems to remember herself. She knots my shawl awkwardly over her breasts so it veils her stomach.

'Sit down.'

Obediently, she perches on a wooden stool and leans forward.

'Y'know, I don't know what to call you. You're my grandmother, but it doesn't seem right to say Granny. D'you know what I mean?'

It hardly matters what she calls me. It's a long time since I have been anything except Mum-reese or Dr Black. 'My name is Iris.'

'Is that what you want me to say?'

I rest my head on the cushions and close my eyes.

After a minute, maybe more, she murmurs, 'Iris?'

The line of sunlight is creeping towards us. I rouse myself again.

'Have you told your mother where you are? You'll have to go back home right away. It's very inconvenient this . . . this appearance in my house. You must telephone her at once, tell her where you are, and say I told you, to . . .'

A shadow crosses the child's face.

'Yeah. I know, I know. Thing is . . .' She half stands and rummages under the shawl in the tight pocket of her trousers. She produces a small silvery object. 'My mobile doesn't work out here.'

'Is that a telephone? You can use the one here, I suppose. It's through there. Mamdooh will show you.'

'Right. OK. Um . . . I'm really hungry, though. Is there something to eat, maybe, before I call home and tell them everything's cool?'

'Auntie is bringing it.'

Auntie and Mamdooh arrive together. Auntie's quite lively with curiosity now but Mamdooh is offended, I can see from the way he puts down the tray with exaggerated care and doesn't look at the girl. It doesn't matter. She'll be going back where she came from, maybe not today but certainly tomorrow. What was her name?

It comes back to me surprisingly easily. Ruby.

Ruby's eyes lit up at the sight of breakfast. She was very hungry indeed, and here was a bowl of fat purple figs and—lifting a little beaded cloth that covered a bowl—thick creamy yoghurt. There was a basket of coarse bread, a glass dish of honey and a plate of crumbly, sticky little cakes. There was also a battered silver pot, a tiny wisp of steam rising from the spout.

'Thank you, Mamdooh. Thank you, Auntie,' Iris said. 'We'll look after ourselves now.'

Ruby drew her stool closer.

'Pour me some tea, please,' Iris ordered. Ruby did as she was told and put the glass on the table beside her.

'Mm,' Ruby said, after a long swallow. 'That's so good. What is it?'

'Don't you know? Mint tea.'

'I like it. We don't have it at home. Can I try some of this?'

Iris nodded. She watched as the girl spooned honey onto bread and ate, biting off thick chunks and chewing with strong white teeth. After the bread and honey she turned her attention to the figs.

'How do you eat these?'

Iris showed her, slicing open the skin to reveal the velvet and seed-pearl interior. Ruby ate, her smudged eyes screwed up in a comical spasm of pleasure.

'Aren't you going to eat anything?' she asked.

'I'll have one of those.' Iris pointed to the triangles of baklava. Ruby put the pastry on a plate and set it next to Iris's glass of tea. Then she stretched out her legs, sighing with satisfaction as she looked around the little courtyard.

'It's another world. Glorious Araby.'

'What did you say?'

'When? Oh, that. It's from a poem or something, isn't it? Don't ask me who wrote it or anything. I suppose I read it or heard it. You know how some things just stay in your mind? And other things you're supposed to remember, however hard you try it's just like, *phhhhht*, and they're gone? Stuff you're supposed to learn for exams, mainly?'

'If it matters, you will remember it. You have to hope for that.'

'Depends on what you reckon matters.' Ruby laughed, then caught sight of her grandmother's face. It had fallen suddenly into lines of anguish and the powdery skin under her eyes looked damp with tears.

She bit her lip. 'Did I say something wrong?'

Iris reached inside the sleeve of her robe and brought out a handkerchief. She dried her eyes carefully and tucked the hanky away again.

'I am becoming forgetful myself,' she said. She made a little gesture with her hands, swimming them through the air and then closing them on nothing. It made Ruby think that memories were slippery, like fish.

'That must be frightening, sometimes,' she ventured.

'It is.'

'What can you do?'

Iris turned her head to look full at her. 'Try to . . . try to capture what you can't bear to be without.'

Ruby didn't understand this but she nodded anyway. The sound of water splashing from the little spout filled the courtyard.

Mamdooh came through one of the arches and stooped beside Iris's chair. It was time to move it further into the shade. As she watched him helping her grandmother and settling her again Ruby noticed he wore the same tender expression as last night, as if Iris were a little child.

While they were talking quietly together, Ruby stared up into the parallelogram of sapphire-blue sky. She could just see the tips of towers, topped with slim bulbs of stone and spikes bearing crescent moons. There was a whole city on the other side of these walls. Now that she had found her feet she was longing to explore it.

'Mamdooh is going to the market now,' Iris said.

Ruby leapt up so eagerly that her stool fell over. 'Can I go with him?'

Iris lifted her hand. 'You will have to ask Mamdooh.'

'Please may I come with you?'

He had round cheeks, rounded eyelids, full lips the colour of the breakfast figs, but his bald head was all speckled and his eyes were milky. His stomach made a sizable mound under his long white robe. He didn't look as old as Iris or Auntie, but he wasn't young.

'To the market, Miss?' He sounded doubtful.

'I'll, um, put a cover-up shirt thing on? I've got one in my bag. I could help carry the shopping, couldn't I?'

'I do this for many years, thank you.'

'I'd really like to come.'

Iris closed her eyes. 'Show her the market, Mamdooh, please. She will be going home to England tomorrow.'

He bowed. 'Of course.'

When she came downstairs again with a man's shirt buttoned up over her vest, Mamdooh was waiting for her. He had a woven rush basket over his arm, and a faded red flowerpot hat set squarely on his head. A black tassel hung down towards his left eye.

'If you are ready, Miss?'

They went out through the blue-painted door and the sun's heat struck the top of Ruby's head. She took the few steps to the corner and looked up at an ancient crenellated wall, a cluster of smaller domes surrounding the large one and the three slender towers.

'What is this place?' she called to Mamdooh, who was making stately progress in the other direction.

'It is the mosque of al-Azhar. We are going this way, please.'

'It's very old.'

'Cairo is a place of history.' The way he said it told Ruby that he was proud of his native city and his reverence made her want to know more of it. She quickened her pace to catch him up again, and they swung down a narrow street and out into a much broader one. Out here there was a roar of traffic and hooting and tinny amplified music, and they were caught in a slow tide of people before Mamdooh ducked down into a tiled modern subway not much different from the one beneath Oxford Circus. When they surfaced again, Ruby blinked.

'Khan al-Khalili bazaar. Follow close to me, it is easy to be lost here.'

He was right. It would be the easiest thing in the world to lose yourself in this maze of tiny alleys leading away from the almost-familiarity of the main street. There were canvas awnings looped overhead, and in their welcome shade the brightness of the crammed-together shops and stalls was dazzling. The merchandise was piled up and hung in tiers so it seemed to drip stalactites of hectic colour. One shop was crammed with interesting-looking brass, another niche was festooned with belly dancers' costumes gaudy with nylon fringing and glass beads. Next door hessian sacks spilled ochre- and saffron- and pearl-coloured grains.

The footpaths between the stalls were choked with people and wooden carts and porters with boxes piled on their heads. There were men in Western clothes, and others in *galabiyeh* and tarboosh, a faded red flowerpot fez, like Mamdooh. There were women robed in black from head to toe, others in trousers and sturdy blouses with just a scarf wound over their hair.

The shopkeepers competed for Ruby's attention as she went by.

'Lady, look-see. Just looking, no charge. Very good prices.'

Urchins plucked at her shirt, holding up novelty lighters and boxes of tissues and bottles of water. Even in the shade it was hot, and the air felt saturated with moisture. Her shirt was soon sticking to her back and thick hanks of hair plastered themselves to the nape of her neck.

An even smaller capillary led away from the alley of shops, this one enclosed by rickety houses. There were wooden benches lining the house walls, all heaped high with vegetables and fruit. Mamdooh stopped, surveying the merchandise.

Stallholders surrounded him at once, thrusting up polished aubergines and bunches of white onions for his attention. Some of the offerings he waved away, others he condescended to pinch or to sniff at. Once an item had received his approval, there was a convoluted exchange obviously relating to the price. Finally, at length and with ceremony, a purchase was wrapped in a twist of paper in exchange for some coins and Mamdooh stowed it in his straw basket before moving on.

Ruby had never seen shopping taken as seriously as this. She found a space against a dusty wall and watched in fascination.

Mamdooh glanced back once or twice to check on her. When he realised that she wasn't going to wander off, he gave her a small nod of approval. And then, when his shopping was complete he tilted his head to indicate that she was to follow him.

They threaded their way back through the porters and tourists and stallholders and customers, a slow mass of hot humanity that made urgency impossible.

Slanting sunlight just ahead revealed an open square. There were walls of sepia-coloured stone, the dust-coated leaves of rubber trees casting patches of shade on broken pavements, and a pair of faded sun umbrellas rooted in pillars of concrete. At two tin tables, bare except for ashtrays and a folded newspaper, sat a handful of old men.

They raised their hands or mumbled greetings to Mamdooh, who responded with two or three brief words. Several pairs of eyes, red-rimmed or milky, turned towards Ruby.

She understood the situation at once. Mamdooh came out to do the household's shopping, then retired to this café with his friends, and her presence was an impediment to this pleasant interval in his day.

She said hastily, 'I can find my way back, you know, if you want to stay with your friends for a bit.'

Mamdooh looked genuinely shocked at this suggestion.

'That would not be at all right, Miss. We will be going home at once.'

Farewells were exchanged with the old men and Mamdooh sailed across the square. But now, Ruby sensed, she was walking with him rather than in his wake. The impression was confirmed when he remarked, 'Market, very old also.'

'How old?'

'Seven hundred year.'

'Ha. Just think of all the buying of things.' Centuries, Ruby thought, of leather and herbs and perfume and figs.

'Selling,' Mamdooh corrected her. He rubbed his thumb and forefinger together. 'Selling, very important.'

They were walking companionably towards Iris's house when an extra-loud volley of hooting caught their attention. There was a black-and-white taxi parked where the alley finally became impassable to cars. The faded blue of the door was just behind it.

'Lady, lady! We look for you!' a voice shouted.

Nafouz was leaning out of the driver's window.

Mamdooh moved fast for a man of his bulk. He streaked across to the taxi and shouted at Nafouz, flapping his big hand towards the open end of the alley. From the passenger side of the car another young man climbed out. He looked like Nafouz, but younger.

Nafouz slid out of the car. He appealed direct to Ruby. 'We are friends, yes? I bring you, last night.'

'No.'

'Lady?' Nafouz's eyes were wide, hurt pools.

'Yes, I mean, you drove me from the airport. That doesn't make us friends, does it?' She had kicked him, for one thing.

Nafouz turned away to burrow inside the car. Ruby looked at the other young man. He had the same slicked-back hair as Nafouz and a similar white shirt. He smiled at her.

'I bring this for you.' Nafouz had re-emerged. He was holding out a CD case with a hand-coloured insert, a pattern of swirls and tendrils in red and black ink. Ruby looked at it. Jas had painted the insert, and he had burned the CD inside it for her. It was one of his own mixes, just about the last thing he had made for her before . . . Before he . . .

The CD must have fallen out of her bag as she scrambled into or out of the taxi. She would have been sad to lose it. 'It's only a thing, baby,' Jas would have said. 'Things don't matter, people do.'

'Right. Well, thanks,' she muttered, taking the case.

'You take a tour? I show you Cairo. Special Cairo, my brother and me. Not tourist places. Real city.'

Mamdooh had now mounted the steps and produced a key for the blue door.

Ruby hesitated. She would have loved to pile into the taxi and go cruising through the streets with them. 'Another time, maybe,' she said lamely. There were priorities, other matters she had to deal with first.

The younger brother came round to Nafouz's side of the car.

'I am Ashraf.'

The door was open, Mamdooh was waiting with the basket of vegetables at his side. The brothers were waiting too.

'My name's Ruby.'

Their faces split into identical white smiles. 'Nice name.'

'I've got to go now. But I'd like to take a tour. Have you got a . . .?' She made a scribble movement in the air for a pen, but Nafouz dismissed it.

'We find you.'

'Miss?' Mamdooh said, holding the door open wide. His forehead was serrated with disapproval once more.

'See you, then.' Ruby marched up the steps.

In the cool hallway Mamdooh blocked her way. 'It is important to have some care, Miss. You are young, in this city there are not always good people. It is important that you make no risks. Do you understand what it is I am saying to you?'

He was treating her like a child. In London, Ruby did what she wanted. Lesley and Andrew didn't know what that involved, nor did Will and Fiona who were Andrew's brother and his wife. She was supposed to be their lodger, but—well, after a while they had given up on telling her what to do and what not to do. That was because of Will. Even though Fiona didn't know about him, the three of them had ended up in this kind of silent contract, where nobody saw anything or said anything in case it led to somebody seeing and saying everything.

And there had been some bad interludes. The memories came back in the night, and Ruby would twist and turn under the covers to try to make them stop and go away. She even wished for Lesley to come and tell her it was all right and she was safe.

But usually in the end she fell asleep somehow, or the daylight would come and she'd wonder what she had been so afraid of.

Luck or cunning, Jas had said. That's what you need to survive. She could see him breathing out a snaky ring of blue smoke as he spoke.

So Ruby understood exactly what Mamdooh was saying.

'Yes,' she said stonily. She stood and faced him, giving no ground.

Mamdooh tucked the handles of the basket over his arm.

'Mum-reese resting now. Later, she will speak to you.'

And order her home. Ruby knew what he meant her to hear, but she gave no sign of it.

Left to herself, she wandered through the house.

It was less opulent than it had looked in last night's darkness, and even more neglected. The great lamps that hung from the vaulted roofs were furred with dust, and cobwebs spanned the corners. The rooms were barely furnished with unmatching chairs and tables that looked as if they had been brought in by an incoming tide and just left where they landed. There were no books, ornaments, or photographs—none of the cosy decorator's clutter that Lesley arranged in her own house and those of her clients. There was nothing, Ruby realised, that told any stories of Iris's past. She was quite curious to know why.

This morning, Iris had told her that she was becoming forgetful. She had made a swimming movement with her old hands, as if she were trying to catch fish. And there had been tears in her eyes.

Didn't framed photographs and bits of china and books help you to recollect? Ruby frowned, trailing her finger through the grey film on a wooden chest and recalling her grandmother's words. She had said something about capturing what you can't bear to be without. It was the word capture that resonated.

When she was small, Ruby distanced herself. She couldn't read and write as well as girls in her class, and she was endlessly in trouble. A way of making sense out of her confusion had been to collect things. By piling them up in her room she could make herself bigger than they were, so even if what she collected represented only a strand of the world's abundance, it had still seemed to offer a measure of control.

But if you wanted to capture memories that threatened to swim away like fish? How would you do that?

An idea came to Ruby. It was a very neat, simple and pleasing idea that would solve her problem and at the same time be valuable to her grandmother. It was the perfect solution and she was so taken with its economy that she ran up the nearest of the house's two flights of stairs towards the door that she had worked out must be Iris's. She hovered outside for a moment, with her ear against one of the dark panels.

Then she tapped, very gently. When there was no answer she rapped more loudly.

'Auntie? Mamdooh?' Iris's voice answered.

'It's me. Ruby.'

There was a long silence. Then the voice, sounding much smaller, said, 'You had better come in.'

She was sitting in the same low chair as last night, a rug over her knees. Ruby read bewilderment in her face.

She stooped down beside the chair and put her hand over Iris's thin, dry one. 'Am I disturbing you?'

'No.'

'I went shopping with Mamdooh. I think I got in the way of his routine, but it was really interesting. He told me there's been a market there for seven hundred years.'

'Yes.'

The monosyllable came out on a long breath. Iris was obviously almost too tired to speak and her fragility gave Ruby a hot, unwieldy feeling that she could only just identify as protectiveness. She wanted to scoop up her grandmother and hold her in her arms. But even as she chased this thought to its logical conclusion—Iris would not appreciate being handled like a rag doll—the old woman seemed to summon up some surprising inner strength. She hoisted herself upright against the cushions and fixed Ruby with a glare.

'Have you spoken on the telephone to my daughter?'

Ruby quailed at this sudden direct challenge. 'Um, no.'

'Why have you not done so?'

Ruby withdrew her hand and took a breath. 'It's really because I don't want to go home. I was hoping you wouldn't make me.'

Iris studied her. Her gaze was very sharp now, all the weariness and confusion seemed to have evaporated. 'Why is that?'

'It's quite a long story. If I could stay here with you for a while, I could maybe tell you . . .'

'That is not possible.'

Ruby bent her head. The sonorous, amplified chanting that had woken her this morning suddenly filled the room again. 'What is that?'

'The call to prayer.'

'Oh. All right, I'll ring Mum and tell her where I am and there'll be a mega fuss and outcry, and I'll go home. But if I could stay here, just for a few *days* or so, then maybe I could help you.'

'How do you think you can help me?'

Now it was Ruby who made a small gesture with her hands, as if trying to catch darting fish. 'You told me you are sometimes forgetful.'

'Yes. So?' Sharply.

'I walked round the house this afternoon, and you don't seem to have any belongings, the kind that help you to remember the past.'

'I have lived a long life, in different places. Most of them primitive. I have learned that so many material possessions are just that, material.'

She was saying almost the same as Jas; *it's just stuff, baby*. There were connections here, twining around herself and Iris and the old house and even Mamdooh, and Nafouz and his brother. Ruby wanted to stay, more than she had wanted anything in a long time.

'I thought, I wondered, if you told me what you want to . . . to capture, maybe I could be the keeper of it for you. I could be the collector of your memories. I could write them down, even. I could be your am . . . what's the word?'

'Amanuensis.'

Ruby's pale face had been animated, but now a heavy mask descended. Iris hadn't seen her look sullen before.

'Not that, maybe. I'm dyslexic. Bit of a drawback.'

'Are you?'

'It's not the same as being thick. But sometimes it might as well be.'

'Thank you for making that clear. You don't seem thick to me.'

'But maybe we could tape-record you? Like an oral history project. We did one at school, with the old ladies from the drop-in centre, about the Blitz.'

Iris laughed at that. Her hands loosened in her lap, her face lost its taut lines and her eyes shone. Ruby suddenly saw a young girl in her, and she beamed back, pleased with the effect her company was having.

'How useful to have previous experience.'

'I didn't mean to compare you.'

'Why not? I remember the Blitz. The beginning of it, anyway. Then I came out here, to Cairo, to work.'

'*Did* you? How come?'

'That's the beginning of another long story.'

They looked at each other then, as the last notes of the muezzin crackled and died away.

It was Iris who finally broke the silence: 'Go and talk to your mother. You may use my telephone, in the room through there. And when you have finished I will speak to her myself.'

Ruby stood up and went through the interconnecting door to Iris's bedroom. It was very bare, containing nothing more than a bed swathed in white curtains and a couple of wooden chests. A telephone stood on the table on one side of the bed, and on the other there was a framed photograph. A young woman, certainly Iris herself, stood with a tall man in an army shirt. Her back curved against him, his arm circled her waist. Their bodies seemed to fit one against the other, like a carving or sculpture. Ruby walked round to the opposite side and picked up the receiver. After two or three attempts, she was listening to her mother's mobile ringing.

Lesley answered immediately, of course.

'*Ruby*? Ruby, are you all right? Thank God you've called. Tell me, what's happened? Where are you?'

Ruby spoke, briefly.

Her mother's voice rose. 'You are *where*?'

When I replace the receiver I see that my hands are shaking.

I return to the other room where the child is waiting for me.

'What did she say?' she asks.

The anxiety in her round face tells me how much she does not want to be packed off back to England. I sit down to collect my thoughts. I can give her the gist of my conversation with Lesley, but there is so much else that I would find harder to put into words.

'Your mother has been worried about you. I told her that I thought you would be safe enough here.'

At once, the anxious expression breaks up into a smile that contains glee and satisfaction and a measure of triumph. I am beginning to understand that Ruby's innocence is shot through with calculation. And I realise that the notion interests me more than anything has done for quite a long time.

'So I *can* stay for a bit?'

Our separate conversations with Lesley have had a further curious effect, of course. That she is in opposition to both of us makes partial allies out of Ruby and me.

'I would like a drink. Will you call Mamdooh?' I say.

I am stalling for time because with part of myself I fear the loss of privacy that having her here will inevitably mean. I want to be alone to concentrate on the past, in order to hold on to it for as long as I can. Yet maybe the offer of help that Ruby made is less naive than it sounded; maybe there is something in her idea.

Mamdooh brings in a tray with two glasses, a jug of water and a decanter.

Ruby accepts her glass with small enthusiasm. 'I don't like whisky.'

'What do you drink?'

'Depends. Vodka and Red Bull?'

'What's that? I'm sure it's disgusting. I don't have anything of the kind anyway, so you'll have to make do with Scotch.'

We both laugh and Mamdooh peers at us in surprise.

When we are alone again she draws up a stool and sits close to my chair. As I taste my drink, I am thinking about Lesley.

It is some months since I have spoken to my daughter. Whenever we do talk there are always polite words that fail to build a bridge. And the space between us, that has always been there. From the very beginning.

Lesley was born in the middle of a grey English winter. My pregnancy had been unplanned; my husband and I hastily bought a house to be a home for our unexpected family. In this house, the baby and I spent long days alone together while my husband was working in the City.

Lesley cried unceasingly. I had completed my medical training by that time, and, raw as I was as a doctor, I knew that she was not ill or even failing to thrive, but she was never a placid or contented baby.

I don't deny the probability that she absorbed my unhappiness and reflected it back at me. I tried to hold the infant close, tried to soothe her yelling by rocking her in my arms as I paced through the silent house, but she would not be pacified. When Gordon came home he would take her from me and she would whimper and nuzzle and then fall asleep, exhausted. The silence came like a blessing.

As soon as I could, I found a nurse for her and took a job at the local hospital. And from there we have gone on.

'Well?' Ruby demands. 'Can I stay?'

I turn my glass, looking at the dimples of light trapped within it.

'What did your mother say to you?'

An exasperated sigh and a shrug. 'She said she was about to call the police and report me missing. She said I am irresponsible, and thoughtless, and that I should go home and get a job and be a different person. I've heard it all before, about five zillion times.'

'She was worried,' I repeat.

We look at each other over our whisky glasses.

'You see, the trouble is that I'm crap at everything,' Ruby quietly says. 'At least, all the things that Lesley and Andrew rate. Not that I'd admit that to very many people, actually.'

'I don't think you are,' I tell her.

'Thanks.' Her tone is dismissive but her eyes implore me.

'All right,' I say slowly, because it is dawning on me that I do rather want her to stay. At least, I don't want her to go right now. 'I will telephone Lesley again, and ask if you may have her permission to spend a few days with me.'

She hugs her knees and rocks on the stool. 'Fantastic.' She grins.

I finish my whisky first. My hands are steady now.

Lesley answers the telephone. 'Hello?'

'It's Iris,' I say again.

'Mummy, tell me what's really going on?'

I never felt comfortable with *mummy*; it was Lesley who always insisted on it.

Into the space I say careful sentences about it being a pleasure to meet Ruby, how Lesley would be doing a favour to me if she were to allow her to stay for a few days in Cairo. Now that she's here, I say, we might as well turn it to advantage. The Egyptian Museum. An outing to the Pyramids at Giza. Ancient history, archaeology. And so on.

Although nowadays I hardly leave the house, I find myself almost believing that Ruby and I will make these excursions together.

'If you agree, that is, Lesley. You and . . .'

Her husband; second husband, not Ruby's father. I have met this one two or three times but I find that I can remember nothing about him, not even his name. It's impossible to work out whether it is my forgetfulness that is to blame, or his unmemorableness.

'Are you sure it won't be too much for you, having Ruby there?'

'I don't think so. If it turns out to be, I promise I'll say so.'

'Well . . . it's kind of you to do this for her. Thank you. After she's just turned up like that, uninvited. Andrew and I had no idea, one minute she was here and the next she'd vanished. It never occurred to me . . . she bought an air ticket, just like that, took her passport . . .'

'Enterprising of her. As I said, she'll come to no harm here. Boredom will set in before too long and then you'll have her home again.'

'I expect so. We'll see.' I can hear that Lesley badly wants Ruby to go home, but she knows better than to insist on it. I find myself admiring her adroitness. 'Thanks again for taking her in.'

'What else would I have done?'

'I don't know, Mummy.'

The bridge of careful words begins to creak and sway, and we both step hastily backwards.

We quickly end the conversation. Now, and for the next few days, I am responsible for Ruby.

My mother, my daughter, Lesley thought as she put down the telephone.

I don't think my mother ever loved me, otherwise she wouldn't have left my father and me.

I love Ruby more than anything and she doesn't want my love. It chafes her, just like when she was a little girl and I took her to have her hair cut. The tiny ends of her hair worked their way inside her vest and itched and itched. Even though I undressed her and gave her fresh clothes, the memory of the itching still made her scream. I am the cut hairs, for Ruby. Part of her but not part of her, and an irritation.

Iris and Ruby.

Motherhood, or actually the denial of it, is the thread that connects all three of us. I wanted to spin a better, finer filament for Ruby and me, a gossamer link that wouldn't drag between us and trip us up the way that Iris's and mine always has done. But all I seem to have created is a different kind of unwelcome tie.

Or look at it another way: perhaps we are like the poles of a magnet, Ruby and me and Iris and me, always driven apart. And by the same analogy Ruby and Iris have leapt together, irresistibly attracted.

Iris and Ruby ate dinner together, in a small room through an archway off the double-height hall. As Ruby gazed upwards into the dim, cob-webbed heights, Iris briefly explained to her that the celebration hall was where important male guests would have been entertained. The musicians would have taken their places on the dais at the end and there might also have been a belly dancer. The women of the household would have watched the party from the upper gallery, hidden from the men's view behind the pierced screens.

'Why?'

Iris frowned. 'Do you know nothing about Islamic culture?'

'Not really.'

'The women occupy the *haramlek*, a part of the house reserved for them, where men may enter only by invitation. There is a separate staircase, a whole suite of rooms including the one where you sleep. And the other half, where the men may move freely, where visitors come, is the *salamlek*.'

Ruby listened, and ate hungrily. The meal was a simple affair of flat bread and spiced beans cooked with tomatoes and onions, of which Iris hardly touched anything.

Mamdooh and Auntie came back to remove the remains of the meal.

'Ya, Mamdooh, Auntie. We have decided that Ruby will be staying here with us for a few days, before she goes back to her mother in England. We must make her welcome to Cairo.'

Mamdooh's expression did not change as he nodded his head, but Auntie's walnut face cracked into a smile.

After the shuffle of their slippers had died away Ruby sighed. 'Mamdooh's got a problem with me, hasn't he?'

'He is set in his ways, that's all. We both are. Do you know, when I was about your age, Mamdooh's father was our house *suffragi*? He looked after us. Sarah, Faria and me. The three flowers of Garden City. I remember our Mamdooh when he was a plump little boy who followed his father to work. So we have known each other for sixty years.'

Ruby waited for more, but Iris seemed to have lost herself. At last she shook her head.

'We are set in our ways. It will do us good to have a change in our routine. Give me your arm, please. I think I will go to bed now.'

I lie still, watching the various textures of the darkness. If I turn my head, I can just see the glint of reflected moonlight on the corner of the silver picture frame.

On the evening of his first telephone call, I scrambled to finish dressing for dinner before he arrived to pick me up. The dress was one I had had in London before the war, dark coral-pink silk with a full skirt and a low bodice. I had just enough time to pin up my hair and paint my mouth before the doorbell clanged. I looked at myself in the dressing-table mirror as Mamdooh went to answer it.

The most important time in my life was about to begin. I knew that, even if I didn't know anything else.

Mamdooh had shown him into the dimly lit drawing room. Xan was standing with one hand on the back of a sofa, staring through the part-open shutters into the fading sunlight. He was wearing uniform, his face was deeply sunburnt. He turned round when he heard me come in.

He said, 'I came as soon as I could.'

'I'm glad.'

Then he took my hand and led me to the window so we could see each other's faces. There was a second's silence when everything in the world seemed to stop and wait. Xan very slowly lifted my hand to his mouth and kissed it.

As I looked at him his eyebrows drew up into amused peaks. 'Where shall we begin, Miss Black?'

I had thought I remembered everything, every single thing about him, but the fun in him struck me afresh.

I pretended to consider. 'Let's think. You have to ask me whether I would prefer dinner at Le Petit Coin de France or Fleurent's. Then you say something about maybe looking in afterwards at the Kit Kat Club.'

'Of course. Out in the desert, one forgets these essentials.'

'So we might have a drink here first, while I try to make up my mind. I'll probably decide to change my outfit at least once before we leave.'

Xan grinned. 'I am at your service.'

I mixed gin and tonics from the tray Mamdooh always left ready.

We sat down together on the sofa and I raised my glass.

'To wherever it is you have been, and to having come back.'

His face clouded for a moment and he took a long swallow of the gin. 'I will tell you about it, but not this evening. Do you mind?'

'No, don't let's talk about the war this evening.'

I knew nothing, then, about what he had seen or had to do, but even in my naiveté I understood that what Xan needed tonight was to forget, to be made to laugh, to put down the weight of wartime.

I said, 'So. What will happen is that by the time I am dressed, and have decided on Fleurent's, and we have got there in a taxi, they will have given our table away to a brigadier. But there will be at least two tables packed with people we know, and so we will squeeze up with them. There will be a lot of laughing and even more drinking, and then we will all decide that we are having so much fun that we must go on somewhere else. We will all pile into taxis and in the confusion you will be in the taxi behind. When we arrive at wherever it is we are going we will be unable to find each other for at least an hour. By which time I shall be very tired and will insist on being taken straight home.'

Xan laughed. 'You lead a rackety life, Miss Black. It's not a very convincing plan of action in any case. I shall not let you get into a taxi without me, and I will not let you out of my sight for one minute, let alone a whole hour. And we are not going to Fleurent's, or the Kit Kat Club. Why should I share you with every soldier in Cairo?'

'Then where are we going?'

He took the glass out of my hand and set it on the red and black marble table top. 'Wait and see.'

Mamdooh brought my Indian shawl and wished us a very good evening as we went out together.

The sky was almost dark, a heavy velvet blue with the first stars showing. There was a car waiting a few steps away, with a driver who got out quickly and opened the door for us. He was tall and hawk-faced, dressed in Western clothes but still looking like one of the Bedouin tribesmen who lived in the desert.

'This is my friend Hassan,' Xan said quietly.

'Good evening, Hassan.'

The man nodded at me.

We sat in the back of the car and I watched the shuttered streets gliding by. Excitement and anticipation chased through me and I found that I had to remind myself to breathe.

'I live there,' Xan said, pointing up at some balconied windows.

I craned my neck in an effort to see more. 'Alone?' I asked.

He laughed. 'With some other men. You never know quite who's going to be there. When someone comes back from a picnic in the desert it's a matter of taking a look around to see if there's a bed that looks more or less unoccupied. You dump your kitbag and hope for the best. It's pretty empty at the moment, actually. Not all that surprising, if you know what I mean.'

I knew what he meant. We were both quiet as we thought about the recent Allied defeats in Crete and Greece as well as Cyrenaica.

'Does Jessie James live there too?'

'Jess? Yes, when he's in town. But the Cherry Pickers are away now.'

Jessie's famous cavalry regiment had charged with the Light Brigade at Balaklava. Now, with armoured vehicles instead of horses and cannon, they were in the line east of Tobruk.

Xan glanced at me as we crossed the English Bridge. We were heading towards Giza and the desert.

'You're at GHQ, aren't you? Who do you work for?'

'Lieutenant-Colonel Boyce.'

Xan's smile broadened. 'Small world, the army. May I drop in and see you in the office one of these days?'

'I'll make you a cup of GHQ tea. It's a treat not to be missed.'

His finger rested on my wrist for a second. 'I'll hold you to that.'

We were passing through the fields and scrubby mud-brick settlements and lines of palms that marked the western edge of the delta.

I had thought perhaps we were heading for the Mena House Hotel, a popular destination near the Pyramids, but then the car turned in an unfamiliar direction down a narrow unmade track.

After a while Xan leaned forward and murmured something in Arabic to Hassan.

'We're nearly there.'

Directly ahead of us I could make out the smoky glow of a fire, and the black silhouettes of a handful of palm trees. There were some tents and a few people moving between us and the fire. Camels were tethered in a line. We were coming to a tiny oasis.

Hassan brought the car to a halt. Xan and I stepped out where the shingle-and-sand camel track petered out in a sea of fine, soft ripples.

'Welcome,' Hassan said to me. '*Mahubbah*. These are my people.'

A circle of men sat close to the fire on upturned oil drums. One of the men stood up and came towards us. He was old and had a white beard. He was wrapped in a coarse woven blanket.

'*Mahubbah*,' he murmured. He touched his forehead to Xan who returned the salute, then the two men embraced each other.

'Abu Hassan,' Xan said respectfully.

I stood in the sand, and fine cool trickles ran into my shoes. I felt strange in my coral-pink silk evening dress with the chill desert breeze blowing strands of hair across my face.

The old man bowed to me and Xan took my arm. He murmured in my ear, 'Hassan and his father welcome you. They would like you to know that their house is your house, and they are your servants.'

'Will you tell them I am unworthy of their generosity, but I am proud to be their guest?'

'Exactly,' he said warmly, and I listened again to the clicking of unfamiliar Arabic.

Hassan and his father bowed once more and retreated towards the circle of seats and the firelight, leaving Xan and me standing alone.

'This way,' he said, pointing into the darkness. 'Wait a minute, though.'

He reached into the boot of the car and produced a bag that he slung over his shoulder, and an army greatcoat which he held out to me.

'Wear this for a moment or two, in case the cold gets too much. Will you take my hand?'

I did so and the warmth of his fingers enveloped mine.

The ghost of a path curved round a swelling dune. I stumbled a little in my dancing shoes, but Xan held me tightly. After a few more yards I saw a dark smudge ahead of us, then the glow of lights caught within it.

The shape resolved itself into a tent, a little square structure made of some kind of woven animal hair. There were long tassels hanging from the four corner poles, their filaments lifting in the breeze. Xan drew back the tent flap and stood aside to let me in. The tent was lined with hangings in broad strips of green, black, cream and maroon, and the floor was covered with rugs and piled with embroidered cushions. Lit candles on flat stones burned everywhere, and in the centre of the little room, under a hole in the roof, stood a metal brazier full of glowing embers. It was as warm inside the tent as in Lady Gibson Pasha's ballroom, and in the candlelight it was a hundred times more beautiful.

I caught my breath in a sharp *oh* of surprise and delight, but then Xan came close behind me and put his big hands over my eyes.

'Are you ready?' he murmured, and his breath was warm against my ear. He turned me through a half-circle again, so that I was facing the way we had come in.

'Ready,' I answered and his hands lifted.

I blinked, and stared. Ahead of us, framed and cut off from the rest of the world by the dunes, lay the Pyramids. I had never seen them from this viewpoint and it was as if the three great tombs were ours alone.

Xan took the greatcoat from my shoulders. The fire was warm on my ankles and bare arms.

'Do you like it?' he asked.

I turned my head from the view, meeting his eyes, trying to find a word. 'Yes,' I whispered.

He undid the canvas bag he had brought with him and took out a bottle of champagne tied up in an ice bag. He peeled off the foil and eased the cork. Then he burrowed in the bag again, produced two tin mugs and handed them to me. I held them out as he popped the cork and the silvery froth ran into the mugs. We clinked them together.

'Sorry about the glasses. But this is the desert, not Shepheard's Hotel.'

'I would rather be here with you, looking at the Pyramids and drinking champagne from a tin mug, than anywhere else in the world.'

'Really?' His face suddenly glowed in the candlelight.

'Yes.'

I was amazed that Xan had taken such pains to surprise me, and that this evening was so important to him. He had planned it so perfectly that we stepped straight from the Cairo cocktail circuit into another world, and he was as eager for my approval as a young boy.

In actual years Xan couldn't have been more than twenty-five or -six, just three or four years older than me, and I guessed that in other important ways we were contemporaries.

He was probably more experienced with women than I was with men, but neither of us had ever felt anything as momentous as this.

We were not-quite children together. And we were also immortal.

How could we not be?

I lifted the tin mug to my lips. 'Here's to us,' I said.

'Here's to us,' he echoed.

He took my arm and drew me to the heap of cushions next to the brazier. 'Are you warm enough? Are you comfortable?'

Ripples of coral-pink silk were crushed between us. I rested my head partly against the cushions and partly against Xan's shoulder, and saw how the Great Pyramid of Cheops sliced an angle of pitch blackness out of the desert sky.

'Yes.'

'Good. Iris?'

This was the first time he had spoken my name, rather than teasingly calling me Miss Black.

'Mm.'

'Talk to me. Tell me. Let me listen to your voice.'

This moment was a part of Xan's dreams. Perhaps when he lay in a scraped shelter in the desert, hungry and cold and suspended between remembered horrors and stalking danger, this was what he had allowed himself to imagine. It was the intimacy of talking with nothing held back, the sharp pang of desire mingled with the sweetness of trust. It was a dream that had become real tonight for both of us.

I reached up and touched his temple. A thin blue vein was just visible beneath the sun-darkened skin.

I told him about growing up as a diplomat's daughter, shuttled between embassies around the world with loving but distant parents.

In his turn, Xan told me about his father who had been a distinguished and decorated commander in the first war. In the years afterwards he had come out to Egypt to expand the family textiles empire, and Xan had spent much of his boyhood playing with the children of the family servants.

'So that's how you know Arabic so well.'

'Kitchen Arabic, yes. Then I was sent home to school, and after that on to Sandhurst. My father insisted that I was going to be a regular soldier and I was commissioned in 1938.'

'Where d'you call home?' I asked.

'Home?' Xan mused. The candle flames were reflected in his eyes. 'It's here,' he said at length.

'Cairo?'

'No, *here*.'

I understood that he meant our tent with its coloured hangings, the starry night outside and the two of us. I explored the significance of this, allowing it to swell and flower in my mind. I wanted the exact same thing but I was afraid that it was too much to ask.

'Why?' I ventured to ask and hated the break in my voice.

Xan propped himself on one elbow, his face just two inches from mine. 'Don't you know why, Iris?'

'I am not sure. I want to hear you say it.'

He smiled then, lazily confident of us. 'I saw you walking under the trees at that party, with Sandy Allardyce. I looked at you and I thought that I would give anything to be in Sandy's place. Then Faria Amman brought you across to our table and I felt so damned triumphant, as if it was the sheer force of my will-power that had brought you there.

'When I heard your voice, it was exactly how I knew it would be. Your smile too. It's not that I think I know you—that would be presumptuous—it's more that I have dreamed you. You have stepped straight out of a fantasy and become real. Does that sound idiotic? I expect every man who takes you out to dinner says the same thing.'

'No, they don't.'

I wanted to tell him that I understood what he meant. I wanted to be Xan's dream. The night was so perfect, I even believed that I could be.

'And now I see you aren't a phantom. It turns out that you have warm skin, and eyes brighter than stars. Your hair'—he twisted a lock of it round his finger—'smells of flowers. So this is where I want to be. This is what I want home to mean.'

His mouth was almost touching mine. As I closed my eyes, I heard several sets of footsteps scuffing through the sand outside the tent.

Xan sat up, grinning, and poured more champagne.

'Sayyid Xan?' a voice said, and Hassan's head appeared at the tent flap. I sat up straighter and smoothed my skirt over the cushions.

Two young boys followed Hassan into the tent, and they began setting out dishes and bowls. Hassan lifted the earthenware lid of the biggest pot and a cloud of fragrant steam escaped.

After they had withdrawn again, bowing and smiling, Xan put a bowl into my hands and ladled out the food. It was a thick stew of lamb with beans and tomato, and we sat turned towards each other on our bank of cushions and devoured it. I tore up chunks of bread and mopped the spicy sauce, then Xan took hold of my wrist and licked my fingers clean for me. He kissed each knuckle in turn and I noticed how his hair grew in different directions at the crown of his head. This tiny detail, more than anything else, made me want to touch him. And want him to touch me. I was almost frightened by how much I wanted it.

'Who is Hassan?' I asked. 'What is this place?'

'We played together when we were boys. Now we work together. Hassan knows the desert better than anyone else in Egypt.'

'Work', I guessed, would probably be for one of the secret commando raiding groups that operated between and behind enemy lines.

'That's very dangerous, isn't it?'

'This is a war.'

Both statements were true. There was nothing either of us could add, so we just looked at each other in the candlelight.

Then Xan leaned forward. 'I'm here now,' he whispered. 'We are here.'

I put my hand to his head as he kissed me, drawing him closer, and the whorl of unruly hair felt springy under the flat of my hand.

'We weren't going to talk about the war,' I said at last.

'No.' Xan smiled, then knelt upright and rummaged among the dishes. 'What have we got here?'

There was a bowl of dates, and a little dish of plump shelled almonds. He made me open my mouth and popped the food in piece by piece.

'Stop. I'll explode.'

In an old Thermos flask there was strong black coffee, and when everything else was finished we drank that from our tin mugs.

'Hassan and I have to leave again very early in the morning. I'll take you home now.'

I smiled at him, then leaned forward and gave him a lingering kiss. It took a serious effort of will to pull back again.

'That was the very best evening of my life,' I said.

'Was it? Do you mean that?'

'I do.'

'There will be more,' he promised. 'Hundreds, no, thousands more. A lifetime of evenings, and mornings and nights.'

I touched my fingers to his lips, stalling him for now. I couldn't ask where he was going, or when he would be back. All I could do was to send him off with the certainty that I would wait for him.

chapter two

RUBY SWUNG HER LEGS out of bed and went to the window. The view of the street was already becoming familiar.

Humming as she turned back again, she picked up a T-shirt and a pair of trousers from yesterday's heap that she had tipped out of her rucksack. She pulled on the clothes, then opened a drawer and scooped the remaining garments into it. The absolute bareness of the room was beginning to appeal to her; it looked much better without a bird's nest of belongings occupying the floor. She even straightened the covers on the bed before hurrying down the passageway to her grandmother's room. Her head was full of how she would start helping Iris to record her memories. They could start talking this morning, while they were eating their breakfast.

The door to Iris's room stood open. She skipped up to it, ready to call out a greeting, then stopped in her tracks. The window was shuttered and the only light came from a lamp beside the bed. Iris was lying on her back and Auntie was reaching over her to mop her forehead with a cloth. The air smelt sour, with a strong tang of disinfectant. When

Auntie moved aside Ruby saw that Iris's face was wax-pale, and the cheeks were sunken. It was as if she had died in the night.

Ruby's cheerful words dried up. She hovered in the doorway until Auntie half turned and saw her. At once she came at Ruby, making a shooing movement with her hands. Iris lay motionless.

'What's the matter? What's happened? Is she ill?'

The answer was a few mumbled words in Arabic and a push away from the door. Ruby could only retreat and head downstairs in search of Mamdooh. She found him in the kitchen at the back of the house.

'Is my grandmother very ill?'

Mamdooh pressed his lips together. 'Mum-reese has fever.'

'What does that mean?'

'Fever,' he repeated. And then, making a concession by way of further information, 'Doctor is coming. Now she must sleep.'

'Will she be all right?'

'*Inshallah*,' Mamdooh murmured, flicking his eyes towards the ceiling.

'Is there anything I can do to help?'

'Nothing, Miss.'

'All right.' She sighed. She knew something about sudden death but she had no idea about illness; it had never played any part in her life.

Ruby wandered out into the courtyard and sat for a few minutes on the stool next to Iris's empty chair, watching the way that sunlight turned the trickling water into a rivulet of diamonds. Soon she realised that she was very hungry indeed, and decided that it would be simpler to go out and buy herself something to eat rather than trying to negotiate Mamdooh and the kitchen. She checked that she had money in her trouser pocket and let herself out of the front door.

As soon as she started walking the heat enveloped her, and sweat prickled at the nape of her neck and in the hollow of her back. She kept to the shady side of the alleyway, following the route that Mamdooh had taken the day before. She had noticed plenty of little bakeries and coffee shops in the bazaar, she would buy some breakfast there.

The underpass led her to the edge of the maze. She hesitated, looking back over her shoulder as if someone might be tailing her, then hurried into the nearest alley where coffee was one of the stronger elements in the thick tangle of smells. But the narrow shops and piled barrows here were all crammed with plastic toys and knick-knacks.

A man blocked her path. 'This way. Just looking, very cheap.' When she tried to edge past him he caught her elbow and she had to shake him off. He yelled after her, 'Just looking, why not?'

She felt like shouting back that she didn't want a plastic tea set, that was why not, but the effort seemed too great. She pushed past the people immediately in front and a wave of protests washed after her. She turned hastily right and then just as quickly left, at random, trying to get away from the toy vendors.

In this area of the market the stallholders were selling clothes and shoes. Barrows were stacked high with Adidas nylon track suits and white trainers, and the walls were festooned with racks of shiny blouses and pairs of huge pink knickers and bras with bucket-sized cups. There were more women shoppers now, all with their heads and throats swathed in grey or white scarves, all with long-sleeved tops and skirts that hid their legs. The tourists she had noticed yesterday were conspicuously absent. Ruby was sure that everyone was staring at her. She felt increasingly grotesque. Her hair obscenely sprouted and frizzed in the damp heat and her breasts and arms seemed to bulge out of her T-shirt. She was too tall. Her skin was too pale and she was clammy with heat and rising panic.

She pushed forward, telling herself that somewhere not too far away there would be someone selling bottles of water. The shouts of the vendors and quarter tones of loud fuzzy music banged in her head.

She was gasping for breath as she stumbled out into a square that looked familiar. It was familiar—it was where Mamdooh had come yesterday, to meet his friends. There was the same coarse, dusty foliage and a pair of sun umbrellas rooted in pitted concrete cubes.

A group of men was gathered at an empty tin table. They weren't eating or drinking—that was because of Ramadan, Ruby had been told. But they weren't talking either. They just sat in a horseshoe, looking out into the hot white light. Looking at her.

She walked forward, thinking she could ask for help because they had seen her with Mamdooh. But none of the faces betrayed even a flicker of recognition. She hesitated, not sure now whether these really were Mamdooh's friends. Maybe it wasn't even the same square.

Ruby turned full circle, trying to work out which of a half-dozen alley mouths to make for. She had no idea.

Her glance passed across someone leaning against a wall a few yards away, then jerked back again. Here was a face she recognised. Where and when had she seen it before?

Yesterday, that was it. It was Nafouz's younger, handsomer brother.

He was slouching, one knee bent with the foot pressed against the wall behind him. He was also openly watching her.

Ruby marched up to him.

'I'm fucking glad to see you,' she said, trying to hide just how relieved she actually was. 'I'm completely, totally bloody lost.'

He looked slightly shocked at her language, but also pleased and—surprisingly—rather shy.

'I think you are lost,' he agreed, his nice smile showing his good teeth.

'Are you *following* me?'

'Why would I do that?'

He was still smiling so that she didn't know whether it was a straight question or a mocking one.

'How the fuck should I know?'

'You swear very much for an English girl, Ruby.'

'D'you have a problem with it?'

'It is not problem for me, no.'

'Right. Look, now you're here, can we go somewhere and buy a drink? I'm really thirsty.'

He pushed away from the wall. 'Of course. Please come this way.'

They made their way down a thin passageway with the old walls on either side leaning inwards so they seemed almost to touch at the top.

Ruby said, 'Um, I'm really sorry. I've forgotten your name.'

'It is Ashraf. You can call me Ash.'

'OK, then, Ash. Where are we going?'

'To a place the tourists like.' His smile flashed at her over his shoulder. He was definitely mocking her now, but she was too thirsty to bother with a response.

After a few more corners of the maze, they came to an entire lane that was filled with rickety chairs and tables, spilling out of the open doors of a café. Waiters with trays held at shoulder height threaded between the tables, plonking down cups and bottles and bills. Ash had been right about the tourists, because almost all of the people crammed into the alley were Westerners with cameras and bags of bazaar purchases. Mucus-faced urchins and Egyptian women with dark faces and glittering eyes worked the tables, trying to sell purses and lighters and packets of tissues. Ash took Ruby's hand and towed her through the crowd to a just-vacated table.

A waiter was already looming over them as she sank into a chair. She asked for a bottle of water and a cup of coffee and some yoghurt and then gestured to Ash. He shook his head without speaking.

'Sorry. Forgot,' Ruby sighed.

When the waiter came back, Ruby downed half the bottle of water.

'Why are you in Khan on your own?'

Ruby told him.

'I am sorry for your grandmother's illness,' he said. 'She will be well soon, *inshallah*.'

'Yeah. I hope so.'

Once she had quenched her thirst and spooned up some yoghurt, Ruby sat back and looked at Ash. He was very good-looking, with fine, almost feminine features and thick, long eyelashes. She reached out to the pack of Marlboro that showed in the pocket of his shirt.

'Can I bum one of these?'

'You are a woman. It is better not smoke in public.'

Ruby snorted, then clicked Ash's lighter to the cigarette. After inhaling deeply she said, 'So. No swearing or smoking. What am I allowed to do, according to you?'

Ash raised one eyebrow. 'Maybe come for a ride with me?'

'You've got a car?' It was an entrancing idea. She was dying to see Cairo beyond this isthmus of ancient streets but after her experience in the bazaar she would have preferred not to try it alone.

'I have my moby. You can be pillion passenger.'

'Moby? Oh, one of those bikes with engines. OK then.' Ruby scraped the last of the yoghurt out of the jar.

'You are still hungry I think.'

'Yeah, I am, actually.'

Ash stopped the waiter and asked him for something. While they waited they smoked and watched the tourists come and go.

A plate was put down in front of her. There were two fried eggs and a basket of flat bread. 'Perfect,' she crowed, and Ash looked pleased.

While she devoured the food he told her that he worked at night as a telephonist in a big hospital. 'Very good job,' he said.

He was also trying to improve his English, and saving up to pay for a computer study course. Nafouz was helping him, but they had to give money to their mother and younger brothers and sisters. Their father had died more than two years ago.

'May he rest with God,' Ash added.

Ruby put her knife and fork down on a clean plate, and picked up the bill the waiter had brought. She frowned at the blurry numerals.

'I would like to pay for you, but this place is not cheap,' Ash said awkwardly.

'Why should you pay for me?'

'Because I am a man.'

'I can pay for myself,' Ruby said. 'And you haven't eaten anything. Shall we go?'

They left the café and Ash led the way back to the underpass. It was surprisingly and disorientatingly close at hand.

Ash's bike was locked to a grille in the wall at the end of the narrow street leading straight to Iris's house and the big mosque.

'What's it doing parked right here? You *are* following me,' Ruby accused. 'Did you tail me all the way round that bloody bazaar?'

He only grinned and straddled the machine's seat, sliding his hips forward to make room for Ruby on the pillion. 'You are coming?'

'I suppose so. Just for half an hour. Then you've got to bring me back to check how my grandmother is, right?'

She sat primly upright at first, but then the little machine shot forward and she had to grab Ash round the waist in order not to fall off the back. He sped into the traffic, weaving in and out of taxis and buses.

'You like?' Ash howled at her over his shoulder.

'I hate,' she screamed back, but he only laughed.

They emerged into a vast square set about with tall buildings and with an inferno of endlessly revolving traffic trapped within it.

He waved a reckless arm at a low pink block. 'Egyptian Museum. Very famous.'

A moment later they shot out into slightly clearer air. Ruby saw branches and leaves against open sky as Ash swung the bike in a flashy circle and cut the engine to bring them coasting up against the kerb. Ruby sprang off, coughing and rubbing her eyes, and Ash locked the bike to a puny sapling rooted in the wide pavement. They were in a boulevard lined with trees. On the other side, beyond several lanes of traffic, was a low wall and then seemingly empty air.

'Come,' Ash commanded. He took her wrist and they darted into a gap between thundering buses.

Below and beyond the wall, there was water. It was a wide, swirling, grey-brown river and on it sailed a dozen little boats with slanting masts and graceful sails like unfurled handkerchiefs. Ruby leaned far out over the wall, looking at the vista of bridges spanning the water, towers and distant trees.

'Nile river,' Ash said at her side. 'That way'—he gestured— 'Alexandria. Then Europe. And that way'—he swept his left arm in a stately arc along the river—'Egypt.' For Ash, it seemed, the name was enough to convey the magnificence of his country.

'It's beautiful. I like the boats.'

'One evening I take you sailing in a felucca. At sunset. Very romantic.'

They began walking, their hands occasionally brushing together. They passed beneath a huge, ancient-looking tree, its trunk a mass of writhing tendrils for all the world like dun-coloured snakes.

'Banyan tree.'

They stopped and looked up into the canopy of coarse leaves. Ash's throat was smooth, his skin pale brown. Ruby stepped up close, put her hands behind his head and pulled his mouth down to hers. She kissed him hard.

She saw the flash of dismay and disbelief in his eyes before he stepped sharply backwards.

'Why you do that?' he demanded.

'Didn't you like it?'

He had liked it, of course, but it was not what he had planned.

Ash had intended to make a play for the English girl, that went without saying, but he had expected to chase her and when she finally gave way the triumph would all have been his. Now she had taken the initiative and he felt diminished. He had no idea what to expect next.

They were now both aware of the breadth of experience and expectation that separated them, and they were uncomfortable.

'You have boyfriends,' Ash said flatly.

Ruby tried to give a careless laugh, but it came out sounding harsh.

'Yeah. What do you expect? Yes, I do. Have had.'

He nodded. 'I see.'

She didn't like his disapproval and tried to startle him back into sympathy with her. 'No, you don't. My boyfriend died. In an accident.'

'What? Accident in a car?'

'No. He fell. He fell off the balcony of someone's flat. It was late at night, a party. He had been drinking and taking stuff. I didn't see how he fell. Maybe he jumped, I don't know. He was a bit fucked up. His name was Jas.'

Ash shook his head. This information was almost too much for him, but he took her hand gently and led her a few steps to a bench facing the river wall. They sat down with their backs to the traffic and stared at the ugly cylinder hotel across the water.

'Did you love him, this Jas? Did he love you?'

He asked this so simply and tenderly, and his directness seemed to flick a switch in Ruby. She almost heard the click. Without any warning tears welled up in her eyes and poured down her face.

'Maybe. Yes. It wasn't like you think.'

'I think nothing,' Ash said.

Ruby knuckled her eyes and sniffed hard. She tried not to cry, as a general rule. Not about Jas, or anything else. She usually tried not to think about Jas being dead either, except as a bare fact, but now she couldn't stop the thoughts—or the images that came with them.

The flat had been on the ninth floor of a tower block on the edge of a no-man's-land of railway sidings and warehouses. There were a lot of people in the flat. Two girls had been arguing about the music that was playing, and one of them had snatched a CD and flung it at the wall. Her boyfriend had given her a shaking and when he pushed her away from him, she fell sideways on one of the mattresses on the floor.

Ruby was sitting on the other, with her knees drawn up to her chest like a shield. She had been wanting to go home for a while, or at least somewhere that wasn't this place, and wondering how to negotiate an exit. She was dimly aware that Jas had moved away but she felt too out of it herself to pay any attention to what he might be doing. The next thing was a shout, and a ripple of movement as several people stumbled towards the door onto a balcony.

Ruby found herself following them. Cold air blew towards her, and the few steps seemed to take a long time. The balcony was small. The walls were brick, topped with gritty stone. A white-faced bloke was holding on to the stone as if he was on a ship in a bad storm, and a girl was half turned away with her hand over her mouth. Ruby walked very slowly to the wall and looked over.

A long way down, Jas was lying on his side with his head and his arms and his legs all at weird angles. There was a dark pool spreading round his head. Just in one glance you could tell he was dead.

The girl took her hand from her mouth and started to babble. 'I just sort of turned. I saw his legs and his feet, falling.'

When the police arrived, there wasn't much she could tell them. It was that that shocked her, really. She knew his name, and the address of the house where he squatted. He came from Sunderland, and he liked curry and Massive Attack. He had made her a CD compilation and decorated the insert with red Biro swirls.

It wasn't very much. It wasn't very much for a life that was now over.

The police drove her back from the police station to Will and Fiona's house in Camden. She hoped that no one would be awake yet so she could slide into her bedroom without being seen.

But Will was up. He was coming down the stairs, wearing a suit and a blue shirt and red tie, his cheeks and jaw shiny from his morning shave.

'Fi's still asleep. Where have you been all night?'

He was in a position to ask the question because he was her stepfather's brother, so she was part family as well as part lodger. But they were also conspirators because when they were alone Will didn't always treat her like family. Ruby thought he was rather pathetic, but she had taken advantage of the situation in the past. Being in a conspiracy with

Will meant she could get away with things that he and Fiona, as a fully united front, would never have allowed.

But not any longer. Not after this night.

She blinked, and her eyes burned with the image of Jas lying at the foot of the high-rise.

'Um. I went to a party.'

Will looked angry, in his plump way. 'It's five to six in the morning and you're supposed to go to college today.'

'I know,' Ruby mumbled. 'Sorry.'

He sighed. Then he put his hand under her chin and tilted her face so he could examine it. She felt too numb to break away from him, or to do anything but stand there. Will sighed again and then his hand slid over her bottom but he gently pushed her away at the same time, as if it were she who had come on to him. He was very good at making things appear the opposite of what they really were.

'Go on, then. Go upstairs and get into bed, before Fi catches you. I've got to get to the airport.'

Ruby went up the stairs, very slowly. Her feet felt as if they had rocks tied to them. In her bedroom she took off her clothes and crawled under the bedcovers and pulled them over her.

As soon as she closed her eyes Jas was lying there with the black puddle spreading round his head.

She told Ash briefly about Jas. It wasn't right, she realised as soon as she had begun, to use it as a way of getting his sympathy. Her tears were drying up, leaving her eyes feeling sticky in the heat.

'Anyway,' she said, and shrugged. She stood up quickly, pulling at her clothes where they were glued to her skin. After a second he got up too, still looking at her with gentle concern.

'That is very sad. I am sorry,' he said. 'What would you like to do now? Do you want to go back to your grandmother's house?'

She didn't want to cry again, for one thing, didn't even want to think about crying. It was all too dangerous.

'Can we just go on with what we were doing before?'

They walked on, under the dusty leaves, in and out of patches of shade. Ash waited for what she would do or say next.

'Don't you have a girlfriend?'

He considered carefully. 'Of course, there are some girls I like. But it is not quite the same thing, I think.'

His solemnity made Ruby laugh. She still wanted to make him like her and the wish surprised her.

'It was only a quick kiss, back there, you know? I just thought it would be nice. Sorry if it was the wrong thing. I get things wrong all the time, it's the way I am. You'll have to get used to it if we're going to be friends.'

Ash stopped again. He looked over his shoulder at the traffic and at the passers-by, then he steered Ruby into an angled niche in the river wall where an ornate street lamp sprouted.

'*I* would like to kiss *you*, now, please.'

She leaned back. The stone was hot against her ribs and spine.

'Go on, then.'

'Wait. To me, these things have importance. They are not just a quick this, or for nothing that. Perhaps you think to be this way is funny?'

'No,' Ruby said humbly. 'I think it's lovely.'

'All right.' He came nearer. Close up, there were all kinds of different textures and colours visible in the dark brown irises.

He kissed her, an experimental meeting of mouths that seemed, to Ruby, very tentative. Then he pulled back again.

'Good,' he said.

'Thank you.'

Feeling rather pleasingly chaste, she resumed her walk at his side. After a little way they turned aside from the river and wandered through a quiet area of curving streets with enclosed gardens. Ash and Ruby let their hands brush more often as they walked.

'This is Garden City. Nice place, for rich people.'

'Where do you live? Is it near here?'

Ash laughed, a little awkwardly. 'It is not like this, my home.'

'I don't know anything about Cairo.'

'I will show you.'

Later they came out alongside the river again. An island, separated from the mainland only by a narrow channel, lay directly opposite. Ash told her it was called Rhoda, pointing out the landmarks and telling her little pieces of history. Ruby nodded dutifully. They had been walking for a long time and the sky was already fading from blue to pale grey.

'It's time I went back,' she said.

They turned north, walking towards the Tahrir Bridge. When they reached the place where Ash had left the bike, lights were beginning to twinkle on the bridges and the buildings across the river. The sunset sky was streaked with gold and pale green.

'It's beautiful,' Ruby sighed.

Ash took her arm. 'I have an idea. A special, very special Cairo view, just for you. You have to tell a small lie, but I think you can do that?'

She gave him a warning look. 'Maybe.'

He was marching her through the torrent of traffic and through a gateway into some gardens. A huge hotel loomed over them, and a line of shiny cars snaked up to the doors.

'You stay in places like this?'

'I have done,' she admitted.

'So you know what to do.'

As the revolving door disgorged them into a glass-and-marble lobby, a doorman in a tarboosh and white baggy trousers worn with a sash and a red waistcoat stepped in front of them.

'I am staying in the hotel. Room 806,' Ruby said firmly.

'Good evening,' he murmured and stepped back again.

Heads up, they walked past the brocade armchairs and the fountain to the lifts. Ash was chuckling.

They swept up to the top floor and stepped out into a mirrored lobby. There was a murmur of voices, tinkling piano music and glasses.

'Please close your eyes,' Ash ordered.

He took her hand and led her from carpet to paving. They were outside again, with a breeze fanning Ruby's face. A little spasm of fear ran down her spine as she wondered how close the edge was.

'You are safe,' Ash breathed in her ear. He steered her a few more steps, then halted. 'Now, open.'

She looked. They were in a garden on the roof of the hotel. Below them, far below, was the dusk-blue higgledy-piggledy mass of Cairo. The sun had set but the sky was blazing gold and orange.

'Do you see?' Ash murmured. His arm was round her shoulders, she could smell his skin.

'Yes.' She thought he meant just the view. But then, at the exact point where the dusty glitter of the city met the fiery sky, she saw three sharp triangular cut-outs pasted against the glow. '*Oh.*'

Ruby leaned forward, taking in her first glimpse of the Pyramids. They looked so close, almost part of the city itself. She had always imagined the Pyramids surrounded by empty seas of sand.

'You like it?'

'Yes. I like it very much.'

The sky was fading. The pianist in the rooftop bar played more loudly and guests in evening dress drifted out to look at the view.

'We have to go,' Ash muttered.

Outside on the street again, it was night-time. Hand in hand, Ruby and Ash walked back to the bike. She felt quite comfortable this time, sitting close up to Ash with her arms tight round his waist, as they swooped through the traffic on the way home.

He stopped where Nafouz had drawn up in the taxi, only forty-eight hours ago.

'Thank you for a nice day,' Ruby said, realising with a shock just how long she had been out.

He touched her cheek with his fingers. 'I will come again?'

'Yeah. I mean yes, I'd like you to.'

'I am your Cairo boyfriend?'

When Nafouz made the same suggestion she had laughed at him. But Ash's wanting to set out the terms in this way made Ruby feel shy in a way that she hadn't done since she was twelve.

'If you want to be.' I am *blushing*, she realised.

He leaned over and kissed her in the same tentative way.

'How will I hear from you?' she asked.

His eyes widened. 'I will be here. I find you.'

'See you, then.'

She rapped hard on the sun-blistered door of Iris's house, and heard Ash accelerating away.

The door swung open.

'Miss. You have been away many hours,' Mamdooh said.

'Sorry. I . . .'

'Sorry not good enough. You make Mum-reese worry, Auntie worry, and myself.' He was breathless with anger.

Auntie came down the inner staircase and darted straight at Ruby. Ruby braced herself for another rebuke, but Auntie took her hands and lifted them, pressing the knuckles to her own mouth. Her eyes were almost hidden in the fans of wrinkles but there were tears at the corners.

'I'm really sorry,' Ruby began.

She had said the same words often enough before, but Auntie's tears made her feel something different. Or maybe it was remembering Jas, or all the impressions of the day piling up inside her. Without warning she started crying again herself, beginning with a dry sob and then the tears breaking out as if something hard had burst inside her.

Instantly, Auntie gathered her in her arms. She held Ruby like an infant, murmuring in Arabic and patting her hands and rubbing her arms. Mamdooh put a very big, clean handkerchief into her hand.

'You have had trouble today? Someone has tried to hurt you?'

'No, no. I made a friend. His name is Ashraf, his brother is the taxi driver, and he . . . he works in the Bab al-Futuh Hospital. He showed me Garden City and a view of the Pyramids from the top of a hotel. I didn't mean to stay out so long. How is my grandmother?'

'She is resting.'

'Can I go up and see her?'

The old people held her between them now, one on either side.

'First you must have food. After, you can take some tea for her. It is better you are not crying.'

Ruby understood the sense of that. And the breakfast of two eggs she had eaten in Khan al-Khalili was a long time ago.

The kitchen was quite cosy in the light from a pair of oil lamps, and there was a good smell of food. Mamdooh laid out spoons and three brown bowls, Auntie brought out a blackened pot from the oven. Flat bread was laid on a wooden platter, and coarse salt in a smaller bowl.

They all sat down together. Ruby reached for the bread at once, then realised that the two old people were watching her, waiting for something. She wondered blankly what it could be, and then it struck her.

'Forwhatweareabouttoreceive,' she mumbled, 'maytheLordmakeustrulythankful.'

This seemed to fit the bill. They were being respectful of her religion. Mamdooh nodded gravely, then lifted the lid off the pot.

It had been quite a day, one way and another, Ruby thought. She had been kissed as if she had been playing Spin the Bottle at a kids' party, and she had said grace.

Mamdooh noticed the smile that transformed her. 'That is better. Now please eat some of this very good food.'

It was good. Chickpeas and tomatoes, and some thick but tender meat. In reply to Mamdooh's questions she told them a little about Ash and where they had spent the day.

Afterwards, Ruby carried the plates to the sink and Auntie showed her how they were to be washed and dried, and where to put them away.

Mamdooh prepared a tray. There was the little silver teapot and a bunch of fresh mint leaves, sugar and a glass cup in a worn silver holder. There was also two medicine bottles, a glass and some pills.

'You like to come up now, Miss, to Mum-reese?'

Ruby said good night to Auntie, who wrapped her arms round her again and showed her few remaining teeth in a wide smile. Ruby guessed that they had both forgiven her.

The lamp was on beside Iris's bed, but the rest of the room was dim. Her eyes had been closed, but as soon as Mamdooh came in with Ruby behind him she opened them. At first, the expression was blank. If there was anything in the depths, it was bewilderment. But then Iris saw Ruby. Her lips moved and she tried to sit up against the pillows.

'There you are,' she said.

How long have I been ill this time?

I have had the lurid, monstrous dreams of a high fever, but not so many of them. I am sure it was only this morning that the doctor came, the young Frenchman called Nicolas Grosseteste. He thinks I am old and frail, but I am not quite as frail as he believes. My immune system is weakened from many years of living in equatorial climates and I am susceptible to fevers. But I feel better tonight. Seeing the child makes me feel better.

Mamdooh gives me a glass of tea. I take the medicine bottles from him and read the label. There is a broad-spectrum antibiotic, and linctus for my chest. So Nicolas doesn't think that I am about to die either.

'Thank you. Ruby will sit with me, Mamdooh. She can help me to get ready for bed.'

He wishes us good night and goes away, closing the door. I sip my tea. Ruby looks less sulky than she did—when—yesterday?

'Talk to me,' I order. And then it comes over me, warm, loosening my limbs like a shot of pethidine, the luxury of it.

Talk to me. How long since I have said that to a living soul?

'Um. What about?'

'Whatever you like.'

'Well. You know what? I saw the *Pyramids* today.'

'You went out to Giza?'

'No. I don't think so. From the top of a hotel by the Nile.'

'Ah, yes. What did you think?'

'Amazing. I didn't know they were in the middle of all the houses, though.'

She looks so pleased with this adventure. I reach for her hand and at once she sandwiches mine between hers.

'They're not, not really. When I am on my feet again, we'll go out to Giza. I'll show you a different view.'

'That'll be cool.'

We sit here, hands linked, considering our different visions of the pharaohs' tombs. I am suddenly overcome with tiredness and ask Ruby to help me into bed.

Only a week after our dinner overlooking the Pyramids, Xan took me to a fancy-dress party. We had seen each other every day, for swimming at the Gezira Club and cocktails at Shepheard's, and for dinners in restaurants that we both agreed came nowhere near our tent in the desert for food or ambiance. We went dancing, and we met one another's friends. We also sat for hours in quiet corners, holding hands and telling each other our histories.

Xan and I decided to go to the costume party as Paris and Helen of Troy. Xan went to the toy department at Cicurel's and acquired a tin breastplate, a shield and a helmet with a stiff red horsehair plume. He completed the outfit with sandals, a toga made from a bedsheet and a cavalryman's dress sword.

My costume was a white strapless evening gown borrowed from Faria and accessorised with the long metal pole that Mamdooh used to open the top shutters in our flat. From one end of the pole I hung a little carved wooden ship with the number 1 painted on each side. At the other end was a much bigger model launch, also borrowed via Faria from one of her numerous nephews and labelled 999. I wore a huge hat made of two cardboard cut-outs of the *Queen Mary* that Xan had spotted in the window of a travel agent's near Shepheard's, with 1000 painted on the sides.

The party was given by three of his friends in a flat in Zamalek, quite near where Xan himself lived. We were surrounded by familiar faces. Sarah was there, dressed as Little Bo-peep with her blonde hair in ringlets, and brandishing a shepherd's crook. Sandy Allardyce wore a cardinal's robes and even Roddy Boy loomed into view, wearing an eye-patch and with one arm tucked inside an admiral's coat.

'Hello, there,' my boss greeted me, dodging the pole and the dangling ships. 'Most appropriate costume, Miss Black, if I may be so bold.'

'Thank you, Colonel.'

'Are you a friend of David's?' he boomed. David was one of our hosts, an associate of Xan's with a mysterious war job.

'I've only just met him. Xan Molyneux brought me along.'

Roddy Boy's eyes flicked over me. 'Ah. Yes,' was all he said.

Jessie James floated up. From somewhere, somehow, in the middle of Cairo in the midst of a war, he had acquired a choirboy's white surplice and starched ruff.

'Darling, beautiful Helen of the thousand ships. Can't we run away together and leave that bastard Molyneux behind? Or at least come and dance with me to this vile music?'

'Evening, James,' Roddy Boy said.

'Hello, there,' Jessie murmured as he swept me away. We propped my pole of dangling ships in the corner and edged into the throng of dancers.

So Xan and I were surrounded by friends and people we knew, but we were in another place too. It was a small, sweet, vivid and waiting world that contained only the two of us. As the party separated us and then washed us together again, we would catch one another's eyes and everything else faded into monochrome.

On one occasion, when I had battled my way to the kitchen for a glass of water, Xan came up behind me. His hands slid down on my hips and his breath fanned my neck.

'I want to touch you all over. I want to taste every inch of you. Are you going to make me wait, Iris?'

I turned round to face him, stretching on tiptoe to bring our eyes level. 'No,' I said. 'I can't wait.'

We emerged into the short-lived, dewy cool of predawn and walked hand in hand through the deserted streets to his flat. The place was empty and silent. It was the first time I had been there and I took in its temporary, makeshift atmosphere.

'Except for Jessie, everyone is away at the moment,' Xan said.

We touched our fingertips together, briefly, superstitiously.

His bedroom was bare, the bed itself narrow and hard.

Then he took me in his arms. His tongue traced a course from my mouth to my collarbone, lingered there and then moved downwards.

I had had several lovers, Xan more than several, but for me what followed was nothing like sex with the polite, awkward boys I had half enjoyed in London. It was unlike anything I had ever known, and it was wonderful. I didn't know you could laugh and cry at the same time, and feel that strangeness of another body within yours and yet love and trust every fibre of it.

Afterwards Xan gathered me against him and we looked a long way into each other's eyes.

'I love you, Iris Black,' he said.

'Xan Molyneux, I love you too.'

The next afternoon, Ruby opened the front door, which had been firmly closed by Mamdooh before he came to tell her she had visitors, and found Ash and Nafouz waiting at the foot of the steps.

'Ruby, hello,' said Ash, running up the steps. 'We come with my brother's car. We take you for a tour, you know?'

'We-ell . . .' Ruby longed to go, but then she thought of leaving Iris on her own. 'I can't. My grandmother kind of needs me right now.'

'I am sorry. Your grandmother is ill today also?'

'No, she's much better. But she should have some company.'

Ash smiled. He really was good-looking, Ruby thought again.

'Then this is not a problem. Nafouz?' He beckoned his brother forward. 'Nafouz and I, we like to take you *and* the lady for a nice ride.'

Ruby blinked at this. It was certainly the first time any of her boyfriends had offered to double-date with her grandmother.

'Please to ask her,' Nafouz joined in.

'OK, then. Hang on here. I'll go and find out if she wants to.'

Iris was sitting in the garden, where Ruby had left her.

'You probably won't want to do this,' Ruby began, but Iris tilted her head and looked sharply at her.

'Whatever it is, I think you should let me decide for myself.'

Ruby told her about Ash and Nafouz and the taxi. Iris listened carefully and then her face split into a smile.

'A very good idea,' she said briskly. 'I shall certainly come. Will you call Auntie for me?'

Five minutes later, with her head swathed in a white scarf and a pair of black sunglasses hiding half her face, Iris declared that she was ready.

Auntie and Mamdooh came out with them. Mamdooh had put his tarboosh on his head to walk down the steps, and was trying to get Iris to lean on him for support.

'I can walk,' Iris insisted.

Ash and Nafouz had been lounging against the wall opposite, but when they saw Iris and her retinue they stood respectfully upright.

'How do you do?' Iris said clearly, sounding rather like the Queen and making Ruby begin a cringe. But the two boys bowed and murmured their names and pointed to the black-and-white taxi.

'Please to come this way, Madam,' Nafouz said.

'We shall be back later, Mamdooh, thank you,' Iris said. She let Nafouz escort her to the car. She sat up in the front seat beside him, Ash and Ruby scrambled into the back.

'Where would you like to go?' Nafouz asked Iris.

'Downtown, I think,' she answered. She settled back in her seat and drew her scarf round her throat.

I do leave the house of course, once in a while, but this time feels different. There is the charming but no doubt opportunist brother beside me, Ruby and her beau whispering in the back seat, the air thick with the speculative negotiations of youthful sexual activity. This should make me feel old, but it has the opposite effect.

As we turn into Sharia el Bustan I am thinking that I must discuss contraception with Ruby. I never had such a conversation with Lesley. Or if I did I have forgotten it, along with everything else. Maybe I can be a better grandmother than I was a mother.

Maybe it is the recognition that there is still something I can learn how to be that makes me suddenly feel so buoyant.

Avoiding the feeder road for the Tahrir Bridge the boy swings the car left down the Corniche and a minute later we pass in front of the walls of the embassy. Once, the gardens stretched down to the bank of the Nile. Here are the trees that shaded the afternoon tea parties of my childhood. I half turn to tell Ruby this but she and the boy are murmuring together, deaf to everything else.

Now we turn left again. I know these shuttered, curving streets so well. The boy raises one eyebrow at me and I nod.

He has me neatly pigeonholed. He knows Garden City is where I lived, it is where most of us British lived in those days. Tended gardens, elaborate wrought-iron gates and grilles, ceiling fans turning the humid air in the afternoons. The car rolls slowly past the ghosts, past the blind windows that shield more recent histories.

I am glad when we emerge again into Qasr el Aini and this time head over the bridge. The sun is going down, and coloured lights glimmer in the river water as we reach the island.

'I have forgotten your name. Forgive me?' I say to the driver.

He flips me a smile. A flirtatious smile, for God's sake. 'Nafouz. What is yours?'

'Dr Black.'

'You are medical doctor?'

'I was. I am retired now.'

'I am taxi driver only but my brother Ash is working in hospital, operating switchboard.'

'You both speak good English.'

'We try,' Nafouz agrees. 'We learn.'

The layout of these Gezira streets is familiar, the buildings less so. The ugly lattice of the Cairo Tower looms on one side, on the other is the wall of lush trees that shade the Gezira Club grounds. Nafouz turns left and we approach the gates. Sixty years drop away and I am in a taxi on my way to meet Xan.

I remember cotton sundresses and shady hats, uniforms and cocktails and the *plock* of tennis balls, Xan waiting for me in the bar as I arrived from a day's work at my desk in Roddy Boy's outer office.

Xan saying, 'Darling, let's have a drink. I've got to go away again tomorrow. It's a bit of a bore, isn't it?'

The enclave of empire that I knew, the shady mown-grass sanctuary of British assumptions and attitudes has vanished long ago. The people are all dead. I am still here but I am as much of an anachronism as tea dances and air-raid warnings.

I am still here. Instead of making me sad, the thought fills me with a reckless appetite. I pull off my sunglasses. 'Let's go to Groppi's,' I say.

Nafouz asks, 'Are you sure, Doctor?'

I insist, very brightly, 'Certainly I am sure.'

So the four of us find ourselves sitting at a table in the little café garden of Groppi's.

Once, everyone in Cairo who could afford it came here. Ladies in furs sat at these little round tables drinking tea with men with silky moustaches, and officers ordered cream cakes for their girls.

It's dusty and neglected now, with an unswept floor and waiters in dirty jackets. The two boys are hungry and Ruby looks bored.

'What would you all like? What shall we order?' I say encouragingly, looking at the menu, a dreary plastic-laminated affair sticky with fingerprints. The two boys are smoking, giving each other looks out of the corners of their liquid eyes. Ruby leans forward to help herself from one of the packs on the table.

'Does Lesley let you do that?'

She gives a sharp cough of laughter and smoke pours from between her teeth. Her odd mixture of childishness and bravado tickles me, and I find myself laughing too. The atmosphere changes and we order toasted sandwiches, and coffees and pastries and bottles of Coca-Cola. It is after sundown so the boys break their Ramadan fast with gusto and the strange meal somehow becomes what I wanted, a celebration.

They tell me about their family. Father dead, several younger siblings whom they must help their mother to support. Ruby's beau is the clever one, the one they are banking on. He looks very young to carry such a weight of responsibility.

'I learn to speak English, and also some computer studies. But it is not easy to pay for teaching.'

And he meets my eyes. They have seen where I live and they probably think I am rich. In fact I am poor, certainly by European standards. I murmur in Arabic, a conventional piety.

The table top is pooled with coffee and there are still little cakes glistening with sugar to be eaten but Nafouz is tapping his watch.

'Time for work. We are both night shift.'

I call for, and pay, the enormous bill. It is a long time since I have been to a café, much longer since I have paid for four people at once. Before everyone stands up I say, 'Thank you for this evening, Nafouz. Thank you, Ash. I enjoyed it very much.'

This is the truth. It has helped me to see the today versions of yesterday's places. The old Groppi's I knew, like Cairo itself, has been overlaid by the present version. Because I am here, seeing it as it is now, I realise that there is nothing mysterious or fearful in this. Of course I can't catch and keep everything. I can only strive for what is important; my memories of Xan.

On the way back to the taxi the boys take my arms, as if I am their own grandmother. I am glad of the support because I am very tired. On the way home, I look out at the lights and the thick crowds in the streets. Nafouz has yet another cigarette clenched between his teeth.

Behind me, I can hear Ruby and Ash whispering on the back seat. When we reach the house they say goodbye to each other offhandedly, in the way that the young do, not making another arrangement because it's understood that they will meet again just as soon as possible. I feel a thin stab of envy, and then amusement at the nonsense of this.

Mamdooh and Auntie seem actually to have been waiting in the hall-way for our return. At any rate, they spring from nowhere as soon as Ruby and I come in.

With the afternoon's change of perspective I notice how we have become interdependent, the three of us, over the years. I need them and they need me to need them.

'We have had an excellent outing. A drive, then Groppi's.'

An idea has just formed in my head and I keep it fixed there as I unpin my headscarf and hand it to Auntie. 'We'll have some tea later, upstairs. Ruby, Mamdooh, will you come with me?'

Ruby shuffled in their wake to Iris's study. Mamdooh was trying to insist that Mum-reese should rest, Iris sailed ahead with the absent but intent look on her face that Ruby was beginning to recognise.

'I think there is a box in there.' Iris pointed to a pair of cupboard doors painted with faded white birds and garlands of leaves.

'A box?' Mamdooh frowned, opening the doors.

'Exactly. There it is.' Iris pointed.

Mamdooh lifted a pile of dusty books, some sheaves of printed music and an old-fashioned clothes brush off the lid of a dark green tin box. It had handles on the sides and he stooped and puffed a little as he hauled it off the shelf. The dust that rose when he dumped it on the desk indicated that it hadn't been disturbed for a very long time.

Iris undid a bolt and threw back the lid. Ruby glanced at the disap-pointing jumble inside. Among brittle newspapers were a couple of tar-nished metal cups, a big bunch of keys and a brown envelope. There was a musty smell of forgotten times.

'Can you carry it upstairs, or is it too heavy?' Iris asked, turning her face up to Mamdooh.

'I can carry,' he said at once.

Mamdooh put the box on a wooden table in Iris's sitting room and closed the shutters, then turned to see that Iris was already burrowing through the contents. He gave Ruby a look that suggested she was responsible for all this disruption and backed out through the door.

Ruby settled herself among the cushions on the divan and picked up the manila envelope. A handful of curling black-and-white snapshots fell out and she examined them eagerly. This was more like it. They weren't very interesting, though. In one, a group of white men stood in front of a low mud-brick building. In another some black men were putting a roof on what looked like the same building.

'What are all these?'

Iris glanced up from her excavations in the box. 'Let me have a look. That is Nyasaland in, I suppose, 1958. That building is a clinic, and those two men are the district commissioner and the regional medical director. I worked in the clinic for six years.'

'Lesley was four. She told me.'

'Yes. She was born in '54.'

Ruby had heard Lesley talk about how she was brought up by her father and nannies, while her mother 'looked after black kids in Africa'. When she mentioned her childhood, which wasn't very often, Lesley tended to look brave and cheerful.

Ruby felt suddenly curious about an aspect of her family history that had never interested her before. 'Why did you go to work in Africa when you had a husband and a daughter in England?'

'It was my job,' Iris said.

'But didn't you miss them?'

'I had home leave. And once she was old enough Lesley would come out to stay with me in the school holidays.'

'She told me about that. She said her friends would be going to like Cornwall, or maybe Brittany, while she would have to make this huge journey with about three changes of plane and at the end there would be a bush village and terrible heat and bugs, and not much to do.'

'That sounds like it, yes.'

It occurred to Ruby then that there was an unbending quality about Iris that being old hadn't mellowed at all. She would always have been like this. Uncompromising, was that the word?

'You remember everything,' Ruby said, softly but accusingly.

Iris seemed to have found whatever it was she had been looking for in the depths of the tin box. She pounced and her fingers closed over something. Then she lifted her head and Ruby saw the distant expression that meant she was looking inside herself.

'Do I?'

'Nyasaland, the men and dates, everything.'

Now Ruby saw in her grandmother's face the grey shadow of fear.

'Those things are only . . . Like so many plain cups on shelves. You can reach for them, use them without thinking. Most of them don't matter, like what I remember of those photographs. Sometimes you lose your grip on one of them and it falls and smashes to pieces, and you shrug and say to yourself, what a pity.

'Then you reach for a cup that you use every day, one that you love and use so often that as you stretch out your hand it is already making the shape that fits its curve. You are certain that yesterday it was in its proper place, but now there is nothing. Just air. You have lost something that was so familiar, so much a part of your life that you were not even looking for it. Just expecting it to be there, as always.

'That's the way the important memory feels, the one you don't want to lose. And it's the fragment of your past that explains why you have lived your life the way you have done. And made the mistakes that you have made. Do you understand any of this?'

Ruby hesitated. 'A little. Maybe.'

'You are very young. There's not much on your shelves and you don't know what's going to be precious. It's not until you're old that you find yourself hugging the cup all day long. Afraid to put it down.'

That's what she's doing, Ruby thought, when she goes into a trance and doesn't hear what you're saying to her. She's holding on to the precious cup, in case it's not there the next time she goes to look for it.

Ruby suddenly stood up. She left the room, and Iris seemed too wrapped in her own reverie even to notice. Her head lifted in surprise when Ruby came noisily back, as if she had actually forgotten she had ever been there. Ruby held out the framed photograph that she had taken from its place beside Iris's bed. 'Who is this?'

She was half expecting an evasion, because whoever he was, the man in the photograph was important. Most definitely he wasn't Iris's husband, Ruby's grandfather Gordon.

Instead, something remarkable happened. Iris's face completely changed. Warm colour swelled under her crepy skin and flushed her throat as she held out one hand for the picture. The other fist was still closed round whatever she had taken from the tin box.

Very carefully, Ruby passed the photograph to her. Iris gazed down into the man's face.

'Who?' Ruby persisted.

Instead of answering Iris opened her hand, the one that didn't hold the picture. In the palm lay a toy ship carved from some dark wood. A white numeral 1 was painted on each side.

'The first of a thousand ships.' Iris smiled. Now even her voice sounded softer and younger, with the vinegary snap gone out of it.

Ruby had no idea what she was talking about. She knelt down and examined the ship as it lay in her grandmother's palm. It was old, but it didn't look remarkable. She picked it up and placed it carefully on the arm of Iris's chair. Then she took the photograph back, noticing how Iris gave it up with infinite reluctance. She studied the two young faces and saw that they were dazzled with happiness.

Iris said slowly, in her different voice, 'His name was Alexander Napier Molyneux, Captain in the 3rd Hussars, on secondment to Tellforce. That picture was taken in October 1941, on the day that Xan asked me to marry him.'

Ruby was delighted with this information. 'Did you say yes?'

'I did.'

She waited for more, but Iris was silent. Gently Ruby put the photograph aside and folded Iris's hands in hers.

'Are you afraid of forgetting him?'

'I never kept diaries, you see. I was so certain of my mind. And now it's going. Sometimes I reach and there is nothing there.'

Ruby tightened her grip on Iris's hands. 'You *can* remember. I know you can, because of the photographs and the ship. You told me about those without even thinking. You've just told me about Xan Molyneux, haven't you? It's there, Iris, I know it is. And I know what we have to do. It's just *talking*. You have to tell me the stories and I will remember them for you. I'm really good at that, my friend Jas told me. I remembered all kinds of things about people we used to know back in London, and he was always amazed. But I did it automatically. I told him it was like collecting anything. I used to have these collections, you know, when I was a kid. Shells, insects. Hundreds of them. I used to know exactly what they all were and where to find them in my room, although Lesley was always going on about mess. All you have to do is tell me. And then, if you do forget, I can tell your memories back to you, like a story.'

She massaged Iris's cold hands, trying to rub warmth and certainty into them. 'Do you see?'

Iris's colour had faded and the tight lines pursed her mouth again. 'Maybe,' she said uncertainly.

Ruby smiled. Confidence and an idea of her own value swept through her, and she leaned up to kiss her grandmother's cheek.

'Definitely,' she insisted.

chapter three

BEFORE THE WAR Colonel Boyce's office at GHQ had been a spacious bedroom in a substantial villa. By the time I came to work there the room had been partitioned into three cubbyholes. Roddy Boy had one cubbyhole, and as his typist I occupied a walled-off slice of the corridor outside the bedroom. My desk was wedged between a pair of tall tin cabinets in which I filed the endless succession of pinks generated by interdepartmental communications.

Roddy's head poked out of his office. 'Miss Black? Could you take this along to Brigadier Denselow?'

I took the sealed folder marked *Secret* and walked down two sets of stairs and through a pair of temporary doors into what had once been the villa's kitchens.

Brigadier Denselow's assistant, Captain Frobisher, was sitting with his feet on his desk reading a novel from the Anglo-Egyptian Club library.

'Hello, light of my life,' he greeted me routinely.

I handed over the folder and Martin signed the docket for it. In answer to his entreaty I told him that no, I wasn't free for dinner.

'You never are,' he sighed. 'What's wrong with me?'

'Nothing. But I am in love with another man.' Whom I had not seen, nor even heard from, in seventeen and a half days.

When I returned to my desk I saw that Roddy's door was firmly closed, with the 'Do not disturb' sign hanging from the knob.

I had been painstakingly typing for perhaps half an hour before Roddy's door opened again. I saw my boss's knife-creased trousers emerge first. He was followed by a pair of sunburnt legs in khaki shorts, very stained and dusty.

My heart lurched in my chest. I looked up at the owner of the legs and Xan smiled down at me. Behind the smile he looked exhausted.

'You promised me a cup of GHQ tea, remember?'

'So I did. Milk and sugar?' I laughed because I knew perfectly well how he took his tea.

'Let me think. Do you know, maybe it isn't tea I want at all? Perhaps a drink instead? At Shepheard's?'

Roddy gave us his pop-eyed stare. 'Ah, yes. You two know each other, don't you?'

'We have met,' I said demurely. The last time I had seen Xan was as he was leaving my bed, at dawn, before heading away into the desert on one of his mysterious sorties.

'It is lunchtime,' Xan said, consulting his watch. 'Colonel Boyce, may I take Miss Black away from you for an hour?'

'Harrumph. Well, yes, all right. Only an hour. We are extremely pressed at the moment, you know.' The green telephone on his desk rang. 'Ahhhm. The Brigadier. Excuse me, please.'

The door closed behind him and Xan immediately seized my hands and kissed the knuckles. 'Christ. Come on, let's get out of here.'

We went out into the afternoon heat. It was the beginning of October 1941, but there was no sign as yet of cooler weather.

'Xan . . .'

He held me back a little. 'Wait. Are you free this evening?'

I pretended to consider. 'Let me think. I was planning to go to the cinema with Faria . . .'

'Oh, in that case . . .'

'But maybe I could chuck her. What do you suggest instead?'

'Bed. Followed by dinner, and then bed again.'

'Do you know what? I find that I am free tonight, tomorrow night and every evening for the rest of the year.'

We walked on to Shepheard's, past the beggars and amputees and ragged children who held out their hands to the Cairo grandees passing up and down the steps of the hotel.

Shepheard's was out of bounds to other ranks. The bars and terraces swarmed with a lunchtime crowd of fashionably dressed civilians and officers of all the nations who had forces in Egypt. We found a table on the verandah overlooking the street and ordered buffalo steak sandwiches and Stella beer from one of the waiters.

It felt strange to be sitting on the verandah at Shepheard's with Xan, patiently waiting for our beer, when only an hour ago I had no way of knowing even if he was alive or dead. And if it was strange for me, I reflected, how much more disorientating must it be for him?

I said quietly, 'Am I allowed to ask where you have been?'

He jumped, as if his thoughts had been a long way off. He did smile at me, then rubbed his jaw with one hand. 'On a patrol.'

'Was it bad?'

'I have had better experiences.' He spoke lightly but the taut muscles round his mouth revealed his distress.

The waiter returned and put the beers down. Xan's had hardly touched the table before he swept it up and finished it in two long gulps.

'Sorry,' Xan said after a moment. 'I'll liven up once I've had something to eat.'

I leaned forward and touched his hand. 'It's all right.'

He did revive when he had eaten his sandwich and most of mine. He sat back again in his chair and grinned at me. 'Now all I need is a bath and some sleep, and you.'

'All three shall be yours. Xan, it wasn't a social call you were paying on Roddy Boy this morning, was it?'

'No, it wasn't.' And then, after a pause, 'How much do you actually know about what he does?'

In theory, I was only supposed to handle routine typing, filing and administration. But Roddy had long ago decided that I was trustworthy. Quite often, he asked me to collect or deliver signals in clear to the cipher clerks because the junior staff officer whose job it should have been was inclined to be too busy for this menial task.

I had lately started reading everything that passed through my hands, greedy for the smallest crumb of information, good or bad, that might have anything to do with Xan. So I now knew the names and quite often the general whereabouts of most of the commando forces who supplied us with intelligence from deep behind enemy lines.

'A fair amount,' I said cautiously.

'And so you have heard of Tellforce.'

The sun struck splinters of light off Xan's empty glass and cast hard shadows over the white field of the tablecloth.

'Yes. I have heard of Tellforce.'

Another shadow fell across the table. We both looked up and there was Jessie James. The two men exchanged a glance that excluded me.

'I didn't know you were back,' Jessie murmured.

'I got in a couple of hours ago.'

Then Xan was on his feet and they exchanged a brief handshake. Jessie hauled over a chair and sat down beside me, telling me that I shouldn't hide myself away just because Xan was always off fooling around in the desert.

The sombre mood that had descended on Xan and me lifted again. Xan and Jessie drank more beer and I ordered a tiny thimbleful of thick, sweet coffee. Jessie was full of the latest gossip and funny stories about people we knew. One of his fellow Cherry Pickers had won a mule in a poker game with a group of Egyptian traders. He had ridden the mule home from the card game and installed it in the garden of his rented house. He had bought it a straw hat with a hatband in the regimental colours, and he took the animal and its hat with him to polo games and race meetings at the Gezira Club.

'No,' I protested.

Xan laughed and Jessie blinked at me. 'The two of them are very happy together. I'd call it a marriage made in heaven.'

I finished my coffee and looked at my watch. 'I'd better go,' I said reluctantly.

Xan lightly touched my wrist. 'What time will you be free?'

'About eight.'

Later that day, after we had made love, Xan and I lay in my bed. My head rested on his chest and I listened to the slow rhythm of his breathing. Faria had gone to a big dinner that was being given by Ali's parents, and Sarah was in her room. She had been ill a month earlier with one of the debilitating stomach complaints that were Cairo's special weapon, and was taking a long time to recover.

Xan sighed and shifted position, combing his fingers through my hair. I felt the weight of happiness, almost tangible, defined even more sharply by the constant counter of anxiety and by the certainty that we would have to part again very soon.

'Before Jessie arrived this afternoon you mentioned Tellforce,' I began at last. The name of the secret force had been in my head all afternoon. I didn't want to hear how closely Xan was associated with it, but I couldn't unlearn what I already knew.

'This is between us,' Xan murmured.

From what he told me that night, which was only the bare facts, together with what I knew already, I was able to put together the picture.

Tellforce was an irregular group of officers and men who had been recruited for their knowledge of the desert and the ways of the desert. Before the war the officers might have been mining engineers or hydrologists or Arabists, but now their job was one of the most demanding of all the special operations. They drove patrols of heavy specially adapted trucks deep into the desert, moving far behind enemy lines and spying on their manoeuvres. They kept twenty-four-hour roadside watches from the sparse shelter of wadis or patches of scrub, and from these uncomfortable hide-outs they counted every single truck, tank and car that passed, and estimated the numbers of occupants. Collecting these snippets of information meant that Tellforce patrols were always at risk of being spotted by enemy convoys or aircraft.

They were also known as the desert taxis because they delivered commando raiders to their targets and then brought the survivors out again. And they made their own lightning strikes whenever an opportunity for sabotage presented itself.

'I see,' I said at last.

'Don't worry,' Xan said. 'Hassan is always with me.'

I remembered the impassive tribesman who had driven us out to the oasis beyond Giza.

'We have been at Kufra,' Xan continued. 'We were out on a patrol and spotted some unexpected enemy tank movements. Mark III Panzers. They just materialised out of nowhere, fifteen of them.'

I listened, keeping my breathing even to counter my apprehension.

'We were half of our patrol, just five trucks and a command car. We had been moving mostly at night and were about to leaguer under camouflage for the day when the forward vehicle signalled a halt. Luckily we had dune cover so we held up and watched them go by.'

Xan slid his arm from under my head and fumbled for a pack of cigarettes from the pocket of his discarded shirt. He lit one and leaned back against the pillows. I waited for what seemed like a long time.

'That was what I had to tell Boyce.'

Relevant information gleaned from enemy signals traffic or human intelligence reports from reconnaissance patrols like Xan's were Roddy's raw materials. It was his job to assess and collate them, then build up a picture for the central command of our section of Intelligence.

'We watched them go by and waited. I started to hope that they must have missed the other half of the patrol too, but after fifteen or twenty minutes we heard the Panzer cannons start up.' Xan exhaled.

'I gave the order to the men to hold off. We could have pushed forward after the tanks and done what we could, but . . .'

The silence uncurled between us. Doing what they could would have meant only one possible outcome.

'The firing stopped after a few minutes and then we did move in.'

Xan described the scene in only the barest and most unemotive words. At first it was impossible to see anything through the smoke and churned-up dust. Then, as his little convoy crawled in the tank tracks, they came upon all that was left of the second half of the Tellforce patrol. Most of the men were dead, the others badly wounded. The tank commanders probably assumed that they were coming up to the outposts of a more significant force. They had smashed straight through the isolated patrol and rolled on in search of bigger objectives.

Xan left one detachment of men to dig graves for their dead companions and with Hassan and the wounded survivors he set off towards the distant first-aid outpost at Kufra. Among the injured was the captain, whose legs had been blown off at the knees.

'Burke and I were commissioned on the same day. I sat in the back of the truck with him, giving him sips of water from my bottle. He kept saying, "Damn nuisance, Molyneux. Damn nuisance. I need feet in this game." He died with the truck bumping over the sand. Bled to death.'

Xan stubbed out his cigarette with little jabbing movements. When I was sure that he had finished I put my arms round him and made him lie down again beside me.

'I drove back to Cairo with two other badly wounded men. Somehow Hassan kept them alive until we got them to hospital here.' It was 500 miles. 'Then I came straight in to see Boyce.

'Boyce said the Mark IIIs couldn't have been where they were. There was no intelligence relating to them, therefore they can't have existed. So in the view of GHQ, half of my patrol was wiped out by a mirage, eh?'

I had never seen Xan angry like this before. I held him, trying to draw some of the rage out of him. There was nothing I could say that would really mean anything. 'It will be over one day. It will be done, and it will have been worth doing.'

He closed his eyes, then forced them open again, as if he didn't want to contemplate what lay behind the lids.

After a moment I realised that Xan had fallen asleep, just in a second. I hadn't realised the depth of his exhaustion.

He slept for twenty minutes, stirred in my arms, then jerked awake again. As soon as he remembered where he was a smile of pure relief broke across his face and he looked like the Xan I knew.

'I've been asleep. Bloody awful manners. Will you forgive me?'

I kissed his nose, then his mouth. 'Yes.'

'I feel better. I'm sorry about before. What's the time? Come on, let's go out to dinner. How about Zazie's?'

It was ten thirty. Most of us in Cairo kept eastern Mediterranean late hours, although some of the British still insisted on dining at seven thirty, as if they were at home in Surrey. I was already scrambling into my dressing gown and heading for the bathroom. If Xan wanted to go out drinking and dancing, that was exactly what we would do.

Zazie's was packed, as it always was. Xan had to slip several notes into the palm of the maître d' to secure us a table. We chose our food from the elaborate menu, and Xan ordered a bottle of champagne. We lifted our glasses to each other in a toast that contained no words, only wishes.

By 1 a.m. the club was a hot, smoky mass of people who had come in from dinners and other more sedate parties. Xan and I shuffled in the crowd packed onto the tiny dance floor. I spotted Sandy Allardyce at a table with a handsome much older woman.

'Who is that with Sandy?' I murmured in Xan's ear.

'Haven't you met her? That's Mrs Kimmig-Gertsch. She is Swiss, or claims to be. A widow. Her husband was in armaments, I believe.'

'What does she do in Cairo?'

'Oh, she lives here. She has a lovely house in the old city, right beside the al-Azhar mosque.'

'And what is she doing with Sandy?'

Xan grinned.

At 2 a.m., when we emerged from Zazie's, the night air was full of the reedy smell of the Nile. We were now part of a big, laughing group of people that contained Sandy Allardyce and his widowed lady, and it soon became apparent that we were heading back to the widow's house to continue the party.

We streamed up some worn stone steps, following behind Sandy and Mrs Kimmig-Gertsch. An anonymous door in a blank wall swung open and an immense Nubian in a snow-white *galabiyeh* with a royal-blue sash bowed to us as we marched in.

Xan had been right, the house was beautiful.

It was very old. The windows were set in deep embrasures that revealed the thickness of the walls, and the stone floors were gently hollowed by centuries of slippered footfalls. We were shown by bowing servants into a grand double-height hall, panelled in wood. A huge wrought-metal and crimson glass lamp in the Moorish style hung on chains from the central boss of the roof. Way above our heads a gallery circled the upper part of the hall, with exquisitely carved and pierced hinged wooden screens that would have shielded the women of the household from the eyes of male visitors. The room was simply furnished with low carved tables and divans piled with kilims and embroidered velvet cushions.

The party spread itself out and settled on the cushions, with Mrs Kimmig-Gertsch sitting in a slightly higher chair at the end of the room. Someone found a gramophone behind a door in the panelling and put on a recording of a plaintive Arabic love song that rose and fell as a background to the talk and laughter. The servants brought in silver pots of mint tea and little brass cylinders of Turkish coffee, and set them out beside crystal decanters of whisky and brandy.

After a while, I wandered out of the room in search of a bathroom. None of the servants was in sight so I chose a likely doorway, but found that it led out into a little loggia that gave in turn onto a courtyard garden. There was a scent of flowers and damp earth, and the sound of trickling water. By the light from the open doorway behind me I could just see the turquoise and emerald tiles lining the walls. Above was a quadrilateral of dark velvet sky, and the triple towers of the mosque. It was the most perfect and peaceful little garden I had ever seen.

I stood there, admiring and—yes—coveting it, until one of the servants coughed discreetly behind me and asked in Arabic if I was in need of anything. I murmured my request and was shown the way.

It was four in the morning when the Nubian major-domo ushered Xan and me out into the grey predawn. I didn't think about the time; I just wanted to get home again and lie down with my lover.

Xan slept for just an hour, then slid away from me. 'Go back to sleep. I'll telephone you later,' he whispered.

At seven thirty I was making myself a cup of tea and swallowing aspirin for my headache when Faria appeared in her cream silk robe, grimacing at the earliness of the hour. She did a little voluntary work for her mother, who with two other Cairo society ladies ran a charitable club for servicemen. She took the aspirin bottle out of my hand and shook two pills into her mouth, and asked where I had been the night before.

I told her and she raised her eyebrows.

'There is a rumour that Mrs Kimmig-Gertsch is a German spy.'

'Why is Sandy running around with her?'

Faria gave me a look. 'He is a British spy. Didn't you know that?'

In spite of our headaches we both laughed at the idea of the two of them locked in a steely pas de deux of espionage and counterespionage over cocktails and card table.

On my way out of the flat I met Sarah. She had a small suitcase in her hand and she told me that she was going to Beirut for the weekend. I said that I was pleased she was feeling better, ordered her to have a good time and kissed her goodbye. Then I walked to work with the hundreds of soldiers and civilians heading to their desks in GHQ.

It was a long day. When I emerged at eight o'clock there was the usual crowd of boyfriends and hopefuls waiting to meet their girls. To my delight, Xan's black head was among them. I ran and he caught me in his arms and whirled me off the ground.

'Come with me?' he begged, after we had kissed.

I asked where, expecting that he would say Shepheard's or another bar for a cocktail before I went home to change for dinner. But he tucked my hand under his arm and led me to the car, the same one in which Hassan had driven us out to Giza.

As we drove out into Qasr el Aini, Xan said, 'I'm going to look in at the Scottish Hospital to see one of the men I brought in yesterday. Is that all right?'

'Of course it is.'

The Scottish Military was just one of the places where wounded men were taken when the hospital trains and ambulance convoys reached Cairo. Xan parked the car and we ran up the steps. The hallways and stairwells were crowded with soldiers, bandaged and on crutches or in wheelchairs, and the wards we passed were crammed with long rows of beds. On the first floor we found a ward where most of the occupants lay face down, what was visible of their faces like sections of pale carved masks, as motionless as if they were already dead.

Xan stopped beside a bed in the middle of a row, then leaned over the man who lay in it. 'Hello, old chap. You look quite a bit better than you did this morning,' I heard him say.

There was no answer. There could hardly have been, because the lower half of the soldier's face and his neck were a white carapace of dressings. A tube led from where his mouth would have been. Xan sat down on the edge of the bed and talked in his ordinary voice, about how another soldier called Ridley had made it too, and how there was a cinema just down the road from the hospital that was air-conditioned, cool as a winter morning, Xan said, with padded seats, and they would go and see a picture, the three of them, and have iced beer afterwards.

I don't know if the soldier understood or even heard him, because he gave no sign. Xan just went on talking.

There was a strong, sweetish smell in the ward with a whiff of suppuration in it. Sweat broke coldly on my forehead. It occurred to me that I was going to faint, or maybe to vomit.

I walked quickly away, heading down the ward without any idea where. I pushed blindly through a pair of swing doors into a sluice room, past a row of sinks and into a lavatory cubicle.

When I came out again, wiping my face with my handkerchief, a nurse was there rinsing out a kidney bowl at one of the sinks.

'Are you all right?' she asked.

'Yes. Thank you.' What I felt now was shame for having responded like a swooning Victorian maiden to the spectacle of other people's suffering.

The nurse briskly set down her metal bowl, took a glass out of a cupboard and poured water from a jug. She handed the glass to me and I sipped carefully from it.

'I'm sorry,' I said pointlessly.

To my surprise she smiled. 'It can take people that way at first. You get used to it, though.' Her voice was attractive, with a distinct Scottish burr. 'Do you want to sit down for a bit? Your friend's still talking to Corporal Noake.'

'I'm fine. I will be, in a minute.'

She held out her hand. 'I'm Ruth Macnamara.'

'Iris Black.'

We shook.

'If you're sure you're all right, I'd better get back to work. See you around, eh?'

'Yes,' I said to her departing back. 'I hope so.'

I walked slowly back up the ward. Xan was still talking. I went round to the other side of the bed and looked down into the soldier's eyes.

'Hello, there. I'm Iris, Xan's friend.'

I didn't know how much was left of the lower part of his face but the man himself was still there. His eyes flickered, moved, then fixed on mine. Just perceptibly, he nodded. I took his hand and sandwiched it between my two and he clung to me with his eyes.

After a minute, Xan said easily, 'We'll be getting along now, Noake. I'll look in again tomorrow, if they haven't packed us off by then.'

We left him among the other carved men.

When we reached the car again we sat and lit cigarettes and stared out at the darkening sky.

'Will you really be going tomorrow?' I asked.

'I don't know. It won't be long, though. There's the big push coming.'

We all knew that. The Germans and Italians knew it too.

'What happened to Corporal Noake, exactly?'

'His lower jawbone was partly blown away.'

'Poor man.'

'He was luckier than Reggie Burke,' Xan said grimly.

'Yes.'

We finished our cigarettes and the last of the daylight drained out of the western horizon as if the desert sand were drinking it up.

'Where would you like to have dinner?'

I didn't want food, or whisky or dancing. I wanted Xan, and Xan safe, and the end of the war.

'Let's go home,' I said.

'Will you?' Xan repeated.

It wasn't that I didn't want to answer, just that happiness momentarily flooded my throat and turned me mute.

We were reclining on a rug in the shade of a tree, and had been watching a polo match. As well as Xan's low voice I could hear shouting and ponies' hoofs drumming on the turf and then the sharp crack of a stick on the ball.

I turned my dazzled face to his.

'Yes,' I managed to say. 'Yes, yes, yes. I will. More than anything.'

So, incoherently, I promised to marry Xan Molyneux. The leaves and the chinks of light and all the rest of the world were blotted out as he lowered his head and kissed me.

Jessie James was the first person we told. He came to meet us still in his white breeches and shirt soaked with sweat from the match.

'Did you see that?' he called.

'No,' Xan said bluntly.

'But it was the very best goal I've ever scored. What kind of friend are you, Molyneux?'

'A very happy one. Iris says she'll marry me. Can you believe that?'

Jessie stopped in his tracks. A smile split his face, but he pretended to be dismayed. 'Oh, no. Iris is going to marry *me*, once she's realised what a hopeless apology you are. Tell him that's so, Iris, won't you?'

I put my hands out and grasped his. 'Wish us luck, Jessie.'

His smile faded into seriousness then. 'I do. I wish you both all the happiness and all the good luck in the world.'

Later that afternoon Jessie took a photograph of us, using a camera airily borrowed from a man called Gordon Foxbridge who had been watching and taking pictures of the polo match. Major Foxbridge was a staff officer at GHQ, and an enthusiastic amateur photographer.

Major Foxbridge offered to take the photograph himself, but Jessie wanted to do it and so the Major obligingly handed over his Leica. With Xan's arms wrapped round my waist I let my head fall back against his shoulder and laughed into the lens.

'Watch the birdie!' Jessie sang.

It was Gordon Foxbridge, though, who developed the picture in his own darkroom and then delivered it to my desk in a brown manila envelope marked 'The engagement of Miss Iris Black and Captain Molyneux' as if we were in the Tatler.

Wherever I have travelled since, through all the years, the photograph has come with me. And this is the picture that Ruby asked me about.

What answer did I give? I can't remember.

How can I find the words to tell her, my grandchild, all this history? I can't even catch hold of it myself. If I try to stalk it, it floats away out of reach. So I have to be patient and let the memories and the dreams come, then try to distinguish them.

But I have never been a patient woman.

Ruby's quaint offer touched me, and so did the way she set it out with assurances about her shells and beetles. I can imagine her as a smaller child, dark-browed and serious, walled up in a bedroom decorated by Lesley and poring over her collections.

She is an unusual creature. Her coming is an unlooked-for blessing.

That same evening we went back to the Scottish Military Hospital to see Corporal Noake before heading out to dinner with Jessie James, who wanted to set in train one of the long evenings of Cairo celebration.

We started with cocktails at Shepheard's and then dinner on a boat moored on the Nile, where Jessie proposed a toast and a circle of faces glimmered at us over the rims of champagne glasses. Faria was there, with the poet who was looking more mournful than usual. Sarah was still not back from her trip, but there were some of the Cherry Pickers.

'How heavenly for you both,' Faria said. 'When's the wedding?'

Everything did happen very quickly in Cairo. There was no reason to put anything off even until tomorrow or indeed to deny ourselves any of life's pleasures, because there was always the likelihood that the war would intervene, but I murmured that we hadn't decided yet. I wanted to tell my parents, and Xan's parents would need to hear the news.

There was another reason too why Xan and I had not talked about a wedding day. He was going back to the desert and we both knew it would be very soon. Perhaps in only a few hours' time.

'I'll be in Cairo again by Christmas, darling, at the latest.'

'Promise?'

'Cross my heart. We're going to drive Rommel all the way out of Africa, I know we are. And after that you and I can make our plans.' He was optimistic for my sake and I tried to believe him.

As the hours went by, our party gathered momentum until it rolled under its own impetus through the Cairo nightspots. By two in the morning we were at Zazie's again. Xan and I danced and I felt the heat of him through my satin dress, and we convinced ourselves that the night was endless. Leaving for the desert was no more than a little dark unwinking eye at the vanishing point of a long avenue of happiness.

Sandy Allardyce materialised. He held my hand, rather damply, his round red face was very serious and I realised only belatedly that he was making a confession of love.

'. . . a good man. Reckless, but a fine field officer. But, you know, wish it could have been different, Iris. Just wanted to tell you, you know?'

I shook my head, confusion and sympathy and a shaming desire to laugh mounting in my throat. 'Sandy. I *didn't* know, honestly. Had no idea. I never . . . let you believe anything I shouldn't have done, did I?'

'No. Never a single thing. Perfect lady, always.'

Sandy took my hand and pressed his mouth to the knuckles. 'Won't speak of it again. Rest of my life. Promise you, on my honour.'

From her front-row table Mrs Kimmig-Gertsch glowered at us.

The night did end, at last, with Xan and me in a taxi going back to his flat. The sun was up and the street sweepers were working, and donkey carts loaded with vegetables plodded to the markets. I was beyond being drunk and I wasn't tired, and the light had a hard, white, absolute brightness to it that suggested that this day was a crystallisation of everything that had gone before. I already knew that it was one of the days I would remember all my life.

It is the memory of making love on that airless Cairo morning, when we had drunk and danced ourselves sober again, that I hold most close. We were so sweet and shameless, and so powerful in our innocence.

Even now, when I am eighty-two and losing my mind, the recollection of it can catch me unawares and turn my limbs to water.

Xan fell asleep in the end, and I lay and watched the impression of his dreams.

I didn't go to work. I called Roddy Boy and told him I had gippy tummy, and bore the sarcastic slice in his voice when he told me that he hoped Captain Molyneux was taking good care of me.

In the afternoon, after we had eaten some recuperative pastries and drunk coffee in the shady garden at Groppi's, Xan took me to a jeweller's in the old quarter to buy a ring.

The merchant unlocked the safe and brought out his velvet trays for us and we let the raw stones trickle in cold droplets through our fingers. In the end, I chose a smoky purple amethyst and ordered a plain claw setting for it. Xan led me out of the shop again and tucked my hand under his arm.

'There. Now, what would you like to do?'

'Where is Hassan?'

'At home with his family, I should think. Why?'

I thought how perfect it would be to go out to the Pyramids again, and watch the sun setting behind Hassan's hidden oasis.

As soon as I told Xan he smiled at me.

'You have only to command. But I'll have to go and beg for a car.'

We walked until we came to a tall, anonymous house in a neglected street that ran westwards towards el Rhoda. I was just reaching the conclusion that this must be a headquarters of some kind for Tellforce when a figure detached itself from the shadow of the broken buildings opposite and ran towards Xan. It was Hassan.

I waited, knowing that whatever was to come would not be good news. Hassan stepped back again, briefly inclining his head towards me.

I could already tell from Xan's face what was coming.

'I have to go,' he said.

'When?'

'Now. I've got to be in place beside the road out of el Agheila with my patrol, tonight.'

By my half-informed reckoning this was about 400 miles west behind the enemy front line, on the Libyan border.

'*Tonight?* How? Isn't it . . . a long way?'

'Wainwright's here with the WACO.'

Tellforce had a small two-seater aircraft, usually piloted by the Tellforce commander himself, Lieutenant-Colonel Gus Wainwright.

'He's waiting at the airfield.' Xan took my face between his hands. Hassan had turned away and stood like a stone statue, guarding the steps and the dingy house and—I saw—Xan himself. I also saw that a glitter of excited anticipation had kindled behind Xan's eyes. Now it was here he was ready to go. He *wanted* to go, he was already rushing towards the adventure. I felt cold, even with the afternoon's humid weight pressing against the nape of my neck. But somehow I smiled, my mouth curling against his as he kissed me.

'I'm sorry,' he murmured.

Against all the impulses, which were to cling to him like an importunate child and beg him to stay, I pressed the flat of my hands against his shirt. Somehow, as the kiss ended I stepped out of his arms and put a tiny distance between us. Hassan edged closer by the same amount. First and most importantly it was the two of them now, not Xan and me.

'Come back when you can,' I whispered. 'Go on, go now.'

Hassan was already moving towards the Tellforce staff car that I saw parked under the shade of a tree. Xan turned away, then swung back and roughly pulled me into his arms again, and there was the raw bite of his mouth against mine.

'I love you,' he said.

'And I love you. I'll be here. Just go.'

Hassan reached the car and slid into the driver's seat. Xan sprinted after him, then slowed again and shouted back over his shoulder, 'Will you go and visit Noake and Ridley for me?'

I had already decided that I must do this. 'Of course I will.'

He wrenched open the passenger door and sketched a salute. With one hand I shaded my eyes against the sun, and I touched the fingers of the other to my lips and blew him a kiss. The skidding car tyres raised puffs of dust that hung in the air long after the car itself had vanished.

When I reached the hospital I went first to ask after Private Ridley. I was directed to a voluntary aid supervisor in an unventilated ground-floor office that reminded me of my own slice of working corridor. The woman was French but she explained in neutral English that the soldier had died early that morning without regaining consciousness.

'I'm sorry. Was he a relative? Or a friend, perhaps?'

'Neither. A friend of mine is, was, his commanding officer.'

'I'm sorry,' the Frenchwoman said again.

I left the office and found my way up to the ward.

Noake was lying propped against his pillows, the lower half of his face masked with fresh dressings, but when he saw me he lifted his hand in a little flourish of greeting. I sat down in Xan's place. I wouldn't tell him about Ridley's death, not yet.

'Hello, there. You've only got me tonight, Mr Noake, I'm afraid. Captain Molyneux's been whisked back to the desert, by *air*. Colonel Wainwright flew in today to get him, what d'you think of that?'

I could see what he thought of it. Beneath the bruised and puffy lids his eyes glimmered with interest.

'I don't know when he'll be back,' I blurted out.

To my surprise, Noake's hand crawled across the sheet, found mine and grasped it tightly. He was letting me know that he sympathised with the anguish that I suffered on parting from my lover.

For a moment, I had to keep my head bent.

I didn't know how much I was supposed to know, or how much Noake should know that I knew. But he wasn't going to be able to tell anyone and I longed to talk about Xan.

'There's a big push coming, everyone's talking about it. I'm concerned for him, because I know a bit about what Tellforce does. But Xan's got to do his job like everyone else, like *you* did, Mr Noake.'

And like Private Ridley did. I looked into the injured man's eyes, remembering the involuntary kindling of excitement I had seen in Xan. 'It must be hard for you, to miss what's going to happen.'

Noake nodded, his fingers still tight over mine.

'We'll have to keep each other company,' I said.

A starched apron came into view on the other side of the bed. Ruth Macnamara was standing there with an armful of fresh bedding.

'Here you are again. Can't stay away from us, Albie, can she?'

I was glad to know his first name. 'Albie? May I call you that, too? I'm Iris, d'you remember?'

He blinked his agreement.

Ruth asked me, 'Where's your friend tonight?'

'Fiancé.' The word was out before I considered it. Blushing, I rushed on, 'I was just telling Albie. Gone. Called back to the desert in a hurry.'

'Oh. Oh, look, d'you want to have a cup of coffee or something after I finish work? I'm off shift in half an hour.'

'Yes, let's do that.'

She hurried away and I went on talking to Albie Noake. I had no idea what he wanted to hear but I told him about Faria and Sarah and the apartment in Garden City, and about Mamdooh and his son who followed him to work and sat on a stool in the corner of Mamdooh's cubbyhole near the front door. I talked about Zazie's and Mrs Kimmig-Gertsch's house, and Roddy Boy. Once or twice Albie's eyelids closed and I thought he had fallen asleep, but as soon as my murmuring stopped they snapped open again.

'She can talk enough for both of you, can't she?' Ruth demanded when she came back.

I disengaged my hand gently from Albie's and stood up.

'Good night, Albie.'

I followed Ruth out of the ward and down some stone steps. Outside a door marked 'Nursing Staff' she said briskly, 'Wait here.'

Three or four minutes later she re-emerged and I blinked at her. The nurse's starched cap had always hidden her hair, and now I saw for the first time that it was a rich, dark red. It turned her pale skin translucent and took the slightly pinched severity out of her face.

When I was driving with Xan I had noticed a small café on a street corner, within walking distance. I suggested that we might go there and Ruth nodded briefly.

'Anywhere we can get something to eat. I'm pretty hungry.'

At the café, Ruth ordered eggs and *fuul*, and I asked for a plate of fruit. We drank mint tea while we waited for our food and as soon as a basket of 'aish baladi was placed in front of us Ruth tore off a chunk of the warm, coarse bread and chewed ravenously.

'Sorry. I don't get much time to eat during the day. Usually I like to get the bus straight home from work and have a meal. The person I live with cooks, or if I'm on my own I throw a few ingredients together.'

'Do you share with another nurse?'

'A doctor.'

'Where does he work?'

Ruth lifted an eyebrow. 'She.'

Then she named one of the other military hospitals.

I was blushing at my own assumption. 'That was stupid,' I said.

'No, it wasn't. How many female surgical anaesthetists do any of us know? But Daphne is one. She's pretty good.'

'I'd like to meet her.'

Ruth didn't say anything to that. A hot pan full of eggs and chopped peppers arrived and she dug her fork into it. I ate slices of melon and mango and watched her eat. When rather more than half of Ruth's plate was empty, she finally looked up again.

'That's better. So. Your fiancé is Albie Noake's commanding officer?'

'His name's Xan and when he was called back to his . . . unit, this afternoon, I said I'd go on visiting Albie instead of him.'

'That's good. The men get medical attention, of course, the best we can provide, but they don't get many of the other things that they need. Company, especially women's company. Although the VADs and the other voluntary organisations do what they can. Albie's lucky.'

'What will happen to him?'

'Mine is an acute trauma ward. He'll stay there until he is stable. Then he'll be moved to a longer-stay ward, where they'll try to repair his mouth and reconstruct his jaw. Or maybe that will be too complicated and he'll be sent by ship back to England for the work to be done there.'

'Will he be able to speak again?'

'It will be a manner of speaking.'

'Poor Albie.' He was twenty-eight years old.

She went on eating. 'At least he's alive.'

Ruth was unsentimental and I could see how the work she did would absolutely require that, or else it would be unbearable. And as well as being distressing I could also guess how fascinating and even noble it must be, compared with what I did. I envied her.

'Xan brought in another of his men who was badly injured at the same time. He died this morning, but I didn't tell Albie. Maybe I should have done, though.'

'Yes, I think you should,' Ruth agreed.

The food was finished. Ruth and I sat facing each other across the rickety wooden table.

I took a piece of paper out of my handbag and scribbled my telephone number on it, then passed the slip across to Ruth. She took the pen out of my hand, folded my slip of paper and tore it very neatly along the fold line, then wrote her number in return.

'Maybe if Daphne and I ever get the same day off, you could come and have something to eat with us,' she said.

'I'd love to,' I said. I was drawn to Ruth Macnamara. I hadn't met anyone quite like her before.

I started to walk towards Garden City but the day had begun to seem like a very long tunnel. Riding home through the dawn with Xan felt like a week ago. A taxi loomed towards me and I flagged it down.

I gave the man the address, fell inside and dozed until we jerked to a stop outside the apartment.

Inside I found Sarah sitting in a circle of lamplight, her knees drawn up and her bare feet on the crimson sofa cushions. She looked pale, but her hair was freshly washed and there was a slick of lipstick on her mouth.

'Sarah! You're back. You look much better.'

Sarah held out her arms to me. 'Here I am. And *you*. Faria told me your news. I'm so happy for you, Iris. Come on, give me a hug.'

I sat down beside her and we hugged and kissed each other. Sarah smelt of her favourite perfume but the bones in her shoulders seemed much more prominent, and there was a veil of sadness in her face.

'Are you really all right?' I asked.

''Course. And you're going to be Mrs Alexander Molyneux. *How* exciting. Are you completely thrilled?'

'I am.'

'Can I be your bridesmaid?'

'Of course. You and Faria.'

'What heaven. Not pink, please don't say pink. Maybe palest mint green, what do you think?'

'Where is Faria?'

'Oh, out.'

'Ali?'

'Jeremy, I think,' Sarah said. She must have bitten her lips from inside because they went pale under the lipstick. Then she jumped up with a little laugh. 'Let's have a drink. A drink to you and Xan.'

She poured us a significant measure of gin apiece and tilted her glass.

'To the two of you. Happy for ever,' she called, and drank.

Where?' Iris asked sharply. 'Where are you taking her?' Ruby and Ash shuffled a little awkwardly under her gaze.

'To al-Qalaa. To Citadel, Ma'am,' Ash answered politely.

To *where*? Ruby was going to protest, but decided that she would save it until they were alone together.

'I see. You will tell her some of the history?'

'Of course. I am proud of this.'

'Good.' Iris approved of Ash, and even Mamdooh had opened the front door and shown him through into Iris's garden without any noticeable signs of objection. 'Go on. Off you go. Make sure you bring her back here by six o'clock on the dot.'

'Of course.' This time, Ash even bowed.

'*Creep*,' Ruby whispered under her breath.

The moby was outside. Ash pulled his sunglasses down over his eyes, flicked back his hair and gestured to the pillion.

'Where *are* we going?'

'Didn't you hear? To Citadel.'

'Don't I even get consulted? Maybe I don't want to go there.'

He frowned at her. 'Why not?'

Ash never backed down and Ruby liked that. He was also looking particularly fit today. She flicked a grin at him and bounced onto the pillion seat. 'Oh, come on then. Let's get going.'

He kicked the starter and they plunged out into the traffic. By now, Ruby was quite confident on the back of the bike. She pulled a scarf across her mouth and nose to filter out the dust and fumes, as she had seen other women passengers do, and wound her arm round Ash's waist. Above them, monopolising the skyline, were the sand-coloured walls and turrets of the old Citadel. The way to it curved upwards along a series of wide, sunbaked avenues, past gaudy tents and littered fairgrounds on Midan Salah ad-Din. When they reached the entrance at Bab al-Gabal they left the bike padlocked to the trunk of a struggling sapling and continued on foot, into a walled and crenellated maze of turrets and domes separated by glaring empty spaces that trapped the afternoon's heat. Treading over hot stone and dust-lapped patches of lawn, Ruby began to lag behind Ash.

'Why are we here?' she demanded irritably.

'History. First fort built here, nine hundred years old. By Salah ad-Din.'

'Yeah?'

'You know who this is?'

'Should I?'

He frowned at her again. 'You are educated English woman and you know nothing, it seems. He is a great leader and warrior against your Christian Crusaders. You have heard of *Saladin*?'

She sighed. This did ring a faint bell. 'Yeah. Look, I'm crap at history, always was. And geography and maths and biology, you name it. But I'm not at school any more so it really doesn't matter, does it?'

Ash looked dubious. 'Learning is important. It is a way to make a life better for yourself and your family. You don't believe this?'

Ruby squinted against the light. 'Yes, I believe it, but that doesn't mean I have to do it.'

He gave her his white crescent of a smile. 'You are funny. And you are very pretty today.'

That was better. 'Am I?'

Ruby had stopped making up her eyes with black lines and dark smudges, and she had also stopped gelling her hair into spikes because she had run out of gel. It flopped over her forehead in a shiny fringe.

'Yes,' he said. He took her hand and turned it over to look at the veins on the inner side of her wrist. He glanced round to make sure that no one was watching them, then touched the tip of his tongue to the place where her pulse beat.

A second's giddiness made Ruby close her eyes.

'Come on,' Ash whispered at last. 'I show you something.'

The enormous mosque enclosed at the heart of the Citadel could be seen from almost every corner of the city, but from close at hand Ruby thought it was disappointing. The domes were covered in dull tin and the pale walls were stained, and a fat snake of tourist visitors lethargically coiled in front of the huge doors.

'What are we looking at?'

'This, the mosque of Mohammed Ali. Two hundred years ago, he ruled this country. He made Egypt modern. I must go inside to pray.'

At the mosque doors there were guardians policing the tribes of tourists. Ash and Ruby exchanged their shoes for felt slippers and Ash lightly twitched the sleeves of her shirt to cover her arms. He lifted the folds of her scarf and draped her head, and then they passed inside.

The domes and half-domes soared above them, like the insides of a giant's eggshells studded with thousands of precious stones. Chandeliers and huge glass globes hung from the dim heights, and there were screens of latticed metal and borders of scalloped gold. Ruby stood with her feet together and her hands pressed against her sides.

Ash stepped forward onto the intricate patchwork of rugs that scrolled away in front of them. He knelt and pressed his hands and then his forehead to the floor.

As she waited Ruby felt an absence inside herself, a strange whisper of sensation that was more a negative balance than a physical reality. Her only belief, since she had been old enough to reach for one, and which had been thoroughly agreed with Jas, was that she didn't want to believe in anything. And yet now she found herself parched with the need for whatever kept Ash's head bowed to the dusty rug.

Ash's narrow back arched like a cat's and then he unfolded himself to the vertical once more. They walked out of the mosque and reversed the shoe procedure.

'Do you believe in God, then? Allah, whatever?'

'It is what I must do.'

Ruby was left in doubt whether the compulsion was from piety or social pressure or as an insurance policy.

'Must?'

'Yes, Ruby. This is simple for me, more easy than you think.'

Ash took her arm and they followed the angle of the perimeter wall. To the east of them were the brown ribs of the Muqqatam hills and ahead, stretching north, another landscape of brown diggings and ragged buildings, blistered with a few domes, a low-rise reflection in miniature of the other city.

'Shall we visit something else?' His face was serious.

Ruby sighed. What she would have liked was to sit or lie down with Ash somewhere quiet and private and have him put his arms round her and press their foreheads together, not even needing to talk, as she and Jas used to do. Since that plainly wasn't going to happen, they might as well pass the time in some other way.

'If you want.'

They went back and unchained the moby. It was a short ride to the sepia walls of the low-rise mirror city they had seen from the heights of the Citadel.

The bike threaded on a narrow dirt road between what looked like very small square-built houses, with arched open doorways and lattice-screened windows. A line of children skipped across in front of them and Ash called a warning, then they came into a paved yard where a flock of long-haired white and brown sheep bumped at a wooden feed trough. Between a pair of dusty acacia trees Ruby saw a high domed canopy sheltering a pair of stone tombs, and to the side of the pillars supporting the canopy there were more stone blocks, the same shape as the houses but smaller, just big enough for one person to lie within. A child's ball and a pink plastic doll, legs askew, lay in the dirt.

'What is this place?' she murmured.

'Cities of the Dead.' He grinned, flicking an eyebrow at her.

All the little houses were tombs. But the whole place was busy with the living, too. There was an old man in a blue *galabiyeh* and a white headcloth, minding the sheep. A little boy sat on a step, stirring the dust with a stick, and his mother looked out of the doorway behind him and tipped a bowl of dirty water into the gutter.

'A place to live,' Ash added.

Ruby kept quiet, half guessing why he had brought her here.

'My family. You can meet them. Not Nafouz, he is with the taxi.'

He wheeled the bike and they walked down an uneven street of tomb houses. They reached an ochre-painted building with a single stone step, none of it very old-looking. Ash led the way and she followed, ducking her head beneath the lintel. Inside there was light from a single electric bulb, a table with an oilcloth, a very old woman sitting with a child in her lap. Ruby stared, trying to make sense of what seemed so unlikely. In the middle of the small space was a raised stone covered with incised inscriptions. It was unmistakably a tomb, and above and around it lived Ash's family.

'Misa' al-khairat' (evening of many good things). The old woman beamed and the child scrambled off its grandmother's lap and ran to him. Ash swung it up by the hands and kissed its brown cheeks.

'Habib, habib.'

Then everyone's eyes slid towards Ruby.

Ash said her name and added, my friend. Ruby carefully skirted the tomb, and went to stand in front of Ash's grandmother.

'Ahlan w-sahlan,' she said, with her bird-eyes on Ruby.

'Ahlan biki,' Ruby muttered, as Ash had taught her. She was rewarded with a wide smile. Ash's grandmother folded Ruby's hands between her own two. It was all right, Ruby thought. She couldn't look quite as disconcerted as she felt. Holding the child in one arm, Ash was hunting among the jars and packets that stood on a shelf. Like Jas, she thought, or Ed—searching for something to eat as soon as he came home. This was a home, but the grave drew her eyes.

A woman came in with a thin blue plastic carrier bag in either hand. There were shops too, then, in the Cities of the Dead.

'Ummi,' Ash said. He kissed her, and unwound the handles of the plastic bags from her fingers. He dumped the shopping on top of the grave.

Ash's mother was small and thin, with the same dark eyes as her sons. Ash introduced Ruby and they went through the same greeting, but Umm Nafouz (Ruby knew she must call her by the name of her oldest child, Ash had told her that too) was busier and less cordial than the grandmother had been. She turned away quite quickly and began to take bags of flour and tinned food out of the shopping bags.

Ruby gazed at the room's centrepiece. It had plain stone walls and a slab on top with the lettering. How many people were buried within, and how long ago? The dead were too close. She looked quickly away again.

Ash's mother was laying out pans and food, preparing to make a meal. There was a gas bottle with two ring burners beside the table, a radio and cassette player on a shelf, and a curtained doorway at the back of the room that must lead to where the family slept.

There was warmth in this place that more logically should have felt cold and gloomy. The child wriggled between her legs and Ash's, and put its hands over its eyes, then lowered them just far enough to be able to peep over the fingertips. She was inviting Ruby to play the game.

Ruby hid her own eyes briefly then exposed them again. 'Boo,' she said and the child laughed.

It was dark outside. Ruby looked quickly at her watch.

'It's half past five. Iris said six o'clock, remember?'

Ash said, 'You are right. I will take you home.'

Ruby put her hands together and bowed to Ash's mother and grand-mother. '*Masa' il-kheer*,' she said.

'*Masa' in-nur*,' the two women replied.

Ash wheeled the bike and Ruby walked close beside him.

He said, 'You are quiet. You think it is a strange thing.'

'It's only strange . . . to me. That doesn't mean it *is* strange.'

'It is my family tomb. When we were young we came here once every week to visit, to have picnic among our dead, to celebrate the *moulid*. It is not a place of fear for us, but of memory and respect. Then after my father died . . .' Ash shrugged. 'It is a home to live in. And the dead and not-yet dead, we are company all together. Why not? The dead do not harm us, only the alive.'

Ash's lips brushed Ruby's cheek. 'You were polite to my family. Like Egyptian girl. My mother will not be so unhappy.'

Light spilled inside Ruby, a brightness so easy and careless that she wanted to laugh. It was partly to do with wanting Ash and his narrow, brown body, of course it was, and she was surprised by how much she did want him, but it was also the opposite of the negative balance that had troubled her in the mosque of Mohammed Ali. There was a posi-tive here, glimpsed in the tomb house of Ash's family and in the way that life continued among the remains of other lives. It was very strong in Ash himself.

'Was this what you meant, when I asked you if you believed in God and you said *it is what I must do*?'

Ruby's hand travelled through an unseen arc, to take in the Cities of the Dead and the people who had to live there.

'God is good. He takes care of each of us.'

'I wish I believed that.'

Ash laughed. 'Infidel.'

Ruby pressed her head against his shoulder, ran her hands down the curve of his back to the hollow above his hip bones. He was beautiful.

'But, you know, it is not a free ride. I work hard and go to school, English, and I hope computers. I told you this, learning is important. Nafouz and I, we must look after our mother and brothers and sisters and we will live in a better place. But for now . . .' His shoulder twitched against hers. '. . . For now, we can enjoy too sometimes. Why not?'

Ruby laughed. She still felt the lightness inside her. 'Yeah.'

Ash was vital, springing with energy. He wasn't bored or disgusted with everything, as she quite often felt in London, and he was different from Jas. Jas used to lie on his bed for days at a time, smoking weed and listening to music.

'So now you have made a tour, eh? Citadel, my family.'

'Yeah.' The shock of the tomb houses still reverberated. She needed some time to absorb what she had seen.

'Ruby, it is not possible for everyone to live in a house the same as your grandmother.'

'I know that,' Ruby said.

'Now. It is time. I take you back.'

'Will we go out again soon?'

'Of course we will.'

They rode back to Iris's door. When she looked up at the high wall, with not a light showing anywhere, Ruby thought of Iris sitting alone inside with only the two old people to look after her. Ash's grandmother seemed the luckier, with her daughter and grandchildren around her and the dead too, everyone together.

Why was Iris cut off from her own daughter, and Lesley from her mother? She would ask, Ruby decided. She would find out.

The child has been to the cemeteries. As we are drinking our tea together she tells me about it and I can see that the experience has shocked her.

'People live on top of the graves. In the little tomb houses. There are sinks and electric lights and kids' toys, just like anywhere else.'

'The cemeteries are poor areas, but they are quite respectable. There are schools, sewerage, clinics.'

'Ash said the one they live in is his family tomb.'

'That's right, it would be.'

'But . . .' She shivers a little. 'All the dead people.'

'Are you afraid of the dead? Of death?'

Of course she is; she is young.

'No. Well, not of ghosts or . . . djinns. But I wouldn't like to sleep the night in a cemetery.' Her face changes, a shiver passing over it like wind across still water. 'I don't want to die.'

'Someone close to you has, haven't they?'

I was expecting to hear about a family dog, or perhaps even a school friend in a car accident. Her answer surprises me.

Ruby tells the story quickly, without embellishment, but her mechanical delivery hardly disguises the depths of horror. The last image of the crumpled boy with his head in a pool of dark blood will stay with me, too. I am filled with concern for her.

'Ruby, who knows about this?'

'I told Ash.'

'No one else? Not your mother or father?'

'No.'

'Why not?'

'The thing is, Lesley and Andrew didn't really know about Jas. He wasn't the kind of person they would go for. Don't get me wrong, there wasn't anything bad about him, he just wasn't plugged in to things most people care about, like money and jobs. I suppose some people might have thought he was a bit messed up. Lesley would have done.'

Ruby sighs. 'Lesley likes everything to be in order. She's really controlling. I suppose it's partly her way of keeping us safe, looking after us. But it can be a real pain. For example we've got some glass shelves in the kitchen at home, and all the mugs are kept there. But they have to be in a straight line and they have to be *plain white*. You know? They're just mugs for drinking tea out of, but if there's a patterned or coloured one it has to be kept out of sight in a cupboard. You can't really drop someone like Jas in the middle of a world like that.

'So I kept him separate. I liked having him all to myself, anyway. I'd just go off from Will and Fiona's place and stay with him. He had a room in a squatted house, but he'd made it nice. He'd decorated it with postcards and pictures of flowers and leaves and trees, cut out of magazines, stuck all over the walls, so the whole room looked like a garden that had exploded. We'd just lie and look at it. He used to say, "It's just the two of us, babe. Just you and me. This is our Garden of Eden." I loved that. But then, after he . . . died, it was like he'd never been there. I didn't want to think that he was so close to nothing.' Her voice sinks to a whisper. 'As if I was the only memorial he had.'

Now I can see the shape of ideas crossing her mind.

'Are you afraid of death?' she asks me.

'No. Nor will you be, I hope, when you get to my age. But I am afraid of what might intervene between now and then.'

'I know. Of forgetting.' Her eyes flick briefly towards the open door of my bedroom where Xan's photograph stands on the table next to the bed. 'Has anyone close to you died?'

'Almost everyone,' I say drily.

She laughs and then guiltily catches herself, reckoning that amusement is inappropriate in this context. What she is trying to do, as gently as she knows how, is to give me the opportunity to talk about Xan. She's curious about him on her own behalf, but it's also part of our odd bargain. I am supposed to reminisce and she will remember for me.

But it is *hard*.

Ruby put it well. I wanted to be the memorial, not to Xan himself because his family and his friends and his regiment remembered him too, but to our love. I had nothing else of him, and for a long time looked for nothing else.

For sixty years, the best part of a lifetime, I have jealously guarded these memories. I never spoke of them to my husband, or to my daughter, and I am aware that that was an act of selfishness. Lesley always knew, with the inarticulate, visceral intuition of a child, that I withheld myself from her.

Ruby is watching me, trying to work out where I am, waiting for me to say something. I have forgotten what we were talking about.

In the end she prompts me. 'Iris? What happened? Why don't you and Lesley get along?'

I want to answer her, but the words and reasons and recollections jumble together and then swirl away, out of my reach . . .

. . . No. That won't do. It would be easier to take refuge in the windy spaces of forgetfulness, but this truth is still sharp enough in my memory and I have to admit it: I didn't want to be a mother. Not then, not to Gordon's child, not to Lesley.

Maybe I never was cut out to be anyone's mother. Even if everything else had been different, my lack of maternal inclination might have been the same.

'I think Lesley and I respect each other,' I say.

Ruby feels rebuffed, I can tell. Silence spreads through the room as I try to work out a way to undo this.

Outside, the sky is overcast. Winter is coming, and it brings a damp chill that seeps through Cairo like mist off the Nile. I try to ward off the automatic shiver. Ideas suddenly jostle in my head and I clap my hands, making her jump.

'When did you get here?'

She looks startled. 'Um, it was twelve days ago.'

'You have been in my house for nearly two weeks and I haven't taken you anywhere, or shown you anything except for that one outing with your friends, and it is high time that I did. I promised your mother that I would educate you.'

I clap my hands again, louder this time.

'We'll go out now. We'll have an excursion. I know, we'll go to Giza. We'll drive out there, visit the Pyramids and then watch the sun set over the desert. Will you call Mamdooh? Tell him I will need the car.'

'You have a car?'

'Of course I do. Hurry up, or we will miss the sunset.'

Mamdooh's face was dark.

'Mum'reese, it is not a good idea. For Miss, I can arrange to make a visit with a guide who will speak English. Tomorrow, or even better the next day.'

Ruby followed Mamdooh through the kitchen, both of them in Iris's wake. He had given her one furious glare, indicating that all this must be her fault, and Ruby had done her best to signal back that it was nothing to do with her.

'Where is the key? Mamdooh?'

'It is here.' Auntie stood aside and Mamdooh took a set of keys out of a drawer in one of the old cream-painted cupboards.

'Very good. Come on.'

Auntie picked up a duster and polishing rag. In a small procession, with Ruby at the back, they passed through a door she had never seen opened before. It led from the kitchen into a small scullery. Mamdooh slid several bolts and opened another door. Ruby saw that it led into a cobbled alley at the back of the house.

Iris stood expectantly beside a pair of wooden doors secured with a chain and padlocks. Mamdooh very slowly went about the business of unlocking and withdrawing the chain. Finally he folded back the doors.

And there was a car.

Auntie moved first. With her bunched-up duster she made a little swipe over the bonnet. Under the thick coat of Cairo dust and gritty sand, it was just possible to tell that the car had once been black.

Iris looked mystified. She opened the driver's door and leaned into the interior, dust rising in little puffs under her fingers as she twisted the steering wheel.

'Not any insurance, not any service, oil, *benzene*,' Mamdooh muttered. 'Look, tyres all flat.'

Ruby wandered round to the back and rubbed the rear insignia plate clean. It was a Volkswagen Beetle, not so very different from the new one owned by Lesley in which Ruby had learned to drive.

Now Mamdooh stood back with his fists clenched on his hips. 'It is not possible to drive this car.'

Iris gently closed the door again. 'I bought it in the seventies, when I was living in Swakopmund. When I moved up here to Cairo I drove all the way, and everything I wanted to bring with me fitted into here.' Absently she patted the hood, her fingertips leaving little marks like the blurred footprints of birds.

Reluctantly Iris stepped away from the car although her hand still stretched out as if she didn't want to relinquish the memory and promise of adventure that went with it.

'We'll get a taxi instead.'

'Mum-reese, it is too late today. When you get to Giza it is dark.'

He had outflanked her, but Iris wouldn't be deflected. 'We'll go somewhere else, then. The museum. We'll go to the museum.'

Within half an hour a black-and-white taxi, much newer than Nafouz's, drew up outside the dark pink block of the museum. Iris sat up in the front next to the driver and Mamdooh, who had insisted on coming with them, was in the back next to Ruby.

Mamdooh negotiated for tickets, then they walked inside.

Ruby tilted her head to look upwards. Dim galleries rose round a central well crowned with a span of murky glass. Radiating away from where she stood were tall wooden cases filled, heaped, overflowing with a wild profusion of exhibits. She drifted down the wood-and-glass avenues, gazing at the displays. There were tiny carved wooden figures from tombs and huge imperious pharaonic statues. There were primitive boats and earthenware pots, broken shards and scratched hieroglyphs and curled papyrus, massive jewellery in gold and cornelian and glass, amulets and bracelets, and humble leather sandals that looked as if they had been discarded only a day ago. The artefacts were all dusty and most of the labels were written in scratchy, faded Arabic, but for Ruby this only added to the appeal.

Mamdooh shuffled and huffed at her shoulder.

'Miss, to come this way, please.'

Go away, she wanted to shout. But Iris was beckoning to her too.

'Where are we going?' Ruby asked.

'Upstairs.'

Reluctantly she followed them up shallow stone steps to the first-floor gallery, all the time wishing that she could have this treasury to herself without the distraction of Mamdooh and Iris.

There was a crowd of visitors in one room, and past the craning heads she caught one brief glimpse of the serene funerary mask of the boy king.

'Here?' she pointed.

Iris shook her head. They came to a side gallery, with rows of polished wooden benches in the anteroom.

'I will wait here,' Mamdooh announced.

The room beyond was hushed and dimly lit. The mummified remains of the royal pharaohs lay in sealed glass boxes.

Ruby crept along the line, lingering beside each enclosed mummy. Here were a queen's dark ringlets and hooked nose, here was a skull showing through skin like dried leather, long yellow teeth bedded in the jawbone, a withered arm circled with a coil of gold. Iris moved in step with her, murmuring the names: *Seti I, Ramses II, Tuthmosis IV*. Some of them looked as if they were merely asleep, others were withered and collapsed, a bundle of remains more touching than macabre. What struck Ruby most was that these were just people, with wrists and nostrils and fingernails. Outside in the halls were the decorated sarcophagi and tomb ornaments, but here were men and women. They had lived and known glory, and then they were dead. She was alive and they were not, and nothing but a heartbeat separated her from them.

She understood why Iris had brought her here. The dead were just the dead, neither awful nor remarkable. History separated out these individuals and preserved their names where others were obliterated for ever, but there was no real difference between this hushed room and the tomb house where Ash's family lived.

I watch Ruby as she tiptoes past the glass cases.

This is death in formal guise, like in the Cities of the Dead. Inevitably it makes me think of its antithesis, tumbled and shocking and finally forgotten in the sand.

Xan was away, out of my reach. As I had promised I would, I went to the hospital and up the stairs to the ward full of carved men.

'Hello,' I said quietly to Albie Noake. The upper half of his face had more colour in it now and he was propped higher against his pillows. Within his reach lay a notepad with a pencil attached to it by a piece of string. His eyes followed me as I moved a chair to the head of the bed, where I could sit with my mouth close to his ear. By the time I put my hand over his where it rested on the bedsheet I knew that he knew what I had come to say.

'Mr Ridley died without gaining consciousness. I'm so sorry. I wish Xan had been here to tell you.'

Briefly, his eyes closed. I wondered how much they had seen and been through together, Albie and Xan and Private Ridley.

Then Albie's hand twitched beneath mine and he indicated with a tilt of his head that I was to pass him the notepad. He wrote carefully and a bead of sweat appeared on his forehead.

Thank you for telling me, he had written. *Poor old Ridley.*

I lifted my head and met his eyes again. There was a look in them that begged me to stay and talk about life and hope, anything that was nothing to do with dying in the desert.

I talked until I forgot he couldn't answer.

'Do you have children, Albie?'

He picked up the notepad. *No, not married.* And *Missed my chance with you! Mr Molynew beat me to it.*

'I bet there's a girl or two waiting for you at home.'

There sending me back soon on a hospital ship.

'When? Albie, that's good news. They'll repair your jaw, they can do all kinds of amazing surgery nowadays. You'll be as good as new.'

We'll see. Will you come again before?

'Of course I will. I'll come every day, if you can bear it.'

I can. Thanks.

He looked tired, and he made no objection when I took the notepad out of his hand and awkwardly tried to settle his pillows.

'Good night, Albie. See you tomorrow.'

I hadn't seen Ruth, but she came up behind me as I left the ward.

'I told Albie that his friend died.'

'How did he take it?'

'Stoically.'

Ruth nodded. 'Look, as it happens Daphne's off this afternoon and I'm going home in an hour. Would you like to come out to the flat and have some food with us? It won't be anything very grand, I'm afraid.'

It occurred to me that Ruth must think I was grand. I blushed and mumbled that I'd love to come.

'Fine. About half past eight?'

I told her that I would look forward to it very much.

After their slow tour of the mummies they came back to the doorway. When Iris raised her eyebrows in enquiry, Ruby took one more glance back over her shoulder at the quiet figures.

'Thanks,' she said.

Mamdooh's bulk rose up from the bench. They made their way down the stairs once more.

'I think we can go back home now,' Iris announced. Mamdooh summoned a taxi from the waiting line.

Back at Iris's house, Ruby helped her off with her coat. Iris's face had gone papery with fatigue, but there was a gleam in her eyes.

'You were interested in that, weren't you?'

'Yes.'

'I thought you would be,' she crowed.

On impulse, Ruby took her grandmother in her arms and hugged her. At first Iris held herself rigid, pulling away, but then she relaxed.

'I loved it.' She planted a kiss on top of Iris's head. 'And death, after all, when it's right there it doesn't seem too huge and terrible to let into your mind. That was what you meant, wasn't it?'

Iris went to bed early, fussed away into her room by Auntie. Ruby wandered into her own bedroom and took out Jas's CD. She lay down on top of her covers and thought about him, and for the first time since the night at the top of the tower block it wasn't his crumpled shape in a halo of blood that superimposed itself over all the others. She saw him in his exploded garden of cut-out flowers instead, and heard his slow mumbling voice explaining to her just what the music meant.

chapter four

WE ARE SETTLED in our routine now, Ruby and me, and although the rhythm of my days is not much changed the house has a new life beating in it. In the mornings, when the sun has risen high enough to warm the air, we sit in the garden and drink coffee together. Ruby cuts up fruit and passes the pieces to me one by one, or breaks off strips of flat bread and dips them in honey before arranging them on my plate. As if I am the child, she the attentive parent.

When she is at home I hear her moving about, her feet on the stairs and the small creaks of her bedroom furniture. Then there is the bleat of a motorcycle horn from down in the street and she is off with her friend. I don't insist on knowing where, although quite often she tells me anyway.

Ashraf took her out to see the Pyramids and she came home comically disappointed. So many people, she frowned, and queues and dusty souvenir shops and tour guides holding up umbrellas.

'Was it like that in your day?'

'Not quite, it was wartime. But all the soldiers went out there to take a look, you could get a gharry at sunset when it was cooler, and there were young boys selling picture postcards and camel rides. The British Army had padded the Sphinx's head with sandbags to protect it.'

Ruby has also started making solitary visits to the museum, spending hours there at a time. She comes home to relate her discoveries, speculating about Nefertiti's beauty, wondering about the significance of the sphinxes, and telling me that a metre-long piece of the beard of the Sphinx at Giza is in the British Museum.

'I think we ought to give it back. Don't you think that would be satisfying, fitting it back on his chin like putting a piece in a puzzle?'

'Yes, it would, rather.'

We discuss the case of the Elgin Marbles, of which she has never heard. Lesley might even be pleased, I think, with the cultural content of some of our debates.

The child is also picking up some Arabic—a slow but steady accretion of basic words, *bread*, *water*, *scarf* and so on, and the phrases of polite greeting and thanks and blessing. When I compliment her on her quickness she looks surprised and pleased.

'Thanks. Ash teaches me. I try to learn something new in Arabic each time to say to his mother, to keep on the right side of her. She asked me to stay and eat some food with them last night so it must be working.'

'Ruby . . .'

Her face changes. 'I know, I know. It's rude to say no, and hospitality means that even if they haven't got much they try to give everything to the guest and go hungry themselves. So I just had a mouthful or two and chewed for a really, really long time.'

She mimes the effort of registering delighted appetite and at the same time swallowing next to nothing, and I laugh.

'I like being able to say a few words to Auntie, as well. I come out with something in Arabic and it cracks her up, she goes *tee hee hee* as if it's the best joke she's ever heard instead of just me asking for more soup.'

'Auntie's very reserved and she doesn't take readily to strangers, but she liked you straight away.'

'Yeah? Did she? Pity about Mamdooh, then.'

'Mamdooh is just doing what he sees as his duty, which is to look after us. He is the protective male in a house full of feeble women.'

'You're not feeble, and neither am I. Nor is Auntie, come to that.'

'Ruby, you don't have to take issue with every single thing. Mamdooh is the way he is, just accept that and try not to outrage him.'

She looks as if she is about to take issue with me, but she bites her tongue and sighs instead. 'Mamdooh's OK. Hey, you know your car?'

'My car?'

'I was telling Ash about it, Ash and Nafouz. You know, about how it's just sitting there in the garage falling to pieces among the cobwebs, and Nafouz said he's got a friend who's a brilliant mechanic who could maybe look at it and get it going again? Then we could go out for drives together. What do you think?'

She loves pomegranates and has been peeling one as we talk. The skin falls away in a neat coil to uncover pith that she slits to get at the glowing heart. I shake my head in answer to her silent offer; the seeds stick in my teeth.

'I'll think about it.'

She nods, eating pomegranate off the blade of the fruit knife. Five minutes later she jumps up and kisses the top of my head and five minutes after that she has gone out. Silence seeps slowly through the house, filling the corners and the dark angles of stairways.

I sit in my chair, and pick up another thread.

After the visit to Albie Noake I went home to Garden City to get ready for my evening with Ruth and Daphne. Mamdooh told me that there was a package for me on the hall tray.

I knew what was in the package and took the little square box into my bedroom and closed the door.

Xan's amethyst was opulent in its simple claw setting. I slipped it onto to my third finger and held my hand up in happy amazement.

I was an engaged woman; I was going to marry Xan Molyneux. I wanted nothing else in the world.

Later, I caught the Heliopolis bus. It was packed like a sardine can and smelt of tired bodies, and when we finally reached Ruth's stop I clambered down with relief. Following Ruth's directions, I found myself in a nondescript enclave of low modern houses with concrete balconies and outside staircases. The upper windows of Ruth's house stood wide open and loud dance music boomed out. I stared in surprise, then realised that the concrete stairs led up to a separate apartment. As I tapped the door knocker there was a crash and a bellow of laughter from above.

Ruth's face appeared. 'Sorry,' she murmured, opening the door wider.

'Some French officers live up there, they make a terrible racket at all hours. Come on in.'

Their sitting room was small, but they had made it look beautiful with handwoven rugs and Bedouin cushions in the colours of the desert, and unframed abstract paintings on the white walls.

'Hello,' a voice said from behind Ruth. 'I'm Daphne Erdall.'

I shook hands with Daphne. She was older than I had expected, perhaps in her early forties. She had a tanned face with broad cheekbones, a wide mouth and clear grey eyes, and her fair hair was so thick it stood out almost horizontally from the crown of her head. She was one of those people you look at and think, this is *someone*.

I had brought a bottle of whisky, a real Scottish malt. I gave it to Ruth.

Her face lit up. 'My God, Daph, look at this. Nectar from the god of the glens. Can we drink some, Iris?'

'That's pretty much what I brought it for.'

'You're very generous. We've only got local gutrot,' Daphne said. She poured us each a measure and we held up our glasses. 'To friendship,' Daphne proposed in her direct way. Pleased, I echoed the toast.

'It's a nice flat,' I said. Another crash sounded from above.

Daphne laughed. 'Apart from Gaston and his cronies, that is. Actually they're all right. Our hours don't overlap much. I'm going to see to the food for a minute; Ruth'll take care of you.'

'I'll show you the rest of the flat,' Ruth offered.

There wasn't much to see. In the kitchen a square table was already laid with three places and Daphne was at the stove stirring a pan of couscous. There was a narrow bathroom with a hip-bath, and a bedroom with shuttered windows. And there was one double bed, smooth under a white cotton coverlet.

Belatedly, the penny dropped.

Ruth was leaning in the doorway. 'Are you surprised?'

I was, but I tried not to show it. 'No. Well, yes, a bit. I haven't met . . . But actually, it's none of my business, is it?'

She raised one eyebrow. 'You'd be surprised at how many people think it is their business. Either to be nosy or comical about.'

'It's ready,' Daphne called from the kitchen.

When we sat down at the table with the candles lit and Daphne poured from a jug of red Lebanese wine, there was an air of celebration.

'It's a special occasion. You are here, and Ruth and I hardly ever get a chance to sit down and eat a proper dinner together,' she explained.

We drank the raisin-flavoured wine, ate roast chicken and couscous spiked with fresh herbs, and we talked. My hosts were good company, but they were serious-minded. I quickly realised that I couldn't rely on the superficial cocktail chatter that did for the rest of my social circuit.

As at every dinner table in Cairo that night, we discussed the war. But even the familiar assumption that the war itself was right and justifiable, made automatically by all my circle, was called into question here. Although Ruth and Daphne didn't call themselves pacifists, that is effectively what they were. Every day they saw the damage that combat did to men like Albie Noake and Private Ridley, and they spent their working hours trying to repair it.

'You've seen my ward,' Ruth said quietly. 'In a week's time, or whenever the push for Tobruk comes, we'll be caring for twice as many severely wounded. Or three, four, five times as many. The corridors will be full of stretchers. And it will be the same in Daphne's and every other hospital in Cairo. Is any strategic gain, any military advantage whatsoever, worth that amount of loss and suffering?'

'If we don't attack, the Axis forces will push across the western desert and on to Cairo. We have to defend Egypt,' I said.

Daphne's clear eyes rested on my face. 'For our own ends, not Egypt's. This isn't our country, yet we behave exactly as if it were and as if the people are our servants and inferiors. Farouk is the King of Egypt, but our ambassador is the ruler.'

'So why are you here?' I demanded.

'Because I love this country. I was here before the war, working with a village medical programme. When the war is over I'll go back to it. In the meantime I'm a surgical anaesthetist and I treat each individual on the operating table as a life we can save. There have been a lot of injured men, and you heard what Ruth said. There are soon going to be thousands more.'

Under the tablecloth, I twisted Xan's amethyst on my third finger.

I turned to Ruth, pushing away the thought of a dam about to break and release a tide of blood. 'What about you? Why are you here?'

'I love Egypt too. And I love Daphne. I want to be where she is.'

Smiling again, Daphne refilled my glass with the last of the wine. Ruth stood up to collect the plates.

'And you?' Daphne asked me.

'I work at GHQ. Clerical administrator.'

'Iris has just got engaged,' Ruth said mischievously.

Young women like me, as the cynical wisdom of Cairo put it, came out here either to find a husband or to escape from one. I hadn't been guilty of either intention, and Sarah and Faria had often teased me at the beginning for not being interested enough in having fun, yet in

Daphne's and Ruth's company I couldn't help feeling frivolous.

'Congratulations,' Daphne said. 'What is he doing?'

'He's a cavalryman, seconded to one of the special ops groups.'

'Ah.' There was warmth and sympathy in Daphne's shrewd look. She knew what special ops work was likely to entail, and she left it at that.

I cleared my throat. 'I've been thinking lately about what else I could do here. I've been wondering about hospital work.'

Again, there was an appraising look. Ruth put the malt whisky bottle back on the table.

'I could ask the Director of Nursing at the QM, where I work, if she could find a niche for you,' Daphne said. 'It'd only be voluntary work, mind, but there might be something more interesting than reading to the men or rolling bandages.'

The Queen Mary was the biggest of the Cairo hospitals now taken over by the military.

'Would you? I'd like that very much.'

'Leave it to me,' Daphne said.

The three of us raised our whisky glasses and this time the toast was a silent one. Now not only did I have intimacy with Xan, I had the luxury of this congenial female company. Warmth, unconnected with whisky, ran through my veins. I had been lonely, I realised, and now suddenly I wasn't.

'*My darling girl,*' my mother wrote. '*Your father and I were so excited to hear your big news, and we are so very pleased for you both. What do you plan to do? You won't think I'm too sentimental, I hope, if I tell you that I have dreamed of my girl's wedding in an English church on a midsummer's morning, with her father to give her away. And her mother shedding one tear in the front pew. Of course this war has changed that for everyone, not just you and your Alexander.*

You do not mention a date, and it may not be your intention to wait at all. I know that 'quick' wartime ceremonies are quite normal nowadays—but, darling, I should so like to see you being married. Perhaps after Christmas, or even in the spring, your father and I could somehow find a passage out to Cairo to be with you? What with coupons and everything in such short supply here, it may even be easier to put together your trousseau out there.

What a lot there is to think about. Daddy is well, and sends all his love, as do I. The vicar has asked me to help out with the garden effort, we are turning some of the park over to vegetables.

God bless you both. Ever your loving Ma.

I read her letter at my desk, in a brief lull. GHQ was in turmoil. The
offensive had begun two days earlier as twenty-mile lines of Allied
troops and armaments poured across the frontier towards Rommel's
Panzer Group Africa, and Tobruk.

The original offensive by the three brigades of the 7th Armoured
Division and supporting artillery and infantry had developed into the
confusion and horror of the battle of Sidi Rezegh. Thirty thousand
British, German and Italian tanks and other vehicles milled and circled
in a flat, exposed desert landscape of dust, thorns, smoke, burnt-out
tanks and dead men covering 3,000 square miles. On the ground, it
was often impossible to tell friend from enemy. Every vehicle that
loomed in sight could be a threat or a reinforcement. Signals trucks
were captured and whole formations seemed to evaporate because the
next link in the chain couldn't communicate with them. Supply dumps
and entire headquarters were lost, and men of different units formed up
together and fought on in the whirling chaos of smoke and sand.

Roddy Boy and his staff sweated to interpret and transmit back to the
field commanders the intelligence that poured in from the shattered
forces, while the cups of tea I carried in to him turned cold and orange
on his desk. A new admiration for him dawned in me.

In the midst of this, in the rare moments of relative calm, I read the
word *trousseau* and the incongruity of it made me smile before Roddy
Boy appeared in front of me with yet another sheaf of paper and the
order snapped over his shoulder, 'As quick as you can, Miss Black.'

Then, on November 24, Rommel suddenly gathered together the
remaining Panzers of his army and broke eastwards towards the thick-
ets of wire that separated Libya from Egypt. Beyond Egypt, only time
and the conquests of Palestine and Syria would separate him from the
oilfields of Iraq and Persia.

I had no idea where Xan might be. I tried to stop myself from fitting
Tellforce operations into the floods of intelligence that washed over me.
All I could do was work, snatch an hour's sleep, and work again.

After two days of confusion, intelligence confirmed that in Rommel's
absence the British had taken the opportunity to attack Sidi Rezegh
once more, so he reversed his momentum and pulled back to a point
east of Tobruk. In his wake the Panzers rolled back from the wire to re-
engage, but these were the last throes of the battle and it was hardly a
victory for either side. Eighteen thousand British and Allied troops had
been killed, wounded or captured. Rommel had lost all but forty of his
tanks, and German shipping losses in the Mediterranean meant that it
would probably be weeks before he could replace them.

GHQ drew breath.

On December 7, Axis losses around Sidi Rezegh forced Rommel to withdraw to the west of Tobruk and the 242-day siege of the harbour and garrison was lifted. On the same day Roddy came out of his office after a short telephone call and told me that the Japanese had bombed Pearl Harbor. 'Now the Americans will be in,' he said.

The next evening I went to the Scottish Military again. The entrance was blocked by a line of ambulances, as it had been for days, and inside the hospital the corridors were packed with lines of walking wounded. Albie Noake had been moved off Ruth's ward and into one where patients shuffled about on crutches and played cards at the centre table.

Yanks are in. All over soon? Albie wrote.

'I don't know. I hope so.'

Any news from Mr M?

'No. Not yet.'

Bet there having some fun, wherever they are. I bloody hate missing it, scuse languige.

I put my hand on his, trying to smile. 'I know you do. They'll be missing you too.'

Still coming to see me off?

Albie's place on the next hospital ship sailing for England via the Cape had been confirmed. He would be leaving in two days' time.

'I asked my boss for an hour off to come to the station. He acted as if I'd asked for a month at the seaside, but he said yes. I'll be there.'

They need the beds. It's gone mad here.

Our eyes met. 'Yes.'

The railway station was in chaos. Egyptian railway officials dashed up and down the platforms trying to direct the medical orderlies who surged through the metal gates carrying stretcher cases. Trains waited to ferry the injured to the ships waiting in the Gulf of Suez. There were wounded men everywhere, in wheelchairs and on crutches, or slowly limping in twos and threes through the engine smoke and stale hissing steam towards their numbered carriages. Pedlars and street boys ran around between them, hawking fruit and cigarettes.

I couldn't find Albie. I knew the number of the MTC transporter that would be bringing him from the hospital, but I couldn't see it in the line. Five minutes later it trundled round the corner. Two orderlies jumped out and folded down a step, and the men began to emerge. Albie was walking now, unsteadily but unsupported. Waving my arms in the air so he would see me, I ran towards him.

'I thought you'd decided to stay after all,' I panted.

I picked up his kitbag in one hand, gave him my other arm and we set off in a shuffle through the crowds.

Then, at the end of the platform, turning from side to side as he searched through the throng, I suddenly caught sight of a man who looked like Xan. I was used to this. In every crowded street in Cairo I would catch sight of someone who resembled him, and my heart would jump into my throat. But this time, as we drew closer together, instead of the likeness disappearing he looked more and more like Xan.

I gave a shout that made heads turn to look at me: 'Xan.'

Albie saw him now too, and made the squawk of vowels sound that was all the speech that was left to him.

Xan sprinted through the crowds. With one hand he caught hold of me, the other he held out to Albie.

'You're here,' I said stupidly.

'I flew up this morning with Colonel Wainwright. I heard that Corporal Noake was on the way home, so I raced across to wish him bon voyage. You look better than you did when I last saw you,' he told Albie.

Albie gave him the double thumbs-up.

Xan looked just himself, tired and dirty but as happy and full of laughter as he always seemed. Gratitude washed through me. Xan took the bag from me and with one of us on either side we walked Albie on down the train until we found a carriage with an empty seat in it.

I stood back while Xan helped him up the step, hoisted his bag onto the luggage shelf and settled him into his place. His head bent close over Albie and he talked quickly into his ear. I knew that he was briefly telling him whatever it was he had missed, in the desert with Tellforce. Doors began slamming all down the train. A guard in a sweaty uniform held a green flag furled under his arm. I hopped quickly onto the step and leaned past the crammed soldiers to kiss the side of Albie's face that was still there.

'See you back in England,' I said.

The flag was being unfurled. Xan and I jumped back down onto the platform. The train clanked forward and we walked and then ran alongside the window of Albie's carriage, waving and calling goodbye until we couldn't keep up any longer.

We dropped back and fell into each other's arms.

The car was repaired.

The work was done by Nafouz's friend Husain who was a garage mechanic, and when it was finished Nafouz and Ash returned the car to the alleyway behind Iris's house. The pitted chrome had been polished as far as possible and the patches of bodywork not consumed by rust were black again.

Iris made a slow tour from the back to the front of the car, touching the door handles and running her fingertips over the rust that bubbled around the sills. She stroked the bonnet's slope and completed the circuit. Then she looked Nafouz straight in the eye. 'I will put my car in the garage now. Then you may come into the house and speak to me.'

'Lady, Doctor, I will put away . . .'

'No, thank you,' Iris snapped. She opened the driver's door and slid into the creaking seat, grasping the wheel with her freckled hands. Then with a crescendo of revs she stamped on the clutch and scraped the gearstick into first. The car strained until she remembered the handbrake, and then it sprang forward and Iris spun the wheel to bring it coasting into the garage. She switched off the engine and stepped out, pocketing the car keys at the same time.

'Mamdooh will show you the way,' she told Ash and Nafouz.

Iris and Ruby reached the inner garden first. Iris's cheeks were flushed and she looked as excited as a child. 'I wasn't sure I could do that.'

'You didn't have any trouble at all.'

'I didn't, did I? It's going to be fun.' She took the keys out of her pocket and flipped them into the air, just managing to catch them again. Ruby thought she was like a teenager who had coaxed the use of the car out of her father for a Saturday night, and the idea made her smile.

Mamdooh escorted the boys out into the garden and stood like a sentinel with his hands clasped in front of him. Ash and Nafouz shuffled a little, staring around them without wanting to stare. The pots of greenery gave off a warm scent of leaves and earth, and the water splashed into its glazed bowl.

Iris sat down and indicated a bench facing her chair. Nafouz took his place but Ash hesitated, and Ruby hovered beside him instead of drawing her chair to its usual position close to Iris's.

'And so what do I owe you and your friend for servicing my car?' Iris asked pleasantly.

Nafouz leaned forward, making a deprecatory flat-palmed gesture. 'I would like to say nothing, this is done for friendship only.'

'Thank you. But?'

'My friend is a poor man. He has a wife, children.'

'Of course. Go on.'

Nafouz mentioned a large sum, in Egyptian pounds, with a mournful shrug.

Equally regretfully, Iris named a third of the price.

Ash and Ruby looked at each other and she saw that Ash was smiling. It was clear that Iris and Nafouz understood each other perfectly.

'Come with me?' she murmured to him, tilting her head the way they had come. Mamdooh frowned, but he couldn't follow them and stand guard over Iris at the same time. Auntie was presumably preparing the inevitable tray of mint tea and sweet pastries. Ash and Ruby slipped back into the house while the negotiations continued their course.

Ash walked through the celebration hall, gazing up at the carved panelling and painted ceilings and the screens shielding the gallery.

'All this house belongs only to your grandmother?' he whispered.

Through his eyes, Ruby saw the grandeur of it instead of the dust and cobwebs. She answered awkwardly, her voice sounding much too loud in the shadowy space, 'I think so. I never really asked her.'

'Do you live in a house also like this in England?'

'No. God, no. Nothing like.' She laughed, again too loud, and then bit her lip. Nothing like the tomb house, either. There was suddenly a thin shaft of mystified envy splintered with embarrassment between herself and Ash, and she didn't know how to deal with it. It was as if Jas had been pitchforked into the middle of one of Lesley's dinner parties.

She grabbed Ash by the wrist. 'Come on.' Maybe in her room he would just look into her face and not see anything else.

At first he followed willingly, then he realised that they were heading for the inner stairway.

He stopped dead. 'I cannot.'

'I thought you were allowed if one of the women of the household *invited* you.'

'Even then it is only for brothers, cousins. Not for stranger.'

Ruby reached up and cupped his face between her hands.

'You are not a stranger,' she whispered. 'You're my friend.'

He blinked, but didn't move.

Then she pulled his head down so that her mouth touched his.

'I'd say you were my brother. But actually I love you,' she said. At the same moment it occurred to her that this wasn't a blandishment or even a veiled threat. It was the truth, as close as she had ever got to it.

Ash looked amazed. His eyes widened and he pulled her closer as he kissed her. Afterwards he let her lead him up the stairs and along the gallery to her room and crept inside.

'My bedroom,' Ruby said superfluously.

He stood with his hand on the latch and looked at the austere space. There were two or three books on a chair, a small squared-off pile of CDs, the cover on the narrow divan was pulled straight. Everything else was tidied away into the chest. It was the way Ruby liked it, now.

Ash grinned, and she saw that he was recovering himself.

'I have not visited a girl's bedroom before. I did not think you would be so tidy, Ruby.'

She aimed a kick at his shin, and he caught her wrists to stop her punching him. They scuffled like puppies, laughing and puffing until they stumbled against the divan in the window arch, then they flopped onto their knees and peered down into the street.

'After the first time with Nafouz, I came back and I thought this was your window. I saw the light here, just the one, shining in all this big wall. I stood down in the street and looked up, trying to see you.'

'You *were* spying on me. And that time in Khan al-Khalili you'd followed me all the way, hadn't you? Some people might think that was creepy, you know.'

'Creepy? What is that?'

Ruby hooked her fingers and distorted her face into an approximation of creepiness and Ash recoiled.

'I am not like that in any way,' he said seriously.

'I know that *now*. I told you what I feel now, didn't I?'

'Yes. I am surprised and I am also pleased of course. But, Ruby, it means that we are not playing any more.'

They knelt upright, facing each other.

'Is that bad?'

Gently he put his hand to her waist, stroked it upwards, splaying his fingers so they rested in the indentations between her ribs. 'I am Egyptian boy, you are English girl. I am poor boy, you are rich girl. I am telephone worker, you are . . . *phhh*. I do not even know. You can be anything you want, I suppose.'

'I'm not anything very much. No . . . wait, Ash, don't contradict. It's the truth. I ran away from home to come here because Jas died and because my uncle really *is* a creep and my mother and her husband think I'm a failure, and I just woke up one morning in England and looked around me and I thought that if I didn't do something soon they'd be right. I came here to Iris's house, thinking it didn't matter where I was just so long as it was a different place to feel nothing much in.

'Then I met you. You took me to the Cities of the Dead and I saw your house and family and you showed me places and . . . this is going to sound properly cheesy, but it made me understand some things I hadn't worked out before. I don't think you should feel sorry for yourself unless there's good reason, and I really haven't got one, but I was still feeling sorry for myself without properly acknowledging it. So I was angry as well. But being here with you and Iris and Auntie, and yeah, even Mamdooh, has made me feel different. I like going to the museum because it makes me feel small, and yet part of it all, like we all are, you and me and Iris and all the people in her history, and mine and yours and everyone in the Cities whether they're alive or dead, and that's really comforting.' Ruby sighed. 'I want to do something now it's my turn, not be useless. I just don't know what it is, yet.'

Her face broke up into a smile that made Ash tighten his grip and draw her closer to him. Their faces were almost touching.

She whispered, 'What you were saying, about you being Egyptian and me English, rich girl and poor boy?'

'Yes.'

'I think the only words that matter out of all of them are *girl* and *boy*.'

'Perhaps you are right.'

Face to face and hip to hip they had begun to slide down onto the bed. A sharp rapping on the door jerked them upright again in a tangle of legs and arms.

'*Miss* Ruby?' Mamdooh shouted.

Ash exclaimed in Arabic and leapt to his feet, staring wildly around him for an escape route.

'It's OK,' Ruby said. She strolled to the door and opened it, and Mamdooh loomed into the room.

'This is not correct,' he spluttered. Ash was already sidling past him in an attempt to get away but Mamdooh moved with surprising speed to cut him off, and Ash shot an imploring glance at Ruby.

'What's wrong?' Ruby innocently asked Mamdooh.

His big face was puffed with rage. 'You bring shame.'

Ash began a protestation but Ruby hushed him.

'Shame? What right do you have to say that?'

Mamdooh wouldn't look at her. 'You are Muslim boy,' he said to Ash.

Ruby darted round and stood next to Ash. 'Yes, he is, and he has never done one thing wrong or *shameful* as you call it ever since I have known him. I might have, but he hasn't. You should apologise to him.'

'Ruby,' Ash miserably whispered.

Mamdooh frowned from one to the other. 'Is this truth?'

'Yes.'

'In this country, in this house, it is not for boys to visit the bedroom of a young girl.'

'In England we figure that if people are going to do something they'll find somewhere, bedroom or not.'

'You are being rude,' Ash told her.

Ruby whirled round, ready to take him on too, but he held her gaze. After a long moment her shoulders dropped. 'I'm sorry, Mamdooh, OK? I promise I won't bring any boy up to my bedroom again. Will that do?'

Majestically, he inclined his head and stood aside to let them file out of the door. 'Mum-reese waits for you.'

Iris and Nafouz were sitting in the garden, drinking mint tea and looking like the best of friends.

'There you are,' Iris called when she saw them. 'Have some tea, both of you.'

Ash accepted the glass Ruby gave him but he would only sit on the edge of the bench.

'It is time for Nafouz and me to go. I am glad car is fixed, Madam Iris.'

Iris smiled gaily at him. 'You must come for a drive.'

As she saw them out, Ruby asked Ash when they were going to see each other again.

'Soon. I have to work, Ruby, you know this.'

Ruby watched the two brothers until they reached the end of the street and disappeared in the direction of Khan al-Khalili. She stood on the top step and breathed in the thick scents. Animals, diesel fumes, spices, pee.

It came to her that she liked Cairo.

After the battles for Sidi Rezegh and Rommel's withdrawal to the line at Mersa el Brega, there came a lull in the desert fighting. Many of the officers and men of the 8th Army came back to Cairo on leave, and for Xan and me and our friends Christmas 1941 turned into a series of wild parties, where we danced to the gramophone and drank whatever we could lay our hands on.

Sometimes it would have been easy to forget there was a war on at all. Some days were officially meatless, even in the smart restaurants, because enemy control of the Mediterranean meant that meat could no longer be imported and local supplies were rationed, so we just ordered shellfish or cheese soufflé instead. Grain shortages drove the poor in Cairo to attack the bakeries in attempts to steal what they could no longer buy.

As she had promised, Daphne Erdall found me volunteer work at her hospital. It wasn't nursing, which was what I had naively hoped for, but at least it was something. For three evening sessions a week I sat at a desk in the almoner's office and filled in forms with the details of British casualties; name, number, rank, regiment, injuries, date of arrival, supervising MO, ward, notification of next of kin. I typed letters addressed to wives in the Home Counties and mothers in Yorkshire and Scotland, and passed them on to the proper authority for signature.

I saw Daphne sometimes, and although at first I was a little in awe of her we slowly began to be friends. If I was early for work and she was finishing a shift, we would have a cup of tea together in the medical staff canteen. Daphne would tell me about her day's list of operations and if they had lost a badly wounded soldier on the table her eyes would darken with sadness and frustration.

I tried inviting Daphne and Ruth to some of the parties we all went to that Christmas, but they were rarely off duty at the same time and when they were they preferred to be alone together.

But then, oddly enough, they appeared at Mrs Kimmig-Gertsch's New Year's Eve party.

The lovely panelled hall was decorated with a pine tree that blazed with dozens of real wax candles and its sharp, resinous scent perfumed the whole house. Mrs Kimmig-Gertsch herself stood in front of it, shaking hands with an impressive turnout of Cairo society. She inclined her head to us when we reached her. She was wearing a white Grecian-style evening dress swathed and draped across her stately bosom. 'Have you planned a wedding day?' she demanded, her eyes on my amethyst.

'Not yet,' we murmured.

'Don't leave it too long,' she ordered. Xan bowed just a shade too theatrically and I concentrated very hard on not giggling.

Xan put his hand under my arm as we turned into the room. 'Look at this,' he whispered. There were jewels and furs, pale or sun-flayed European faces and haughty, sallow Levantine ones, medals and moustaches and feathers and coiffures mixing with the dress uniforms of a dozen armies. 'And we are in the middle of a war.'

It was hard to believe.

It was then that I saw Ruth and Daphne. The screens of the upper gallery had all been opened up for the party and they were leaning over the carved partition and looking down on the heads of the crowd.

I pointed them out to Xan. 'I'm surprised. I'd no idea they knew Mrs Kimmig-Gertsch. Would you like to come and meet them?'

'Yes, very much.'

We found the stairway that led up to the gallery and made our way towards them.

'Ruth? Daphne? May I introduce my fiancé, Xan Molyneux?'

Xan said, 'I've heard a lot about you both.'

'Likewise,' Ruth agreed.

'I wanted to say thank you for nursing Albie Noake. I heard from Iris how expertly.'

'It's my job,' Ruth said, but a faint blush betrayed her pleasure.

Two by two, we made a slow circuit of the gallery, Xan with Daphne and me with Ruth.

'How do you know her?' I asked, as we watched our hostess sketch a curtsy to an Egyptian royal princess.

'Not me, Daphne. Before the war she was involved in a charity that was considering a major donation to Daph's village medical project. The money never quite materialised, actually, but we seem to have made it onto the guest list anyway. What about you?'

I told her about Sandy.

Below us a group of men in distinctive red trousers were dancing a noisy conga line through the crowd. It was the Cherry Pickers.

'Is Jessie here?' I asked Xan.

'Of course he is. I think he's marking the mule's dance card.'

My new friends and Xan liked each other at once. He could talk as fluently as Daphne did about the war and about bread rationing and the predicament of Cairo's poor but he also teased her, and Ruth, about their serious-mindedness.

'It's New Year's Eve. No irrigation project can be got under way tonight, can it?' He hoisted two glasses off a passing tray and put them into their hands. 'Let's concentrate on irrigating ourselves. Here's to 1942,' he said.

They echoed the toast and I looked at their bright faces outlined against the swirl of party guests. I was pleased and excited to be with the three of them and I drank to celebrate.

We danced, and I picked at some of the cold lobster and creamy gateaux laid out in the dining room, and danced and drank some more. I held on to Xan's wrist and he steered me through the crowds as familiar and half-recognised faces swam up and sank back again. Much later, I found myself following him and a crowd of other people through the kitchen regions of the house and out into a narrow cobbled alley somewhere at the back. The cool air made me stumble in my high heels and Jessie James put his arm round my waist. The famous poker game mule, that had become the constant companion of one of his officer friends, was patiently standing outside a pair of stable doors and his owner was tugging at the bridle.

'Come on, darling. Don't be coy, come and greet your public.'

The Cherry Pickers all cheered. The mule was wearing a sable wrap with the tails hanging round its forequarters and an orchid corsage was tucked into the bridle's headpiece. The mule lifted one hoof, stepped delicately forward and crossed the cobbles to the door that led into the house. The rest of us formed a ragged column behind it.

'What's happening?' I mumbled to Xan.

'He wants them to see in the New Year together.'

A little group of musicians had been playing on the low dais facing the giant Christmas tree. Now the leader stood up, tucked his violin under one arm and made a little bow. A noisy group was counting down the seconds to midnight. *Twelve, eleven, ten . . .* As the mule made its entry through the tall doors it was stricken by the bright lights and the surging crowd. Its legs splayed and its head reared back, setting the sable tails jiggling.

Five, four, three . . .

Everyone was shouting now. The mule gave a terrified snort.

Two, one, hooray . . .

There was a popping of corks like gunfire. The band scraped into an approximation of the first bars and the crowd swayed dangerously as everyone crossed arms with their neighbours. Ruth and Daphne were singing, I could hear their voices through all the clamour.

We'll take a cup of kindness yet, for . . . auld lang syne.

The mule broke free and dashed through the room, scattering women in satin and diamonds, and sending chairs crashing over. His owner chased behind and cornered it beside the Christmas tree.

'Dash it,' he cried, 'don't you know the words?'

'Happy New Year, Iris, darling.' Xan laughed as his hands cupped my face. 'Nineteen forty-two will be our year. We'll make it our year.'

chapter five

AS WE LEAVE THE CITY behind the darkness thins.

There is never a precise moment in the desert when you can say *now it is dawn*, but the day comes swiftly and without drama. Suddenly the single-storey mud villages and irrigation canals stand out on either side of the road in the flat grey light and the rigid black silhouettes of date palms subdivide monochrome fields of crops. We overtake a buffalo cart, and an old man riding a donkey with empty panniers dragging at its haunches.

We are going to see the sun rise at the Pyramids, I remember that much, but now that we are on the road I want to be back in my house, inside the familiar place. If we go on, the harsh sun and the wind over the dunes will obliterate me.

I turn to the driver. 'Daphne, stop.'

Ruby noticed a scruffy little café at the side of the road where the owner was putting out tin tables and his wife was sweeping dust off the concrete standing with a palm leaf brush. A cup of coffee might help, she thought. This excursion was already turning out to be a bad idea.

'Let's stop here, shall we?' she said to Iris.

They sat down on metal chairs with the battered table shielding them from the road.

'I would like some hot coffee,' Iris said. She looked pale but calmer.

Ruby was hungry. She ordered bread and eggs and a dish of fruit while the café owner yawned and scraped his jaw with the back of his hand. It was still very early.

'Iris? Who's Daphne?'

Iris sat quite still, gazing along the road that led away from Cairo. At first, Ruby thought she hadn't heard the question. A tin pot of coffee and two thick white cups were banged down on the table in front of them, followed by a bowl containing slices of greyish bread. Ruby poured coffee and pushed one of the cups close to Iris.

'Daphne Erdall,' Iris said clearly.

'Go on.'

There was no answer this time, but this was the technique, Ruby had learned, when Iris drifted into one of the lost places.

You kept prodding her with questions and disjointed answers were doled out in response. Then—not always, but sometimes—the fragments occasionally coalesced into chunks of intelligible narrative.

Only two days ago, when Ruby was taking Iris out for a walk in the sunshine, the sight of a mule with a small boy had made her stop short and give a little laugh that turned into a gasp. She wouldn't say what was funny or painful, but she had clasped Ruby's hand more tightly as they made their slow turn to the end of the street and back.

But then, when they were inside the house once more, Iris had suddenly come out with a story about a mule being led into this hall because its owner wanted it to sing Auld Lang Syne at a New Year's party.

'Were you living here then?' Ruby asked, puzzled.

'Oh no. That was the beginning of 1942. The house belonged to Gerti Kimmig-Gertsch in those days.'

'So did you buy it from her?'

'Of course not. It's a much more interesting story than that.'

'I'm all ears,' Ruby said, but Iris only complained that she was tired and would Ruby please send Auntie upstairs to her.

Then yesterday afternoon Iris had suddenly had the idea that they should make a dawn excursion to the Pyramids.

'The museum, and the Pyramids. Essential for all visitors to Cairo. What would your mother say if I didn't take you out there?'

Ruby shrugged and said she had already been out there with Ash and Giza had been crowded with a million tourists and touts and taxis, but Iris dismissed her with an impatient wave of the hand. They would get up very early and go out to see the sun rise.

Yesterday evening, out walking with Ash, she told him about the plan for the morning.

'No difference, early or late. Always many people.'

'Yeah. But my grandmother is thinking of sixty years ago.'

'You will take care, Ruby. I would come with you, but I must work.'

'It's fine. What can happen?'

'Going to Giza only, I suppose nothing. You will take Cairo taxi?'

'I'm going to drive the Beetle.'

Now Iris and Ruby sat at the roadside café watching the morning traffic build up. Iris finished her coffee and drank some water, dabbing her mouth afterwards with a folded handkerchief as Ruby chewed her way through bread and hard-boiled egg chopped up with onion.

'Have some breakfast.' She pushed the bowl of bread an inch closer but Iris ignored her. 'Or tell me about Daphne Erdall.'

Surprisingly, Iris responded at once. 'She was a doctor. A very good doctor, a surgical anaesthetist here in Cairo, and her friend Ruth Macnamara was a nurse. I was very young and silly but I learned a lot from the two of them. It was because of Daphne's example that I decided to study medicine myself, once the war was over. I married your father when I was coming to the end of my clinical practice at St Bartholomew's.'

'My grandfather, you mean.'

Iris glared at her. Her lips were compressed into a thin line emphasised by radiating creases. 'Don't tell me what I mean. Yes, your grandfather.'

Ruby thought of the soldier in the photograph beside Iris's bed, the only photograph on display in the whole house, the soldier who was definitely not Grandfather Gordon. 'What happened to Captain Molyneux?'

Iris considered for a moment before answering. Then she cleared her throat and said precisely, 'He was killed in the desert. In May 1942.'

In the following silence Ruby did the arithmetic. Sixty-three years ago; remote history, almost. 'That's sad,' she said.

'Sad. Yes.'

Iris sat with her hands folded, looking straight ahead of her at what Ruby could not see. There was something practised and impenetrable about her absolute stillness.

As Ruby tried to think what to say next she noticed that the world had acquired colour. The walls of the café shack were sunflower yellow, the crops in the field across the road a pale, watered-down green. Somewhere behind them, beyond the Suez Canal, the sun had risen.

'Would you like some more coffee? Or shall we move on?'

In the absence of any response she beckoned the surly café owner and asked for the bill. Then she followed him into the dingy interior and took two litre bottles of water out of the chiller cabinet, fumbling with dirty pound notes as she paid for everything. Outside again, she took Iris by the arm and led her back to the car. It was now much too late for seeing the sunrise at the Pyramids, but they headed on anyway in the steady flow of traffic towards the dun-coloured fences and loop roads and coach parks that surrounded the Giza complex.

Then Ruby glanced at Iris and saw that she was weeping. Tears ran down her face and into the seams round her mouth.

Ruby pulled in to the side of the road once more. Then she put her arms round her grandmother and tried awkwardly to draw her close. The handbrake and gearstick got in the way.

'Iris, stop. Please stop.'

Iris felt so fragile, too small and brittle to contain such grief. Ruby could do nothing except hold her and wait for the tears to stop. She stroked her thin hair and murmured pointless words that were intended to be comforting.

At last Iris's shuddering sobs petered out and she was quiet. 'Ridiculous.' She sniffed. 'Give me a handkerchief, will you?'

Ruby didn't go in for keeping handkerchiefs tucked into her sleeve or folded into a pocket, the way Iris did, but after some rummaging she found Iris's own for her and put it into her hand.

'Were you crying because Captain Molyneux died?'

'After sixty years? No, I don't believe so. I've grieved enough for his life cut short and for mine for running on for so long with so little in it. It's weakness now, but I suppose I am crying out of a general sense of loss. Maybe I am mourning for the human condition.'

'That sounds a bit . . . what's the word? Grandiose, is that it?'

To Ruby's relief, Iris laughed. 'Yes, you are probably right. On the other hand, wherever you look there is so much loss and folly to contemplate, and we are so frail in the face of it that it's hard to do anything other than mourn. But you're young, Ruby. For you everything carries a twin charge of novelty and infinite possibility. Whatever novelty I shall experience is unlikely to be pleasant.'

Ruby considered. 'Well, I turned up, didn't I? That was a novelty, and you said you were pleased about it.'

'Yes, Ruby. You did, and I am.' Iris sighed. 'I have had a long life and I have been useful. I enjoyed my work, very much, for many years. I have a home and people to care for me. I am afraid of losing what I have always valued . . .'

'The cup on the shelf?'

Iris looked startled. 'Did I say that to you?'

'Yes.'

'I had forgotten. You see? Yes, there is that, and there is also the sense that I have had a hole at the centre of my life. It has been there for a very long time.'

Ruby pressed the flat of her hands against the steering wheel and arched her back. 'This *hole* in the centre? It's not really Captain Molyneux, is it? Would I be right in thinking it's actually Mum?'

There was a pause. 'Lesley.'

'Yeah. Your daughter, my mother.'

Ruby was thinking, she's not going to answer and she won't say anything else.

But Iris did nod her head, very slowly, as if it hurt. 'Maybe.' She took a long breath, raised her chin again and glared out at the file of traffic. 'Where are we going?'

If she didn't want to talk, Ruby couldn't make her. 'To the bloody Pyramids, supposedly. Do you still want to?'

'I . . . would like to go for a drive. Out into the desert a little way. Can we do that instead?'

'Of course we can.'

They rejoined the column of traffic, but instead of being drawn with it towards the three triangles magnetically pasted against the whitish southern sky, they broke free and headed on, westwards, with the sun rising higher at their backs. Out here there were only low sand dunes that glittered where the sun caught them and trapped broad scoops of donkey-brown shadow within their concave arms.

'There is a tiny oasis out here somewhere,' Iris said. 'With a view of the Pyramids that you don't get from anywhere else.' She looked back over her shoulder, searching for a glimpse of it.

'Do you want to turn back and try to find it?' Ruby murmured.

'I only went there once.'

The Beetle hummed along, its tyres swishing through the skim of sand on tarmac. Ruby and Iris both fell into a contented silence, watching the endless rise and fall of the empty landscape.

For the first three months of 1942 I worked at my GHQ job in Roddy Boy's office and spent whatever time I had to spare at the Queen Mary. I saw how the medical services dealt with the constant stream of casualties brought back from the front as Rommel recaptured Benghazi and pushed eastwards again, and my admiration for Daphne and the others who worked with her steadily grew. When we met outside working hours, I began to ask her and Ruth more and more questions about medical and nursing techniques. But I didn't confide to them what I had begun to plan for the future, although I did talk about it to Xan.

'After the war, when we're married and back in England . . .'

'Yes, darling. I'm going to buy myself out of the army and find a job. What do you think I could do? Stockbroking? Or insurance salesman. I'm sure I could persuade people to buy life insurance. Anyway, whatever I do won't matter, will it, because we'll have each other?'

'What shall I do?'

'Have babies. Dozens of 'em.'

'Well, yes, but there's something else. I want to train to be a doctor.'

'Do you?' He stretched out his arm and hooked me closer to him. 'My clever, ambitious wife-to-be. In that case I won't need a job at all.'

'Xan, be serious.'

The playfulness faded out of his eyes. 'I don't want to be serious.'

I could have bitten my tongue. I had seen very little of him since New Year's Eve and when he did appear in Cairo, with Hassan or on occasional flying visits with Colonel Wainwright in the WACO, he was filthy and exhausted and he flatly deflected all my questions about what he had been doing.

We held each other tightly. After a moment he said, 'I'm sorry. It's hard, and it's getting harder, to move between . . . war and being with you. It's like walking a tightrope between hell and heaven.'

'I can only try to imagine.'

'Don't. I don't want you even to begin to imagine it. Iris, if you want to study medicine after the war, then you shall. We'll make it our priority.'

'Good.' I smiled at him.

'That's settled, then. What's the news from GHQ?'

'GHQ is the same as ever.'

'Unfortunately.'

Intelligence gathered by Roddy Boy's section had in the past been employed to assure field commanders that the enemy had not been reinforced with men or arms, and then the opposite had turned out to be true. Now I heard from Xan that there was more concern. Xan's Tellforce and some of the other commando groups were discovering that the enemy had developed an uncanny ability to predict when and where their raids were to take place.

'What does that mean?' I asked, although I knew the answer.

'A security leak.'

'From GHQ? That's not possible, surely?'

'Maybe not. But who can say for certain? Or maybe it's the Americans. It seems only to have been happening since they came in.'

We were sitting together on a rug spread under a mimosa tree at the club. I drew up my knees and wrapped my arms round them.

'Maybe it's Sandy Allardyce.'

'Trading military secrets while locked in the arms of Mrs K-G?'

Deliberately we both laughed but it was anxious laughter with a note of wildness in it.

'No, it's not them,' Xan said, rubbing his thumb over the amethyst on my ring finger.

'You will be careful, won't you?' Uttering the words made me feel weak and imploring, but I couldn't help myself.

'Yes,' Xan promised, because there was nothing else he could say. His arms slid round me and he drew me down to lie beside him on the rug.

'Don't worry too much,' Xan said gently. He was smiling.

'Worry? What about?'

He kissed me and we rolled over, laughing. Always laughing.

A few days later, when Xan had gone away again with Colonel Wainwright, I woke up with a flat taste of metal in my mouth. As soon as I sat up I felt sick, and I perched on the edge of the bed for a moment and rested my feet on the cool floor tiles until I could contemplate getting dressed. Sarah was sitting at the dining table with a cup of coffee, and the smell of the coffee immediately made me feel worse.

'Are you all right?' she asked.

I made a face. Food in Cairo was becoming scarcer and restaurant fish was not always reliably fresh. I had eaten shellfish the night before. Quickly, I left the room.

I felt better once I had been sick. Sitting at the table with Sarah, I drank some weak tea and nibbled on a piece of toast.

The sickness continued into the next day and by the time a week had passed I was having to accept that there might be another explanation for it than a mild dose of shellfish poisoning.

I mentioned my suspicion to Ruth and Daphne.

'I'm not a gynaecologist but it sounds like pregnancy to me. Weren't you using anything?' Daphne asked.

'Not invariably.' I coloured a little, remembering the urgency of some of the times.

'Well, there you are. I can arrange a test for you, at the hospital.'

'What do you want to do?' Ruth asked.

Before I could formulate the answer, I knew without any whisper of doubt what I wanted to do. I wanted to have Xan's child. Xan's son.

'Xan said he wanted babies, dozens of them. I'm going to have the child, of course.' My face split into a smile.

'Ah. Then there's no problem, is there?' Daphne looked pleased.

I was babbling now and grinning at them both. 'None. It's a bit early and it'll mean my mother probably won't get the big wedding she's been dreaming of. We'll just get married, with our friends around us, and I want you two to be godparents. Will you?'

'I think you should come in and see my colleague Esther Reisen,' Daphne said briskly. 'She is a gynaecologist. It might be a good idea to be positive before you appoint the godparents, don't you think?'

'I will. Then I can tell Xan it's definite.'

A few days after that I had the confirmation from Dr Reisen. I was pregnant. I had no idea how to contact Xan; in the past I had just waited for him to materialise. There was nothing in the intelligence traffic—at least, none that I was party to—that gave me any clues about Tellforce patrols. In the end I wrote a brief note, saying in the most general language that Xan should contact me as soon as he was able. I sealed it in an envelope and addressed it to Captain A. N. Molyneux, and walked to the house near where Hassan had been waiting when Xan and I came back from choosing my amethyst, and I strolled up and knocked on the door. It was opened by a smart-looking Indian NCO.

'Yes, Madam?'

'I have a message. For a Tellforce officer.'

'What is this Tellforce?'

I looked rapidly up and down the deserted street, then stepped quickly past the NCO and into the house. I produced my envelope and held it out to the soldier.

'This letter is for my friend, and fiancé. It's a personal matter, but it is urgent. I am going to give it to you, here . . .' I held it out and reluctantly he took it from my hand. '. . . and I hope very much that you'll be able to help. If there's a way of getting it to Captain Molyneux I will be very grateful, and so will he.'

'I don't know, Madam,' he said, but his nod contradicted his words.

'Thank you, Corporal.'

I told Faria and Sarah that I was going to have a baby.

Faria was dieting before her wedding in order to fit into the wedding dress that had already been made and stitched with thousands of seed pearls. She put down her cup of hot water in which floated a slice of lemon, the only aperitif she was allowed in place of the usual large gin and tonic, and sympathetically blinked at me.

'Oh, no. Poor darling. But you know, there are things you can do, I can tell you someone . . .'

'I'm pleased. I want the baby, I should think Xan and I will just get married a bit sooner.'

Sarah didn't say much. Once she understood that it was a welcome pregnancy, she murmured a word of congratulation, and jumped up and left the room. Faria shrugged and lit another Turkish cigarette, then went back to flicking through a magazine. When I went to look for her I found Sarah in her room, sitting at her dressing table, staring at her reflection. I thought she might have been crying, but she denied it.

'Don't be silly. It's so heavenly for you both. A baby, just imagine.'

Two nights later I lay awake in my bed. Faria was with Ali at some pre-marriage formal celebration and Sarah was out with the middle-aged French diplomat with whom she had recently started a half-hearted affair. It was a hot night and the ceiling fan stirred the air without cooling it. I heard a small click, and then what might have been the lightest footstep in the corridor outside. The hair prickled on my head and my eyes snapped wide open. As I held my breath the door silently cracked open and I saw a black profile against the blackness beyond. It was Xan.

'You're here,' I whispered and held out my arms. The bed springs creaked as he slid down beside me and his mouth was warm on my neck. 'Did you get my message?'

'I did, this morning. Therefore I am here, but only for a couple of hours. Tell me.'

He smelt of sweat and tobacco and oil and dust, and I buried my face against his battledress. In the darkness he seemed bigger and more solid than I remembered, full of recent events and escapades that I could only guess at, and knowing this made me want to hold him even more tightly.

'I am going to have a baby.'

There was a small gasp of indrawn breath, a silence, then a whoosh of exhalation that swelled into a shout. It was a shout of pure happiness and my face creased into a quiet, relieved smile.

'Are you? Are you certain?'

I told him about Daphne's colleague, Dr Esther Reisen at the Queen Mary.

His hand came to rest on my belly. 'How do you feel?'

'Not bad. Sick, some of the time, but that won't last more than another three or four weeks. Are you really pleased?'

He kissed my hands and my neck and my mouth. 'I can't believe it. Yes, I'm more pleased than you can imagine. Let's get married. Straight away. As soon as we can arrange it. Never mind the cathedral and the dress and the guard of honour. I'll ask the colonel for two days.'

'Yes,' I agreed. 'Yes, yes. Now, put your arms round me. Here. Touch me. Take this off. Wait. I'll undo it . . .'

There was a tangle of his clothing and my nightgown, and the creak of his Sam Browne belt and a shocking clatter as his service revolver fell onto the floor, and then we were naked and enveloped in each other.

Afterwards he lay with his fingers tangled in my hair, holding my head against his heart.

'Do you have to go?' I whispered.

'In a minute or two, yes.'

'Where?'

'Back.'

'Can't you tell me anything?'

'Have you heard of the Qattara Depression?'

'No.'

'It's a huge hollow, thousands of square miles of it, scooped out of the desert floor about forty miles south of the coast and the railhead at a place called el Alamein. The northern sides are too steep for tanks to descend and the bed is treacherous soft sand. If Rommel advances that far, he'll be caught in a bottleneck between the sea and the Qattara and this will be the best place to try and hold him before the frontier.'

'How is Tellforce involved in this?'

Xan's mouth came close to my ear, as if even here in my bed we might be overheard. 'Hassan and I think there is a way through the Qattara. Not an easy way, but I believe it can be done. If we can somehow reconnoitre a route for the heavy armour, without the enemy knowing about it, we can hook around and come in at them from the south where they will never expect to be vulnerable.' Against the thin skin beneath my ear his mouth curved in a smile of anticipation, and I shivered.

'It's time,' he murmured now. Then he sat up and began to gather his clothes. I reached to turn on the light beside my bed and lay with my head propped on one hand, memorising him.

When he was dressed, Xan sat down again beside me and picked up my left hand. He kissed the knuckles and pressed his lips to the amethyst, and smiled as he held my face between his hands. "Bye, darling. Will you find out what it takes to get us married with indecent haste?'

'I will.'

He kissed me on the lips. 'Look after yourself, and the baby. I love you both. I'll be back again soon.'

He knelt down and retrieved his revolver from under the bed, slid it back into its holster and stood up. The door opened, closed behind him with a swift click and he was gone.

'**W**hich way?' Ruby asked after a while.

Iris didn't say anything and Ruby drove a little further, wrestling with the wheel without knowing quite what to do when the steering broke away from her. The car's bonnet slewed disconcertingly across the snout of the dune ahead before she brought it under control again.

Iris was humming to herself. It was time to turn back, Ruby decided. She checked automatically in the rearview mirror and there was nothing there. Not only no other traffic: nothing except the dunes and the sky.

'Right. Home time.'

She braked and the car slithered. The reassuring road had dwindled into a rough track and even that was almost invisible; there was a wind blowing that sent a fine swirl of sand fuming over the ground and covering everything. Their tyre marks were already fading into twin blurred furrows. Ruby swung the steering wheel hard right and the car ploughed a slow half-circle.

She drove another 100 yards, but the track was gone. The veil of blown sand was harried by the wind, and it was getting harder to keep the tyres turning. She would have to stop and get her bearings.

Iris turned her head. She was smiling disconnectedly. 'Why are we stopping?'

'I want to take a look, make sure of the way back.'

'Back?'

'Yes,' Ruby said loudly.

She opened the car door and stepped out, and the wind tugged at her. Blown sand stung her ankles. She scrambled to the low crest of the nearest dune, surprised by how steep it was and how deep her feet sank. From the top she had expected that she would see the main road heading out to the oasis, whatever it was called, and the insect progress of trucks and buses. But there was only a vista of close identical dunes, rippled by the rising wind.

She ploughed down the slope and back to the car. The floor and her seat were already thinly coated with sand. She slammed the door and wound up the window, then sat with her hands on the steering wheel.

Ruby said, 'I don't know where we are.'

The sun was now only visible as a dim eye, pale as wax, behind a thickening veil of greyish umber haze. The wind steadily rose, whipping sand off the crests of the dunes like spray off a breaking wave. The desert was shifting, unleashing itself. The wind was scouring up sand and flinging it against the windscreen and the door panels, making a noise like tiny hailstones drumming on the metal.

'It's a sandstorm,' Iris said wonderingly.

'Looks like it.' Ruby's throat was dry and tight, and her eyeballs still stung just from the dash she had made to the crest of the nearby dune.

'A desert sandstorm can be very dangerous, you know. We should turn round and drive straight home.'

'It's too late for that. We'll have to sit here until it blows itself out.'

'Sit here?'

'Yes.' Ruby formed the word crisply, raising her voice a little, lending herself a conviction that she was far from feeling. It might have been her imagination but the car seemed to rock and shudder under the force of the wind. Let's think, Ruby advised herself. Decide what to do for the best. She tried to be rational, but fear prickled down her spine.

At the same moment a huge gust of wind sliced the entire top off the nearest dune and flung it against the car and for a second they were in darkness. Then more wind stripped the sand from the car windows. The light when it did come back was clotted, yellow-brown, swirling like soup. There was nothing to think about, she realised, not until this storm was over. Driving even another yard was unthinkable.

'A desert sandstorm,' Iris repeated. 'The men used to fear them. Even Hassan.'

'I'm not surprised.'

Inside the partly sealed car it was now uncomfortable to breathe the dust-laden air and Iris coughed, gasped for breath, then coughed some more. Ruby burrowed in her grandmother's bag, brought out her white headscarf and wrapped it round the lower half of her face for her. She pulled up her own T-shirt to cover her mouth and nostrils.

'Ruby?' Iris's voice was very quiet and muffled even further by the folds of her scarf. 'I'd like a drink of water.'

There was an instant's panic when Ruby thought *we haven't got any*, then with relief she remembered the two bottles she had bought at the café. She reached into the back of the car for one, twisted off the cap and handed it to Iris. Iris pulled back her scarf and gulped thirstily.

'That's better,' she said, and handed the bottle back to Ruby.

The car seats creaked as they both sank lower, covering their noses and mouths, and preparing for the wait against the wind.

'Hassan?' Ruby prompted, almost automatically now.

'Yes, Hassan. He was Bedouin. Xan used to say that he knew the desert as well as his mother's smile. Even the Qattara Depression. That was the key to it. The route across. Everyone said it couldn't be done.'

'Why not?'

'Soft sand, impassable to tanks. That's what the generals all thought. Xan showed them.'

'Did he? How did he do that?'

It was difficult to talk through the face coverings and harder still to hear what was said. The cracks and gaps in the old car were mouth-pieces for the wind, and it sighed and blared and moaned across them. Iris didn't try to answer. Her chin drooped on her chest and after a little while Ruby saw that she had fallen asleep.

Ruby sat and stared at the opaque world. She made some mental calculations about the two bottles of water and the fruit that Auntie had pressed on her when they had left that morning. That already seemed ages ago. How long would these minimal supplies last?

A day, two days at the most. But they wouldn't be here for anything like that long. Once the wind dropped, they would be on their way again.

We were going to look for Xan, driving deep into the desert in search of him: we had to hurry or he would be gone and I would never see him again. The anxiety was intense and my eyes stung and burned with the effort of searching the monotony for the smallest sign of him.

Either I imagined this, or I dreamed it. And now I am awake and I remember that I am with the child, and we are caught in a sandstorm.

'Ruby, how much water have we got?'

Wide-eyed, she studies my face. 'Two litres, minus what you drank earlier. Some fresh fruit, some dried apricots.'

'You had better drink some. Go on. Let me see you do it.'

She opens the bottle and tilts it to her mouth. I see the muscles convulsively clutch in her pretty throat, and the effort it costs her to lower the bottle long before her thirst is quenched. She holds the bottle out to me and I take a few swallows. When I hand it back she screws the cap on very carefully and stows the bottle out of our sight on the back seat.

'Are we in trouble?' she asks in a flat voice.

'I don't think so.' I peer out of the windscreen. There is nothing to see but yellowish murk, but it seems to me that this is now dust hanging in the air rather than sand torn off the dune backs. In time it will settle. 'Mamdooh and Auntie will send someone to look for us.'

'But they don't know where we are. I avoided seeing Mamdooh this morning, I didn't want the hassle. I talked to Auntie in the kitchen and she talked to me, but she didn't know what I was saying. And I told Ash that we were going to the Pyramids. No one knows we've come out here.'

I try to remember how we reached this place, but it has gone.

I'm very tired. I rest my head against the window and see how everything is coated in dust. The backs of my hands are grey, my lap, my knees, the metal curve of the dashboard.

If no one knows where we are, no one will be coming to look for us. There is an inevitability in this that does not particularly disturb me.

'Don't worry,' I say.

After Xan slipped into my room that night and then slipped away again, I began making preparations for our wedding. From the embassy I found out what it would take to obtain a special licence for two British nationals to marry at short notice and made the application.

Xan was in a camp at the fringe of the Qattara, although I deduced this by guesswork rather than from anything he told me. We communicated by letters. His scribbled, creased pages reached me erratically, dropped off by the Tellforce plane whenever it touched down in Cairo or carried by the infrequent messengers who travelled between GHQ and his patrol. The smart Indian NCO called at Garden City to deliver them, and there was always a batch of my letters waiting to be taken away. So Xan and I planned our wedding.

We would be married by an English chaplain in a side chapel at the cathedral, with a tiny handful of friends to witness the ceremony. Xan wanted Jessie to be his best man. Ruth and Sarah would be my attendants; Daphne was unlikely to be able to take the time off from the hospital and Faria would be on her honeymoon. It was comical that Xan's and my minimal preparations were being made neck and neck with the final elaborate arrangements for Faria's and Ali's huge wedding. Our marriage would take place just five days after theirs.

Gus Wainwright has promised me at least twenty-four hours' leave, Xan wrote. *It may only be a short honeymoon, darling—but we will have a whole life together afterwards.*

A whole life. A very long time and it is no wonder that I am tired.

The child is twisting in her seat.

'It's four o'clock.'

'Is it?'

'It's going to be *dark* in an hour or so.'

'Yes.'

'That means we're probably going to have to spend the night here.'

The desert night; the sky a bowl of darkness, stars dimmed by the dust from the storm. Very cold at this time of year and as silent as space.

Xan's resting place.

It was getting colder. They had no warm clothes to put on and as the time crept by the night air seeped into the car until they were shivering.

'Let's get into the back seat. We can cuddle up,' Ruby said at last.

They moved into the cramped space and pressed close together. It was a comfort to hold her grandmother's light-boned body in her arms and hear her breathing. Ruby rested her cheek on the top of Iris's head and watched the slice of black sky visible through the rear window. The red and white lights of a jet descending to Cairo airport blinked in the distance and this vision of normality made Ruby forget their predicament for a second, but then it dawned again with renewed intensity. The planes were too high; the Beetle would be just a speck in the limitless sand.

Iris was dozing. Although her limbs ached with cramp and her throat and mouth were parched, eventually Ruby fell asleep too.

She woke up with a thirst like a high fever and shivering uncontrollably as if her bones would crack. Iris had been stirring and mumbling; it was the sound of her voice that woke Ruby.

'What did you say? Are you all right?'

'That was the day.'

'Never mind. God, your feet and hands are freezing. I'm going to turn the engine on and run the heater for a few minutes to warm us up. I should have thought of it before. Sit still.'

In the driver's seat, Ruby groped for the ignition key and turned it. There was a grinding noise, the strangled wail of the starter motor clogged with sand, then silence. Ruby let her hand fall into her lap. The silence spread, rippling away from the immobilised car. The Beetle might as well have been a pharaonic relic, she thought, or just a lump of rock sticking up out of the sand, for all the use it was going to be in getting them out of here. The only way that they were going to survive was by walking, or by waiting to be rescued.

What were the odds, either way? she wondered.

Then a flash of hot, white certainty shot through her brain. She didn't want to die. Life was too good, too precious and too untasted. It was clear to her that she loved everything about it. The garden at home, with all those dumb plants that used to yield her beetles. Ed and Dad and even Andrew and Will, and especially Lesley. There were things that she still wanted to do, an incoherent mass of them like making love to Ash and going to Ayers Rock and to that Inca place in Peru, and most of all saying to her mother that she was sorry they always quarrelled. Weirdly but definitely, most of all that.

'Are you awake?' she whispered into Iris's hair.

Iris nodded her head, but she didn't say anything and Ruby wasn't sure if she had really heard.

'I love you,' she said.

It was simple. In the morning she would go for help.

The rapid dawn briefly raised their spirits. After the darkness, even in the monochrome light, even the empty dunes were reassuring. Soon the sun would flood warmth into the world.

They drank some of the second litre of water, trying to hold the blessing of it in their mouths for as long as possible. Then they clambered stiffly out of the car and eased their joints by stretching out in the sand. Iris looked frighteningly pale and shaky, and Ruby peeled an orange for her, placing the segments one by one into her mouth as if she were feeding a child. Iris sat propped up against the shaded side of the car with her mottled bare legs stretched out in front of her. Ruby took one last gulp of water, then half buried the bottle in the sand beside Iris and put the basket containing the rest of the fruit and the dried apricots within reach. She made sure that her grandmother had her hat and her scarf, then she squatted down directly in front of her, looking into her eyes to see if she took in what she was telling her.

'I'm going for help. I'll be as quick as I can. Stay here in the shade, don't move away from the car. Drink a sip of water once in a while, and—look—here are two oranges and two pomegranates. Iris?'

'I am not deaf. You will look where you're going, Lesley, won't you?'

Where was she, in her unreadable confusion? 'Yes.'

Ruby leaned forward and quickly kissed her. Her feet and head felt heavy, but her heart was racing with adrenaline. The sooner she went, she reasoned, the quicker she would be back again.

She began walking, towards the flaming ball of the sun. From the crest of the first dune she looked back. All she could see were Iris's feet sticking out beyond the car and her own footprints leading away, already fading, like a betrayal.

She scrambled up a dune, down into the hollow beyond and up again, always heading into the sun. It was hard work and she was soon out of breath. The next dune was higher and she had it in her mind that once she was on the summit of this one the road would be there in the distance, with trucks and tourist buses catching the sunlight and winking rescue at her.

As she laboriously climbed, the sand carried her backwards. Sweat ran into her eyes, and she flopped onto her hands and knees to crawl the last few yards.

She poked her head over the ridge. There was no road in sight. Only more dunes, in every direction, identical.

On her knees Ruby shuffled in a circle. A breeze fanned her face but it also stirred the sand. The tracks leading backwards and linking her to Iris were blurred hollows, becoming less distinct with every puff of wind. As soon as they were rubbed out Iris would be lost to her.

It was unbearable, unthinkable to leave her lying there alone.

Ruby staggered to her feet and began running back the way she had come. Already it was hard to distinguish the footprints from the natural dimples worn by the wind.

Oh, please, let me find her. Please, please let me.

Faria's wedding was exquisite. Every detail proclaimed the wealth of both families and their satisfaction at this dynastic amalgamation.

The wedding feast was held at Faria's parents' mansion. The bride and groom led the way from the church on foot, accompanied by the *zaffa*—a long parade of drummers and belly dancers who played and sang and danced around them. The enormous reception hall of the house was decorated with tall sheaves of green wheat, representing fertility, tied with ribbons of gold representing—I supposed—money. Ali and Faria sat between the wheatsheaves under a golden canopy to receive their guests.

There were no field officers from any of the Allied armies. Rommel's long-awaited attack had begun two days earlier.

Out in the desert, after an Italian feint towards the north of the Gazala Line, the Panzer Army had hooked south around Bir Hacheim and were now fighting their way up through General Ritchie's armoured brigades towards Tobruk. The armoured cars and infantry of the German 90th Light, meanwhile, ploughed into the exposed communication lines of the Allied rearguard.

I wandered through the glittering rooms, into the supper room. The tables heaped with food stretched into the distance; much more food than the hundreds of guests could ever eat. I turned aside from a swan sculpted in ice that lifted a crystal trough of beluga caviar between its wings, and saw Roddy Boy coming towards me.

He took my arm. 'Iris, come with me.'

'Where?'

'I have something to tell you.'

I knew. I already knew.

There was a niche at the far side of the supper room. I sat down on a gilt Empire sofa and Roddy Boy put his hand on my arm.

'Please tell me at once,' I said.

'I have some very bad news. I am afraid that Captain Molyneux was killed in action two days ago, in the Qattara.'

I must have asked for more information.

A few feet away from us, Ali's and Faria's guests were scooping lobster and caviar on to white-and-gold porcelain plates. The wedding banquet was in full swing.

I listened to Roddy Boy's words as if I had already heard them.

He told me that Xan and his Arab scout had been leading a small exploratory detachment over the route that their patrol had devised as a means of bringing Allied armour in on the southern flank of the 8th Army. It was a highly secret operation, known to very few people outside Special Operations Executive. But as the little column wound its way through the wind-sculpted buttes and mesas of the Qattara, a formation of five Italian Macchi aircraft had appeared and homed in on them with a level of accuracy that ruled out coincidence. Most of the men had been mortally wounded by machine-gun and cannon fire, and several of the vehicles had burst into flames.

The heavy armoured trucks and cars had been drawn from the 11th Hussars, the Cherry Pickers, and their second-in-command was Captain James. Captain James had been very seriously injured but he had been brought in from the desert and was now in the Queen Mary Hospital. It was Jessie James who had given an account of the skirmish, and of Xan's death, to a staff officer from GHQ.

'I am so sorry,' Roddy said. 'As soon as I heard I came straight here.'

Somehow I spoke. The words sounded as though they came from someone else. 'Thank you. Colonel Boyce, how could the enemy have known that Xan's patrol was in the Qattara?'

'I am afraid I can't answer that, Iris. I wish I could.'

Can't or won't, I thought. There was a security leak, exactly as Xan had suggested. Roddy's eyes flicked towards the door of the supper room. He was under unusual pressure and there were heavy demands on his time; he had broken the news and he wanted to be gone.

'I'll go to the hospital,' I said.

'Are you sure you want to do that?'

I was already on my feet, walking unseeingly through the crowds of guests and past the sheaves of green wheat for fertility.

'I've got a GHQ car,' Roddy mumbled as he tried to keep up. 'You could take it, I'll walk.'

'Thank you,' I said again, not even looking back.

In the car, on the familiar route, I stared at the people in the streets who were walking and talking as if nothing had happened. It was impossible that Xan was dead. Xan, who had been more alive than any of them. My mouth moved and I found I was saying his name.

Jessie James was lying behind screens in a ward full of men who had just been brought in from the battle. His face was paler than the dressings that covered his upper torso and his light hair was dark with dirt and blood. At first I thought he was unconscious but when I took his bloodstained hand and held it his eyes opened.

'Iris.'

'Yes.'

His lips moved but his voice was barely audible. 'Xan. I'm sorry.'

'Shh.'

There was a silence while he summoned up a reserve of strength.

'Air attack. Out of nowhere.'

'Roddy Boy told me.'

'I saw . . . came straight at us.'

'Jessie. I have to ask you this. Are you certain he is dead?'

'He was in the lead truck. The rest of us were spread out on a broad front behind. Xan's vehicle took the brunt of the fire. The truck burst into flames. A ball of fire. None of them got out.'

Jessie's eyes closed. A breath sighed out of him. He didn't say anything more and I sat there with my hand linked in his as the life seemed to recede, from his fingertips, from his arms and legs, until it was just concentrated in a flutter round his heart.

The screens parted and I looked up to see Daphne. I watched as she put her fingers on Jessie's neck, then shone a small torch into each of his eyes. Her expression didn't change.

'Well?' I demanded.

She shook her head.

'Xan is dead,' I said.

She came to my side of the bed, unlaced my fingers from Jessie's cold ones and pulled my head against her.

'Xan is dead,' I repeated. I knew I hadn't begun to register what the words meant.

'Iris. Listen to me. You have to go home and rest. Remember the baby.'

Since the moment when I saw Roddy Boy heading towards me, I had not given it a thought. I had forgotten that I was pregnant.

Another dune and her gasps for breath keep a rhythm with the words *please, let me find her*. Her outward tracks were barely discernible.

Ruby crested the dune and the Beetle lay in the hollow below. Her legs wobbled and she sat heavily down in the sand, slip-slithering to the bottom. Iris seemed not to have moved at all, but there were tears running down her face and glimmering in the sun.

Ruby knelt in front of her and gathered her up into her arms. 'It's all right, here I am, you're safe, we're going to be all right, I won't leave you again, Ash will find us, Ash and Mamdooh and Auntie, I promise, they have to find us, don't they?' She attempted the reassurance out of a complete absence of conviction, and she thought how frail and improbable the words sounded. But in any case Iris was staring at her, through her tears, as if she had never set eyes on her before. She wasn't crying over their plight, or out of fear at being left alone. She was crying for something inside her own head and Ruby couldn't reach that.

It was for the best, probably, Ruby thought. Let her be, with her memories. Better that than be aware of this reality.

Lesley had been in the garden for most of the afternoon, sweeping fallen leaves off the herringbone brick paths, but now it was getting too dark to work.

In the kitchen she washed her hands and filled the kettle. She could hear Andrew talking on the phone. Then he appeared in the doorway.

'There's some French doctor on the phone from Cairo. It's about Ruby.'

Lesley's hand reached up to her mouth. 'Is she hurt?'

'He says your mother and she went out yesterday morning and they haven't come back.'

Lesley took two steps to the kitchen phone. French, her mind obstinately retained that. She cleared her throat.

'*Bonsoir? Je suis la mère de Mademoiselle Ruby Sawyer . . .*'

'Good evening, Madame. I am afraid there is some anxiety concerning your daughter and your mother,' the doctor began in accented but perfect English.

When Lesley replaced the phone her hands were shaking. Andrew was still standing in the doorway.

She said, 'We'll have to fly out. Tomorrow, as soon as we can.'

He nodded. 'I'll see what flights there are.'

Under a sky blown clear of cloud, the temperature dropped as soon as darkness came. Ruby helped Iris into the back seat of the car again and held her with her head cradled in her lap, stroking Iris's hair. Iris folded her arms across her chest and drew up her knees to fit in the cramped space. They were both shivering but the cold was only a partial distraction from their thirst.

Ruby decided that they would share the remaining pomegranate when the sun rose again, then she would plan what to do.

But *what to do* suggested a breadth of choice belonging to the precious world that had just slipped out of her reach. Go out, stay in. Smoke a cigarette, or not. Tea or coffee, pizza or curry, cinema or telly—mundane choices that she had never bothered to savour. Choice. She had been considering the stark options that would be open to her when the sun rose again.

They could sit here and hope to be found. But, realistically, how long would it take for Mamdooh and Auntie to summon the rescuers? Most probably Iris would be dead before anyone came.

Or she could set out again, as she had done this morning, and this time instead of losing her nerve and turning back she would have to keep on and on walking until she found help or until she dropped.

Either, or. The richness of the whole world reduced to a choice that was not a choice at all, but a sentence.

Mamdooh walked through Qarafa with the folds of his *galabiyeh* drawn up round his ankles, following the ragged boy who dashed ahead of him. In the City of the Dead the flat brown tombs and the colourless dust darkened, and their sharp edges were picked out with the silver-bright tracery of rising moonlight.

A few more turns brought them to a closed door and the child wordlessly pointed to it. He held out a hand and Mamdooh tipped a couple of coins into his palm. Then the child vanished into the dusk.

Mamdooh banged hard on the door. It opened by a crack and Nafouz's face was revealed. Mamdooh reached in and grasped him by the collar of his leather jacket. With unsuspected strength he hauled him out into the open and in the crack in the doorway the faces of Nafouz's mother and his grandmother immediately appeared instead.

Mamdooh shook Nafouz and poured out a stream of questions, and Nafouz shrilly insisted that Ashraf was at his work at the Bab al-Futuh Hospital, and had been at work the night before too, as usual, and he had not seen Ruby for two whole days.

The two women emerged from the protection of the tomb house and now they all stood in a little circle in the indigo dusk. Mamdooh turned on them and demanded to know if this was the truth.

It was, Ash's mother protested. Several times Ashraf had brought the young girl to this place, but not in the last two days. And yesterday afternoon he had said that he would go to meet her but he had come back and told his family that the girl was not in the usual place at the agreed time. Today, the same thing.

What was Ashraf to do about that? she demanded. Was her son to blame if an English girl was not reliable?

Mamdooh retorted that what her son should now do was tell the truth to the police. He then told them that the police were looking for Miss and for Dr Black, her grandmother, who was missing also. The young girl's mother and father were coming from England to take charge of the search. They would all want to speak to Ashraf, and to the rest of his family too, and it would be advisable if they remembered every smallest thing and spoke nothing but the purest truth.

Mamdooh walked away, back in the direction he had come.

Ruth is stroking my hair.

After Xan died I went through the motions of living, although I felt hardly alive myself. On what would have been our wedding day and for two weeks afterwards I did my job for Roddy Boy, went to the hospital for my voluntary shift and came home again to Garden City. It was a meaningless triangle and at each point of it I longed to be at either of the others because surely the pain there would be more bearable than at the present one. But it never was.

Ruth and Daphne did their best to look after me. Daphne drove me out to the flat on the Heliopolis road one evening, and I sat in the same chair as on my first visit and accepted the last of the malt whisky that I had brought them as a present. I tried to think back to the happiness that had suffused everything then, but I couldn't grasp it.

A belt of pain tightened round my middle. 'I'm so sorry,' I heard myself mumble as I put my head down and tried to assimilate the pain.

Daphne put one hand to my forehead and held my wrist in the other. When I could stand up, I went into the bathroom and found blood. There was a thin stream of blood running down the inside of my leg and dark droplets on the tile floor.

My friends made me lie down on their bed. I was very thirsty, burning up with thirst. Ruth sits beside me and strokes my hair again, but there is nothing to drink and I am too parched to ask for water. The stroking soothes me, but I am cold, shivering. It's dark and my arms and legs are bent and hooked in a narrow space.

Ruby did not sleep. Between wishing for and dreading the dawn it was the longest night she had ever known.

At last the stars began to fade and a pearl-grey line touched the horizon. As the light came again Iris stirred and moaned. Ruby helped her to sit up, then held her face between her two hands.

'Iris, listen. Look at me. I've got to go for help, otherwise we are going to die.'

Iris's cracked lips twitched as she tried to speak. No sound came out.

'I don't want to leave you, but I don't know what else to do.'

Then Iris nodded, very slowly but definitely.

'I'm going to set out as soon as it's properly light.'

Again the nod.

'Let's share this,' Ruby said. The hoarded pomegranate was dull with dust. She tore the peel, careful in case of spilling even a drop of juice. She gave two-thirds to Iris and dug her teeth into the remaining third. There was an ecstatic second as the seeds split on her tongue and yielded a few drops of liquid, but then it was gone.

The sun was not yet up and the air was still cold, but it was light. Ruby climbed out of the car and sank up to her ankles in chilly sand.

'Let me make you comfortable before I go.'

She took Iris's hands and helped her from the car to sit in the sand beside it, putting one arm round her waist and lowering her gently. Iris was very weak now. Ruby knew that if she didn't go immediately, she would not be able to leave her. She leaned down and kissed her on the forehead. 'I love you,' she told her. 'I'll be back very soon. Just wait for me, all right?'

She was straightening up when Iris grasped her wrist. 'Just go. Don't worry.'

She knew what Iris was telling her.

'I'll be back,' she repeated angrily.

She pulled herself away and began to walk.

She didn't look back until she reached the crest of the nearest dune. The Beetle looked even more like a chunk of the desert than it had done yesterday.

Only *yesterday*.

Ruby turned her back on the car and her grandmother, and trudged eastwards through the sliding sand, as fast as she could, while the sun still told her which way to go.

Daphne called a taxi, and she and Ruth took me to the Cairo Hospital for Women and Children, run by the nuns. In a shuttered white room there I miscarried my sixteen-week pregnancy, Xan's son.

The placid, smooth-faced nuns nursed me. For two days I wouldn't see anyone except Ruth, who came after she finished work and sat with me for a few silent minutes.

Xan was dead and now I had lost the precious link to him. I remembered his delight when I told him that I was pregnant and I grieved twice over, for myself and for Xan too because it was his child as well as mine that was lost. It seemed beyond bearing that I could not share my desolation with him. It was incomprehensible that I would never share anything else with him, and I wept until no more tears would come.

On the third day one of the sisters made me sit up and wash my face and comb my hair.

'There's a different visitor to see you,' she said.

'I don't want a visitor.'

'Yes, you do,' she told me. The door opened and Sarah came in. She had a bunch of marigolds and cosmos in her hand, flowers that made me think of my mother's garden.

'Oh, darling,' she cried. 'I'm so sorry.'

She put the flowers in a toothmug, then sat down in the chair beside my bed and took my hand.

To see Sarah made me feel, for the first time since I had lost the baby, that there was a chink of light in the world. As well as the flowers, her pale complexion and pale eyebrows and even the neat collar of her starched blouse all seemed to stand for Englishness, and a distant, quiet normality separate from this present agony. The continuity that she represented gave me an inkling that I might be able to go on living.

'I'm glad you're here,' I whispered finally.

Sarah let me weep again, and in the end I shouted and sobbed at her, 'If I can't have him, why couldn't I at least have had his son?'

Sarah bent her head. 'Listen to me, Iris. It's hard, but you do know that Xan loved you. You were loved, passionately, by a man you deeply loved and admired in return. You conceived a child together, out of love and hope, and now it's ended you can at least mourn them both without feeling ashamed.'

The grief that had blinded me shifted a little and I was able to take a glance beyond it. It was suddenly plain to me that she had suffered a loss too, although I had never seen as much before now. 'What happened?'

'I wasn't loved,' she said simply.

'Who didn't?'

'Jeremy.'

Jeremy the poet, Faria's helpless and hopeless admirer.

'But he was in love with Faria . . .'

'I know that. It didn't make any difference. When she was too busy for him—well, then there I was. It was much better than nothing, for me. Iris, can you understand that?'

I hesitated. 'In a way.'

'Faria wouldn't sleep with him, of course. But I did. That was better than nothing for *him*, do you see?'

Her sadness cut my heart. 'You love him.'

'Yes. Terribly. And then, I was pregnant.'

'What did you do?' I asked, already knowing the answer.

'I told him, of course. What was I hoping for? That he would say to me that this changed everything, ask me to marry him. He just said that he was very sorry and he would do everything he could to help me. So I had an abortion. I went to Beirut, do you remember?'

In my self-absorbed happiness I had accepted the story that Sarah had had gippy tummy and had gone on holiday to recover.

'I'm so sorry,' I said. 'I wish you'd felt that you could tell me.'

'I couldn't tell a soul,' Sarah whispered. 'I am only saying this now because I can't bear to see you so stricken.'

We held each other and cried, and I hoped that I was not only crying for myself. Then Sarah sat upright in the chair and wiped her eyes.

'What are you going to do?' she asked, taking a powder compact and a lipstick out of her handbag.

I might have replied that I didn't know, or care, but I stopped myself. 'I'm going to come home to the flat as soon as I can. Could you bring me some clean clothes, perhaps?'

'Of course.' Sarah liked to be given a defined job. 'There's a bit of a flap on, even more than usual, actually. Women and children are being evacuated. The embassy's in charge of allocating places on the Palestine train. People are pulling strings all over the shop, just to get a seat. It's chaotic. What do you think you'll do?'

I had no idea. I had no sense of purpose and I couldn't think where I would go if I were to leave Cairo. Heavily I said, 'Go back to work again, if Roddy Boy wants me, I suppose. What about you?'

'I'd like to get out to Palestine. Why wait to be invaded? Mamdooh says half the shopkeepers in town have got German swastikas and bunting all ready, to welcome the troops when they arrive.'

'They would do.' I smiled, against the odds.

Sarah promised that she would bring in my clothes the next afternoon. We clung briefly to each other before she left.

'Thank you for coming.'

She patted my shoulder. 'Got to stick together, eh?'

I suddenly wanted very much to be back at the Garden City flat, the nearest approximation I had to home. I thought again about returning to London, after the war, to study medicine. I would not be Xan's wife, but I could make myself useful somewhere.

But first I knew I must write to my parents, telling them the news about Xan and the baby.

I am tired. I would like to surrender and sleep, but I know that I can't because there is more to be done. The child was right when we talked about an empty place at the centre. I try to swallow on a throat full of sand and the parade of memories starts up again.

The line held at el Alamein.

After twenty-eight days of almost continuous fighting the battle ended in a stalemate, but the Panzer divisions had been halted and the enemy forces never reached Alexandria or Cairo.

The city streets filled up with soldiers once more. People filtered back from their refuges in the delta, and the bunting disappeared from the shop windows as quickly as it had appeared.

I remember the exhausted sense of anticlimax that descended after the days of the flap, and the terrible July heat that weighted every movement. My second summer in Cairo was long and painful.

Sarah's French diplomat boyfriend was posted to Baghdad and she decided that she would follow him.

'Why not?' She shrugged. 'What else should I do?'

Jeremy had left Cairo for Palestine at the height of the crisis, without taking the time to say goodbye to her.

Faria came back from her honeymoon and settled into Ali's opulent house. I went once or twice to dinner with the newlyweds, but the other guests were mostly business associates of Ali's and Faria herself was uncommunicative.

'That is very sad,' she sighed, when I told her about the baby. 'But maybe in the end, you know, it is for the best?'

I began to look for somewhere else to live, without having any heart for it. And then one day at work, Roddy Boy put his head out of his office and announced that my father was on the telephone and wished to speak urgently to me. I took the receiver and in the familiar dingy office environment of spilling folders and metal cupboards I heard my father saying that my mother was ill and maybe I should consider returning to England as soon as possible. I knew he wouldn't suggest such a thing unless it was serious.

'I'll be sorry to lose you, Miss Black. But your family must take precedence,' Roddy told me. And apart from Ruth, Daphne and my inessential voluntary work there was nothing else to keep me in Egypt.

I booked my passage home on a ship sailing via the Cape and then, when my belongings were packed and I was waiting out the last few hours in the empty Garden City apartment, Mamdooh came to tell me that I had a visitor.

'Who is it?'

In the dim hallway with its overelaborate furniture, a tall dark-faced man was standing.

It was Hassan, who I believed had been killed beside Xan in the Qattara Depression.

Shock rooted me to the ground and my voice dried in my throat, but Hassan slowly extended his hand to me and I reached out and grasped it. I hung on to him as if he were a connection direct to Xan, and Hassan bent his head and touched his fingers to his forehead in greeting.

'You are alive,' I croaked. 'How? Wait, don't stand here. Come in, sit, let me give you some tea. Mamdooh, will you bring some?'

If it seemed foolish to welcome a man back from the dead with a glass of mint tea, I didn't know how else it should be done. I took Hassan into the drawing room where the furniture was already partially shrouded in dustsheets and we faced each other across an inlaid table.

'I come to pay respect, Madam,' Hassan said. 'The Captain my friend. From a boy, Bedouin and British man, friend.'

'I know. You must have known Xan better than anyone else. Will you tell me what happened?'

Hassan described how the planes had come from nowhere, out of an empty sky, straight at them. Xan's driver had swerved, trying to avoid the fire, and they had fired back at the aircraft, but they had stood no chance. The truck hit a patch of soft sand and sank down to the wheel arches, and Hassan dived out and began to run. When he looked again he saw that Xan was trying to pull the driver, who had been shot in the back, out of the burning truck. He shouted at him to run, but Xan wouldn't leave the wounded man. Then the ammunition and the fuel stored in jerry cans in the back of the truck had exploded in a huge fireball.

Hassan had turned from the scene of his friend's death and melted into the moonscape. It had taken him many days to make his way back.

'I did not know if to come here,' he explained at the end.

'I am so glad you did. I'm happy that you are alive. Thank you.'

He stood up then and bowed his head once more.

'What will you do now, Hassan?'

His eyes met mine. I remembered the desert oasis and the men gathered round a fire, just as they must have done for hundreds of years. He said quietly, 'Like you, I believe I will continue my path, but I will keep a memory always.'

Hassan had brought me a connection to Xan that I longed for and now I knew how bravely he had died. When we reached the door I caught his arm once more.

'Hassan, I would like you to keep this. Xan gave it to me when he asked me to marry him, and I would be happy to think that it will stay here in Egypt with you.'

I took the amethyst off my engagement finger and put it into his hand. He held it in the cup of his palm and we both looked at it.

'Madam?'

'Please take it. It will be a link between us, you and me and him.'

Hassan touched his lips to the ring. Slowly, he took a worn leather pouch out of a fold of his clothing and put the ring into it.

'Goodbye, Madam,' he said. 'May God be with you.'

'And with you,' I answered.

The next day, my goodbyes already said, I left Cairo by train for Suez. It was Major Gordon Foxbridge, the photographer, who drove me and my luggage to the station. It happened that he had the morning free, he told me, and he had a staff car at his disposal. As we parted he asked if he might have my address and, grateful for his assistance, I gave him my parents' address in Hampshire because I had no other.

It was thirty-five years before I saw Cairo again.

My mother recovered from her illness and I spent a few months nursing her. But she died suddenly a year later, in September 1943, from bronchial pneumonia.

Under the terms of her will I inherited a share of her family trust and with this money to live on, I began the long battle to get into St Bart's medical school.

I kept in touch with Daphne and Ruth, and from time to time I also heard from Sandy Allardyce. He married Gerti Kimmig-Gertsch and they moved between Cairo, Italy and Zurich.

My father died in 1946, and not long afterwards I agreed to marry Gordon Foxbridge. I didn't love him but I liked and respected him, and I didn't expect ever to fall in love again. I had had my great passion and that was more than many people would ever know. I had my memories and I continually returned to them. For sixty years I reached up to the shelf and took the familiar cup down, wrapping my fingers round it and letting the warmth nourish me.

My second pregnancy was unplanned. Gordon was overjoyed and we bought a house outside London in a hurry.

Lesley was born in 1950.

I shift my legs in the sand and my head rolls against the metal flank of the car. I want to sleep, to slide under the surface of consciousness, but a hand holds me back. The clutch torments me even more than thirst and the white eye of the sun.

My daughter clings on to me. I try to creep backwards, like a hermit crab pulling into its shell, but it is Lesley who follows me into my refuge. She stands there with her hands on her hips; her face is screwed up with childish accusation.

'What do you want?'

I must have mumbled the words. Small stabs of pain radiate from my cracked lips, a flash of agony explodes beneath my cranium and subsides in a series of throbbing waves. At the periphery of my mind I know that I am experiencing the effects of extreme dehydration. Quite soon, if I am lucky, delirium will be succeeded by unconsciousness.

I am apart and looking down at myself, an old woman lying in the sand, thin hair spread like the wing feathers of a dead bird.

Lesley is still there, staring at me as if she is waiting for something.

There is still more to be done.

Andrew went out to see the police.

'I'll come with you,' Lesley said, but he insisted that she should stay in the house in case there was any news.

'I'm going to meet a senior officer. It's nearly three days since Ruby and your mother disappeared, and they are taking it seriously. After that I am going to the British embassy.'

There was nothing for Lesley to do but sit and wait.

The gaunt, dusty house was impressive but uncompromisingly

austere; Lesley tried and failed to imagine the solitary existence that her mother must lead here. It was as if she were speculating about a stranger, not the woman who had given birth to her, yet Ruby had made a connection with her at once.

Whenever the telephone rang, the manservant Mamdooh answered it. He spoke Arabic, and after the call was finished he pursed his lips and shook his head. 'I am afraid no news, Madam.'

Lesley was in Iris's sitting room when someone came to the door. She heard Mamdooh bringing him up one of the house's several confusing sets of stairs and jumped up to see who it was.

'Good evening,' a suave little man said. 'I am Nicolas Grosseteste.'

'I'm so pleased you have come. My husband's gone to the police and the embassy. I'm so worried and sitting here is making it worse.'

The doctor shook her hand. 'It is a matter for concern. The police will do everything they can, I assure you.'

'Have they been kidnapped?'

'I think that must be considered as one possibility. But myself, I believe it is more likely that they have got lost, or stranded.'

'Why do you think that?'

'Your mother has been ill.' He left a delicate, interrogative pause that Lesley did not try to break. 'But since your daughter arrived in Cairo I have noted a great improvement in her health and her state of mind. The two of them appeared to share a remarkable rapport and it is my guess—my hope—that they have embarked on some excursion together. This may have gone wrong, but your daughter is a young lady of considerable energy and resource. I would place trust in her.'

'I see,' Lesley said.

She was on the point of asking the doctor whether he would like a drink, but Mamdooh was already at the door with a silver tray and a small glass of wine. The two men murmured in Arabic while Lesley looked on. A pulse beat in her neck. It was her role always to be excluded, she thought. Andrew was the master at it; now her daughter and her mother had established a *remarkable rapport*.

It didn't matter. She would volunteer at this moment for an entire lifetime of emotional isolation, so long as Ruby could be found safe.

Mamdooh left them together again and Nicolas sat down with his glass of wine. There was nothing to do except wait and the silence pressed in on them. But then a moment later Mamdooh was back and this time he was showing a young man into the room. He was thin, with slicked-back black hair and smooth skin. He looked from one to the other and burst into a torrent of words.

'This man Mamdooh tell me the police look for me. I don't hide. Ruby is my friend,' Ash said hotly.

'I am Ruby's mother. Who are you?'

'*Umm* Ruby,' the young man said. He bowed to her and Lesley understood that this was a polite greeting. 'My name is Ashraf. Ruby is my friend and I show her Cairo and we speak English together. I would not do to her any thing that would harm one hair of her head. I take her to meet my own mother.'

Lesley saw that the boy was on the verge of tears.

'It's all right. We are friends here. You had better sit down, Ashraf, and tell us whatever you know.' They were an incongruous group, sitting in Iris's underfurnished room.

Andrew found them there when he came back to the house. He told them that the police had talked to a café owner on the road to Giza, who said that Iris and Ruby had stopped there for breakfast two days ago at dawn. Another roadside vendor reported that he had seen the old Beetle a little later, beyond Giza, heading out on the desert road.

A police search would start in the morning.

Ruby no longer had any idea what she was doing.

She moved slowly, dragging up the ridges and sometimes falling down the other side. She was too exhausted to think about the world that had slipped away from her. All she was left with was a dull awareness that she must keep going or Iris would die. As the day drew on, even that certainty began to fade. She couldn't go much further. Her body was shrinking but her tongue had swollen. Soon it would fill her mouth and throat and choke her.

Soon it would be dark again.

She reached the top of another dune, slid down the other side. From this hollow she could see off to the right, where the shoulders of the dunes overlapped in a series of leaves like a deep stage set. The way between them looked almost like a track and she began to hurry along it with hope clicking on like a bright light. But only a few steps showed her that there was no track, only the illusion of one.

The despair that followed was complete. Ruby stopped walking. She sat down in the sand and her head dropped to her knees.

A rest. She would just rest for a while, staring at the infinity of sand between her feet.

When she did look up again she saw a camel.

It paced between the dunes ahead, close enough for her to hear the small jingle of its harness bells. There was a man in a *kuffiyeh* on its back. Behind the first camel came another, its haughty head up, rolling with its steady camel gait through the solid waves.

Ruby staggered to her feet.

Now she saw that there was a string of camels, some with riders and others carrying baggage.

She shouted, but no sound came out of her scorched throat.

She began to run, waving her arms, zigzagging through the sand with the breath like a razor-blade in her lungs.

'*Stop. Someone's coming.*'

'*Lindy, wait . . .*'

'*What's happening?*'

They had seen her. It was all right.

Ruby stopped running and her arms dropped to her sides. Her head was pounding as if it would explode, but there was also a *whoosh* inside her as colour and possibility and the future flooded back to her.

'Help,' she managed to say. 'Help my grandmother.'

She dropped to her knees in the sand.

The camel train came to a halt. It seemed neither likely nor particularly improbable that the riders were speaking English, or even that they sounded like her mother. There were four women and they were all dressed like Lesley, talked like Lesley. The nearest one slid down from her saddle and came towards her.

'What's wrong? Are you in trouble?'

She was wearing a water bottle in a kind of woven holster on a shoulder strap. Wordlessly, Ruby held out her hand for it.

The water dripped on her tongue and then flowed. She huddled in the sand and drank and drank until the bottle was empty.

The Lesley-voices were babbling. 'Hammid, I think she's lost.'

The Arab man in the *kuffiyeh* knelt down in front of Ruby. 'Where have you been?' he demanded. 'Where are you going?'

Ruby grasped the man's arm. 'My grandmother. You have to find her.'

'Where is your grandmother?'

She pointed to her tracks emerging between the dunes.

'How long have you been walking?'

With a struggle, she put the words together. 'I left her in our car early this morning. We have been lost for three days. She's got no water.'

The man pushed back his head covering, reached inside his blue robes and pulled out a mobile phone.

The women closed in on her. It hadn't been a hallucination: they were speaking English, and they did look and sound like her mother. As she listened to the guide's rapid Arabic, Ruby took in the women's linens and khakis, their broad-brimmed hats and sunglasses and pearl ear studs, and on the camels' backs saw their baggage with the words Ideal Desert Safaris in white stencil lettering, decorated with a palm tree.

She saw the man fold his little silver mobile and tuck it back inside his robes, and she registered the incongruity of it.

'Help is coming,' the guide said.

'Hammid is a wonderful guide. He'll find her,' said a woman who was holding Ruby's hands.

'How far is it? How far are we from the road?' Ruby mumbled.

Hammid looked up. 'From here? Maybe three miles.'

'That's quite close.'

'But you were walking away from it.'

Lesley and Andrew and Dr Grosseteste were still waiting.

Ash had explained that he must go to his switchboard night shift at the hospital but would come straight back to the house in the morning, as soon as he had finished work.

'Thank you for coming.' Lesley tried to smile. Mamdooh appeared and escorted Ash down to the front door.

Andrew turned to Nicolas. 'How on earth do you deal with this place on a daily basis?' he asked.

'Cairo?' The doctor looked at him, then gave a delicate shrug. 'One learns the technique.'

Andrew's mobile rang. Lesley and Nicolas stared at each other in equal hope and dread as Andrew took the call.

'Yes. Yes. I see. That's good. Thank you.'

Lesley shouted at him, 'What is it? What did they say?'

The police reported that Ruby had been found by a group of camel trekkers, wandering in the desert not more than a mile or so away from a little-used track leading back to the Fayoum oasis road. A search party was about to set out to look for Iris and the car.

'Oh, thank heaven.'

Lesley leapt out of her chair and blindly ran to her husband. He held her while she fired questions at him. 'Where is she now? Is she hurt? Can I talk to her?'

Andrew kept one arm round her shoulders and rubbed the free hand over his sagging face. 'Ruby insisted on going with the searchers.'

Ruby crouched in the back of the four-wheel drive. Her head bounced against the canvas roof as the vehicle swayed to the crest of a dune and tipped over the other side. It was fully dark now, and the headlamps raked over an unending slice of rippled sand that just showed the faintest impression of her footsteps. The police driver and Hammid next to him were hunched in silence, intent on their task. To the left and right of them were two other trucks, covering as broad a sweep of the desert as possible.

The driver said something and the truck came to a halt. Hammid jumped down and Ruby watched as he walked round the front of the bonnet. He crouched down in the beam of the headlamps and studied the rampart of sand as the other trucks stopped too. Ruby scrambled from her seat and ran to shake his shoulder.

'Why have we stopped?'

But she could see why. As they followed the tracks they had become progressively fainter, to the point where there was nothing to see at all.

Hammid swung a torch in a circle, and only the smooth silent expanse of the desert was revealed. He shook his head. 'We will go back now and wait for daylight.'

Ruby took a breath, mustering her last reserves. She looked up and overhead were the winking lights of a plane dipping towards the airport. She gripped Hammid's arm and begged, 'Please. I know it's near here. I *know* it is. If we give up now she might die before the morning.'

'You don't know the desert. We could search all night and miss by a few yards. It is much better with daylight and more people. A helicopter can come.'

Ruby clenched her fists and raised her voice until she was shouting, her own urgency almost deafening her. 'If you won't go on, I'm not going back with you. Give me as much water as I can carry and I'll search until I find her. Understand me?'

Hammid considered. A small breeze fanned across the sand. At last he said, 'Very well. We go one more hour.'

Ruby ran back to her seat before he could change his mind.

The trucks started to roll again.

They drove on, up the curved dune faces, down the other side. The grind of the engine in low gear vibrated all the way through Ruby's bones. They teetered at the crest of yet another summit, hanging in a vacuum before plunging into the descent.

Then Hammid's head jerked forward and he called out. Ruby pitched forward to look down, over his shoulder, into the depth of darkness below.

There was the car, almost submerged in sand on its windward side.

Ruby flung herself out of the truck before it had stopped moving and ran, sinking up to her ankles as the sand tried to the very end to hold her back. She threw herself down and pressed her head to Iris's rib cage, praying to hear a heartbeat or feel the faint exhalation of a breath.

There was nothing, but Iris's skin under her clothes was still warm.

Lesley and Andrew were in the anteroom where Nicolas Grosseteste had advised them to wait.

Ruby and Iris were both alive, they would be here soon. Lesley would have liked to hold her husband's hand for the warmth of it, but he was checking his mobile. She sat and studied the hem of her skirt instead, smoothing it over her knees and listening to the passing footsteps.

A pair of feet eventually stopped in front of them and an orderly in a grey overall led them down cracked corridors to a cubicle with a bed in it. They saw her before she saw them: Ruby was sitting on the bed with her head hanging and her upturned hands resting on the sheet beside her, the fingers loosely curled. She looked utterly exhausted.

'Ruby.'

Her head came up when she heard her mother's voice. 'Oh, Mum.' The words came out of her as a choked whisper. Lesley folded her arms round her and cupped her head against her shoulder. 'I'm so glad you're here.'

'It's all right, it's all right now.'

Ruby was crying. Her tears were hot against her mother's neck. This was a much younger Ruby, without the metal studs piercing her skin and with her eyes unpainted, and her hair flattened and gritty like a child's in a sandpit.

Lesley held her, and as Ruby clung to her she felt a surge of happiness so sharp and complete that it came close to ecstasy.

Nothing else mattered. Not Andrew, not loneliness, not even Edward nor that her own mother might be on the point of death. Ruby was here, the smell and the solid shape of her, and she was safe. The fuse that lit the bright delight for Lesley was Ruby, it always was. And the flare of delight itself now was that Ruby was vulnerable and knew that she needed her mother and hadn't concealed it.

'You're safe, I'm here,' she said.

'I was so stupid. I didn't mean it,' Ruby sobbed.

'No, darling. You weren't stupid. It isn't stupid to be young,' she murmured to console her.

'I drove the car off the road, didn't I?'

Lesley understood instantly that she was meaning the desert misjudgment had been stupid. It wasn't a bigger acknowledgment than that; in her own eager haste she had misinterpreted it. It wasn't that

Ruby had looked back over the years of rebellion and defiance, and finally seen them for what they were.

'Oh. Well, yes.'

Hot dismay flashed through her at the thought that Ruby might register the scale of her misunderstanding. The white light faded to grey and she was heavy again, feet locked to the floor.

'You didn't know,' Lesley said quietly. She let her arms fall, then took Ruby's hands in hers. 'What happened?'

Ruby twisted in her grasp. It was still too close to be talked about. 'I got us *lost*. We could easily have died.'

A doctor told them that Iris's condition was serious. They were briefly allowed into a room where she lay hooked up to bags of fluid, the tubes taped to her thin grey forearms. Her eyes were closed and her mouth hung open, and there was a tube in her nose as well. Andrew and Lesley stood one on each side, and Ruby briefly hovered at the bed end. Each time Iris took a breath it was like a snore; then it subsided and it seemed that she was never going to take another. Go on. *Breathe*, Ruby furiously and silently commanded.

There was nothing further they could do, the doctor said. The next twenty-four hours would tell. Nicolas had gone home, but he had left them a message to say that he would see them in the morning.

'We all need some sleep,' Andrew said.

Ruby squashed into the back of a taxi between her mother and stepfather. She put her hand awkwardly on Andrew's sleeve, realising that at the hospital she had hardly acknowledged his presence. 'Thank you,' she said humbly. 'I'm really sorry.' She had parroted that often enough. But this time she meant it.

'You're in one piece. That's what matters.' He leaned forward. 'Do you think this driver is taking us all round the houses?'

'No. This is the right way. Where's Ed?' she asked Lesley.

'Staying with his friend Ollie. It was the best we could do at short notice.'

'Are we ever going to get there?' Andrew muttered.

'It's just down here.' The sight of the three minarets touching the sky made Ruby's stomach turn over with renewed anxiety for Iris. 'You don't think she's going to die, do you?'

'No, I don't,' Andrew said.

In that moment she loved him for always having to know best and for always having an opinion to express, right or wrong. It was weird, that, because it was one of the things about him that had always annoyed her most. Lesley didn't say anything. She had been very quiet since they had left the hospital.

Mamdooh opened the door almost as soon as Ruby knocked. His moon-face was heavy with gloom. 'Miss, you are safe. And Mum-reese?'

'They're looking after her,' Ruby said.

Auntie appeared and swept Ruby into a flutter of hugging and patting. She was rapidly murmuring in Arabic and Ruby couldn't understand her any better than she ever had done but she whispered back just the same, telling her that she was sorry and it was all her mistake and Mum-reese was in the hospital and being cared for and they would all have to hope and pray that tomorrow she would begin to get better.

'*Hasal kheir*,' Auntie said. Ruby did understand that, it was one of the phrases Ash had taught her. It meant something like, it could have been worse and we should be thankful that it was not.

'*Inshallah*,' Ruby added. That it might not yet turn out to be worse.

Turning back to Andrew and Lesley she noticed how lost and incongruous they appeared in the dim, bare, stone heart of Iris's house, flanked by Mamdooh in his *galabiyeh* and Auntie with her white-shawled head. She felt a weight dropping off her as she looked at them. They were only people, as kind and as blinkered and as likely to be correct or mistaken as any others. Maybe the weight was resentment.

'It's late. You should go to bed,' Ruby said, as if they were the children.

Lesley nodded her head obediently, and then collected herself. 'But you need some food, and remember what they said about fluid intake.'

At the hospital, Ruby had been examined. She was dehydrated and hungry and sunburnt, that was all.

'Auntie will fix me something in the kitchen. Have you got a bedroom?'

'If we can find it.' Andrew peered up into the shadows of the gallery.

'Good night, then.' Ruby hugged them both and thanked them, as best she could. The words were just words but she meant them. Lesley held on to her for a second and then turned away in Andrew's wake.

In the kitchen it was warm and quiet. Mamdooh sat in his chair next to the stove with his hands laced together over his belly, as he always did, and Auntie laid out an earthenware bowl and a dish of flat bread. Ruby tore off papery chunks and soaked them in bean soup, and crammed the rich hot mush into her mouth. There was no need for any of them to speak. Their thoughts were with Iris.

The metal clash and footstep squeaks of hospital. Familiar from layers of memory and experience, but I can't place myself in any of them.

Pain at the periphery, or rather within a separate place that I don't want to re-enter. So I am the patient, not the doctor.

I open my eyes and pain shoots through my frontal lobes.

In my immediate field of vision there is a doctor's face. Beyond him, standing against a window so that it is haloed in light, is another figure. A woman in a flowered dress, not a nurse. The woman steps forward, away from the sunlight.

It is Lesley.

'She's awake,' the doctor says, in English. My wrist is lifted and turned, then my head. I close my eyes against the intrusion.

When I look again, Lesley is close at hand. Her face leans down over me, her forearms are resting on the bedsheet. The doctor has gone. Lesley lifts a hand and touches her fingers to my forehead. She is smiling, rather tremulously, her characteristic smile that might at any moment melt into tears.

'It's all right,' she whispers. 'You're going to be all right.'

I look past her, to where an IV pack hangs on its stand. The tube is taped to my arm. They're putting in fluids, that's all. We were in the desert, I remember, without water. The pain is mostly in my head, I realise; the aftereffects of severe dehydration. Lesley is correct, then. I am not going to die today, or even tomorrow.

A shadow falls for a moment, a compound of weariness and exasperation. But then I look back at my daughter's face. I don't know why she is here and the effort of working it out is too much. But I have the sense that Lesley has been in my mind. It was her absence that was like a butcher's hook, holding me up and stopping me from slipping down and away. Now the negative is reversed to positive, absence has become presence, and I realise that I am profoundly glad.

I make an effort of concentration and lift the fingers of my left hand. The plastic IV tubing faintly chafes my skin and Lesley sees the movement. She takes my hand and laces her fingers with mine.

I say her name. The smile flowers all over her face.

'I'm here, Mummy. Everything is going to be all right. I love you.'

Love. The wide sea that one word conjures up, all the currents and tides and storms and oily swells of it. But I manage to nod my head.

As soon as she woke up Ruby knew that she had been asleep for a long time. The light was bright behind her half-closed shutters and Auntie was at the door of her bedroom. She was bringing morning tea; at least, a glass of hot water with a Lipton's tea bag laid in its yellow envelope in the saucer. A cup of tea English-style, a special treat.

Mamdooh eased into the doorway and decently hovered there. Ruby hoisted herself upright, keeping the sheet pulled up to her chin.

'Mum-reese?'

'Today better. She is weak, but now awake. Your mother's with her.'

The cup and saucer rattled. 'God. Oh, what a relief. That's so good. She's going to be all right, isn't she?'

'God is merciful,' Mamdooh agreed. 'Your friend has called to the house. He waits for you outside.'

'Ash?' Ruby wanted to see him, very much. She began to get out of bed and Mamdooh hastily withdrew. Auntie dipped the tea bag into the hot water and pressed the glass of cloudy brownish fluid into Ruby's hand. She was very thirsty, sticky-mouthed with the taste of sand and the residue of bean soup, so she drank it in a single draught.

Ruby pulled on the nearest clothes that were not actually in the reeking desert heap, raked her fingers through her hair and leaned to open the shutters. Ash was standing against the opposite wall, one knee bent and the foot propped under him. He was wearing his leather jacket and a red Coca-Cola T-shirt. She rapped on the window to attract his attention but he was smoking, and looking away down the alley.

She ran down the stairs and out of the front door.

Ash straightened up and threw his cigarette aside. 'You look very terrible,' he said.

She stopped short. 'Well, thanks very much.' Ruby pulled angrily back but then she realised he was only shocked at the sight of her. She hadn't bothered to consult a mirror and wondered briefly just how bad things were.

'I've been in the desert. Three days. It was . . . it was . . .' She stopped there and shrugged. She supposed that in time she would develop a routine for describing the experience, it would become her desert story, but she was nowhere near that yet. 'Can we go somewhere? I want something to eat.'

'Come, then.'

He took her hand. They went down the alley and into the street that led to the busy road. Ruby looked all around her, at the crowds of people in which each person had his own precious history, and the peeling walls and telephone wires and glinting traffic and exuberant density of ordinary Cairo, and she was almost overcome with gratitude for it.

At a café on the edge of Khan al-Khalili Ash pulled out a chair for her and Ruby quickly sat down. Immediately the usual crowd of newspaper vendors and shoeshine boys and children trying to sell lighters and bottles of water swarmed around them. Ash waved them away, and from the waiter in a stained white jacket he ordered yoghurt and coffee and fried eggs with flat bread for Ruby, the same as he had ordered for her first breakfast in the bazaar.

Ruby helped herself to one of his Marlboros. Inhaling the smoke brought a wave of giddiness.

'The *suffragi*, and your mother and father, they think I have taken you and Madam Iris and done harm to you,' Ash blurted out.

'Did they? Why?'

'How should I know this? The *suffragi* came to Nafouz and my mother, and talks about the police. And then of course, to help in any way I come to the house as soon as I can and your mother and father—'

'My stepfather,' Ruby interrupted, but Ash only stared at her.

Angrily he said, '—They look at me as if I am guilty for something. Why do they think that when I am your friend and you are mine? I tell you why. It is because I am Egyptian boy and you are English girl.'

They looked at each other across a gulf that had not been there before.

'I'm sorry for whatever it was they said, or did. It was probably worrying about me that caused it, and my stepfather's like that with pretty much everyone, not just you. My mother always tries to do the right thing. And weren't you concerned about what had happened to us, or were you only thinking about yourself?' she snapped back at him.

'Ruby, Ruby. What do you think, since you know me?' Ash reached out and took her hand. He was very good-looking, especially when he was angry and serious. She felt raw and needy, and the need translated itself into wanting him. She held on to his hand, turning it over and studying the flat purplish ovals of his fingernails. 'I was afraid that you were dead,' he muttered.

'I was afraid that I was dead.'

She said it in such a way that he caught her hand more tightly and hauled the rest of her closer to him so that their mouths awkwardly met across the table. He kissed her very hard and it was the more startling because Ash never made demonstrations in public.

The waiter came and banged down the plate of fried eggs. Ruby looked at the clouded yellow eyes and the brown lacework at the edge of the glistening white and her mouth watered. 'I'm so hungry.'

Ash smiled at her, a sunny smile from which the anger had melted away. 'Eat, then,' he said.

Lesley sat beside Iris's bed, letting the time pass.

'Hello?' an English voice said.

Lesley looked up and saw a woman in a khaki T-shirt with the Land Rover logo on it, only it had been changed to read SandLover instead.

'Hello,' Lesley answered uncertainly.

'How is she?'

'A bit better. She woke up about an hour ago.'

'That's good news. And your daughter?'

'She was asleep when I left the house. Um, do we know each other?'

'I'm sorry, my fault. I was in the group who found your daughter last night, or perhaps she found us, I'm not sure which. She was marvellous, you know. We just wanted to make sure everything had turned out all right. I'm Ros Carpenter, by the way.'

Lesley came round the foot of Iris's bed and shook the woman's hand, and the woman gave her a friendly hug and said that she was sure Iris would soon be on the mend. The other members of the group were having coffee at a place round the corner, actually, and would she like to take a break for a few minutes and come and meet them?

'Well . . .' Lesley hesitated, looking back at Iris. Then she decided quickly, why not? Ruby was marvellous, this woman had said. She smiled at her. 'Just for half an hour. I want to say thank you to all of you. My name's Lesley Ellis.'

The other three women were gathered round a table, and they waved them over and shuffled up their chairs to make room.

'This is Lesley,' Ros announced proprietorially. 'Her mum is recovering and our desert wanderer is at home fast asleep.'

There were exclamations of relief, and the largest of the women cheered. Lesley looked around the table, touched by their warmth.

The blonde one said, 'Your daughter was very brave. She was exhausted, terribly thirsty, sunburnt—she had walked all that way, but she didn't think about herself at all. The one thing she had in her mind was to get help to her grandmother. Our guide tried to send her to the hotel with us but she just stood there and shouted at him until he said she could join the search.'

Lesley smiled. 'Yes, that's Ruby.' It was, too. It came to her that her beloved child was a different person from the one all her misgivings and anxieties had rested upon.

A woman with sunglasses pushed up on her head took Lesley's hand and patted it. 'This must have been a horrible few days for you.'

They gave her coffee and a croissant, introduced themselves, told the story again of how Ruby had stumbled from between the sand dunes and almost collapsed at their feet.

'Our guide, Hammid . . .'

'Lindy's in love with Hammid.' The one called Clare laughed. 'Can't stop saying his name.'

'No, I'm not. I'm just saying that *he* said you should always stay put if you lose yourself in the desert, but if Ruby had done that it might have been too late.'

'She did the right thing in this instance,' Jane agreed.

Lesley looked at her watch. 'I'd better go.'

The women all hugged her and Lesley thanked them once again.

When she reached Iris's side ward again, Ruby was sitting in the visitor's chair. She looked clean and almost her normal self, apart from her cracked and swollen lips.

'Darling, you're here. Did you sleep? How do you feel?'

'Mum. Where did you get to?'

'I went for a cup of coffee with the camel trekkers, they came to see how you both are. How did you get here?'

'Really? That was nice of them. I'm fine, I woke up and had breakfast with Ash. Then I had a shower and he gave me a lift on his scooter. Iris was awake a minute ago. She looked around and asked for you.'

'She asked for me?'

'Yes. I told her you'd be back soon.'

Lesley sat down quickly on the other side of the bed. She took her mother's hand, so thin and small, and held it tight. Ruby was quiet, sitting with her head propped against the back of the chair, and Lesley sat watching her and letting the wordless phrases of gratitude rise slowly through her mind, like bubbles in the sea.

chapter six

I AM RECOVERING. The figures coming and going at the edges of my awareness gain definition as the pain recedes. I recognise the nurses, who do what they must with reasonable efficiency, and the doctor, who when he leans over me smells of coffee and tobacco overlaid with cologne. And I have four visitors. Nicolas is the easiest. He sits in the chair beside my bed and reads to me, paragraphs from the *Egyptian Gazette*. When Mamdooh comes he brings a covered basket of food, cooked by Auntie, which I cannot eat. He sits for a few minutes, uncomfortable, too large for the spindly chair, and anxiety radiates out of him.

And then, my daughter and her daughter.

Lesley's expression is hesitant and at the same time expectant. Ruby looks as if there is a light behind her eyes. The future offers her everything, by right. She has only to reach out and take whatever she wants.

I am too tired to say more than the occasional word, but I like it when they are here, separately or together.

Now they have put more pillows behind my back and slipped their arms round me for further support. Ruby is holding a cup and Lesley dips a spoon into it and pushes the tip against my lips. I open my mouth and taste, like an infant feeding, and then I swallow. It is warm, sweetened porridge. The first solid food I have eaten in—how long? I have lost track.

'I want to go home. I want to be in my own home,' I say. At home I will be able to concentrate on what I have to do.

'**D**o you like them? They're my favourites.'

Ruby and Lesley were at the museum standing in front of a series of statues with enigmatic sloping faces and massive bellies and thighs.

'They are certainly impressive. Who are they?'

'Pharaoh Akhenaten. About 1300 BC. And his wife, Nefertiti.'

'Really? That's Nefertiti? You are very knowledgeable, I must say.'

'I am interested,' Ruby said, faintly reproving.

She pointed out a carved panel, calling it a stele, that showed the pharaoh cradling a child and his wife nursing two smaller infants. The domestic intimacy of the scene was in sharp contrast with all the funerary pomp and symbolism elsewhere, and Lesley lingered in front of it.

She became aware that Ruby was shifting at her side, preparing to say something.

'I'd like to stay here, you know.'

'To do what, darling?'

'Look, Mum. You've got to go back home soon, haven't you? Ed needs you, and so does Andrew.'

Andrew had returned to England four days earlier. Ed had insisted that he was fine, he came home from school and made himself some cereal and did his homework, and then Andrew came in and they had supper together. Takeaway, sometimes, he had added with satisfaction.

But Lesley would have to go back soon.

Ruby continued in a voice of calm reason, 'On the other hand we can't leave Iris here on her own. She'll be out of hospital in a day or so, and I can't really see her packing up and coming back to Kent. Can you?'

'No,' Lesley conceded, although that was more or less what she had been anticipating.

'So I thought, like, the best thing would be for me to stay on. Seeing as it's what I want to do anyway. I could maybe study Egyptology? Or something like that,' she added.

Carefully, Lesley said, 'You want to stay here, look after Iris, and be a student?'

Ruby met her eye. 'Yeah. That's it, pretty well.'

Lesley's back and feet ached.

'Let's sit down.' She pointed to a bench against a wall, out of the stream of visitors. Ruby followed her and they sat, Ruby shuffling herself sideways a little so that she could go on looking beyond a pillar at the Akhenaten statue.

She's my daughter, the refrain started up. I love her and I don't want to lose her to Cairo and Iris and pharaohs. What will she get up to if I am not there to restrain her? The thought of the desert and what had nearly happened blew a hot blast of fear straight into her head.

'It's certainly worth thinking about,' she temporised.

Ros Carpenter and the others had given Lesley a picture of a different Ruby, one who had been notably brave and who had only thought about rescuing Iris. What if it was this *other* Ruby who had been the real one all along, Lesley speculated, while as her mother she had kept a deficient version of her in her heart for her own purposes?

To fortify herself, by seeming strong in comparison?

To convince herself that she was needed?

And if this was possible maybe something similar, some other faulty construct, might also be at the heart of her relationship with Iris?

'Do you think I have been a good mother?' Lesley asked abruptly.

The question was out before she could stop it or even edit it and she disliked the imploring note it sounded.

Ruby sat on her hands, revealing her discomfort.

'*Do* you?'

'Mum, I don't know. You gave me plenty to kick against. Well, yes, of course you've been a good mother, like you came out here to rescue me. You've always been there, doing the right thing.'

Doing the right thing: how dull it made her seem.

Ruby added seriously, 'There are all the good people in the world, and you are one of them. Then there are all the other people, and they're Iris and me. D'you think that's true?'

Iris and Ruby on one bank, herself on the other, and the river of opportunity and experience flowing between them. She was stricken with a sense of absolute isolation. 'Maybe,' she whispered.

Ruby turned from Akhenaten and saw her mother's face. 'Oh, Mum,' she whispered. 'What's wrong?'

Lesley shook her head. Not here, she pleaded with herself. Don't cry in front of a hundred Dutch tourists and a haughty statue of Nefertiti.

Ruby slid back along the bench and put her arm round her shoulders. 'What is it? Is it about Iris?'

Lesley pressed her lips together, then retrieved a tissue from her bag and blew her nose. 'In a way it is.'

'What way is that?'

'I haven't ever understood why she was never there.'

Ruby chewed the corner of her lip; the cracks and fissures had healed, and the swelling had gone down days ago. Her face was smooth and her mouth was her own again. Lesley saw her making the connections as clearly as if the chain of thoughts were projected on a screen.

'You wanted to do it differently for Ed and me. You wanted to be there every hour of the day.'

'Yes.'

She nodded. 'I understand. Haven't you ever asked her why?'

'No.'

'Then you must. Before she forgets everything.'

Iris came home. They went to the hospital together and brought her back in a private ambulance. Iris tried to insist that there was no need for such a thing, but she was shaky on her feet and she walked very slowly with the aid of a stick. Her wrists and ankles looked like twigs.

Mamdooh and Auntie were waiting for her in the hallway, under the red glass of the big lantern. They swooped on her and tried to take her arms as if she was going to be lifted up between the four of them and carried up the *haramlek* stairs.

But Iris held up her hand. 'Wait.'

She stood still instead, propped on her stick. Her head rotated, then her chin lifted as she gazed upwards into the painted rafters.

They all hovered, watching, ready to dash forward if she fell.

'I love this house,' Iris said.

Then she consented to be helped upstairs and put to bed.

Two weeks before Christmas and Lesley announced that she had booked flights home for herself and for Ruby.

'I am not coming,' Ruby said immediately.

It was a chilly, grey afternoon but the three of them were in the garden. Iris had grown stronger since coming home and she liked to sit out there until the winter twilight fell.

'It's Christmas,' Lesley repeated.

'You and Ed and Andrew can have Christmas. You don't need me.'

'Yes, we do. I do.'

'I don't want to leave Iris. Iris doesn't want to leave Cairo.'

'You will do as your mother tells you,' Iris said precisely.

'But . . .'

'Remember, you stay in this house only at my invitation.'

'Well, yes, I know, but . . .'

'That is enough. You will go back to England for Christmas, because that is what Lesley wants you to do. Will you call Mamdooh, please? I would like to go inside.'

Later, Ruby slipped into Iris's bedroom. Auntie had put Iris to bed and she was lying back against pillows with the sheet folded across her chest. The picture of her and Xan Molyneux stood on the bedside table, as always, with the little wooden ship with the numeral 1 painted on each side placed alongside.

'Can I talk to you?' Ruby asked.

'Yes.'

'We were quite happy before I got us lost in the desert, weren't we?'

'You did not lose us. If anyone was responsible it was me, because I know the country and the desert and you do not, and I should have taken proper precautions instead of letting you joyride into nowhere. I can't even remember how it happened.' Iris gave an exasperated sigh. 'In any case, no harm was done. We are both here now.'

'No harm? No *harm*? We could both be dead. You were in hospital for days. You could easily be dead instead of lying here.'

'The shame is rather that I am not. Death is not an unthinkable prospect for me, remember.'

Ruby shouted, 'How can you say that? What about Lesley? What about *me*? I've only just found you. I've only just begun to know what you are like and I've hardly found out anything about your life, and yet you say that it's a shame that you aren't dead?'

Iris stared at her. 'I am sorry,' she said in the end, through pale lips.

'Don't say it ever again.'

'But I am old. Death will come as a relief.'

'Not to us left behind.'

'Don't shout. It is my life and the end of it is mine also. I am selfish, but you are the same.'

Ruby considered this. 'Am I? Actually, yes, I suppose so.' There were the good people, like Lesley, and then there were the others. 'It's quite funny, isn't it?'

They looked at each other and suddenly it was funny. They laughed, Iris wheezing and runny-eyed and Ruby uninhibitedly, showing her white teeth and with her hair springing back from her face.

'It's weird that we're alike, since we hardly met until a few weeks ago.'

'Not so strange, really. There is the matter of genetic connection.'

'But Mum's so different.'

'That's true.'

Their amusement subsided.

'Have I got to go home for Christmas? Won't you let me stay here with you?'

'No, I won't let you. I prefer to spend Christmas as I always have done in this house. And I have a lot to remember.'

'The cup on the shelf?'

'Yes, something like that.'

'All right. I'll go. Can I come back in the new year?'

'You may. I would like that, if you are sure.'

'I'm certain,' Ruby said firmly. She grasped Iris's hand and held it. 'There's something else, as well.'

'Oh dear,' Iris sighed.

'It's Mum herself.'

The muscles tensed once more. 'Yes?'

'She wants something, I don't even really know what it is but it's to do with you and her and the past.'

'I know.'

'Can you give it to her?'

There was a silence compounded of reluctance and denial and apprehension. Deliberately, Ruby let it stretch.

'When is it you are supposed to go back to England?'

'In two days' time.'

'That's sooner than I expected. I might give you and Lesley a farewell party. A dinner,' Iris said grandly. 'I could ask Dr Nicolas and your two young men. I like them.'

'A dinner's a very good idea. I think, though, it should be for just two guests. Me and Mum.'

Ruby and Lesley confirmed their flights, and Ruby collected a few belongings and stuffed them into a rucksack. Most of her possessions she left as they were, tidied away in her spartan bedroom. The more she left behind, she reasoned, the more certain her return would be.

The day before their departure was dark and windy. Rain swept in from the north in unpredictable gusts and the garden became an unwelcoming space of dripping water and slippery glazed tiles. Auntie dusted the table in the domed room that led off the hallway and put fresh candles in the candlesticks, Mamdooh took deliveries from local shopkeepers, and the two old people retreated into the kitchen.

At breakfast time, Iris told them that they were to join her for drinks at 6 p.m. She spent the rest of the day in her room.

At six o'clock precisely, Ruby and Lesley were both waiting under the lantern in the hall. Mamdooh had climbed the stepladder and placed tea lights in the crimson glass lights, and a smoky reddish glow now suffused the bare space.

Iris came slowly along the gallery. They caught a glimpse of her as she passed an open screen. A moment later she turned the corner of the stairs, descending one step at a time, leaning on her stick. Ruby moved forward instinctively, but she held up her hand.

'Thank you,' Iris said. 'I can manage.'

She came to stand between them, upright even with the stick, but her gaze slid past them to the other end of the room. There was a long pause.

Iris was looking at the spot where a mule wearing a sable wrap and an orchid corsage had stood in the first minutes of 1942.

'Mummy?' Lesley said softly.

Iris turned her head, very slowly. Her eyes finally settled on Lesley's face. She looked startled.

'I was thinking of something else. Something reminded me . . .' It was the candlelight. With an effort she came back to the present. 'We are going to drink a toast,' she announced.

Wearing his tarboosh and a red cummerbund, Mamdooh brought in a tray and three glasses and a bottle of French champagne.

Iris raised her glass. 'To the future.' They echoed the words, and drank with eager smiles and murmurs.

Iris soon tired of standing and so they led her through to the dining space where the candles flickered in the faint draught. She clapped her hands at the sight of the napkins and glasses and polished cutlery.

'How pretty. Isn't it pretty? Now, you here, Lesley.' Iris took the head of the table and Lesley the foot, with Ruby in the centre of the long space between them. Lesley quickly finished her champagne and drank a second glass, the rim clinking faintly against her teeth and betraying that her hand was shaking.

Mamdooh brought in an earthenware dish and served with great for-mality. Auntie had made chicken stew. He uncorked a bottle of red wine and poured that for them too, then he withdrew.

Ruby thought, God, what are we going to talk about?

Iris picked very neatly at her chicken, then touched her napkin to her lips. The candle flames shivered and sent up thin trails of smoke.

Lesley made a bold effort. 'Do you know, Mummy, I was thinking about this while you were in the hospital. You've never told me how you and Daddy first met. Was it during the war?'

Iris's cutlery clinked as she laid it down. Don't say anything mean to her, Ruby silently begged. But to her surprise Iris suddenly smiled.

'He was a major, working in Intelligence here at GHQ Cairo. We knew him a little in those days. Then, after the war, I met him again in England.'

Lesley smiled back over her glass. 'Go on.'

I can remember the day, almost the exact date. It was in Hampshire at the end of June 1946. My father had died a few weeks earlier and was buried next to my mother in the village churchyard.

I was at medical school in London, spending long hours in lecture halls and dissecting rooms, then coming home on the bus to sit with my textbooks until bedtime. One weekend, telling myself I must make the time sooner or later, I took the train down to Hampshire, to begin the job of clearing my parents' house. Among the post that had accumulated there I found a letter addressed to me. It was from Major Foxbridge.

'He had your address, then?'

'I gave it to him as I was leaving Cairo. Your grandmother was very ill and I was rushing home to be with her. It was the middle of the war. We didn't automatically expect to see people again.'

'You don't have to make excuses for giving your address to a handsome major,' Lesley teases.

I look at my daughter through the candle glow. She has her tremulous look. The child watches us both.

'I don't know about excusing myself. I saw that Gordon's address was not very far away from your grandparents', so I sat down at my father's desk to telephone him. It was a Saturday and he was at home. The result was that he drove over, perhaps twenty miles, and we had a drink in the garden and then he took me out to dinner.'

'The rest is history,' Lesley says.

'History?'

'Tell us some more,' Ruby says quickly.

I am a little dizzy with champagne, but suddenly I find the words.

'The Qattara Depression.'

'What's that?' Lesley asks.

'Mum, just let her tell it in her own way.'

'When I lived here during the war, Lesley, I met a soldier and I fell deeply in love with him. We were going to be married. His name was Xan Molyneux and he was killed in 1942 in the desert, a few days before our wedding, in a place called the Qattara Depression. He was on a special operation with his commando group and six Italian aircraft came out of the sky and shot them to pieces. Only two members of the group survived. One died three days later in hospital, the other was an Arab scout who escaped by walking across the desert.

'Before he went out there Xan told me that the enemy forces had developed an uncanny ability to pinpoint Allied movements in the desert. He suspected that there must have been an intelligence leak.'

Gordon was by that time out of the army and working in the City.

I remember that he took me to the restaurant of a local hotel, where we sat at a table next to some open French windows overlooking the garden. We drank beer, and talked and talked about the war and Cairo and people we knew. It was a joy to be with someone who shared those memories. And we talked about Xan, of course.

During that talk, Gordon told me what I could not have learned as an ordinary civilian, that the US military attaché in Cairo had been responsible for allowing a stream of top-secret information to fall into Italian and then German hands.

Every night, between September 1941 and the middle of 1942, Colonel Bonner Fellers used a code called the Black Code to relay information about Allied movements in North Africa to Military Intelligence in Washington. It was the Colonel's bad luck that the Italians had broken into the US embassy in Rome, stolen the black notebook in which the code was written, copied and returned it before anyone noticed it was missing. The Italians wouldn't share their prize with the Germans, but they did pass over decoded transcripts of early messages and Fellers's encryptions, always starting off and ending in the same way, meant that the German cryptographers soon cracked the code for themselves.

Rommel referred to these priceless bulletins as 'my little Fellers'.

Among countless other pieces of information the intercepts would have revealed the covert movements of Tellforce, plotting their surprise route by which heavy armour might strike northwards towards el Alamein. And so the Italians had been able to direct their air attack straight at them.

Gordon's light hazel eyes met mine across the dinner plates. He had a tidy moustache, slightly receding dark hair, well brushed. The dining room had emptied out and we were alone.

Slowly but very deliberately he reached for my hand. 'Has it upset you, to know more about why Xan died?'

I thought about it for a moment. 'No. Anything that makes it easier to understand makes it a little easier to bear.'

From that night onwards, Gordon Foxbridge pursued me with single-minded determination. He told me he had loved me even when he took Xan's and my photograph on that breathless afternoon at the Gezira Club, and after Xan died he resolved that if he couldn't have me he didn't want anyone.

'Why?' I was amused and rather impressed.

'Why do we love one person rather than another? There is no recipe, only certainty that has its own logic.'

True, I thought.

At length, after more than two years during which I readily became his lover but always refused his proposals, Gordon's kindness and considerateness wore me down. Exhausted with the end of my training that meant long hospital hours, and vulnerable to the stability and security he offered, I finally agreed to marry him.

I gather my breath again. I have talked so much, more than I have done for years. My food lies cold in front of me, almost untouched.

Lesley deserves the truth. It is all I can offer her.

'I shouldn't have done it. Shouldn't have married him.'

'Why ever not?'

'I didn't love him. I loved Xan Molyneux.'

'But he was dead.'

'And so was the child I was expecting. I was going to have his baby but I had a miscarriage. I lost them both in the space of two weeks; you might say that I lost everything. But it was wartime, and I wasn't alone in that.'

Lesley's gaze wavers and drops from mine. I can see her mind working. Ruby has cupped her chin in her hands. She looks concerned but not very surprised.

Then Lesley lifts her head again. There are spots of high colour on her cheekbones and she is more than half drunk. She is angry, not sympathetic in the least. Not that I am looking for sympathy.

'So all the time, all those years, when you left Daddy and me behind and went off to look after other women and their children in bloody Africa, you were wanting the family you lost instead of the one you actually had? You discarded us because we made the mistake of being still alive, not a heroic memory?'

She pours herself another glass of wine and drinks deeply. Ruby begins a move to restrain her, but I shake my head. If it takes alcohol to get Lesley to unbutton and say what she feels, instead of smiling with the corners of her mouth and hiding it all, then the headache and the nausea will be worth it.

There is still more that I have to say.

'No. I have had long enough to think about it and I believe that it isn't quite as you see it.'

I need a drink myself. I take a mouthful, choking a little as the fumes go to my head.

'Perhaps if Xan and our son had lived, it wouldn't have been so very different.'

'What do you mean?'

'Death preserves an ideal. Ideal love, lover, infant. Can you follow that? In the end, Xan, Gordon, your brother or you, I might not have been so different. I might have betrayed them, neglected them too. I did what I did and I am the person I became. Bad, good, flawed. Indifferent. Better alone, preferring to be.

'An ordinary life didn't mean enough, it wasn't precious enough, after Xan died. I found the rigour I needed in practising medicine. I was passionate about my work and the detachment in me became an asset, not a shortcoming. You need to be able to stand back a little, when you do work like that. I don't think, Lesley, I would have lasted in the role of good mother or proper *wife* to anyone. Maybe . . .' My voice is beginning to fail me. '. . . Maybe not even to Xan Molyneux.'

I raise my hand and let it fall again. I am utterly exhausted by this confession, because that is what it is.

'Gordon deserved better than I gave him. And so did you, my dear.'

Lesley stares. Then she stands up.

I get to my feet too.

'I'm sorry,' I say.

Lesley's face swims, then tears slide down her face. She reaches out to me, and we shuffle into an awkward and unpractised embrace.

I don't know how long we stand there. I am aware of Ruby still sitting at the table, picking the wax runnels from the candles and frowning as she moulds them in her fingers.

'Iss all right,' Lesley says in the end. There are black marks under her streaming eyes and she is tending towards maudlin. 'Got to go on, haven't we? Life goes on.'

'Yes.' But I disagree.

Now Ruby stands. 'You ought to go to bed,' she says, into the space between us.

Lesley and I take each other's arm and we move slowly, unsteadily, towards the *haramlek* stairs.

chapter seven

CHRISTMAS IN ENGLAND. Christmas with all the re-enactments of family tradition, performed in the same way for as long as Ruby could remember. The difference was that this year she noticed how hard her mother worked to make it look effortless.

Lesley lifted her antique glass tree ornaments out of their cotton-wool nests and hung them on the guaranteed-not-to-drop tree. Presents were bought and wrapped and handed over. Will and Fiona and their children came to stay.

She participated in all this and even, to her surprise, enjoyed approximately half of it. At the same time she thought constantly about Iris and about Cairo like a parallel world that was waiting for her to slip back into it. The knowledge that she had a separate resort, another place to which to retreat even if it was only in her mind, made it easier to forgive the shortcomings of the present one.

On Boxing Day when Fiona and Lesley took the wound-up children out for a walk and Andrew immediately fell asleep, Will followed her into the kitchen and casually dropped his arm round her shoulders. He tilted her chin in order to gaze into her eyes.

'How is my special girl?'

Ruby considered, giving herself plenty of time to do so, while Will's finger traced a line down her neck to her collarbone.

I don't need to have any kind of weird contract with you, not any more. You can't confuse me any longer with your creepy blend of authority and sleazy secret advances.

'I am not yours,' was what she said. She was pleased with the splinters of ice in her voice.

She detached his hand from her shoulder and let it fall, then she added, 'I don't want you to touch me ever again. And if you do, I will tell my mother and your wife about it.'

As an afterthought she picked up the tea cloth and pointed to the washing-up.

'Here.' She smiled at him, putting the cloth into his empty hand. Will had not cleared up a plate or a glass throughout the whole of Christmas. That was women's work.

When she came back from the walk Lesley said, 'Ruby, darling, you've done the saucepans. Thank you.'

'Not me. It was Will,' Ruby told her.

'Thanks for doing all the cooking and shopping and everything,' Ruby said to her, when Will and his family had at last gone home. Andrew and Ed were watching the football. 'Everyone enjoyed themselves.'

'Did they?' Lesley said eagerly. 'Did you?'

'Of course I did. I never thought about it before but Christmas works like glue, it keeps us all sticking together, eating the turkey and playing the games and going for the walk. Now we've done it and that's it for another year. But I understand why you wanted me to come home for it and I'm glad I did.'

They looked at each other and a slow smile curved Lesley's face.

Ruby said, 'You never got an answer, did you?'

Lesley knew instantly what she was talking about.

'In a way I did. It wasn't exactly a revelation that Iris wasn't a good mother. But it helped to hear her admit that she probably wouldn't have been to anyone else either. That it wasn't just me who had somehow failed to capture her interest, which was what I always felt.'

'You didn't know about her great love affair, and the lost baby?'

'No. Nothing at all.'

'I'm pleased she told us. She must have wanted to, the way it all came out in a great rush.'

'Did you talk a lot, when you were there together?'

'She told me a few stories, but they never connected up, not the way they did when she told us about Granddad and the Black Code and the Qattara Depression. Now I come to think about it, most of the time I talked and she listened. I probably moaned about how unfair life was.'

'Was?'

Ruby grinned. 'I'm saying nothing more at this stage.'

'Of course not.'

Abruptly, Ruby asked, 'When can I go back there?'

'Can you tell me why you want to, so much?'

Ruby considered window-dressing her proposition with more assurances about language courses and pharaonic studies. She was eager to do those things, but she was afraid that concealing the real reason for going back to Cairo would be to deny Iris herself.

'To be with her. She's old.'

'I know that.'

If Ruby went to Cairo she would be doing what Lesley would have been glad to do herself—but Iris wouldn't want that. She wouldn't look for Lesley's company now, any more than she had done before. But at least Ruby could be there. Ruby would be the thread. And if Iris's condition worsened—past the point, Lesley secretly calculated, when she would be able to exert her iron will—then it wasn't so far for Lesley to travel to be there herself.

Lesley beckoned and Ruby took a sideways step, to come under the shelter of her arm. They stood close together, their cheeks touching.

'I think you should go,' she said at last.

Ruby's head lifted at once. 'Thanks, Mum,' she said.

This time, she knew exactly how much to pay the taxi driver for the ride in from the airport. The smell of diesel fumes and frying offal, underpinned with the amalgamated spicy, rotting, fermented odours of Cairo itself, was perfectly familiar.

The door in the high wall opened and Mamdooh's shape was outlined against the dim light within. 'Miss, you are here again,' he said. It was impossible to tell whether his gloomy tone was lightened by a briefly welcoming note.

Ruby stepped inside and he took her bag. The quietness of the house struck her again. It was all shadows and arches, muffled with dust, populated by ghosts. Auntie hurried out of the kitchen and grabbed her hands, looking up into her face and talking volubly.

'How is Mum-reese?' she asked them.

'Dr Nicolas has visited her. She is tired, but she waits to see you.'

The door to Iris's sitting room stood open, letting a slice of light out into the dim breadth of the gallery. Ruby stepped inside.

'You are here at last,' Iris greeted her.

In her own room, Ruby sat on her bed and stared into the darkness outside her window. Just in the space of a month Iris had become much smaller, frailer, except for her eyes which appeared huge in her shrunken face. Ruby didn't know if she had been able to conceal her shock at the sight of her.

She would have to talk to Dr Nicolas, find out from him what treatment or medicine Iris could have that would make her better. And even as she resolved to do this, the recognition of its futility crawled up her spine to grasp the nape of her neck.

Iris wasn't going to get better. She was dying.

No . . .

I won't *let* her die, was Ruby's first reaction. It isn't fair. I didn't let it happen in the desert and I won't now.

'You like pomegranate,' Iris announced as triumphantly as a child.

'Yes, I do.' Ruby gnawed the seeds from their caul of pith and burst them between her teeth.

The light in Cairo even in January was bright after the English murk, and the sun was gentle on the tops of their heads.

'Would you like some yoghurt, look, with some of this honey? You haven't eaten anything, hardly,' Ruby insisted.

'I'm quite happy.' Iris smiled.

It was true, she did seem happy. They sat in the garden together as they had done before, and if Iris wasn't too tired they talked.

'Tell me more about Xan Molyneux?'

'Ah, Ruby. If you had only known him.'

'How did you meet him?'

In Lady Gibson Pasha's garden. Dancing with Xan and then falling and spraining my ankle. I had been drunk on whisky and champagne, and then drunk on Xan himself. The child's eyes as I talk, round in surprise. She thinks as all the young do—as I thought myself, when I was her age—that passion is their own invention.

I find that I am laughing because I remember the night and the joy of it, when it was the loss of memory I feared more than anything else.

Hassan at the wheel and Xan in the back beside me. Holding my hand in the creased coral-pink silk folds of my dress.

The Bedouin tent pitched in the shelter of the dunes, the view of the Pyramids and champagne frothing into tin mugs. The first time I understood the split in Xan, and Jessie James and all the others, who had to confront the unthinkable every day in the desert and who only wanted to laugh and get drunk and make love when they left it behind.

'Was that the first time you and Xan made love?'

'No, not that night. That came a little later.'

And I can remember it as if I have just stepped out of his arms. The joy of it.

Ruby is still looking at me, with a strange expression now.

'The cup on the shelf,' she says again.

'That's right,' I tell her. I have the sudden certainty that when I can no longer hold it, when it has slipped out of my hands, it will not be smashed into a thousand pieces.

Ruby will be holding it for me.

Ruby *is* the cup.

When Iris was resting in bed, Ash and Ruby resumed their long walks.

When Ruby returned to the old house, the unbreathing silence seemed to unfurl within her head. She would almost run through to the garden or up the stairs, her chest tight with anxiety, looking for Iris.

'Here you are,' Iris would murmur. 'Sit down, don't loom over me.'

'Do you want to talk? Or are you too tired?'

'What about?'

'You never told me how you came by this house.'

'It was a legacy.'

'From whom?'

'Sandy.'

Poor Sandy Allardyce. Never had children, with Mrs Kimmig-Gertsch or anyone else. Lived here alone the last ten years of his life and died in his sixties. He inherited the house from Gerti Kimmig-Gertsch, then left it to me, of all people, in his will; a letter from his solicitor reached me months afterwards, me in my rented two rooms next to the clinic in Namibia. I hadn't seen Sandy since I left Cairo in 1942, but we exchanged letters once in a while.

'He was in love with me.'

'**H**e was in love with me,' Iris said.

Ruby caught a sudden sideways glance, darting under her grand-mother's lashes, a look of coquetry, utterly knowing and triumphant.

Iris remembered how she had once been. Maybe, Ruby thought, she even felt today as she had once done. Capable of rousing men to passion. Eager, with the man she loved, to return it.

'What was it like, the first time with Xan?'

Iris gave a small sigh, her chest just perceptibly rising and falling under the covers.

'It was like going to heaven.'

Iris had fallen asleep. Ruby stood up, very carefully, so as not to disturb her, and slipped out of the room.

Now I am alone. That's right. Silence rests on my head, reaches into the ear, swelling in the chambers and pressing against the delicate bones.

Nicolas. Nicolas witnessed my scrap of a will.

I have nothing to leave, only this house with its serene Ottoman arches and the garden where it is cool even in the summer's heat.

I do not want my Ruby, my precious gem of a Ruby, to retreat here, to be caught here, with secondhand memories for company.

The house will be sold.

And whatever money it realises, a great deal of money I think, because people have tried to persuade me to sell it, will be divided into three.

One-third for Mamdooh and Auntie.

One-third for Ruby, which will be something but not too much.

One-third for Ashraf, so that he can go and study.

Two-thirds for Egypt, one-third for England.

That's good, I think.

And Lesley, my poor Lesley . . .

She will not want my legacy. Let it pass on to Ruby, who has love from both of us. Who is more like me than Lesley ever was.

More like me. Miss Iris Black, Mrs Xan Molyneux as never was, Mrs Gordon Foxbridge, returned to Dr Black again.

Ruby woke very early with a cold premonition in her heart. She blinked in the dim light, trying to identify what was wrong. Then in one movement she sat up and pushed back the covers. She ran down the corridor, her warm feet leaving faint prints on the bare floor.

Iris was lying on her side, facing the photograph.

Ruby hesitated in the doorway. When at the beginning of her time here Iris had fallen ill, she looked into the room to see Auntie sponging her waxy forehead and had feared for a moment that her grandmother had died in the night.

It was not like this.

Without taking a breath Ruby crossed to the side of the bed.

She touched her hand to Iris's arm and it was cold.

Iris was gone.

Ruby slipped down to her knees and put her arm round Iris's shoulders. She had left in her sleep, alone.

Gently, Ruby leaned forward and kissed her cold temple, where the blue veins showed under the skin. She knelt there for a few minutes, holding her, then she stood painfully upright again with all her body aching. The absence was complete.

In the kitchen, Mamdooh stood up from his chair by the oven as soon as he saw her face.

Ruby took both his hands. 'My grandmother died in her sleep.'

Auntie was standing beside the sink. A rising wail of grief broke out of her, loud as the first call of the muezzin. Ruby briefly hugged her, then she turned away. She would have to telephone Dr Nicolas, Lesley; she would have to perform the tasks that those who were left behind always had to perform, in one way or another.

But not yet, first she wanted some time to be alone and to think about Iris.

Ruby left the house. She turned the opposite way from the front door and walked the few steps that led into the courtyard of the great mosque. She had only looked inside a handful of times, peeking at the sea of praying men who pressed their foreheads to the holy ground. But now the great space was deserted. She walked slowly, under a sky heavy with rain, the pebbles sharp under the thin soles of her slippers. The court was as vast as the desert and the smooth rhythm of the arches was like a rolling sea. Ruby tipped her head back and the first raindrops needled her face.

She wanted to hear Iris's voice, but she couldn't summon it up. Not yet. The image of the empty shell that she had left behind was too clear.

The three minarets topped with crescent moons soared towards the sky.

It was like going to heaven, Iris had said. Suddenly Ruby glimpsed the look that Iris had shot at her. The knowing, confident, amused look of a passionate woman. Maybe that's what it was like, Ruby thought.

She hoped so.

A sudden gust of wind swept across the open court, bringing rain from the north, down from the reeds and water of the delta.

The rain on the pebbles smelt strangely, yet familiarly, of England.

Rosie Thomas

When Rosie Thomas's marriage ended in divorce, she decided that the time had come to start leading a very different kind of life. For twenty-three years she had been a traditional wife and mother, writing her novels from home so she could always be there for her children and husband. 'When marriages end, the important thing is not to be destroyed. I was adamant that I was not going to become bitter. My life used to be utterly conventional and unadventurous. Now it's anything but.'

Newly single and independent, Rosie swapped her Victorian home in North London for a trendy penthouse flat in the City and threw herself into experiencing as many new challenges as possible. She discovered a love of travelling and mountaineering and has now climbed in the Alps and the Himalayas. She has also competed in the Peking to Paris car rally, and spent a month living and working on a tiny Bulgarian research station in Antarctica—adventures that have all been inspirational for her novels. In fact it was Rosie's own 'lost in the desert episode', as she calls it, that led to the dramatic climax in *Iris and Ruby*.

'My partner Theo and I went on a three-day trek to the Fish River Canyon in Namibia and had hired a local guide. But on the second day the guide fell behind and we never saw him again. We were lost in the desert, with little water, little food and no map, for two and a half days. I really thought that we were going to die.'

Rosie set *Iris and Ruby* in Cairo and travelled there for her research. 'Being a woman alone in Cairo is most uncomfortable. It is very much a male society and, as a Western woman on my own, I was seen as fair game—every taxi driver wanted to be my "Cairo boyfriend". But Cairo is a truly beautiful city, full of contrasts. Iris's home in the novel is based on an actual house that was owned by a Major Gayer-Anderson, and is now a museum, and it is quite, quite beautiful. I also visited the Egyptian Museum, which is organised in such a haphazard way that it feels as though the artefacts have only recently been dug up and just thrown onto the shelves.'

I asked Rosie if, in all her travels, she had a favourite destination? 'Favourite? That's difficult. I like different places for different reasons. Last summer I was completely stunned by Afghanistan—even though there were still tanks on the streets. I was surprised by how beautiful it was; how amazing the people are, after centuries of conflict rolling over them, and how they truly believe that life will get better, especially if tourists start to visit their country. I would love to go back.'

Rosie's next life-enhancing experience will be competing in the 2006 London Marathon on behalf of Saving Faces, a charity set up to help people suffering facial trauma caused by illness or accident, and of which she is a trustee. 'Saving Faces does not receive any government funding at all, yet facial trauma can devastate people's lives completely. I am not a runner—just the occasional jog around my local park once or twice a week—and the longest distance I'd ever run before was probably six miles, so training for the Marathon has been intense.

'Unfortunately my training regime has had to go on ice these last two weeks because I sustained an injury. I've had treatment, though, and I'm hoping it will be all right. My doctor told me that I could have an MRI scan, and then a cortisone injection into the site of the injury. "You won't feel a thing on the day," he told me, "but by God you'll know about it afterwards." I decided to decline—I think I'll just stick to the Nurofen!'

One of Rosie's running partners is her agent, Jonathan Lloyd. 'It's so funny. He purports to be the most genial and laid back of men but he has a competitive streak in him that you would never believe. Whenever we run together, he has to put on a sprint in the last hundred metres in order to beat me!'

After the London Marathon, Rosie is taking some time off to attend a friend's wedding in Bali. 'Well, it should have been just a holiday but I'm thinking of changing the setting in my next novel from Pakistan to Bali—I've been told it needs more colour. It's daunting to change things so late in the day, but it's also part of the writer's challenge. When I bought my ticket, I discovered that it's cheaper if you keep going all the way round the world, so I'm heading off for a month's backpacking via Japan and Mexico. Apparently it's called a "grey ticket" and they sell more round-the-world tickets to people of my age than to youngsters. So I'm obviously not the only one in their fifties taking on new experiences and challenges!'

Jane Eastgate

DOROTHY KOOMSON

my best friend's girl

It's Kamryn's birthday and she is going to enjoy it to the full—even if it is her thirty-second! Well, if you can't celebrate your birthday what can you celebrate?

Kamryn has the day planned to perfection, from a champagne breakfast to a fun-filled evening with friends. But as she opens her pile of birthday cards, there is one that will change not just her perfectly planned day, but also her whole life.

Prologue

TO BE HONEST, I'd been tired for so long I don't remember, not accurately, when I realised something serious was wrong with me. No matter how much I slept I was always tired. It wasn't until Tegan asked me to go to the doctor that I realised. My four-year-old had got tired of me being too exhausted to play with her. Of me having nosebleeds. Of me being breathless after even the smallest amount of exertion. 'Mummy, if you go to the doctor she can make you better,' she said one day out of the blue. Just said it, and I did it.

I sat in the doctor's, told her what was wrong, and she did a blood test. Then called me in for more tests. More tests with names and words I'd heard on the medical shows on telly, then words that never had a happy ending on TV. Then, I got the call saying I had to go see my doctor straight away. And even when she told me . . . When she said she was sorry and then started talking about treatments and prognosis, I just didn't understand. Not why. Not how. Not me.

It took a good few days for what I'd been told to sink in. Every second counted, they said, but I still couldn't comprehend. I kept thinking they were wrong. You hear about it all the time, people finding out they had glandular fever instead of . . .

About a week later, on my way to work, I got to the train station early, and a woman came and stood beside me. She got her mobile out of her bag and made a call. She said, 'Hello, it's Felicity Halliday's mother here. I'm calling because she's not very well and she won't be coming to school today.' I fell apart. Just broke down in tears. It hit me then, right then, that I would never get the chance to make a call like that.

Everyone was terribly British about it all and ignored me as I cried and sobbed and wailed. Yes, wailed. I made a hideous noise as I broke into a million, trillion pieces.

Then this man, this angel, came to me, sat down, put his arm around me and held me while I cried. The train came, the train left. As did the next one and the next one. But this man stayed with me as I cried. He waited and held me until I stopped wailing. Then he gently asked me what was wrong.

Through my sobs, all I could say was, 'I've got to tell my little girl I'm going to die.'

Chapter One

THE POSTMAN JUMPED as I snatched open the front door to my block of flats and eagerly greeted him.

'Special day, is it?' he said.

'It's my birthday,' I grinned.

'Happy birthday,' he commented, and handed over the post for the four flats in our block. 'Twenty-one again, eh?'

'Nope, I'm thirty-two and proud,' I replied. 'Today I get to wear gold sequins and high heels and brush gold dust all over my cleavage.'

'Well, have a good day then, love,' he said.

I shut the door and slung the letters that weren't for me, but had the audacity to arrive at this address today, on the floor of the hallway. I took the stairs two at a time back up to my flat.

In my bedroom I had already laid out my birthday breakfast feast: fresh croissants with smoked salmon, three chocolate truffles and a glass of Moët. Everything had to be perfect today. Everything. I'd planned it that way. After I'd devoured my special brekky, I'd stay in bed until midday, opening birthday cards. Then I had an appointment at the hairdresser to get my hair washed, deep-conditioned and cut. I was going for a radical change—ditching my usual chin-length bob for a style with long layers and a sweeping fringe. After that, I'd come back home and get dressed up. I really was going to wear a dress of gold sequins that set off my dark skin in a spectacular fashion. I was going to squeeze my feet into gold high heels and I was going to brush gold dust over my cleavage. And then a few of the girls from work were coming round for drinks and nibbles before we went into town to dance the night away.

I slipped carefully under the sheets, not wanting to spill any of the special spread, then took a swig of champagne before I tore through my cards like a child. Around me the pile of brightly coloured envelopes grew as I tugged out the cards and smiled at the words written inside.

It wasn't dim of me, then, not to notice it. It was like all the others. Slipped in among the bundle, innocuous and innocent-looking. And, like all the others, I didn't really look at it, didn't try to decipher the handwriting on the envelope, I simply opened it, eager to receive the message of love that had been scrawled inside. My heart stopped. I recognised the handwriting before I read the words with a racing heart.

Dear Kamryn, Please don't ignore this. I need to see you. I'm dying. I'm in St Jude's Hospital in central London. Yours, Adele x

PS I miss you.

Slamming it shut I registered for the first time that the card had 'I love you' on it instead of one of the usual birthday greetings.

I slung the piece of glossy cardboard across the room as though it had burnt my fingers. It landed on the wicker laundry basket and sat there staring at me, daring me to pretend the words inside weren't carved into my brain.

I took a slug of my champagne but it tasted like vinegar in my mouth. The croissant, carefully sliced and filled with smoked salmon, was like sawdust as I chewed. The truffles were paste on my tongue.

Still the card stared at me. Goading me. *Ignore me if you can.*

I threw back the covers, got out of bed and went over to the card. Dispassionately, I tore it in half. Then tore those pieces in half again. I stomped into the kitchen, stamped on the pedal bin to open it and dropped the remains on top of the rotting vegetables. 'There. That's what I think of that! And you!' I hissed at the card and its sender.

I returned to my bed. That was better. Much better. I sipped my champagne and ate my food. And everything was all right again. Perfect, even. Just like it should be on my birthday.

Nothing could ruin it. No matter how much anyone tried. And they were bloody trying, weren't they? You don't try much harder than with that message, dressed up as a birthday card. Very clever. Very bloody clever. Well it wasn't going to work. I wasn't falling for that nonsense.

The door was ajar and didn't protest as I gently pushed on it.

From her place among her white pillows she smiled as I stepped into view. 'I knew you'd come,' she whispered.

Dolce & Gabbana. Even now, at what was probably one of the darkest hours of her life, Adele wore designer clothes—a white D&G T-shirt. She always did have more style than sense.

At one time, that thought, twisted as it was, would've been out of my mouth—callously uttered to her because she would've appreciated it. I couldn't today. Things had drastically changed between us. Firstly, I hadn't seen her in two years. Secondly, the last time I saw her, she had her fingers buried in her hair, mascara was running down her face and snot was dribbling out of her nose. She was talking, saying things I didn't want to hear. I was grabbing my clothes and my bag and blinking back tears and trying not to collapse in a heap. Things don't go back to being normal after you part on those terms. Thirdly, she was ill.

We didn't speak as a nurse fussed around Adele, noting the readings on the machines, checking the lines on the drips. The nurse had a round, friendly face with big brown smiling eyes. She reminded me a lot of my mother. She grinned at me as though she knew me, told Adele not to talk for too long and left us to it.

Still we didn't speak. 'Hi' seemed a pretty insufficient way to greet someone I'd sworn never to communicate with ever again.

'That nurse reminds me of your mum,' Adele said when the silence had started to drown out even the hum of the machines.

I nodded in agreement but couldn't bring myself to talk. I just couldn't. This wasn't the Adele—Del as I called her—I'd come to see, this wasn't the Adele I'd braced myself to talk to after all this time.

I don't know what I expected, hadn't really thought about it when I got on that train to travel two hundred miles from Leeds to London, but I didn't expect her to look like this. I could close my eyes and see that mass of curly honey-blonde hair, which was always trimmed to shoulder length, that smooth, healthy glow of her creamy-white skin. Her eyes, which were the blue-grey colour of highly polished steel; her smile, which would always light up everything around her. Behind my eyelids, the real Del would be there. So perfect and three-dimensional I could reach out and hug her.

With my eyes open, Del Brannon was different. Altered.

The Del who was propped up in bed had skin that was a blotched patchwork of grey, white and yellow. Her face was hollowed out from her weight loss, and under her sunken eyes, conspicuously missing their eyebrows, deep dark circles were scored. Around her head was tied a royal blue scarf, probably to hide her lack of hair. My body went cold. Her beautiful, beautiful hair was all gone. I didn't know she'd look like this. Frail. Like an anaemic autumn leaf—so dried, brittle and fragile that one touch would crumble her into a million pieces.

'It's good to see you,' she said, her voice a low rasp that was probably as painful to create as it was to hear. 'I'm glad you came.'

'What's with the voice?' I asked.

'It's the treatment. Makes my mouth dry and my tongue feels like it's grown shagpile.'

'God, remember when we felt like that because we'd actually enjoyed ourselves by getting drunk the night before?' I commented, then mentally slapped myself. I didn't mean it the way it sounded—I was trying to express sympathy but it'd come out wrong.

Del's dry, cracked lips pulled up into a smile. 'Trust you,' she said. 'No one else has dared say something like that to me. Too scared of making me cry, I suppose. Too scared that I might break down and die on them.'

'It wasn't intentional,' I replied, shamefaced. 'Just being myself.'

'I wouldn't want you any other way,' she said.

'What's wrong with you?' I asked. That sounded wrong, too. Harsh. Unfeeling. Admittedly, part of me was still that woman who was picking up her belongings and swearing to herself she'd never be that hurt again, but most of me was brokenhearted. I was used to solving problems with action and here I was, staring at someone who was in pain, knowing I couldn't do a damn thing about it. That's why I sounded so harsh. I was helpless and I didn't 'do' helpless very well. 'I mean, you said you were . . . What are you ill with?'

'Leukaemia,' she replied.

'I thought only children got that,' I said before I could stop myself.

'That's what I said!' she exclaimed. 'You know, when the doctor told me. It went down like a cup of cold sick, I can tell you.'

'Glad to know it's not only me who says inappropriate things.'

'Yep, even when I'm at death's door.' She said that so blithely, calmly. I had an urge to shake her. Violently. How could she be so laid-back about it? So comfortable with the notion? I was still struggling to understand how someone who was my age, who went to the gym, who ate relatively healthily, who had never smoked, woke up one day to find there was a clock ticking over her head.

'It's all right, you know, I've accepted what's happening to me,' Del reassured me, as though reading my thoughts. 'It took a while but I'm here. I know it's going to take you a while to catch up.'

'Only a little while,' I said sarcastically.

'I had to get here quickly,' she continued, ignoring not what I'd said but how I'd said it. 'I had to make plans. It's not just about me. So, no matter how much I wanted to pretend it wasn't happening, I had to remember the most important person that needs taking care of.'

Tegan. She was talking about her daughter Tegan. How was she taking this? If I was having problems dealing with it, how was a clever little five-year-old coping?

'I suppose you've worked out why I wanted to see you,' she said after another long silence had passed.

'To make me feel guilty for ignoring you for two years?' I replied.

'Apart from that,' Del said, a sly smile playing around her grey lips.

'Well then, no.'

'After I'm gone . . .' Del paused, 'I want you to adopt Tegan.'

'What?'

'I want . . . No, I *need* you to adopt Tegan after I die.'

I could feel the frown creasing my forehead, and my face twisting itself into an 'Are you mad?' look. 'You're joking, right?'

'Do I look like I'm joking?' she replied, exasperated. 'No, *Kamryn*, I'm not joking. I want you to adopt my daughter when I die.'

'All right, *Adele*, if you're serious, I'll give you a serious answer. No.'

'You haven't even thought about it.'

'There's nothing to think about. You've always known that I don't want children. I told you enough times, I'm not having kids.'

'I'm not asking you to have kids, just my one.' Del inhaled deeply, a move that seemed to take all her strength and added to her grey colour. 'I've done all the hard stuff, morning sickness, labour . . . You just have to look after her. Be her mother. Love her.'

'Just' look after her. 'Just' be her mother. Like that was easy. And anyway . . . 'Del, we haven't even *spoken* in two years and now you're asking me to adopt a child? Can you see what's wrong with this picture?'

'Tegan isn't "a child",' she snarled, instantly enraged. 'She's your god-child. You loved her once, I refuse to believe that's changed.'

I couldn't argue with that. I had loved Tegan. I still loved Tegan.

I glanced at the photo on her night stand. It was in a plain glass frame, a big close-up picture of Tegan and Del. Tegan had her arms linked around her mum's neck; they were both grinning at the camera. Tegan was a miniature version of her mother in every respect except her nose. The shape of her nose she inherited from her father.

'Kam, I still think of you as my best friend,' Del was saying. 'And you're the only person, the *only* person on *earth* I'd trust with my daughter. She was like your child once. And, I'm sorry to lay this on you, but I don't know how long I've got left, I can't afford to mess about. If you don't take her . . . What will happen to her? There's no one else. There's no one—' The whites of her eyes darkened with red and her chest started to heave. 'I can't even cry,' she whispered between heaves, 'because I'm not producing enough tears.' Instead of crying, she started to choke, each cough convulsing her thinned body.

I laid a hand on her forearm. 'Please don't,' I said, desperate to stop her. 'I'll think about it. But I'm not promising anything, all right?'

Del kept inhaling deeply until she'd calmed down. 'You'll really think about it?' she said when she was calm enough to speak.

'Yes. I'll think about it.'

'Thank you,' she whispered. 'Thank you.'

We lapsed into silence.

'Kam,' she began. The way she said my name made me look at her and I knew instantly what she was going to say next. I didn't want her to say it. I wanted her to leave it. 'About what happened—'

'Don't,' I cut in, a warning note in my voice.

'You never let me explain,' she pleaded.

'Don't,' I warned again.

'Kam, listen to me. I didn't . . .'

'I SAID DON'T!' I shouted so suddenly and brutally that I even frightened myself. 'I don't want to think about it, I don't want to hear about it, and I *certainly* don't want to talk about it. It's over with. *Leave it.*'

It was a wound that hadn't healed. She'd been picking at a scab that skimmed the surface of an injury so deep even the slightest jolt would have it gushing blood again. Del did as she was told and refocused her line of sight on the picture on her night stand. She half smiled, but I could see the sadness tugging around her eyes. Tegan was everything to Adele. Everything. The idea of leaving her must be more than she could bear. And how do you explain to a child that you're leaving them?

'Where is she?' I asked in an attempt to diffuse the tension.

She closed her eyes briefly, as though pained, before delivering her next bombshell in a quiet voice. 'With my father and his wife.'

My heart skipped a beat. Were things so bad she'd really left Tegan with them? 'And how's that been?' I asked diplomatically, instead of screaming 'Are you mad?' at her.

'Awful,' Adele replied. The whites of her eyes reddened again; she'd be crying if she could. 'They don't let me see her. Since I've been in here they've brought her to see me once. Once in four weeks. I miss her so much. And I can tell every time I call her that she's becoming more depressed. My father and his wife don't want her there and she knows it. Kam, I've only got a little while and I want to spend it with her.' She looked at me, her steel-blue eyes beseeching me.

'Isn't there anyone else she can stay with?' I asked. I knew Adele had no other family but surely she had some other friends? Anyone but her father and stepmother.

'No. When I first realised I was seriously sick, I wrote to you to ask if you could take care of Tegan for a while but you never replied.'

'I never opened the letter,' I replied honestly. I'd shoved it at the bottom of my knicker drawer like all the other correspondence from her—I was too indignant to open them but too cowardly to bin them.

'I guessed you didn't. I tried a couple of other people, but they couldn't take on such a big responsibility, so it had to be my father.' Del always called him that, 'my father'. To his face she called him 'Father'. Never did she call him 'Dad' or 'Daddy'. There was always a level of formality between them. 'When we moved in he was so hard on Tegan, but I didn't have the strength to fight him and his wife.'

'Do they still live in the same place, down in Guildford?'

'Yes.'

'OK.' I took a deep breath. *Can't believe I'm about to do this.* 'What if I go down and see her?'

Del's face brightened. 'You'll do that?'

'I'm not saying I'll adopt her or anything, I'll just go see if she's all right. OK? Just a visit.'

'Thank you,' Del smiled. 'Thank you, thank you, thank you.'

'Will she even remember who I am?' I asked.

'Course. She still draws you in pictures. Talks about you. And those anonymous cards and pressies you send on her birthday and at Christmas, I always tell her they're from you. She always asks when you're going to come back from holiday.'

'Holiday?'

'You left so suddenly I told her you had to go on holiday for a long time. Because then she'd think you were coming back. Neither of us could've stood it if there wasn't at least the hope that you'd come back,' she said. Her eyelids suddenly shut and stayed closed.

'I'd better go,' I said. I stood up, hoisted my bag on to my shoulder.

'Give her my love.' Del's voice was as weak as tissue paper. 'Tell her Mummy loves her.'

'I will,' I said. 'Course I will.'

I paused at the doorway, waiting for Del's reply. I got nothing. I turned to her and saw that she was asleep. Then I walked out.

Adele and I had known each other for nearly half of our lives—fourteen of our thirty-two years. We'd met in the first year at Leeds University, when we were put on an English assignment together.

I'd internally groaned when I heard that I was going to be studying with Adele Hamilton-Mackenzie. At eighteen I was a staunch working-class citizen and now I was being forced to team up with someone who was clearly from a well-to-do family, what with her having a double-barrelled surname and everything. Plus, she was bound to be from a public-school with the kind of accent that would make me want to slap her. She turned her blonde head and sought out Kamryn Matika across the class. She smiled and dipped her head at me; I did the same before she turned back to the front. *God*, I thought bitterly, *she's bound to think the world revolves around her. And she'll try to order me about.*

At the end of the class, I gathered up my books and pens, ready to hightail it out of the lecture hall, when I was confronted by a slender eighteen-year-old who was dressed like a fifty-year-old in a blue polo neck and blue polyester slacks. She grinned at me with straight white teeth, and tossed her mass of silky blonde hair.

'Hi, I'm Adele,' she said, her voice as bright and lively as it was thoroughbred. *She's perky as well as posh; can my life get any worse?* I thought. 'How about we nab a coffee and talk about the assignment.' It wasn't a question, more a vague order.

'I think we should go away and think about it and meet up in a few days,' I replied through a teeth-clenchingly fake smile. No one ordered me about—vaguely or otherwise.

In response, Adele's poise disintegrated until her shoulders were hunched forwards and her gaze was fixed desolately on the parquet floor. She wasn't as self-assured as she acted, and I wasn't as brazen and hard-faced as I pretended. I might start off giving that impression, might act cold and unapproachable, but I always let myself down when my conscience kicked in—I had no bitch follow-through.

'Not a fan of coffee to be honest,' I said, trying to sound friendly. 'How about we go get a drink in the college bar instead?'

'If you're sure?' she replied cautiously.

'Yup,' I muttered, feeling suitably manipulated, 'I'm sure.'

'**W**hat kind of a name is Kamryn, anyway?' Adele asked me.

'A made-up one,' was my terse reply. I'd spotted her students' union card—I was sharing valuable drinking time with Lucinda-Jayne Adele Hamilton-Mackenzie. So, her asking about my moniker when she was Girly Two-Hyphen Name was an audacious step too far.

'It's not a spelling mistake? Your name is Kamryn. K A M R Y N,' she spelt it out. 'Not C A M E R O N, Cameron like the boy's name?'

'Actually, it is. I thought it'd be fun to pretend it was spelt differently. I love people asking me about it. You're so wise, you caught me out.'

Adele raised her left eyebrow slightly and twisted her lip-glossed mouth into a wry smile. 'You're not very friendly, are you?'

'I guess not,' I agreed. It'd taken her four drinks to discover I wasn't the sharing kind. Far too many people opened their hearts and lives at the drop of a hat. Why give someone that power over you? Why endow them with the ability to hurt you that much? Let someone in and you were asking for an emotional kicking some day.

'At least you know it,' she said. 'But despite that, I like you.'

'I'm honoured.'

'No, I am.' She placed a slender hand above her left breast. 'Truly.'

She stared at me with such a friendly, open expression that I couldn't help but bite the proffered bait. 'Why's that then?' I asked.

'You're lovely.' She even sounded truthful. 'I haven't met many lovely people in my life. So, when I do, I feel honoured. You pretend you're all prickly but underneath you're simply gorgeous.'

'Are you a lesbian or something?' I asked brusquely.

'No, I'm not,' she laughed. 'But if I was, I'd definitely fancy you.'

'I wouldn't blame you,' I lied. Not even short, fat, ugly men fancied me. And I couldn't blame them: I wore baggy clothes to hide my weight; I had never applied make-up to my dry, spotty skin; I only tamed the mass of frizz masquerading as my hair by plaiting it into shoulder-length black extensions. I had no illusions at all that I was beautiful, pretty or even able to attract the right sort of attention from men. Especially when on top of the paucity in the looks area, I was lacking the *je ne sais quoi* that attracted men to ugly girls: I wasn't funny, wasn't friendly and wasn't going to use sex to get attention.

'You're so full of shit,' Adele laughed. 'You don't believe that for a second,' she continued. 'That's why you're so prickly. You think people don't like or fancy you, so you exude the impression that you don't care what others think. I've seen your type before. I'd say you were bullied at school by boys. And you were probably bullied because you're different from other people. And unlikely to change to fit in.'

I recoiled from her. *How did she know that? How? Is everything that had happened written on my face?* Were the taunts, notes, phone calls, scrawls on walls all there, plain for any passing posh princess to see? College, two hundred miles from where anyone knew me, had been my chance to leave all those hideous years behind and reinvent myself.

Was it all a waste of time? Did I have 'misfit' imprinted on my forehead?

I forced a smile so Adele wouldn't know how close to the bone her words had sliced. *What should I say? How do I retaliate?*

She said, 'One of my friends from school was like you. Bullied to the point where she had no confidence in herself at all and shut out all her friends because she didn't think she could trust them. Actually, she wasn't really a friend. I don't have that many friends if I'm honest.'

'Well you're bound not to if you keep saying things like that,' I sniped. 'What makes you such an expert when you've clearly come from a perfect life with rich parents who could send you to all the best private schools? Huh? What makes you such an expert on crap lives?'

She picked up her drink, slowly swirled it round, then stared down into it. 'My mother died not long after I was born because of complications from childbirth. My father never wanted children, and he blamed me for my mother's death. My father wanted nothing to do with me so I spent a lot of time with a childminder until he married again. His wife is not my biggest fan and she's never made a secret of it.' Adele looked up at me, smiled. 'I don't have many friends because I'm too much. I try too hard, which makes me hard work. But I can't help it. I don't know how not to be who I am. I've spent so much time with people who don't like me, I try to avoid upsetting them. I do know a bit about crap lives. It's not as bad as some but it's certainly not perfect.'

I suddenly felt like an accidental mass murderer. 'Sorry,' I mumbled.

'It's all right,' she said, sitting up, tossing back her hair and flashing me a big, bright smile. 'You weren't to know.'

'Listen, Adele, if we're going to hang around together you've got to cut that out,' I said.

'Cut what out?'

'Being so damn nice all the time. It's not natural.'

Adele's steel-blue eyes lit up. 'You want to hang around with me?'

I shrugged nonchalantly.

She grinned at me in return. That smile lit up her face, put an effervescent gleam in her eyes. The radiance of that smile flowed from her to me and I fell for her. Deeply. I couldn't help but like her. She was going to be an important part of my world. She was going to help shape the person I was to become. I didn't know how I knew, I simply did.

We became almost inseparable because we grew up together. Once Adele settled into college life she found herself and who she was. She stopped dressing like a fifty-year-old, she often had a strop that involved swearing and throwing things. But she finally killed the timid Adele I'd had that drink with when she had her bellybutton pierced.

I, meanwhile, lost weight, smiled more and murdered the Kamryn that Adele had that first drink with when I refused sex with a gorgeous man because he was wearing paisley-patterned Y-fronts. But all that was to come. At that moment, she'd been enormously happy that I'd shrugged my consent at the possibility of us hanging around together, and I was secretly overjoyed that someone thought I was lovely.

Adele became a member of my family. Christmas, Easter and summer holidays if I went home, she came with me. Her father and his wife weren't bothered that she never went home. If she called, which I was always amazed she did, she'd come off the phone in bits. Always crying and on the verge of vomiting, always wondering what she could do, how she could change to make him love her even a little bit.

Mr Hamilton-Mackenzie was never going to change. I knew that when I heard about the depth of his resentment towards her. When we first met Adele would often get falling-down drunk and tell me about her father's quick-to-discipline attitude. About time spent in hospital with broken arms, fractured legs, a cracked jaw as a result of being 'punished'. Once he'd knocked her through a ground-floor window and a piece of glass had lodged itself in her back, narrowly missing her kidney—the glass had to be removed by surgery. Amazingly, annoyingly, depressingly, no one suspected what was going on. Or, if they did, they looked away, not wanting to get involved.

My family weren't perfect but they were bothered—very vocally so— if I didn't go home every few months; they did call me regularly for a chat and, because she was my friend, they accepted Adele into the fold. Adele found a new place called home with the Matikas. It wasn't her real home, it wasn't the love of her father, but every time my mum told us off for waking up the house when we came in at 3 a.m.; every time my dad reached into his wallet and gave her a tenner to buy herself something; every time my sister asked for advice about her love life, it was almost as good as her real home. She felt she belonged.

Obviously, only one thing could possibly come between us: a man.

This was surreal. Being in London, a city I had fled over two years ago. But not just London, this particular area of it. Waterloo.

I wandered across the huge station concourse, memories slamming into me with every step I took. This was the place where I used to come to meet Adele after work for drinks when we were both single. She used to work just around the corner and I used to get the tube here from Oxford Street, where I worked, so we could travel home together after a few drinks.

Waterloo was also remarkable for another reason. This was the place where I met him. At a house party just up the road from here. Him, the man who came between me and Adele.

He wasn't just any man, though. He was Nate Turner, my fiancé.

Nate walked into my life one cold April night and said he didn't want to walk out of it again. I told him to try that line on a woman who might believe it. 'I'm going to win you over,' he'd stated seriously.

'Better men than you have failed,' I'd replied equally seriously.

Eighteen months later we decided to get married. And three years after that we set a date for the following year. We didn't have the perfect relationship, more a perfect understanding. He put up with a lot from me, had to deal with my issues.

My 'issues' weren't immediately obvious. By the time I met Nate my outward appearance was that nothing bothered me, that year after year of being called fat and ugly hadn't done a thing except to spur me on to success. No one, except maybe Adele, knew that beneath my adult veneer, beneath my confidence and great job and ability to sleep with good-looking men, beat the heart of a terrified girl.

The outside world, and even to an extent Adele, was taken in by my outward appearance; the impenetrable, polished image that I diligently maintained. People truly believed I was cool and haughty, confident and capable. Nate had seen through me. He discovered almost straight away the thing that terrified me more than anything else: people.

It'd started before the bullying at school. I suspected it was what triggered the bullying—those who terrorised me saw that there was something not right about me, that I didn't fit in, that every conversation was underlined with the fear that they'd discover I wasn't like other people, and they exploited that terror.

I didn't seem to have that thing that binds us, makes us human. I struggled to make those connections, form relationships, even platonic ones. I grew up in a big family, was close to my siblings, but for some reason I never quite knew how to react in certain situations. I was so worried about saying the wrong thing, of inciting wrath, that communication became an exercise in terror. And it made me seem standoffish, judgmental and, in later years, a hard-faced bitch. It wasn't that I didn't want to relate to others, it was just that I didn't know how.

Then I met Adele and found I could communicate. I started to believe that I wasn't defective. Broken. I could form relationships.

I'd been seeing Nate for a few weeks when he told me he knew my secret. We'd gone to one of his work parties and from the moment I walked in I knew I didn't fit in. I wasn't dressed as classily as the other women, I didn't radiate their insouciant style and I didn't work in broadcast media. I tried to make polite conversation but I knew with every word I was confirming how different I was. When, three torturous hours later, Nate said, 'Shall we go?' I was out the door and hailing a taxi before he'd finished forming 'shall'. Later, Nate wrapped himself around me like a cat curls around its owner's legs and said, 'People terrify you, don't they? That's why you're so cold. I saw you tonight, you were trying to talk, to connect with people, but you had such fear in your eyes.'

I sometimes think people can see that I'm defective, that there's nothing there. Behind the job and clothes and make-up there's nothing to know. I sometimes think I'm this shell and I can't work out why people like me. And when I'm with strangers it reminds me of that. That I'm insubstantial. I didn't say that to him, of course I didn't. Even if I could get the words out, why would a casual fling want to hear that?

To my silence he added, 'You don't have to be scared. I'll always look after you. I think you're amazing. You're everything to me, babe.' That upset me so much I got dressed and went home.

Nate didn't seem to care that I wasn't a hundred per cent strong all the time, that he was with someone who had the potential to become needy and dependent. He took me as I was, loved me whether I was nice or nasty. He dealt with everything I threw at him, and then some. It wasn't one-sided though. I put up with a lot from him, too. He came across as laid-back and infinitely secure, but he was a mass of neuroses that I took on once I decided to give it a go with him. We had balance, Nate and I. A perfect symmetry of love, honesty and trust. With him, as I confessed to Adele after about six months, 'commitment' and 'for ever' weren't only concepts, they were a reality.

It was a Saturday night two years ago. Del and I had put Tegan to bed with the intention of doing some wedding planning, seeing as my 'big day' was only two months away, but we'd been waylaid; distracted by wine and a packet of cocktail sausages. I'd had to borrow a T-shirt from Del because Tegan's bath earlier had resulted in me, my top and my bra being soaked through.

Rather than sorting out the seating plan, we were talking about Del's dating. She'd recently met a man and interest wasn't as yet waning.

'He does this thing with his hips and it's . . . Wow,' she revealed. 'It blows my mind every time.'

'Nate does this thing with his mouth,' I revealed. 'He starts off licking my inner thighs really slowly, then he does this thing with his mouth . . .

It's . . .' I grinned and sighed. 'Amazing. I'm getting shivers down my spine just thinking about it.'

'Hmmm, I know,' Del agreed. Then froze. Everything about her froze the second those three words came out of her mouth.

My heart had stopped mid-beat. Time seemed to stand still.

Del's eyes edged over to my area of the room, two discs of blue steel, now branded with terror. *She'd been there. She'd done it. With Nate. She'd done it with Nate. His tongue had licked her inner thighs. His lips had . . .*

'When?' I asked, forcing the word out of my mouth.

'Long time ago,' she whispered, her eyes never leaving mine. 'Long, long time ago. Way long time ago.'

The breath caught in my chest again and I inhaled to try to get it moving, but my body was immobile. Frozen. Nothing would go in, nothing would come out, it hurt too much. 'How long for?'

'Once. Only the once.'

Tears pricked behind my eyes and my jaw muscles clenched. Once. Only the once. The words didn't have any meaning. Did once make it any better than twice? Or fifty times? I blinked but my vision was still blurred by tears.

Del sat hunched forwards on the sofa, staring at the laminate flooring. Then, she lifted her eyes, glanced at the picture of Tegan that sat on top of the television before returning her gaze to the floor.

It was an instinctive thing, a little thing that gave everything away. 'No,' I gasped, more to myself than to her.

Del's head snapped round to me as she heard my gasp. My eyes darted from Del to the photo to Del. Our eyes locked and her face drained of colour. I shook my head, trying to dislodge the thought. My eyes flew back to the picture. From that smiling snapshot, Tegan's nose was a dead giveaway. She was Nate's child.

Everything fell into place. Now I knew why Tegan looked so familiar. It wasn't because she was her mother's double, which she was in most ways, it was because she had the same ski-slope nose as her father, the shape of his large eyes, his sardonic twist of the lip. I'd seen those features all along, of course, but my mind hadn't made the connection.

I'd asked Del who the father was when she first found out she was pregnant. She'd tearfully told me that it'd been an accident, that he was a married man she'd met through work. 'He didn't mean for it to happen. Neither did I, it was an accident. No one's to blame.'

I was the surrogate father. The one who went to antenatal classes, who'd been in the delivery room almost gagging at what I saw, who helped out as much as I could—all the while encouraging her to tell the daddy, that even if she didn't want him to know, he had a right. And, I often said, Tegan might want to know.

I was a prize idiot. A big fat festering idiot who'd been lecturing her, pushing her to tell the love of my life that he'd knocked her up.

I launched myself off the sofa but once on my feet I found I was almost doubled up from the red-hot searing pain in my stomach.

Nate had a child. Nate had fathered my best friend's child.

I started to gather up my things: with shaking hands I pulled the wet top I'd taken off earlier over the white T-shirt. Then remembered the T-shirt was hers. My lying, cheating friend's. I ripped the top off, pulled off the T-shirt and threw it on the ground, then tugged on my damp top.

'Kam, let's talk about this,' she pleaded. 'Please, Kam, let's talk.'

It was a halfhearted plea. I wasn't a talker when I was upset. I was the ignore-it-in-the-hope-it'll-go-away type. Besides, what was there to talk about? How good my fiancé was in bed? Ask if he knew Tegan was his daughter and was he still going to marry me? He'd done this awful thing but was planning to say 'I do' in eight weeks—EIGHT WEEKS. He was going to stand up in front of everyone we knew and declare that he loved me; that he was going to forsake all others. Except he wasn't, was he? He certainly hadn't in the past so why would he in the future?

'He doesn't know about Tegan,' Del said. Her voice was strong. When it came to Tegan, she wasn't going to mess about. 'I don't want him to know,' she continued. 'I don't want to upset Tegan's life. Whatever else you do, don't ruin Tegan's life. It's not her fault.'

I wish I had it in me to call her names. To slap her face and pull out her hair. The best I could do was to walk out. And never go back.

'I'm here to see Tiga,' I said to the woman who answered the door to the five-bedroom house a fifteen-minute taxi ride from the centre of Guildford. She looked at me blankly and then I remembered I was the only person who called Tegan 'Tiga', as in tiger. 'I mean, I'm here to see Tegan.'

A spark of recognition ignited in Muriel's eyes. She was Del's step-mother. A slight, fragile woman, she seemed so respectable, normal, even docile. However, pure evil pulsed through this woman's veins.

Del had shown me what this woman was capable of. I'd seen the silvery welts on Del's thighs from where her stepmother had put out cigarettes on her. The little finger on her left hand that hadn't grown straight after this woman had wrenched it out of its socket.

'I'm Kamryn. Tegan's godmother?' I said, flattening out my voice to hide my hatred. 'Lucinda-Jayne's friend?' Del had dropped 'Lucinda-Jayne' the second she got to college in favour of her middle name, Adele. When we graduated from college she changed her surname to Brannon, her mother's maiden name. We'd had a big celebration when she finally changed her name by deed poll. Her father still called her Lucinda-Jayne and she wouldn't dream of correcting him.

'Yes, I remember who you are.' A slur streaked Muriel's voice. Was it sherry, wine or gin and tonic she'd been spending time with today? They'd been her constant companions when we'd met years ago.

'So, can I see Tegan?' I asked.

'She's not receiving visitors,' she replied.

'A five-year-old isn't receiving visitors?' I replied, irritated and incredulous in equal measures.

Muriel sneered down her nose at me. 'The little madam is being punished,' she said contemptuously, 'if it's any business of yours.'

'It is my business.' Every one of my words was carefully modulated to prevent me screaming. 'I'm her godmother. I've been asked to look after her if anything happens to her mother.'

'You will have to call another time because, as I explained, she is being punished.' The woman moved to shut the door, and all the hatred and anger simmering inside erupted through the surface of my placidity. I lunged forwards, every muscle in my body tensed as the flat of my hand slapped against the blue door and held it open. 'Punished for what?' I asked, a snarling edge to my voice.

Muriel said nothing.

'I'd like to see her. I'm not leaving until I see her.'

She lowered her voice. 'I can't let you in. You don't know what Ronald will do to me if I let you see her.'

'You obviously don't know what I'll do to you if you don't,' I said in a tone that was menacing and scary, even to me.

Muriel increased the poison in her glare and I hardened the expression on my face. I knew what she was capable of but only when dealing with a defenceless child, while she had no clue what I was capable of.

Muriel's body relaxed in resignation as she let go of the door, turned and headed up the large staircase, muttering just loud enough, 'It's not even as if we want her here.'

The house hadn't changed much since I'd last come here eight years ago. Del and I had made a flying visit to get the rest of the clothes and books she had left here, which had been an excuse. Del had returned to make peace with her father, to reach out to him one last time. He'd been ultra-polite because she'd had a guest with her but also excessively dismissive. It was one of the most chilling things I'd ever seen.

When we climbed into the back of the taxi Del didn't have to tell me she intended never to return there, I knew it. She'd done her best to reconnect with her family and now she had to leave it.

Muriel stopped outside a white panelled door. There was a key in the lock, which she reached for. *They'd locked Tegan in?*

Tegan's room was twice the size of my living room. Two of the walls were lined with white bookcases and on each shelf sat dolls, play bricks, cuddly toys, teddies and books. None of them looked as if they'd been played with. In the centre of the room was a small red plastic table and a yellow plastic chair, and at the table sat Tegan.

Even from a distance I could see everything was wrong. She sat stock-still on her chair, her small body rigid with fear. Her pale blonde hair hung around her face in dirty clumps, her pink top was grubby. And her eyes were fixed on the plate of food in front of her.

Shock punched me a fraction below my solar plexus. The last time I saw Tegan she'd been a child that took nothing sitting down, lying down or standing still. She was always wanting to run or play or laugh.

'Tiga,' I whispered. I moved slowly across the room towards her. 'Tiga, it's Auntie Kamryn, do you remember me?' I bobbed down beside her and looked at her as I waited for her to reply.

A few seconds passed before she nodded. Nodded but kept her eyes forwards, fixed on her plate. The plate was loaded with age-greyed boiled potatoes, dried and shrivelled peas and a desiccated pork chop that was covered in a skin of white mould. The smell of the rotting meal assaulted my nostrils and I drew back, half-retching.

'So you do remember Auntie Kamryn?' I said, fighting the gagging.

Tegan nodded again.

'That's brilliant. And did Mummy tell you that you might come and stay with Auntie Kamryn for a little while?'

Tegan nodded.

'How do you feel about that?'

She raised her shoulders. Then a tiny, hoarse voice said, 'Don't know.'

I slowly reached out to tuck a lock of her unwashed hair behind her right ear so I could see her face, but before I made contact she flinched away from me into a cringe, her hands flying up to protect herself.

I recoiled too, my heart racing with fear and horror. She thought I might hurt her. Then I noticed her right hand—three red lines were streaked across its swollen palm. Around her right wrist were blue-black-purple bruises that looked like large handprints, as though someone had held her hand open as they whacked her with a cane.

It was those red lines marking her young skin that did it. I was angry.

Completely, totally angry. I suddenly knew what I had to do.

I clambered to my feet and marched across to the chest of drawers. I yanked open the top drawer, checked inside. I grabbed a handful of tops, then opened another drawer, gathered another bundle of clothes. I yanked open the third drawer and took the vests and pants in there.

'What are you doing?' Muriel shrieked.

I ignored her. I went to my holdall, wrenched back the zip and shoved everything inside.

'You can't do this!' Muriel screamed at me as I opened the wardrobe and reached for a couple of coats and some shoes. 'I'll call the police.'

My head whipped round to glare at her. 'Be my guest. I'd love to hear you explain why Tegan hasn't been washed in days, why she's sat in front of rotting food and how she got the marks on her hand. Actually, hang on, I'll call the police myself.' I chucked Tegan's clothes in the general direction of my holdall, reached into my coat pocket and pulled out my mobile. 'Do you want to press "call" or shall I?'

'Take her, we'll be glad to see the back of her,' Muriel spat before turning on her heels and storming out of the room.

When the door shut behind her I turned back to Tegan and bobbed down beside her. I didn't get too close for fear of scaring her again. 'Do you have a favourite toy?' I asked her.

She nodded suspiciously.

'OK, go get it and anything else that you love and bring it to me.'

Her eyes widened in alarm.

'We're going away,' I explained. 'You're going to come and stay with Auntie Kamryn.'

Tegan, although clearly tempted by the idea of getting out of there, was nobody's fool and continued to regard me suspiciously. We didn't have time for this. For all I knew Muriel was calling her husband.

'Come on, Tiga, get your stuff and we can go see your mummy tomorrow.'

'Mummy?' Her pale face brightened. 'Mummy?' She stood up, went to her bed, got down on the floor and from under it she pulled a multi-coloured rucksack. She held the rucksack out to me. I grinned at her.

Time passed. I don't know how much, but by the end of its passing I was standing on the corner of a street in a town I didn't know very well, a child in my arms and half a dozen bags at my feet.

'Do you know what today is?' I asked Tegan. 'It's my birthday.'

'Happy birthday,' she whispered.

'Thanks,' I replied.

It's also the day I'm going to be arrested for kidnapping.

Chapter Two

LIGHT, THE COLOUR of twice-used bath water, strained through the gaps in the beige curtains, trying to brighten my hotel room. My eyes ached as I stared at the world that was coming alive outside. I could hear the birds tuning up for their dawn chorus, cars speeding by, plus the occasional police siren. I'd stopped thinking those police sirens were coming for me a couple of hours ago but my mind was still racing at a hundred miles an hour—it had been for most of the night . . . Eight hours earlier, I'd been let into the room by a porter who brought up our bags, then quietly shut the door behind him. I'd checked us into a hotel that was within walking distance of St Jude's Hospital. The room was sparse and small, but it had a double bed, a small cot bed for Tegan and a television—everything we needed.

As the door closed behind us I walked over to the cot. Tegan was like an anvil in my arms; my biceps were frozen in pain because I'd been holding her for so long. The second we'd got in the back of the taxi that would bring us into central London, Tegan had climbed into my lap and fallen asleep. The whole sixty-minute drive into town she hadn't stirred, nor when I talked the receptionist through the registration form, nor when we came up in the lift to our room.

I laid her gently on the cot bed, then nearly jumped out of my skin as her eyes flew open and her pale oval face slid into a mire of fear. She was terrified. Wide awake and terrified.

Join the queue, honey, I thought. I was terrified too. The implications of what I had done were only just starting to hit me.

'What's the matter?' I asked cautiously. My fear that she might burst into tears outweighed all my other fears. I had no clue how to handle a crying child, except maybe to scream 'Shut up!'

Tegan's visage of terror didn't slip, not even for a microsecond.

'Do you want to sleep in the big bed?' I asked, taking a wild guess at what might be troubling her—apart from being abducted and being held hostage by a woman she hadn't seen in two years.

Tegan nodded.

'OK, but let's have a bath first, all right? And maybe something to eat?'

She nodded. 'OK, good.' That was a plan. A good plan. I could work with this. Bathe her, feed her, get her to go to sleep. I picked up the laminated menu card and scanned it for something that she might like. It was clear that she wasn't going to speak to me so there was no point in asking her. Burger and chips seemed the easiest choice. Then I searched through the bags, found her blue checked pyjamas, lay them on the big bed and went to the bathroom. I pinned back the white shower curtain, then sat on the side of the bath to push the plug in and turn on the taps. Once the bath was half full, I drizzled in some bubble bath.

I went back to Tegan and knelt down in front of her. 'Can we take off your clothes then?' I asked gently.

She hesitated, then slid off the bed and stood in front of me, patient and passive. I took off her jacket, then gently tugged her grubby pink top over her head. I had to stop myself from recoiling in horror. She was reed thin, she hadn't been fed properly in weeks. And it wasn't just her thinned body. Her skin . . . Tears punched at my eyes. Her beautiful skin was blotched and dappled with dirt and bruises and welts. My mind caved in on itself. How could they do this? I never knew this sort of thing went on. I mean, I knew it existed, and I knew it was awful. But it wasn't real because I'd never seen it. I'd heard it all from Del, I'd seen her scars, but I couldn't know, I couldn't *believe* until this moment. Fat tears swelled in my eyes.

Stop it, I ordered myself. *Don't let her think you're disgusted by her, that it's her fault.* It was all over her: the dirt, the bruising, the marking. Once her last item of clothing was off, I wrapped her in a big white towel and enveloped her in my arms. 'You'll be all right, sweetie,' I told her. 'I'm going to take care of you, OK?' She didn't react as I tried to hug away her pain. How still and silent she stood in my arms made me pull her tiny body closer to me.

While I bathed her I was constantly reminded of the last bath I'd given her, where she'd soaked me through and I'd had to borrow a T-shirt from Del. I was reminded because it was so different: there was no boisterous splashing, no giggling. She sat still, her eyes fixed on a point on the tiled wall, her body not resisting any swipe of the flannel.

Her blonde hair fell in straight golden waves to her shoulders when I'd dried it and she was pretty damn cute in her blue checked pyjamas. Cute, but silent. A knock at the door made both of us jump. After a few fraught seconds I realised it was probably room service with our food.

I took the burger, chips and Ribena to her. She tentatively reached out and picked up the burger. Before she bit into it she looked up at me, silently checking it was OK.

I conjured up my brightest smile then nodded at her. She cleared her plate and drained the carton, then sat back, staring at me with big scared eyes. Tegan took all her cues from me, unsure what to do next— a case of the completely lost leading the completely lost.

'Are you tired?' I hazarded.

She nodded. Good, she was sticking to the plan: bath, food, bed.

'OK, come lie down.'

The corners of her mouth turned down, then her jaw started trembling as her eyes filled with tears. *No, no, not crying! I can handle anything except crying.* 'What's the matter, Tiga?' I asked.

'I'm scared on my own,' she whispered, then cringed as though she expected me to explode at her.

'Do you want me to lie with you?' I asked gently. She slowly nodded. 'OK, you lie down and I'll take my shoes off.'

Tegan nestled down under the blankets, made sure I was lying facing her, closed her eyes, then fell asleep. Just like that. Out like a light.

I blinked unseeingly at the window. How had I got myself here? Here. Where this thing called adoption was a serious issue.

Me and child. Kamryn and child. Never meant to happen.

Children had never been in my sphere of destiny, not on my list of things to do. There were lots of children in my life—eight of them courtesy of my two brothers and sister—and while I loved each one of those little people with all my heart, they weren't enough to make me want to partake. You had to be prepared to give up everything for children. *Everything.* Time, space, affection. I wasn't that altruistic and wouldn't pretend I was that way inclined just to look 'normal'.

When I was younger, most people thought my lack of interest in children was because I hadn't met the right man. When Nate and I started talking about marriage, everyone—Del included—thought I'd change my mind. People constantly asked me when Nate and I would be having children and I replied, 'Erm, never.' There was, without exception, surprise then sympathy at my response, then I'd get a variation on, 'Are you sure you want to marry Nate when he doesn't want children?' I usually informed these people: 'Nate and I aren't having kids. It's one of the fundamental things we agree on. You know, no voting Conservative, no buying Oasis CDs and no children.'

I lay facing Tegan, examining the contours of her face, seeing Nate. A smile spread across my face as I remembered the amount of times I'd done that to Nate over the years we were together: lay in the middle of the night, watching him sleep.

My parents, out of everyone, were hurt the most by me cancelling the wedding. That phone call, the one I made from a hotel room in Leeds two days after I found out what had happened between Nate and Del, the one that went 'Nate and I have split up, the wedding's off and I'm moving to Leeds' was a typical Kamryn move as far as they were concerned. I could never get it right. I'd always dressed shabbily, I was never pretty, I'd never had boyfriends, I'd never fitted in, and now, the one thing, the *one* thing that would prove I was normal, was off. My siblings—both the older one and the two younger ones—had managed it, had got married, had settled down, had reproduced, so why couldn't I? What was wrong with me? Although they never actually said it, I knew they were thinking, *What did you do wrong, Kamryn?*

My siblings and my friends were more understanding. Most of them said that if it wasn't right, it wasn't right, but I knew they all wanted to know the real reason for our split. Everyone was supportive but I knew I could never be honest with them. I could never say to another human being: 'My fiancé and my best friend made a child.'

That was what Adele and Nate had done. I wasn't simply hurt by them having sex, I was humiliated, disgraced and, ultimately, isolated. When you can't be honest with people, you can't ever relax with them in case you let something slip. I couldn't have stayed in London, among the friends and elements of that life, even if I wanted to. It would have been too hard on a daily basis hiding what had happened.

Tegan stirred and I held my breath in case she awoke, then she settled back into sleep.

Del knew what a ginormous thing she was asking of me when she made the request to adopt Tegan. She knew I couldn't look at Tegan the same way ever again. I sent her presents and postcards, all from a distance. At no point did I have to look at her while I made those little contacts. To look at her would be to remember what my two favourite people had done. And to remember how I hurt the day it had all come out. How I'd hurt every day after that.

I gently brushed a stray strand of hair away from Tegan's face. Could I adopt the child of the man I had been two months away from marrying? In sleep she looked so much like him. In waking life she had shades of him too. She might become more like her dad every day. Could I bear that? Every day, day after day, for the rest of my life staring at mini Nate, being reminded of my best friend and my fiancé making love.

This was all academic, though, wasn't it? There was no going back now. I'd taken Tegan from her grandparents in Guildford. I'd had to. That meant I'd said yes to adopting her.

Kamryn and I had a lot of sex without love or even real emotion in our younger days. Of course, it wasn't the done thing, us being women and all, but we had our reasons. My reason: weariness. I, Adele Brannon, was weary. Tired of meeting another new man, of hoping he was The One, then finding he wasn't. So I decided to take the far more appealing route of chasing lust, on the way to love. I believed in love, so while I waited for its arrival in my life I concentrated on having the best sex with the best-looking men in London, just to pass the time, you know.

Kamryn, on the other hand, didn't believe in love. She'd experienced every type of being screwed over by men there was and had decided to give a little back—in kind. Years and years of being told you're ugly and fat will do that. She was careful not to talk about the years before we met, but sometimes I'd catch her off guard and she'd reveal how deeply she'd been scarred by the things people used to say to her. When I met her she was a good-looking woman, but as she got older, she got better-looking; grew into her features and went from good-looking to striking. She had huge dark eyes, long eyelashes and this amazing smile. The tragedy being she never saw it.

I remember more than once she confessed that no matter how much weight she lost, how many times she was called beautiful, she would look in the mirror and see a fat, ugly person. Years of hearing the same thing had done that to her and that made me cry. I wasn't surprised she was wary of people, didn't know who to trust. And that no matter how many times you told her, she wouldn't believe she was beautiful.

The worst part was the better-looking she got, the more she attracted men who seemed to be after one thing—to make themselves feel like real men by putting down a gorgeous woman.

It was the nice ones, the ones who'd sucker me in too, that hurt the most. They'd start off being lovely, treating her well, then they would erode her confidence, put down her looks, try to douse her spark. After she'd dated another creep for six months only for him to suggest she diet to trim down her size fourteen frame so she could fit into the size ten dress he wanted her to wear to his work do, Kamryn changed. He was the last of the men who would make her feel like nothing. After him, Kam refused to show her soft side to another man. She didn't have to say it for me to know that this went back to her school days. All the things people had called her during school and sixth form— Man-Ryn, Fugly (Fucking Ugly) and Mike Tyson—had left the type of scars that would never completely heal. All the men she dated during and after college seemed to prove her school 'mates' right: they made her believe that there was something fundamentally wrong with her and that love was going to pass her by. The only thing for it was to use men for sex and never let any of them get so close they could hurt her.

About eight years ago, everything changed. We were out clubbing and as usual we stood out—she with her curves, dark skin and pretty black hair, me with my slender frame, pale skin and masses of blonde hair. This club was a new one but seemed to be full of the same old disgusting men. I had to drink to compensate for the lack of talent, while Kam dispatched every man who approached her with her acid tongue and acrid expressions.

I was the drunkest of the two of us so in the taxi back to our flat in north London I was allowed to lay my head on her thigh and fall asleep while she stayed awake to get us home.

'I'm going to do it with Nate,' Kam said.

'I thought you'd already shagged him,' I replied, not opening my eyes.

'I have,' she said. 'No, I mean, I'm going to go out with him. Date him. I . . . I think I might like him.'

My eyes flew open and I sat bolt upright. She'd met Nate at a party a few months earlier and since day one she'd been giving him the run-around. He'd call and she'd screen calls, only phoning back days later. If she did answer the phone she'd be very vague about when they'd next meet up. Most shockingly, even for her, she shagged him after their first official date—which was afternoon coffee in north London—because she'd been convinced it would get rid of him. Not Nate. He hung in there. He'd dismantled her defences.

'What?' I said.

'I think I might like him,' she repeated, studiously staring out of the window.

Bloody hell! Those six words were her equivalent to 'I'm falling in love with him.'

'Really?' I said to her.

She nodded but wouldn't look at me.

'Wake me up when we get home,' she said. She was embarrassed and vulnerable, she'd exposed a part of herself that hadn't been seen in years: she was unsure about a man. Kam closed her eyes and pretty soon she was asleep.

I watched her sleep as the cab made its way through the dark London streets. I was still reeling. Kam was in love. Wow! I suddenly felt sick. What if he's a bastard? What if he loses interest once he's got her undivided attention? Kam will never recover. I had to do something. And that something was to tell the taxi driver in hushed tones to head for another address . . .

After three rings of the bell, the door of the house in Tufnell Park was answered. I'd dropped Kam off here a few times so I knew it was the right house.

'Adele?' Nate said as he opened the door. He was wearing jeans and a T-shirt, and even though it was 3 a.m. he didn't look as if he'd been asleep. Nate was good-looking. Strong features, sexily messy brown-black hair and big navy blue eyes. 'Is Kamryn all right? What's happened?'

'She's in the taxi. I tell you—' I poked him in his chest—'if you hurt my

friend, I kill you. You treat her right or I kill you. Proper kill you.'

He didn't say anything but even in my drunken state I could tell he didn't believe me. 'I'm serious,' I reassured him, just as the heel of my left shoe slid off the step . . . For the longest microsecond of my life I was falling then Nate's strong hands were on my forearms and he was hauling me inside. My legs had turned to rubber so he had to practically carry me to the lounge doorway. He grabbed his wallet from the side. 'Wait here,' he ordered and disappeared outside. He returned a few minutes later followed by an extremely pissed off Kamryn. I'd graduated from standing in the lounge doorway to lying in the middle of the floor. My legs had stopped supporting me.

Kamryn threw herself into one of the armchairs and sat glaring at me.

'I'm so pleased to see you both,' Nate said pleasantly.

'You owe Nathaniel for the taxi,' Kamryn said, her arms tightly folded.

'I had to tell Nate to treat you proper,' I explained. 'Or I would kill him.'

'You got that message across,' Nate reassured. 'Thank you.'

'You should have seen how many men tried it on with sexy Kamryn tonight,' I said to Nate. 'All the men in the club were after her. But she didn't do anything. She said, "Nooooo, I've got a boyfriend."'

'Del . . .' Kam threatened.

Nate turned to me. 'She said that?'

'Oh yes. She said, "I've got a new boyfriend, he's called Nate and he's so sexy, I really love him."' I pointed at him. 'She loves you, she loves you.'

'Del! Shut up!' Kam said, outraged.

'She loves you, she loves you.'

Kam leapt up. 'She thinks you're so lovely,' I shouted before she got to me. 'She said you're so funny and sexy. And you've got the biggest . . .'

'SHUT UP!' Kam screeched, then she was on top of me, started tickling me. After a few seconds, Nate came over to us and hauled Kam off me.

'Enough!' he decreed, holding back my angry best friend. 'Kam, I know Adele's making it all up—I've accepted that it's illegal for you to say anything nice about me. And, Adele, thanks for trying but I've got a pretty good idea of how Kam feels about me, so don't try to make me feel better.'

I clamped my hands over my mouth. Kam had stopped fighting in Nate's arms and was staring at him. I think what he said had jolted her, the fact he knew she wouldn't ever say anything nice about him even though she liked him had thrown her. He smiled at her with deep affection.

Since I've been in hospital I've had a lot of time to replay bits of my life. That night is often dusted off and played. Especially the bit where she says, 'I think I might like him.' She'd told me first that she loved him—she didn't even say it to Nate until months later. I was so honoured: it showed how much she thought of me. I still hate myself for ruining what they had.

Hoodwinked. Conned. Duped. Whatever you called it, it had been done to me. I hadn't realised it until this morning when Tegan and I had shown up at the hospital. I'd opened the door to Del's hospital room and as Tegan ran in and scrambled up onto the bed, Del smiled at me in a way that said she knew my answer was yes. That I was going to take on her child. The cheeky minx had already had the legal documents drawn up, naming me as Tegan's legal guardian. She'd also sent off for the relevant forms so I could get the ball rolling to adopt Tegan. These papers were stashed in the wooden locker by her bed, waiting for me to put my moniker to them.

'You might as well sign them now,' she said with a grin.

'Yeah, I might as well,' I replied. I was trapped: I couldn't take Tegan back to Guildford; I couldn't leave her to grow up in care. I had no other choices; no way out. I had to do this. This was my little Tiga, after all. I'd held her minutes after she was born. I'd helped name her. How could I not want to take her on?

Very easily, actually, the thought popped into my head before I could stop it. *You are a bad person*, I chastised myself. *A bad, bad person.*

A transformation had come over Tegan when we'd arrived. She didn't seem to notice the tubes and machines around her mother and had practically leapt onto the bed, throwing her arms around her mother's neck. Having hardly said anything to me since Guildford, she was chatting at super-speed, pausing constantly to kiss her mother's cheek.

I slipped out to give them time alone together. I'd forgotten about the bond between them. They were best mates. How the hell was Tegan going to cope when . . .

What if Del got better?

I seized that thought, clung to it like a life buoy in the sea of despair and self-pity I was currently drowning in. Del would live. I'm sure it wasn't my imagination that she was looking better. Less grey. That was probably Tegan's influence. Having her around obviously made Del feel a million times better, so we could build on that.

About half an hour later Nancy the nurse took Tegan for a walk to the canteen so Del and I could talk.

'You could get well again,' I blurted at her. I still hadn't mastered the tact-in-front-of-an-ill-person thing. 'I mean, you could get better.'

Del shook her head slightly. 'No.'

'Come on, Del, you can't give up. You can still beat this thing—'

'Kam, it's too late,' Del cut in.

I wasn't going to be deterred. 'There are lots of new treatments, alternative therapies. Have you tried acupuncture, or—'

'Kam,' her voice was stern enough to halt my wild chatter. 'I've come to accept this, you will too.'

'But you've got to fight,' I whispered.

'I have been fighting. That's why I'm still here. Kam . . .' her voice trailed off. 'I want to live. *God* I want to live. I want to see my daughter grow up. But I'm not going to. I have to accept that or I'll be frozen. And I have to make as many plans as I can for Tegan. Do everything I can to make sure her life is sorted. And being with you is the start of that.'

I sniffed back my tears but still they broke free, tumbled down.

'I've written her a load of letters,' Del was saying. 'Got twenty birthday cards. Twenty Christmas cards. I've written them all. It's amazing how much there is to say, even when you're writing them for the future. But the letters, they're for things like her eighteenth birthday. And her twenty-first. And when she's deciding whether to go to uni; some are just for those times when we'd have a chat.'

I bit down on my lower lip and dipped my head as she talked. She wasn't going to be here in a few years. In twenty years. In five years. Even in a year. That was a horrifying thought, knowing someone you loved wouldn't see the future. Del was going to die.

'I didn't want to make a video. I don't want her to forever think of me like this. I want her to remember me as the healthy woman in the pictures. So, the letters will help. I hope.' Del's eyes reddened. 'You've got to love her. Promise me. Even when she's really bad, or says something horrible, you've got to love her. Promise me.'

I brushed brusquely at my tears. Who did she think I was? *What* did she think I was? Of course I'd love Tegan, if I didn't I wouldn't even be considering this. 'Del, just because I stopped talking to you doesn't mean I didn't still care about you both.'

'I'm scared she won't have unconditional love. And that's all a mother wants for her daughter. Promise me that's what you'll give her—unconditional love.'

I nodded. 'I've always loved her. Why do you think I sent her pressies? And look—' I scrambled about in my bag for my wallet, pulled out the red leather purse, opened it and showed it to her.

Del opened my wallet and saw a picture of Tegan. I'd taken it on her third birthday, just weeks before I left London. 'You've always carried this?' she whispered. 'Even after . . .'

'Yep,' I cut in. I'd put that picture in there when I moved to Leeds. I wanted, no, needed a reminder of her because in all of it, in all my hurt and anger and shock, there was one truth that was clear to me: it wasn't her fault. Besides, 'I've always adored Tiga. You know that, you said it yourself the other day. I couldn't stop loving her just like that.'

Del's body relaxed, almost as though one of her concerns, one of the things on her list of things to worry about, had been dealt with. 'One more thing you must promise me,' Del said.

'What's that then?'

'When you adopt her you'll change her name to yours, won't you?'

'Probably. To be honest I haven't thought about it in that much detail.'

'All right. Then you've got to let her call you Mummy, if she wants to.'

'You what?' I shrank back in my seat, stricken. 'Come on Del, that's . . . No. No. I can't.'

'Why not? I want her to feel as though she's got another mother, that she's got someone who'll do all the mummy things with her.'

'She will have. But it's not right, her calling me Mum. It's not . . . It's not natural!'

'That's the best argument you've got?' Del mocked me.

Rather shamefully, it was. What I was trying to say was, you couldn't replace a human being that easily and it wasn't right to try. Tegan might love me, but she could never love me like she did her mother. Asking her to try would be wrong. It'd tear her apart, it'd confuse her. I wasn't going to be responsible for screwing her up.

'You know that's not all I'm trying to say,' I replied.

'Come on, Kam, what do you think adoption means? It means you're becoming her mother, you're adopting a role. I want her to think of you as her mother. And I want you to think of her as your daughter.'

'I will.'

'Not if you won't let her call you Mum.' Del stopped talking suddenly, resting her frail body. Her eyes slipped shut. 'If someone calls you beautiful often enough you believe it.' Her voice was as fragile as tissue paper. She slowly opened her eyes. 'If someone . . . If they tell you something often enough you believe it. Self-fulfilling prophecy. I want that to happen to you and Tegan. If she calls you Mummy often enough you'll believe it. She'll be a part of you that you'll never . . . you'll never want to let go. She'll become your daughter. Please. Just think about it.'

'OK. I'll think about it. Only think though. I'm not promising.'

Silence came to us. Silence that she broke with, 'Kam, about Nate—'

'Del, please, don't,' I interrupted. 'I can't deal with talking about that on top of everything. I'm just about coping with all this. I can't handle talking about that as well. OK? Please. We'll sort it out another time.

Look, you said you had a few months . . . I'm going to get time off work. If the doctors agree, I'll find a place to rent for the three of us and you can come home. I'll learn how to take care of you and you can come home. You know, till . . . till . . .' I couldn't say it. 'I want to be there with you at . . .' I swallowed. 'I want to be with you.'

'You'll do that?'

I nodded, my face buckling with emotion. I'd baulked at the thought of taking care of a child; could I really sit with someone I loved and watch the life ebb out of her? I'd have to. Of course I'd have to. She had no one else. And she'd do the same for me if the roles were reversed. 'Of course I'll do that, Del,' I said. 'Of course I will.' Our eyes met and for a second I felt like I was back in that college bar, back where I fell for her. Everything good about her, all her inner beauty radiated outwards at me.

'Count yourself lucky, mind,' I said with a cheeky smile. 'You know I wouldn't do that for anyone else, don't you?'

'I'm honoured,' she replied with a laugh. 'Truly, I'm honoured.'

'No, I am.'

Chapter Three

I'D BEEN IN LONDON a week, and it was almost as if I'd never left. In that time, Tegan and I had slipped into a routine. A loose one, but still a routine. We'd wake at fifteen seconds past the crack of dawn, dress, drop by the hospital for an hour or so until we'd exhausted Del, then we'd go house-hunting for a nice three-bedroom ground-floor flat that would give Del her own space and Tegan and I our own rooms. Today was the day we were going to find somewhere, I could feel it in my soul.

Everything else I needed to change to fit my life around this situation had slotted into place. I'd asked for a six-month sabbatical from work, but they'd suggested I have the preceding week and the next two weeks as my annual leave, then work from home—home being the place I rented with Del and Tegan—three days a week. We'd get email, I could easily work from the London office of the department store I was

National Marketing Manager for, and if I needed to go to Leeds then they'd schedule midday meetings so I had time to get there and back in a day. I'd find an estate agent to sort out renting my flat in Leeds. It was all going to work out. We just needed somewhere to live.

Despite my conviction about finding the right flat, today hadn't exactly started well. My five-year-old charge hadn't roused from bed yet because she'd been up late, fizzing with excitement about the future. About the three of us being together. She'd begun to relax with me in the past eight days.

Her latest idea was getting a cat. It'd been one of the first things she brought up when we went to visit her mother yesterday evening.

She'd opened the door to Del's room, ran in, leapt up onto the bed and began her ritual of kisses. Tegan never seemed to notice her mum wasn't looking well or that she was connected to machines. And, yesterday, I wasn't surprised. Del looked amazing: colour was back in her face and the sparkle was back in the steel-blue windows to her soul. She was almost normal.

'How you doing?' she asked. Her voice sounded far more substantial than it had been only three days ago, and my grin widened.

'I'm fine. I'm always fine,' I said. 'You look so well.'

'I feel a lot better. You, on the other hand, look exhausted.'

'I'm fine, really.' I *was* tired, couldn't remember the last proper night's sleep I'd had, but hey, let's get everything in proportion. Terminally ill, a bit knackered—who should be complaining here?

'Can we get a cat?' Tegan interjected.

'You'll have to ask Kamryn,' Del said, passing the buck rather neatly to me, even though she knew how I felt about all things furry.

'Can we?' Tegan asked me.

'Not right now, sweetie. We'll talk about it another time.' *As in never.*

'If we get a cat, can we call it Pussy Puss?' Tegan asked sleepily.

'Pussy's a good name for a cat,' Del said, trying to hold back her laughter.

'Yeah,' I said, 'it certainly is.'

'Can you imagine walking around the neighbourhood calling "Pussy, Pussy"?' Del giggled.

'Why are you laughing?' Tegan asked, as her mother and I snickered like two schoolboys.

'Your Auntie Kamryn is just being silly, that's all. Don't mind her.'

'No sweetie, don't mind me.'

Tegan had a snooze while Del and I thought up the rudest names for pets that we could wander around the streets shouting out. Our favourite had been Your Hairy Butt ('Your Hairy Butt, dinner time!'), which made Del laugh so much I thought she was going to pass out.

When we got back to the hotel, Tegan, wide awake after her snooze, had been keyed up about getting a cat, about her mum coming home, about having fish fingers for dinner . . . Nothing was too trivial for her to chatter about. Less than a week ago she wouldn't talk to me, now she couldn't stop. When she'd finally fallen asleep it'd been pushing 3 a.m.

I checked her sleeping form. *Maybe I'll leave her a bit longer*, I thought, when a knock made me jump. My eyes went to the LCD display on the clock radio by the bed: 07:55. Far too early for callers. I opened the door.

Nancy, Adele's nurse, was stood on the other side. I knew. The moment my eyes settled on her face I knew. But I also didn't know, I wasn't ready.

'Hello, Kamryn,' she said with a smile. Not her usually bright, sunny one, this one was warm but subdued.

'Hi,' I said back.

'Where's Tegan?' she asked.

'She's asleep,' I replied.

'OK, good. May I speak to you in the corridor?'

We walked to the end of the corridor. 'I'm sorry, Kamryn,' Nancy began, and the bundle of butterflies that had been fluttering around my stomach plummeted through my body. 'Adele passed away in the night.'

'But she looked better yesterday,' I said through the thick lump of emotion that had filled my throat. 'She said she felt better.'

'Adele looked better but she had been deteriorating for a long, long time. We were all surprised that she survived this long.'

This didn't make sense. We'd been laughing yesterday. Joking about pets called Your Hairy Butt. 'She wasn't on her own, was she?' My eyes frantically searched Nancy's tired face. 'Adele didn't die alone?'

Nancy shook her head. 'No, I was with her. She said to tell Tegan she loved her and to tell you goodbye.'

'I should have been with her. I said I'd be with her.'

'She didn't want that,' Nancy said gently and laid a hand on my arm. 'She'd asked enough of you already. And, she was happy.

'Adele had been holding on because she didn't know what was going to happen to her baby. But when you came she was happy because her child would be taken care of and she could let go. That's why she was looking better, she wasn't as worried. She knew yesterday that she was near the end—after you had gone she said that if she passed away in the night, not to tell you until this morning. She didn't want to spoil the last memory you had of her laughing and joking by you watching her go. She just wanted you to remember the laughing.'

'That sounds like Adele, a control freak till the end,' I whispered, anger tingeing my voice. If I had known, I could've said a proper good-bye. I could have kissed and hugged her. Told her how much I loved her. *I hadn't said that, had I? Not once in the past nine days did I say I loved her. And I never said I'd forgiven her. Had I forgiven her? I don't know. I didn't want to talk about things, I know that, but had I forgiven her? Even if I hadn't, shouldn't I have said it? Shouldn't I have put her mind at rest?*

'She didn't suffer. She went to sleep and didn't wake up. I was holding her hand as she fell asleep, she knew she wasn't alone.'

'I didn't want her to be alone,' I whispered. *I thought she had months left, not days. I should have listened to what she had to say, let her unburden her mind. I didn't want her to die thinking I still hated her.*

I turned to Nancy. If she had been with Adele then she had probably been up all night. 'Thank you, Nancy,' I said. 'For everything. For being there all these months, for being there at the end, and for coming to tell me yourself. Thank you.'

Nancy left. I watched her walk down the corridor and suddenly my legs gave way. My knees were pressed into the faded paisley corridor carpet. It started as a small nugget of pain deep inside but it grew and grew until it was a huge choking ball of agony. She was gone. I was never going to see her again. The first wave of tears came spilling forth. She'd left me. I'd left her, but she'd left me. For ever. My best friend was gone.

My body lurched again as another flood of tears poured out. I'd wanted to cry like this the day I found out about her and Nate, but hadn't been able to; even on the day of what would have been my wedding I hadn't been able to cry completely. Now it was all coming out, coursing through my body in painful waves.

The next emotional block dissolved. The block that had stopped me breaking down when I got that card on my birthday, and had found myself neck-deep in memories about Del and Nate, disintegrated and the shock, anger, resentment came gushing out.

Next came the outpouring caused by seeing her lying in that hospital bed. The horror of finding out she was the shell of the woman I loved. I'd hated myself at that moment for letting her down. When she needed me most I'd turned my back on her. And she'd dwindled to that. To nothingness. I'd wanted to cry then but hadn't.

Then came the tears for what had happened to Tegan. I could've saved her from all that pain, all that violence, if I'd opened just one of

Del's letters. Every bruise and mark and welt on Tegan's thin little body was scarred on my soul. I'd fought those tears when I first bathed her because I had to be strong. Now, though, all that was left was a big pool of sobbing.

Tegan was still asleep. I'd been lying next to her for what felt like an eternity. I didn't want to wake her. If I woke her, I had to tell her.

I'd calmed down. I wasn't calm, just *calmer,* no longer hysterical. I hadn't realised until I started crying how unbalanced I'd felt, how I'd spent two years on the edge of hysteria, always wanting to let it out but unsure if I started if I'd be able to stop.

Tegan opened her eyes suddenly, making me jump. She always did that. 'Why are your eyes red?' she asked.

'I've been crying,' I replied.

'Why?' she asked.

'I'm sad.'

'Why?'

I inhaled deeply. 'I'm sad because of your mummy.'

'Mummy?' Tegan sat up. 'Are we going to see Mummy today?'

I shook my head. 'No, sweetie,' I said.

'I want to see Mummy.'

'Tiga, when your mummy said you were going to live with me, where did she say she'd be?'

'In heaven with Jesus and the angels,' Tegan replied. Just like that. As though heaven was only around the corner.

'Did she say why?'

'Because she was ill and Jesus and the angels would look after her.'

'I'm sorry, your mummy's gone to be with Jesus and the angels.'

Tegan shook her head. 'No she hasn't. She's in the hospital.'

'She was yesterday. But today she's gone to heaven.'

'When is she coming back?'

'I'm sorry, Tiga, she's not coming back.'

'I DON'T BELIEVE YOU!' Tegan shouted and I recoiled at the volume of her voice. She leapt off the bed. 'I don't believe you. I want to see my mummy. I want to see my mummy.'

'I'm sorry, you can't,' I said quietly.

'I want my mummy,' she screamed. 'I want to see my mummy!' Her cries got louder and more anguished. I kept repeating that I was sorry but Tegan didn't hear me. She just screamed, stamping her feet and flailing her arms about. On and on. 'I WANT MY MUMMY, I WANT MY MUMMY, I WANT MY MUMMY.'

I slipped my arms around her even though she fought me. 'I WANT MY MUMMY, I WANT MY MUMMY.'

She bucked and twisted, but I held on to her until her rage subsided and she went limp in my arms. 'You've still got me,' I said.

'Don't want you,' she whispered in a tiny, hoarse voice, 'want my mummy.'

The handle to the door of my former bedroom turned and the door slowly opened. I watched as more of the corridor of my parents' house came into view and Tegan stepped in. She was dressed in a calf-length, black satin dress with a full skirt my mum had bought her. The black was tragically striking against her whey-coloured skin and pale gold hair. Her beauty brought a lump to my throat because she wasn't going to wow people at a party but was attending her mother's funeral.

The day after Adele . . . The day after it happened, Tegan and I moved to my parents' house in Ealing, the outskirts of west London. The plan was to return to Leeds a few days after the funeral. After today.

Tegan had reverted to the fearful silence that had shrouded her when I'd taken her from Guildford. She refused to speak to me unless absolutely necessary, but I always had to be in her sight. If I left her company for too long, she'd seek me out, apprehension smudged onto her face, until she could touch me, just to make sure I was real. Solid. There. I'd find her sitting outside the bathroom if I went for a shower. The day I nipped down the road for a bottle of water, I'd returned to find her sitting beside the front door, her eyes like two chips of dark sapphire on a snow plain. She'd curled her arms around my thigh when I walked in, and I accepted that I couldn't leave her alone again.

Tegan stood in the corner of the room, waiting for me to finish getting ready. My dress wasn't as beautiful as hers—it was a simple straight up and down, ankle-skimming linen creation with a V-neck and short sleeves that I'd grabbed in a dash to Ealing Shopping Centre.

'I like your dress,' I said to her.

Tegan said nothing. I looked down at my shiny black shoes, trying to control the expression on my face. It was hard enough coping with everything else, and the funeral would be a nightmare, but it'd be a million times worse if Tegan continued her campaign of silence against me.

It wasn't her fault, though. She didn't know how else to be. What do you do when you're five years old and your mother dies? And in her place is a strange woman who you haven't seen in two years, claiming she'll take care of you?

I stood, painting a smile on my face. 'What do you think of my dress?' I asked. Since this question required more than a nod for an answer, she didn't tell me. 'Do you like it?' I rephrased.

She nodded and turned the corners of her mouth up, nearly managing a smile. I almost wrapped her up in my arms as a thank you for acknowledging me, for taking this small but significant step on our road back to verbal communication. 'OK, I'm ready, finally. Let's go.'

Adele Brannon
(formerly Lucinda-Jayne Adele Hamilton-Mackenzie)
died recently after a valiant battle with leukaemia.
She is survived by her daughter, Tegan Brannon.
The funeral will be held on July 31 at 4 p.m.
St Agnes's Church, Ealing.

In the grey-brick Catholic church Tegan sat motionless and impassive beside me, watching the people who stood in the pulpit talking about her mother. The church vibrated with the presence of *hundreds* of people. Adele had thought she'd be lucky if she got enough people to make a football team turning up. 'One of my biggest regrets is that I don't know that many people. I wish I'd made the effort to touch more lives.'

She had touched lives, I wish she'd known that. The church was filled to capacity, with two rows of people standing at the back. I'd only contacted a couple of the places where she worked, put notices in her local paper, another in a couple of the media trade magazines, and one on our university's website. Word of mouth must have done the rest.

My whole family was here; even my older brother who lived in Japan had flown in. Nancy, Adele's nurse, had come and brought her husband.

Adele's father wasn't there. Wasn't there, didn't want to be there, hadn't even sent flowers. He didn't care. That was the stark reality of it.

I'd rung Mr Hamilton-Mackenzie to tell him what happened on the day Adele died, and after a long silence he'd said, 'Thank you for letting me know.' He hadn't asked about Tegan and I guessed it was the shock.

'I'll let you know about the funeral arrangements,' I'd said and he thanked me again before hanging up.

A week later, three days ago, I called him again.

'Kamryn,' he'd said warmly when he answered, 'how are you?'

I'd been thrown; thought for a moment I'd dialled the wrong number. 'As fine as can be expected in these circumstances,' I said cautiously.

I heard something catch in his voice as he said, 'I know. I'm still coming to terms with this myself.'

'I'm calling about the funeral,' I said, the evil thoughts I'd had about him melting away like ice left out in the noonday sun. I was right, death had made him accept that he loved his daughter. 'It's on Friday. I've done almost everything that Del couldn't do herself . . .'

'Del?' he interjected, his voice stern.

'I mean Lucinda-Jayne. She made most of the arrangements—she wanted to be cremated—and I've sorted out the details. But if you want to add any readings or hymns let me know and we can work it out.'

Silence. I fancied I could hear him pulling himself together. 'I won't be attending. Neither my wife nor I will be attending.'

'Why?' rose up in my throat as a protest, but I stopped myself in time. I'd nearly fallen for it. Fallen for his game. This was why Del was always broken up after every phone call. He knew how to lure you in, to con you into thinking you were conversing with a decent person—then he'd turn on you.

I took a deep breath. 'OK,' I exhaled. I had no strength to argue with him, nor even to talk to him. What was there to say to this man?

He had no idea how difficult the preceding week had been. That one of my many tasks was identifying Adele's body. I hadn't flinched in the morgue when I was asked to confirm that the person lying motionless in front of me was the friend who had once rugby tackled me for the last packet of crisps in our flat.

I'd stared at her, lying on a hospital trolley, serene and delicate, frozen and frail. The first dead body I'd ever seen was of my best friend.

'It's not right that I should have to bury another member of my family,' he was saying in a voice designed to break the heart of anyone who didn't know how many times he'd put Adele in hospital. 'Lucinda-Jayne was the last of my family and I can't say goodbye. You understand, don't you, Kamryn? Don't you?'

'What about Tegan?' I replied, my voice as even as a sheet of glass. 'Isn't your granddaughter a member of your family?'

He paused. The pause elongated itself into silence, which became a yawning chasm of arrogant righteousness: he was right and nothing would make him think otherwise, not even the truth.

'Goodbye,' I eventually stated, and hung up. That was it. The end. He'd never challenge me if I tried to adopt Tegan. He'd never try to get in touch, and, while I was relieved and grateful, that was when the sadness had started to stab at me. *Why didn't he love his child?*

I slipped an arm around Tegan's shoulders and refocused on the priest, listening to his speech about life and death, and Adele. He hadn't known my friend, he was repeating what I'd written for him. But he went beyond what I'd noted, he talked about the warmth he felt when he spoke to those who knew Adele. How wonderful a friend she must have been because so many people had come to pay their last respects. He moved on to explain about her being a mother, saying he was sure that Adele's daughter would be in good hands.

I wouldn't count on it, mate, I thought before I could stop myself. That would have made Adele laugh. 'Trust you,' she'd have guffawed. 'Only you would think like that at my funeral.'

The final prayers were said, the final hymn sung. I got up with the rest of the congregation and turned to follow the four men—two of them my brothers—who picked up the oak coffin and began carrying it out of the church. As I gathered my mind together, I saw him. His tall frame dressed in a black suit with a black shirt and tie, his grief-bleached skin, his agonised features, his softly spiked-up brown hair. I gasped, my body momentarily rigid with shock, before he disappeared out of the doors. Nate.

There was a small service at Ealing West Crematorium that only my family came to. Slowly the box was pulled away from us, pulled away behind the heavy black curtain. It was over. I bit my lower lip and didn't move out of my seat as everyone filed out. Once I was alone— Tegan had gone with my mum and dad—I stepped out of the pew and stood in front of the curtain, where she'd disappeared.

A million thoughts were speeding through my mind, each leaving a burning groove where it ran. Adele. Tegan. Work. Death. Life. Nate.

I was ashamed to admit I'd been thinking about Nate.

What was he doing there? He was at a friend's funeral. *How did he know she was gone?* He probably saw the notices in the trade press—he was a radio producer. Every question had an obvious answer. It hadn't occurred to me that he'd turn up. Did it mean anything? Was he in love with her? But they both said it was just the once. And I'd assumed they hadn't seen each other in the two years since I'd left them.

I'll never know for sure, of course. Never find out what really went on . . . What was wrong with me? Why was I thinking about this stuff? I should be thinking about Del. But Nate kept wrestling his way into my mind. I could remember the last time I saw him more clearly than the last time I saw Del. I remember how he'd stared at me with haunted eyes as I walked out of the door. I'd been expecting everything to end with a row but it was depressingly quiet. I'd collected my belongings; looked back to take in his unshaven chin, unwashed hair and sleep-deprived eyes. I listened to him say, 'Don't go', then I walked out.

I had no grand finale with Adele, no curtain call or fade to black. I'd racked my brain and still I couldn't remember what I'd said to her. Did

I say goodbye? Did I hug her? I couldn't remember and it was breaking my heart. I knew I didn't have much time left with her, so why didn't I take in every detail? Why didn't I hang on to every second?

The ball of pain in my stomach contracted suddenly. I doubled over, clutching my stomach, trying to hold myself together. *How would I have said goodbye if I knew that was the last time I would see her?* I don't know. I would have looked at her, I know that. Had I anyway? Did I turn around and look at her? *I can't remember*.

Nate. I was thinking about Nate, too, because I didn't want to think about what came next.

I wish I was a better person, could embrace the idea of taking on a child. All I could see were bleak times. Hardship. Sacrifice. Years and years of being responsible for someone else. A hundred and one things would have to change about my life so that I could slot Tegan into it. So that I could make her a new home.

Footsteps on the blond wood floor made me straighten up, scrabbling to recreate the serenity I'd been projecting for the past few days. Everyone thought I was being strong, that I was brave and undaunted; the reality was Kamryn Matika was faking it.

I jumped slightly as a hand slipped into mine. I looked down. Tegan's big blue eyes were fixed on me. Then she spoke, her voice small and wavering as each word came out. 'Are you my new mummy?'

I nodded. 'Yes, sweetheart, I am.'

Chapter Four

'WHAT DO YOU THINK of your new home?' I asked Tegan.

She was sitting at the very centre of my cream sofa, clutching a rag doll called Meg she'd had since she was a year old.

'It smells,' Tegan replied honestly.

The girl on the sofa was right. My flat reeked of fish and the other rubbish from the bin, having been neglected for the six weeks I had been in London. From the doorway I surveyed the room. The place seemed to have grown horribly messy.

'Hang on,' I said. I left the living room, clambered over our bags that littered the long, narrow corridor and entered the kitchen. I recoiled at the stench. Holding my breath I took the rubbish to the black wheelie bin outside, then returned to wash my hands in the bathroom. Another finger of shame needled me as I noticed the dental floss stuck to the side of the basin. This messiness had to stop, I realised. I returned to the kitchen and opened the window. The smell would soon disperse.

On the sofa, Tegan was doing that thing she did so well—sitting still and silent. Waiting. Waiting for me to tell her what came next. The tragic part being I really didn't know. Life had become a list of events I had to get through: identifying body, funeral, collecting Adele's belongings, moving back to Leeds. And here we were, in Leeds. That also meant the plan had stopped. What came next? Life, yes. But how?

'This will be your room,' I told Tegan. 'We'll take out the sofa, put it in the smelly kitchen. Except I'm hoping it won't be smelly by then. We'll get you a bed, and we can paint the walls whatever colour you like. I'm sorry, you can't have wallpaper because it'll end in tears—when I was little, my mum and my dad almost got divorced over wall-papering . . .' Tegan watched me as I rambled. 'Anyway, I'll put the desk in my bedroom, and we'll use the kitchen as a living room as well as a kitchen. It's big enough, thankfully. Does that sound all right to you?'

We'd got the train to Leeds this morning. I'd hired a man with a van who had set off before us with Adele's boxes, our biggest bags and everything else we couldn't carry. The boxes were piled up in the communal hallway downstairs. When I'd arrived at the storage facility, I'd been horrified that her whole life, her thirty-two years, had fitted into ten boxes. Most of the boxes contained things she wanted me to pass on to Tegan.

'Listen,' I went on. 'We need some food and some other bits like shampoo for you, so how about we go shopping? How does that sound?'

Conspiracy. There was some kind of conspiracy. Who knew you could get so much shampoo? Since I got my shampoo from the hair salon where I had my hair straightened every six weeks, I'd never needed to know what types of shampoo there were out there for white hair. And how it related to a small white girl's hair. *Why didn't Adele tell me about things like this?* I thought, anxiety clawing at me. Was this the thing that was going to crack my veneer of calm? It wasn't simply shampoo, though, it represented much more. How little I knew of my young charge. She had likes and dislikes that I hadn't a clue about. Television shows she didn't want to miss, food she was allergic to, events that would cause her temper to flare. I leant against the trolley, visually

ransacking the shelves; each second that passed stoked the fires of inse-
curity burning inside me. 'Do you remember which shampoo you used
to use?' I asked Tegan. She shook her head.

From the corner of my eye I saw a supermarket helper approaching.
'Excuse me,' I said. 'I'm trying to find the best shampoo for a child's
hair.' I indicated to Tegan who dutifully smiled at her. 'I was wondering
if you could tell me which is the best one?'

'Oh, um . . .' the woman began, turning to the shelves.

Before she could finish her reply a voice cut in, 'Don't you know?'

We looked to the source of the voice and a mumsy-looking woman,
about forty, was staring at us.

'Sorry, were you talking to me?' I asked.

'Yes. Don't you know which shampoo you should be buying?'

What's it to you? I thought. 'Erm, I've never bought it before,' I
replied, turning back to the supermarket helper.

'Why didn't you ask your employer before you came out?'

I ignored her for a moment, then what she said filtered into my
mind. I spun back to her. 'Why would I ask a marketing director about
children's shampoo?' I asked with a frown.

'Her parents will obviously know what shampoo they use.'

Oh, it was suddenly clear: a black woman with a small white girl,
could only mean that I was staff; an au pair. *Do I look like an au pair?* I
glanced down at myself: I was wearing baggy navy blue jeans and black
trainers. If you didn't know me, you wouldn't look at me and think I
was a successful thirty-two-year-old National Marketing Manager, that
was true. But why couldn't I be her parent? Why did this woman look
at me and instantly think employee? I could be Tegan's stepmother, for
all she knew.

'Well, her parents don't,' I said through tight lips. The supermarket
helper sidled away, perhaps to get security in case things got physical.

'Where are her parents?' the woman asked.

'What's it to you?' I asked calmly, although a rivulet of indignant
venom ran through the words.

'What are you doing with that child?'

'If you must know,' I snapped, 'she's my child. I'm her parent.'

'You?'

'Yes, me.'

'Do her parents know you're trying to pretend she's your daughter?'
The woman raised her voice, drawing attention to us.

'I'm not pretending anything,' I hissed.

'Then what *are* you doing?' she said, just as loudly.

What am I doing? I'm doing my best not to break down in tears because I can't find the right shampoo. I'm just about managing to stop myself from opening a bottle of vodka every night and drinking until my best friend is alive again, my fiancé isn't a cheat and I'm still living in London being Regional Marketing Manager of the company I've given seven years of my life to.

Tegan tugged on my jeans just above the knee until I looked down at her. 'I like this one,' she said, holding a bottle of shampoo in a bright orange container up to me. I grinned down at Tegan who, surprisingly, smiled back up at me, before I dropped the shampoo into the trolley.

The woman's question, 'What are you doing?', still hung in the air. I looked back up at her and smiled sweetly.

'What am I doing? I'm buying shampoo.'

Tegan slipped her hand into mine and, pushing the trolley, we strode away. My heart was racing in my chest. This was going to happen a lot in the coming weeks, months and, probably, years. Outsiders weren't going to instantly believe I was Tegan's legal guardian, her 'parent'. Since I'd sent the adoption papers off, I'd found out that it wouldn't be straightforward to adopt Tegan. It'd take months, possibly years. I had an array of official hoops to jump through, but even then it might not be enough. Cross-racial adoptions were very rare, especially this way round, a black woman adopting a white child. I had to do it, though. I had to adopt her, make her part of my family. Be her mother like Adele wanted. From what I'd found out so far, however, I might not be allowed to.

'Mummy Ryn,' Tegan said, making me jump out of my thoughts.

'What did you call me?'

'Mummy Ryn,' Tegan repeated, as though it was every day she called me 'Mummy' when she'd been calling me Auntie Ryn most of her life.

'Why did you call me Mummy?' I asked.

Her little face looked for a moment as though it was going to scrunch up in tears. 'You said you are my new mummy,' she whispered, her royal blue eyes filling with tears, her voice accusing me of lying to her.

I crouched down to her height, willing her not to cry. 'I am,' I reassured her pale face. I stroked her hair and tried a smile to calm her.

She shook her head, 'But you are not my real mummy. My real mummy has gone to heaven. And she's not coming back.'

A lump rose in my throat. 'That's right,' I agreed quietly.

'So you are not Auntie Ryn no more.'

'I suppose not.'

'You are Mummy Ryn,' she concluded. I was impressed with her reasoning skills, it proved how intelligent she was.

'OK, I'm Mummy Ryn. What did you want to ask me?'

Tegan sniffed, wiped at one of her teared-up eyes with the back of her hand. 'Am . . .' she gulped. 'Am I allowed to have some chocolate?'

'Yes, but only if you eat all your vegetables as well.' Responsible adults were meant to say things like that, weren't they?

Her heart-shaped face suddenly brightened. 'We haven't got no vegetables,' she giggled, pointing to the food in our wire-framed trolley.

It'd been so long since I heard her giggle, there was no way I could force vegetables on her now. 'You've got me there,' I agreed with a grin. 'No vegetables today. But tomorrow, we're going to start eating healthily. OK?'

She nodded. Then she slipped her arms around my neck, gave me a quick squeeze, then let me go.

Violent nausea rose and fell in my stomach. *What will we do if I'm not allowed to adopt her?*

I had this life before I inherited Tegan. It was a life of work. Nothing but work. My job title was National Marketing Manager for Angeles, the department store. The chain had begun a hundred years ago as a haberdashery store in Leeds and the head office was still based there, not in London. We had branches in every major British city. I'd started in the London store as a regional marketing assistant and had worked my way up to my current position as second-in-command for the entire company's marketing department—main role: running the in-store magazine, *Living Angeles*. I'd helped the National Marketing Director, Ted Payne, set it up and, two months before my non-wedding, the plan had been for me to spend a month in Leeds coordinating the magazine's launch. After I left Nate and Adele, I'd asked Ted if I could accept the job as National Marketing Manager that he'd been offering me since we'd met.

When I'd finally bought my flat in the Leeds suburb of Horsforth, three months after I left London, I had to force myself to go back there, night after night. All my life I'd lived with people: my family, then Adele, then Nate. I wasn't cut out for living in silence and solitude. I knew I had two choices: buckle under the strain of it all or spend as much time as possible at work. I'd get into work for 7 a.m. and leave around 10 p.m. I'd even work weekends, just so I wouldn't be alone in the flat.

As time wore on, of course, I eased off the manic work schedule and made some real friends at work. One of them was Betsy Dawali, who I shared a glass-walled office with. The other was my boss, Ted Payne.

Ted was fifty or so and exceptionally attractive. He had an unwavering decency too, and a calm, straightforward way of talking that made him incredibly sexy.

The night he came to visit me after my return to Leeds he'd been unsettled. I didn't like to see him like this. He'd always been steady and strong, not hesitant and nervous. He always knew what to do in any situation. Ted had been the one who had arranged everything when I'd asked for a sabbatical so I could take care of Adele—he'd come up with the idea of me working from home. When I told him I'd fostered a child, he'd organised for me to have compassionate and maternity leave.

Ted studied me for a long moment. 'Kamryn,' he began. 'I have some news. I didn't want to worry you while you were away. I'm . . . I'm leaving. Ava and I are moving to Italy, starting again over there.'

He was leaving me, he was walking out of my life.

'That's . . . It's great for you. But I'll miss you.'

'You'll hardly know I'm gone,' he said with a laugh.

I didn't laugh. Ted knew how much he meant to me.

Since we'd met six years ago Ted had been offering me a job as his second-in-command. Just over two years ago, when I'd asked if the position was still open, he'd been shocked, but he'd asked me no questions, simply told me what I'd have to do to formally apply and gave me the job almost straight away. When I'd stepped into my new role, we were setting up *Living Angeles* so we worked many a late night together, would order in food and then he'd walk me back to my hotel.

One particular Friday night he walked me back to the hotel, wished me a good weekend and left me in reception. I went to the room that had been my home while I was meant to be finding a flat and sat on the edge of the bed in the dark, unable to do anything except wring my hands. Minutes later there was a knock at the door. It was Ted.

'Kamryn,' he said, his face creasing in concern, 'are you OK?'

'I'm meant to be getting married tomorrow,' I confessed. 'But it's over. I'm not getting married. I'm all alone.'

He folded his arms around me and I crumpled. He led me to the bed and lay with me all night, holding me as I swung between silence and quiet sobbing. In the morning, I looked at him to say thank you and understanding swelled between us. He kissed me and I decided to go with it. I knew he was married and that while he and his wife, Ava, had split up recently they were talking about getting back together, but I was tired of feeling loss and pain and loneliness. I wanted to feel something else. I reached for the button on his shirt but he stopped me. 'I-I . . .' he stuttered, 'I'm sorry. I'm back with Ava. I'm sorry.'

I was relieved. I hadn't been sure I could go through with sex and now, thankfully, I didn't have to. Ted left, and although we never mentioned the night again, we were closer. He'd seen a fragile side of me and I saw the same side of him six months later when his wife left him again.

'It's going to work out with you and Ava, then?' I asked.

'Absolutely.'

The troubled expression belied the conviction of his reply. 'So, what's up? What aren't you telling me?'

'There's no easy way to say this. They've already found my replacement. I've been working with him on a handover for the past couple of weeks.'

'You mean I've not even been given the chance to apply for the job? Don't they think I'm up to it?'

'It's not that, Kamryn, you know you can't do this job now that you've got a child, not with all the late nights and travelling.'

The heat of indignation burned its way up through my body to the tips of my hair. 'That's why? Because I've got a child?'

'No one has said that officially. They want someone new, someone who's going to be able to put in the hours, look at the company's marketing strategy with a fresh eye and make some big changes.'

'This wouldn't be happening if I was a bloke, would it?'

'I'm not saying what they've done is right,' Ted stated calmly, 'but would you really want to miss out on the time with Tegan? Especially when she's just lost her mother and will need you.'

Although he was right, the resentment still thudded through my veins. 'That should have been my choice. Who are they to make decisions about my life? I've worked for Angeles for seven years and this is how I get treated?'

'It's a testament to how much the company respect and like you that they were willing to let you work from London, then gave you all this time off for compassionate and then maternity leave,' Ted reasoned.

'That's also what alerted them to the fact that my priorities might have changed. God I'm pissed off,' I stated. It wasn't simply the job. It was the sense of powerlessness. First I couldn't do anything to stop Adele . . . *going*. And then I didn't stop Tegan from being hurt by her grandparents. I had motherhood forced upon me and now my job had been snatched away from me. I wasn't mistress of my own destiny any more.

'What's the new Marketing Director like, then?'

'Luke Wiseman? He's ambitious,' Ted stated diplomatically. It got worse. 'He was head-hunted for the position.' And worse. 'From a management consultancy firm.' And worse. 'He's a Harvard Business School graduate. He's got lots of ideas, which is what Angeles needs.'

'I suppose you're right.' My whole body slumped in resignation.

Tegan stood with a paintbrush in one hand, a pot of red paint at her trainered feet and a mix of happiness, excitement and apprehension on her face. 'Am I really 'lowed to paint on the wall?' she checked again.

'Yep, any colour you want.'

I'd taken us to a DIY store yesterday and we'd bought a host of stencils—animals, stars, moons, suns, dolphins, fish—and paints in red, blue, brown, yellow and green. It was marginally cheaper than painting the whole room again. I'd moved all the furniture into the middle when Tegan had been asleep in my room last night. I'd dismantled my desk; old white and cream sheets covered the furniture.

'Can I paint a fish there?' She pointed under the window. 'Red.'

'Go on, then,' I said. I picked up the fish stencil, attached it to the wall with tape, then stepped aside for the artist to do her work, flicking on the radio as I did so.

Tegan made a stroke in the middle of the stencil. Each of her strokes were carefully placed so she wouldn't go outside the edges. The fish looked bereft on the wall, one lone splash of colour in the wide ocean of cream-white. 'OK, who's next?' I asked.

'An elephant,' Tegan decided. 'Blue?'

'If the lady wants blue, the lady can have blue.'

It took most of the afternoon to encircle the room with animals, then we stood beside the covered furniture and looked at our handiwork. It was pretty. Tegan's ark of multicoloured animals. She was good at painting, it had to be said. Probably got it from her mother. But then her father had been good at art too. Nate was always scribbling things on pieces of paper. Since I'd seen him at the funeral, Nate had been inhabiting my mind.

'Like A Virgin' came on the radio and shoved Nate aside, replaced the image of him in black with the image of Madonna in white, gyrating. I held my hand out to Tegan and she slipped her blue, red and green splattered fingers into my palm. I started rocking my hips; I moved her hand with mine and she followed suit. Our bodies moved in time to the music. I grabbed her, pulled her into my arms and started jiggling around the room with her. She started laughing, throwing her head right back and rocking her body in my arms as though she was dancing too.

'Like A Virgin' segued into Cyndi Lauper's 'Girls Just Wanna Have Fun', and I put Tegan down as we both simultaneously threw our arms in the air and started moving our bodies side to side.

'This is my mummy's favourite song,' Tegan laughed. And then stopped as she realised what she'd done: she'd brought up her mother when neither of us had mentioned her in the past week.

I stopped dancing too, my heart drumming hard in my chest. Tegan and I stood staring at each other, every word of the song like shards of glass scraping across our skins.

Moving stiffly, I went to the radio and flicked it off. The silence was sudden and brutal. I didn't know how to handle moments of sudden remembering like this one. I'd done the best I could to read up on how to help a child deal with death but reading was no substitute for experience, of which I had none. And none of the articles had explained what to do in moments of sudden remembering. When you were having fun even though your mother, your best friend, was gone. None of them explained how to handle the twin emotions of guilt and resentment. Guilt at forgetting for a minute that this horrible thing had happened; and resentment at your loved one for leaving you. I didn't know how to explain to her that she was allowed to be angry, upset, confused, hurt. And that laughing was permissible.

I pointed to the expanse of cream-white on the chimney breast. 'OK, so what are we going to do there?' I asked.

Tegan shrugged. Her eyes glistened; the corners of the mouth that had been pointed upwards in a grin seconds ago, were turned down.

'How about a sun?' I said. Her eyes stared back at me. 'A big yellow sun. And some green hills?' She nodded. 'OK. Anything else?'

'A tree,' she whispered.

'OK, trees. I think I can paint trees. What else?'

'Chocolate flowers.'

'Do you mind if I make the flowers into those red and white swirly sweets instead? We won't have enough brown paint after the trees.'

She stared at the wall for a few seconds, then nodded in agreement.

'I think your mummy would have liked the sun and the hills and the trees and the flowers that are really sweets,' I said. We couldn't just pretend Del didn't exist. We had to find a way to talk about her, no matter how painful. 'She'd be able to paint them a lot better than me,' I added.

Tegan's damp, inquisitive eyes stared at me for a long, quiet minute. 'My mummy drawed lots of pictures,' she eventually said.

'Yup, she certainly did. And she was very good. Come on then,' I said. 'Once we've done this, we'll go buy you a bed.'

'Is this really my room?' Tegan asked, from the doorway. It'd taken us another week to get ourselves sorted out. Betsy, the woman I shared an office with at work, sent her brother, Brad—a sulky fifteen-year-old—to come around and help me shift furniture. The cream sofa was moved into the dining end of the kitchen; my beanbag was placed in the corner at the bottom of the alcove, where I'd built in book shelves. Brad helped me move the twenty-eight-inch telly into the kitchen, too. Betsy was the grateful recipient of the large dining table. There was no way I could keep it. Instead I got a small table that marked the living area from the kitchen.

The computer, printer and other paraphernalia had been relegated to my bedroom. The real problem had been my books. I had over five hundred of them on shelves in the living room. In the end, what didn't fit onto the book shelves in the alcove was piled up on the floor beside the telly. The only other storage I had were five cupboards that were flush to the wall in my corridor, but half of them were now filled with Adele's boxes. The small telly that had been in the kitchen was now in Tegan's room.

The room she stood staring at. Her new bed was made up with a single duvet that had a light blue sky and cloud scene. Beside the window stood a light wood wardrobe. Under the window sat a matching drawer unit. I'd used carpet tape to fix two large red and white rugs to the laminate floor. On the other side of the fireplace sat a large toy box. She also had a shelf for books. To finish off I'd spelt out 'Tegan' on the door in brightly coloured letters.

'Yup, it's all yours. You can do anything you like in here,' I replied.

She took tentative steps into the room, then sat on the bed.

'Now I thought you might like to try sleeping in your own bed tonight, but if you want to still sleep in with me, that's fine too.'

'I like this bed,' she proclaimed. 'It's big enough for Tegan.'

'Cool. Now, I'm going to make a cup of something to drink. Why don't you try out your television and video?'

Tegan nodded eagerly, then scuttled across the room to the small television that sat with a new video player I'd shelled out for.

Shelling out was something I'd been doing a lot of recently and it was scaring me how expensive everything was. I hadn't been the most sensible person when it came to money nor, despite my job title, was I raking it in. I'd always lived with an overdraft and a credit card. (Nate had been the sensible one when it came to money, but few of his frugal ways had rubbed off on me.) Now that I had two mouths to feed, clothe and take care of, I was struggling.

Del, much as I loved her, had been appalling with money. *Irresponsible*. There, I'd thought it. Del was irresponsible. She loved her daughter, but she hadn't provided for her in any way.

She had no savings—just a great clothes collection. I suppose, like me, she thought she had all the time in the world to start being a financial adult. Things were going to be tight for us.

I took my time making the drinks, giving Tegan the chance to familiarise herself with her new space. 'I like this room,' she informed me as I returned with a cup of Horlicks.

'I'm glad, Tiga,' I said. 'I've got something for you.'

'A present?' Her eyes lit up.

'Sort of,' I said. I went back to the kitchen to retrieve the memento I'd dug out when Tegan was asleep last night.

'I know this might make you sad at first, but I think you should have it up anyway.' I held out the picture of Adele and Tegan that Del had kept on her bedside stand in the hospital, the two of them beaming out from behind the plain glass frame. Tegan hesitated, her eyes wide and scared. 'You don't have to put it up, sweetheart,' I said to her, frightened that I'd pushed her too far too soon. 'I'll put it to one side if you want.'

What had I been thinking? I didn't want to look at pictures of Adele all day, why would she?

Tegan stood, went to the television and placed her picture on top of it. 'I think it should be there. Is that OK, Mummy Ryn?'

I nodded and smiled. 'That's perfect, sweetheart.'

Rustle, *flick* went the papers as the headmistress leafed through them. I watched her while Tegan, of course, was still and silent in the comfy chair beside me, clutching her rag doll, Meg. *How had they got so many papers, so much information, when I hadn't provided it? Nor filled in any forms.* In fact, when I'd called the school to find out how I went about registering a child for the next term, they had said I had to give them my child's name, former address and the name of her former school—but I didn't need to fill any forms in.

Fundamentally, it seemed wrong. I had been raised finding it difficult to join any kind of group—Girl Guides, students' union, bank, jobs—there were always forms to fill in, information to dole out. This should be harder. As a result, I'd asked to meet the headteacher because I needed to make life difficult for myself. And I didn't want to launch Tegan into a new environment without seeing it for myself first.

I'd had to keep letting go of Tegan's hand to dry sweat off my hands as we walked from our flat to the primary school. I couldn't remember approaching any kind of meeting with this amount of trepidation.

'Mrs Matika . . .' Mrs Hollaby began as she raised her head to me.

'It's Ms Matika,' I cut in.

'Ms?' she replied, the slight inflection in her voice questioning my marital status. Was I divorced or one of those *liberal* women?

'Call me Kamryn.'

Her face creased into a professional, practised smile. 'Kamryn.' She made my name sound like a statement. 'It's a shame your partner wasn't able to come along.'

'I don't have a partner,' I replied quietly.

Mrs Hollaby frowned. 'You are, then, Tegan's only parent?'

'Yes,' I said.

Rustle, flick went the papers as 'Miss' searched them again, trying to explain why Tegan with her white skin and blonde hair had brown-skinned, raven-haired Kamryn for a parent.

I had to enlighten her; those in charge had to know what had happened for Tegan's sake.

'I'm Tegan's legal guardian,' I glanced at Tegan, making it known that I didn't want to discuss this in front of her.

'Miss' understood and reached out her long hand for the phone receiver. I watched her fingers tap in a number, then she asked for someone to come into her office. A few minutes later a young woman entered the room. After a short conversation with Mrs Hollaby, she bobbed down in front of Tegan and introduced herself as Maya. She asked Tegan if she wanted to come and meet some other children at the playgroup.

Tegan's head snapped around to look at me, her eyes wide.

'You're allowed—do you want to?' I smiled encouragingly.

She nodded.

'Go on then,' I said. 'I'll come find you later, OK?'

Her lips moved up into a smile, 'OK,' she replied before she slid off the chair. Holding Maya's hand she left the room.

I watched them go, another kick of fear almost winding me: what if I never saw her again? I didn't know anything about this Maya person.

'She'll be fine,' Mrs Hollaby said to the back of my head.

I resettled myself in the chair, faced her. 'I know. I just worry.'

'I can see that.' She arranged her face into a concerned expression.

From a place deep inside me I sighed as I resigned myself to letting a complete stranger into my life. Since Nate and Adele, I hadn't opened up to people. Share too much and someone could hurt you. 'I'm Tegan's legal guardian,' I began. 'Her mother, my best friend, died recently. I've inherited Tegan. I'm responsible for her. I'm going to adopt her.' No one else knew that. Everyone thought that I was taking care of her. 'Her mother only d— left us a few weeks ago, but I've got to get moving with adopting her.'

'This must be very difficult for you,' she said.

'Am I that obvious?' All bravado in my voice was ruined with a quiver of emotion; this was more difficult than I thought it would be.

Her eyebrows knitted together in concern. I looked away, to protect myself from her sympathy. I would have no strength when faced with the kindness of strangers.

'Do you have a social worker?' Miss asked.

'I, erm, haven't had time to do that yet,' I said, still not looking at her. 'I've been trying to sort out the flat so that Tegan could have her own room. I've only had time to do this. To register at a school. I thought that if I got her into a school you might be able to recommend a play-group or something that she can go to during the summer holidays for when I go back to work. But I will get a social worker. I promise.'

She touched my hand. 'I'm not berating you, Kamryn. I was asking because they can help. That's what they're there for. Not only with the adoption, but also with any problems you're having. They'll also help you find someone for Tegan to talk to.'

What does Tegan need to talk about? I wondered as alarm bells sounded in my ears. 'Grief is hard on everyone,' she stated. 'If Tegan is finding it hard to express that, she might need someone else to talk to. You will need a social worker for the adoption, however.'

'OK. Yes. I think I knew that.'

'There is help available, you simply have to ask for it.'

I couldn't ask for help, it was all I could do to explain my situation; revealing I was struggling as well would be impossible.

'So, do we, I mean, does Tegan get in? Does she have a place here?'

She nodded. 'Yes, she lives in the area and it's been a pleasure meeting her, she seems a lovely child.'

'She is. And about the playgroups?'

'Yes, of course. We have a playgroup here. It runs from eight to six-thirty. We give the children breakfast, lunch and a light snack in the afternoon before they are picked up.'

'It costs, right?'

'Yes.'

No matter what the cost it wouldn't be as expensive as a childminder. I'd crunched and crunched the numbers, stripping back our budget, and a playgroup was the only thing I could afford. I would simply have to work through lunch to ensure I left on time every night, and then take work home to do after Tegan was asleep. 'Do you have places?'

Mrs Hollaby smiled. 'We'll make a place for Tegan.'

I threw my arms around her neck, squeezed her in gratitude, as I cried, 'Thank you! Thank you so much!' Something had gone right.

Mrs Hollaby's body stiffened in my hold and I caught myself. 'I mean, thanks, that's great,' I said calmly. 'Shall we go find Tegan now then?'

The sun almost blinded me as I crossed the threshold into the playground, its brightness causing me to squint. I scanned the corners of the playground for Tegan. I couldn't see her. My heart jumped in fear, then I spotted her standing with four girls. The five of them were engrossed in an intense conversation. Tegan looked up. Our eyes met and she beamed at me. She lifted Meg in her right hand, waved the rag doll at me, then submerged herself in the conversation again.

'Looks like she's fitted right in,' Mrs Hollaby commented.

'I met lots of people,' Tegan said. She held onto my hand and swung it as she skipped along the pavement. 'I met Crystal. She's got a brother called Cosmo. And I met Ingrid and she's got a big brother called Lachlan. I haven't got a brother, have I?'

'No,' I replied.

'And I met Matilda. She's got lots of brothers and sisters. She's got a sister called Marlene. And a sister called Maree. And she's got a brother called Declan. And a brother called Dorian. And a brother called Daryl.'

'That's a lot of brothers and sisters.'

She nodded, her ponytail bobbing. 'I know. Matilda said was I coming back tomorrow. Am I going back tomorrow, Mummy Ryn?'

'Not tomorrow, next week. Did you like it there, then?' I asked.

'Yes.' She was excited. 'I've got lots of friends. Crystal and Ingrid and Matilda.'

I never made friends that quickly as a child, I didn't make friends that quickly as an adult. Tiga? No problems.

'Are you going to come and play next week?' Tegan asked.

'No, I'm going to work.'

Tegan stopped. 'Why?' she asked, panicked.

'Because I'm an adult and adults have to go to work. But you can play with your friends all day then tell me about it later.'

'Are you going to come later?'

'Yes, in the evening. And then you can tell me who else you met.'

'Do you promise you'll come afterwards?' she asked.

'Yes, I promise.'

'Double promise for ever and ever amen?'

'Yes, I double promise for ever and ever amen.'

Tegan grinned and started skipping again. 'Guess what?' Tegan asked.

'What?'

'Crystal's got a cat.'

Chapter Five

I HESITATED OUTSIDE the ninth-floor office, my hand raised to knock.

On the other side of the door was Luke Wiseman, the new Marketing Director of Angeles. He'd summoned me via email to his office to have a 'chat' (his word, not mine) the third day of my return to Angeles.

On my first day back at work (the thought of which had turned my emotions into a pendulum that swung constantly between fear and excitement) Tegan, who hadn't been blighted by nerves on her first day at playgroup, had given me an extra big hug at the school gates. 'Have fun at your work,' she'd told me, like I was the child and she was the adult.

The train ride into Leeds city centre after that had been nerve-racking; all I could think about was not being intimidated by Luke Wiseman—my first ever work nemesis, the only colleague I'd known to get a job I should have been given. By the time I'd reached my tenth-floor office I was flitting between wanting to throw up and deciding to slap him to show who the real boss was around here. I'd found out ten minutes later that he was in London until Friday. Today.

Once I knew I wouldn't be forced to deal with my arch enemy, I relaxed at work, enjoyed people dropping by to tell me their news, to find out what I had been up to. Betsy, who'd been alone in our office for nearly two months, spent the day offering to make the tea and running around the desk to engulf me in bear hugs. 'You could have me up for sexual harassment,' she said at one point, 'I'm so tempted to snog you.'

'The feeling's mutual, mate,' I'd replied, a little surprised but immeasurably happy that I'd been missed.

Ted had left yesterday in his usual dignified, understated manner. 'Goodbye, Kamryn. I'll keep in touch.' And that was it, no more Ted.

Now I had to conquer Luke. I took a deep breath, steeled myself, then knocked on the door. Seconds later, a baritone voice bid me enter.

The man behind the desk didn't stand as I entered. In fact, he sat back in his chair, stretched his tall body and made no attempt to hide the fact he was sizing me up. I was more discreet as I scrutinised him. His features, strong and well defined, looked as though an artist had spent hours chiselling them smooth into his clear, tanned skin. The black hair on his head had been razored to a grade one, which made his face all the more striking. Around his succulent lips was a thin, line moustache that ran down the sides of his face into a beard. What stood out about him, though, were his eyes—a bright, clear, burnt orange-hazel colour. From the stretch of his body I knew he had a gym-made physique. I recognised his type: he was Mr Career, dynamic, thrusting, über-ambitious, and anyone who worked with him had to give 150 per cent or he would take it as a personal insult and finish their careers.

While I appraised him, Mr Wiseman's hazel eyes flicked over me, took in my raven-black hair; my dark brown eyes; my unmade-up mouth; my slender neck; my body hidden beneath a plain red shirt and straight-leg black trousers. His eyes hardened with distaste. Clearly he wasn't impressed with what he saw.

'Sit down,' he ordered.

'Why, is this going to take long?' I replied, matching his hostile tone.

He smiled suddenly. 'Please, Kamryn,' he said warmly, as he indicated to the seat opposite his desk, 'take a seat.' *It's too late for the charm now. I saw the revulsion in your eyes, I know what you think of me.*

'I'd rather stand,' I said, returning his charming smile with one that was a hundred per cent fake. 'I've got a lot of work to do.'

My reply wiped a layer of shine off his glossy smile. He studied me for a moment. 'What are you doing tonight?' he asked.

'Sorry?' *Is he asking me out?* Had I read him wrong? Had that expression really been his way of covering up his attraction to me?

'I've been having dinner with all the heads of departments to pick their brains about what they think of the marketing of Angeles, see if they have any ideas on how we can improve things. You're the last on my list . . . Of the marketing department. So I thought, if you're not busy tonight, we could get it out of the way.'

I was impressed at the number of insults he'd managed to cram into that minuscule monologue.

1. 'Last on my list.' *Just in case I doubted that I would be last on every one of his lists.*
2. 'If you're not busy tonight.' *Of course, I was bound to be dateless and friendless on a Friday night.*
3. 'Get it out of the way.' *I was like a smear test to him: unpleasant but necessary.*

'Dinner tonight should be fine,' I said, through my fake smile.

'I'll meet you in the foyer at six-thirty,' he said.

I arrived in the foyer at six thirty-two, according to the huge clock that sat above the receptionist's area. Luke was there, all six foot two inches of him, wearing a beige mac over his trendy clothes. When I emerged from the lift he looked at his watch before shooting me another of his fake smiles—anyone would think I was a couple of hours late.

'I'm not late, am I,' I stated as I halted in front of him.

'Just a couple of minutes,' he replied curtly. 'I've booked us a table at a restaurant around the corner for—' he paused to look at his Rolex—'seven minutes' time. We'd better hurry if we don't want to be even more late.'

After handing our coats to the maître d', Luke and I were seated at a table for two in the centre of the crowded restaurant. When the waiter arrived, to Luke's credit, he requested a pricey bottle of red wine. To his detriment, he didn't ask me if I wanted wine, let alone the colour I might prefer. I hated red wine, so asked for water instead. We ordered, gave our menus to the waiter and then sat back.

'So, Kamryn, tell me about yourself,' Luke said.

'What do you want to know?' I asked, keeping my line of sight focused on the stem of my glass to avoid meeting his eye. Every time I glanced at him I saw the naked disgust on his face. Something about me repulsed him. I wasn't sure why he'd taken against me, particularly when he had the job and I didn't, but he made no effort to hide his dislike of me.

'Anything you want to tell me.'

'All right, I'm thirty-two. I've worked for Angeles for seven years now. I set up *Living Angeles* with Ted. It actually came from my idea, but I don't like to brag. I love my work and I'm sad that Ted has gone.'

Mr Wiseman's left eyebrow slowly arched. 'I meant, tell me about you,' he said patronisingly. 'Your life. Not your work. Are you married? In a long-term relationship? Do you have kids?'

I'm supposed to know that's what you meant, am I? I thought. 'No, I'm not married,' I replied sarcastically, 'I don't have a boyfriend and I don't have— JESUS CHRIST!' I leapt up, knocking the chair over. I grabbed my bag, then ran out of the restaurant, not bothering to say another word to Luke. Tegan. I'd forgotten her. I'd actually forgotten her.

I ran out onto the pavement while one hand ferreted about in my bag for my mobile. I pressed the 'on' button and nothing happened. The battery was flat, obviously why the school hadn't called me.

What will they do with her? Will they leave her on the pavement until someone arrives? She'd be sat there, waiting, thinking I'd forgotten her. Which I had. I was choking on my guilt. *How? How could I forget?*

I spotted a yellow taxi light on top of a car and almost threw myself under the wheels as I bellowed, 'TAXI!' He screeched to a halt in front of me and I leapt into the back seat telling him where to go. I added, 'And I'll pay you double if you get me there in under fifteen minutes.'

The imposing red-brick building of the school was deserted when we arrived. Fear squeezed my heart. I ran to the school gates and tentatively pushed one, found it was unlocked. I sprinted the short distance to the big blue door and with a gentle push that opened too.

'Tegan?' I called. My voice echoed down the emptiness and I had another clutch of fear. *What if she isn't there? What if someone took her?*

Her blonde head poked out of a classroom at the end of the corridor. Her face lit up as she saw me, then the smile evaporated and her face slunk into sullen disappointment. I ran to her, threw myself to my knees and then scooped her up. 'I'm sorry,' I said into her hair. 'I'm so, so sorry.' Tegan stayed silent and motionless in my embrace.

Maya, the teaching assistant, emerged from the classroom. 'She thought something had happened to you,' Maya explained. 'Especially when we couldn't get you on your mobile.'

'The battery's flat. I'm so sorry. I got caught up at work. I'm sorry. It won't happen again. I didn't realise the time until it was really late.'

Maya bobbed down to our height, stroked Tegan's hair. 'We were all right weren't we, Tegan? We drew some pictures.'

'I'm sorry I've taken up your time as well,' I said to Maya.

'These things happen,' Maya replied, adding with her tone: *But it'd better not happen again.*

'OK, Tiga, come on, let's go home.' I gazed into her five-year-old face, her eyes strained with sadness and fear. I'd done that. Made her think she'd been abandoned. 'I promise I won't do this to you ever again.'

Silence like that day I took her from Guildford. She was scared of me again. Wondered if I would let her down, especially after she'd made me double promise for ever and ever that I would come back every evening. Tegan wasn't sure if I'd be there when she needed me. Nor if this part of her life was going to unravel like the life she had with her mum—and all because I wasn't used to letting anyone know what my plans were. That had to change because this couldn't happen again.

'I am sorry, all right?' I said to Tegan, as I shook cornflakes into a white bowl and placed it in front of her. She said nothing, simply stared at her breakfast and waited for me to splash on milk. She was five and already an expert at the cold shoulder. 'Look,' I pulled up a chair beside her. 'It won't happen again—I promise. I . . . I'm sorry. You see, there's this nasty man at my work called Luke. He's my new boss.' Tegan spooned orange-yellow flakes into her mouth. 'I had to go for dinner with him and he's awful. So arrogant. He's horrible.'

'Like a monster?' she asked, finally acknowledging me. I was obviously speaking her language.

'Yeah, exactly like a monster.'

'Oh,' she said and nodded with some sympathy for my predicament.

A knock at the front door made us both jump. We looked at each other, wondering who it could be. The person knocked again and I hurried to answer it. Luke, tall and imposing, stood outside my flat. He'd poured himself into a pair of loose-fitting blue jeans and a white T-shirt that skimmed over his muscular chest. His D&G sunglasses were hooked into the neck of his T-shirt.

'Luke! Oh f-f-damn!' I'd all but forgotten that I left him sitting in a restaurant having ordered an expensive meal.

'Yep, that's the effect I like to have on a woman—especially one who enjoyed my company so much she ran out of a restaurant.' In his arms he carried what looked very much like my red mac.

Before I could start to explain, Tegan appeared beside me, linked her arms around my right thigh and stared up at Luke.

'Who's this?' Luke asked, crouching down to Tegan's height.

'This is Tegan,' I replied. 'Tegan, this is Luke from my work.'

Luke smiled, a genuine smile that moved his eyes into friendliness, one that was yet to be aimed at me. Tegan had that effect on adults. 'Pleased to meet you, Tegan.'

Tegan blinked back at him, then turned her head up to me. 'He doesn't look like a monster, Mummy Ryn,' she informed me. Luke turned his face up to me too and raised a questioning eyebrow; I glanced away.

'I just wanted to check you were OK,' Luke said. 'Your mobile was off, so I asked your friend Betsy for your address. I hope you don't mind. Oh, and I thought I'd return this.'

I relieved him of the red rain mac. 'Thanks, and yes, we're fine.'

'We're going to the zoo,' Tegan piped up, her eyes fixed on Luke.

'Are you?' Luke asked her.

'Yeah, are we?' I said.

'You said we could go to the zoo,' Tegan accused.

'Yes, sometime. Not today.'

'I'll leave you to it, then,' Luke said.

'Mummy Ryn,' Tegan said, 'Luke can drive us to the zoo in his car.'

'No he can't,' I replied quickly.

'Why can't I?' Luke asked indignantly.

'You might not even have a car.'

'How do you think I got here?'

'I'm sure you've got better things to do on a Saturday.'

'Nothing that can't wait.'

I had to do this, didn't I? I had to let her have her way on this because I'd terrified her last night. It was the least I could do. 'Thanks, Luke, a lift to the zoo would be great,' I managed through gritted teeth.

As expected of a sunny Saturday during the summer holidays the zoo, which was about fifteen minutes outside of York, had hordes of people flocking towards it—and it wasn't even midday when Luke pulled up into the overflow car park.

Tegan had done most of the talking during the ninety-minute drive, asking Luke questions about the zoo. I was silent in the front seat, trying not to slump into a sulk at having to spend the day with this idiot.

Fluffy pink candy floss was installed in Tegan's hand and she flitted away into a world of her own, staring at the creatures behind glass and high fences.

'I take it she's the reason you left last night,' Luke murmured.

'Yup,' I replied.

He checked Tegan wasn't listening, whispered, 'You forgot her?'

I nodded and he jerked in disgust. 'I take it you haven't been doing this very long.'

I looked him squarely in the face, I'd already been shamed by a five-year-old, he couldn't make me feel any worse. 'You take right,' I said.

He returned my gaze, steady and straight. With the sounds of animals as a backdrop, our mutual dislike grew. A few more hours and this feeling between us would blossom into full-on hatred.

'Mummy Ryn,' Tegan said, tugging on my hand, forcing me to break the confrontational eyelock with Luke, 'can we go see the monkeys?'

'Absolutely,' I replied.

We set off for the monkey enclosure on the far side of the zoo.

'About work,' Luke said as we walked. 'Do you mind if we talk now seeing as our conversation was cut short last night?'

'Course not,' I mumbled. Actually, I did mind. This was Tegan time, but I couldn't say that. I had to prove to my new boss that a child hadn't slowed me down, that I was efficient and capable.

'You and Ted had a very close working relationship . . .' Luke stopped, allowing the statement to hang in the air, a big black stain of accusation I was expected to be desperate to scrub away.

'Yes, we did,' I replied without shame.

'I see.' My reply had, apparently, confirmed his suspicions.

'Of course, most people thought we were at it at every given opportunity,' I whispered so Tegan wouldn't hear.

'I never accused you of anything,' Luke defended himself. 'I'm simply concerned that the marketing department won't work as well now that Ted has gone.'

'You mean you'd heard the snide remarks about how Ted carried me in this position then presumed I'd done the deed to get my job.'

We stopped at the chimpanzee enclosure and Tegan's eyes almost doubled in size. 'Monkeys,' she breathed.

'With you being head of marketing, I'd have expected that you'd go out of your way to get on with your second-in-command, not judge them before you've even met them,' I said in hushed tones.

'If you'd been around to meet maybe I wouldn't have had to rely on gossip about your morals to make my assessment,' he hissed back.

'Yeah, you're right,' I admitted. He *was* right, but I wasn't going to use Adele as a sick note. 'You want to know the worst part about the rumours? Ted is, and always has been, devoted to his wife,' I went on. I gave Luke a long up and down look. 'He's a decent man.'

Luke tried to force me into another eyelock. Ignoring him, I crouched down beside Tegan. 'A baby monkey.' Tegan pointed. I followed her finger to where a female chimp cradled a baby chimp in her arms. 'That's her mummy, isn't it?' she said.

'Yes, sweetheart,' I replied. Everything started closing in on me. I was drowning, being submerged in a reminder of my best friend and what had happened to her. That she was gone.

'Her mummy hasn't gone to heaven to be with Jesus and the angels, has she?' Tegan murmured, her voice low and matter-of-fact.

'No, sweetie, she hasn't.'

The diminutive blonde inhaled. Her eyes glazed over as though she was calculating something. I wished she would talk to me, tell me what she was feeling. The intense agony of being suffocated by the reminder of Adele's death I'd just felt was probably nothing compared with what she felt. I wanted her to tell me, to let me know how she felt.

'Can we see the snakes?' Tegan asked, coming out of her reverie.

'OK,' I said, standing up.

'I'll get the ice creams,' Luke said.

'Mummy Ryn wants chocolate ice cream,' Tegan told him. 'She likes chocolate.'

Luke gave me a derogatory once-over. 'Yeah, I can see that.'

'Right, so, Kingdom of the Snakes,' I said. 'Go on then, Luke, take us to your leader.'

We spent most of the day like that, Tegan dictating the order in which we saw the animals, Luke and I discussing work in hushed tones and taking every opportunity to snipe at each other. Tegan was happy, oblivious to the atmosphere between her two accompanying adults.

In the car back to Leeds Tegan came up with the idea of a picnic in the park. It was late afternoon and she was too buoyed up simply to go home. 'How about we save the picnic for another time, sweetie?' I replied. 'We'll have a mini one when we get home.'

'O-OK,' she replied, disappointment in her voice. 'Can Luke come?'

'If he wants to,' I replied, knowing he would. Knowing it'd be too much to hope for him to slink away.

'Do you want to come to our picnic at home?' Tegan asked.

Luke's eyes flicked to the rearview mirror, and his face once again lit up. 'That would be lovely, thank you, Tegan,' he said.

I let us in to our flat and Tegan led Luke into the kitchen area. I busied myself making the picnic while Tegan and Luke sat at the dining table. They made a hundred-piece jigsaw, and then Tegan got out her papers and pens and pencils and they drew pictures of the animals we'd seen. In the depth of their playing, the picnic was forgotten. I left the sandwiches, salad and pop beside them on the table and flopped onto the sofa to watch television. Luke was taking this seriously. Had thrown himself into playing with Tegan with the same intensity he would devising a new marketing strategy for Angeles. Had it been anyone else, his interest would have been endearing, but because it was him, I decided it was nice that Tegan had someone her own mental age to play with.

The second the clock hit eight o'clock I flicked off the television, stood up and announced, 'OK, Tiga, bedtime.'

'Do I have to?' Tegan whined before letting out a huge yawn.

'You can hardly keep your eyes open. Come on, bed.' I turned to Luke. 'You'll have to go, Tegan really does have to go to bed.'

'OK,' Luke said, putting down his red pen and standing up.

'Will you come back tomorrow?' Tegan asked Luke.

'If I'm allowed to,' Luke replied.

'You have to ask Mummy Ryn if you can come back tomorrow,' Tegan informed him. Her mouth opened, gaping into a yawn. 'She won't get cross. Mummy Ryn never gets cross, not even when I painted on the wall.'

'Is it OK if I come back tomorrow?' Luke asked.

'If you've really got nothing better to do,' I replied.

'Nothing that can't wait,' he confirmed.

Don't do us any favours, eh, mate? I thought. 'Right, that's settled. Bye then, Luke.' I moved to Tiga and picked her up from the chair.

Reluctantly, Luke moved towards the door. 'Bye, Tegan,' he said.

'Bye-bye,' she whispered. 'See you tomorrow.'

As the door shut behind Luke, I placed Tegan on her bed, tugged off her clothes and replaced them with her gingham pyjamas. 'Na-night,' I said.

'Na-night,' she whispered. 'You don't like Luke.'

Maybe she hadn't been as oblivious to our animosity as I'd thought. 'He's all right,' I said.

'I like him,' she stated. 'Can he be my friend?'

If he must, I wanted to say. Instead, I held my tongue. Waited and waited . . . Soon her chest was moving slowly up and down in sleep.

We'd had fun today. Despite Luke, we'd had the first bit of fun since Adele left us. I thought again of Luke. Tall, handsome and incredibly charming—to Tegan. I had to admit, she'd had fun *because* of Luke. Tegan had taken to him instantly. Maybe there was good in him; somewhere beneath his arrogance and his dislike of me there could be a decent person. One I could warm to. If Tegan liked him, then maybe I could too.

I awoke and the house was shrouded in middle-of-the-night silence. I blinked, groggy and exhausted, confused about where I was. My face was damp, I realised. I'd been crying in my sleep. Again.

I sat bolt upright. Tegan. Was the house so quiet because something had happened to her? I went to Tegan's bedroom door. Carefully, I pushed it open. She was all right. Still here.

Being a parent was exhausting. How anyone with a child closed their eyes at night and went to sleep when the world was beset with danger, I didn't know. I staggered to the bathroom at the end of the hall, and rinsed my face in cold water. As I straightened up, I caught my reflection. My face was clean but I could still feel the slick of tears on my cheeks, a residue of the pain that had leaked out when I was asleep.

The sleep crying had to stop. It was no good for my eyes, no good for my skin. No good for my mind because I woke up more exhausted than when I went to sleep. Sleep crying came, of course, from not being able to control myself. Once I entered dreamland, I couldn't ignore the guilt that shadowed my every thought. I'd let Adele die with unresolved issues between us. Anguish wrenched through me whenever I thought that Adele's last moments on earth might have been filled with her wishing I'd let her explain. It ached physically to think that when she asked Nancy to tell me goodbye that for a flicker of a moment she wondered if I still hated her. If I still blamed her.

The thought was so unbearable I had to shove it aside and bury it in thoughts of work and making our money go further. Anything to avoid the gut-wrenching, big-dipper feeling that I had wronged my best friend.

Even if I couldn't forgive her, I could at least have let her explain. Because I'd never believed she was in love with Nate when she slept with him. Nor that she even fancied him. *I did a bad thing in not giving Adele a chance to explain.* I stopped looking at myself in the mirror, couldn't gaze at the face of someone so awful any longer. *I am a bad person.*

'**S**o, this is where all the cool kids hang out,' Luke commented as he reclined on my picnic blanket. The last Saturday of the summer holidays, a few select members of Tegan's playgroup had a picnic in Horsforth park. They played rounders, ate food, drank pop. I'd basked in the reflected glory of Tegan's popularity. I'd never been part of the cool or popular anything, but Tiga was. The other children—Crystal, Matilda and Ingrid—were the core gang, and with their brothers and sisters, we ended up with nearly twenty children. My basking had lasted right up until she demanded Luke's number to invite him.

'Do we have to?' I'd whined.

'Yes, he'll really like it,' she'd replied. He had, of course, accepted and said he would bring the food. It looked like he'd picked up his local Tesco and emptied several varieties of sandwiches, dips, crisps, sausages and biscuits into a picnic hamper. It was sufficient for everyone at the picnic with enough left over for dinner for the rest of the week.

Despite that, it hadn't made me like him. There was very little my boss could do to endear himself to me. The feeling was mutual. Relations between us had declined in direct proportion to the amount of time we spent together. 'I've never seen two people who dislike each other as much as you two,' Betsy commented after a meeting with Luke.

'It's not my imagination then, it is a two-way thing?' I asked.

'Too right! He's perfectly pleasant to the rest of us . . . Why does he hate you so much?'

'He thinks I look like a dog,' I replied. My stomach flipped as I voiced this thought. I'd always known it, the look in his eyes the first time we met had told me so, but I hadn't named it. Now I had, I couldn't deny it. His sole reason for not liking me was he thought I was ugly.

The worst part was, I couldn't leave him at work, because Tegan kept asking him to come back. Three Saturdays and two Sundays in a row he'd dropped by to play with Tegan. I suspected he'd started visiting because he wanted to check I was treating Tegan properly, but now he just liked coming over to see her. Tegan hadn't been this taken with anyone for as long as I could remember so I found it impossible to turn him away. I had grown to respect his friendship with my five-year-old. There was nothing about him that suggested he had an ulterior motive for hanging around, and while I didn't leave them alone together, it was mainly because there weren't too many places to go in my flat, not because I feared what he would do. Despite how much he disliked me, I could glean that Luke was one of the good guys.

I lay back on the tartan blanket, my head up so I could see the kids running around.

'Why does Tegan call you Mummy Ryn?' Luke asked.

I refocused on him. 'Because I am. I didn't give birth to her but she thinks of me as her mother.'

'I meant the Ryn part. Why Ryn and not Kamryn or even Kam?'

'When Tegan was tiny, people often called me Kam. I was always correcting them, saying, "Ryn. My name is Kam*ryn*." Tegan thought my name was Ryn because she heard me say it so many times.'

'That's a good story,' Luke said, he even managed a small, genuine smile. 'What do her friends call you?'

'I don't know, "That Weird Lady Who Lives With Tegan"?'

Luke's face creased up as he laughed out loud, which made me laugh. We both laughed while looking at each other. Maybe he wasn't so bad. 'You know, you should smile more often,' he mused. 'Your smile suits you. And if you lost a bit of weight . . .'

My expression hardened as my grin evaporated. I jerked myself upright, raised my knees, hunching forwards, trying to hide my frame. I stared down at the blanket, my face hot with embarrassment, my eyes burning with a desperation to start crying. He thought I was fat as well as ugly. But I didn't understand why it hurt when this man said those things. I'd heard them all my life: and I'd white noised them. But this man could hurt me. Was it because no one had been so blatant about disliking me in years?

'I didn't mean that the way it sounded,' he justified, not recanting it: he might not have meant it the way it sounded, but he still meant it.

I hid my face and my hurt from him. I wasn't going down this road again. It'd taken years for me to build up some confidence, to believe I was worth something, I didn't need to let this man do this to me.

Trying to blank him from my mind, I glanced up, just as a yellow tennis ball whizzed through the air towards us. Luke jumped up to his feet and sped off across the grass to join the game. Once he was gone I relaxed. He had that effect on me, every time I was with him I was on edge, waiting for the next insult, for the next look. I lay down on my side, propped up on one elbow, watching Tiga. Every few minutes she would take her eyes off the game and seek me out. As we made eye contact a toothy smile would spread across her face, she'd lift her right hand, wave it briskly at me, wait for me to wave back and then return to the game.

There might be better ways to spend a Saturday, but at that moment I couldn't think of a single one.

We've got a long walk home, I thought once the game had broken up. Tegan looked as if she was going to fall asleep where she was kneeling, helping me to pack up the leftover food. Luke had headed off in the direction of the park's loos when the game had finished, and I was eager to leave before he returned.

'Excuse me, Mrs Brannon?' a female voice said from somewhere above us. Tiga and I both glanced upwards.

Beside us stood one of the mothers from the picnic, one of the people I often saw when I arrived at the school to collect Tiga. I got to my feet, brushing bits of grass and dried dirt off my hands. 'I'm not Mrs Brannon. I'm Ms Matika—Kamryn Matika. Tegan's guardian.'

'I see,' she replied, although lines of confusion crisscrossed her eyes.

'It's complicated,' I said. 'And you are?'

'Mrs Kaye, Della Kaye.' She paused. 'I was wondering . . . You see, Matilda—I'm her mother by the way—she keeps asking if Tegan can come to her house, I mean, our house.'

'Of course,' I said, then realised I'd been hasty. Who was this woman? Where was their house? 'I mean, Tegan's never mentioned . . .'

'I know you're really busy at your work,' Tegan deflected.

'I wouldn't mind you going to your friend's house,' I said. 'You can go any time you want.' I turned to Mrs Kaye. 'When would be convenient?'

'I was thinking,' Mrs Kaye began, 'what if I take Tegan when I pick up the girls and she stays with us for a couple of hours every afternoon until you come home from work? It'll be easier for you when school starts again next week and the kids have to be picked up by four o'clock.'

'Erm,' I replied, hijacked by the kindness of the offer.

'Really, it's no problem. We'd love to have Tegan over.'

'And you wouldn't mind?'

'I look after six children already, one more won't make a difference.'

Tegan was looking fearful, maybe she didn't want to go to Matilda's house, which was the real reason she didn't mention it. 'How about I talk it over with Tegan and then get back to you?'

Mrs Kaye seemed pleased with this, then after giving me their phone number and saying her goodbyes, she walked away.

As I watched her leave, a heavy, lead feeling filled my mouth. Why hadn't Tegan asked me this? I unfolded the blanket, sat down then patted the area of wool beside me. 'Let's sit and talk a minute,' I said. 'Tiga, you know you can tell me anything, don't you? I don't mind if you want to go to your friends' houses for a few hours after school. You just have to tell me and we'll arrange it.'

'But I know you're busy,' she said in a small voice.

'That doesn't matter . . .' My voice trailed off as I realised that she'd probably missed out on more than a few birthday parties because she hadn't told me about them. 'I'm not cross,' I clarified. 'Not even a little.'

Her shoulders fell suddenly as she relaxed.

'Do you want to go to Matilda's house after school, then?' I asked. It would save us a lot of money on the after-school club if she did.

'Would I be 'lowed?' she asked.

'Yes, sweetheart, as long as you want to.'

'OK, I want to go.'

I grinned at her. More than anything I wanted her to have a friend apart from me. And not just Luke. A child as gregarious as Tegan needed people outside of our little unit, even I could see that.

'Good, I'm glad,' I said. 'And I'll make sure Mrs Kaye knows that you have to ring me every day at four-thirty.' This was our agreement since the incident where I forgot her. Every day she rang me to find out what time I was going to pick her up. In other words, to make sure I never forgot again.

'Right, come on,' I said, moving to the picnic basket. 'Let's get packed away before Luke reappears.'

'Can Luke come to my house for his dinner?' she asked.

'If he wants,' I replied.

'I'm sure he will,' Tegan said firmly. She exhibited an unusual bold-ness where Luke was concerned, she wouldn't ask me if it was all right to go to a friend's house, but with Luke coming to dinner, no hesitation.

'Like I say, we'll see if he wants to.'

'You'll see if who wants to what?' Luke asked, causing my heart to lurch. I looked at him. Even after rounders he looked immaculately turned out, his shorts without so much as a hint of a grass stain. His legs, covered in light brown hairs, had tanned a little in the summer sun.

'Erm, we were wondering if you wanted to come for dinner?'

Luke's face lit up in uncensored delight and I got a glimpse of what he must have looked like as a child when given the Christmas present he'd begged for. What happened, I wondered, to turn that delight-filled boy into this abundantly arrogant man?

'That'd be great!' he proclaimed.

Since my return to work, I'd noticed that the office I shared with Betsy had become a drop-in centre for the other women who worked in the non-retail departments. I think it had started while I was away, people coming by to keep Betsy company, and it hadn't stopped. Especially when they realised that my work-machine days were behind me. I had changed. I did a good job—I'd soon be out on my ear if I didn't, Luke would see to that—I simply didn't become involved in work. Not like I used to. The marketing director's job going to Luke was only part of it. The main part, the other ninety per cent, was a feeling of futility. I knew it was connected to Adele, but I hadn't allowed myself to examine it.

'The thing is,' Betsy was saying on the Monday after Tegan's school picnic, 'I think I could fall in love with him.' She was talking about a man she had met a week earlier. She'd just shown Ruby from the accounts department, one of our most frequent visitors, a text from this man. 'I think he might be The One. He's so gorgeous.'

A memory stung my chest as I watched Betsy. Adele had said that more than once, with that same expression on her face.

'Oh please, you always say that,' Ruby dismissed.

'I do not!' Betsy protested. She stuck out her lower lip in a huff.

'Oh bless you,' I said with a smile. 'I do know what you're talking about. But looks aren't everything,' I paused for effect. 'Agility and imagination in the sack are.'

'Glad to see you're using company time to discuss important market-ing issues, Kamryn,' Luke's deep voice stated. None of us had heard him approach our office, nor enter, because he hadn't bothered to knock.

My stomach spiked with ice as I looked at the vision in charcoal grey in our office doorway. The first time I step out of my work persona within the walls of Angeles and he, of course, was around to witness it. This would become another piece of evidence that I was the unprofes-sional, unsuitable underling that he had to get rid of.

Ruby scuttled out of the office without uttering another word; Betsy sat frozen, staring at me. 'Betsy, would you mind giving Kamryn and me a moment alone, please?' Luke said, firing her a smile of pure charm.

Reluctantly, Betsy exited. Luke entered the spacious office and stood beside my desk, effectively towering over me. As usual, his eyes flicked over me in an unimpressed manner, and I immediately felt dishevelled: my black hair wild; my black trousers unflattering; my body lumpen and unappealing. Luke had the effect of making me feel unkempt and unattractive; being with him reminded me of being at school, hearing all those things they used to say about me all over again.

'Yes?' I asked, straightening up to exude confidence.

'Look, Kamryn,' he began, 'we got off to a bad start.'

I paused, peered at him in surprise, 'Pardon?'

'I said, we got off to a bad start.'

'Yes, I suppose we did,' I replied, wondering when the bollocking would begin.

'We've got to work together and see each other outside of work because Tegan likes me being around.'

I contemplated him in cautious silence.

'After Saturday . . . With the dinner invite . . . I was so incredibly touched. And I got to thinking about all this and how stupid it is. And I hoped we could work out our problems; see if we can find a way to get on.' I must have looked sceptical because he said, 'All right, maybe not get on but not wind each other up.'

'OK,' I replied.

'Right then.' He paused. 'I'm sorry for acting as though you couldn't do your job. I'd just heard so much about you that I thought you'd be this dynamic, pretty young thing who was eager to please. Instead . . .' his voice trailed away and he grimaced slightly, as though he couldn't believe he'd begun to expose his uncensored thoughts again.

'Oh, please, don't stop now, I want to hear it all. "Instead . . ."?'

'Instead, you turned up and you seemed kind of scatty. Not what I expected at all. So, sorry, I shouldn't have judged you like that.'

I said nothing.

'And I'm sorry, also, for listening to those ridiculous rumours about you and Ted. That's not the way I usually work.'

'Thank you for saying all that, it's very gracious of you. And I want to apologise for calling you a small-minded, tiny-dicked, arrogant wanker who got his job by licking arse rather than by hard graft,' I replied, even though my heart wasn't in it. What Luke had said had hurt and I was disgusted with myself for letting it needle me.

'You never called me that,' he pointed out.

'Oh, I did. In my head. In fact . . . Sorry, I just did it again.'

Luke's expression softened a little, a sliver of amusement danced around his lips. 'So, we wipe the slate clean and start again?' he said.

'Yup, I believe that is what we have agreed.'

Luke smiled, not a charming one but not a caustic one, either. 'I do mean it, you know.'

I returned his smile. 'Me too.'

When I returned from a meeting with the head of the children's department later that day, I found a Twix bar on my desk with the note: *Tegan said you like chocolate, Luke.*

Chapter Six

LIGHT FLOODED MY SENSES as I opened my eyes a fraction. I had to snap them shut again immediately. It was too painful. My mouth and my head and my eyes all felt swollen and tender. I had the beginnings of a migraine; I could still think, so I wasn't in the grip of a proper one—yet.

I didn't have time for a migraine. I had a child to prepare for school; I had to get ready for work. The fist around my temple tightened.

Maybe Mrs Kaye would come over to take Tegan to school? I wondered before dismissing the idea. She had six children to sort out, she couldn't take on another at such short notice.

I gasped as the fist clamped tighter around my head.

Or maybe Luke? He'd come and take Tiga to school—he'd do anything for her. And for me too, it seemed.

He'd been true to his word about starting again and in the two weeks since the picnic hadn't snapped at me or dismissed any of my ideas out of hand. He'd also suggested we have daily meetings in his office to discuss our revamped marketing strategy. I felt involved again, and the feelings of futility eased. Luke and I weren't friends or anything, just colleagues. He had started to accept that I really did know my job and that if I'd been given the chance to apply, I would have been a serious contender for his position. The times we saw each other outside of work we did actually speak about non-work things. In the spirit of our newly negotiated peace I was sure if I picked up the phone he'd be straight over to take Tegan to school. All I had to do was pick up the phone.

Time passed. And I still couldn't move. The alarm went off and I didn't even have the energy to shut it off. I must have fallen asleep again because the next thing I knew, Tegan was stood by my bed.

'Mummy Ryn, it's time for us to get up,' she sing-songed.

'I- I can't,' I replied. 'I'm not feeling well,' I managed.

'You're sick?' she asked.

'Yes, Tiga, I'm sick. I'm sorry.'

Her eyes doubled in size and she turned and fled. Even though I could barely lift my eyelids, I had to find out what was wrong.

Summoning all my strength I gripped the edge of my sheet and pulled it back. That small movement sent spikes of pain shooting behind my eyes. I had to rest for a few seconds before I stood up, and had to hold onto the bedside table to steady myself.

I grabbed on to the wall and moved across my bedroom, keeping myself upright by holding onto the wall with the flats of my hands. I headed along the corridor, which was mercifully straight. I held on to the cupboard fronts as Tegan's bedroom, my target, loomed into view. One more step, one more step. I launched myself away from the wall and made it—I was finally standing in Tegan's doorway.

She was sitting cross-legged on her bed, rocking back and forth, her face contorted with the pain of unshed tears.

'Tegan, what's the matter?' I said, leaning against her door frame.

'You're ill and you're going to heaven to be with Jesus and the angels.'

'What?' I asked.

'You're going to heaven like my mummy,' she accused.

'Tiga, I'm not, it's only a migraine, a headache, it will go away. It w—' My words were cut short by a knocking at the door, which caused agony to explode in my head. I couldn't ignore it; if it sounded again, it would probably finish me off. 'Hello,' I said through the wood.

'It's Luke,' the voice said.

What's he doing here at the crack of dawn? I let him in.

He was wearing the same blue shirt, navy blue tie and black suit he'd been wearing at work yesterday. He was brandishing a smug grin and a twinkle in his eye. 'Hi, I was seeing someone in the area and thought you might like a lift to school and wor— Jeez, you look awful,' he said. 'Kamryn?' His voice sounded as though he was whispering at me from the end of a long tunnel. 'Are you going—'

More pain exploded in my brain, and the world was suddenly an array of pulsing pink lights. Then everything was white.

Slowly, I prised open my eyes, and didn't instantly snap them shut. The light didn't puncture my head with stars of agony like it did earlier. Something cool and damp lay across my forehead: a flannel.

'Ahhh, you're awake.' Beside my bed, Luke sat on one of the kitchen chairs, a book in his hands. He examined me with concerned eyes.

'Where's Tegan?' I croaked.

He indicated to the space on the bed beside me. I turned my head: she was curled up like a cat in the depths of sleep.

'She didn't want to leave you.'

'I passed out?'

Luke nodded. 'When you keeled over she was hysterical. She started screaming about you going to heaven like her mum. She refused to go to school, said if she left you would go to heaven without her.'

I stared down at her, watching her troubled little face as it slept. Suddenly her eyes flew open. She sat up. 'Are you better?' she asked.

'A little bit,' I replied, trying to make my voice sound normal.

'Hey, T, why don't you go get Kamryn a drink from the kitchen? I've put one on the table,' Luke said. To me he added, 'T said you had a migraine so I rang the doctor and she said you should get lots of fluids.'

The second she disappeared, Luke threw himself forwards in his seat. 'I take it Tegan's mother died recently?' he said in lowered tones.

I nodded.

'How recently?'

'Very.'

'Kamryn, you can talk to me.'

We had ceased hostilities, we had pleasant conversations and, at some point, he and I could become real friends, but right now he was getting nothing out of me.

Tegan returned to the room, holding a glass in both hands, walking slowly and carefully so as not to spill any of the contents. I took the glass, lowered my head, drank. 'Thank you,' I said.

'Are you going to be better?' she asked, rocking from one foot to another, twisting her petite hands together. It never occurred to me that she would make the connection between my illness and death. That she'd think I'd go the same way as her mother. But why wouldn't she?

'I'll be better in no time,' I said. Tegan twisted her mouth to one side, and regarded me with suspicion—convinced she was not. Tegan needed someone she could rely on, I realised as I watched her reaction to my reply. Someone who'd be there when I wasn't.

'I'm going to be fine,' I reassured Tegan, reaching out my free hand to her. She slipped her small hand into mine and I was transported back to the day of the funeral. The day I held her hand in mine, suddenly frightened at this new responsibility. I had to ensure she reached adulthood, that she was happy and healthy and intellectually stretched as she made that journey. Single parents were constantly being held up as pariahs in society, but they should be hailed as heroes—bringing up children on your own without falling apart was a miracle to me. I'd only been doing it for a couple of months and I was struggling. Much as it grated my self-sufficient mind to admit it, I needed someone.

Luke patted his legs. 'Jump up, T, and we can read to Kamryn before she goes back to sleep.' He started reading, encouraging Tegan to follow the words with her finger. I closed my eyes.

When I awoke again Luke was still sitting by my bed, reading. 'Hi,' he said. I moved my arm but Tegan wasn't beside me.

'I convinced her to go watch telly,' he said.

The spikes of pain were blunted now, only a dull throb signalled my earlier torture. 'Thanks, Luke. Thanks for everything.'

He leaned forwards, picked up the glass of water and handed it to me. 'I called Tegan's school earlier, explained the situation, and I told work we wouldn't be in for a couple of days. You're sick, obviously, so I'll work from home.'

'Why?'

'It's clear that you need someone to take care of you both.'

'I don't *need* anyone,' I snapped.

Luke gripped his lips together rather than rise to my anger. 'Well, I thought I'd stick around if that's all right.'

'Everyone at work's going to think we're shagging now.' I pulled the covers up to my neck, I was braless in a white T-shirt in front of a man who had issues with my body.

Luke glanced down, embarrassed. Something occurred to me. He lived in Alwoodley, so for him to be in Horsforth meant he was travelling in the wrong direction for work. 'Why were you in the area again?'

'I, erm, was visiting someone.' We made eye contact and I knew exactly what he meant.

'Blonde or brunette?'

'Blonde. Pretty. Amazing body. Not afraid to use it.'

'Good for you.'

'I think we should talk. Kamryn, I'm well aware I've been a pig to you, but you haven't been the easiest person to get along with. And now I'm beginning to understand why—you're grieving.'

I stopped looking at him, stared at my off television.

'I don't pretend to understand any of what you're going through, but I do know that bottling it up isn't good for you or for Tegan.' That touched a nerve—was I hurting Tegan by not being honest about my emotions? 'Seriously, Kamryn, you can talk to me. It'll go no further.' He paused; I said nothing.

'OK,' he said with a sigh. 'I was engaged to be married. I met her at Harvard. I've travelled a lot so we've been together on and off for ten years—whenever I returned to New York we got back together. This last time we were together for three years.' Luke reached into his inside pocket, pulled out his wallet and showed me her picture. Long blonde hair, immaculate skin, shaped eyebrows, soft pink lips. She was stunningly beautiful. 'Her name is Nicole and we'd actually set a date for the wedding. Then I was offered a job in London. I assumed she'd want to come with me but she said no. When I decided to turn the job down she told me not to because London wasn't the issue, her feelings for me were. She wasn't sure it would work out between us. So, I came alone. We speak every week and I still carry her picture, and . . .' He stared at the carpet for a few seconds. Then he raised his eyes. 'And I cling to the hope she'll change her mind about us. There. No one else in England knows that. I'm trusting you to keep it to yourself because even eighteen months down the line it still hurts. I still want her back.'

While he'd been talking, I had to hide my horror at Luke, my boss, humanising himself right before my eyes. He had shared with me. Me. That must have taken him a lot to do. He'd done it, though, to get me to do the same. But opening up . . . It terrified me. Especially to him. But this wasn't about me, it was about Tegan. She loved this Luke man. And today proved I needed a back-up person; he was it. I stared at him for a moment, my heart racing in my chest. *This is for Tegan.* 'OK,' I began. I told him the tale. Starting with the night I found out about Adele and Nate to the moment he walked into our lives.

When I'd finished, Luke nodded his head. 'You've been struggling to cope with all this on your own?' he asked. He whistled long and low. 'I'm surprised you haven't had a complete breakdown, no wonder you've been such a prickly bitch.'

'What's your excuse for being an arrogant bastard?' I replied.

'It's my nature,' he shot back.

I smirked at that.

'If you let me, I'd like to help out.' His sincerity surprised me. Yes, his story had made him human, but this was making him a nice human.

'Why?'

'Because I like Tegan.'

'There's got to be more to it than that.'

'Maybe there is, maybe there isn't. I'll tell you about it one day.'

Luke was saved from further questioning by Tegan, who came bounding in and leapt up onto the bed. 'Are you better?' she asked.

'Much, much better. I can even get out of bed.'

Tegan slowly led me to the living room where we collapsed on the sofa together. 'While you're up, put the kettle on, Luke,' I said.

'Yeah, put the kettle on, Luke,' Tegan giggled.

'What did your last slave die of?' he mumbled.

'Answering back,' I replied.

He glanced at me over his shoulder and I managed a smile. Holding my eyes with his, he grinned back. *I could grow to like this man*, I realised.

'If you could just wait in the other room while Tegan and I have a chat.' The social worker was good. She made what she said sound as damn close to a request as you could get, but we both knew it was an order.

I moved out of the living area, which, like everything else in the flat, had been polished and wiped to within an inch of its life. After the cleaning I'd put on a pale pink silk dress, the most expensive item in my wardrobe, to impress that social worker. Tegan had bunches in her hair and was wearing her favourite outfit: an A-line blue denim dress.

In my bedroom, I sat on the bed, accepting the fact that the social worker had to find out if I was ill-treating Tegan. But then, would Tiga say anything even if I wasn't in the same room? She was funny and gregarious, but also incredibly closed. She'd never mentioned what happened in Guildford; would she admit if she was unhappy with me?

My stomach flipped a little as I wondered what the woman would ask. Would she ask leading questions, try to get things out of Tiga? Like me forgetting she existed that one time? And what about collapsing a few weeks ago and scaring the living daylights out of her? I hadn't done that on purpose either, but that didn't mean it hadn't scarred her for life. I chewed on my lower lip. What if Tegan hated being with me?

Thirty torturous minutes later, I was allowed back in. Tiga was grinning as I sat down on the sofa. She climbed into my lap and made Meg kiss me on the cheek. 'Meg loves you today,' she said, climbed off my lap and wandered out of the room. I turned my attention to the social worker. She was thirtyish, with thin lips and flat eyes. I couldn't read her.

'So, do I pass muster?' I asked.

'That wasn't the reason for my visit,' she replied.

'What was the reason for your visit, then?' Had she been instructed to steer clear of the fact that Tegan was white? There was nothing they could do about me taking care of her because it was a request in Adele's will, but they could turn down my adoption application and never say that our different colours was the real reason why.

'How are you finding all this?' she replied, avoiding my question.

'Fine,' I replied.

'It's not a strain?'

'No, not really.'

'How are you finding working full-time and taking care of Tegan?'

'Fine.'

'It must be tiring?'

'Must it?' I replied, facetiously, remembered who she was and added, 'It's fine.'

'Picking up Tegan from school isn't a problem with your hours?'

'No, she goes to a friend's after school and I pick her up from there.'

'Children often fall out, what if that happens with her friend?'

'There's an after-school club at the school. I'd have to leave work earlier to pick her up by six but then I'd just work through lunch.'

'And you wouldn't mind that?'

'Are you trying to say I should give up work or something? Because I can't afford to—and if I work part-time things would be even tighter than they are now.'

'Are you struggling financially?'

'Who isn't in this day and age?' I was becoming riled. Why was this woman determined to twist everything I said?

'Who's Luke?' she asked, changing tack.

'He's my boss,' I replied cautiously. 'He's a good guy.'

'Tegan said he was her best friend,' the social worker stated.

'They do get on . . .' *So, he's her best friend, huh?* I thought jealously.

'She also said that you never get cross with her.'

'Did she?' I replied. 'Is that bad?'

'No, simply unusual. Do you seriously never get cross with her or are you holding back?'

'Tiga's the best behaved child in the world, she hasn't done anything to make me cross with her.' I paused to consider this. 'Not ever.'

'You think she's holding back?'

'Maybe . . .' Fear spiked in me. 'I've never thought about it. She just always does what she's told. I never considered she wouldn't disagree because she's frightened of me. That's what you think, isn't it? That she's scared of me. I wouldn't hurt her, though. Not ever.'

'I didn't think for a second you would,' the social worker said. 'I just wonder if she needs counselling to help her come to terms with her mother's death.'

'That's not a thought, is it? It's an order,' I said.

'I wouldn't say that.'

'What would you say? That if I don't get her counselling, you're not going to recommend that I be allowed to adopt her?'

'Why don't you think about it?' she said, not answering my question. *Deliberately* not answering my question. *Again.* She stood. 'I'll schedule another meeting with you in a couple of months, see how the pair of you are getting on together. It was lovely to meet you both.'

Bitch! I kept thinking. She'd said, without saying it, that I wasn't taking care of Tegan properly. That we needed to bring more people—counsellors—into our lives. And that she would screw me over if I didn't comply. In my more rational moments, of course, I knew that she was only thinking of Tegan and how counselling would help her, but most of the time since that woman had left had been crammed with the urge to scream 'BITCH!'. I knew I wasn't doing brilliantly before she showed up but now I knew I was doing it all wrong. I wasn't helping Tegan to deal with her mother's death, I was holding her back, damaging her.

'Mummy Ryn,' Tegan asked.

'Yes?' I snapped, then heard my voice and stopped. Took a deep breath. She'd been sat at the table painting pictures. She didn't look damaged; her body wasn't tensed, her eyes weren't filled with fear, but who knew what pulsed beneath the surface? 'Yes, Tiga?' I repeated.

'What time is Luke coming back?'

'About ten o'clock.'

'But that's after my bed time.'

'I know, but he's driving up from London, there's no way for him to get here earlier. He might come over tomorrow.'

'But I'm painting him a picture.'

'Then give it to him tomorrow.' I stared into the cupboard of tinned food, waiting for inspiration to strike. I heard scuffly sounds behind me as Tegan climbed down from her place at the table.

'What if he doesn't come tomorrow?'

'He probably will. He usually comes over on Saturday.'

'But what if he doesn't?'

I don't know! I almost shouted. I took a deep breath; this wasn't her fault, I reminded myself. I spun towards her and found she was right behind me, clutching her bowl of dirty paintbrush water. And as I turned, my legs knocked the bowl free of her fingers. The contents splashed over my lap. Tegan gasped before she fell into a terrified silence.

I stared down at my dress. I'd spent so much money on this dress. It'd been my first purchase when I'd moved to Leeds, it represented me starting again. I loved this dress. Now it was ruined. Just like the rest of my life. Ruined. Destroyed. Nothing I could do would fix it.

'I'VE HAD ENOUGH OF YOU!' I screamed.

Tegan froze—literally petrified by my anger.

I wanted her to go away. I *needed* her to go away, to get away from me before I said something that couldn't be taken back.

'Go to your room,' I whispered, controlling my voice.

Without a protest, she left the room. I didn't move, I was frozen with fear for what I almost said . . . that if it wasn't for her, I wouldn't have social workers looking down their noses at me. I would be Marketing Director of Angeles, it'd be me travelling up from London right now, not Luke. If she wasn't here, I'd be free to do what I wanted. And I wouldn't always be wondering if I was going to fall at the next hurdle.

Tears swelled in my eyes, I covered my face with my hands, trying to rock myself better as I thought about how many more ways I could screw this up.

'Tiga,' I whispered later as I pushed open her door. 'Tiga, I'm sorry.' She sat on her bed, her knees pulled up to her chest, clutching Meg. 'I didn't mean it—' I stopped speaking as I noticed her drawers and wardrobe had been emptied of clothes. Her multicoloured holdall had been retrieved from under her bed and sat open on the floor, a few clothes already in it. My heartbeat quickened. Had the social worker told her that if she didn't like living with me, she could go live elsewhere?

'What's going on?' I asked, panicked. 'Why have you started to pack?'

'Please don't make me live at Nana Muriel's house,' she whispered, then cringed down, lowering her head to be close to Meg.

'Why would I make you live with Nana Muriel?' I asked.

'Because I was naughty,' she replied. 'I don't want to go to Nana Muriel's house. I want to stay with you.'

'Is that why you got your clothes out?' I asked.

She nodded. It had never occurred to me that Tegan thought returning to that hell in Surrey was an option. Was that why she was always so good? Never arguing, never throwing a tantrum? Because she thought I might send her back to being beaten and starved?

'Tiga . . .' I paused as her face creased up in absolute terror. 'Tiga, you're going to stay with me until you're all grown up.'

The lines and creases of her face relaxed a fraction.

'You never have to see Nana Muriel again.'

Her eyes eased up to look at me at last.

'I'm going to look after you for ever and ever,' I stated. That thought once again sent panic stampeding in my chest. 'Tiga, this is your home. Even when you're all grown up, wherever I am will be your home. I . . . I'll always want to take care of you. Do you understand?'

'Even if I'm naughty?' she asked.

'Even then,' I said. 'Not that I'm encouraging it,' I hastily modified.

'I'm sorry I was naughty,' she said.

'You weren't naughty, it was an accident. And I'm sorry for shouting at you.'

'Luke won't see your pretty dress now,' she stated.

I was puzzled for a moment. She stared back at me, oblivious. She didn't know that since my migraine four weeks ago, something had fundamentally changed between Luke and me. He'd not only become human, he'd become a man in my eyes. He'd often stick around after Tegan went to bed and we'd stay up talking until four o'clock in the morning. Tegan didn't know that I'd started to have unsettling thoughts about him and, yes, all right, sex. No, he wouldn't see me in my pretty dress and that was good. The thoughts I had weren't to be encouraged, let alone indulged. 'That's probably for the best,' I admitted to her. 'So, are you going to stay with me?' I asked, banishing Mr Wiseman from my mind.

Tegan scrunched up her nose as she nodded.

'Good. I'm really, really glad.'

Tiga reached out with Meg and made the rag doll kiss my cheek. 'Meg loves you a lot today,' she explained.

'I'm starting to get that. Shall we put away your clothes, sweet pea? And, as a special treat, you can stay up and see Luke.'

Her eyes widened with the delight. 'Really and truly?'

'Yup,' I replied, knowing she'd be asleep before nine, tops.

The allure of seeing Luke was, in fact, the strongest stimulant known to Tegankind—she was wide awake at ten fifteen when he buzzed.

He entered bearing gifts. Like a dad who felt guilty about having to travel for work, Luke always bought Tegan something when he went away. This was his biggest hoard yet, though—he was weighted down with five plastic bags in each of his big hands.

'Jeez, how much have you spent?' I asked as he bustled past me.

'Erm, not much. One of my friends works for a toy company.'

I raised an eyebrow at him. 'Oh yeah? She sounds like a great friend.'

Luke glanced away the second I said 'she', then studiously avoided making eye contact. Guilty as almost charged, obviously.

'Come on, T,' he said. 'Let's see what's in the bags.'

Happiness flashed up in Tegan's eyes like twin beacons in a storm. All the jealousy I'd felt at how he'd come by his bounty was replaced by gratitude. She needed this, needed someone to make a fuss of her, to buy her presents and make her feel special.

Item by item, Luke emptied the bags in front of her, and—I could have kissed him for this—most of the toys were educational, and, if not educational, then books.

'Thank you!' she screeched and launched herself at Luke, who was knocked backwards, caught unawares as we both were. She started bouncing up and down on his abdomen, not seeming to notice the 'Ouf!' sound he made every time she connected with his stomach.

'Look, Mummy Ryn! I'm jumping on Luke!' she giggled. I smiled.

This was the old Tiga. Affectionate, lively, bouncy. Luke brought that out in her; he was like a time machine for her personality. No wonder she wanted to be with him all the time—he made her joyful again. 'Mummy Ryn, am I 'lowed to kiss Luke for a thank you?' she said.

'If Luke doesn't mind.'

Tiga looked at Luke. 'Course I don't mind,' he said, winded.

She leant forwards and planted a smacker in the middle of his forehead, then sat back, looked expectantly at me.

'What?' I asked, wondering what I'd missed.

Tegan sighed theatrically. 'You have to kiss Luke too.'

I took a horrified step back. 'I'm sure he doesn't want to spoil your special kiss with mine.'

'Coward,' Luke mouthed at me, his eyes shining with humour.

'I think you should give him a few more bounces for me, though, Tiga.' Her face lit up and his contorted in horror.

'**H**ave you been crying?' Luke asked over an hour later. He'd read Tiga four stories and listened to her rabbit on until she'd fallen asleep. Now he sat down; I was on the other end of the sofa.

I'd checked my face in the mirror before he'd arrived and my eyes weren't red or puffy. How could he know? 'Why do you ask?'

'You've got that look in your eyes. You used to have it a lot when we first met. I used to think it was disdain but now I know it was because you were crying a lot in those days—because of Adele.'

I couldn't tell him why I'd been crying, no one could know about it. Especially not him, he who could make Tegan so happy. I didn't want him to know I didn't have his skill with her.

'So, who was this woman you were shagging in London?' I asked.

Luke paused as a host of emotions—shame, delight, embarrassment, guilt—flitted across his features. 'I take it the social worker's visit didn't go well,' he ploughed on, determined to get me to open up.

Not as determined as I was to keep shtum, however. 'I'm guessing she was a new conquest judging by how much she heaped on you?'

Luke's eyes remained fixed on me for a moment as he calculated something. 'I didn't mean for it to happen,' he said, admitting defeat, it seemed. 'I liked her but she's not my usual type. I've been thinking a lot lately about what my type is and if I've been a bit rigid and I guess I got my emotions jumbled up with my logic and—'

'I shouted at Tegan,' I blurted out. I couldn't bear to hear any more.

'Is that why you were crying?'

I nodded.

'It's OK, you know, we all lose our tempers every now and again.'

'You don't understand, I lost it. I said I'd had enough of her. I . . . I almost told her that she'd ruined my life.'

'But you didn't, that's what's important.'

'So it's not important that I think that?'

That stumped him. 'Ryn'—I liked that since we'd become friends, he'd taken to calling me Ryn too—'it's a horrible fact, but she has ruined your life. The life you had before has been dismantled, so it's been demolished, ruined. But that doesn't mean it's bad ruined. There are good ruins—look at those on the Acropolis. They're good ruins.'

Bless him for trying.

'What did the social worker say?'

I gave him a brief run-down.

'Bitch,' he spat at the end of it. *Ah, I might have given him the Kamryn-spun version.*

'Maybe she didn't actually say that Tegan only likes me because she's got no other option and that she's just grieving for her mother so counselling might help her to see that,' I conceded.

Luke smiled. 'I didn't think she had but she obviously added to you being upset earlier, that's why I called her a bitch.'

Over the past few weeks, I'd learnt more about Luke's story. He'd grown up in Birmingham but had gone to college in London. After university he moved to Boston to study at Harvard Business School, then he settled in New York to begin working in banking. He'd returned to London, then moved to Scotland, then Japan, then New York again and began working in management consultancy; and then returned to London working for the same American company. Then he was head-hunted by Angeles. From the sound of it, his thirty-five years had been unsettled, he was always moving, trying new things. Part of me admired that pioneering spirit, part of me wanted to ask what he was running away from. Asking such personal questions wasn't allowed though. Support was: and he was offering it to me.

'She was so scared,' I said, shaking my head, trying to dislodge the image of her face. 'I did that. I nearly gave her a nervous breakdown.'

Luke edged across the sofa, placed his hand on my face, stilled my head. 'It's going to be OK,' he reassured, his warm hand on my face punctuation for his words. 'You're a good person.' His voice dropped a fraction. 'You're a great person.'

My eyes traced the contours of his face. *I like him.* The thought hit me like a mallet on the head. This was more than sexual attraction. I liked him. His hand on my cheek quickened my heartbeat. I liked this physical contact, it was comfortable and comforting.

Luke traced the outline of my face with his eyes, too. I hadn't changed from when we first met, but he didn't look at me the way he used to. The disgust had gone. Replaced by what would seem to the untrained eye, the eye that wasn't privy to the history between us, affection.

The silence fizzed with expectation. His head was meant to move closer and his lips were meant to meet mine and my day would be complete . . . A complete and utter disaster. I was pretty certain he liked me, but he wasn't attracted to me like I was to him. And he still loved Nicole.

'I'd better get on with the washing-up,' I said. He didn't move as I went to the kitchen area. 'Have you eaten?' I asked over my shoulder.

'Erm, no,' he replied. I heard him get up.

'There's pasta left, if you want some?' I retrieved a dinner plate from a cupboard, heaped on the penne pasta in a homemade tomato sauce. Luke took his dinner from me then went to the table. He moved to pick up his fork, realised he didn't have one and turned just as I held one out to him. We exchanged intimate smiles, the type that couples gave each other, and I felt that kick again: more than lust, less than love; a reckless cocktail of emotions that would end in fantastic sex—and trouble.

Two minutes later, I refilled the sink with plates; Luke appeared beside me holding his plate, nothing but streaks of pasta sauce on it.

'Did you inhale it or something?' I asked.

'I didn't realise how hungry I was until I started eating—and although your pasta deserves to be savoured, I couldn't help myself. I never can.'

What? 'Is that your way of saying I'm a good cook?'

Luke turned fully to me, his face innocent and sweet, especially now it had become beard-free. 'Not a good cook, a great cook.'

He's flirting with me, I thought with a mental smirk. That in itself was comical. The fact he was so bad at it made it hysterical.

'Wash or dry?' he asked when I didn't respond to his ridiculous statement. 'I ate so I help to wash up.'

'OK, dry.' I handed him a tea towel and we worked in a companionable silence for all of thirty seconds before he broke it with, 'You're such a good mother, I don't know how anyone could ever doubt you.'

I gave him another sideways glance and found he was vigorously drying off a plate. He was nervous. Mr Arrogance himself was nervous.

'Tegan is such a lovely child and that's mostly thanks to you. You're a great influence, you care so much for her and you encourage her. It's—'

'Stop,' I said, dropping the plate I was cleaning. 'You make me sound like Mary Poppins. I'm not. I'm Kamryn. Who keeps screwing up.'

'You're so hard on yourself,' he commented with a shake of his head.

'You don't give yourself enough credit for how fantastic a parent you are. And how much of a difference you've made in Tegan's life. And the difference you've made in my life. I've changed so much because of—'

'Are you flirting with me, Mr Wiseman?' I injected.

He slid a plate onto the worktop. 'Are you winding me up, Ms Matika?'

'You're an easy target when you keep chucking such over-the-top compliments at me,' I said. Before I could wonder what he or I would do next, I felt Luke's strong hands on my waist, spinning me towards him and suddenly his lips were on mine in a swift, breathtaking kiss. Taken aback, it took me a couple of seconds to respond, to kiss him back. While his lips parted mine and his tongue pushed into my mouth, Luke's muscular body pressed mine against the sink, and his hand moved up my top, slowly caressing my lower back.

We broke apart, our chests heaving. 'Bed?' he whispered.

I nodded.

The moment I shut my bedroom door Luke grabbed me again, kissing me ferociously while my hands explored the smooth, firm contours of his body. Each touch exploded more desire in my veins.

There was no doubt about what was coming next as Luke took off his shirt, revealing the defined muscles of his chest and arms. I gasped inside not only at the perfection of his body but also at the thought that I was going to have sex. With Luke. The Boss. All those rumours circulating at work about him and me would become true.

He climbed on top of me, lifted my white T-shirt and pressed a kiss on my belly button. My body jerked with the intense pleasure. I closed my eyes, arched back my body and sighed as I gave in to bliss, courtesy of Luke Wiseman . . .

'**W**hy have you got your clothes on?' Tegan's voice asked in my ear.

'Hmmmm?' I replied.

'Mummy Ryn,' she persisted. 'Why have you got your clothes on?'

I'm never, ever going to have a lie-in again. I thought with sadness.

Tegan's small fingers gripped my forearm, shook me. 'Mummy Ryn, why have you got your clothes on? Did you sleep in them?'

I slipped an arm down and felt my legs. They were indeed covered in my jeans. I definitely had my bra on because I could feel it digging into my ribs. And I had my T-shirt on. *Hang on, didn't Luke take that T-shirt off?* I wondered through my drowsiness. *LUKE!* I glanced down to my right. The bed was empty.

'Do you always sleep in your clothes?' Tegan asked, climbing up onto the bed. I absently helped her up as I ransacked my memory. The last thing I remembered, Luke was covering my body in hungry kisses. We were going to have sex. That obviously hadn't happened.

'No, sweetheart. You've seen my pyjamas,' I said.

'Why aren't you wearing them?'

'Because I was too tired to get changed.' I cringed at the thought of it: I'd been lying under an incredibly good-looking, semi-naked man and I'd fallen asleep. The last person I'd had sex with was Nate, more than two years ago. In that time, I'd been so intent on working out who I was since I'd become Kamryn Matika: single and best-friendless, that sex became something I'd do when I'd pieced myself back together. And love, which was always lagging behind sex for me, wasn't even a consideration. The first hurdle would have been allowing myself to be intimate with someone new. I'd thought that would be easy, but obviously not. Because when sex came a-knocking, I sparked out.

'Who is your letter from?' Tegan asked, pointing to the bedside table. A piece of folded paper was propped up against my bedside lamp. I picked it up and found it was in fact two pieces of paper—the one underneath had *Tegan* on it. I read it out loud.

> *'Dear T, Thank you for the picture of me at the zoo. I hope to see you soon. Look after Ryn, she is very tired. Love, Luke.'*

I looked down at my own note and read it silently.

> *Hi Ryn, I decided it was best I leave in case Tegan came in—there'd be a lot of explaining to do if she found us asleep together. Thanks for dinner. Let's wash-up together again some time, yeah? See ya, Luke.*

'Is that from Luke as well?' Tegan asked.

I bit down on my lower lip and, with a half smile, nodded. Each time I thought about our first kiss lust deliquesced my insides. I could have done it with Luke. That was a liberating thought. It meant I had moved a step along the road to getting over Nate.

Tegan frowned at me. 'Do you like Luke?'

'Yes, I like Luke,' I replied, curling my arm around her.

'More than you like me?' she asked.

'Of course not!' I screeched. 'Tiga, I love you.' That was the first time I'd said it to her. 'I like Luke, but I LOVE you. I'll not love anyone like I love you. Not ever.'

'We won't do anything,' Tegan said.

I raised an eyebrow at the little girl sitting on Luke's lap. He in turn was sitting on my big red beanbag. They were both staring earnestly at me as I stood in the living room/kitchen doorway.

'You expect me to believe that?' I replied.

'We honestly won't do anything,' Luke said, in the same tone she had used. It'd been a fortnight since Luke and I first kissed and then didn't have sex because I'd fallen asleep. The morning after, he'd shown up and acted as though nothing untoward had gone on between us. He'd taken us out for a drive and chatted away like normal. Even when Tegan fell asleep while we were driving home he avoided all chat about the night before. By the time I let us into the flat I started to wonder if he *had* started to undress me.

After Tegan had been bathed, read to and convinced to go to sleep, Luke had flopped down on the sofa beside me. 'She's knackering,' he said.

'I know,' I replied. 'Right, I'd better get on with the washing-up.'

Before I could get up, he grabbed my wrist. 'Oh no you don't.' He pushed me against the armrest and kissed me. 'I knew I had to keep it together today. If I mentioned it or even looked at you too long I knew I wouldn't be able to control myself.'

I sighed in relief. 'Thank God. I started to wonder if I imagined it all.'

'No, you didn't.' He kissed me again, deep and slow. 'I'd like us to go to bed, but only if I won't send you to sleep.'

'Are you going to hold that against me for ever?'

'Not for ever, but for a while, I think I'm entitled.'

And that was it. We went to bed and I didn't fall asleep until after Luke had gone—I wouldn't let him stay because I didn't want Tegan to find us in bed together.

Adele had been so cautious about men and Tegan. Very few men met her daughter—Adele didn't want her to become attached to a man who would be gone if the relationship ended. Once again I'd screwed up; had gone about this the wrong way. 'My' man was in our lives before I'd bedded him. If it didn't work out, we'd still have to see each other because Tegan would think the world was coming to an end otherwise. So, even after two weeks, we were keeping things under wraps, trying to work out if we had anything beyond sex going for us.

All the signs were good. He spent at least three nights a week at our place. I enjoyed his company. And his body. But every touch, every nice word skimmed the surface of my heart, none of it penetrated. He had yet to break through to who I was. Still, it was great to have him around. Today Luke had offered to sit with Tegan. I was going to wash my hair. 'Are you sure you'll be all right?' I asked again.

'We're not going to break anything,' Luke reassured me.

Now why did he have to say that?

I sighed silently and slunk away to the bathroom. If Luke was sticking around, I had to trust them, didn't I? I knelt down, put my head over the bath and drenched my hair. *Gosh*. The thought swept through me as I lathered up. *Gosh*. I was relaxed. It was such an alien sensation.

I was always so frantic, rushing: trying to fit lots of things in while thinking of Tegan, and if she was all right, if she was hurting, whether I should let her start Saturday morning karate classes like she wanted. And relaxing at the office wasn't an option, either, especially now the new marketing director (Luke) had brought in a host of initiatives and ideas that had doubled my workload. We were going to be expanding *Living Angeles* to have separate magazines for the homes, clothes and children's departments. Plus an on-line shopping guide. I was overseeing these things. Since all this extra work had started, I rarely took a lunch break; after Tegan was in bed I'd spend more hours on the computer until Luke lured me to bed. My life was frantic.

I vigorously washed out the shampoo and slathered on the conditioning treatment. I had to wait ten minutes for it to fulfil its promise to give me beautiful hair. I could go check up on those two . . .

Walking in bare feet meant they couldn't hear me approach the living room. I stopped to watch them. They were still sitting in the position they had been ten minutes ago. On Tegan's lap sat my globe. Luke was pointing something out.

'It was very hot,' Luke was saying. 'So hot, in fact, I got sunstroke.'

'What's sunstroke?' Tegan asked.

'It's when you spend too much time in the sun and you get ill.'

'Did you nearly die?' she asked.

'No, but I was poorly.'

'My mummy died,' Tegan said.

My heart stopped. She hardly ever mentioned her mum to me. I wasn't sure if I should bring Adele up, either. Everything I'd read about bereavement and children said to let the child come to you with their questions, but sometimes I wanted to check how Tegan was doing. To ask if she wanted to talk about Adele. Fear of upsetting her—fear of upsetting myself—stopped me. I wouldn't know what to say. Would Luke?

'She's gone to heaven to be with Jesus and the angels,' Tegan added.

'I know,' Luke replied, 'Ryn told me. Do you miss her?'

Tegan bit her inner lip, then nodded. 'Sometimes,' she said in a small voice. 'I want to tell her things and I can't. I wanted to show her my homework with the special star because I did it so good. But I can't.'

'Have you told Ryn this?'

'No,' she said in such a whisper I had to lean my head closer to the door to hear her. 'She cries about my mummy going to heaven. I don't want her to be sad.'

How does she know I cry about Adele dying? I never did it in front of her. I never cried in public. It was always in the dead of night. Maybe, like Luke, she picked up on the emptiness in my eyes after I'd cried.

'I know Ryn is sad, but she'd be sadder to know that you're not telling her something that upsets you. If you want to talk about your mummy, then tell her. She won't mind. She loves you. Promise me?'

Tegan said nothing for a moment, then nodded. A short, decisive nod. 'Yes, Luke,' she said.

'Good girl.'

Luke's six-foot-two body wrapped around my five-foot-six frame was something I'd started to get used to. That night, he was even more clingy, his face cosseted against my neck. 'Ryn,' he began.

'Hmm?' I replied. I steeled myself because his voice, low and hesitant, told me he was about to say something awful.

'I'm sorry for how I treated you,' he blurted out.

'Eh?' I replied. That was the last thing I expected to hear. I'd been preparing myself for terminal illness or being transferred abroad.

'The things I said to you, how I used to look at you, the things I thought . . .' He paused, wincing as though replaying them in his head. 'I'm sorry. I'm so sorry. I was so wrong. You're beautiful. Inside and out. You're beautiful. I look at what you've done for Tegan and how you treat me despite what I was like . . . I'm sorry, I'm truly sorry.'

'Ah, it's over with. And you were probably right. I am a bit of a—'

'Don't,' he cut in sternly, putting his fingers over my lips. 'Don't make a joke of it. I couldn't bear it. I hate myself for how I was.'

'It's all right,' I hushed. 'You weren't the first, I doubt you'll be the last.'

'How do you bear it?'

'It's been the same all my life, I don't let it bother me.' Luke's arms tightened around me. 'Seriously, it's not a problem. I've developed a thick skin where I don't believe anything that anyone says. That way, I know that no one can get to me because if it's not true, it can't hurt me.'

'Does that apply to good things, too?'

I thought about it. About how it took me ages to accept anything that Nate said—and he always said the loveliest things. From day one he called me beautiful. More than once he'd told me I was his dream woman. But it was years before it sunk in that he meant it, and when I accepted he genuinely loved me, I started to rely on hearing his compliments, which made it all the more painful when they were gone. 'I suppose.'

'That means you don't let yourself feel anything.'

'No, I feel plenty. I just don't let other people's beliefs upset me.'

'So you don't believe that other people like you?' he asked.

'I didn't say that, I said I don't let it affect me. If people like me, that's fab but it doesn't stop me from existing. If they don't, that's fab too 'cos I don't care and still I'm existing.'

'That's such a sad way to live.'

'Luke, if you grew up being told *every day* that you're ugly, fat, stupid, a man, a dog, you can either grow a second skin and not rely on anyone else for your happiness and self-definition, or you can let it bury you. Guess which I did? I had to. It was a survival instinct.'

'But you don't need that survival instinct any more.'

'Yeah, you say that, but I met this bloke not too long ago who took against me because I'm not very pretty and I'm not thin. Now if I'd discarded my survival instinct I'd have been a mess at a time when I needed to be strong.'

'I'm sorry. And you are pretty. You're *gorgeous*. And your body is divine. You're divine.'

'You don't have to say that. It's all right. It doesn't bother me.' *Much. It doesn't bother me much.* I never said that out loud because I never wanted that modifier to be real. And if I said it out loud it became real. It would bother me more, a whole lot more.

'I grew up in a children's home,' Luke said.

'Really?'

'That's why I know that living with a survival instinct is a sad way to live.' *That's why you were so keen to help out.*

'Oh.'

'Both my parents are alive, you know? They just put me in a home. You see, my mum's English and comes from a very rich family. She met my dad, who's Spanish, when she was sixteen. When she got pregnant her family threw her out. My dad was only eighteen but they tried to make a go of it. It was too hard though and when I was about two my mum left, went back to her parents. My dad kept going for years and we did have some good times. I remember he'd take me to the zoo. And we'd go see some of his relatives who lived near us, have these brilliant Spanish meals. I felt like I belonged somewhere. He'd always pretend to his family that he was doing OK, but a lot of the time we were just about getting by. He wouldn't get out of bed for days. Now I know he was depressed but at that age, I didn't. I tried to keep going.

'When I was seven, social services took me away because I hadn't been to school for weeks. I'll never forget that day, I was crying and calling for my dad but he didn't do anything. He just sat there.'

A sudden need to protect Luke, the little boy taken from his family, rose in me. I rolled over and held him close.

'When they took me to the home, I was terrified. They found me foster homes, lots of them. Some were good; some were awful. But it didn't matter either way because I always behaved badly so I could get sent back to the home. It's stupid, but I thought that if I was at the home, my dad would come get me. He'd know where I was.

'When I got to ten, no one would foster me. No one wanted a troublemaker. And because of that, I stayed at the home. That's when I realised my dad wasn't coming for me. So I decided not to rely on anyone, just to focus on doing well. And when I left the home at sixteen, I was in a good way: I'd done ten O levels. I left there, got a bedsit, got a part-time job, managed to do four A levels and got into university.

'I'd also learnt other lessons. Like, that my mum didn't want me.' He paused, inhaled to control himself. 'I found out that she'd moved to Australia years earlier. I wrote to her, telling her about myself, and she wrote back saying she'd moved on. She'd put all that stuff—she actually called me "stuff"—behind her, and told me not to contact her again.'

I gasped at her cruelty.

'I took that pretty hard. I couldn't work out what was wrong with me. Why she didn't want me. It took me another two years to get up the courage to call my dad. He agreed to see me, but he wasn't interested, either. He'd remarried, had two young kids and he didn't want me in his life. That was worse. I'd spent so much time with him.'

'Oh, babe . . .' I said. This explained so much about Luke. His arrogance, his constant strive for perfection, why he'd moved so much— Luke never felt wanted.

'Sorry,' he said.

'Don't be sorry, I understand.'

'No, you don't. I'm so in awe of what you're doing. Despite how Tegan came about, you're still looking after her.'

'Thanks.'

Luke's fingers took hold of my face. 'I mean it. I want you to believe me. You're awesome. You've stopped Tegan becoming me.'

'You're not so bad,' I replied. Luke was a damaged man, I realised. He'd never felt he belonged anywhere, so work and being successful had become his reason for living. I pressed a comforting kiss on his mouth and he kissed me back, hard. His desperation and sadness came through in the way he started to make love.

Afterwards, I was tempted to ask him to stay. He shouldn't be alone

when he'd revealed so much of himself, but I couldn't risk Tegan finding us together. Luke took the decision out of my hands by getting up,
getting dressed. 'I'll see you,' he mumbled over his shoulder as he
walked out the door. That was the type of disposable goodbye you'd
say to a stranger you never expected to see again. If Luke left like this,
we might lose him. He would feel so vulnerable that in this time alone
he might decide to put us at a distance to protect himself.

From my bedroom window, I watched Luke leave my building. He
opened the door to his black car and got in. He leant over the steering
wheel, cradled his head in his hands and started to cry. As I watched his
broad shoulders shaking, I was slowly tugged back to the hotel room,
holding Tegan as she screamed her heart out because her mother had
left her. I'd been overwhelmed then by a need to protect her. That feeling was back. I wanted Luke to know someone did want him.
Someones—Tegan and I—would be lost without him. I picked up my
mobile and dialled his number. He picked up after the fourth ring.

'Come back,' I said.

'But Tegan . . .' he protested.

'You can leave before she gets up. Just come back.'

He came back and fell asleep in my arms.

'Is Luke your boyfriend?'

I was putting Tegan to bed. 'Why do you ask that?' I replied, laying
aside the book we were reading. She was tucked up under her rainbow
duvet, her clean hair hidden under a pink silk headscarf. Like most
black women, I wore a scarf at night to protect my hair from the rav-
ages of sleep; when Tegan saw mine she had wanted one too. She
wouldn't believe me when I told her she didn't need one. Her face, like
the rest of her, had filled out a bit of late so she had five-year-old cheeks
that plumped up when she smiled.

'Because Regina Matheson said that if a man and a woman see each
other all the time they're boyfriend and girlfriend.'

'Does she now,' I replied. There was no way of getting out of it now, I
had to tell Tegan the truth. But how? The other reason I'd been delaying,
had let six weeks pass without telling her, was that I didn't know how to
explain it to her. 'Would you mind if Luke was my boyfriend?' I asked.

'No!' she giggled. 'Do you kiss him?' she asked. 'Like on TV?'

'Sometimes,' I replied cautiously, unsure if I should be having this
kind of conversation with a child. 'Goodnight now, Tiga.'

'Is he still my friend?' she asked.

'Of course,' I stated. 'He'll always be your friend.'

'Are you still my new mummy?'

'Yes, sweetie.'

'But you're not my real mummy, are you?'

'Why do you ask me that?' I replied, terrified of what she might say.

'Because Regina Matheson said you can't be my real mummy because we aren't the same colour. You're black, and I'm white, aren't I?'

Deep inside, a rage started to burn. I wanted to meet this Regina and order her not to fill Tegan's head with such terrors. That things were bad enough without her telling Tegan that she didn't belong with anyone.

'And she said I don't have a real family because I don't have a daddy.'

The rage exploded into flames. 'You know what, I bet Regina Matheson doesn't know if her mummy wants her all the time,' I said.

Tegan's eyes widened in wonder.

'Her mummy is stuck with her. So's her daddy, for that matter. No matter what she does, they have to keep her, but I chose to have you with me. And I don't have to keep you but I want to. I want to keep you all the time and no matter what happens I'll always want to keep you with me. Do you understand?'

Tegan nodded.

'I'm sure Regina's mother loves her very much, but she didn't choose her. She got what she was given, while I picked you.'

'Are you glad you picked me?' she asked in a quiet voice.

'I'm not only glad, I'M ECSTATIC!' I fell on Tegan, tickling her, and the lovely sound of her laughter filled the bedroom.

'My mummy tickled me,' Tegan said, still giggling.

'I know,' I said, trying to smile. My throat constricted suddenly and my eyes began to sting, like they did whenever I thought of Adele. I swallowed the feelings and thought of something else.

'What does heaven look like?' Tegan asked, her voice sleepier now.

I slowly shook my head. 'I don't know,' I replied.

'Does it look like that?' She pointed at the picture on the chimney breast opposite her bed. The emerald fields, the green-topped brown trees, the big yellow sun. The picture was as good a scene of heaven as any, I suppose.

'Maybe, sweetheart. But I don't know.'

'My mummy would like it if it was.'

'Yes, she would, but I think she'd like a few clothes shops, too.'

Tegan nodded and laughed. 'Na-Night, Mummy Ryn.'

I wandered into the living room and started as I found Luke watching television. I was so surprised I couldn't help, 'Oh,' escaping my lips.

'Oh?' he replied cautiously.

We had an honest friendship—*relationship*—but no one would take kindly to being told you'd forgotten they existed. And I had. In the talk of Adele, I'd forgotten he was in the flat.

'I mean, oh, you've washed up,' I covered.

'Wasn't I meant to?'

'It's not that . . . I'm tired.'

Luke stretched. 'In other words, you want me to go.'

'I didn't say that,' I protested halfheartedly.

'You didn't have to, your face says it all.'

'Yeah, well, my face has been lying for years, so I don't know why you choose now to believe it.'

Luke put his head to one side and his hazel eyes narrowed slightly. 'How about you go cry in the bedroom, I wait here until you're calmer and then we start again?'

'Don't patronise me,' I spat.

'Or, you could tear a few more strips off me but let's do it in the bedroom so T doesn't hear.'

'Or you could f-off home.'

'Or I could f-off home.'

Nate used to do this. Used to ride out my moods with an incredible amount of stoicism, refusing to rise to any type of bait.

'I feel so guilty,' I stated. Talking. That was the best move. Sharing.

'For?'

'For everything. For not being there when Adele needed me. For being so bad a mother I forgot Tegan that time. For not being able to raise her how her mum would have done and all the while there's some silly bint of a child at school telling her that I'm not her real mother and I never will be. So obviously she's going to feel abandoned because not even I'm her real family . . .'

'OK, let's deal with these things one at a time. I know this isn't what you want to hear, but counselling could be the step forward you need.'

'Counselling for me?' I said, when I finally realised what he meant.

He nodded. 'Tegan's not the only one who has lost someone she cared about. And, unlike Tegan, you had a lot of unresolved issues. You need to talk them out, to someone who isn't me. A professional might be able to help you put it all in context. Which might alleviate some of your guilt.

'OK, Tegan missing her mum is natural. There's nothing anyone can do about that, but you worrying about her not thinking of you as her mother—she calls you Mummy. And not just to you, by the sound of it. For this girl at school to have said this about you not being her mum, she must be calling you Mummy Ryn when you're not there. She truly thinks of you as her second mother.' I must have looked unconvinced because he added: 'There is one way you can fix that.'

'What, go back in time and give birth to her?'

Luke rolled his eyes. 'Ryn, I know the social worker freaked you out, but I think you should focus on adopting her again. Get T counselling, get the relevant forms, do whatever it takes to make her a Matika.'

I sighed internally. It was all right for him to say 'do whatever it takes' because he didn't know what it would entail. He didn't realise that to adopt Tegan, I would have to contact Nate.

Chapter Seven

WHOSE IDEA WAS IT to come up to town on a Saturday? We were pushing our way through the crowds of central Leeds, having been driven into town by His Royal Highness Luke Wiseman. He who had decreed that we should come up here for the day. 'It'll be fun,' he said, in hearing range of Miss Hedonist herself, Tegan Brannon, knowing that once she was on side I wouldn't refuse. I was in the filthiest mood known to womankind but holding it in, trying not to show my irritation that a trog in a miniskirt—despite it being almost NOVEMBER—hadn't said 'Excuse me' to get past, she just shoved me out of the way.

'I want to look at furniture in John Lewis,' called Luke.

I held the door to Angeles's biggest rival up north for Tegan and Luke, who were right behind me, then crossed the entrance. I was striding towards the escalator when another woman in a micro-mini who didn't seem to know it was winter, bashed into my shoulder with her shoulder while, at the same time, her plastic Tesco bag, which had something heavy and glass in it, connected with the bony bit of my shin. Pain knocked stars behind my eyes. Instead of apologising, she shot me a filthy look then stalked on.

Bitch. I bent to rub at my damaged shin, then straightened up, managing to knock into another solid human form.

Does anyone else want to knock me about, or what? I screamed inside, swivelling my glare to the latest person to make my hit list. My body was jolted again, this time not in pain but in shock. Nate.

Like twin beacons of astonishment, my name flashed up in his eyes: Kam. He said it too; breathed the single-syllable word: 'Kam.'

Weeks had passed since Luke had convinced me to refocus on adopting Tegan and I still hadn't made steps towards contacting Nate.

He was exactly as I remembered him: his brown-black hair softly sculpted into short peaks away from his face. His skin still smooth. His navy-blue eyes that could effortlessly unearth my deepest-kept secret. His nose, straight with its small upturn at the end.

'It is you, isn't it?' he asked when I didn't speak.

I moistened my lips, ready to attempt a reply, when Luke—Tegan sitting on his shoulders—appeared. He looked at me, saw the shock on my face, and turned to the person I was focused on. Luke took in Nate's wide forehead, his big eyes and the full-size version of Tegan's nose, and his heartbeat almost visibly tripled. 'We'll wait for you over there,' my lover mumbled, then navigated the pair of them away from us.

'Nathaniel,' I finally uttered. 'What are you doing here?'

'I live here,' he replied.

'What? In Leeds?' I recoiled, he couldn't, he just couldn't.

'Yes. No. I mean, no. I live in Tadcaster. Halfway between Leeds and York. I, erm, got a job as group scheduler at Yorkshire and Pennines FM. Erm, about a year or so ago. Obviously you still live up here,' he said.

'Obviously.'

Nate's expression changed, the shock was whisked away, replaced by sadness. 'How are you coping since . . . ?' his voice trailed away. Since . . . Nate like everyone else, me included, avoided those words.

I shrugged. 'I'm fine, I guess. How are you?'

'Much the same. I did think about getting in touch,' he said carefully. 'I didn't know how you'd react, though, if it'd just add to it all.'

Enough Adele talk, I decided, lowering my head. Nate couldn't understand how lacerated I felt most of the time, no one except possibly Tegan could understand. How every day that I didn't simply stop, frozen with grief, was an excellent day. I was holding myself together with strands of denial, by ignoring the pain. If I visualised my feelings, the pain of them would be like long deep grooves scored onto the surface of my mind by guilt and regret. And if I allowed myself to glimpse the unfathomable acuteness of my feelings, I wouldn't be able to carry on living. So I constantly consigned my feelings to another place, another time, a debt I'd pay at a later date. The interest was mounting, but I had no resources to pay right now. Nate, simply by being there, was asking with menaces for me to pay some of what I owed. Talking about it would result in a breakdown.

Understanding almost straight away that I wasn't talking about it any more, Nate changed the subject. 'Boyfriend?' he asked. He inclined his head in Luke and Tegan's direction. I followed his line of sight. A little way away, Luke was holding onto Tegan's hands and bouncing her on his shoulders. She giggled loudly.

'Yeah,' I smiled, proud.

'And that's his daughter?'

I tore my gaze from them to frown at Nate, searching his face for a sign that he recognised her. Nothing. I wasn't surprised. Nate wasn't interested in children. He would watch Tegan performing one of her dances if we made him, but he'd always have one eye on the television.

'No,' I replied. 'He's looking after her.'

'Oh.' He smiled slightly at me. 'Cute kid.'

I moistened my lips, ready to utter, *Your kid*, then realised that it wasn't the right setting. *Should I tell him anyway?* I wondered, staring up at him. What if Nate wanted in on her life? Not likely, considering his apathy towards children, but it still worried me. He was her father though, and Tegan had a right to know him, to have him in her life.

In the years before I left, I had repeatedly lectured Adele on Tegan's need to know her father. Now I knew how simplistic—unenlightened— I had been. I'd had no idea of what living under the threat of Tegan having a father was like. Even if 'daddy' didn't want to lure her away, he could reject her, which would permanently damage her. Besides, Tegan, right now, had the complete family set. My parents were her grandparents—she called them Nana Faith and Grandpa Hector, my brothers and sister were her uncles and aunt, their children her cousins. When she went to visit my sister's children in Manchester she always came back regaling me with tales of the fun they'd had together. Nate was blood though. Blood and genes, her connection to the great biological pool of life. We couldn't give her that. Even if I didn't want him in my life any more, I owed it to Tegan to tell him.

'Look,' I said, 'we should talk, properly . . . About everything.'

Surprise leapt onto Nate's face. 'You really want to?' he asked.

I nodded. 'Have you got a number I can reach you on?'

He delved into his coat, removed a business card and handed it to me. I pocketed it as we said brief, stiff goodbyes. I walked towards Tegan and Luke without looking back.

'Who's that man?' Tegan asked as I approached them.

'He's a friend I knew from a long time ago,' I replied.

'Did he know my mummy?' she asked unexpectedly.

'Yes, he did.'

274 | Dorothy Koomson

'Does he know she's gone to heaven to be with Jesus and the angels?'

'Yes, sweetheart, he knows. And he was sad, but he's glad he knew her before she went to heaven.'

Tegan beamed at me, which threw me. I'd expected her to be upset, instead she seemed happy; completely unfazed. 'He's a nice man. Can we see him again?'

I felt Luke's eyes burning symmetrical holes into my face as his expression echoed, *'Well, can we?'*

'Maybe,' I replied, ignoring Luke's unwavering gaze.

Eight years ago, I entered a café in north London and found Nate at a table engrossed in a newspaper. I'd come down here for our first date, having met him a month earlier; there was a mass of fidgety, agitated butterflies crawling over each other inside me. 'Hi,' I said.

My date glanced up. A grin expanded his friendly face, crinkling up his eyes. 'Hi,' he said, still grinning. 'You're more beautiful than I remembered,' he said.

I stopped myself checking over my shoulder to see who he was talking to, then allowed myself to slide into the compliment. 'What, this old face?' I joked. 'I've had it years.'

We ordered coffee and a chocolate-chip muffin to share. And we talked. When he nipped to the toilet some time later, I caught myself smiling as he walked away—and was horrified. His charm and his wit had begun to win me over. But I knew what was going to happen. At some point, he'd want to change me, control me, or leave me, and it'd be worse if I'd invested emotion in him beforehand.

By the time he returned I had formulated a plan. I knew how to eject him from my life. 'Coffee back at your place, then,' I stated.

Nate sat back. 'Um . . .' he mumbled with a slight grimace. After all his confidence and 'you're so beautifuls' was he rejecting me?

I sat forwards in my seat. 'Um?' I repeated.

His grimace creased into a complete face cringe. He *was* rejecting me. *Did I imagine the full-on flirting, the shy smiles and the lingering looks?*

'You don't want me to come back with you?' I asked.

'No! God, no! I mean yes! I do! More than anything, I do. It's just my house is a mess and I don't want you to judge me on that. And I don't have any milk or sugar or coffee—'

'Nate,' I cut in, 'do you have condoms?'

He nodded.

'Then I don't care what is or isn't in your kitchen. Shall I put it like this, if we go back to your place you're going to get lucky.'

Later, much later, Nate pulled me towards him, wanting to cuddle before sleep. The plan had gone a bit wrong. My scheme: shag him, leave, wait for him never to call, hadn't worked. Instead of the detachment that accompanied a one-night stand, I was *feeling*. Affection. Passion. Tenderness. Every time I glanced at Nate's face the word *inamorato*, 'lover', came to mind. The one you loved, with your body, your mind, your soul. Which was insanity—I'd met Nate twice in my life.

I'd never had sex like that in my life, though. Our first kiss had been tentative—after that it'd been a one-way trip into pleasure.

I didn't want this confusion. I didn't want to be feeling for him. I slipped out of his hold and frantically started getting dressed. Nate realised what I was doing and sat up. 'Are you going?'

'Yes, I'm going. Places to do, people to be.'

'Oh, OK.' He rested on his elbows watching me search for one of my socks. 'I had a great time, Kamryn. I haven't talked like that for years.'

'Uh-huh,' I replied, locating my errant sock under his bed.

'There's a Sherlock Holmes retrospective down at the National Film Theatre. I know you like Sherlock, so we could go along?' As he talked, I was tying up my shoelaces.

'Kamryn,' he said gravely, as though it'd finally dawned on him what my departure meant. 'Will I ever see you again?'

That threw me. I'd expected that this would put an end to it. That he'd think I was a slut because I slept with him on the first date and then would tactfully avoid mentioning us making contact again. Which was why I was so upset at enjoying sex with him. I wouldn't see him again. And that had hurt, more than I expected it to.

'Will I see you again?' he repeated. I looked at the man in the bed. He was delicious: *Inamorato*. I could do this again. In a heartbeat. *What if he's playing me for a fool?* I wondered. Then I thought, *He's worth the risk.*

I kissed the palm of my hand, then blew the kiss at him. 'We'll see.'

'That was him, wasn't it?' Luke said as I flopped down onto the sofa beside him. 'That was *Tegan's father*.' He whispered the last two words in case madam, who had pin-sharp hearing, was still awake.

'Yes,' I stated.

'Did you tell him?'

'I don't think John Lewis is the place, do you?'

'Are you going to tell him?'

'Probably.'

'So you're going to see him again?'

'Yes,' I replied.

He closed his eyes momentarily. 'Why?'

'If I'm going to adopt Tegan, I have to get Nate's permission.'

'His *permission*?' he repeated, affronted. 'Are you joking?'

'I never knew this until after I got all of Adele's things but his name is on Tegan's birth certificate. And because I know where he is—that he's still alive—I need to get his permission. He's Tegan's surviving parent so he has to sign away all rights to her.'

'Why didn't you mention this before?'

'Because the last thing I wanted to do was contact Nate. I knew I could get hold of him through his parents if I wanted but I didn't want to.'

'You still feel a lot for him,' Luke stated. 'That's why you didn't want to get in touch with him, you were scared of your feelings.'

'That's ridiculous,' I replied.

Luke studied my face, uncertainty billowing in his eyes before he glanced away. I knew how he felt: jealous. Scared. Unworthy. I used to feel that way about him when he'd open his wallet to pay for something and I'd spot the picture of Nicole, his gorgeous fiancée; reminding me that he still had feelings for someone else. That while we had great sex and spent a lot of time together, Nicole was Plan A, and I was Plan B. A few weeks ago, I noticed Nicole had left his wallet. And her spectre stopped hanging over our relationship. I'd been able to relax, to concentrate on building a relationship with my boyfriend, to work towards allowing him to penetrate my heart. And I his. Now he was in a similar position, although while I'd been wrestling with memories, Luke would be grappling with a human presence.

'That doesn't change us,' I said to reassure him. 'I . . . I love you.'

I didn't. Of course I didn't. I cared for him but it was too soon to tell if it was love. I'd learnt about love from being with Nate, and I knew it wasn't this; it wasn't constant doubt. With Luke there was always disquiet. Should we be together? What would have happened if it were not for Tegan? Without her we'd still be sniping at each other. And if he hadn't decided to change his type, he wouldn't have kissed me. I was never sure which came first—his changing of type or him liking me and deciding to change type. I was never brave enough to ask, either.

I didn't look at Luke and think *inamorato*, but I was fond of him. And, he was a part of my life. I could love him. I just didn't. I had to say it though. 'I do, you know?' I repeated to his sceptical eyes, 'I love you.'

'That's good to know,' he said, his whole body finally relaxing.

There were lots of things you were supposed to say when someone tells you they love you but 'That's good to know' wasn't one of them. A chill breezed through me. Maybe I was wrong, maybe I was still Plan B.

'I like your orangey dress. Where are you going?' Tegan asked, swinging happily from her position under Luke's arm.

'I told you already. I'm going to dinner with that man we saw in John Lewis,' I said, aware that every word slashed at Luke's already fragile ego.

'Where's he taking you again?' Luke asked.

'I told you, I'm meeting him at the restaurant where you and I had our first disastrous dinner, remember?'

My boyfriend hadn't said it, but he feared I'd leave the flat his girl-friend and return Nate's fiancée, that I was thinking of this as a date. I wasn't. The only make-up I'd applied was a little mascara, my 'orangey dress' was a silk number that Luke had bought me to replace the dress destroyed by Tegan's dirty paint water. I'd worn it not because it was flattering—it wasn't particularly—but because Luke had bought it. There was nothing else I could do to reassure Luke short of not going. And I was going to do this. I had to see Nate.

'Right, I'd better be off. Baby, make sure you behave yourself . . . And thanks for Tegan-sitting, Luke, I really appreciate it.'

Luke stepped out into the gloomy corridor with me. Seconds crawled by and he was silent. 'See ya,' I finally said and turned away.

'Ryn,' he said, pulling me back. He touched a tender kiss on my mouth. 'I love you,' he said as he pulled away. He hadn't said that before. Not since I'd said it. In fact, I'd decided that his reply, 'That's good to know', had made his feelings clear: he didn't love me and I should get used to it. Now he'd upended my certainty about his feelings by saying this. And I would always wonder *why* he'd said it. If he'd been motivated by genuine feelings or because he was scared I was going to sleep with someone else. Did he love me or simply want to control me?

Luke stood waiting for my reply and I knew I had to reconfirm I loved him. I opened my mouth and replied, 'That's good to know.' My answer was a reminder that whether we loved each other or not, he wasn't the only one who could be cruel and withholding of their affections. He wasn't the only one who had feelings.

He recoiled in surprise and hurt. And I left without looking back.

Hazy. That's the best way to describe events following my departure from Adele's flat after her accidental confession. I recollect making it home and feeling safe because Nate was out drinking with his ex-house mates. I vaguely recall deciding to go to Leeds because I was meant to be going up there in a couple of days anyway for my four-week stint setting up *Living Angeles*. My clearest memory was of the note I scrawled in blue ink on the telephone note pad and left on our kitchen table: *I know what you did*. Five words that would explain everything: why I had to go and why I wasn't coming back.

The next time I came to, I was lying fully clothed on my hotel bed in Leeds, staring blank-eyed at the television. The phone had rung for a few minutes before I realised what the noise was, and answered it. 'There's a Mr Turner to see you, madam,' the receptionist informed me.

Nate stood as I approached him in the hotel's reception. He looked fragile, as though one harsh word would shatter him.

'I called every hotel in Leeds until I found you,' he explained.

'Let's go into the bar,' I replied, my voice calm and controlled.

'Come home,' Nate said the second we had taken our seats. 'Come home and we'll talk and sort this out.'

'There's nothing to sort out. I know what happened with you and . . .' My voice snagged in my mouth. It was too horrible to name.

'We weren't having . . . It was once. Just once.'

'You cheated on me and it's over,' I hissed.

'We can't be over just like that,' he implored. 'We've been together six years, we're getting married in two months. We have to talk about this.'

'OK, let's talk. Was she better than me? Sexier? More willing? Up for—'

'Stop it,' he cut in. 'It wasn't like that.'

'What else is there to talk about?'

'How much I love you? How much I want you back? How I'll do anything to make it right between us. Anything.'

'Anything?'

'Anything.'

'Then go away and leave me alone.' I got to my feet, tiredness made my head swim. 'I want nothing more to do with you.'

Nate closed his eyes as though he couldn't believe he'd walked into that one.

'I'll come back for my stuff soon. I'll want half the flat money so I can get somewhere of my own. And please, if you ever felt anything for me, please don't tell my parents why the wedding is off. Please. I'll die if anyone else knows. And, and, I think that's it. Bye, Nate.'

I walked away. The last time I saw him was when I went to get my stuff three months later. It was only as I was leaving that he spoke. He said those two words, 'Don't go,' and I stopped, turned to look at him because I knew it was the last time I'd see him, and then I walked out.

Nate rose from his seat as I approached him at the restaurant table. 'Hi,' he said, moving around the table to me and kissing my cheek. He looked good. His thirty-five-year-old face was strong and lacking in any excess fat. His brown-black hair now looked more black because he'd gelled it up into more pronounced spikes than the last time I saw him. His skin was that smooth, gold brown that always surprised me because his parents—and Tegan—were a very pale white.

The waiter arrived with menus; we ordered food. Nate sipped his water, I played with the base of my wine glass. Both of us were silent, waiting for the other to speak first.

'This is like being on a first date,' Nate said with a slight laugh.

'Yeah, except we never really went on dates, did we?'

'We had coffee!' Nate protested.

'That ended back at your house.'

'I thought all my Christmases had come at once,' Nate said. 'Even then we both knew we were meant to be together, didn't we?' He was serious. When it came to us, Nate always said things like that and meant it because, according to him, Fate had thrown us together.

'No, Nate, that's what you thought,' I clarified. 'I had altogether different motives—namely putting you off me.'

'What?' He drew back, alarmed and distressed in equal measures.

'I thought—hoped, I suppose—that you'd think I was easy 'cos I slept with you straight away and you'd disappear.'

'Oh.' Nate sat back, stared down at the white tablecloth. That was cruel and unnecessary, I realised. I'd purposely dismantled what was obviously a good memory for him. I opened my mouth to add that I'd only done it because the fact that I liked him had scared me, but his eyes darted up from the table, silencing me. 'Nothing you did could have put me off you,' he said. 'I'd already fallen for you in a big way.'

It was my turn to focus on the white cotton tablecloth. That was typical Nate: if he wasn't combating one of my moods with stoicism, he'd be earnest about how he felt. And that would make me feel awful.

Our starters arrived. Neither of us moved towards our food even when the waiter had gone. 'That night was pretty confusing for me, too,' I confessed. 'When I got home I knew I had to see you again, and soon, because no one had ever touched me in the way you did. I never slept with anyone else after that night.'

'I thought . . .'

'Yes, I gave you the impression that I had a couple of other men on the go but I didn't. I couldn't think about being with anyone else.'

Nate's face softened into a smile of surprise. He was still grinning as he started to eat. The memory of crying when we decided to get married came back to me. Crying because I'd finally realised what unconditional love felt like. Not only to receive it but to feel it. That meant I wasn't broken, I was like other people, I could feel, I could connect.

Nate glanced up from his soup, caught me watching him and beamed at me. I grinned back and the tension lifted.

We talked and talked about nothing. I know it was nothing because when the waiter brought us the bill we knew virtually nothing new about each other: he didn't know about Tegan, that I'd seen him at the funeral, nor that my boyfriend was called Luke. I didn't know how he'd found out about the funeral, if he was seeing someone, or why he had slept with Adele.

'May I walk you home?' Nate asked.

'You can't walk me all the way to Horsforth, that's miles. And how will you get back to Tadcaster?'

'Details,' he dismissed with a wave of his hand.

'All right, we walk until we get tired, then we can get a cab.' We stepped out onto the street into a navy black night, and walked along in silence. It was past midnight and I hadn't come even close to doing what I'd set out to do. I stole a look up at Nate.

'I can feel you watching me,' he said, and halted, turned to me. I stopped too. 'I remember how often you used to do that, especially when you thought I was asleep.'

'You knew? Why didn't you tell me?'

'Because I liked it. Why would I stop something that I liked?'

Nate took a step closer, still staring at me, his hands reached out. 'Look at you,' he murmured, his white breath curling up and away into the night as he spoke. I expected him to take my face in his hands; instead, he pulled my collar from inside my coat. He patted the wide triangles down in place, all the while staring into my eyes. I was hypno-tised by him. His smile widened, turning him into the man I'd lived with. 'Look at you,' he breathed again. His hands slid down between my breasts to the top button of my coat. 'You're done up wrong.' I glanced down. I'd done up my coat buttons incorrectly.

I looked up into his eyes. 'Oh,' I said with a small laugh.

His eyes fixed on mine, Nate's nimble fingers gently undid the first button, then the next, until my coat was open. Nate pulled it together again, then slowly buttoned it up.

'Thanks,' I murmured, my breathing laboured from, I told myself, the thinness of the cold air. Not from lust and longing.

'Not a problem,' he said. He moved closer. He dipped his head, 'Kam,' he whispered as his lips touched mine.

'Ryn,' I said automatically, pulling away. 'No one calls me Kam any more, it's Ryn.'

'I'm not going to call you what he calls you.'

'It wasn't him who started it,' I replied.

Nate's lips grazed mine again and for a second I wanted to fall into it. To let it happen. To kiss him. I pulled back again. 'Nate,' I interrupted, 'I need to tell you something.'

'After,' he replied, moving in to continue the kiss.

'No.' I moved my head. 'I need to tell you something,' I insisted.

Nate rubbed his face. 'I don't want to hear that you're going to marry him,' he said, clenching his fists.

'This has nothing to do with Luke,' I said, seeing him flinch at the mention of my lover's name. 'I think we need to sit down.'

'OK,' he agreed. 'There's a park down the road.'

We walked the ten minutes to Hyde Park in silence, then sat on a bench not far from the entrance. The wind swirled around us, nipping at our already chilled skin. 'It's about Tegan,' I began.

Nate swivelled towards me, a frown on his face. 'Adele's daughter?'

I nodded, paused, hoped it'd sink in right then and there.

His eyes suddenly lit up with knowledge, dispersing the frown. 'Oh, God,' he murmured. 'I'm such an idiot.' He slapped his forehead. 'That was her, wasn't it? That little girl the other day. How is she after . . . ?'

'She's OK. We have our off days and our better days, I'm meant to be getting her counselling.'

'*You're* meant to be getting her counselling?'

'Tegan lives with me. I'm bringing her up. I'm her legal guardian.'

'*You* are?' Nate was incredulous.

I bristled. 'There was no one else. And I'm her godmother. I had to take on the responsibility. She was always precious to me.'

'You're a better person than I am. It's more than I could do. Is that what you wanted to tell me?'

I shook my head. 'It's about Tegan's father.'

His eyebrows lurched up in surprise. 'Her father? Is he around? Did you find out who he was?'

I nodded.

'And is he going to be involved in Tegan's life?'

'I don't know, I haven't told him yet. I don't know how he'll take it.'

'Not very well, I'd imagine,' Nate mused. 'Do you want me to come with you? Is that what you're trying to say? Because I will.'

'Oh my God, Nathaniel, when did you get so thick?' I snapped.

'I don't understand,' he said.

'Nate, it's you. You're Tegan's father.'

Tegan's face moved in sleep. Her lips were slightly open, her hair hidden under the pink silk scarf. I turned away, a lump in my throat. Awake she was mini-Adele, slumbering she wore her father's face.

It was past 4 a.m.; I'd let myself into the flat a couple of minutes ago and sneaked straight in to check Tegan was all right. She was, of course. I sniffed. Conflicting emotions were fighting to be released as a torrent of tears. I reached into my pocket for a tissue, and my fingers nudged up against my tights, which I'd hastily shoved in there before I got a cab home from Nate's place. *How am I going to explain all this to Luke?*

Nate had stared at me, his expression had frozen the second the words 'you're Tegan's father' had made sense in his head. No air came in or out of his mouth or nose, so I knew he wasn't breathing. All of a sudden, his upper body lurched and he was taking big gulping breaths. 'Wha . . . ? Huh . . . ?' he began. 'What are you saying?'

'Nate, it's true. You're her father.'

Nate launched himself off the park bench, stood stock-still, sat down again. He rubbed his palms over his cheeks, then they went to his eyes. 'No kids. We always agreed, no kids. And now you're telling me, what? I've *got* one?'

I nodded.

'You're wrong. It has to be some kind of mistake. It's not possible.'

'Did you use contraception when you slept with Adele?' I asked.

Nate grimaced, closed his eyes, shook his head in shame.

'Well, then it is possible,' I replied, my voice clipped and icy.

'But she always said it was a married man she met through work. A one-night thing with a man who wasn't capable of loving . . .' Nate's voice trailed away as it dawned on him that what she'd said pretty much described him. Even the work thing because they had run into each other a few times at media parties before I met him.

'It didn't occur to you that she had a baby nine months after you slept with her?'

'No. Why would it? She never gave me even the slightest hint . . .' He pushed his hands against his face again. 'How long have you known?'

I lowered my head, concentrated on my hands.

'That's why you left,' he said. 'I never understood why you wouldn't let me explain. You found out and you didn't bloody tell me, you just . . . What the fuck!' He was off the seat again.

'Adele didn't want you to know,' I stated. 'She didn't want Tegan's life disrupted. She said not to tell you.'

'WHAT THE HELL ARE YOU TALKING ABOUT?' he shouted. 'YOU

WERE WITH *ME*, NOT HER, *ME!* YOU SHOULD HAVE TOLD ME!'

I was off the seat as well. 'LIKE YOU TOLD ME YOU'D SLEPT WITH MY BEST FRIEND, YOU MEAN?' I shouted back.

He glared at me, then hissed, 'Fuck off,' and he stalked away, the dark night greedily gobbling him up as he went.

My instinct was to leave him to it because he needed time to get used to things. Then sanity returned: I was alone, in a dark park. I propelled myself after my ex-fiancé. 'Nate,' I called. 'Please! Stop! Please!' He didn't stop. 'Nate! Just let—' I was cut short by my heel skidding on a patch of ice, taking my legs from under me.

I sat in a heap on the stony ground, the cold seeping in through my clothing. After a few seconds I pulled up my throbbing left ankle, cradling it in my hands. My tights were in shreds around my right knee, stained with blood from where the cold ground had split my skin. More tears sprang to my eyes as arrows of pain tore up my legs.

This was the perfect ending to a traumatising evening: I was stranded in a park with no way of getting home. The person who had been seeing me home hated me and had stormed off. And I was in an extraordinary amount of pain for such a small fall. I allowed myself a wallow in self-pity before I accepted I had to call Luke to come and collect me. But he'd have to wake up Tegan, put her in the car, drive—

'Are you OK?' Nate asked, stopping in front of me.

I lowered my head so he wouldn't see the tears in my eyes as I nodded at him. Holding on to Nate, I limped over to a nearby bench. He gently lifted my legs up and stared down at my gashed knee and swelling ankle. From his pocket he pulled out a tissue. 'Don't worry, it's clean,' he said as he wiped grit and blood from the wound.

'She was my friend, too,' he went on, his voice loaded with sadness. 'She was one of my closest friends and she's gone. And no one told me. I had to read about it in some trade magazine.' He stopped dabbing at my knee. 'Why didn't you tell me? Do you hate me that much?'

'I don't hate you. Nate, I didn't think. It was hard enough getting through every day after she died, and there were lots of things that didn't occur to me. Telling you was one of them. It all happened so suddenly. She told me she would die but I didn't quite believe it. Still don't to some extent.'

Nate nodded. 'The last thing I ever said to her was that she'd ruined my life. And I'd hate her for it as long as she lived. How's that for not thinking someone would die?' Nate closed his eyes. 'After you'd gone, I rang her and asked why she'd told you. She said it was an accident but I didn't listen. I shouted at her. Told her she was a jealous bitch.' He shook his head. 'I want you to know it wasn't planned.'

I lifted my face to the night sky and the cold wind rushed over my features. 'Nate, I don't want to talk about it.' His fingers closed around mine as I lowered my head to him. 'When I first moved up here, I used to throw up every time I thought about you and Adele . . . I still do sometimes. Occasionally I look at Tegan and I have to turn away because I'm so overwhelmed by how she came about. Not her—*I love her*—the circumstance. It hurts. I don't mean it makes me cry. It does- n't. It actually rips away at me inside . . . And I can't talk about it.'

'Why tell me about Tegan, then?'

'Because you deserve to know. And, there's something else. Adele wanted me to adopt Tegan. But, if the adoptee has one living parent, then the prospective adopter has to get permission. I need you to sign over all rights to being Tegan's parent to me so I can adopt her.'

Nate shook his head. 'I only just found out that I've got a child and you're asking me to give her up?'

'You don't want kids, you said it yourself not five minutes ago.'

'Neither did you but you're doing it.'

'I had to. I was always the other person in Tegan's life, you know that. But you don't have to. You can just . . .'

'No,' Nate cut in. 'We can't talk here. Come home with me. Please.'

'**M**ummy Ryn,' Tegan's voice insisted as she tugged at my arm.

'Yeah?' I mumbled.

'Why have you got your clothes on? Did you sleep in them again?'

I groaned. Had I fallen asleep during sex again? That'd be bloody stupid, especially when I hadn't had sex with Nate in years. NATE! My eyes flew open and I found I was hunched up on the sofa.

Images of the night before flashed through my mind: going back to Nate's; him cleaning up my knee; us drinking tea, not talking; him call- ing me a taxi. I'd insisted on going home. For both our sakes. After checking on Tegan when I'd come in, I'd stood in the corridor, unsure whether to climb into bed with Luke or not. It'd wake him up and we'd either talk or make love, neither of which was appealing. I'd ended up curling up on the sofa and falling asleep.

Luke was at the stove, cooking—from the smell of it—bacon and eggs. There was toast on the go as well. He was avoiding looking at me.

'See, you've got your clothes on,' Tegan confirmed.

'Leave Ryn alone,' Luke said to Tegan. 'She must be knackered. Come sit down, eat your breakfast. Why don't you go to bed for a little while?' he said to me. 'I'll bring you some breakfast in an hour.' He still wasn't looking at me. I had to make this right with him; he had to understand I hadn't been unfaithful.

'Your orangey dress is all creasy up,' Tegan commented.

Luke's eyes dared to stray to me, taking in my crumpled appearance, then flinched with pain when he spotted my tights shoved in my coat pocket. His eyes darted away as though scorched by the thought of why my tights would be in my coat pocket, what it implied. 'Go on, get to bed,' Luke ordered. 'I'll bring you a bacon sarnie.'

'Thanks,' I mumbled. The moment to reassure him had passed. And I might not get another one, he might go on believing I had betrayed him.

I opened my eyes and found Luke perched on the bed. 'Thought I'd better wake you up before I go,' he said. 'I've got stuff to do. See you later.'

I reached out, grabbed his arm, held him back. 'What's going on?'

He finally turned his gaze on me. 'You tell me.'

I said nothing, unsure what to say.

'Look, Ryn,' he said after my long silence, 'I'll be honest, I don't know how to handle this. You know how I feel about you and Tegan, the pair of you have become my life. But he's her real father and there's obviously something going on between the two of you.'

'There isn't!' I protested.

'No? Why didn't you come to bed last night? Why were you walking funny? I'm hoping you didn't sleep with him but I wouldn't be surprised if you did because I know you still love him.'

'I told you, I don't any more.'

Luke ploughed over my correction. 'I can't deal with this. It's best I go and we talk about it when I'm less angry.'

'OK.' There was no getting through to him that I hadn't been unfaithful. Instead of leaving, he sat stock-still, asked, 'Did you?'

'No,' I replied. Some people would have been offended to be asked, but I'd ask if I was in his situation. It wasn't a lack of trust, it was a need to know. It was also a way of telling that person you trusted them to tell you the truth. 'I didn't even kiss him, Luke.'

'Did you want to sleep with him?' he asked, then braced himself.

Without hesitation, I replied, 'No.'

'Really?'

'Yes, really. I told him about Tegan and we had a row in the street, then I fell over, hurt my leg—that's why I'm limping. I went back to his place to get cleaned up—that's all. Then I got a taxi home. I didn't come to bed because it was 4 a.m. and I didn't want to disturb you.'

'Is he going to sign?'

'I don't know. He was so freaked out by what I told him, he couldn't deal with anything else.'

'And you seriously didn't want to sleep with him?'

'Seriously.'

'OK. OK. Budge up,' he said, and lay down beside me. I wrapped my arms around him, closed my eyes and let myself drift away into sleep.

I'd been telling him the truth. I didn't want to sleep with Nate. I wanted to kiss him. Hold him. Make love to him. And afterwards, I wanted to go back to watching him as he floated in dreamland, but at no point did I actually want to sleep with him.

I couldn't tell Luke that. Luke wouldn't understand that last night was like stepping back into an old Kamryn suit that I'd never been given the chance to grow out of. Wanting Nate last night had nothing to do with longing for another man at Luke's expense, it was about wanting another me at this me's expense; wanting another time and being willing to sacrifice this time to get it.

Luke wouldn't understand that. And anyway, I wasn't going to see Nate again—I was going to send him the papers and that would be it. So it didn't matter what I'd felt last night, now was the important thing.

Chapter Eight

RAT-A-TAT-TAT! I glanced at the front door to my flat, wondering who was knocking. Luke, who was out with Tegan, had a key. I cautiously opened the door and peeked out.

Nate.

I hadn't heard from him nor seen him in the week since our dinner. 'What are you doing here?' I asked, my voice shaking.

'I wanted to see you.'

'How did you know where I live?'

'I heard when you gave the taxi driver your address.'

'What do you want?' Hostility and fear tainted my voice.

'Like I said, to see you. And to see Tegan.'

My body contracted in terror. 'What? Why?'

'She's . . . Look, do we have to do this on the doorstep?'

'No, no.' I stepped aside to let him in.

Nate surveyed my living area. 'Where is she?'

'Luke took her to the park to feed the ducks after her karate class.'

'Take her out a lot, does he?' he snarled. I'd never heard that low, accusing, vicious tone to his voice, it scared me slightly.

'Nate, stop it, please.' I touched his arm. 'This isn't you.'

His whole body relaxed with a deep exhalation. 'No, no it's not, is it?' He shook his head. 'I'm all over the place right now, most of the time I don't know what I'm doing or feeling.' He parked himself on the sofa.

'What are you doing here?' I asked again.

'I wasn't lying, I want to see Tegan. I have to accept responsibility for her.'

Oh, no. I couldn't live without her now. 'Why? You don't want kids. Are you going to try and get custody of her?'

Nate drew away in horror, his features stricken. 'God, no!'

'So why do you want to see her?'

'Kamryn, she's my daughter. What sort of person would I be if I didn't even try to get to know her before I gave her up?'

'You don't understand, they won't let me adopt her if you're still around. That could be seen as you being capable of looking after her, which would mean I won't be allowed to adopt her.'

His eyes studied me for a few seconds. 'Were you expecting me to sign away my parental rights then walk away like it was nothing?'

When he put it like that, what I asked of him sounded callous— something he wasn't. 'No, course not . . . I don't know.'

'Kam . . . *Ryn*, we haven't even started to talk about what happened between us, I'm not going away until we have.'

That thought filled me with terror. While I didn't know why he'd done it, I suspected I knew. My suspicions haunted me, night and day. They were part of those grooves of guilt and loss in my mind. I didn't want those thoughts confirmed. Didn't want any of those grooves to become a permanent fixture of my personality.

'This isn't about us, this is about Tegan,' I said. 'I need to give her the stability that her mother would have given her and to do that I need to be able to adopt her.'

'And you haven't thought about the possibility of us getting back together and bringing up Tegan as her parents? Us being a family?'

Terror punched the air out of my body in one vicious blow and I turned away from Nate, clutching my stomach. 'Don't take her away from me,' I begged. 'She's all I've got left. Please don't take her away.'

His arms slipped around me. 'Why would I take her away?' he asked.

'I was only saying that if we gave it another go we could be a family.'

'But you won't sign unless I say yes,' I replied.

'I never said that. And I didn't mean it to put pressure on you. I just want us to talk properly. We need to sort things out.' Nate ran his fingers through my hair. He knew that would calm me. My two favourite things were having my hair stroked and my neck kissed. Nate knew that; Luke didn't. 'I want to make things right between us. And I need to accept this new responsibility . . . How are you doing for money? Because I should start paying for her.'

This wasn't what I wanted to hear. I needed him to be uninterested because they wouldn't let me adopt her if he was on the scene. This was what Nate was like, though: honest and noble. A good guy.

'I could manage about two hundred and fifty pounds a month.'

I crumpled again. That money would be a godsend. Even though Luke tried to help out, I resisted his attempts to pay for Tegan—she was my responsibility, not his, and I didn't want to rely on something that could be taken away at some point. Luke and I might not be for ever.

Nate engulfed me in a hug. 'Is that enough? Maybe if I give you a lump sum from my savings, then the two hundred and fifty would go a bit further. About three thousand? With no ties. I'll set up an account for her and I'll see if I can give more as she gets older. Well, actually, I have to pay more as she gets older, there's no two ways about it, is there?'

'Nate, I . . . thank you.'

He lifted my head. 'Ryn . . .' he began but was silenced by the sound of the key in the lock. We both instinctively jumped up. I quickly wiped tears from my eyes.

'We're back!' Tegan chorused as she and Luke bustled in. Tegan, swaddled in her red winter coat, her furry black hat on her head, paused in the doorway when she saw a tall white man standing beside me. Luke, who was two steps behind her, stopped short too.

'Did you have a nice time?' I asked, sniffing away the rest of my tears.

'Yes,' Tegan grinned. 'Who's that?' she asked.

'This is Nate. Remember I told you he was an old friend of mine?'

'You had a pretty dress,' she said to Nate.

Nate frowned comically. 'No, I've seen some lovely dresses in my time but I've never worn one. Promise.'

'Not you!' Tegan giggled. 'Mummy Ryn. She had a pretty dress 'cos she was going to be married.' She pointed. 'To you.'

Shock stumbled into the room, rendering us mute.

'That's right,' I said, recovering first. 'I didn't know you remembered.'

Tegan grinned. 'I did.'

Luke glared questioningly at me. 'Luke, this is Nate. Nate, this is my boyfriend, Luke.' Nate came around from the sofa and reached out his hand. Luke begrudgingly shook it.

'Are you Mummy Ryn's boyfriend?' Tegan asked, in case she hadn't unsettled us enough already.

'A long time ago I was,' Nate replied. 'But Luke is now.'

Tegan seemed pleased with that, she nodded her head in agreement. Luke looked like he might punch Nate just for the hell of it.

'We fed the ducks,' Tegan said.

Nate's face softened and he focused completely on Tegan. 'Oh, wow,' he said. 'What colour were they?'

'Duck colour,' Tegan giggled.

'Oh, were they bright yellow?'

'No!' Tegan squealed.

'Well, that's the colour the duck in my bath is.'

Where had Nate's ability to talk to a child come from? He used to run a mile when asked to stay with Tegan while I went to the loo if we were babysitting.

'There wasn't that many. They were brown. And green and purple with yellow around the neck. Luke said they fly away for winter.'

'Right, I'd better go,' Luke said.

Nate glanced away from Tegan, made uneasy eye contact with Luke for a moment, then he swung to me. 'I'd better get off. Got a work thing tonight. Bye,' he said to me. 'Luke.' He held out his hand and Luke shook it. 'And Tegan,' he bent to Tegan height, 'I'll see you soon, OK?'

The door shut behind him.

Luke's eyes flicked from me to the corridor, accompanied by a small jerk of his head. I followed him to my bedroom and he shut the door behind me. 'I don't like him being here,' Luke hissed.

'I didn't ask him to come, he came of his own accord. But it's my flat.'

'Did he try it on with you?'

'No, he didn't and even if he did—which he didn't—nothing would have happened. I'm with you.'

'What did he want?'

'To see Tegan.'

Luke quailed. 'He wants her?' He sounded as panicked as I felt.

'I don't know. That's why I was crying when you came in. I was terrified because he wants to take responsibility for her and that could mean all sorts for my adoption application.'

'Shit.' Luke sat on the bed.

'I'm scared, Luke.' I sat beside him and he put his arms around me.

'I'm scared that he's going to fall in love with her and then he's going to want her and I'll lose her and I'll let Adele down.'

'It'll be all right,' he said without conviction.

He didn't understand, I wasn't only scared about losing Tegan. Seeing Nate with Tegan, how he'd made an effort with her, had made me wonder if we could make it as a family—Nate, Tegan and I. I was scared because I was having doubts about Luke's place in our lives.

I pushed my way through the huddle of bodies standing in the trendy bar Paragon, in central Leeds. I'd forgotten how packed these places got. Since I'd inherited Tegan I didn't like going out—I felt I didn't give her enough attention, but she'd get none if I wasn't home at all. Also, the thought of leaving Tegan with a stranger was too scary. Which was why I was so lucky to have Luke at times like tonight, my first after-work drink in months. They were at home now, probably making dinner—wrecking the flat in the process. I searched through the smoke-tinted atmosphere for Nate. We were having a drink because he was meeting friends in Leeds that evening. I spotted him at a table in a corner, staring into a pint, a glass of white wine for me opposite him.

I'd barely swallowed the first mouthful when Nate asked, 'Are you going to tell Tegan I'm her father?'

'I don't know,' I replied. 'Tegan's a smart girl, she knows you're hanging around for a reason.' Twice Nate had dropped round to our place since his unexpected visit last Saturday—first of all to give me the details of the bank account he'd set up for Tegan. Two nights later he'd brought round the cash card that came with the account. Tegan had been cautious around him, Luke hadn't been happy.

'Is that how you see it, me hanging around? Like a bad smell?'

'Don't be like that, Nate. I just don't know if she's ready to hear that you're her father. For Tegan, "Daddy" is something she didn't have and now . . . "Daddy" is Luke. Not that she's ever said that, he's just stepped into that role in her life. She's completely devoted to him.'

Nate raised his head, pinned me to the spot with his navy-blue gaze. 'I'm seeing someone,' he said.

I'd been bringing my wine glass to my mouth and this revelation caused me to bash it against my teeth. I wasn't expecting that. 'Oh,' I uttered.

'I've only been seeing her a couple of weeks,' Nate revealed.

Since he saw me again. Oh God. Did that mean seeing me must have reminded him that reality doesn't match fantasy?

'She's one of the producers at the radio station.' She saw him every day. They probably flirted over the kettle. 'She's nice, you'd like her.'

'Let's not play this game, Nate, it makes us both look pathetic.'

'All right,' he agreed, dropping his gaze.

'Why are you doing this, Nate?' I asked, nudging the conversation in a safer direction. 'Why are you so interested in Tegan?'

'Well, it's not that I'm using her to get to you.'

'I don't think that.'

'Right, and that never crossed your mind, did it?'

I lowered my gaze as shame burnt up my face. He was right, of course. That thought had occurred to me, but deep down I knew it wasn't true. It was a way of making life simpler. Thinking that classified Nate as a calculating bastard who would never be as good as Luke because he was using his own child. The reality was Nate wasn't like that. He wasn't devious by nature. That was why I had been destroyed by what he'd done. I couldn't comprehend, couldn't compute how Nate—solid, dependable, adoring Nate—had cheated on me.

'I'm doing this because she's my responsibility,' Nate enlightened me. 'I take my responsibilities seriously. I even take responsibility for that night with Adele. She tried to blame herself but I was there too. I . . .' Nate stopped talking, probably because I was trembling. The thought of Adele had set me off: I was lurching into grief. Today was a bad day. A pain day. Most of the time I could put that debt to grief to one side and carry on, but on days like today, even thinking about Adele could paralyse me. The memory of her lying still and cold would crowd out all other thoughts and I would start to shake. 'Sorry,' Nate whispered. 'I didn't mean to upset you.'

'Did you talk about it a lot then?' I asked, calming myself.

'No, it wasn't like that. I was going to . . .' He stopped again but his expression—shocked by what had come out of his mouth—revealed all.

'You were going to leave me.'

'We have to put this into context, Kam. Ryn. Emotions were way off the scale; my head was all over the place. Me and you were . . .'

'You were going to finish with me? For Adele? You wanted to be with Adele?' My voice rose with every word. She never told me this.

'Kamryn, stop it,' Nate commanded, his voice stern with barely restrained anger. 'I was going to finish it because you were in love with someone else. Or have you forgotten that?'

I was like a rabbit caught in headlights: unable to move, unable to believe what he'd said. 'This is why we need to talk about this properly,' Nate said gently. 'We can't discuss things out of context. There were so many things going on, and I was so low at that time.'

'But . . .' I began, then realised I couldn't deny it without lying.

It was a stupid flirtation with someone from work. He came from our Edinburgh branch to work with us for six months. We clicked almost instantly and we became friends. We went to lunch and flirted with each other, but nothing more. When he returned to Scotland we didn't even keep in touch. It meant nothing and I hadn't realised that Nate had picked up on it. That he had any clue I'd had feelings for someone else. 'I never cheated on you,' I reassured him.

'I know you didn't,' Nate replied. 'But I thought I'd lost you and I wanted to cut my losses and get out. Adele convinced me not to.'

What, by sleeping with you?

'Not by sleeping with me, I know that's what you were thinking. She said some simple but truthful things. And that made me decide to not give up. She's so wise . . . She *was* so wise. I keep forgetting she's gone . . .'

'So do I. I'll be carrying on as normal, and then I'll get a call from Tegan and I'll remember . . . I don't get to speak to her ever again. And you don't realise how long for ever is until you can't do something. Especially when . . .' When I caused so much heartache by not speaking to her. I had right on my side when I cut her out of my life. She'd hurt me. Adele had no one else, though. I'd robbed her of the one person she relied upon. Adele's last few months were empty and lonely when they shouldn't have been. That was my fault.

Anguish settled on Nate's face. 'Adele texted me six months before she died, asked me to come and see her. I wouldn't. She rang me then, and asked if I could look after Tegan for a while because she was going into hospital. She said there was no one else. She was begging me and I wouldn't.' He paused, swallowed a mouthful of emotion. 'I said there was no way on earth I'd do anything for her. She kept saying she was sorry and that if I'd give her a chance she'd make it up to me, she just needed me to do this one thing. That's when I told her I'd hate her till the day she died.'

I couldn't imagine Nate being so nasty. He had the capacity for it, obviously. We all had the capacity for it. But to be so vicious to someone and mean it . . . I couldn't imagine that from Nate.

'That's the other reason I'm doing this. I want to make up for how much I let her down. We were like a family once, the four of us, and now I'll do anything I can do to make her daughter's life easier.'

'You're not doing this because she's your flesh and blood?'

Nate cast his eyes to the table. 'I'd love to say it was,' he admitted, 'but no. I do like her, she's a good kid, but there's no genetic pull . . . But that might change, the more time I spend with her.'

'So you're sticking around?'

He nodded slowly. 'For now.' He pushed his chair out. 'Hadn't you better be getting back? Tegan and Luke will be wondering where you are.'

As I watched Nate shrug on his coat, *inamorato* flashed into my mind. I was jolted. The slide of his lips, the shape of his eyes, his nose all still gave me a kick deep inside, and even though he wasn't, he still felt like *inamorato*. I bet his new woman felt this too. Was it the same for him? Was he in love with her, too? Actually, I realised, that's probably why he wanted to meet for a drink, he was killing time before a date.

'So, you've got a hot date tonight then?' I asked.

'I wouldn't exactly call it "hot", we're going to dinner.'

'OK, have a nice time.'

'Nice isn't the word I'd use. I've got to tell her that it's not going to work out between us.'

'Why not?' I replied, failing to keep that note of hope out of my voice.

'You know why,' Nate replied. 'There's someone else.'

I don't love him. *I do love him. I don't. I do.*

It was the middle of the night and I couldn't sleep. I hadn't been able to sleep for days. Not since I bumped into Nate in John Lewis, if I was honest. Or was it before that? Had I slept properly since Adele died? I couldn't remember it, if I had. Recently the problem had moved from bad to chronic. It'd take me hours to drop off and then after an hour or so I'd wake up again, lie in the still of the night, trying to sort out my thoughts from my feelings. Trying to work out if I loved Luke or not. We'd been going through a rocky patch of late, because neither of us knew where we stood with each other—I knew he was suspicious of my feelings for Nate, and I was just as suspicious of Luke's feelings for me. Things for me had changed since I said 'I love you' and he waited a week to say it back. It had made me doubt everything I thought he felt for me.

I don't love him. I do. I don't.

Luke snuggled into me. 'Hmmm,' he said against my neck. I wanted to push him off. *I just want to be alone.*

Soon he was deeply ensconced in dreamland again, so I slipped out of his hold, then out of the bedroom. Halfway down the corridor I stopped and opened one of the cupboards. I'd shoved Adele's boxes in them after we'd come back to Leeds and hadn't looked at them since.

I pulled out one box Adele had labelled *Clothes*, carried it to the sofa and peered in. The item on top was soft and furry and instantly I knew what it was: my black velvet jacket. I'd lent it to Del for a work do years ago; it'd been quite big on her but she'd been coveting it since the day I'd bought it, so she hadn't cared. How beautiful she'd been. That night and every night. I buried my face in the material, expecting it to smell of Del. Of course it didn't. The party had been over four years ago.

As I moved the jacket it crackled, a dry, papery sound. I shoved my hands into the jacket's pockets, and in the left one there was a folded-up envelope. On the front, in clear letters, it said, *Kamryn Matika.*

With a rapidly increasing heartbeat I unfolded the sheets of paper, all written in Adele's handwriting.

Hey, Beautiful, the letter began. I could almost hear her voice.

> *Let me start by saying, I love you. I'm sure I never got the chance to say that to you before I died. I know I'm dead because you wouldn't have this if I wasn't, would you?*
>
> *I love you, Kam. I've only ever been loved by two people in my life—you and Tegan—and I love the pair of you more than anything. But I know what you're like, Kamryn Matika—you're a stubborn bitch. I know you won't have let me explain what happened with Nate. And you need to know, Kam, you really do. It wasn't what you thought, it wasn't an affair . . .*

It wasn't what Kamryn thought, it wasn't an affair. I never longed for Nate romantically or sexually, he was such a precious friend, it was just, when it happened, it was a time when everything was so mixed up.

Kamryn never understood how much Nate loved her. She loved him back, of course, but he'd do anything for her, his love for her was limitless, I think. Unconditional. And it must have been love from the outset because she was awful to him. Even when they got together properly. The shit I went through to become her friend was nothing compared to how she treated him. How sarky she was, and downright rude. But, he stuck it out. Cut through all her bullshit and proved every single day how much he cared. She often said that I didn't know him, that he needed her to prop him up, but she didn't say that resentfully, I think it was her way of showing that it was a two-way thing. That while he loved her unconditionally, she cared for him in ways that weren't immediately obvious. I thought I was going to die with happiness the day she said they'd decided to get married.

Even then, though, Kamryn didn't quite believe that Nate was for real. She'd always wonder if he'd mutate into one of the controlling bastards who'd plagued her past. She worried, constantly, that he'd find someone else.

The time it happened, Nathaniel was so torn up. He'd just come back from driving Kam to Leeds, where she was going for business. He often did that, would drive her up there, she never asked him to, he simply wanted to do it. Anyway, he dropped by my flat on the way back because Kamryn had told him to. She worried, you see, about me being on my own if she wasn't around, so she'd told him to go check on me. He was knackered, but there was something else. He was troubled, hurting. I could see it the second I opened the door. He said he wouldn't stay long, just wanted to make sure I was all right.

'I'm fine, but you're obviously not—what's the matter, Nathaniel?'

He rubbed his hand across his eyes, stared into space for a moment. Then he exhaled. 'I think Kamryn's going to leave me. She's found someone else.'

'Don't be silly,' I said, trying to be honest.

'She has. I can tell. She's definitely met someone else. She can hardly look me in the eye nowadays and she won't talk to me—not even to snipe at me.'

'Nathaniel, she wouldn't even look at another man.'

He shook his head. 'You're terrible at lying, Adele. But thanks for trying.'

'She really hasn't done anything,' I reassured him. 'And she wouldn't. Kam's not the cheating kind.'

'No, she's not. She wouldn't physically cheat but I reckon I should end it before she leaves me.'

I was horrified. I had to make him understand that it was a glitch. 'Look, Nate, she's not going to leave you. Now, say, hypothetically, she's met someone. Maybe at work. And, say she clicked with this person and they started to spend lunchtimes together, had a laugh. That is all it would be. A laugh. Kamryn would never give you up. She's never loved anyone but you.'

'Yeah,' Nate breathed. He raked his fingers through his hair. 'I'm so confused . . . Do you mind if I lie down for a second before I go home?'

Nathaniel went to lie down in Kamryn's old room. Hours later, I went in to check on him. He was sound asleep when I crouched down by the bed and, bless him, he looked so peaceful. His eyes flew open and he was suddenly staring at me. I don't know if it was because he'd looked so beautiful in his sleep, if I'd forgotten who he was, or if I'd just taken leave of my senses, but I did it. It was all my fault. I kissed him.

Nathaniel looked surprised, then jerked his head away. That shocked me back to reality. I turned to run away, horrified that I'd kissed my best friend's fiancé, but he grabbed my arm, stopped me. I was scared as I turned back because I knew what was going to happen. We kissed again, and then it happened. It wasn't frantic and lust-fuelled. It was slow. Loving, gentle, beautiful. I'm sorry, it's not what Kamryn would want to hear but I want to make it clear that it wasn't about feelings building up over time that we couldn't ignore. It was about two people who had different reasons for doing what they did. No man had been nice to me like that in a long time. And for that little while, I could pretend that the person I was with cared about me, was making love to me rather than just fucking me. It wasn't real but it felt real, for a little while.

When I woke up, Nathaniel was fully clothed and sat on the edge of the bed. 'I'm really sorry,' he whispered. 'So, so sorry.' Even in the dark I could *see how ashamed he was. I was too. 'What have I done? How am I going to make this right? I've done the worst thing possible,' he said. I knew how bad he was feeling because I felt that same anguish. 'When she gets back,' he was saying, 'I'll finish with her and move out. She doesn't want to be with me anyway, so I'll tell her what I've done. But I won't say it's you. This doesn't have to ruin your friendship.'*

I couldn't let him take the rap for this. We'd both done it. We talked and talked until we agreed we'd put it behind us. And it worked. We didn't fancy each other, neither of us had any wish to repeat it, so it didn't become an issue.

Then I found out I was pregnant. I knew straight away he was the father and I knew I couldn't tell anyone. Not Kamryn. And definitely not Nathaniel. He would have confessed and Kam would have left me.

When it was over, I sat on my sofa staring into the mid-distance. *Why? Why had Nate done it?* I now knew it was an impulse for Adele. That was what she was like, impulsive, spontaneous. But Nate thought everything through. He said the other day he was feeling low at the time it happened; was that one of the ways he made himself feel better? Imagining making love to Adele? I had to know. I picked up the phone and stared at the buttons. I couldn't call him, not with Tegan and Luke in the house. I launched myself off the sofa, grabbed my coat, crept down the stairs and outside into the bleak midwinter night. I dialled his number, and after its fifth ring his sleep-musty voice croaked, 'Hello?'

'Why did you do it?' I asked, louder than I intended. 'Why?'

'Kam?' He coughed to clear his throat. 'It's 4 a.m., what are you doing?'

'I have to know. She told me. She told me what happened; I know why she did it. But I don't know why you did. Why?'

'Jesus, Kam, what are you doing? Where are you?'

'In the street.'

'What?' I could hear him wake up, sit up suddenly. 'The street where?'

I sniffed. 'I had to come outside because they're asleep . . . Why? Was I that terrible? I was, wasn't I?' Suddenly it felt as though my internal organs were being crushed. 'I'm sorry,' I gasped. 'I was such a bitch. I knew you'd leave me one day because I was such a bitch.'

'Kam, I'm coming over. Stay where you are. I'll be there soon, OK?'

Nearly thirty-five minutes later the silver Audi driven by my ex drew up outside my building. He crossed the pavement towards my flat as I came down the path to meet him. We met at my gate, his face a mix of confusion and worry and sleep. Unbidden, wild uncontrollable anger spiked through me. Before I knew what I was doing, my arm was raised and I'd slapped him across the face.

Nothing was said for a few seconds, then Nate raised his hand to his slapped left cheek. 'That's been a long time coming,' he said.

I wanted to hit him again, but was scared of hurting him. Because the rage in me was enough to cause him permanent damage. 'Why?' I asked. 'Why did you pull her back? I know what she's like. She would have kissed you and not meant it. But why did you pull her back?'

Nate stayed huddled in his silence.

'Why Nate? What did I do? Was I that awful? I didn't mean to be.'

Nate looked up then, took me in his arms. 'Shhhh,' he hushed. 'I always thought you didn't care that much. I thought you'd gone because of the betrayal. I never thought it had hurt you that much.'

'Of course I cared. I just couldn't speak about it because it'd make me fall apart. So why did you pull her back?'

'Because . . .'

I tensed in his arms, knowing he was going to say it was because I was rubbish. In bed and out of bed. That I was so rotten to him that he had to pay me back somehow. This had always been my terror: what happened confirmed that I was different. Broken.

'Because right after she kissed me and I pulled away from her, she looked so terrified and that simple action reminded me of you. That time when we first had sex. Afterwards you were about to go home and I asked if I'd see you again, remember? You said, "We'll see," and left. You had that same expression on your face. You looked so scared, so surprised, and it was so honest that I fell for you. And, that night with Adele, I was so confused about us, I knew we were almost over, and I saw that look again. It reminded me of that moment I fell for you. I wanted it back. I wanted to make love to the you I fell for, not the one I'd been existing with for the past six months. The whole time I was thinking about you. I used Adele to make myself feel better. And then I was a complete bastard to her when she told you what we'd done. Do you have any idea how much I hate myself for not making things right with her before she died?'

'Yes,' I replied. 'Because I hate myself more.'

Nate pulled away from me slightly. 'You didn't sort things out with her? But how did you know what happened that night?'

I pulled the letter from my pocket. 'I just found it,' I explained. 'I thought you knew that I didn't know.'

'You never talked to her? Why not?'

'I couldn't think about it, let alone talk about it. And then there was Tegan. You two had something that I could never be a part of. I hated you both for that. I never wanted a baby but if I did want one, it would have been yours. You're the only person on earth I'd want to have a child with and you did it with someone else. Someone I loved. That's why I had to leave.' I was incoherent. Every thought in my head rushing to come out at once. 'And I thought I had a few months to get used to the idea of having her back in my life, and then one day we'd have that conversation. But she died so suddenly . . .' I pressed my palms onto my eyes. 'I didn't get to say goodbye. I didn't tell her that I was sorry. That I didn't hate her, I loved her. I walked away not knowing that was the last time I'd see her.' Nate held me up as my strength disintegrated. 'I'm such a horrible person. She was dying and I didn't let her talk. I was too scared to hear it. But I wanted to say goodbye.'

Nate didn't say anything as he held me together. He'd never had to do this with me before. I was the strong one with Nate and me. 'Babe,' he whispered in my ear as everything I'd been feeling for weeks came gushing out in a tidal wave of emotion. 'It's OK,' he reassured me.

Eventually the tears stopped. 'I'm sorry,' I whispered, so tired I could hardly form words. 'I didn't mean to do that.' I mustered enough strength to push him away. 'Nate, this is so messed up. I can't be breaking down in front of you. I've got a boyfriend, whom I love. He's the one I should be crying with, not you. I just wanted to know why, that's all.'

'Don't push me away,' he pleaded.

'You are away, Nate. The sooner we both get used to that, the better.' Even I lurched inside at the coldness in my voice.

He nodded slightly, abject misery on his face as he turned away.

'I'm sorry,' I blurted at him. I couldn't let him go like that. What if it was the last time I saw him? What if it was like Adele all over again? 'I'm sorry for saying that. And for hitting you. I'm sorry for all of it.'

He stopped opening his car door. 'I'm sorry too. I never said that but I am. For breaking up our relationship. For wrecking your friendship with Adele. For hurting you so badly. I'm truly sorry.'

I nodded. 'I'll talk to you soon,' I said.

'Yeah,' he replied. His car started as I opened the main front door.

Upstairs, I quietly opened the front door to my flat, crept into the bedroom. I jumped when I found Luke, fully dressed, sitting on the bed. 'I saw Nate outside,' he stated quietly. 'What's going on?' His face was angry but also afraid. I climbed onto my bed, lay down.

'Give us a cuddle,' I asked.

Luke hesitated, then did as I asked, curled up around me. I relaxed against him. 'What's going on?' he murmured, anxiety in his voice.

In short bursts, I told him.

Chapter Nine

'MUMMY RYN,' Tegan said quietly.

I knew what she was going to say because over the past couple of weeks Tegan had changed. Her appetite had halved, she'd retreated into quietness, and she'd taken to drawing pictures of a woman who could only have been her mother, but if I asked who was in the picture she'd shrug and whisper, 'Don't know.' I knew what she was thinking because I was thinking it too. I too had become edgy and restless—my insomnia had gone from chronic to critical; during the day I could barely summon any energy and I didn't return any of Nate's emails and calls.

'Yes, Tiga?' I replied. I patted my lap.

'You know it's Christmas?' she said cautiously as she settled in my lap. I nodded. Christmas was in just under three weeks, she'd finish school in five days and would go to the Kayes' house during the day. It was Christmas outside and in the flat—we had a tree; decorations were up; every day Tegan opened the chocolate advent calendar that Luke had bought—but inside us where Christmas excitement should be was an ache. Memories. We hadn't discussed what we were doing on the big day yet, and every time Luke tried to bring it up, I put him off until Tegan and I could talk properly. We hadn't been able to do that until now, when Luke was in New York for a week on business. I'd decided to leave the start of the conversation to Tegan, to wait and see if she'd properly remembered or if I was worrying about nothing.

'It's . . .' Her voice died in her dry throat.

'It's your mummy's birthday,' I finished for her.

She nodded.

'I know,' I said. Adele's birthday was Christmas Day.

'Do they have birthdays in heaven?' she asked.

'Erm . . . Maybe,' I replied carefully. 'I don't see why not.'

'If I sent her a card, would she get it?'

'I don't think so,' I replied gently.

Tegan curled up against my torso. Her shoulders started to shake. Her sobs slowly became audible. She hadn't cried in front of me since her mum died. I didn't know this would be the thing that would set her off, that revealed the rivers of pain that flowed through her.

'Why isn't my mummy coming back?' Tegan asked through her hiccuppy sobs. 'Was I a bad girl?'

'No, sweetheart,' I said. 'Your mummy was just ill.'

'I want her to come back,' she insisted.

'So do I.' A thought blossomed in my mind. 'Tiga, have you been thinking that your mummy is coming back?'

'Yes,' she whispered. She hiccupped a few more tears. 'She might not like heaven and come back. She might like Leeds more.'

Adele and I did a great job of explaining death to her, didn't we? 'I'm sorry, baby, your mummy isn't coming back. Not ever.'

The gulps and their accompanying wail increased in volume and distress. It tore through me because I knew how she felt. I held her warm body close to me, trying to envelope her in comfort. 'I rocked you like this when you were little,' I said into Tegan's hair. 'You were so funny-looking when you were born, I thought, Gosh, have they given us the right baby? But then you smiled, and you looked just like your mummy, and I knew you had to be hers. Ours. Because you were mine too, you know? You were my little Tiga. Even when I was away for all that time I thought of you. I had your picture in my purse and when people said, "Who's that?" I'd say, "That's my little Tiga."

'I'm sorry your mummy's not here, Tiga. I know it's going to be hard to get used to. Why don't we call Christmas Day, Adele Day? Adele was your mummy's name, you know that, don't you?'

'Yes,' she whispered.

'OK, we'll have Adele Day. We'll make special Adele Day cards and send them to everyone we know. And we can draw pictures of her and I'll show you some of the pictures in my photo albums. Hmmm?'

'Is Luke going to come?' She'd stopped crying, that was something.

'No. It'll just be me and you. No boys allowed!'

'What about Mr Nate?' she asked.

'Yeuck! No! He's a boy! And, just so we don't miss out on Christmas, we can have it the next day. And open our presents then.'

'Luke can come to that one, can't he?' Tegan asked.

'If you want him to,' I said.

'I do. And Mr Nate.'

'Really? Why?' He was nice to her, the three or four times she'd seen him since their first meeting, but he wasn't Luke. And each time he'd dropped by, it'd been for ten minutes at the most; why would she want to spend such an important day with him?

'You like him,' she said simply, sniffling back tears.

'But he doesn't have to come to our Christmas Day if you don't like him.' There was a note of panic in my voice. I hadn't seen him since our confrontation in the street a fortnight ago.

'I do like him. He's funny.' That surprised me even more. What had he done to make her say he was funny?

'All right, I'll see if he can come. He might not be free, though.' I cuddled her closer. 'It's all right to cry, you know,' I said. I'd stopped her doing that. Not intentionally, but I'd felt better when she did stop. But crying was better than that build-up of resentment that grew from not letting your emotions out. I didn't want Tegan to grow up angry and bitter because she'd been denied the opportunity to express her grief. 'If you feel sad about your mummy or you miss her, you can cry any time you want. You can talk about her any time you want to as well.' I stroked the long, fine waves of her hair. Poor fragile Tegan. My poor, poor baby.

What and what?' was Luke's reply when I told him the plan for Christmas Day. I'd been dreading telling him and decided away from Tegan was the best plan, which meant doing the deed at work once he'd returned from America. He stood over my desk, arms folded, imposing in his charcoal-grey suit. The unusual hazel colour of his eyes added a flint-like quality to the stare that burned accusation and displeasure at me. He wasn't simply upset, he was deeply aggrieved. 'I don't get to spend Christmas Day with you two, but I do get to spend Boxing Day with your ex?' Luke said.

'I have to do this for Tegan. It has to be just us on Christmas Day. And she's the one who suggested Nate come on Boxing Day, not me.'

'What if I come over in the evening?' he asked.

'Luke, no. This is for Tegan. It's her mum's birthday, the first since Adele . . . *died*. I can't believe you can't see how important that is.'

'I do. It's just . . . I don't have a family, either, remember? I usually spend Christmas in New York with friends, but this year I turned them down because I thought I had a family to spend it with.'

'And you have, just not on the twenty-fifth. What do you want me to do, Luke? Put you before my child?'

For a moment, he was going to say yes. I could see it on his face, in his eyes, in the way his lips twitched.

'Is that the sort of person you want me to be? The sort of woman you want to date?' I added to stop him saying something he didn't mean. 'I don't need this, you know? It's going to be a hard enough day without worrying if you're going to dump me because you can't be there. I'm sorry, Luke, but Tegan comes first.'

The phone on my desk rang. I picked it up. 'It's me,' Nate said.

'Oh, hi,' I said. The temperature in the room rose suddenly. I pressed my phone closer to my ear so that Luke wouldn't hear his voice.

'I know you're at work so you can't talk for long, but you don't return my calls to your mobile or reply to my emails,' he said. He spoke without accusation. 'I wanted to talk to you about Christmas. I know it's Adele's birthday, and I was wondering what you were doing? It's going to be hard on you and Tegan.'

'I was going to call you about that actually. Tegan and I are spending the twenty-fifth alone but she was wondering if you were free on the twenty-sixth, when we're having Christmas Day.'

'Is Luke going to be there?' Nate asked.

'Of course.'

'Then I don't think it's a good idea, do you? How about I come over on Christmas Eve and give you your presents then?'

'OK,' I said, relieved. Greatly relieved. Not only because Luke would have spent the whole day in a foul mood, but because I didn't want to spend time with Nate. The elements of our deceased relationship had altered with the knowledge of why he'd slept with someone else. He hadn't done it out of malice, he'd been driven to it by loneliness. That meant a lot of things about me. My constant fear that I'd driven him to do it was right, but I hadn't bitched him into it, I'd abandoned him, left him lonely. Of course, he didn't have to sleep with someone else, but he was only human. I understood a little more about Nate now, and that modicum of knowledge was dangerous.

'Christmas Eve, then,' he said. 'Can I see you before then?'

'Erm, I don't know if that's a good idea,' I replied, after a sideways look at Luke.

'What about Tegan? Do I get to see her before then?'

'If you want. I can drop her off at your place for an hour or so.' There was no way in hell I would do it but this was a test—did he really want to see Tegan or to see me?

'Or I could come over and you could go out for an hour?' he replied. 'Less disruptive for her?'

'You know that's not going to happen, don't you?'

'Not now, maybe, but in time, it might. I do genuinely want to see her. And you, of course.'

I sighed. 'OK, I'll call you, maybe you can come over at the weekend, I'll see if Tegan's up for it. Bye, Nate.'

'OK, babe, love you, bye.' Click went the phone as he hung up. BOOM! went my mind as I repeated what he said in my head.

'Is he coming for Christmas?' Luke asked.

I shook my head, afraid to look at him in case my face betrayed what was going on in my mind. Nate had said it so easily. It's what he always said when we were together. 'He's, erm, busy. He's going to come over on Christmas Eve instead, just to drop off Tegan's presents.'

'Ryn?' Luke began. I turned to look at him. 'I'm sorry for being such an ass earlier. I do understand, I'm just disappointed.'

'I know.'

'No, you don't know. For the first time in my life I've got a family. I never had a child I could spoil at Christmas. Do you know how excited I was? Christmas is a time for families. But the twenty-sixth will be OK. It'll be great, in fact.'

I nodded.

After checking no one could see, Luke kissed me. 'See you tonight.'

He left my office. And when he left, the thumping of my heart at what Nate said increased. He'd said he loved me. Did I love him? If I did, what would it mean for our lives? And it would be *our* lives. Whom I chose to be with wasn't only about whom I wanted to be with, Tegan's feelings counted as much as mine. If she wasn't around, I knew whom I'd choose.

My mobile bleeped. When I opened the message from Luke, it said: *Forgot to say, I love you :).*

Do I really know whom I'd choose? Do I?

Adele Day dawned and Tegan was out of bed before light managed to peek through the night sky.

Her head popped round my door. 'Am I allowed to come in?' she asked.

'Course,' I replied. She climbed up on the bed and under my covers. I encircled her with my arm. 'Do you want breakfast first or your present?'

'I'm allowed a present?' she asked.

'Yes, of course, Madam. This is Adele Day. Afterwards we can have breakfast and you can ring Nana Faith. It's up to you.'

Tegan's eyes widened as she thought about what to do. All the possibilities. 'Present,' she whispered after much rumination.

'OK,' I said. I opened the drawer of my bedside table and pulled out her present, a gold box with a red ribbon around it. 'Here you go.'

Tegan's eyes widened. 'What is it?' she asked. Any other child would have ripped the box open by now, but not Tegan, she had to think it through. I was like that, always a bit cautious; Adele would've had the box open the second she saw it was for her. That's what came from having romance in your soul, I suppose. You believed in things like love at first sight and perfect presents.

'Open it and find out,' I advised.

Tegan cautiously lifted the lid of the box and gazed inside. 'Is it really for me?' she gasped. I nodded.

From its bed of blue silk padding she picked up the gold necklace with a disc hanging from it. She stared hard at the disc and the dark, holographic picture on it. 'It's me and my mummy,' she said eventually.

'It sure is,' I replied. I'd had a photo of Tegan and Adele copied onto the disc.

'Can I wear it all the time?' she asked, staring at the necklace.

'If you want to. It's up to you.'

She held it out to me to put on. I instructed her, 'Lift up your hair so I can hook it up at the back,' before I slipped the chain around her neck. 'There,' I said. She let her hair fall back into place, and I wondered as her blonde locks touched her shoulders if I should get her hair cut. I liked Tegan with long hair, but what would Adele have wanted? Her daughter's hair had always been cut when it reached chin-length. *Does it matter?* I thought, mutinously. *She's not here.* Guilt skipped close behind those rebellious thoughts.

Luke had planted those seeds of mutiny in my mind a few days ago. I'd been pondering aloud what school to send Tegan to when she was older. I explained to Luke that I didn't know if Adele would want her daughter to go to an all-girls' school or a mixed school.

Luke had replied, 'You're not Adele.'

I'd been offended. Did he really think I was stupid enough to believe I could replace her in Tegan's life? 'I know that,' I replied.

'Then stop trying to be her,' he'd said. 'You call Tegan your daughter, so act like she is. Stop trying to second-guess what Adele would have wanted and do what you want. She's your responsibility, not Adele's.'

I'd frowned at him. 'I know she's my responsibility,' I eventually said.

'I'm not saying you're not taking responsibility for her, babe, it's just that you could worry so much about what Adele would want that you do nothing. And it's the ultimate fall-back, isn't it? If things go wrong, you don't have to accept you made a bum decision because you can say it was what Adele would have wanted and not you that messed up.'

'I'm doing the best I can,' I replied, feeling chastised and caught out, even though I seriously hadn't ever thought like that. But he had a point—she was my baby now. My burden. My hope. My love. Everything, good or bad, was down to me.

I looked down at Tegan again. At moments like this, moments when she was so completely reliant upon me for not only her physical well-being but also her emotional well-being, it hit me again. I was in charge. Of it all. All the time. For ever.

'Come on then, missus, let's make some calls and have breakfast.'

In the living room, I handed Tegan the phone.

'Hello, Nana Faith . . . Fine . . .' Tegan laughed a little tinkly laugh and replied, 'You said Happy Adele Day.' Her grin got even wider as I heard the soft tones of my mother talking to her down the phone.

When I'd told my mum about Adele Day, she'd been a lot more sup-portive than Luke had been. She'd said she'd make us a cake, but I'd declined: it was nice but not necessary. Just as I'd said goodbye, Mum had said, 'You know, Kamryn, your father and I are very proud of you.'

'Pardon?' I replied, shocked that my mum had said that about me. Our relationship had been defined by me embarrassing them in front of their friends and our wider family by not getting married.

'Tegan is a big responsibility,' Mum continued. 'You are doing very well, though. Very well.' Mum often rang to speak to Tegan, and Tegan often called my parents. They loved her. Everyone loved her.

'Thanks,' I mumbled.

'Ever since you didn't get married—' We'd never talked about it— 'we were worried about you, but now you have someone.'

'You mean Luke?' I asked.

'Tegan. You've got a family now. That makes me very happy.'

Tegan finished talking to my mum, then spoke to Grandpa Hector. Then she asked if she could call my sister, Sheridan, and her kids. By the time she'd spoken to all our family, I'd made us breakfast.

Adele lay on her back, sunglasses hid her eyes; her skin was shiny with sunblock. She was pouting up at the camera, her long hair that fuzzed around her head in curls the only thing, she thought, that distinguished her from Marilyn Monroe.

Tegan flipped over the page in one of my college photo albums. There was a picture of me slumped over my desk. I'd been cramming for my finals and Adele had caught me asleep on the job. Also on the page, Adele and I were being hieroglyphs in front of the pyramids in Egypt at sunset. The opposite page, Adele and I were graduating. In the background my parents were uneasily talking to Adele's father and his wife. When Tegan spotted her grandfather and Muriel, she snapped over the page quickly. We moved on to another album, later pictures of Adele and me and Nate. There was Nate and I sitting on the sofa in

Adele's and my flat. There was Adele, nine months pregnant. Tegan in Adele's arms, minutes after she was born. Me holding Tegan. Nate holding Tegan, having been threatened with no sex for a week by me if he didn't. Tegan evolving from lying to sitting to crawling to walking to running to dancing. All the while laughing, giggling, smiling. Happy.

We looked through all the pictures, then an exhausted Tegan asked to go to bed at six o'clock. 'Goodnight, Tiga,' I said after I'd switched off the light beside her bed.

'I want my mummy,' she whispered.

I'd decided not to read Tegan the card Adele had left her for Christmas Day, nor any of the other letters she'd left just yet. It'd only confuse her, make her think there was a chance Adele would return.

A small sob escaped her lips, 'I want my mummy,' she said again as she slid into sleep.

Had I done the wrong thing today? Had I screwed up? I should go back to what I was doing before—not talking about Adele. I slipped into bed myself, even though it wasn't even seven o'clock.

I woke up again when I was being nudged aside in bed: Tegan. She snuggled against me. Within minutes she was breathing gently and slowly, asleep.

At least she knew she had me. I wasn't her mum, but I was there.

One of my favourite parts of the day was the time right before Tegan went to bed, when she had her bath.

Two months after Adele Day, Tegan and I had settled into a routine. It'd been seven months since Adele'd died and Adele Day had cemented in both our minds that she wasn't coming back. We had to get on with life and with each other.

Normality had settled on our lives. Luke spent almost every weekday here and even at weekends he didn't go to his place in Alwoodley. Nate also came around a bit—he would drop by, have a cup of tea, chat to Tegan, ignore Luke's seething in the corner. Luke asked me a few times if Nate was going to sign the papers. I hadn't asked Nate what his plans were because I didn't want to push him. My heart did skip every time Nate walked in, but I knew that would stop as I got used to seeing him again. There was only one fly in our ointment. Or rather a huge elephant sitting on the table that every adult pretended they couldn't see.

Tegan scooped up a handful of white bubble-bath foam and dumped it on my hand. I'd lowered my head to blow the bubbles at her when she decided to point out the elephant by asking, 'Is Luke my daddy?'

I struggled to keep my voice steady as panic streaked through me. In all this time I hadn't worked out what to say to her. 'Why do you ask that?'

'Regina Matheson said that everyone has a mummy and a daddy. I said I only had a Mummy Ryn and a mummy who was in heaven. Then she said maybe Luke was my daddy. Is he?'

I am going to hurt this Regina Matheson, if I ever meet her.

'Luke isn't your daddy.'

'But I do have a daddy, don't I?'

'Yes. Yes, you do, Tiga.' My mouth dried.

Tegan stopped chasing bubbles. My shaky voice had alerted her that something was wrong and she asked, cautiously, 'What's his name?'

I sighed as I bit my lower lip. 'Nate,' I said quickly.

'Mr Nate?' she asked, blinking at me in surprise. 'Not Luke?' She was disappointed.

'Nate is your daddy.'

'Do I have to live at Mr Nate's house?' she asked after a tense silence.

'God, NO!' I screeched. 'You're with me for ever, Tegan.'

'And Luke. Are you going to marry Luke?'

'I don't know, I haven't thought about it.'

'If you married Luke, would he be my daddy? Would he be Daddy Luke?' She didn't hide her happiness at that prospect.

'I suppose so,' I replied.

'Are you going to marry Mr Nate?'

'No.' Nate and I were not getting married. Or back together. It wasn't even a possibility, no matter how my heart skipped when he was around.

'Why not?'

'Because Luke's my boyfriend.'

'Why is Mr Nate my daddy?'

Did I really have to do the birds and the bees? 'Erm . . .' I began. 'Do you mind Nate being your daddy?' Ask a diversionary question.

Tegan shrugged. 'I don't know. Mr Nate is funny.' She scrunched up her nose. 'Mr Nate looks at you. Sometimes, he smiles at you. You don't see him or nothing. He likes you more than he likes me.'

'Nate likes us both.'

'Do you like Mr Nate or Luke more?'

Now if I knew the answer to that question, I'd be sleeping better at night. I wouldn't have this constant guilt at wanting them both. Luke for being here now, for having not known Adele so not being a constant reminder of her. Nate for being a reminder of the person I used to be. The Kamryn who was sometimes nice and who often laughed. 'I like them both,' I informed Tegan. 'But I like Tegan the most.'

She broke into a smile. 'Mummy Ryn, I'll think about this. I don't know if I want Mr Nate to be my daddy,' she explained.

I nodded. And I would have to think about how to tell her, that, like it or not, want it or not, Nate was her daddy.

Nate was hunched over a cup of coffee in the Horsforth Coffee House. When I'd rung to arrange this meeting, I'd suggested we meet in central Leeds but he'd said he didn't mind driving over to my neck of the woods.

I arrived at his table and he raised his head. My stomach flipped in horror. He looked like a ghoul. The dark scores under his eyes told me he wasn't sleeping, his cheekbones starting to poke through his skin meant he probably wasn't eating. And his slow, lethargic movements showed that just sitting up was an effort.

I sat down. Close up the devastation was more marked, more ingrained into him. This had been building up for some time.

'Are you OK?' I asked.

He nodded, dismissively. 'I'm fine, gorgeous. So, what was the serious tone on the phone about?'

I hesitated. The state he was in, this was the last thing he needed to hear, but I had to do this. 'Nate, I want you to sign the papers to allow me to proceed with adopting Tegan.'

Nate sagged in his seat, staring at the table in misery.

'I know you like her, but not enough to be her full-time dad. I just want to give Tegan the sort of stability where she knows that I'm not going to leave her. You understand, don't you?'

Nate nodded his tired head.

'So you'll sign?'

Another tired, dejected nod. 'Can I still come and see her?'

'Of course,' I said. 'It'd traumatise her if you disappeared. I mean, she's still freaked out that you're her father, but she likes you, Mr Nate. A lot. I don't blame her.'

'Don't,' he muttered with a shake of his head. 'Please don't be nice to me. It just reminds me how much I screwed things up.'

'I never thought I'd see the day when you asked me not to be nice to you. Phrases you never thought you'd hear, or what?'

'Ryn, do you really think I'd have stuck around if you were as nasty as you seem to think you were? You were so incredible to me. You were always looking after me, encouraging me. I sometimes used to wonder why you didn't want children when you were so good at taking care of people; not just me, Adele too . . .' He closed his eyes.

'Nate, let's not . . . What you described was this perfect relationship and it wasn't. I drove you into someone else's bed. I made you—'

Nate slammed his hand onto the table top. 'Stop being so hard on yourself,' he snapped. 'That was what drove me crazy about you. Always blaming yourself for things you had no control over. You didn't make me do anything—I cheated on you. It wasn't your fault.' He calmed himself with a few deep breaths. 'I did it, I screwed things up.'

'Anyway, I'm meeting Tegan and Luke down at the park,' I said. I wasn't talking about this now. If I carried on thinking about these things, I'd start to crack up again. Before Christmas I'd been on the verge of a breakdown; crying in Nate's arms had been a part of it. Thankfully I'd been able to shut the door on my emotions again before they took over, before the deep scores of grief on my mind were allowed to overwhelm me. 'So I'd better be off.'

'OK,' Nate replied. 'Do you want me to drive you?'

'Sure.'

We left the café, and walked under a grey sky mottled with rain-swollen clouds towards Morrisons car park where Nate had left his car. As we reached his silver Audi, Nate spun to me, pulled me into a hug. 'Do you ever think about us being together?' he murmured.

I more than thought about it, I hoped, I wanted . . . Nate's mouth grazed against my neck. He knew I had no resistance to kisses on my neck. My knees weakened and he pressed my body closer to his. Nate's hand went into my hair as he kissed my neck harder. 'I won't leave a love bite,' he murmured and reality slammed itself against my head.

'Stop,' I said, pushing him away. 'This can't happen, not ever.'

'I know.' He pressed the heels of his hands on his eyes. 'It's all going wrong . . . I've been forced to take two weeks off work because I was messing up. Not concentrating.' My heart lurched for him. He was always professional, so for him to have been signed off . . . I hadn't realised how fragile he was. 'I don't know what I'm doing most of the time,' he blundered on. 'Instead of sleeping I lie awake at night thinking about us. Wanting us to be together again . . . I know you're with him. And that's the worst part. I like him. He hates me, I know, but I like how much he cares about Tegan . . .' Nate collapsed into a crouch. 'Do you remember our first huge row? You went storming round to Adele's. Remember? I came round after you. She went, "If you two split up, neither of you will get custody of me—I'll go live with Kam's parents." Do you remember?' I nodded to his bent head, I remembered. 'It doesn't seem right that you're back in my life and she's not around.'

Nate was grieving. I hadn't even thought how Adele's death would affect him. She was like a member of his family and she had died. Of course he'd be mourning. The guilt of his last words to her must have been consuming him; burning him up from the inside out.

How had I missed that? Especially when he'd been trying to tell me he was suffering. He'd told me the night we went to dinner; when he offered to pay for Tegan; when I asked him why he was making an effort with Tegan; the night we had our confrontation in the street. Nate had been asking me for help and I hadn't heard him.

I bobbed down beside him, slipped an arm around his shoulders. 'Come on, let's go to the park, take our minds off all this.'

'What's he doing here?' Luke demanded in a low angry whisper.

His eyes had doubled in size when he saw me arrive at the park with Nate, and once he'd helped Tegan off the swing he'd glared at me until I went over to him, leaving Nate and Tegan together. Nate sat on the red swing Tegan had vacated, staring at the ground.

'Nate's had a bit of a breakdown,' I muttered. 'I've got you to support me, Nate hasn't got anyone. So I have to be there for him. He was one of my best mates once, I can't let him down.'

Luke sighed. 'I know,' he conceded. 'I don't like it but I do understand.' As we returned to the swings, we saw Tegan staring at Nate.

'What's the matter, Mr Nate?' she asked quietly. 'Are you ill?'

Nate shook his head. 'No, I'm just tired.'

'Oh. Do you want to sleep in my bed? It's very pretty.'

Nate smiled at her. 'Thanks, Tegan, but I've got a bed at my house.'

The weather started to break. 'All right, I think it's time we went home, boys and girls. It's going to start raining,' I said.

'O-OK,' Tegan said. 'Are you going to come to my house for your dinner, Mr Nate?' she asked. Nate looked up at Luke. Luke shrugged and glanced away; that was as close to 'Come over' as he'd get.

'OK, Tegan, I'll come.'

'Come on then.' She held out her hand to him. 'You can call me Tiga, if you want,' she informed him, nodding to emphasise her point. 'Not T, Luke calls me T. But you can call me Tiga.'

'OK, Tiga, thanks.'

Nate started spending a lot of time at our place, almost always at Tegan's request. She hadn't elevated him to Luke status, but he had become like the ducks in the park she was always wanting to feed. Almost every other night we had to call Mr Nate to ask if he would come round for his dinner. If he couldn't make it she'd want to know what he was going to eat. As a result of the time he spent with us—the realisation that he wasn't hated by me or Tegan—Nate slowly got back to normal. As normal as he could. He moved into the phase where it hurts but you can function. He started to sleep, eat properly, and we even had conversations about Adele. 'Remember that night Adele came to my house and threatened me?' Nate asked once when the four of us were in the park.

I smiled as the memory returned to me.

'She told me she'd "proper" kill me if I ever hurt you.'

'She was funny.'

'No, she was serious. I quickly realised that Adele was a part of our lives. I was just waiting for that day when you would say, "Why don't we buy a house so she and Tegan can live with us?".' I grinned because the thought had crossed my mind. 'Yeah,' Nate said, 'I knew it!'

The fact that I could talk about Adele without breaking down also meant that I was getting better. I was dealing with what had happened. I'd had to force myself to. The realisation that I was falling for Nate again had scared me. It meant I wasn't paying enough attention to Luke. I'd started saying 'I love you' every day to Luke, because I did. He was the one I was with, the one I'd chosen to be with and I was going to prove that to both of us. I'd decided upon the perfect way to do that.

'This is like being proper boyfriend and girlfriend,' Luke said. We'd snuck out of work separately to meet up for lunch. Although most people suspected we were together we liked to keep it quiet.

'I know,' I smiled. I'd asked him to come out to lunch because I wanted to talk to him, wanted to do the thing that would prove beyond a shadow of a doubt that it was him I wanted to be with.

'OK, Mr L, I was wondering if you fancied moving in with us? I know you live with us anyway but what if we make it official? Then you can give up your other place and we could start saving together and buy a bigger place. Maybe even a house? With a garden for Tegan.'

Luke's reply was to glance away and retreat into silence. A quiet that deepened into a hush that promised to haunt our relationship for years. I'd messed up by bringing this up. 'This is a big step,' Luke finally said. 'I'll have to think about it.'

That's it? I thought. It was the whole, 'I love you'/'That's good to know' scenario all over again; another slap in the face when I showed him my heart. 'OK,' I mumbled. How many times was I going to let Luke do this before I accepted that I wasn't meant to be opening up to him? That maybe he wasn't thinking we'd last the distance.

'That's not a no,' he added. 'It's just, well, it's a big step.'

'You said.'

'I do see my future with you and T. I just need to—'

'It's OK,' I interjected. 'You don't have to give me an answer straight away. Take as long as you want.' As far as I could see, this meant Luke wasn't in love with me. There was no way he would have reacted like this if he were.

'You're very quiet,' Luke stated.

'Just thinking,' I replied.

Luke sighed. 'You wouldn't want me to agree to something I wasn't sure of just because it's what you want to hear, would you?' he asked.

'Course not. But I am allowed to be disappointed and hurt that you've not jumped at the chance to make things permanent,' I pointed out.

'Ryn, I'll be honest. I've been thinking about asking you to marry me but . . . we've been together less than a year. We can't be getting married after less than a year. It's not the sort of thing I do, I'm not that impulsive. Us buying a house together would be a halfway step but I don't know if I want to do things in half measures. Which brings me back to getting married . . . Which is impulsive. Do you understand why I need to think about this? It's not that I don't love you, it's not that I don't see my future with you, I've just got to work out what's best. I've done this before, remember, and it didn't exactly work out.'

'Yes, Luke, I remember you've done this before. And so have I. I almost got to the altar so I'd have thought you'd at least have thought to talk to me about marriage if you were thinking about it.'

'You didn't talk to me about buying a house.'

'What do you think I was just doing? I haven't been looking at houses, or planning where we should live, I brought it up so we could talk.'

'If I had proposed, you would have said no?'

I nodded. 'I'd have thought you'd know by now that I'm someone who needs to talk about these things. It's my future too, and you being ready for marriage doesn't mean I am. Especially when I've got a child.'

'I see what you mean . . . We're not doing a very good job of planning a future together, are we?'

'I guess not.'

'But I do want us to have a future, though,' Luke said. 'I'll think carefully about moving in, OK?'

'OK.' As he held me close, a small treacherous inkling began in my mind: that whole conversation would have gone so differently if I'd had it with Nate.

A couple of hours later I was with the assembled members of the advertising marketing teams in our weekly round-up meeting. Luke's PA, Carla, was finishing the diary check where she listed all the meetings the departments had in the coming month to ensure there were no clashes. 'And I've just had confirmation that the Edinburgh direct marketing campaign roll-out meeting will take place on the fourteenth, Luke. Shall I go ahead and confirm your attendance?' she asked.

The fourteenth? Hang on. I glanced up at Luke who had paled.

'Luke?' Carla asked when he'd been silent for a full minute. 'Shall I confirm your attendance and book the hotel?'

'Erm . . . Erm, sorry, Carla. Yes. Please confirm my attendance.'

My fingers closed in a death grip around my pen, tight enough to crush the plastic case as the heat of anger burnt through my veins.

'If there's no other business then let's end there,' Luke said. 'Thanks, guys.' Everyone filed out of the boardroom. I remained in my seat, rage stampeding through me. Luke stayed in his seat as well.

'I can't believe you're going away on the fourteenth,' I said, my voice quiet and measured, a far cry from the bile I wanted to scream at him.

'I was never meant to,' he said, trying to placate me. 'I was hoping this wouldn't turn out to be the only time in May we were all available.'

'But you're not available, it's Tegan's birthday. You've known about it for months. We've been planning her party for months.'

'Ryn, you remember what it was like to have a career, what extra you have to put in. I can't say that I've got a child's birthday party so I can't make the meeting.'

Remember what it was like to have a career? I still had a career, I was still in charge of the magazines and they were bloody good even if I did say so myself. *The extra you have to put in?* I was always putting in extra. The only other people who worked as many extra hours as I did without the glory, without the recognition and chance of promotion were other mothers who had to do it to keep their heads above water. But what made me want to swing for Luke, though, was 'a child's birthday party'.

'A child?' I said, venomously. 'Since when has Tegan been "a child"?'

'That came out wrong.'

'Really. Well, this certainly won't come out wrong—I'm taking back asking you to move in,' I said. 'We can't live with someone who can put his job before the girl he's been treating like his daughter for the best part of a year, then dismiss her as "a child". She thinks of you as her dad.'

'I didn't mean it like that.'

'Don't care.'

'I'll see if I can change it.'

'Don't do us any favours, Mr Wiseman. I wouldn't want you to have to look uncommitted in front of your colleagues, what with you having a *career* and everything.' I got to my feet. My heart was beating at triple speed in my chest as I walked the length of the room.

'I'll see you tonight,' he said as I fumbled with the door handle.

'Not at my flat you won't,' I replied without looking round. 'Why don't you go back to that flat you were so desperate to hang on to earlier and plan some more meetings.'

I stomped down the corridor, rage pulsing in my temples. I was as angry with myself as I was with Luke. Because I understood why he'd chosen to go to the meeting. There was a time when nothing would have stopped me working. He'd always been über-ambitious. And, much as he loved Tegan, she wasn't his daughter, wasn't his responsibility, so he was allowed to put his career before her, before us.

Chapter Ten

THE DAY TEGAN'S BIRTHDAY DAWNED Luke wasn't there. He was at work before he left for the meeting we'd been silently rowing about for three weeks. 'When you get to the end of your life, I'm sure you'll be grateful that on the day Tegan turned six you were off at a meeting,' I said to him the night before he left.

'Please . . . I feel bad enough as it is, Ryn. I'm sorry.'

'Tell it to your kid. Oh, I mean, my kid. The "child".'

Luke drew back, his face pinched as though he might cry, and I knew I'd gone too far. 'I'm sorry,' I said, 'that was an awful thing to say. I know you don't think that. Let's call a truce, OK?'

'You're right to be angry, I was out of order. I do think of Tegan as my kid. You know that, don't you?'

I nodded. 'Course I do.'

We kissed and made up.

We had hired the community hall down the road for the party and were having a bouncy castle. We'd invited thirty children, most of them from Tegan's class at school. I'd had considerable help from Mrs Kaye when it came to organising the party and, where Luke would have been, Nate stepped in. He took me to the supermarket the day before and we'd spent nearly two hundred pounds on party food. As a concession to healthiness, I'd bought strawberries, pears and apples to make a fruit salad. The fridge was crammed with food, and Nate'd said he'd arrive early to help make the sandwiches.

I'd been up since five o'clock buttering bread by the time Tegan ran into the kitchen at seven, screaming, 'It's my party day!'

'I know!' I said and scooped her up into my arms. 'Does Tegan want her present now or would she rather wait for her party?'

'Now!' she squealed.

We moved to the sofa and I pulled out the parcel that I'd hidden. It was wrapped in gold paper and tied with a red bow. 'Open it then!'

She examined the parcel, looking for somewhere she could open it without tearing the paper, then looked up at me in bewilderment.

I found where I'd taped down the gold paper, and peeled it back carefully so as not to distress my obsessively neat child. 'There you go.'

With glee, Tegan opened up the parcel and her mouth fell open, her eyes wide. 'Wow,' she said and pulled out a white dress with red spots. It had a full skirt, long sleeves and a red ribbon around the middle. 'It's a dress!' she exclaimed. 'It's very pretty.'

'I thought you might want to wear it to your party.'

'Am I 'lowed? Really and truly?'

'Well, yeah. Although, I think you should see Luke's present as well.' I untaped a box-shaped parcel, she pulled off the paper and revealed a shoe box. She opened it and found white shoes with red spots on them. 'It's the same as my dress!' she said.

'So you can wear them today.'

'Thank you!' she said and threw her arms around my neck. 'I love it.'

'There's one more pressie for you to open right now.' Another parcel: 'To Tiga, with love from Nate.' She gasped with delight. 'Mr Nate brought me a present!' He'd brought her a small silk bag that matched her dress and shoes.

'It's a bag, so you can carry things in it today.'

'It's very pretty,' she decided. 'I wish my mummy could see me.' She scrunched up her face but, instead of looking sad, she seemed fine.

'So do I. But, I do have something from your mummy.'

Tegan's already wide eyes widened even more. 'She sent it from heaven?' she gasped.

'No, sweet pea, she gave it to me before she went to heaven.'

I'd known she was ready to get this; she seemed so much more settled than when we'd arrived in Leeds. I took the card from my dressing-gown pocket and handed it over.

She stared at the white square before cautiously pulling out the card.

'Happy Sixth Birthday' the front declared. Tegan opened it.

My darling Tegan, Happy Birthday. I'm sorry I can't be there with you today but I'll always love you. Never forget that, OK? Mummy loves you. I'm sure you'll have a fabulous time today. Have a dance for me. I hope you're being good for Kamryn. Love, Mummy.

A smile lit up her face as she turned to me. 'My mummy loves me,' she stated. 'She said so. In my birthday card.'

'I know.'

Her smile grew. 'You are Kamryn, aren't you, Mummy Ryn? Am I being good for you?'

'You're being more than good for me, you're being perfect for me.' I leant forwards and took her in my arms. I frequently had a need to hug Tegan these days. I just needed to remind myself that she existed. Our roles had been reversed. After Adele died, Tegan always needed to have me around, now I needed to be reassured that she was real and that she wasn't going to do what Adele had done and leave me.

'Right, baby,' I said releasing her. 'We've got a lot to do before your party. Let's have your bath, and then you can have breakfast.'

She nodded and, still holding the card in one hand, she scooped up Meg. Tegan was going to carry the card around with her all day, as it turned out. She would only forget about it much, much later in the day.

Tegan beamed at her princess cake. She'd been grinning for most of the day and she showed no signs of stopping. With every present, she grinned, with every kind word, she grinned, with every game, she grinned. But her biggest smile of the party so far was reserved for the cake. Everyone crowded round and sang 'Happy Birthday' to her. She paused to make a wish before blowing out the candles in one huge puff. After the cake most of the children ran back to the bouncy castle; Tegan went with them while I took the cake into the hall's kitchenette to cut it up for the goodie bags. This party was going well—during the last two hours only a couple of children had cried, and no one had wounded themselves. The two parents who had stayed for the party followed the children outside, leaving only me in the kitchenette, while Nate sat in the hall, talking to a young lad who hadn't really joined in with the others. Nate had made himself indispensable. He had been on bouncy-castle duty when we'd first arrived, then he went round picking up rubbish. He'd whizzed back to the flat a few times to grab things I'd forgotten. No one would guess that he didn't like being around children.

In the kitchenette, I paused in cutting up the cake and, through the serving hatch, watched Nate. He was dressed in dark green combats, he'd recently cut his hair, and he was looking handsome. Healthier, stronger, *delicious*. I'd had no *inamorato* moments with him, but I did . . . I quashed that thought before it became even partially formed. It would do no one any good to start thinking like that.

Nate glanced up suddenly, spearing me to the spot as our gazes collided. His lips slid up into a smile and a treacherous streak of excitement tore through me. I tried to quash that as I smiled back.

'Mrs Brannon,' a girl's voice said beside me.

'I've told you before, Regina, I'm not Mrs Brannon. You can call me Ryn or Tegan's mum, not Mrs Brannon.'

This child, this Regina Matheson, was everything I'd expected her to be: bossy, overbearing and arrogant. Her freckled nose wrinkled up as she considered what I had told her about my name. Eventually she shrugged. 'There is rather a lot of junk food at this party,' she stated. 'My mum says too much junk food is bad for you.'

'Does she? Well, I'm sure just this once won't hurt. There is some fruit, though. Strawberries or fruit salad. Why don't you have a strawberry?'

'OK, Mrs Brannon,' she said and skipped off to harass someone else.

I had returned to cutting up the chocolate cake for the goodie bags when Nate entered the kitchenette. 'Can I help you with anything?' he asked. I moved to look at him and found we were almost face to face. His navy-blue eyes stared straight into mine.

'See them bags?' I said. He nodded, not looking at the expensive red-foil party bags. 'These pieces of cake, cake, in those bags would be very helpful. Helpful. You need to wrap them in napkins first, though. Though.' I couldn't speak properly, he was doing that to me.

His eyes travelled from my eyes to my lips, lingered there, then moved up to my eyes again. He was going to kiss me, I realised. Would I kiss him back? Or would I push him off, remind him of my boyfriend? Nate moved slightly closer, parted his lips. 'OK,' he whispered. Suddenly he pulled away, robbing me of his lust. He'd done that on purpose.

He washed his hands before starting to wrap up the chocolate squares in the white napkins. 'This is weird,' he said in a normal tone of voice. 'Me and you, kids, not going crazy.'

'They've started to grow on me,' I replied, matching his normal tone. 'Me too.'

'I saw. You and that boy seemed to be getting on pretty well. It's nice to see you relaxed again, Nate. You seem a lot better.'

'I am. Thanks to you and Tegan and Luke. The past few weeks have really helped . . . Do you think this is what it would have been like if we had decided to have children?'

'Are you broody?' I asked. 'There's no shame in it if you are.'

'No.' He shuddered. 'No, not at all. It's something that crosses my mind nowadays. I wouldn't actually want one. I mean, any more.'

'Me neither. I love Tegan, but I'm not wanting to do it again.'

'What about Luke?' Nate asked. 'Is he all right with that? I get the impression he wants lots of kids.'

'Maybe,' I said. Of course he did. That was our elephant in the corner. We hadn't talked about it, but I knew he wanted to be a dad; he knew that I'd finished with all that when I acquired Tegan. A discussion about more children would end with . . . It would end. Everything.

'Do you love him, Kam?'

I glanced up and nodded. 'I do.'

'More than you love me?'

'My feelings for you are past tense, Nate.'

'You're lying, to me and yourself.'

'You don't know what you're talking about,' I said.

'I'm not saying you don't love him, I think you're torn—you want us both. I love you, Kam.'

My hands started to shake as I moved a piece of cake to a napkin.

'I just want you to know. I want you to be honest with yourself.'

I stared at the table top. If I was lying to myself that was my business. I didn't have to admit to anything. It wasn't fair for Nate to accuse me of this. Especially since I knew Luke thought the same. The pair of them assumed they knew what I felt, and when I corrected them they never truly accepted what I said.

'Mrs Brannon,' Regina Matheson began, tugging at my skirt.

I ignored her. And decided to keep ignoring her until she got it right. 'Mrs Brannon.' She tugged harder. 'Mrs Brannon,' Regina said again.

'What is it?' I snapped, finally turning to her.

'Tegan's turning blue,' she stated.

'What—' I ran towards the doors that opened out to the back of the hall. I ran, but felt I wasn't moving. When I was younger, I used to have a recurring dream where I would be running away from danger and my legs would be moving fast, but still I was moving slowly. Running through tar. This is how I felt as I raced out towards the bouncy castle.

Beside the bouncy castle, all the children, silent and solemn, stood in a circle. At the centre of the circle was a parent who was crouched down beside Tegan. Tegan lay on her back on the ground. Still. Her eyes were closed and her mouth was gently parted, but she was indeed turning blue. Bluer by the second. She was so still. Adele. Adele had been this still the last time I saw her. Still and cold and dead.

I shoved aside the woman by Tegan as I dropped to my knees. I pressed my ear to her chest, listening. *Thud.* Soft, faint, but confirmation her heart was still beating. But she wasn't breathing.

'Nate! Get an ambulance!' I screeched.

'It's on its way,' he replied from somewhere near me.

'Did she choke?' I asked the assembled group of children.

'She put a strawberry in her mouth,' Regina said, pointing. I glanced to the side and there was a strawberry, perfect, untouched. She hadn't taken a bite, hadn't choked; that meant she was allergic. When you had an allergic reaction you needed antihistamines and adrenalin to keep your heart beating. I knew that much. I had to keep her heart beating and get her breathing. I blew into her mouth, then moved to her chest and pushed carefully. Five counts, five gentle pushes. No movement and she wasn't breathing. Back to her mouth, blow. Back to her chest. After the final push, I put my head to her chest. *Thud.* Again, small and gentle. Her heart was still beating. Back to her mouth, back to her chest. I had to keep going to bring her back. I heard Nate's voice.

I breathed into her mouth again and then Nate's strong arms hoisted me away from her. I almost fought him, until two green-clad paramedics took my place. The first paramedic placed an oxygen mask over Tegan's face, the other injected the contents of a syringe into her thigh. Nothing happened. She didn't even flinch. My knees buckled and I landed in a heap on the ground. *It's over,* I realised as the paramedics exchanged concerned looks. *She's gone.*

I wandered blindly along the hospital corridors, physically and mentally numb. I stopped and rested against a wall, trying to hold myself together, until Nate's denim-jacketed arms slipped around me and pulled me towards his body. 'Babe,' Nate whispered in my ear.

'Sh . . . I . . . I thought, I thought she was going—' My voice dissolved. I put my arms around Nate and clung to him.

'Shhhh,' he hushed, 'it's OK. She's OK. It'll all be OK.'

'But it nearly wasn't,' I whispered. She almost died. Tegan, my baby, almost died. A few more minutes and they wouldn't have been able to get her lungs working nor her heart beating properly. She was sleeping now, and breathing on her own. But her fragile body lying in that bed, hooked up to a heart monitor, reminded me of Adele's final days.

Nate looked down at my face. 'It's OK,' he reiterated. 'I hate to say it, but if ever there was a case for eating junk food, this is it—you've never heard of anyone being allergic to a burger, have you?' Nate said, succeeding in making me laugh a little. The beam on his face deepened into a look of affection and concern. 'Hey,' he said, 'how about tomorrow I sign those papers, so you can start the adoption process for real? I know you asked me to do it weeks ago but I kind of put it out of my mind. I'll do it tomorrow. Or tonight, when I drop you home.'

'Really?'

'Yes. I don't know why I've been delaying. Guilt, I suppose, because I shouldn't really give her up, but she's more your child than mine. Even from the day she was born you were like her second parent.'

'Thank you,' I said and pressed my lips against his, in gratitude. There were better ways to say thank you, I knew that, but I didn't care. I just wanted to kiss him because he'd supported me in one of the scariest chapters of my life. Because he was going to give me what I wanted by signing the papers. Because the one person who should have been there wasn't.

As our lips touched, another emotion overrode all the others: shame. It wasn't Luke's fault he wasn't here. I pulled away from Nate. Slowly he raised his hand and stroked his thumb across my cheek. All resistance to him faded with that touch and when Nate pushed his lips onto mine, I let myself glide into it. Kissing him was so familiar. Easy. Simple. It opened up my memories. I loved this man once upon a time. I loved him now. But not like I loved Luke. *Luke.* His face elbowed its way into my head and I pushed Nate away. 'I can't do this, I'm with Luke.'

'Really?' Nate murmured. 'Why are you kissing me, then, *Kamryn*?' He said my name as though it had been dipped in desire, and it had the intended effect of making passion explode in my stomach. I glanced away, desperate not to be seduced by Nate, searching for something to look at that would cool me off. I stared at the coffee machine. At the plastic chairs. At an empty hospital trolley. At Luke.

Luke was standing in the corridor, staring at me. At us. His face was expressionless, as though all emotion had been blasted off with the shock of seeing me kissing my ex. Me doing the one thing he feared most.

'Oh, fuck,' Nate breathed.

I took a step, 'Luke,' on my lips, but he cut in with, 'Is she all right?'

'Luke it's not—'

'IS SHE ALL RIGHT?' He raised his voice.

I nodded. 'She's asleep. The antihistamine and the adrenalin knocked her out. She's going to be fine.'

Luke said nothing. Nate stepped forward. 'Look, it's . . .'

Luke shot Nate a look so deadly it could have been fired from a gun. 'Can I see her?' he asked me.

I nodded. 'She's got a private room, this way.'

Tiga was lying on her side; her face was ashen. Luke stared down at her with a wounded expression on his face. I knew it wasn't because of what he'd seen in the corridor, it was because she was hurt. She'd been hurt and he hadn't been there to protect her.

'How did you know?' I asked from the door.

'I, erm, cancelled the meeting,' he whispered. 'I got up there and turned around and drove back. I couldn't stand the thought of missing T's birthday. I went to the community hall and Mrs Kaye told me what happened . . . Will she be all right? Will there be any side effects?'

'She's going to be fine,' I whispered back. 'She's staying in overnight just in case of complications, but she should be fine.'

Luke took her little hand in his. 'See you tomorrow, gorgeous,' he murmured. 'Sleep well.' He got up from his seat, and stalked out of the room as though I didn't exist. He marched down the corridor at a breakneck pace. 'Luke,' I called, but he speeded up as he heard my voice. I followed him out of the hospital and into the car park. Out there I could raise my voice and I did, bellowing, 'LUKE!' with a ferocity that scared me.

He stopped, then spun to meet me. His burnt-orange hazel eyes raged with something close to hatred.

'What do you want?' he asked, his voice frighteningly aggressive.

'Let me explain,' I said, not daring to move any nearer to him.

He shook his head. 'I don't need an explanation. It's clear what's been going on. You've been playing me for a fool since day one. I was the stand-in; someone to play happy families with until he came back.'

'You know that's not true,' I said, hurt.

Luke nodded, reluctantly. 'Yeah,' he conceded, 'I know that's not true.' He took a step closer. 'But you know what is true? I—' he poked himself in the chest—'love her. I would do anything for her. I WANT TO BE HER FATHER! And he—' Luke pointed an angry forefinger in the direction of the hospital building—'doesn't. He'll never love her like I do.'

Luke was right about that one thing. Nate may have tried but it was always that—trying. *Trying* to love Tegan. *Trying* to understand her. And if he thought there was some chance of him caring enough about her like a father should, he wouldn't be willing to sign away all parental rights.

'He's only around because of you. You really can't see that everything he does is to get into your knickers, can you?'

'At least he fancies me.'

Luke's face twisted in confusion. 'What?'

'At least I know that Nate fancies me. Always has done. He never thought I was ugly or needed to lose weight.'

Luke's eyes darkened, and he lowered his head. 'I can't believe you've brought that up. That was a long time ago. Things were different then.'

'Do you think it doesn't hurt, still? That I could forget?'

'No, I guess not. But I suppose if I slept with your best friend and fathered a child with her you'd forget that, wouldn't you?'

It was my turn to lower my head. This was wrong. I was meant to be apologising, explaining that it was a one-off.

'Ryn, I love you,' he said. His face had softened. 'And I always knew that you and Tegan came as a package deal. I can't understand why you would want a man who doesn't love your daughter as much as you do.'

'I don't want Nate.'

Luke sighed and rolled his eyes a little. 'I don't think that's true,' he said. 'And I'm not going to stick around to find out if it is or isn't.'

'You're leaving me?' I was so shocked I nearly fell over.

'Ryn, you don't get to kiss someone else and still be with me.'

'But it wasn't like that. I didn't . . . I was so scared about Tegan and he was there and you weren't. And I wanted you. And he said that he was going to let me adopt Tegan for real. And I was—'

'Ryn,' he cut in. 'Tell it to someone who cares.'

He turned on his heels and marched away.

'I'm glad you're better,' Luke said to Tegan. 'I was very worried.'

I stood by the doorway of the small hospital room, watching them. The adventures of the day before showed on Tegan's heart-shaped face: her skin had been bleached white by the drugs, dark shadows lurked under her eyes and a greyish tinge coloured her lips.

Luke had brought her another birthday present—a photo album that had a gold embossed 'T' in the bottom right-hand corner. Tegan held the album in her arms, watching Luke with apprehension—she could tell something was wrong. His distress was radiating from him in waves.

'What's the matter, Luke?' Tegan asked.

'Nothing,' he replied, avoiding her eyes.

'Mummy Ryn says that when there is something wrong.'

'OK, there is something wrong,' he admitted. My heart stopped, was he going to tell Tegan what I'd done? 'I have to go away.'

'Go away where?' Tegan asked, her eyes wide at the very idea. My eyes doubled in size too.

'Remember I went to New York last year?' She nodded. 'Well, I'm going back there, to live,' he said. Tegan's face became a mask of horror.

'I went for the interview when I was in New York,' he replied to all the unasked questions circling my brain. 'They offered it to me a few weeks ago. I accepted it yesterday.'

'But why?' Tegan asked.

'Because it's my job,' he said.

'Is it because I was ill?' she asked. 'I won't be ill no more, promise. Double promise for ever and ever.'

Anguish flew across Luke's face. 'Of course not. Baby, even if you were well, I'd have to leave. It's something I have to do. I have to go.'

'Don't you like me no more?' she asked.

'Tegan, I love you. I wish I could stay but I can't. I'm sorry.'

'Are you still Mummy Ryn's boyfriend?' she asked.

I held my breath.

'I can't be her boyfriend if I'm in America.'

'I don't want you to go,' she said, her voice without hope.

'I don't want to go either,' he replied. 'But I have to.'

The corners of her mouth turned down and she stared at her hands. She was trying not to cry, I guessed. She was brave like that. 'And you're never coming back?' she asked.

'No,' he replied. 'But I'll call you. And I'll write to you.' Luke closed his eyes as he hugged her. 'Bye, T. I love you.'

'Bye, Luke,' she whispered.

'I'll be back in a minute,' I said to Tegan as Luke shut the door behind him. I opened the door to go after him. I had to stop him leaving us.

He was a little way down the corridor, leaning against the wall. I slid my arm around his shoulders. 'Let's talk?' I asked.

We sat in the canteen, without drinks, hunched over in our seats. 'Luke, I'm sorry for kissing Nate,' I began. 'And I'm sorry that you saw me, I can imagine that hurt a lot, but it was the only time. I was just terrified about Tegan and all my emotions were mixed up. I would have told you, you know. Luke, you're the one I want to be with. I love you. You've helped me and you've helped Tegan, I don't want you to go.'

Luke's reddened eyes watched me talk.

'It was only a kiss you know, just that one time. I haven't slept with him. I'm terribly sorry. Please don't leave us because of that kiss.'

'Ryn, if Tegan loved Nate like she loves me, would we be even having this conversation? Would you be back with him?'

I paused before answering. I was sick of this. I'd had enough of being the imperfect one with suspect motives, impure thoughts, doubts. If we were going to play the 'what if' game then we had to play it properly. Not just with me in the defendant's seat.

'I don't know, Luke,' I replied. 'But she doesn't and she does love you so I can't answer that question. But if we're going to go down that route, let me ask you something: if it wasn't for Tegan, would you have even thought about going out with me?'

It was his turn to pause. He couldn't even lie.

'And why didn't you tell me you'd been for an interview when you were in New York? And that you were offered the job?'

'Because I wasn't going to take it.'

'But that's why you were so hesitant about moving in with us, wasn't it? You were still wondering if you should take that job.' *And go back to Nicole.*

Another silence when he couldn't deny the truth.

'OK, maybe you'll have an answer to this question. When I said I didn't want any more children, you didn't think I meant it, did you?'

'But you'd be such a good mother . . .' He stopped as he realised what he'd said.

'You don't think of me as Tegan's mother, do you?' I said, tiredly. 'And if you of all people don't, how is anyone else going to?'

'I do. That came out wrong. I do think of you as her mother and I saw how brilliant you were with her, and I wanted you to have more kids. With me.'

'But I told you, I don't want any more. Didn't you believe me? Did you think I'd change my mind or something . . . ?'

'It doesn't matter now, does it?' Luke interjected. 'I'm leaving.' He didn't want to play this game any more.

'Yes, you are,' I replied calmly. He was going, there was nothing more I could do to stop him. I'd apologised, I'd explained, but he'd made up his mind to go and that was it.

'I hope you and Nate are very happy together,' he spat.

'Thank you,' I replied, not rising to the bait. 'Keep in touch with Tegan, please. She's going to miss you.'

Did you say bye-bye to Luke?' Tegan asked, clutching her photo album.

I nodded. I sat by her bed and put my head on her lap. 'I'll miss him,' I said. In less than a year I'd lost three people I loved. First Adele, then Ted, now Luke. Too much loss in a lifetime, let alone a year.

'Mummy Ryn, is Luke really going to 'Merica?'

'Yes.'

'Are you sure? Because I think he might go to heaven.'

'He's not, Tiga, I promise you. He's going to America. He had to go.'

'OK,' she said, and patted my head. She started to stroke my hair like I was the cat she'd desperately wanted at one point.

'It won't be so bad with just me and you,' I said. 'We'll be all right. We can go on holiday. Maybe to Italy where my friend Ted lives.'

'Really?' she said excitedly. 'On a plane and everything? Mummy Ryn, that would be fun. And I could take lots of pictures and then put them in the 'bulm.'

'Yeah.'

She smiled, then sighed. 'I wish Luke was coming.'

Rat-a-tat-tat! sounded at the door. 'Come in,' I called.

Meg appeared in the doorway. Tegan's face lit up. 'Look who I found in my car,' Nate said, his face appearing in the doorway too. 'I thought you might want her, Tegan. Was I right?'

'Yes,' she laughed. 'Mr Nate, Luke's gone to 'Merica,' she said as Nate perched on the edge of her bed. 'You're not going to 'Merica, are you?'

'No, I'm not,' he said. 'I'm not going anywhere.'

Nate turned his eyes on me, fixed me to the spot with a steady, intimate gaze and my mouth curled up into a smile because I knew he meant it. I knew that out of everyone in our lives, he'd never leave us.

Dearest Kamryn,

I've asked Nancy to send you this a year after I die. I'm not trying to spook you, I just wanted to make contact with you and to remind you that you're doing a wonderful job bringing up Tegan. How do I know? Because you couldn't fail to do anything else. I know Tegan's in good hands with you and you're in good hands with her—I'm sure you know what I mean.

I hope that you will have found my other letter by now. If not, then I am disgusted, lady! You haven't been through my things? Didn't you even want to see if I had anything of yours?! Well, I did. I had that black velvet jacket—and that's where I put the other letter which explained about me and Nate and why I did what I did.

If you have found it, then now you know and I hope you don't still hate me. I was wrong and I'm sorry. I have learnt, though, that life is too short to bear a grudge. Beautiful, sort it out with Nate before it's too late. Give him the chance to make things right. I know that's all I ever wanted.

Remember that first day we met? You were so instantly nice to me. Yeah, you were prickly but I knew we were going to be friends because rather than follow through with not wanting to come for a drink with me, you did. And you were just lovely—although not in the traditional sense. No one has ever treated me like that before or since. No one has ever taken to me instantly and stuck with me. Thank you for that. I never said it, but thanks for being my friend. Thanks for being you.

I'll go now, beautiful. I just wanted to say goodbye properly, I suppose. I'm pretty sure we won't have had the chance and I wanted to say it. Good. Bye. Not bitter bye, or unhappy bye. <u>Good</u>bye.

All my love, for ever. Adele x

Chapter Eleven

'LUKE!' TEGAN EXCLAIMS with delight in her voice.

I don't look up from the newspaper I'm reading. We're in a café about ten minutes from our flat. It's a haven for parents. You come here and the owners of the place, for a small fee, will take your child downstairs and teach them to cook. They're making pizza today—in about five minutes the supervisors will come up and get the children. I don't look up after Tegan's exclamation because she's always doing it. It's been sixteen months since Luke left and in the early days I did it too. I thought I'd see him, and would go to call out to him, but then I'd realise it wasn't him, and feel stupid. It'd been like that when Adele died too. I'd get a flash of her walking down the street and would have to stop myself calling out to her. Tegan is still doing it with Luke. She swears blind she's seen him.

'All right, T.'

His voice is deep and smooth, and my heart flits over a couple of beats in response. Tegan scrambles up onto her feet on the chair, then wraps herself around him.

'All right, Ryn,' Luke says.

'All right, Luke,' I reply.

He hasn't changed much. He's still tall and muscular. His head is almost shaved; his eyes are still that striking orange-hazel. The only difference is that he's regrown his ridiculous line beard.

'I don't like your beard,' Tegan informs him.

'Why thank you, Madam.' He's talking to Tegan but staring at me, probably thinking I haven't changed much.

'It's itchy. That's not very nice, is it, to make Tegan's face itchy?'

Luke draws his eyes away from me back to Tegan. 'It's gone. The second I get the chance I'll shave it off.'

'OK,' she says. 'Are you going to be Mummy Ryn's boyfriend again?'

'All right, Tiga, it's pizza time, isn't it?'

'O-OK,' she says reluctantly. 'But I want to talk to Luke as well.'

Tegan is unrecognisable from the girl I moved up to Leeds with over two years ago, this lass has no worries about telling me what she thinks.

'You can talk to Luke,' I say, keeping eye contact. 'You just have to go make pizza first. Afterwards, you can come back and talk to him. OK?'

'O-OK,' she replies, realising that she's not winning this round.

'Do you want to go down on your own or shall I come with you?'

'Come with me,' she says, slipping her hand in mine. 'See you later, Luke.' Holding hands we descend the wooden stairs into the huge basement kitchen. As I'm about to leave her she throws her arms around me. 'Thank you, Mummy Ryn,' she says and kisses my cheek. 'You're my bestest friend,' she whispers in my ear. 'Apart from Matilda and Crystal and Ingrid. And Luke.'

'You're my bestest friend too,' I reply. She kisses my cheek again.

I climb the steps, my heart somewhere near my throat. I thought I'd never see Luke again. I'd resigned myself to a life of hearing what he was up to through his letters and emails to Tegan.

When I return to the café area he is sitting in Tegan's chair. 'Well, she's grown up,' he says as I take my seat opposite him.

'But she's also become a little girl again, not having so much to worry about that isn't seven-year-old stuff, which is nice to see.'

The waiter approaches, sets down a large mug of coffee in front of Luke. 'Café mocha, easy on the coffee, heavy on the chocolate, right?'

'That's right, mate,' Luke says with a laugh. 'Glad you remember.'

When the waiter has retreated, I ask. 'Have you been here before?'

'Erm, a few times . . . I, erm, come here most weekends. I used to come hoping to get a glimpse of you and T. Sometimes she saw me.'

So, she wasn't losing the plot: Luke has been stalking us. 'When did you get back from the States?' I ask, ignoring how unsettling that is.

His eyes dart to my left hand then dart away again. 'About three months ago. The job didn't work out . . .' He leaves the sentence unfinished because I know something he knows I know. He made sure I knew, in an attempt at revenge, I guess.

'Did your wife come back with you?' I ask.

Luke married Nicole six months after he left Leeds. We got the news and photos in the office a few days after the wedding. I'd walked into the office I shared with Betsy and saw the picture open on her computer screen. I'd made the right noises to Betsy about being pleased for him and threw up in the staff loos.

'No, she's still in New York,' he reveals. 'She's staying there too. My marriage didn't exactly work out either.'

'I was surprised at how quickly you got married, but then it was to Nicole. I suppose it was easy to pick up where you left off.'

'Not that easy as it turns out, she wasn't . . . How's Nate?'

Our eyes meet, he searches mine for a hint of what I'm about to say. 'He's great. He moved to Leeds, to be nearer to . . . Well, to be nearer. Him and Tegan are good mates, too, she even lets him pick her up from school a couple of times a week so I can work a little later.' I'm still not Marketing Director of Angeles and I never will be, I've accepted that now. For as long as Tegan needs me around I have to put my career second. 'It's funny how she bosses him around and they cook like you two used to—creating a huge mess as they go.'

Luke inhales, 'Does she call him "Daddy" now, then?'

I reach out, cover his hand with mine. 'As far as Tegan's concerned, her only "daddy" is you.'

'Really? Still?'

'Just 'cos you left, doesn't mean she stopped thinking about you.'

'Nate's her father.'

'Yeah, but that doesn't mean he wants to be her dad. He likes Tegan, he cares for her, he just doesn't love her like you did. But, he'll always take responsibility for her. Luke, he's a good guy. He always liked you for how much you cared about Tegan, you know. He's always wanted what's best for her, and if that means letting someone else be her parent, then that's what he'll do. He signed away all rights to her.'

'Really and truly?'

'That day I kissed him, he said that's what he'd do and he did it. And he's sticking around for ever—as her father, not her daddy.'

'Are you and him . . . ?'

'No.'

'Why not? I'd have thought you'd have . . .'

'Been engaged before your plane took off? No, me and Nate couldn't get back together, too much has happened, we've changed too much.'

'So you didn't even . . . ?'

'I'm not a saint, Luke,' I reply. 'Much as I pretend I am.'

It was two months after Luke's departure that Nate and I made love. And, on and off, for a year, we carried on doing so, always stopping before we started a full-blown relationship. Recently we'd stopped altogether, had gone cold turkey because we admitted that we were actually in a relationship. And we weren't free to be boyfriend and girlfriend. Boy had 'cheat' hanging over his head and Girl came with a child. Nate liked, possibly even loved, Tegan but didn't want her full time; I'd forgiven and understood about Adele, but I hadn't forgotten. Those things would always keep us apart. Besides, 'Nate's got a girlfriend now. They've been together three months and it's looking long-term.'

'Do you mind?'

'Not as much as I used to, believe me.' We both had to move on, and he'd been brave enough to take the first step towards that.

'I mind that you mind,' Luke states.

I'll ignore the fact that you got married, shall I? 'Nate and I could never get back together. I mean, I hold my hands up, I fancied him, I still felt stuff for him but I had this amazing boyfriend.'

The old me loved Nate more than anything, he was everything to me; the me who'd been bringing up Tegan loved Luke, and the life—the family—we'd created, more. 'I had this amazing boyfriend whom I adored. And even though I was tempted by this other guy, the only man for me was my boyfriend. And despite the fact he went off and married someone else, I didn't stop loving him.'

'You mean that?'

'Wouldn't say it if I didn't mean it.'

He takes both my hands in his. 'You know, it was only months after I'd left that I realised what you were asking me when we were sitting in the hospital canteen,' he says. 'I thought you were accusing me again of not loving you like Nate did. Then I worked out that you were asking me if I loved you at all. Independently of Tegan. You never thought I did, did you? You didn't realise that yes, Tegan brought us together but I would never have dated you if I didn't genuinely feel something for you.

'I fell for you the day you had your migraine. When I found out who T was to you, it was as though a curtain was lifted and I saw how incredible you were. And that's why it didn't work with Nicole—she wasn't you. Ryn, I did fancy you. You're the most beautiful woman on earth. I love the way you go out of your way to look after people but pretend you don't care; the way you—'

'I've told you before, if you keep saying things like that, I'll think you're flirting with me,' I cut in.

The expression on Luke's face hardens. 'That's why I never said them, though. You told me that, good or bad, you don't believe what others say, so I stopped saying them. I tried to show you how I felt in what I did, not simply what I said. That worked, didn't it?'

'I'm sorry, Luke,' I say. 'I've only ever had one person say those things and mean it. I didn't quite believe there'd be two people who could think them . . . But you always seemed to back off whenever I tried to take a step forwards and then I find out you had your escape plan worked out all along. Are you surprised I didn't believe you loved me?'

'Yeah, but I'm an ass. Things go wrong and I take to the road, that's what I do. And Nate reappearing was the ultimate worst-case scenario. He had more claim on you and Tegan than me; I was preparing for what I saw as the inevitable. Although I have to say, you're an ass if you didn't believe I cared for you independently of Tegan.'

'I'm glad you're back, Luke.' I grin, then recall he hasn't actually said as much. 'You are back, aren't you? Back to be a part of our lives?'

'Yes, but things have to change.'

'Yeah, I know. And the first change is that you've got to be honest with me. Tell me everything, job interviews, plans to get married to me or someone else. Everything. And I'll do the same.'

'OK, I can live with that.'

'The second change is that you've got to accept that Nate is a part of our lives, for better or worse. He's here for ever.'

'OK. But I don't have to like him, do I?'

I sighed. 'I suppose not. But it'd be easier for you if you did. I don't want Tegan feeling caught between you two. She's very clever and as she's got older she picks up on everything, so no nastiness, OK?'

'OK, my condition is that we talk about having more children.'

My heart sinks. 'I don't know . . .'

'We just talk about it. It's not fair on Tegan that she's got no brothers and sisters; you had them, so why can't she?'

'Erm . . .'

'We just talk, Ryn. And if we decide no, then we decide no. It's not fair that we've never talked about it properly; that you've made up your mind and I've got no say in it. That's not what a relationship is about.'

'OK, we talk.'

He grins, leans out of his seat and pushes a languid kiss onto my mouth. I can't help but sigh into it, As he sits back, Tegan comes into view. She's standing by our table, a grin so wide you can hardly see her face. Behind her stands a less than happy cooking supervisor.

'Ms Matika, I really must talk to you about Tegan's behaviour!' she says with barely restrained anger.

'What's she done?' I ask.

'In the middle of cooking she decided to come back up here. When I said she had to finish making her pizza, she told me to "stuff it!"'

Luke swivels in his seat to hide his face while his broad shoulders shake with silent laughter.

'Tegan, say sorry to . . .' I glance at her name badge. *Adele*. My heart skips a beat and a lump forms in my throat like it always does when I think of her or hear her name. 'Tegan, say sorry to Adele.'

'Sorry, Miss Adele,' Tegan says, looking and sounding suitably sorrowful. 'I didn't mean to be horrible, I won't do it again.'

Mollified, Adele crouches down in front of Tegan. 'That's OK, precious. I'll see you next week.'

Tegan nods and manages to keep her sorrowful look until Adele has returned downstairs. When she's gone, Tegan turns to face me. 'I'm sorry for being naughty. I wanted to see Luke. I thought he might go.'

'Luke's going to stick around for a while,' I reply. 'Aren't you?'

'Sure am, gorgeous. I'll be around so much you'll both get sick of me.' She grins. 'Mummy Ryn, can I tell Luke?' she asks.

'Of course, baby.'

'I've got a new name,' she proclaims to her returned best friend. 'My name is Tegan Brannon Matika. I've got the same name as Mummy Ryn. We are family now. Proper, proper family.'

'That's fantastic!' Luke exclaims. 'T, I'm so pleased for you! And you, Ryn. When did you find out you were finally allowed to adopt her?'

'We got the final certificate two weeks ago. It's been two long years, with social workers, counsellors and courts, but we got there, didn't we?'

Tegan gives a short, decisive nod. 'Mr Nate bought us 'hampain but only Mummy Ryn was allowed to drink it. I had fizzy pop.'

It was only as I looked at the adoption certificate that would replace Tegan's birth certificate that I realised what it truly meant. It meant I could stop fretting that I hadn't told Adele I forgave her, because she knew. My best friend knew that I'd love her no matter what because she had left me her most precious keepsake. She had trusted me with her one true love. And adopting Tegan, turning my best friend's girl into my girl, was all the forgiveness Adele would have needed. She hadn't screwed me like I thought she had all that time ago, she'd simply changed my life like I knew she would that first time I met her.

'Guess what, Luke?' Tegan says.

'What, sweetheart?' he asks, smiling at how I cradle my daughter in my arms.

'I think Mummy Ryn is going to let me get a cat.'

Dorothy Koomson

What is your daily life like in Sydney?

From where I live it's pretty easy to walk into the city or just jump into a taxi and get to the Opera House. Although Sydney is bigger than London it actually feels a lot smaller. I've been a journalist for about nine years and I work on a woman's magazine about twenty minutes from where I live. I guess, like everyone else's, my daily life is pretty routine. I get up, go to work and come home, try to do some writing, email my friends in England, because by the time I get home the UK is awake. I'm writing my fourth novel at the moment so I don't go out much after work. And at weekends, in between the weekly shop and weekly cook, I spend a lot of time in front of the computer trying to write my next book, *Marshmallows For Breakfast*.

What took you to Australia?

I came to Adelaide at the end of 2004 for a holiday and liked it here. Then I decided to change my life as things weren't going in the right direction. I remember telling everyone that I was thinking of moving out here and they only paid a little bit of attention. At the end of February 2005 I applied for a job I saw advertised on the internet and got it. About eight weeks later, I was on a plane to Sydney—to a new job and a new life. When I arrived I was also in the middle of rewriting *My Best Friend's Girl* so I was a bit busy. So much so that it's only this year that I have managed to do touristy things like go to Bondi Beach!

Where were you born and where did you grow up?

I was born in London. There are four of us in total—I've got a sister and two brothers and we are all pretty close and always have been. I grew up in London but went to university in Leeds.

When did you start writing?

When I was thirteen. It was a novel called *There's A Thin Line Between Love and Hate.* I used to write a chapter every night in my exercise book and the next morning my school mates would read the latest instalment. I have always loved writing and knew from a young age that I wanted to have something to do with books—but I thought I might become a librarian! I also loved magazines and I'd read as many as possible.

What were your aims in writing *My Best Friend's Girl*?

I set out to write a story about a woman who, in the course of one day, finds herself thrown into motherhood. If you become pregnant you usually have nine months to get used to the concept of being a mother, but the idea of just waking up one day and finding out that you are responsible for a five-year-old child was a fascinating idea for me. And then the rest grew from there. How might Kamryn find herself in this situation? The logical way would be if someone close to her died. And then, what if this child was possibly the last person in the world that Kamryn would ever want to be responsible for? As I wrote the story grew and grew and the themes became more complex. For me, the biggest issue in the novel is forgiveness. Everyone has to learn how to move towards forgiving someone—even if it's just themselves.

Do you cry when you are writing emotional scenes?

I did get a bit teary when Adele and Kamryn are talking and Kamryn accepts responsibility for Tegan. Other scenes I find hard to re-read are when Tegan realises her mother isn't coming back, and when Kamryn has her breakdown in front of Nate.

What do you like to do when not writing?

I don't have as many hobbies as I should have. I love reading—and I do a lot of that. I even started a book club in Sydney so I that I could meet more people. I also try to do yoga, but sometimes don't get up in time, even though my energy levels go through the roof whenever I do get to a workout. I guess writing is both my job and my hobby—I just love it.

What's your greatest indulgence? Chocolate or shoes?

Can't I have both?

Do you have a burning ambition?

It used to be getting a publishing deal and I was totally and utterly focused on that. Then, when it happened, my next goal was to move to a bigger, more established publishing house. Now, luckily, that's happened too. I suppose my ambition now has to be to have the time to write all the other types of novels that I want to write.

Jane Eastgate

Indiscretion

Jude Morgan

When Captain Fortune recklessly loses all

his money, he reluctantly arranges for his

beautiful daughter to take up the position

of companion to a rich widow. But as

Caroline begins to enjoy the racy social

whirl of Regency Brighton, she is soon

dismayed to find that some 'gentlemen'

seek something other than romance . . .

Chapter One

THE WELL-TRAVELLED TRUNKS stood on the dusty floorboards of their new lodgings. The porter was grumbling away down the stairs with his unsatisfying sixpence. Now it was Caroline's familiar task to make their accommodation as comfortable as possible, whilst soothing her father's mind, made gloomy and fretful by the necessity of the removal.

Caroline was so accustomed to this situation, and to making the best of it, that at first she did not notice something more than usually depressed in her father's demeanour. She busied herself with the unpacking, and with making such tactful improvements to the furnished rooms as could be managed. These were the shabbiest lodgings yet, and her own spirits were more cast down than she cared to show.

Still, she was unprepared for the lingering groan that her father gave, just as she was hanging her mother's miniature portrait above the parlour mantelshelf; and for his booming cry of: 'It is all over, Caro—the die is cast—our revels now are ended—we are ruined!'

Caroline turned to find that he had sunk into a chair. 'Come, Papa, don't take on so. It's not so very bad,' she urged, putting an arm about his shaking shoulders. 'Perhaps we aren't as pleasantly situated as we were at Frith Street, but we might do worse.'

'We might do worse, indeed,' her father said hollowly, through his hands. 'Oh, yes. The debtors' prison, Caro—that will be next for me.'

'Oh, nonsense,' said Caroline, who had heard this before.

'You would be better off, my dear, if I dropped myself in the river.'

'No, I wouldn't. For one, I would be no better off materially, because you've nothing to leave me. And more than that, I should be horribly

grieved and miss you sorely. So no more watery talk, I beg you.'
Caroline went to the side-table on which stood their small hoard of
glassware and made him a hock-and-sodawater, taking a little genteel
tipple for herself. When she turned back to her father, he was regarding
her with tragic, bleary, agelessly blue eyes.

'I had hoped,' Captain Fortune said, reaching out for her hand, 'to be
giving you news of a very different kind at this time, my dear—news of
a wonderful turn-about in our fortunes.'

'Well, Papa, that's news you can't give me,' Caroline said, gently yet
firmly. 'The real news, I fear, is very bad, is it not?'

The Captain drained his glass. 'Yes. I very nearly, you know, pulled
off the most remarkable stroke! And instead we are—we are most
damnably high and dry, Caro. In short, we have no money. It's all gone.
I took advice from a smart young fellow I ran into at Tattersall's. Now
everyone knew him for a lodger in Queer Street, and instead there was
the young sprig with diamonds in his tiepin! What was his secret? One
word. Speculation.' From being cheerfully informative, the Captain's
tone took a sudden plunge into desolation. 'And curse my bones that I
ever listened to him, because it has ruined us!'

Her father, Caroline soon gathered, had indeed lost everything and
the rent on this unprepossessing set of rooms in unfashionable
Henrietta Street was paid only for a month.

An observer might not have guessed how shaken she was. But where
Captain Fortune wailed when brought low, his daughter was less prodi-
gal with her feelings.

'Papa, listen,' she said, having mixed him the last of the hock-and-
soda, lit the candles against the encroaching evening, and drawn up a
seat by the sofa where her father was now prostrated. 'This is all most
alarming and distressing, but . . . is there not opportunity here also?'
She drew a deep breath and went on: 'Do you recollect I mentioned—a
little while ago, when we had to leave the house before last—the idea of
governessing?'

'I certainly do.' Her father rose slowly and dramatically to a sitting
position. 'And *you* will recollect, Caro, how damnable I found it.'

'Truly, I don't think we need to talk in these hellish terms. Consider.
If I were to take a post as a governess, I would be comfortably accommodated and secure, and you would have—'

'The satisfaction of knowing I had failed you. To be sure,' said
Captain Fortune, breathing hard. 'You do well, my dear, to reproach me
with it. Oh, but is it not so? Look at these rooms. Poor Marriner will be
sleeping in what amounts to a boot-cupboard, when his loyalty has

already been put to the severe test of living on board-wages. I smell damp in the hall. And that wallpaper is beyond anything.' He pointed a majestically disdainful finger. 'Indeed, it is my one request that you take a sample of that wallpaper, Caro, and paste it upon my gravestone when I am gone, as an emblem of my failure. Your promise, now!'

'Nonsense, Papa,' she murmured, between pain and laughter; but the Captain sprang up, flushed with self-punishing energy.

'This is not what I wanted for you,' he went on, ruffling his hair savagely. 'When I saw you growing up so pretty and accomplished—oh, yes,' he added, as she made a face, 'and accomplished—remember what that music master said of you? What was his name? Signor—'

'Higginbottom.'

'That's the man. And then your drawing—and the most elegant way of carrying yourself, just like your poor mother—well, I thought that when I brought you into society, you'd surely conquer. Conquer! It's not long since I ran into Stanton of my old regiment at Limmer's, and he said he'd seen you and me walking in Hyde Park, and demanded to know when that delicious daughter of mine—his words, my dear!—was going to make her début at Almack's. But without money and without connections . . . Now, Caro, admit that I have failed you!'

'Well, but you don't want me to, Papa—you want me to say the opposite. And that I gladly do. I never did expect a début at Almack's, you know, and I never supposed we were well connected—'

'Ah! but there's the bitter kernel. The connections are there, or should be. In Devonshire my name stands as high as any, but my side have all died out. And then there's your poor mother's family, very comfortably situated. They could undoubtedly do something for you, if they would. But they're a damned hard-faced unforgiving set . . .' He sighed and looked perplexed. 'As for me, I live in a man's world, and there's precious little for you there.'

'Why, I've learned how to play faro, and macao, and hazard, and billiards, and how to make a bowl of rack-punch—'

'Hush, hush—you make me blush for shame. Not that you don't play a devilish hand at cards . . . but I speak of society. When did you last enjoy a genteel social evening, in mixed company?'

'Well . . . when I went to stay with Miss Willis last year.' Caroline spoke reluctantly, for she did not wish to revive that happy memory.

Miss Willis was a friend made at her last school, who had had Caroline to her family home in Hertfordshire for the vacation. There, Caroline had enjoyed all the amusements of gossip, of charades and dinners and picnics, from which her father's raffish life had debarred her. They were not great things, of course—but she would willingly have sampled more of them. But Caroline had made an abrupt and premature departure from that Seminary for Young Ladies in Chelsea upon being told by the proprietress that she must pack her things: six months' fees were owing, and her father's bankers would not honour his last draft. So she had left the school secretly, and had been obliged to borrow five shillings to get her and her luggage by hackney to her father's then lodging in Frith Street.

'Ah, yes, Hertfordshire,' her father said sorrowfully. 'And there, I dare swear, the young men were mightily impressed with you. This—this is where I feel most the lack of a mother's care. For she would know how to put you in the way of a good marriage.'

'Put me in the way? You make it sound like a speeding coach that would flatten me!'

'Well, so it is, in some sort. A happy marriage—a love-match—is something overwhelming, and overpowering.' His eyes grew misty. 'That was how it was with your poor mother and me, at any rate.'

'But, Papa, you spoke of a *good* marriage. And that is something entirely different, is it not? A girl should set her sights on a man who has money; or if not, who can expect to come into money; or if not, who has moneyed connections. That's the order, is it not? But I'm not sure I want to marry on those terms. Or indeed marry at all.'

'Hm. But not to marry? Well, well,' he said. 'I would not have you do aught against your will. But, Caro, don't, I pray you, be caught in narrow notions of love and marriage. Your mother and I made a love-match, yes. But it would also have been a good, sound, prosperous match, if her family had not been so damnably determined to disoblige us. Love and prudence *can* go together. And that, you know, is what I see for you: a good man who loves you, and a comfortable situation.'

Her father beamed at her: he had cheered himself up considerably; and he appeared as proud of this golden vision of her future as if he had ever done anything to secure or foster it for her.

'Well, Papa,' Caroline said, taking advantage of his altered mood, 'the governess notion—it is not so very terrible, is it? And there is nothing against my beginning to make enquiries to that end, at least?'

'Nothing,' Captain Fortune said, 'except this: it will not be needed. Because I have an idea.' He began to pace the narrow width of their parlour, his lame leg thumping on the floor. 'The remedy has lain beneath my hand the whole time. The man who was unanimously declared the finest Romeo ever seen in Bristol—to say nothing of Gloucester—need not fear pecuniary embarrassment. I shall tread the boards again!'

He struck a flourishing pose, and there was no denying that her father remained a handsome man. He was broad-shouldered and upright: his complexion had survived soldiering and port-wine remarkably well. And yet, as for treading the boards . . .

'You doubt me,' he said.

'No, no,' she said hastily. 'Of course not, Papa. But if by some chance this excellent idea does not bear the fruit you hope—then we must consider something else. And that means me doing something for my living, like becoming a governess. Is that agreed?'

Her father gave the eager, smiling, attentive nod that meant he was not listening at all; then limped over to the little store of books she had lovingly arranged on the alcove-shelf, took down his Shakespeare and began excitedly thumbing. 'By heaven, I really cannot conceive why I did not think of this idea before!'

Captain Fortune began the pursuing of the idea the next day, with all the energy and address at his command. When he had an end in view, he fairly drove himself at it; but his judgement as to whether an end was attainable, or worthwhile, was less to be relied upon.

Caroline's father had come from a genteel Devon family, but had alienated their affections by a flamboyantly rebellious youth, which had culminated in his engaging as a strolling actor with a touring theatre company. The names of Garrick and Sheridan might have rendered the stage illustrious: they could not make it respectable; and James Fortune's elderly and conventional parents took their hostility to the grave. At last he had recovered his credit with an uncle, who had settled on his nephew sufficient money to buy a commission in the militia, then embodied against the new-risen threat of Bonaparte. It was thus, as a handsome young officer, that he had met Caroline's mother.

She was then a very young woman of gentle upbringing and untried character, making her first sortie from Huntingdonshire, where her father had a good property, to London. She was very ready to be dazzled; and much worse might have befallen her than the passion for young Captain Fortune, which swiftly led to their elopement and marriage by the Gretna blacksmith. For he loved his bride as steadily as his volatile temperament would allow: nor could he be fairly said to want her for her money, for that was at the disposal of her outraged parents, who withheld it, and still he stood by her.

But she was not cut out to be a soldier's wife, at least not one of those who followed the drum, and when Captain Fortune went with the army to the Peninsula she remained in England, living upon very little. She was by now the mother of the infant Caroline, but her parents remained unreconciled to her marriage: the portion she might have expected was bestowed on her more dutiful sister: and only the fondness of a grandparent secured her a legacy at last.

Captain Fortune returned eventually from the Peninsula, his right knee shot away so that he limped. The restored family were not rich, but with the price of his commission, and Mrs Fortune's inheritance, they had a competence. But the Captain, with his expansive schemes, soon brought them into difficulty. Caroline's mother, never strong, had died when her daughter was twelve, in the unhappy knowledge that there was not much money left, nor much prospect of any more.

To some respectable people as came into their orbit, the Captain had been a shockingly bad father to his daughter. Her education had been fitful, her mode of life unsettled, and her wardrobe was sadly inadequate to set off such beauty as nature had blessed her with; and from long mixing in male company, and that not of the best, she knew far too many curse-words. But Caroline was less severe. Life with her father had been an interesting experience, and that counted for much. In her father the colourful worlds of the soldier, the dandy, and the artist met, and she had glimpsed all of them. In her nearly twenty years she had been nourished by a very rich diet of experience compared with the bland fare served to most young ladies.

Thus there was no bitterness in her, even as she regarded her father with the last veil of illusion stripped and realised she must make her own way. As for his scheme of relaunching himself as an actor, she gave it a tolerant attention, listening to him read Romeo, and even accompanying him to auditions. But the time of year was unpropitious. It was June, when the season ended, and even Captain Fortune's sanguine temper was unequal to the series of rebuffs he met with.

Caroline felt his humiliation, and it spurred her on to making enquiries on her own account for a governess's position. When her father was out of the way, she went to consult with her old nurse, now settled in Marylebone, who directed her to the Petty Register Office where prospective governesses and employers were matched. Caroline was only a little knocked back by the Office's request for references.

This was problematic. The natural person was the proprietress of the Seminary in Chelsea, but the fact that that lady was among her father's creditors cast an unpromising shadow over any application. However, Caroline set herself at once to composing the most artful letter within her power, and had just despatched Marriner to the post-office with it when her father came home with news that changed everything.

He came in breathing hard from negotiating the steep, narrow stairs, and with a pained, wondering look about his brow. She supposed at first that he was sunk back into melancholy reflections, but he surprised her by calling her to sit down by him and, after studying her in the most dreamy and perplexing way for some minutes, said: 'Caro, how would you like to be a rich woman?'

Mrs Catling: such was the name of the person who was to be the agent of this spectacular change in Caroline's fortunes. 'Mrs Catling,' her father said, 'is a splendid woman. Mrs Catling is all that is estimable. I do not base this judgement upon personal acquaintance,' he added. 'I have never met her. But her late husband was colonel of my regiment. You've heard me talk of old Devil's-Eye Catling, perhaps? Everyone was terrified of him. But there was one thing only that he was afraid of.'

'Mrs Catling?'

'Aye! "The commander-in-chief" he used to call her,' Captain Fortune said, with a reminiscent chuckle. 'Well, he's been dead above a year now: the gout did what the Frenchies couldn't; and there's Mrs Catling a rich widow without any children, past sixty, quite alone. She lives mainly at Brighton, but she's been staying in London for the past month. I ran into Stanton again at Tattersall's. And it was he who put the notion in my head. He told me that, as a widow, it's Mrs Catling's way always to look kindly on anyone connected with the regiment. I hear, too, that old Devil's-Eye was cousin to Lord Dereham, and a rich man in his own right, so all in all she's comfortably situated. Except in one regard, my dear—she's solitary. She's in need of a companion.'

Caroline, feeling from her father's benignly smiling pause that she was expected to make a remark, asked if the widow had no relations.

'She does! And here, as Stanton pointed out to me, is the most interesting circumstance of all. There are, I understand, a nephew and a niece, who presume on their expectations from the old lady. But they have quarrelled! Mrs Catling is now minded to look elsewhere for company to cheer her solitude and to be perhaps—who knows?—what she cannot find in her ungrateful kin: a worthy heir.' The Captain took Caroline's hand in both of his, patted it, and added: 'Or heiress.'

'Papa,' she said, staring at the top of his lowered head, 'I can hardly mistake your meaning. But what can we have to do with this lady?'

'She has been seeking a companion in Town—but has not found one to suit. Now you cannot fail to follow me, my dear.'

Indeed she could not. Besides governessing, acting as a paid companion was one of the few occupations open to the unprovided woman. But the profession of toad-eating, as it was unflatteringly called, often amounted to nothing more than placating the capricious temper of a rich old woman.

'Well—this comes as a great surprise,' she answered at last. 'You said you have never met this Mrs Catling?'

'Not beyond giving her a bow from a distance—but I shall soon repair the omission. I took the liberty of sending a little note in to her house at Dover Street, asking if I might wait on her tomorrow, and I received a favourable answer. Now, this commits us to nothing, Caro. But you see the advantage. There's she, disposed to favour the families of the old regiment: there's she, seeking a young lady companion to solace her twilight years of widowhood: there's she, with a great deal of money, and no one to lay it out on. And here—well, damn me for a dunce if I've added the sum wrong, but here's you!'

Caroline, wanting space to think, went to the window and looked out. It was a lively enough scene: carts and wagons coming away from the market at Covent Garden jostled with carriages heading for the fashionable milliners, glovers and button-makers, whilst directly across the way the linen-draper stood out on his doorstep and gossiped with the apothecary next door, each with his hands tucked in the pockets of his tight white waistcoat. But a down-at-heel young drab, supported on the arm of a very young and idiotic-looking buck, served as a sharp reminder that this was a harsh world for the unlucky and unprotected.

She turned back to her father. 'Here am I, as you say, Papa. And I am very willing to consider anything that may—well, in short, I will consider anything. But tell me—is Mrs Catling amiable, do you suppose?'

'Amiable isn't in it!' her father exclaimed. This meant, of course, that he did not know, but his choice of words was discouraging. 'My dear, I am delighted you have embraced your golden opportunity!'

'Well, but, Papa, I'm not going to think of it as such—the golden part, I mean. That's my one condition. If I am to put myself up for this position, it must only be on the same terms as if I were applying for a governess post—that is, employment, and no other expectations. I cannot step into such a place and begin angling for legacies.'

'My dear, I said nothing of angling,' her father said solemnly. 'I speak only of probabilities.'

'In any case,' Caroline continued, 'Mrs Catling may not take to *me*.'

'Oh, pooh, how could she not? There is nothing to take against. You have only to be yourself, my dear Caro, no more nor less! Of course when you do meet her there is absolutely no need for you to mention how your education ended, or to use any slang-words, or give your opinions. Marriner! I'll have my coat brushed—I think I'll step across to Offley's. Well, my love, don't wait up. I shall put your case before Mrs Catling, when I call on her tomorrow. I really have the strongest presentiment of success!'

The morning brought a letter that, short as it was, weighed heavily in the balance of decision. The proprietress of the Chelsea seminary, in a few violet-inked lines, declined altogether to furnish a testimonial to Miss Caroline Fortune.

Perhaps, then, it was fate: so Caroline thought, as she watched her father, a little seedy from his late night, set off for his appointment at Dover Street. He was very soon back: when she heard his limping foot on the stair, she supposed he must have been shown the door.

But no: he was jaunty.

'Ah, she wastes no time, Mrs Catling! Estimable woman! She knew my name at once—she remembers the name of every officer who served under her husband. When she said she'd see you at the earliest opportunity, I suggested this afternoon—like a fool! She soon put me in my place with that one. She does *not* receive visitors in the afternoon, says she. She's a true stickler, that's what: and I admire her for it!'

Caroline could not entirely share his admiration. Captain Fortune, in his gallant way, liked all women, classing them as fine, damned fine, splendid or estimable. She must cultivate a fatalistic patience until the next morning, when she was to present herself to Mrs Catling.

A restless night drove her to an early waking; and before breakfast she spent a disconsolate time laying out her clothes. Frugality at least simplified her choices. If Mrs Catling was a stickler for correctness, then a morning-dress it must be, and of those Caroline had two.

A small foxed mirror that was all she had to dress by, and Caroline was used to seeing only a dim, cramped, and partial reflection of herself. While she did not lack a sense of her own merits, still she thought herself no more than tolerable-looking, and nurtured abysmal doubts about her ability ever to shine in company. She had a quick tongue and a turn for wit, but these she employed, in truth, somewhat as a shield behind which she could shelter.

As for the figure in the mirror, which any observer must approve as tall and slender, she thought it gawky. Her hair, which was of a dark chestnut, coiled at the crown and fringed on the brow with a few curls, she could just contemplate without bitterness. As to her face, the strongly arched eyebrows gave her, she thought, a ridiculously surprised look. The thinness of her nose displeased her, and the waxy fairness of skin caused her to mutter that she looked like a ghost as usual.

The house in Dover Street was imposing and, as Caroline saw when the footman admitted them, elegantly fitted out. Mrs Catling's purse must be long indeed for her to be able to afford such a place as a mere lodging for a Town-visit. So her father proclaimed, in what could only be called a stage whisper, as they were conducted upstairs; and whatever the old lady's infirmities might be, they plainly did not include deafness, for her voice came sharply from the drawing room: 'Yes, Fortune, I'm rich enough, as no doubt you knew very well when you sought me out.'

The Captain composed himself into an apologetic attitude, and went into the room bowing if not quite scraping; but the lady seated there waved at him to desist.

'Stop that mopping and mowing, man, you look ridiculous. Yes, very large and splendid the place is, for one old woman, and that is just how I like it. This is your daughter, I dare say.' Mrs Catling gave Caroline a short, hard look and then extended a hand to her father. 'Well, Fortune, she's as handsome as I'd expect from a pretty fellow like yourself.'

'Mrs Catling'—he bowed over her hand—'you are all goodness.'

No, she was not, as anyone less chivalrous than the Captain would have perceived at once on beholding Mrs Sophia Catling. The relict of the late Colonel 'Devil's-Eye' Catling had herself a penetrating glance and a carrying voice that would have suited the parade-ground; nor was hers a face that promised a charitable disposition. A dark, hawkish handsomeness, heightened more than obscured by her sixty-odd years, was offset by something shrewd lurking about her eyelids and lips.

'Allow me to present, my dear madam, Caroline. My daughter—as you so justly observe. You're like your late husband, Mrs Catling, nothing escaped him: I remember him saying to me, "Fortune," he said—'

'If you behaved like such a fool with Colonel Catling, he would never have spoken a word to you. What is all this nonsense? You're nervous, I think. You probably need drink to settle you—you have that look. There's a tavern in Dover Yard. Go there, man, go. We cannot talk with you standing by. I shall send her to you in thirty minutes.'

Captain Fortune, a great lingerer and ditherer, had never been so smartly got rid of. There was time only for a glance of mutual reassurance, and then Caroline was left alone with Mrs Catling.

'Well, he didn't introduce me,' her hostess went on, motioning Caroline to a seat on the other side of a marble fireplace. 'But then you know who I am, of course. So, why do you want to be my companion?'

Mrs Catling put up her chin as she spoke, and stared Caroline down in a manner that had surely excoriated numerous drapers and ostlers.

Caroline merely returned her look. 'I am in need of a position, ma'am. My father told me of this one, and I agreed that I would try for it. I know of you only what he has told me—'

'Which I doubt can be relied on.'

'Just so—as you can know of me only what he has told you. So we are in like case, ma'am, and may both be wrong.'

Mrs Catling put her head on one side, studying her: a reluctant smile dawned. 'I dare say. I have made enquiries, and your late mother was a Perrymount, I find, from Huntingdon? A good family. Of course they won't own you: it's an old story—your precious father stole her away and spent all her money. And now he's stuck with a grown girl, and no provision for her! Lord, what fools these mortals be. Men most of all; and of all men, soldiers. Dice, wine and trollops is all they are good for.'

'You would know them, of course, from your late husband.'

'Colonel Catling was the exception that proves the rule,' the widow said. 'I will show him to you.' She went to a bureau and took from a drawer a miniature portrait. 'That is Colonel Catling,' she said, placing the picture in Caroline's hand. 'What do you think of him?'

Caroline couldn't be sure, but she didn't think she had ever seen a man so fierce, cross-eyed, and mad-looking. 'It is a face of much decision,' Caroline said, after a short struggle, offering the miniature back.

Mrs Catling did not take it. 'But not handsome?'

'I wouldn't presume, Mrs Catling, to pass judgement on such a matter.'

'Suppose I insisted? What then?'

'Then—then I should think you were testing me out.'

Favouring her with the reluctant smile again, Mrs Catling took the miniature back. 'Quite right. The fact of the matter is I have a horror of flatterers. So you see, pleasing me will not be an easy task. However. At least you did not go into raptures over the late Colonel. Who was certainly not handsome, nor indeed charming. I am not a *lonely* woman, Miss Fortune, and it would be a very great mistake in you to suppose it. I seek a companion to make my life easier. A solitary woman cannot go about freely, or accept invitations or receive company, without a lot of fussing about her solitary state. What I do require is correctness. You must know how to conduct yourself upon every social occasion. I observe you know how to deport yourself, and I dare swear you could dress well enough too. On top of the stipend, there would be an allowance for dress, if I were to take you. This is not generosity: I simply could not bear to have a dowd about me. Do you read novels?'

'I read whatever I can get my hands on,' Caroline answered honestly.

'You play, I hear, a little. And you draw, no doubt?'

'I do. I know that is traditionally the other accomplishment, but I actually do it for pleasure.'

'Well, that I can approve. Now, I will state it unequivocally: I will not countenance your throwing yourself at men. I am no friend to that overprized imp Cupid. Look at what he did to your mother. You don't resemble *her*, I hope.'

'You'll forgive me if I can't join you in that hope, ma'am,' Caroline said, colouring, 'as I have tender memories of my mother, and would be very pleased to be like her.'

'Hey, well, that's loyal of you, I suppose,' Mrs Catling said, with a shrug. 'But my conditions, Miss Fortune, remain. What I will not tolerate is if you are flighty. I may as well add that the same conditions would surely apply if you went to be governess to some merchant's brats, which is your only other recourse. But with me, there would be elegance, society, and rational conversation. The choice is yours.'

'Do you mean—the post is mine?'

'Let me put it this way: I have seen three other young women, and each was on her way home by this time. Well, I suppose you hardly know what to say, and all the rest of it?'

'That would be affectation, as I came here to apply for the post. No, I will say a very heartfelt thank-you.'

'You know, of course, that I live principally at Brighton,' Mrs Catling went on. 'So you must make a removal from London. I come up to Town only once a year, for a small part of the season. For fashion of the first water, Brighton is the place. To be sure, the moral influence of the Prince, making it his favoured resort, is not entirely salubrious. But there is no denying that where he goes, fashion attends. The Colonel knew him, and I have been invited to the Pavilion a few times.'

In her heart Caroline deplored the Regent as the gluttonous buffoon of the public prints, but that did not affect the fascination of that fabulous palace by the sea. 'Oh, ma'am, what is it like? Is it true that they burn two hundred pounds' worth of wax candles a night?'

'Let us just say that reports of the Prince's style of living are seldom exaggerated, Miss Fortune. But come! I leave for Brighton the day after tomorrow. Will you come?'

'I will be very glad to come. I—well, thank you, Mrs Catling.'

The widow waved a hand with a repressive look, as if even this degree of warmth unsettled her. 'Very well. Now, aside from clothes, I do not anticipate you will have much luggage. If there are some books and other small effects, those may travel with us: anything larger will have to be sent to Brighton separately. You will, of course, have your own room there, and the servants will wait on you in the ordinary way. I may send my maid to help dress your hair when we go out. And now there is one last test. My passion, Miss Fortune, is cards. I must have cards every night. Now I am watching your face carefully.'

As this was one area of her education that had not been neglected, Caroline had no fear of what her face might betray.

'So, you do not quail at the prospect of partnering an old woman at whist for years upon years? For I should add, Miss Fortune, that I fully intend to live for ever.' Mrs Catling's eyes took on a hooded look as she said this. 'I hope that does not disappoint you. Does it?'

'I can't fairly answer that, Mrs Catling,' Caroline said candidly, 'so I wonder if it's perhaps not a fair question.'

'Of course it isn't. You have evaded the question neatly enough. In truth I acquit you of any conscious designs on my wealth: I think you are probably too naive for that, and still thrive on the blissful belief that a rich and handsome man will descend from the skies and marry you.' Mrs Catling made a face of distaste, and looked up at the clock on the mantel. 'There—less than thirty minutes, just as I said. Come—shake hands upon the arrangement, Miss Caroline Fortune: and now ring the bell and go and find that father of yours, and tell him the news.'

The footman came and, a little dazed, Caroline found herself following him to the drawing-room door; where he coughed apologetically, and stepped back to Mrs Catling. 'Ma'am,' he murmured, 'Mr Downey is here. I wasn't sure—he would insist—'

'Again? Tell him to be gone,' Mrs Catling snapped; and the footman bowed out of the room precipitately, propelling Caroline before him.

Below, in the hall, a young gentleman was waiting in peculiar agitation, pacing about and swishing his cane. He looked up sharply when Caroline appeared, but then demanded of the footman, 'Well?'

'Mrs Catling is not at home, sir,' the man said, with a suffering look.

'I see.' The young gentleman breathed hard, and clapped his hat on his head. 'And *she*, I suppose'—with a twitch of his cane in Caroline's direction—'has just been here to clean the chimneys.'

'Quite so—and shockingly dirty they were,' Caroline said, moving past him to the front door. Glancing into his face, she fancied a resemblance to the old lady upstairs, for he was rather of the middle height, and square-cut. This, and his hostility, disposed her to think him Mrs Catling's relative; but having no desire to be introduced, she advanced to the door, telling the footman with a smile that he need not trouble.

Bursting with her news, she sought out her father at the tavern in Dover Yard. The sight of him in the tap-room should have dispelled any lingering doubts about how he would get on without her. Within half an hour he had acquired three new bosom-friends, and had moreover charmed them into standing him drinks.

'It will be,' he cried, 'the making of you, Caro!' His speech was a little foxed, of course, and it was noisy in the tap-room—which accounted for her mishearing *making*, for an alarming moment, as *breaking*.

Chapter Two

TWO DAYS LATER, a travelling-carriage stands before the house in Dover Street, ready to depart. A neat equipage, but substantial enough to bear the trunks, boxes, and dressing-cases strapped up behind: the four well-matched bays, the shining harness, the coachman's blue livery with silk facings and gold-laced buttonholes, all produce a smart and spanking appearance in the high June morning.

The carriage belongs, of course, to Mrs Sophia Catling, and offers ample evidence of her wealth, her taste for the best, and her insistence on privacy. Caroline Fortune has never travelled in such style, and she stands regarding the turn-out with admiration. Melancholy, very faintly, tinges her view. She has parted with her father at his Henrietta Street lodging early that morning—Mrs Catling laying a strict injunction on his coming to see them off, for fear of what she called 'theatrics'.

As to what he will do when she has gone, he has airily assured her that he has various irons in the fire, and still has hopes of a return to the stage, perhaps back in the West Country.

Now the coachman steps down and, ambling near to Caroline, quietly comments: 'I thought we might see the danglers today, before she gets off—but no sign of 'em.'

'Danglers?'

'That's what I call 'em. On account of their dangling after her money, you see, which is on account of her having nobody to leave it to but them. That's what they reckon, anyways.'

'This is Mrs Catling's family?' Caroline asks, finding she has adopted the coachman's whisper. 'There's a nephew and niece, I understand?'

'That's them. One is a Mr Downey. And the other's a Miss Downey.'

Oh, she loves keeping 'em dangling better than a rubber of whist. Well, it doesn't look as if they're coming today, but you'll meet them sooner or later, miss. Of course, they won't like *you*, on account of seeing you as another dangler.' The coachman gives a chuckle, then adds, 'I never said any of this, mind,' before sauntering back to the carriage.

No danglers appear, however; and soon Caroline takes her seat in the carriage along with Mrs Catling, and Mrs Catling's personal maid—a little pinched comfit-chewer with a look of lifelong discontent.

'Well, Shrewmouse?' Mrs Catling accosts her. 'You are sorry to be leaving Town, no doubt, just as you were sorry to come here. That's about what I'd expect of you.' The Shrewmouse, whose name is Miss Lott, is drab and dour, and of that class of people whose function in the social sphere corresponds to that of boot-scraper in the domestic.

Caroline is sorry for her; but, Mrs Catling shall not make a boot-scraper out of *me*, is her own silent resolution as the carriage begins to move. She sincerely wishes success, for her new life, and intends that no failure of effort, temper, or spirits on her part will jeopardise it.

'Tell me, Miss Fortune, what was my coachman talking to you about?' Mrs Catling says, peering closely at her. 'Oh, don't fear, you won't get him into trouble. I know anyway. My precious nephew and niece. He thought they might come to see me off. As did I. But even they must have baulked at such a naked display of interested hypocrisy. You will suppose me deficient in family feeling also—but in truth I am not. I am very fond of my nephew and niece, certainly fonder than their conduct towards me warrants. I have one sister living. Her return for being the pretty one of the family was to make a bad marriage. When the man died, and left her with two children and very little else, she considered herself ill-used rather than the author of her misfortunes. She scarcely stirs from her house, which is in no better an address than Golden Square, if you please. The one effort to which she will rouse herself is to remind her offspring, Matthew and Maria, who are now grown, that they have a rich old aunt. The precious pair are most devoted to me. They are forever seeking reassurance as to the state of my *health*.' Mrs Catling utters her scornful laugh. 'And for all that, they are creatures of dreadful caprice—let them fancy that I have slighted them and they get upon the high ropes at once. Dear, dear!'

Caroline sees that a game is being played here, between Mrs Catling and her young nephew and niece—not a pleasant one: she senses resentment, power, and greed as only some of its elements. But what chiefly troubles her is the prospect, which the coachman seemed to hint at, of her being dragged into it.

Well, she thinks, when I meet them, I shall tell this Matthew and Maria at once that I have no designs on their aunt's fortune and that they are not to consider me a rival. But for now there is the excitement of bowling out of London on the Brighton coach road. Mrs Catling's carriage cannot make the pace set by the post-chaises, the sleek curricles, tilburies, chariots and chair-back gigs that pass them with a whirl of red-rimmed wheels, but still they get along at a great rate.

They stop to water the horses and refresh themselves at Reigate, and then at Cuckfield, where they dine. Even with stops they make such good speed that it is still afternoon when they come to Brighton. The resort, seen for the first time in coppery sunlight is brisk, breezy, brilliant—and, for those of a more conservative disposition, a little brash. This may be put down to the Prince Regent, whose patronage has made the town, and whose principal creation rises above it all, strange and splendid and gargantuan: the Royal Pavilion, still unfinished, a cheese-dream of domes and minarets.

Mrs Catling's house in West Street is old compared with many of Brighton's gingerbread villas: but within, all convenience and cleanness. This latter is confirmed by its mistress, whose first action on entering the hall is to sweep a white-gloved finger along the surfaces of a table, a Chinese bowl and a picture-frame. The platoon of servants drawn up at rigid attention evince no surprise at this; but Caroline sees twitches of alarm at Mrs Catling's next proceeding. She takes a straight-backed chair, places it next to the door to the dining room, and instructs Caroline to step up on to it.

'Run your finger along the top of the lintel. Stay—let me see your glove first. Good. Now, up you go.'

Caroline does as she is bid. With dismay, she finds the finger of her glove coming away black, but there is no hiding it or wiping it with Mrs Catling below watching intently. She steps down: Mrs Catling's eyes sparkle at the sight of her glove. 'Dear, dear,' she intones, and taking Caroline by the other hand as if they are beginning a dance, leads her over to the servants, and urges her to display the offending finger.

'I cannot suppose you were not expecting me, as I wrote you with every detail,' Mrs Catling says, addressing her household. 'The only supposition is that you care neither for my opinion nor for your situation, and would gladly forfeit both.' Mrs Catling smiles blandly at the pained silence that ensues. 'Well, well. I am in indulgent mood, for I have been fortunate enough to find a companion—she is Miss Caroline Fortune, and here she is, and you are to answer to her as you would to me; and so I am pretty well contented, and will overlook the dereliction—this *once*.' She turns to Caroline and adds, 'You had better put the glove aside to be laundered, my dear.'

Mrs Catling is all of a sudden in genial spirits, and ordering a maid to show Caroline to her room, cordially hopes she will like it, and urges her to mention anything that is missing for her comfort.

Nothing is: the room is admirably fitted out, if more formal than homely. Caroline turns to the maid, thanks her, and assures her she isn't going to investigate the lintel for dust; but she gets no answering smile from the girl, who scuttles away.

'Well,' breathes Caroline, facing the room and her future, 'I wonder how I shall get used to this.'

A domestic tyrant—that her new employer was, to be sure; and Caroline's first days at West Street offered many further evidences of it. But she found, to her slightly guilty relief, that her own duties were light, and her own treatment by Mrs Catling fair and even generous.

Nothing more strenuous was required of her than taking her employer's arm on daily airings along the Marine Parade, and even they were liable to culminate in jellies and tarts at Dutton's, the celebrated confectioner's. Mrs Catling's chief amusement consisted in observing and satirically commenting upon the people they passed, and there was no one of whom she did not know something discreditable.

Caroline had prepared herself to be bored: she had not prepared herself to be amused and entertained. Her time, beyond one half-day a week, was not her own, but it passed agreeably enough even indoors. Mrs Catling was grown short-sighted, and Caroline took charge of her correspondence, as well as reading out loud to her from light novels and verse. Her employer also relished society and cards. Piquet and vingt-et-un filled the hours between dinner—which Mrs Catling took fashionably late—and supper, whenever they were alone at home; but that was not frequent. At least once a week Mrs Catling had company to dine, entertaining her guests politely, feeding them royally, and after they were gone satirising them comprehensively. Then there was a ball at the Old Ship every Thursday, and card-parties on Wednesdays and Fridays—besides concerts, promenades, and the theatre.

As for the dances themselves, the assemblies and card-parties, Caroline liked them very well. If her status as Mrs Catling's dependant, meant that she was always more looker-on than participant, she was not dissatisfied with this.

But Caroline was twenty years old, and could have been forgiven more sighs than she allowed herself, at the prospect of forever creeping along in the craggy shadow of Mrs Catling. She tried not to repine, but still there were nights when she threw open her bedroom window to gasp the fresh air that was never allowed to circulate in Mrs Catling's house, and to hear the near murmur of the sea, which to her young mind, seemed the very sound of life going on tantalisingly without her.

Mrs Catling's ill-humours were not unbearably frequent, and when they did come the storm was soon ridden out. More unpredictable, and more troubling, were the tremendous fits of gloom to which she was subject, when the wry satire fell away, and the greedy relish, and instead there was only the world and her vast, bleak contempt for it.

It was the arrival of a letter one morning that finally broke through one such spell of cold brooding. Caroline, reading out her correspondence to her, had despaired of any communication raising anything but a scowl—and then she came to a letter that changed everything.

'From Mr and Miss Downey, ma'am.' *Ah, the danglers.* 'Shall I read it?'

'Oh, yes.' All at once there was a light in Mrs Catling's eyes—a very feline, if not kindly light; like a bored cat that hears a mouse in the wainscot. 'Oh, yes, read it. Let us hear what they have to say.'

> 'My dear Aunt,
>
> 'It is in no spirit of trifling formality, but with the greatest earnestness, that Maria and I enquire after your health. That we were not able to satisfy ourselves upon that score, before your removal from London, was owing to our not being informed of your departure. I called at Dover Street, and found you gone two days since. The disagreement there had been between you and me on my last visit, I take to account for your leaving without affording us the opportunity of goodbyes. I fear it was a consequence of our quarrel—which, I hasten to add, was not of my seeking; but the share of blame that is portionable to my impetuosity of temper I willingly accept. You must know, Aunt, that to hear my late father abused is a thing I can never endure—however no more of that.
>
> 'We hear, through mutual acquaintance, that you have found a companion to your satisfaction: it is a satisfaction that finds a willing echo here in Golden Square. We are pleased to think of you no longer solitary. I hope the connection prospers, and that the young woman is sensible of her good fortune. My dear aunt, Maria and I intend coming to Brighton the day after tomorrow, that is Wednesday, on purpose to see you. We shall come on the Eclipse coach, which I hear can complete the journey, most remarkably, in under six hours. We shall wait upon you as soon as we arrive, if we may; and I look forward with anticipation to the final repairing of the breach, of which this letter is the first attempt.
>
> 'Your most dutiful and affectionate nephew,
>
> 'Matthew Downey.'

'Well! Did you ever read such a letter?' said Mrs Catling. 'My nephew is a great one for his feelings. Notice how even such small blame as he will accept he turns to his own account. And a most friendly and disinterested reference to *you*, my dear. They are pleased I have you! Oh, of course they are! And they are not coming to Brighton to make sure that I am not growing *too* fond of you, of course they are not!'

'Mrs Catling, you know I don't want to be a bone of contention between you and your family. It is fair to no one.'

'I know that, my dear. Why, you are all innocence and sweetness, and you shudder at the thought of replacing my family in my favour!'

'I disclaim the innocence and sweetness, ma'am, but as for the rest— yes. If you think I have such designs—'

'But this is delicious! Now *everyone* is protesting their sincerity,' Mrs Catling cried, with her sharp jangling laugh. 'You might add, my dear, that you would be just as fond of me if I hadn't a penny—that's one of my nephew's old favourites, though he hasn't used it in this letter.'

'Ma'am,' Caroline said, studying her acidly smiling employer, 'you truly do not believe I am sincere?'

'My dear Miss Fortune, you must not suppose yourself singled out. I trust your sincerity quite as much as anyone else's. And I greatly look forward to introducing you to that precious pair. Well, so they will be upon us tomorrow! I dare say I should ask them to dine. Friday will do: we have no one else coming.'

'Won't they be staying here, ma'am?'

'Here? Why so?' Mrs Catling's eyes narrowed. 'They do not ask if they can come and stay, and neither were they invited. They merely announce their intention of coming to Brighton. I am not a hotel-keeper. I have a great deal more to think of than their whims and fancies.'

This was of course not true. Nothing else was to be thought of at West Street from the moment of the letter's arrival, which the Downeys must surely know; and Mrs Catling surely knew that they knew—and so on. Such was the game into which Caroline found herself unwillingly drawn.

The Downeys being due to arrive in Brighton on Wednesday afternoon, and promising a call as soon as they did, Mrs Catling made sure that her carriage was ready by noon on Wednesday.

'I need an airing,' she said to Caroline, 'and so, I have decided, do you. A *long* one.'

So they went on a drive. They trundled about the Downs. They drew up above Brighton Camp, and watched some horse-exercise: they went on to Rottingdean and Saltdean, and looked at churches and views while the shadows lengthened. It was evening when the coachman was allowed at last to turn the horses' heads towards home. There, Mrs

Catling had the satisfaction of finding that her relatives had called, and called again, and gone away to their inn much perplexed.

The meeting came at last—the next morning, when Caroline was accompanying Mrs Catling on her usual promenade. A man's voice cried, 'Aunt! Aunt Sophia!' from some distance behind them.

'And now this woman on our left, with the crown of curls, well—'

'Ma'am,' Caroline interrupted her, 'someone is calling you—surely Mr Downey.' She turned to look back, but was steered firmly round by Mrs Catling, who could hear perfectly well, and was determined on a last triumph of making her relatives run after her, and get out of breath, and be generally at a disadvantage.

So they were: Mr Matthew Downey, and Miss Maria Downey, stood panting before them, he that same dark and stocky young man Caroline had encountered in the hall at Dover Street, she a golden-fair, long-limbed, languorous sylph of a girl.

'Matthew—Maria—how d'you do, my dears? We are blessed by the weather again, are we not? Though I do smell a shower in the wind,' Mrs Catling said, with provoking blandness; and gathering Caroline's arm tightly to her, 'This is Miss Caroline Fortune, my new companion—I say *new*, though we are so wonderfully used to each other that I feel as if I have known her all my life! My dear, what are you thinking? Pray put up your parasol—you'll spoil that beautiful skin.'

This mark of affectionate attention was so utterly unlike Mrs Catling that Caroline could not have been more surprised. But it succeeded in its chief aim. Mr Matthew Downey, at least, looked thoroughly put out: he could manage only stiff civility as the introductions were made.

'But, Aunt,' he went on impatiently, 'you must know we have tried to call upon you. And you never at home—we were quite concerned—'

'Were you?' Mrs Catling said, smiling. 'Why? Did you suppose the servants had murdered me, and were concealing the fact? But, my dear Matthew, you forget yourself—here is a gentleman unintroduced.'

This was a tall, fine-figured man who had been accompanying the Downeys, and who, having declined altogether to break into a run, only now came up with them. He was dressed with negligent elegance, his coat fashionably tight across his broad shoulders, his cravat tied with careful carelessness, his patent boots dazzling. He was about thirty, and in his aquiline good looks the best qualities of youth and maturity stood in such striking balance that Caroline turned a little dry-mouthed at the sight. His smile, though, completed him: it had just the right dash of self-mockery in it.

'This is Mr Leabrook,' Matthew said, impatient as before. 'We met on the coach, and came down to Brighton together, and so we became a sort of friends. Oh, hang it'—as Mrs Catling's satirical eyebrows rose—'I don't mean it to sound so. It was *you* we came to see, Aunt.'

'I am flattered,' Mrs Catling said, 'and now you see me, and you might, my dear Matthew, be a little more gracious. I shall be very glad to have Mr Leabrook's acquaintance also. Your name, sir, suggests a Northampton connection . . . ?'

'My family have long been settled in Northamptonshire, yes, ma'am,' said Mr Leabrook, in an agreeable light-toned voice. 'Your own name is familiar to me from the splendid reputation of the late Colonel—also from your young relatives, who have spoken with the warmest admiration of you, this last couple of days. I confess it is I who have stuck to them rather, as I have found such pleasant company. However, here is a family reunion, and I am *de trop*; so I'll wish you good day.'

But Mrs Catling would not hear of that. Mr Leabrook, fashionable and well connected, was doubly welcome as another stick with which to beat her relatives, for by giving him a deal of attention she still withheld it from them. While she plied him with questions about how he liked Brighton, she retained Caroline's arm with every appearance of possessive fondness.

Meanwhile Mr and Miss Downey stood by: she had a pretty, sulky mouth and looked bored, but he was cross and heated, and Caroline felt that the charade had gone on long enough. She disengaged herself from Mrs Catling with the excuse that her bootlace was undone, and hung back, making a long pretence of fixing it. At last she had the satisfaction of seeing her employer walking on with her nephew and niece on each arm, questioning them minutely about the standard of service at the Old Ship, where they were staying. Danglers they might be, she thought, but they had come a long way to see her after all.

'It was well done,' said Mr Leabrook, falling into step with her. 'I caught your name, Miss Fortune, and I have gathered from my new friends the position you have taken up. I do not suppose it to be an easy one. But where do you hail from?'

'I have lived mostly in London. I suppose that is where I hail from, though hailing sounds rather strong and decided for me. I fear I drizzle if anything. Or mizzle. They are the same, I dare say, though I always fancy mizzle as that little bit wetter—not that you can have rain that *isn't* wet.' Caroline listened to herself with rising mortification: if it were possible to blabber worse nonsense, she could not see how.

'I thought you must be London,' Mr Leabrook said, looking at her with great attention, delicately laced with amusement. 'There is an air.'

'Why are you at Brighton?' She meant a polite enquiry: it came out grossly forensic. 'I wonder,' she added limply.

'I am here on a family errand also. I have a younger sister—all of thirteen years younger than me, and she has been at a boarding-school at Hove, and I have come to bring her home. That *was* the plan. It has all gone rather awry. First the pole of my carriage broke while I was in London, the very day before I was due to come here and fetch her away in it. Hence my taking the public coach instead—which, of course, was one of those lucky accidents, as it introduced me to our friends here. And now I find that Georgiana, my sister, does not wish to come home. She is invited to Weymouth for the summer by a schoolfellow, whose father has a pleasure-yacht, and Georgiana has a great fancy for sailing. Our place in Northamptonshire is about as far from the sea as it is possible to be in England, so perhaps that accounts for it. Are they reconciled now, do you suppose?' he added in a lower tone, nodding at Mrs Catling and her supporters. 'Downey has been most anxious about it all. What is the substance of this quarrel, do you know? Of course I realise you must be discreet.'

'I suspect it is one of those quarrels that will always be breaking out, from the pride of either party. But you are right—I must be discreet.'

'Else they will be making *you* the subject of a quarrel, eh? Never fear me, I shall say no more.'

Caroline studied his graceful figure, his clear-cut profile with the grey eye sparked by humour. Here was such naturalness, combined with polish and civility; she suspected he was an accomplished flirt.

'You are wanted, I think,' he said, nodding ahead.

Mrs Catling, obviously feeling she had indulged her relatives enough, was turning herself about, and demanding: 'Where is my Caroline? I am quite lost, you know, without my Caroline—quite lost.'

Caroline, who had never even heard her employer use her first name, let alone decorate it with that fond possessive, tried to keep the surprise from her face. But Mr Leabrook missed nothing. He said quietly, 'My feeling is that if someone tries to use you as a tool, you shouldn't mind it, because it is their choice and folly, not yours.'

'My dear,' Mrs Catling cried, as Caroline rejoined her, 'we must go home soon, and this mantle is all in a twist from the wind, and I must have your delicate fingers. No one can set it right just as you do—here is Matthew making it ten times worse with his fumbling.'

'I can't see much amiss with it, ma'am,' Caroline said, primping.

'Well, upon my word, I tried my best,' Matthew Downey said, fuming and frowning as if she had said something against him.

I shall not try any more, Caroline thought, if they are so resolved upon enmity: I shall just not try. Still, it was disheartening. When Mrs Catling, on parting, invited the Downeys to come later and dine at West Street, Caroline greeted the prospect with inward dismay. She felt she had been hated enough for one day.

What made her feel differently was when Mrs Catling turned to Mr Leabrook, and cordially invited him too.

'That is an invitation I would gladly accept,' he answered, 'if I did not fear that I would be intruding on a family party.'

'Oh, my dear sir, we are not that sort of family, believe me—you see us in one of our rare intervals of not quarrelling—is it not so, Matthew?' Mrs Catling chuckled, to her nephew's obvious discomfiture.

'That I cannot credit, for there is too much amiability on either side. But I shall certainly come if you will have me—it will be a great pleasure,' Mr Leabrook said. His glance rested on Caroline as he said it.

If she was a chief part of that pleasure, Caroline was far from proof against feeling gratified by the compliment; but she hoped she was in no danger of overestimating it either. Mr Leabrook was after all a single gentleman at a loose end. However, the evening brought further demonstrations of his regard; and to his presence also she felt she owed such ease as was established between herself and Mrs Catling's devoted nephew. For while Mr Leabrook set an example of unstinting civility to her, it was plain that the young man looked up to his new friend, and set some store by his opinion.

Matthew Downey's softened manner towards Caroline at dinner was the less surprising, however, after her encounter with Maria, who, on arrival, had declared that she wanted the use of a mirror, and slipping her arm through Caroline's had impelled her upstairs to her bedroom. Once alone, she gave Caroline's cheek a kiss, and sat down on her bed.

'And so you are the terrible creature who is to cut us out of the will!' she said. 'And yet you have but the one head, and no horns that I can see. Well, you wicked minx, turning the feeble mind of our frail old aunt, what have you to say for yourself?'

'I must confess,' Caroline said, laughing, 'that I have been fearing you believe these things in earnest.'

'Lord! Well, I don't. And the kiss is meant to say so—and also, if they do force us into falling out in the end, as a sort of making-up in advance. Because I know them: *she* is a shocking make-mischief, and my poor brother is so susceptible, he *will* work himself up into a pother, though that's the very thing she relishes. Dear, dear—you must think us a sad set!'

There is no beautifier like sympathy, and under its influence Caroline perceived that Maria Downey's mouth was not sulky at all, but rather charmingly indolent.

'I thought you must hate me,' Caroline said. 'And all I want is to keep my position—and, oh, Lord, how soapy *that* sounds!'

They laughed, which felt like an enormous relief to Caroline: laughter in Mrs Catling's company tending only to be an extract of malice.

'Then the best thing, my dear, is to forget all about it. My brother suspects *everyone* of coming between him and his aunt, while I do not give a hang. But how do you come to want such a position? You are neither pruny old maid nor country vicar's clumsy daughter. Though I fancy I can make a guess. Esteemed parents somehow omitted to set you up as esteemed parents are supposed to? Ah, I have smoked it, because I am—well, not in the same boat, but in a vessel very like it. You've heard Aunt Sophia speak of my papa and mama, no doubt?'

'I—yes, just incidentally.'

'Ah, is that a new word for "with scathing contempt"? She despises 'em. Mama, who's her sister, went and married Papa for love, which Aunt Sophia can never approve to begin with. Then Papa, who was a lawyer, set himself to changing the world instead of feathering his nest. He wanted to get into Parliament and reform it, and when that didn't answer, he devoted himself to getting other men in, which all cost him a deal of money. So when he sank into the grave, as the poets have it, there wasn't much left for us. But what vexes Aunt Sophia about my mama is that she obstinately refuses to regret marrying Papa, ever.'

'I begin to see a little more clearly now. It is all a sad pity—and really, would it not be better if Mrs Catling would simply say what she intends, instead of keeping you'—Caroline nearly said *dangling*—'forever in suspense?'

'It certainly would be better. But then she would not have the enjoyment of power. Oh, she has taken Matthew under her wing to some degree. He is studying for the Bar like Papa, and she has contributed an allowance until he is qualified, and I think he is as close to her heart as anyone. I use the word "heart",' Maria added, with a droll glance, 'in the very loosest sense possible.'

'But surely,' Caroline faltered, 'to favour one and not the other—'

'Not me, you mean? Well, you have probably observed, my dear, that Aunt Sophia likes *men* best. But luckily I have another resource. I think this face of mine as bland as butter, but it *can* captivate. There is a gentleman I met at the beginning of the season, who intends making me what he quaintly terms *his own*, as soon as he is able.'

'Oh, I'm so very pleased for you! That is—if he is a *nice* gentleman.'

'He has the requisite number of eyes and teeth,' Maria said, laughing, 'and is good-natured and pleasant, and if he is six-and-thirty I don't mind it. Best of all, he is very comfortably off; and so what my aunt chooses to do with her fortune is up to her—I am thankful to be spared the fatigue of caring any more about it. All I must do is wait: he is gone to the West Indies, and I cannot look for his return at least until the beginning of next year.'

'So long—that must be a sore trial of patience for you.'

'I dare say it would, if I were very much in love,' answered Maria, smiling at her in the mirror, 'but my regard for him is quite manageable, believe me, and hence so is the anxiety.'

This was said with the lightness that Caroline already recognised as characteristic of Miss Downey, and that did not necessarily preclude true feeling. Still, she found herself wondering whether the years of being played on their wealthy aunt's hook had not had a more demoralising effect on both the young Downeys than they realised.

But Caroline for her own part was simply happy to have made a friend where she had feared an enemy. And with Matthew managing to be polite to her, and Mr Leabrook being rather more than that, Caroline found nothing but enjoyment in the dinner. Her employer too was in mellowest mood on moving to the drawing room.

The gentlemen were not long over their wine, but long enough, it seemed, for Mr Matthew Downey to take a good deal of it. His colour, always high, was quite fiery, and his gait was unsteady, which misled Caroline for a moment. He could not surely be coming to sit by her?

But he was. 'Miss Fortune, I must apologise to you,' he said abruptly. 'We have met before, in London—you remember it, of course—at Dover Street. And I fear on that occasion I was deficient in courtesy. Indeed, I believe I was thoroughly rude. The only excuse I can offer is that my mind—my heart also—were much occupied.'

'I hardly remember it Mr Downey. Truly, it is forgotten.'

'By you perhaps—I cannot so easily efface the painful impression. But then it was so horribly like me—when I am overmastered by some great feeling, I become quite blind and insensible in that way.'

Well, he had gone rather swiftly from apology to talking about his feelings, a subject in which she could hardly be expected to share his lively interest. But she concluded that he was surely after making friends, and that any reserve on her part would be churlish.

'I cannot make a fuller explanation,' he said, returning to the point. 'Discretion forbids—and I could not burden you with confidences.'

He looked, though, in his inflammable way, as if he might be going to; and so she said hastily, to divert him, 'Well, and so you met Mr Leabrook on the road, I believe, and were not previously acquainted?'

'Oh! yes, to be sure—a piece of great good luck, was it not? I have made a capital friend in Leabrook. But you must not suppose there to be something flimsy in a friendship so quickly made. Where there is true cordiality and sympathy, an hour can do as much as a lifetime.'

She had meant only a commonplace enquiry: it was rather fatiguing to be taken up like this; but at that moment Mr Leabrook, catching her eye, drew Matthew into a general conversation.

Maria soon transferred the attention back to Caroline, however, for she had found on a table within reach of her sinuous arm Caroline's sketchbook, and now the contents must be admired.

'How provoking—your people truly look like people, instead of dolls in very foldy dresses like mine,' Maria said. 'And hands—how does one draw hands? Mine always seem to have *one* finger too many.'

'Figures I can manage, but they must float in limbo,' Caroline said. 'You see how few are the landscapes, and decidedly not good.'

'I fancy the ability to draw landscape is uncommoner than generally supposed,' Mr Leabrook said, bending over the book. 'I mean to have some views of my estate made, when I find an artist equal to them.'

'Your property in Northamptonshire is large, Mr Leabrook?' Mrs Catling asked.

'It is large enough to content me—and my late father took pains to improve it. I am perhaps less fond of country living than he, or my mother, who is very content to remain there all the year, rearing doves.'

'Rearing doves, you say, Mr Leabrook?' Maria put in. 'I find that enchanting. Everyone used to have a dovecote, didn't they? So pretty and medieval, like mead—which I always fancy as very refreshing but was probably quite odious and sticky—what do you think, Caroline?'

'I think it was probably horrible, and I do not think I could have worn one of those pointed hats with a handkerchief on it, and kept my countenance.'

'True—but you ladies would have been in better case than us men,' Mr Leabrook said. 'Just think—Matthew and I would be in tabards and hose, and that I am sure I could not carry off.'

Caroline, running her eye over his tall lean figure, thought that he would probably look very well in it. She thought him all that was handsome and amiable. 'But that does not mean falling in love with him,' she said to herself—so distinctly, that for a moment of real alarm she thought she had spoken the words out loud.

Chapter Three

THE DINNER-PARTY HAD ended peaceably, in spite of its hostess's best efforts. Caroline's sympathies were now firmly with the Downeys, and over the next week they ripened, for they were much together. Having made her point, Mrs Catling now invited her relatives to socialise every day. With Maria, Caroline continued on excellent terms—no less, and no more: it was hard to imagine so self-contained a nature admitting any deep friendship. With Matthew there was a startling change.

'I wish I knew what you really thought of me!' he burst out one afternoon. They had all gone in Mrs Catling's carriage to picnic at Rottingdean. Matthew had asked Caroline to take a turn along the cliff-path with him. She was just glancing regretfully back at Mr Leabrook when he spoke, so it was with a sort of guilty start that she replied, 'Oh—why—why, I think very well of you, Mr Downey.'

'I would be glad to believe it!' he said, shaking his head with a sigh. 'After our unfortunate beginning you have turned utterly polite and closed-up, and I can't tell what may lie behind your expression. For myself, I am terribly open.' He paused. 'I will be honest—indeed I can be no other—and confess that I suspected you, at first, a schemer. It was unjust of me,' he pursued. '*Now* I realise that we are much in the same boat. You have no doubt heard my aunt abusing my late father. The other day she was talking to me of *your* father, Miss Fortune, and characterising him as a shabby reprobate, who could not provide for his daughter, and so had foisted the little chit onto her in hopes of a legacy. Her exact words. I could not help but feel goodwill to you after them.'

Caroline felt that the exactness might have been omitted, but was prepared to accept the goodwill. 'Well, as to a legacy, or anything of that kind, Mr Downey,' she said, 'if I could sign something—some document—renouncing any claim on Mrs Catling's fortune, ever, I would do it—here and now! Failing that, I do not see how I can convince you.'

He hesitated, and then with a look of genuine frankness said in appeal: 'You must think me very mercenary! Looking only to what my aunt can do for me. I for my part don't see how I can convince *you* otherwise, unless—unless I take you into my confidence.'

'Oh, you don't have to do that!'

'No—but I shall, because there is something about you, Miss Fortune, that invites it. I feel I can trust you.' He had drunk several glasses of champagne at nuncheon, and she wondered whether she ought to remind him of it; but already he was plunging on: 'Tell me, have you ever been truly in love? I don't mean any trifling attachment. So that you are half ecstatic and half tormented, and your heart drums wildly.'

Caroline did not answer. She was ruefully admitting to herself that, for all her thoughts about Mr Leabrook, her heart kept a steady beat.

'Well,' went on Matthew, 'such a love is mine. Oh! it is wonderful to let this out at last—for I can confide in no one. Maria is a dear sister, but she is so dreadfully practical. That day at Dover Street, Miss Fortune, I had just come from seeing my love. I offer this as some explanation for my conduct. I offer you her name also: it is Perdita.'

'Oh, like the mist . . .' The Prince Regent had had a notorious mistress named Perdita Robinson: Caroline realised, just too late, that this would not be a tasteful comparison. 'Like the mist on the sea,' she improvised desperately, 'in beauty, I mean—I imagine her.'

'I was not mistaken in you, Miss Fortune—you have described her exactly!' cried Matthew. 'You do have a feeling heart—and you embolden me to unveil the secret. Oh, a sacred secret. Between Perdita and me burns the purest of flames. It is only my unfortunate situation that renders secrecy necessary. I am but two-and-twenty, and not yet qualified, and I have no money, and no expectations beyond Aunt Sophia. As for Perdita, she is quite without fortune. Her father is a mere apothecary, and he lives at Snow Hill. As for me, my aunt has explicitly told me that if I go rushing after a petticoat, as she terms it, then I can expect no more help from her.'

'Good Lord—how long is such a prohibition to last?'

'I have heard her say that no man should marry till he is at least thirty,' Matthew said, with a grimace, 'and then only from motives of the most careful prudence. The fact is, if she knew about Perdita, my credit with her would be lost. But what about my dear girl? It is intolerably hard on her to be turned into a secret, as if she were something shameful. That day when I saw you at Dover Street, she had spoken passionately of our wretched situation' Matthew tugged out his handkerchief and mopped his brow. 'It was a painful meeting—even though it concluded with what *should* be the happiest thing that can ever come to pass. No. I still say, the happiest. We became engaged, Miss Fortune: secret the bond must be, but solemn it is, and indivisible.'

'Oh . . . I can see how very hard it is for you, Mr Downey. I want to congratulate you on your engagement, and yet one can hardly properly do so! Yet you are plainly devoted to this young lady—and if she is amiable and true, then surely . . .' She had been going to say that surely Mrs Catling might be brought round to a more sympathetic view of the couple's plight; but after a moment's reflection she curbed her tongue.

'There is nothing to be done,' her companion said. 'I must wait: I *can* wait. The last thing I am, I hope, is weak-spirited. And I am relieved to have spoken out. Now you know all and I am content.'

He looked indeed as if a weight had lifted from him. And perhaps as a consequence, all the pleasanter aspects of Matthew Downey's character remained uppermost for the rest of that day.

It would not do to be too obvious about it, and start at once pleading his cause, but she flattered herself that Mrs Catling did set some store by her opinion. So when the card-table was set out for them that night, and Mrs Catling, snapping the seal from a new pack, asked her how she had liked the picnic today, Caroline was prompt with her answer.

'Oh, I never enjoyed a day more, ma'am. Not just the beauty of the spot—there was true ease and cordiality on all sides, and that is very comfortable to my spirits.'

'Is it now? Well, I noticed Matthew paying you a deal of attention. He was giving you his life-history, no doubt, in minute detail, with him as a saintly hero, and with *my* cruel misdeeds painted in glowing colours.'

'Well, we had a great talk; and I must confess I have come to know him better, and I think there can be no doubting that he is warmly attached to you, Mrs Catling, in spite of quarrels.'

'Uff! A proper fiddlestick!' Mrs Catling grunted; yet Caroline, glancing up at her from lowered lids, thought she did not look displeased. And later she had the satisfaction of hearing Mrs Catling speak of her nephew almost indulgently before they retired.

But there was an unlucky sequel. The next day, in place of their usual call, came a note of apology from Matthew and Maria. It was Mr Leabrook who brought it to West Street: he had parted with them at the Old Ship that morning, and remarked pleasantly that Matthew was going to get that haystack hair of his cut, and Maria to shop for some small necessaries. 'So, I said I was happy, idle fellow that I am, to be their envoy,' he concluded, with a genial smile—which faded as he saw the mask of Mrs Catling's black fury descend.

Caroline was used to this, and registered only a weary regret at the hours of ill-temper to come. For Mr Leabrook it was a new and disconcerting experience.

'I want my needle-case,' Mrs Catling pronounced, after allowing Mr

Leabrook to talk himself to a perplexed standstill on every subject under the sun without the slightest response. 'Why you should be so slow to oblige me in this matter, Miss Fortune, I cannot think. It is not simply that your remuneration is ample and your duties light: it is the reflection that any well-disposed person would surely be prompt in such little civilities to an elderly lady that confirms my reluctant opinion of your increasingly *spoiled*, *saucy* disposition.'

Mrs Catling's voice rose on the last words to a soft snarl, which Caroline, jumping up to do her bidding, saw Mr Leabrook's handsome face react to first with amazement then with distaste.

To his credit, Mr Leabrook hung on for a good half-hour, but Mrs Catling's mood did not sweeten after his departure. It seemed she might even deny Caroline her half-day; but as granting it allowed her to appear neglected and ill-used, she let her companion go at last. Caroline descended to the beach and strode along its length very vigorously, the sea-breeze blowing in her face, so that when she came up to the town again, and made for Crawford's circulating-library, she was refreshed and all in a glow. The brilliancy of her complexion caught the eye of more than one visitor to the library, where Caroline's attention was all for the books: the means of escape furnished by reading was grown more vital to her; and she was just exulting at having procured the first volume of Lady Caroline Lamb's *Glenarvon*, which everyone was talking of, when her eye fell upon Mr Richard Leabrook.

He was outside, looking idly in at the bow-window. He appeared bored, but that expression lifted, flatteringly, on catching sight of her; and when she came out, he was waiting. 'Miss Fortune, you may have compelling reasons for seeking the relief of solitude this afternoon—reasons I will no further allude to than to say I entirely understand them—but if we are going the same way, may I walk with you?'

'Thank you—but I have had enough solitude now, and would be glad of your company. You allude very delicately, sir, and yet you need not. Mrs Catling was fierce upon me today, and will be again, no doubt, some other day. I put up with it because that is what I am here for.'

'Well, I had a notion she was formidable, from my friends the Downeys. Whom I saw not long ago, by the by, at Dutton's. I dropped a hint that their absence today from their aunt's had caused a certain acrimony in that quarter. Matthew despaired. It had seemed that the one thing sure to displease his aunt was to call *every* day: he had been reproved for it before on Brighton visits. Poor fellow: now he will have to work at making up lost ground. You do not, I think, share his inflammable temper, Miss Fortune—and yet you are related to the lady?'

'No—not by family. The late Colonel Catling was officer of my father's regiment; and so my father besought Mrs Catling's interest on my behalf, having no other means to establish me.'

'Ah, he was in the Peninsula?'

'Yes, he was made captain before Talavera, and was wounded. I long ago lost my mother, and my father has had to do his best for me. My situation is quite eligible—I do not complain of it.'

'To be sure—and there are no terms short of the utmost respect and honour that may be accorded a hero of the war,' Mr Leabrook said, with a brief bow. 'I have always held the soldier's profession in high esteem, but there is no military tradition in my family. We are squireish. Dare I say, a little too much so? To you, I dare. Because I believe that you, Miss Fortune, are as much attached to the pleasures of the town as I am.'

'Oh, you make me sound like a toper, or gambler, or worse!' Caroline said, laughing.

'Still,' he said amused, 'you do not deny it. Brighton is very well in its way, but now my carriage is mended, and has arrived here today, and that has set me wondering whether I should not be leaving. The luxury of choice, I know,' he added, with a sharp glance at her. 'What do you think I should do?'

'You can best determine, sir, whether there is anything to hold you here,' Caroline replied. She spoke a little more calmly than she felt—but only a little. While he was a most attractive man, and it seemed that this flirtation must shade at some point either into indifference or seriousness, still there was no high excitation or suspense in her.

'May I ask if I will see you at the Castle ball on Monday night?' he asked, as the weather intervened and drenching rain poured down.

'That depends on whether your terrible *ennui* has taken you away by then,' she said, glinting a smile at him before she darted off. 'But I will certainly be there.'

If there were ever any doubt of Richard Leabrook's attending the ball at the Castle, it was resolved by Mrs Catling, who, together with the Downeys and a rather staggery old crony of the late Colonel's, invited him to be one of her party for the evening.

It was now the height of the Brighton season: every lodging was taken, and every species of carriage was to be seen bowling along the Royal Crescent, the Marine Parade and the Steyne.

The ballroom at the Castle Assembly Rooms was magnificent in size, with a ceiling forty foot high, and stately in its mouldings, columns and frieze, all brilliantly lit by great chandeliers. Filled with company, it was, however, very noisy, the violins only a thin filigree of sound around the solid babble of talk, and very stuffy and hot.

Caroline came here with a light heart and a willingness to enjoy herself that was not fretted by any conditions. Mr Leabrook had been much in her mind, and as Mrs Catling had given her permission to dance with any of her party, she looked forward to taking the floor with him. Splendid he looked this evening, in a coat of superfine corbeau-grey, white marcella waistcoat, and cream breeches and stockings revealing a length and shape of leg to make stubbier gentlemen despair.

He engaged her for the first pair of dances, and the third, and was every bit as graceful a partner as she had supposed; and she did not at all dislike the envious glances she received. Still, there could be no monopolising her in such a place; and whilst having to dance a quadrille with the drooling old soldier was something of a trial, she was happy to stand up with Matthew for the fifth.

He was in good spirits; and, on her remarking so, said with a smile, 'Aye—a letter has done that. Such a small thing as a letter is, and such worlds of happiness it can open up! I need not tell you, Miss Fortune, who it is from. The confidences you extracted from me the other day will supply the sacred name.'

'To be sure,' said Caroline, feeling too cheerful to protest that the confidences he had poured out to her had hardly been *extracted*. 'I hope that person is well, Mr Downey.'

'She is,' he said eagerly, 'she is wonderfully well, I thank you. It is a communication so full of warmth and patience that it has truly kindled my spirits. Strange effect from a square of paper!'

'So it is,' she agreed cordially, 'and I found the same effect myself this very morning.' Her father had written one of his rare letters—to her surprise, from Bath. He had fallen in with an old bachelor comrade who was going to try the waters, and had offered him a share of his board and lodging for the price of his company. But Caroline had a chance only of saying a little of this: Matthew smilingly told her that he was very glad, and then reverted to the subject of his own letter.

Soon after this she gladly sat down for a while, so overheated did she feel; and Maria was in worse case, having adopted the fashion of long sleeves, though in truth she looked as coolly composed as ever. Caroline had not been fanning herself long, however, before Mr Leabrook approached and murmured in her ear.

'My wish, Miss Fortune, is to claim you again, but that uncanny perception of mine tells me you are fagged. Come—that chair is narrow—I see a sofa over there by the wall, and I can navigate you to it.'

He led her skilfully through the press, saw her seated on the sofa, then melted away, to return shortly with a glass of claret-cup that was very welcome. While she drank it he sat on the edge of the sofa, watching her in an attentive silence, which at last she taxed him with.

'Are you out of spirits, Mr Leabrook? You are rather abstracted.'

'I was never in better spirits,' he said, gently but distinctly, 'but I have been thinking, and wondering. About you, Miss Fortune.'

'About me?' Caroline said. Something seemed to have changed: Mr Leabrook lounged beside her as composedly as ever, but she felt his attention upon her tightening. And she knew now, if she had not known before, that if he were about to become serious with her, she must deeply regret the alteration: that it was not what she wanted.

Mr Leabrook proceeded in his soft yet precise voice. 'I fancy myself an indifferent good judge of people, Miss Fortune. Dull sticks and prigs and prudes above all I can spot a good way off, because they bore me so. Likewise, I know when I meet their opposite. You, I imagine, would waltz very well, Miss Fortune: you would find nothing shocking about the pressure of a man's arm about your waist.'

'I had no idea I was so transparent,' she said, regarding him doubtfully.

'It depends who is looking. And you and I have the measure of each other, do we not?' Without waiting for an answer, his eyes still fixed on hers, he pursued: 'Brighton is very well, but Matthew and Maria will be leaving soon enough, so I shall not linger once they go. And it occurs to me to wonder—my dear Miss Fortune, why should you be left behind? I have mentioned my carriage. It is fast, and well-upholstered, and you will find it comfortable. Let me take you away in it.'

'Take me away, sir? Where do you mean I am to go?'

'Away from here—from Mrs Catling—from mean subordination!'

'Well: I hardly know whether to be flattered or perturbed, Mr Leabrook. Do you suppose me so fragile that, if I wished to flee Brighton, I could not make my own way?'

'Of course I do not suppose you fragile in the least,' he said, chuckling, 'but you do right to reprove me for not speaking plainer, even though you know well what I mean. The carriage, Miss Fortune, is to contain the two of us—you and I, together. We might even go tonight.'

Caroline found her breath quite stopped in her throat, and when she struggled to speak, there came a gasp. 'Do you mean a Gretna elopement, sir? A romantic fancy—I would say even fantastical.'

'Nothing so conventional,' he said, renewing his smile. 'Conventional—and trite and narrowly respectable—the exact qualities that I do *not* find in you, Miss Fortune. We go—where, who knows?

London, to be sure. There is the greatest felicity coupled with the least observation. We may do as we please: taste all that the town has to offer. I find this a delicious prospect; and so, I flatter myself, do you.'

'"Come live with me and be my love, And we will all the pleasures prove . . .",' she recited flatly. 'I cannot remember the poet's name, but the sentiment is apt, I think.'

'It is very apt,' he said, with warmth, 'and my confidence was not misplaced—you *do* understand me.'

'Oh, yes, I do, sir. I understand very well. Forgive me—I am just trying to recollect how the verses continue. After all the pleasures have been proved, I mean: what then?'

He shrugged. 'What then? I protest against the phrase. Think how much happiness has been lost by a preoccupation with consequences!'

She was now so very disgusted with him that she feared she could not moderate her tone. But she mastered herself: this was the nub of it. Richard Leabrook was well able to dismiss the question *what then*? He was a man, and rich, and independent: the consequences of any such affair must be slight. For her, they must be profound.

'I am not sure how to answer you, Mr Leabrook. When a man asks a woman to go off with him and become his mistress for some unspecified time on some unspecified terms, there is as far as I can see no ready response—certainly none that could do justice to her indignation, or his conceit.'

'Very well,' he said, blinking rapidly. 'You have placed the matter in the worst light possible. But consider what you would be leaving behind. Servitude, no less; and servitude without hope of a prosperous release. For you have told me you have no other hopes or connections.'

Their conversation the other day, in which he had asked with such apparent sympathy about her father and her situation, came back to her with new understanding. Yes, he had made sure of her.

'I have nothing, in fact—that is what you are saying.'

'No indeed: you have charm—wit—taste—beauty—these have engaged my attention from our first meeting; and there was, I thought, something else also—spirit, daring. Without that, I would not have ventured thus. But above all, I did not suppose *you* indifferent to *me*.'

'Certainly there is, or was, a degree of regard, even partiality,' Caroline stated. 'We agreed very well. But that is not enough to throw myself away for. I would have to set a very low value upon myself to do it. And though you represent Mrs Catling as treating me like a servant, in truth you esteem me at even less value than she does. For I am, as you say, without hopes or connections: consider then what my prospects would be once our little adventure was over.'

'So: I am mistaken in you, Miss Fortune.' His tone was dispassionate, but his look was much altered. 'You are a deal more conventional than I supposed: I am sorry for it.'

'Not wholly mistaken, perhaps, Mr Leabrook. I do not say that I could never be persuaded to sacrifice my reputation to passion—only that it would take a great deal more than I feel for *you* to make me do it.'

She got up and walked away from him, the emotions of astonishment, anger, and hurt pride, requiring grim concentration.

The crowds of people around her were a blur, but she did catch sight of the sunflower-like head of Maria Downey, and turned instinctively away from it. She needed a space of solitude: she was unequal to enquiries about her agitated state. She lingered in the card room, on pretence of looking over a game, for as long as she dared, whilst summoning her normal looks and manner. Bitterest of all, perhaps, was her reflection on her own misjudgement; she had liked Richard Leabrook very well.

Mrs Catling was snappish with her on her return: the old lady had put on kid shoes for the two sedate dances she allowed herself, but now wanted them changing back for her overshoes, and only Caroline would do. This was usual enough to be reassuring. And then Mr Leabrook sauntered over, and declared to Mrs Catling, with a great yawn, that he was tired to death and he craved her pardon for breaking up the party, but he simply must return to his lodging.

He was uncomfortable, and would meet no one's eye. Here at least was a satisfaction to Caroline; but it was the only one she could draw from an evening that seemed to drag interminably to its close.

Chapter Four

MR LEABROOK WAS LEAVING Brighton at once: he came to West Street to announce it, coolly and pleasantly, the very next morning. The Downeys were calling at the same time, and Matthew indignantly protested that this was the first he had heard of it.

'It is the first anyone has heard of it, my dear Matthew,' Mr Leabrook said, smiling, 'because I have only just made up my mind to it.'

'But why? We have all been getting along so famously.'

'That is always the best moment to part—before indifference and aversion set in.'

But Matthew was more inclined to labour a point than to take it. He went on declaring himself baffled and disappointed. Mr Leabrook laughed and appeared perfectly easy—but Caroline knew better now than to trust to appearances. And if there were any consolation to be found on this most unpleasant of mornings, it lay in the suspicion that she had wounded his pride more than he cared to show.

Consolation—but not much. Caroline had woken with the unhappy recollections of last night, and was feeling thoroughly miserable. At breakfast her shaking hands had made such a clatter with the coffee-pot and the sugar-bowl that Mrs Catling had remarked that she was more stupid than usual today.

And now here was Mr Leabrook calling, and as elegant and civil as ever. Yet there was a change. He did not address a word to Caroline.

'This is so very sudden,' Matthew grumbled. 'Really, Leabrook, I cannot think why you must be so sudden about it. I had thought of your staying another week at least.'

'Then, my dear fellow, consider—how long before you and Miss Downey must return to London? A fortnight at most? You see, we are all impermanencies here, except your estimable aunt.'

'Who is beginning to wonder at you, Matthew,' said Mrs Catling, with relish. 'For it would seem that when Mr Leabrook is gone, there will be nothing in Brighton you care for.'

Oh, Matthew, don't rise to it, Caroline thought—even as he did so.

'Really, Aunt Sophia, you could not suppose I meant—I only meant that Leabrook's company is, you know, an addition—and that—'

'It will not be the same!' put in Mrs Catling, sighing. 'Yes, I see, Nephew—I see very well!'

'No, no, there is always pleasure in *your* society, Aunt—but the difference I mean . . .'

It was Mr Leabrook who put an end to it. 'Downey, enough: your sentiments do you credit on both sides. Now here's my proposal: you and Miss Downey shall come and stay with me in Northamptonshire, just as soon as you are able, and as soon as it can be reconciled with your aunt's prior claim. What do you say to that?'

'Prior claim? Dear me, you make me sound quite the tyrant,' chuckled Mrs Catling. 'I would not dream of standing in the way of such an invitation: indeed I shall think quite the worse of you, you two, if you do not take it up.'

'There, Matthew,' Maria said yawning, 'it is all handsomely arranged.'

'Well, I never saw a better-bred man,' was Mrs Catling's conclusion, after Mr Leabrook had taken his final leave. 'You might do worse, Matthew, than look to him as your model. There is still time to erase your father's unfortunate influence, and make something of you.' And to Caroline: 'Hm, you're mighty quiet, miss: if going to balls puts you into a mopish mood, I shan't take you to any more.'

Caroline did not much care if she ever attended a ball again. When Mr Leabrook left West Street, he made such a cold, correct and silent bow over her hand, accompanied by such a fleeting, inward twist of a smile, that she suffered a renewed gush of misery.

In this depression of spirits, it might be expected that Caroline would have little energy to devote to pleading Matthew's cause, but it was not so. During the ten days that remained of the Downeys' visit to Brighton, she took every opportunity of acting as his advocate with Mrs Catling. How much of this she could take credit for she could not tell, but by the time of the Downeys' departure for London, Mrs Catling had decided to increase Matthew's allowance, and unbent so far as to say she would miss his nonsensical ways.

Soon, though the resort remained lively enough, a more general exodus was noticeable from the villas and lodging-houses of Brighton, as the chill mists that stole in from seaward once the sun was down told their autumnal tale. And Mrs Catling revealed a new aspect to her character. The first sniffle of a cold transformed her into an invalid.

'My colds,' she informed Caroline, 'are worse than anyone's.' Having made a morbid achievement out of her indisposition, she retired to the drawing-room sofa and devoted herself to it. Her physician, a spruce, obliging little man who knew the value of his fee, prescribed any number of powders and possets, as well as complete rest, and a strengthening diet. Nursing, tender selfless nursing, she must have also: fortunately there was her young companion to provide that.

Recumbent before a blazing fire, Mrs Catling settled herself in for a good long bout of demanding illness. And Caroline was the one satisfying the demands. This was her most testing time so far. Besides the constant attendance of a nurse, Mrs Catling wanted almost as constant amusement—reading, cards, backgammon and, when those failed, talk; and even a moment's distracted silence on Caroline's part was liable to call forth from her employer a growl of self-pity and abuse.

And then there was the mood of gloom to contend with. 'They have not a thought to spare for me,' was her lament, when a week passed without a letter from either of the Downeys. 'I might be on my deathbed for all they care. Are you sure there were no letters this morning?'

Not that morning, or the next, dearly as Caroline wished there were. The desperate idea came to her, as Mrs Catling's despondency grew daily more savage, of forging a letter from Matthew, just to cheer her employer up, and she was on the point of trying the experiment when a letter arrived at West Street that altered everything at a stroke; and the letter was not for Mrs Catling, but for her.

The hand on the cover was quite unknown to her. She never got letters at all except from her father—and it occurred to her, as the paper crackled open, that she had not received one lately.

Mrs Catling, steeped in self-pity, waited for a rheumily breathing minute or so, and then demanded impatiently: 'Well, what have you there? You might tell me, since I never receive any letters of my own.'

Caroline heard herself saying, as if from far off: 'It is a letter from my aunt. We have never met. This—this is my first letter from her.'

'Aunt on the mother's side?' Mrs Catling enquired.

'Yes. My mother's sister. Her name is—her name is Selina—' and then Caroline burst into helpless tears.

'Oh, come,' Mrs Catling said, after an open-mouthed moment, 'come, what's this? I never supposed you so sentimental. What, this aunt wants to be friends with you at last, hey?'

'It isn't that,' Caroline got out through her sobs. 'My father,' she said, 'is no more.'

'No more what?' croaked Mrs Catling above her handkerchief: then meeting Caroline's swimming eyes, said: 'Ah! Ah, dear me. Well, that is a great—a great nuisance for you.' She composed her expression into an approximation of sympathy. 'You'll want to go off somewhere and cry, I should think.'

Caroline did. In the solitude of her room she could give full vent to her grief, where the fact that her father had more often been encumbrance than support to her did not prevent the doleful cry into her pillow that she was all alone in the world. At last the storm had quieted enough for her to sit up and read again the fateful letter.

Gay Street, Bath—September 10th

My dear Caroline,

I pray you will forgive my addressing you thus, when I am scarcely known to you. I am your late mother's sister, and hence your aunt, Selina Langland: I dare swear even the name may not be familiar to you, the family breach having been so complete. It is not the least of my regrets at this long estrangement, that it should only be ended by the sad event I must tell you of. My dear Caroline, your father died here at Bath last night after a short illness—so very short, and mercifully so I think, that there was no time to alert you to its progress.

How I come to be the bearer of this melancholy intelligence I may briefly state. It is simply this: my husband Dr Langland and I have been spending a part of this season at Bath as a result of a slight indisposition on Dr Langland's part, for which the physicians recommended the waters. We make our daily visit to the Pump Room, and it was there, not a fortnight since, that I turned and beheld your father.

We recognised one another at once, though we had not met since my poor sister's marriage. Your father appeared to me little changed from the young captain whom our family once considered—wrongly, I see now—as the destroyer of my sister's happiness. In short, you will see from this that we met cordially. Your father invited us to drink tea with him the next day: I accepted: so simply was the breach of years repaired. Or rather, a beginning was made: of course there was much misunderstanding to be resolved before there could be perfect ease between us.

Yet achieved it was: we met each succeeding day, with increasing friendliness—to the great satisfaction of Dr Langland, who as a man of the cloth has always deplored such familial disharmony. It was your father's greatest delight to give us his account of you, my dear, such was his pride in you; and we looked forward to completing the reconciliation, by meeting you, our unknown niece, at the earliest opportunity. Indeed your father had declared his intention of writing you with the cheerful news, the very night before he was taken ill.

This malady at first appeared a mere ague, there was evidence, according to the surgeon who attended him, of a severe heart-stroke; and though Dr Langland and I waited upon him as soon as we heard the news, he never recovered the power of speech. He left the world, at ten o'clock this morning, with no appearance of suffering.

My dear Caroline, I hope you may find some comfort in the knowledge that your aunt and uncle await you in Bath, to help you in any way we can through the matter of your father's funeral. Dr Langland has such acquaintance among the clergy here, as makes it certain we may procure your father a respectable burial at St Swithin's Walcot. I am aware of your situation, your father having told us all, and understand its dependence. Nevertheless I know you will be released for such an event as this for as long as is necessary. Dr Langland agrees that travelling post would be best, and if, as I suspect, you are not able to bear the expense yourself, do pray assure your employer that if she will arrange it, we will refund the cost to her directly. As for lodging, there is ample room for you here—should you wish it.

Your affectionate aunt,
Selina Langland

Caroline bathed her red eyes, folded her letter and placed it in the bureau, tidied herself in front of the mirror, and then went downstairs.

'Well! You've collected yourself, I see,' Mrs Catling said. 'Very good. You'll find it best: no amount of moping will help, you know. Now, there's the newspaper. Reading will take your mind off it. Oh! This wretched cold: you've no conception how I suffer.'

In truth the mechanical exercise of reading out *The Times* to her employer suited Caroline as well as any activity: there was just enough occupation to keep her from being swallowed up by her grief. But no one could make less allowance for the quiet nursing of emotional bruises than her employer—a woman so greedy of attention that she plainly resented even the consideration that was due to bereavement.

Soon, she snapped at Caroline to leave off reading, sighed windily, and said, 'Well, well, it's plain you're still brooding on your father, so you had better speak of it. Come, what's your concern? I can't think what there can be to make you so untoward.'

'Only that I have lost my father, ma'am,' Caroline said, after an openmouthed moment, 'and I can't help being sorry for it.'

'You might help it, if you exerted yourself. That is, by bearing up.'

'There is one thing, Mrs Catling,' Caroline said, 'if you don't mind my mentioning it now. My aunt is arranging for my father's funeral in Bath, and wants to know how soon I may get there.'

Mrs Catling directed at Caroline such a grey, fishy, unresponsive look that her companion supposed for a moment she had not heard her.

'The funeral, ma'am. In Bath. I might go by the public coach, and willingly will do so, but my aunt says that if I go post, she will meet—'

'Go? I do not understand. My dear Miss Fortune, you have very much mistaken your position here, if you suppose you may gallivant off whenever the fancy takes you: and as for a time like *this*—'

'But it is an exceptional occasion, ma'am. I assumed—'

'To assume is to presume,' Mrs Catling said. 'I will overlook the presumption in this one case, as you are something out of sorts on account of your loss. But you must know that your going to Bath is quite out of the question. You must write this aunt and tell her so directly.'

For a long time afterwards Caroline could only wonder at her own self-control, but she could not curb her tongue.

'Mrs Catling, I want very much to say goodbye to my father by attending his funeral, and I may as well say that I too assumed that I would be freely allowed to do so. I shall go to Bath, ma'am, whether I have your permission or not. I do you the courtesy of telling you this, rather than simply going, because I do feel beholden to you for some kindnesses; but I emphatically refer to past events, and not your present conduct, which is nothing less than that of an unfeeling tyrant.'

Mrs Catling—though she went from white to crimson to white again—also maintained such command over herself that she sounded capable of manslaughter rather than outright murder as she hissed at Caroline: 'Never have I been spoken to like that. I will allow you a few seconds to recover your wits, and then I will hear your apology, and then I may consider—only consider—not dismissing you from your post.'

'You need not trouble with the consideration, ma'am. I am going to see my father laid to rest, and I am going today.'

'Then you will not be returning, Miss Fortune, ever. Pack all your bags, and consider our association at an end from the moment you step out of my door. You will not get a character from me.'

'If you will see fit to give me my wage for this month, Mrs Catling,' Caroline replied, 'then I undertake to be out of your house by noon.'

'Apply to my steward: I'll have nothing more to do with you.' Mrs Catling waved her away curtly; but added with, it seemed, real bafflement: 'You are a fool—a fool against your own interests!'

It was in Caroline's mind to say that her father was too, but at least he would have one sincere mourner at his graveside, and this was one more than Mrs Catling could ever count upon. But that was not a thing to be said to an old woman, even in the heat of battle. So she walked to the door with her head high, in silence.

Chapter Five

THE BELLS OF BATH ABBEY did not ring for the arrival of the public coach in which Caroline travelled, as they did for distinguished visitors in their own carriages, and it was with a feeling not unlike the low light of autumn gold declining now across the squares that she viewed this place, where her father had come to the end of his own eventful journey. But it was proof that her spirits were not quite crushed that she was still curious to meet her unknown Aunt Selina.

As a letter could scarcely have got here faster than herself, Caroline had not written her aunt of her coming, and it was with some nervousness that she climbed out into the yard of the White Hart and directed her bags to be sent to Gay Street. Soon after, equipped with directions given her by a civil ostler, she set out to walk there herself.

The townhouse in Gay Street, where her aunt and uncle lodged, was tall, quiet, neat, a little gaunt and wintry—all epithets that might have been applied to the lady who, to Caroline's amazement, flung open the front door and, pushing aside an equally amazed maidservant, hurried down the steps to meet her.

Not only to meet her, but to throw her arms about her, crying: 'My dear girl, I saw you from the parlour window—oh, my dear Caroline, I am so very thankful that you came.'

'But how could—how did you know who I was?'

'How? Because you are the living image of my poor sister. I never saw such a likeness.' Having embraced her, Caroline's aunt now withdrew to arm's length with an abrupt stiffness. 'Forgive me, this conduct must seem quite extravagant. I haven't even introduced myself.'

'You're surely my aunt Selina,' Caroline said, moved by her reception, 'and I could have wanted no better introduction.'

'That's her again!' the other sighed. 'She would have said the same. I could never—well, what am I thinking? Walk up, my dear, please—you're surely tired after such a journey. You came post, I hope? Dr Langland will reimburse your employer just as soon as—'

'No—no, Aunt, I came by the coach.'

'By public coach? Alone? I never heard of such a thing.' And from the expression on Aunt Selina's long, honest face, it was plain that this was no mere figure of speech. 'What can she have been thinking?'

This simple concern nearly undid Caroline, and, seeing this, her aunt changed the subject, saying her uncle was longing to meet her, and pressing her to walk in. Soon, without quite knowing how, she was in a comfortable parlour having her hand powerfully shaken by a lean, gangling, bright-eyed gentleman in clerical black.

'My dear, I was never more glad in my life—but you must be tired. Hungry and thirsty too no doubt—we'll ring the bell directly. John Langland. Your uncle John no less—I hope you'll call me so—I never knew Selina's sister, of course—not that that signifies—and in short this is quite delightful. Hard to see how it could be better.'

'Perhaps, my dear, it *could* be better,' suggested his wife, tentatively. 'It is not a happy occasion that brings Caroline here.'

'Oh, to be sure, that's true—entirely true, Selina. Dear me, did I speak out of turn? This is rather dreadful. My dear Caroline, I hope you don't think—really I'm quite floored now—and what I did not mean . . .'

Dr Langland's attempts to extricate himself reminded Caroline so forcibly of a carthorse backing out of the shafts that she was as near to laughter as the occasion allowed; and there was such an innocent good nature about him that she hastened to reassure him.

'Now, refreshment you must certainly have, my dear,' her aunt said, pulling the bell-cord by the fireplace. 'Will you have—well, shall I suggest tea? You don't object to taking it at this time of day, I hope?'

'Not at all,' Caroline assured her aunt, who seemed really anxious on the point; indeed she would not have objected to something much stronger, but everything—from her aunt's plain, untrimmed cap, to the penitentially hard chairs where a heap of earnest sewing and a stack of devotional volumes, crowned with a magnifying-glass, attested the twin pursuits of their leisure—was serious.

A maid who, from her look of wholesome scrubbed seriousness might have been identified as the Langlands' maid from a parade of a hundred, appeared noiselessly at the door. 'Jane, will you bring tea and bread-and-butter, if you please.'

'Such a journey,' fussed Dr Langland. 'You didn't post it, my dear? Do I have you right? Surely your employer cannot have refused to advance you the funds. Your late father, during our short acquaintance, constantly spoke of her as a sterling woman. Unless, dear me, she entertained a doubt of *us*, as guarantors for the sum? To be sure we are personally unknown to her, but Selina is of course of unimpeachable family, and as for me a rectorship is surely recommendation enough, though one could add that my late sister was the first Lady Milner. Not that such worldly testimonials have any bearing upon virtue or honesty—they do not. But I am at a loss, my dear. I am baffled.'

'Very well, sir,' Caroline burst out—partly to silence him, but also because she saw it must come out. She had not wanted to begin by telling her new-found relations that she had lost her position. 'The fact is, I have parted with my employer, and so it was scarcely to be expected she would pay for my carriage. Really the coach wasn't so bad. A good stout umbrella protects you against most perils, believe me.'

Her aunt stared. 'You don't mean you rode *outside*?'

'Oh, no—I mean the umbrella is for fighting off the unwanted attentions of gentlemen. A good jab under the ribs usually does it.'

There was such a silence, such a stricken air of consternation, that Caroline could only blunder on: 'Well, that is how it happened, at any rate, but the main thing is I am here now, and so very relieved to meet you both. And yes, I am glad too, very glad, that Fate brought you and my father together before the end, Aunt: we can be friends at last, and that's something to be thankful for, though I miss poor Papa sorely.' She had talked herself close to tears again, but successfully held them back.

'My poor child,' Aunt Selina said, stirring. 'The very thought of what you have been through! I hesitate to pain you any more by alluding to it; but this parting with your employer—a Mrs Catling, I think. I gained the impression of a strong-minded woman, to say the least. Am I on the right road, my dear?'

'Well, yes,' Caroline said; and told her aunt and uncle how she had come to lose her position with Mrs Catling, as briefly and coolly as she could, for she did not wish to seem continually angling after sympathy.

'This is shocking—shocking,' her aunt got out at last, shaking her head and going over to her husband to squeeze his hand. 'To dismiss you because you wished to attend your own father's funeral! It is absolutely inhuman.'

'Shocking,' echoed Dr Langland. 'I never knew there were people so lost to common feeling and decency. Dear, dear me!'

Caroline felt, in fact, altogether uncomfortable, so generous was the pity that enfolded her. Even from the maid, who presently brought the tea-tray, she received a degree of solicitous consideration that embarrassed her. She had never known such people as this, who were kind, gentle, reliable and unworldly. Indeed their transparent good nature was such that it set her wondering. How could the estrangement between the sisters, Selina and Caroline's mother, have been so lasting?

There were indications that Aunt Selina was, at least, conscious of the question. Several times Caroline caught her aunt gazing at her with a brimming look, as if she were on the verge of unburdening something; and when she showed Caroline up to her bedroom, urging her to rest, she seemed almost to choke on her parting words: 'I can't get over the likeness. Too long—really, it's been too long.'

The funeral was all it should have been—a proper and dignified farewell. Captain Fortune's short stay in Bath had produced a long tally of acquaintance—mostly gentlemen of a military, sporting, or lounging type—and they all came to St Swithin's, filling the church with a potent presence of pomade, rum and tobacco.

'Oh dear,' Aunt Selina kept helplessly saying, in spite of Caroline's assurances that this was second nature to her. Caroline was quickly becoming aware how many things in her experience would call forth that 'Oh dear' from her aunt. Yet it was Aunt Selina's presence that got her through the day. She told her so, frankly, when in a rawness of feeling she faced the next morning, and was gently pressed to accompany her aunt on her morning walk to Sydney Gardens.

'My dear, I'm glad I could help,' Aunt Selina at last said, after one of her long meditative pauses. 'All the same, I feel rather a fraud. It's late in the day for me to be a help to my one true niece. My quarrel with my poor sister was bad enough, but to transfer it to you—'

'Well, we haven't quarrelled, Aunt—we've just been apart.'

'Oh, in my heart I have kept up the bitterest quarrel, I'm afraid. Because of what Margaret did to me. There! That sounds thoroughly dramatic, does it not? What can your poor mother have done? When she ran off with your father, you see, that left me: just me, at home with parents who were very fond but very severe and very, very disappointed in their elder daughter—the pretty, graceful one. I resented the burden Margaret had placed on me—the burden of being the *good* one. Dear, dear, I'm shocked to hear myself saying this,' Aunt Selina went on, with a tremulous laugh. 'As if I did not wish to be good. And as for our family's way of living in Huntingdonshire—healthfully situated, retired and quiet, with very little society—why, that suited me too. And so did the prospect of a respectable marriage in due time to a gentleman of the neighbourhood. Dear, dear,' she said again shakily. 'I have never spoken of this to anyone—not even John.' A look of alarm came over her, which was not difficult for Caroline to read: for what did this seem to say about her marriage to Uncle John? 'Don't mistake me, my dear. It could not have turned out better: that gentleman of the neighbourhood who came along in due course was the one man I could have loved.'

'That I can believe. I never saw so well disposed a couple.'

Aunt Selina's look conveyed subtle thanks, but then, shaking her head: 'Ah, you haven't heard the worst of it. I said how fortunate I had been in marriage: we were blessed in all but one regard—we never had a child. And will you believe I envied your poor mother there too?'

'Oh, Aunt, don't think of it.'

'No, no, I'm glad to.' Aunt Selina came out of one of her abstractions with a refreshed look. 'Severe self-examination, even when painful, is one of the best exercises for the soul.'

Caroline was not sure about that, but the confession certainly seemed to have done Aunt Selina good; and when they got back to Gay Street, and Uncle John benignly asked if they had had a good walk, his wife surprised him by saying they had had the best of walks that ever was, and kissing him heartily.

The funeral being over, the question of how long she was to stay at Gay Street was much in Caroline's mind. She had a lively aversion to trespassing on the Langlands' good nature; and when she went to bed, that night and the night after, was strongly conscious of significant looks between her aunt and uncle, and of being talked about after she had retired. Yet at each succeeding breakfast, when she gently raised the matter of her departure, they would put her off with some remarks by producing some reason why she should stay a little longer. One of these was the imminent arrival in Bath of someone called Stephen.

'My young kinsman,' Uncle John said, laying down the letter. 'He writes me from Beckhampton, where he is investigating a new find of antiquities—quite a hobby-horse of his—a Roman pavement no less—and if I know Stephen he will be down in the hole digging himself, regardless of propriety—even of danger. His poor mother used to get into fearful fidgets about it. That was my late sister, my dear,' he explained to Caroline, 'Lady Milner. She married Sir Henry Milner of Wythorpe—my own parish, our dear, dear home ground—and Stephen Milner is their son. He says he will come and call on us while he is down this way—precisely *when* he does not say, which is just like him—but you must certainly stay, my dear, and meet him.'

Knowing their good nature, Caroline began to wonder if the Langlands simply could not bring themselves to tell her to go. She did love being with her hosts, enjoying ever more warm and confidential talks with Aunt Selina during the daily visit to Sydney Gardens, and cementing her cordiality with her uncle by reading out to him of an evening from a very mildly comic novel, but for her own part she had a dread of imposing. She began to have a London newspaper set aside for her daily at a shop across the street, and pored over its advertisements by the light of her bedtime candle.

And she found something that might suit. A lady at Highgate of independent means and infirm health wanted a respectable young person to fulfil the roles of companion, nurse, and general attendant; as no references were required, Caroline felt that this was as good as could be hoped for, and wrote off at once. It was when she came back from posting this letter that she found her aunt waiting for her, with the self-same newspaper in her hand, folded back at the marked advertisement.

'My dear, you'll think me intrusive. I was in your room to put fresh lavender in the chest. And then I saw this and—unforgivably perhaps—I grew inquisitive and looked. And, Caroline, may I ask you—are these your hope?' She pointed gingerly at the advertisements. 'Because—oh, dear, I really shouldn't say it without John here—'

'But I *am* here, my love!' Uncle John leaped into the room. 'I was listening at the door! And I knew what you were going to say. You were going to put to our niece the question that we have been discussing.'

'Too soon, though, I fear,' Aunt Selina said, shaking her head.

'Come, we must grasp the nettle—and pray don't, my dear,' he added, with his glance of confidence at Caroline, 'be put out by that unflattering botanical proverb—it refers not to you but to the question—which is this: my dear Caroline, won't you come home with us?'

Groping for a chair, she gasped out: 'For a visit?'

'To stay!' boomed her uncle. 'To live! To be—why, a daughter to us!'

'Not a daughter,' Aunt Selina put in, wincing. 'Whatever our own wishes, I think we offend against Caroline's recent loss, my dear.'

'True—true—dear me, how shocking, I am quite a fool,' said Uncle John, sagging. 'Still—you do know what I mean—don't you, my dear?'

'Yes, I do. And you are too kind. And my heart is quite full,' Caroline wailed, and was taken into her aunt's arms.

'No, we're not, and so is mine!' cried her uncle, embracing them both, skipping and laughing; so that they played a sort of tearful ring-a-rosie.

'**Y**our room,' Aunt Selina told her as they walked down Milsom Street, 'has lately been papered—a light olive stripe—I hope you will like it. It is at the front of the house, with a pleasant view of the main road through the village, which passes quite close to the Rectory. We have a wall and a little screen of box and holly—no more—and no carriage-drive, though Dr Langland did set up a carriage last year, to spare me from the damps as he said. I must confess we have hardly used it. You will ginger us up, as the saying goes.' Aunt Selina wore a pleased little flush at having used a racy expression. 'We are lucky to have ample room at the Rectory, and the garden and shrubbery are well laid out for walks when the weather fails—not that Wythorpe is often muddy, as we are on the higher ground of the county—you don't know Huntingdonshire, my dear?'

Caroline hardly knew shires at all, except as the names of regiments, but she found the idea of them delightful.

'Well, it is a quiet sort of district, though there is society to be had. Dr Langland and I do not go about much, but even so there are five or six families we dine with. Then there are assemblies at Huntingdon—not that we have attended those in years, but there again you will make all the difference, my dear. Now that reminds me'—they were passing a fashionable milliner's shop—'there is the matter of your dress. Would you rather have an allowance in your own hand for clothes, or leave it to us to settle? I don't mind which—only you'll forgive me observing that you're surely in need of winter dresses.'

Caroline had thought what she had on was a winter dress, but realised after a moment that Aunt Selina was misinterpreting her taste for bare arms and low bosom, and mistaking fashion for lack.

This whole matter of money was an embarrassment, to her at least. It was plain that her aunt and uncle were comfortably situated, and well able to support her, but that did not mean she could contemplate her dependence without discomfort.

'Oh, but you're too good,' Caroline moaned.

'Well, if we are, you needn't weep for it,' her aunt said, with one of her rare laughs. 'What, would you prefer to bed down in the stable?'

In a curious way, she would have, at least for a while: at least until they had had time to accommodate any regrets at their decision.

Soon enough they were deep in preparations for their return to Huntingdonshire, and Aunt Selina pronounced herself very thankful to be going, for 'This frenzied pace of life,' she said as they returned from the usual sedate stroll to the Pump Room, 'it quite wears me out.'

Before their departure, however, there came the promised visit from Dr Langland's nephew. A scribbled note arrived one evening from Mr Stephen Milner at the Bear Inn: *Fagged to death—berthing here for the night—wait upon you in the morning if you'd care to see me—if not run a nightgown up the flagpole as a sign and token—love and what you will* was the substance, in what Caroline gathered was his characteristic style.

She wished she could share her aunt and uncle's pleasure in the prospect: but for some reason Caroline acutely wished this Mr Stephen Milner were not coming. She did not expect to find a man who got excited over Roman pavements sympathetic, and rose the next morning ready to be scrutinised by a whimsical antiquary whom she had pictured right down to the *pince-nez* on his long, disdainful nose.

Or rather, not quite ready. There was one thing that she knew, to her shame, would help her: just a small glass of canary wine, such as was kept in the silver-topped decanter on the table in the front parlour. The door to the front parlour was the first you came to at the foot of the stairs. Going very softly, she slipped in: she would do the fortifying business, then join her aunt and uncle in the back parlour where they breakfasted. Caroline congratulated herself as she took the first sip.

'True—it is rather early for it. Still, I'll join you in one of those.'

Choking, Caroline turned to meet the blearily blinking eyes of a man who had just risen to a sitting position on the parlour sofa.

'Good God! What the devil—?'

'Swearing by both of them,' he commented, with a gaping yawn, ruffling a thick crown of much dishevelled fairish hair, 'has, I'll admit, an agreeable sort of comprehensiveness.'

'You startled me!' she cried defensively. 'And what the—what are you doing here?' She cast a confused glance at the window, but the window was secure, and so too the man's expression—he was quite at home, and apparently untroubled at being surprised in his shirt and breeches.

'What am I doing? Sleeping, or was,' he said, scratching his chest vigorously and reaching for a pair of much scuffed and muddied hessian boots. 'Would you be so good as to pour me a glass, then? It's unlucky to drink alone. You're my uncle John's Miss Fortune, I take it.'

It was hard to tell whether he *intended* the pun on her name that she heard, because his was a face that nature had designed to be satirical. He had strongly arched eyebrows, deep-set grey eyes, broad cheekbones, and a wide, wry, asymmetrical bow of a mouth hooked up at the left corner. A very bad face, Caroline thought, especially disfigured with stubble as it was just now, though oddly difficult to look away from.

'And you are Mr Milner, I take it,' she answered, trying to pour a glass of wine with a mixture of dignity, displeasure, and insouciance. 'I had thought you staying at the Bear Inn.'

'Was. Came away,' he said. 'Heard a din in the yard before dawn. So came here, found the maid a-lighting the fire. "Don't wake anyone," says I. "Let me lie here and finish my sleep."' He tugged fiercely at his boot, then looked up at her brightly. 'Ah, would you give me a shove?'

Stiff with surprise, Caroline found she was going over and doing as he asked, kneeling and pushing at the sole while he pulled at the loops. 'Capital,' he grunted. 'Now t'other.' Booted at last, he stood, a big bony longshanks of seven or eight and twenty, and gave her hand a shake. 'How d'ye do? You're coming to live at Wythorpe—do I have my uncle aright in what he wrote me?' He picked up his wine and gulped it down.

'Aunt Selina and Uncle John have been kind enough to offer me a home with them, yes,' she said, in a voice that even to her own ears came out distressingly niminy-piminy. Really he had very much put her out. 'Well,' she went on, as he shrugged on his short waistcoat. 'I should leave you to your dressing, sir.'

'Why, I'm putting things on, not taking 'em off. It's lucky you woke me, in truth, else I might have slept through breakfast, and I'm prodigious hungry. Mind you, I have had a most unorthodox appetiser,' he added, squinting at her through his empty wine-glass.

'I should tell you,' Caroline said, immediately suspecting that she shouldn't, 'that I am not in the habit of this.'

'Habit of what?'

'The habit of—' She frowned at him as he blandly brushed out his coat. 'Of taking wine at—'

'Five past nine,' he added helpfully, consulting a silver pocket-watch.

'At an early hour. The fact of the matter is I—I have a sore throat. And I find a little canary helps.'

Stephen Milner made a noise in his own throat that, whatever its precise meaning, was decidedly not agreeable. He put on the coat. 'As long as it wasn't to nerve yourself for meeting me,' he grunted.

'Good gracious, why on earth should I do that?'

'Why the devil,' he said, and went carelessly past her to the door.

'Is everyone at Wythorpe as rude as you?' she said to his back; but got only a bare chuckle in return.

Her uncle and aunt were delighted, and not in the least surprised, when Stephen Milner walked in on them at breakfast in the back parlour. Caroline was glad of the opportunity to sit down to coffee and fade into the background while they plied their visitor with greetings and enquiries. There could hardly, she thought, as she bit savagely into a hot roll, have been a worse beginning. When Aunt Selina turned to her, and began to make a formal introduction, Caroline fully expected Mr Milner to seize the opportunity for capricious humour. But he only said: 'We bumped into each other in the hall—but I'm glad, Miss Fortune, to meet you properly,' and shook her hand with great correctness.

'So, Stephen, when do you return to Wythorpe?' his uncle asked.

'Don't know, sir. I've a fancy, while I'm in this part of the world, to go on to have a look at Silbury Hill. Fabulous tumulus, built, according to folklore, by the devil.' Caroline felt his eye light momentarily on her. 'That, or I might travel back with you, if you've no objection.'

'Oh, an excellent notion,' Uncle John said. 'Best to be moving before the autumn rain. And you will surely be wanted at Wythorpe Manor. After quarter day there are all the matters of winter hiring, and stock-keeping, and then Isabella and Fanny will be looking to their winter gowns and dancing-shoes, eh?' he added. 'And all these things, you know, require the presence of the master of the house.'

'Lord, so they do,' Stephen Milner said, in the middle of one of his jaw-cracking yawns.

'Isabella and Fanny,' Aunt Selina explained, 'are Stephen's sisters, my dear. Isabella is about your age—Fanny rather younger—both charming girls. I'm sure they will be good friends to you.'

Caroline, picturing female versions of Stephen, could not quite share her aunt's confidence.

'True—true—that's a blessing,' enthused her uncle. 'What think you of these quaint old bodies having a young girl about the Rectory, hey, Stephen? Won't it be a new lease of life for us?'

'I hope so, sir,' Stephen said, helping himself to ham. 'As for company of her own age at Wythorpe, you forget there's Lady Milner too.'

'To be sure,' cried Dr Langland. 'To be sure!'

'My stepmother,' Stephen informed Caroline calmly, eating away. 'And actually a year or two younger than myself. Curious situation.'

'Augusta too is an excellent creature,' quickly put in Aunt Selina, seeming to leave quantities of things unsaid. 'We look forward to introducing you all round, my dear. Now, Stephen, what did you do with your luggage? And will you stay with us tonight, and dine?'

'I'll gladly stay, Aunt, but if you'll forgive me I'm engaged to dine with a fellow I ran into at the Bear. Name of Beauregard. We were at Cambridge together. You might recall his name from the papers.'

'Beauregard,' Caroline burst out, remembering a piece of gossip that Mrs Catling had chewed on with relish. 'Not the gentleman who ran off with the actress disguised as a page?'

'And disobliged his father, who is a Treasury minister and had him set up to marry the Earl of Melrose's daughter, to their great mutual benefit. Most shocking of all, he has married his actress. Apparently the lady herself delivered the letter announcing the happy matrimonial news to old Beauregard, dressed in her page costume.'

'But surely,' spluttered Dr Langland, 'surely—I cannot conceive—however could a lady pass as a youth?'

'Oh, she was accustomed to it,' Caroline put in, 'for she was well known on the stage for breeches-parts.'

'I see,' her uncle said doubtfully. 'There are one or two such in Shakespeare, of course—though I had not thought the popular stage much enamoured of the Bard in these times.'

'Oh, the play doesn't really signify,' Caroline told him, feeling that Stephen Milner was watching her very carefully. 'The whole point of it is so that the actress shows her legs. I've even seen them work a breeches-part into *Julius Caesar*.'

'Surely this Mr Beauregard must have quite cut himself off from society,' wondered Aunt Selina.

'Absolutely so—he went down to the Lower Rooms for the ball the other night and the Master of Ceremonies refused even to look at him. Fine thing, ain't it?' said Stephen with a sharp laugh. 'So, though dining out is the greatest bore, I said I'd dine with 'em, see if the corruption rubs off on me. You're a lover of the stage, Miss Fortune?'

Taken by surprise, Caroline said, hesitating: 'I—am fond of a play. My father was in the theatre once, so in a way I am bred to it.'

'We were saying how very different she will find our country ways,'

Uncle John said, benevolently patting her arm, 'but she will take to them, I'm sure. The glitter of the great world, you know, is only so much froth and spume: you may look in vain for happiness there.'

Stephen Milner inclined his head respectfully, but said: 'We're all made different, mind, Uncle. You can't feed a cat on carrots.'

'Nor a pig,' said Caroline, 'on cream.'

'Just so,' Stephen said, with a fiendishly delighted look, 'though they both like canary wine.'

'Ah, is this the new slang?' Uncle John said, beaming and wrinkling. 'I do try to keep up with it . . . Oh, Stephen, where are you going?'

'To reclaim my luggage from the clutches of the Bear. I will take up your kind offer, Aunt, thank you.'

'**An** odd creature?' Aunt Selina said a little later, as she and Caroline took their usual walk. 'I suppose he is, my dear, in some ways. Stephen is much addicted to travels—he will think nothing of taking himself off quite alone to tramp about the Western Isles, say, in the worst of weathers—and so he can be a little other-worldly, as it were, in company.'

Well, if Caroline did not quite wish him in the Outer Hebrides now, still she could not be easy with Stephen Milner about the place, though she could not have said why. Back at Gay Street he seemed to take little notice of her until the time came for him to dress for his dinner engagement. Or rather, not dress.

'My dear Stephen,' Aunt Selina cried, 'you're not going like that?'

'Oh, it doesn't signify,' he said, with a negligent glance down at his coat, which was the same he had shrugged on that morning. 'Beauregard don't stand on ceremony.' He turned to Caroline. 'What think you, Miss Fortune? Would you have me at your dinner-table?'

She felt that he was laughing at her. 'I would make allowances for you, Mr Milner,' she answered, coolly.

The household had gone to bed before his return that night—not that this made it so *very* late, for the Langlands were always yawning by ten. He was late down to breakfast too the next morning, and looking profoundly seedy: Aunt Selina, alarmed, hoped he was not sickening.

'Only with a self-inflicted malady,' he grunted, abandoning an attempt at coffee, 'and curable, if one could but find the cure. The wines at Mr Beauregard's table were very choice.'

'You should try hock-and-soda,' Caroline offered. 'Or a raw egg beaten up with pepper-sauce—you swallow it down quick.' She performed an expressive mime, then noticing her aunt and uncle's startled looks went on hurriedly: 'You had a pleasant evening, Mr Milner?'

'From what I can remember of it, Miss Fortune. Beauregard's bride makes a much better hostess than she ever was an actress. So he has lost very little, and she has gained a lot from catching him.'

'It is curious how women are always supposed to be making these lucky catches, and never the other way about,' Caroline said. 'One would imagine we have nothing better to do than sit on the social bank, as it were, forever angling after a man.'

'Precisely what many women do,' he said, with a satisfied smile.

'How dreadful it must be to be a male, forever besieged by these husband-hunting females! But *you* cannot be the object of such pursuit, surely, Mr Milner?'

'No,' he said, unmoved, 'women know I don't care for them, I suppose, or rather ain't taken in by them, and so I'm safe.'

'My dear nephew, such cynicism,' Uncle John reproved him. 'This is only as much to say, you have not met the right woman yet—which is what I heartily wish for you, my greatest wish indeed!'

'I fervently hope the wish will not be fulfilled, Uncle. To marry is to narrow one's possibilities horribly. As no couple can agree so long, they must yawn or fight. You and my aunt are the one baffling exception.' The maid coming in at that moment, he turned to ask her: 'Jane, do you think I might have a raw egg beaten up with pepper-sauce?'

Caroline's prescription seemed to do the trick, but she hardly knew whether to be pleased with her success or not, since a part of her did not particularly want Stephen Milner to be well at all. Mixed feelings was the scarcely adequate term for this vexing, perplexing consciousness when he was about; but perhaps at root was to be found the very simple human desire to know what he thought of her.

Caroline found out, later that day. She had started up the stairs to change out of her walking-dress, when she realised she had left a glove on the hall-table; and returning, overheard her name spoken in the front parlour, where Stephen was talking with the Langlands. Not being a saint, Caroline was soon listening with her ear at the parlour door.

'And she has had to bear up against such a sudden loss,' her aunt was saying.

'Certainly,' came Stephen Milner's voice, 'it's a grief I know myself, and I'm sorry for her. But I'm also sorry for you. I fear you may come to regret this decision to take her in.'

'You alarm me,' cried Uncle John. 'Do you suspect some delinquency in Caroline's character? I cannot believe it—'

'Nor can I,' said Aunt Selina firmly.

'I do not mean that at all,' Stephen said, quite cool. 'I would trust to your judgement of character above anyone's. I am talking about the difference that must exist between her experience of the world, and the new life she is to lead. She has been raised by a rake, and it shows. Place her in sleepy old Wythorpe, and it would be like putting some brightly plumed exotic in a cage of sparrows.'

'Oh, come,' said Uncle John, chuckling, 'there may be a few ruffled feathers—no more than ruffled feathers, my dear boy.'

'But you don't—you don't dislike her, Stephen?' said her aunt.

There came a grunt, so expressive it made the suspensefully listening Caroline flinch. 'Oh,' he said, in a yawning voice, 'I can tolerate her, for your sakes. Well, I think I'll walk to the top of Beechen Cliff.'

'Now? But, look, it's raining quite hard,' Aunt Selina objected.

'So it is: never mind: I want to walk now.' His voice was getting perceptibly nearer to the door. Caroline sprang away, and managed to reach the top of the stairs before he came out.

A small satisfaction, to set beside much mortification. It would have been less if he had described her in terms she could absolutely reject; but Stephen Milner had actually echoed her own secret anxieties, and even amplified them. It would have been less if she had cared nothing for his good opinion; but she found it impossible to be indifferent to him. It was all the more difficult to dismiss his strictures, because he obviously did not much care one way or another.

And that, Caroline told herself, with a sort of mental shake, was exactly the attitude she must adopt. Her aunt and uncle had placed their trust in her, and to *them* she would justify it, come what may—but anyone else could go and boil their head.

While her aunt and uncle were still occupied that day with their painstaking packing, Caroline's was very soon completed. Sitting alone in the front parlour, she dwelt on her father with a sorrow softened now yet still profound. She was jolted out of it by the sudden appearance of Stephen Milner at the door—jolted into wild, unexpected laughter.

'It is coming on to rain,' he pronounced solemnly, while water dripped and pooled around him. The hair hung like seaweed.

'Oh, Mr Milner, I thought you going for a walk, not a swim.'

'Quite refreshing really. In a wretched, dismal, uncomfortable sort of way, I mean. Best change before my aunt sees me—she'll scold.'

'And rightly. You know, you may catch the most shocking cold. But there, you would insist on going.'

'Aye, so I did,' he said, squinting at her through his sodden hair. 'A little hint, by the by, Miss Fortune: when eavesdropping, always bear in mind your shadow.' He pointed to the bottom of the door, then offered her a bland smile. 'Even under a closed door, it can be clearly visible.'

How long she stared at him with her mouth open she couldn't tell—probably long enough to add extra relish to his triumph.

'Well,' she said at last. 'Now you must think me dreadfully underhand.'

Mr Milner gave only a tremendous sniff in reply.

'I will own to the failing,' she went on, 'but must add that I can conceive something much *more* underhand, and that is speaking disobligingly of someone behind their back, instead of to their face.'

'Was I only disobliging?' he mused. 'I thought I was ruder than that. Well, Miss Fortune: I have a lowish opinion of people generally, and I think no worse of you than of the common run—except that, as I shall now candidly state to your face, you do look like trouble.'

It was her turn to sniff. 'I won't say, Mr Milner, what *you* look like.'

'Oh, why not?'

'Because I am too much of a lady.'

'Oh, I don't think so, you know,' he said cheerily, 'not at all. But yes, I really should go and change'—he bowed—'else I shall indeed be rather ill. And I'm sure you would not want that.'

'Certainly not. Horribly ill—distressingly ill—these I would prefer.'

'Ah!' he cried. 'Would you nurse me?'

'Devotedly,' she said, clutching at her heart. 'But that is, of course, if you could *tolerate* me about, Mr Milner.'

He squelched away laughing, leaving Caroline to conduct until dinner a sharp inward debate as to whether she had scored a victory or suffered a defeat. Going down to the dining room after dressing, she was still undecided, and put aside the question to greet the gentleman who was obviously joining them for dinner—and how odd of her aunt not to have mentioned it . . .

'Oh!' she gasped, as the gentleman, turning round, turned into Stephen Milner. He looked with amusement at her outstretched hand.

'A peace offering?'

'No—well, yes, if you like . . . Why are you dressed like that?'

He shrugged. 'I'm dressed for dinner.'

'You know what I mean. Yesterday you went out to dine like a scarecrow, and now . . .' Now, she had to admit to herself, he looked rather well in the swallow-tailed cutaway coat, white silk waistcoat, and starched cravat. 'Why are we so honoured?'

'Well, because yesterday you suspected me of making an affectation of casualness.'

'Did I say that?'

'No, you thought it.'

'You can read minds, can you, Mr Milner?'

'No, only yours. Ah, Uncle John—I should tell you I've decided against travelling down to Huntingdon with you. I've a fancy, while I'm down this way, to visit the old White Horse at Uffington.'

'My dear boy—down this way? That's a good forty miles, surely.'

'Yes, really, Mr Milner,' Caroline said, seating herself, 'all that way just for an inn.'

'The White Horse I mean is a great ancient figure cut into the chalk of the Downs,' Stephen began on a note of stern information: then saw Caroline's ironically raised eyebrow, realised, coughed, and actually—to her infinite satisfaction—blushed. 'As of course you know.'

'I preferred the inn,' she said, with composure, picking up her spoon.

'Yes, yes,' said Uncle John, smiling at them both with benign incomprehension. 'But, my dear Stephen, I do wish we might prevail on you not to postpone your return to the Manor any longer—considering how much you must be needed at the Manor—'

'Considering, Uncle, considering—but considering is what I never do, you know, and I shall return to the fold soon enough,' Stephen said breezily, beckoning Jane forward with the wine.

He drank off two swift glasses. Caroline, observing curiously, wondered what it was about his home that he was so reluctant to face: and came across the curious reflection also, that where previously she had dreaded the prospect of a long coach journey in Stephen Milner's company, now the loss of that prospect did not afford the expected delight.

Chapter Six

CAROLINE'S FIRST SIGHT of her new home was an indistinct one, for they arrived at Wythorpe late on a rainy night after a long journey from Bath that even the conveniences of travelling post could not prevent from being exhausting. Towards the end of the second day, the rain came down, the roads of lowland Huntingdonshire turned bad, and the last lap became a jolting nightmare of mud and wind-whipped darkness.

Through this appeared, at last, lights: Caroline's bleared eyes beheld roofs through trees, a porched door opening to reveal warm welcome radiance, servants with umbrellas. Then, more asleep than awake, she was being ushered on her uncle's arm into a parlour where candlelight, a blazing fire, and a hot, strong posset handed to her by a politely curious housekeeper all conspired to lull her into absolute numbness. Aunt Selina caught sight of her niece's drooping look, and declared that for her there must be no thought of anything but bed.

Ten hours later, she was sitting up in bed refreshed, noticing that despite the olive-striped wallpaper, not everything was as she had envisaged it. For some reason a rectory in a Huntingdonshire village had suggested to her mind creaking, dark-beamed, diamond-paned, even cobwebby age. But neat new sash windows threw the milky light of a clearing day on a whitewashed ceiling. She realised as she dressed on smooth, silent floorboards that the house was quite new.

The Rectory of Wythorpe was, as she soon found, a commodious house of whitewashed brick and red tiles, with two large parlours downstairs as well as a study for Dr Langland and the usual offices, and a stable and coach-house adjoining. At the back, on the south side, a shrubbery of laurels and evergreens divided the kitchen-garden and poultry-yard from a pleasant walled garden of lawns and espaliered fruit-trees. Within, while there was no extravagance, there was some elegance and much comfort, attesting to the fortune that Aunt Selina had brought to her marriage—and which Caroline's mother had forfeited—as well as to the worth of the living. Dr Langland, besides being conscientious about his duties at the little church, whose grey tower could be seen beyond the stable roof, also farmed his own glebe land.

Caroline was eager to explore her new scene, and opportunity came soon, with their first caller. This was Miss Milner—none other than Stephen's sister Isabella; though Caroline would not have guessed it of the slight, trim young woman who stepped sedately into the front parlour, and who put out a tentative hand when Dr Langland made the introductions. Beneath that neat buttery-fair hair was a grave, well-shaped face—quite a beauty indeed, Caroline decided—though in a more solemn style than was usual in a girl of twenty summers. Likewise with the low, fluty voice in which she expressed a hope that Miss Fortune had not taken cold from her wetting last night.

'Oh, no, I am perfectly well, thank you,' Caroline answered, before it occurred to her to wonder how Miss Milner knew about that.

But Uncle John, quite unsurprised, said: 'Ah, you know it was past ten when we got back, then, Bella?' and it soon became clear, from Miss Milner's comprehensive replies, that in Wythorpe everything about everybody was very soon known by everybody else.

'Well, Uncle John, my nonsensical brother wrote me that he had seen you in Bath,' Miss Milner said, after some further friendly exchanges. 'I had some hopes that he might have returned with you—'

'Our hopes also!' cried Dr Langland. 'I said, "Stephen: you have been away too long." Those were my exact words, were they not, my dear?'

'You did tell him so, my dear, indeed, if not in those exact words,' said Aunt Selina, agreeably. 'But Stephen elected to pursue his travels. He spoke of coming home soon: that's all I can tell you, Isabella, I fear.'

'Thank you, Uncle, Aunt,' Miss Milner said, 'and never mind. There are things to do with the wedding that I must consult him about.'

'Oh, you are to be married, Miss Milner?' Caroline said.

'At Christmas, I had hoped,' Miss Milner said, with a faint smile.

'Oh, I wish you many congratulations.'

'I thank you, Miss Fortune,' Miss Milner replied. 'I hope I shall have the pleasure of introducing my fiancé to you presently.'

'Well, and where is your excellent young man, my dear?' Dr Langland enquired. 'Is he at Hethersett?'

'Not yet. He is still away visiting relatives—'

'And acquainting them with his coming good fortune, no doubt!'

'Perhaps,' Miss Milner said, smiling, with a most fascinating blush that began at the back of her neck. 'But we may expect him back soon. Well, Uncle, I hope you find yourself improved by Bath?'

'I do believe the waters have braced my system, my dear. But it would not do for me for long—too much hurry and bustle. I hope that won't disappoint *you*, my dear,' he added with a benevolent pat on Caroline's arm, 'for you are not averse to bustle, I collect.'

'Oh, I have had quite enough of bustle, thank you, Uncle John,' Caroline said. And now she will hate me, she thought, resignedly, as Miss Milner turned her beautiful eyes upon her. Here come I from nowhere, calling her uncle Uncle, and making oh-so-light of my worldly sophistication.

But Miss Milner only said pleasantly: 'I have been at Bath once, when I was thirteen. A fat man trod hard on my toes in the Pump Room. I hope that I may see him again one day. Then I shall stamp on his foot.'

The effect of this, in Miss Milner's quiet, proper tones, was irresistible to Caroline, and she was sure there was a little flinty core of independence under that mild surface, which she very much liked. And something quite different began to displace her belief that Isabella Milner must hate her. Indeed, ten minutes later Caroline found herself putting on her bonnet and preparing to go on a walk with her new acquaintance, who had said she would be delighted to be her guide.

It was now a fine fresh autumn day: the pools of water from last night's downpour made a glittering dapple all about the broad main road of the village, on either side of which clustered the cottages, distinguished by low roofs and peculiarly long, sloping dormer windows. Caroline had conceived this as a flat, bare sort of country, but Wythorpe she found enfolded by a soft swell of hills to the west, and there were venerable trees aplenty, including at the main turning a clump of great horse-chestnuts. She was filled with an absurd happiness, which was not at all diminished by Miss Milner's next words.

'Miss Fortune, I want to say how sorry I am for your loss. I won't allude to it further, except to say I know what it is like to lose a father.'

'Thank you,' Caroline said, pressing the arm which, she found, she had taken quite spontaneously. 'When . . . ?'

'Last December. He was the best of fathers—though of course one always thinks that.'

'Well, I'm not sure mine was the *best*—but I wouldn't have changed him on any account.'

'No, indeed. I *have* heard that he was troubled with—with practical difficulties—that is, Aunt Selina wrote me—'

'Lord, it's no secret,' Caroline said, smiling, as Miss Milner's colour rose again. 'Poor Papa was forever in Queer Street, and even when he wasn't, the money just slipped through his fingers.'

'Aunt Selina did write me, briefly,' her companion said in a rush, 'of her late sister's history—the family quarrel with your poor mother and father, I mean—'

'Oh! my dear Miss Milner. If my parents' marriage was unfortunate, it was so only in the financial sense; and the chief consequence was me, and I am not unhappy.'

Miss Milner gazed long at her. (What a family they are for *looking*, Caroline thought.) 'I think you are very wise,' she sighed at last. 'Tell me, has that hideous blush of mine faded yet?'

Caroline hardly knew how to answer. 'It—well, I do not think it hideous—'

'Thank you,' Miss Milner said, in her gravest tone. 'I have tried to think in that way myself, but it's no use, I still loathe it. If one must blush, at least let it begin in the cheeks, and not at the back of the neck.' Miss Milner caught herself up, and in a reactive flurry asked: 'When you were in Bath, Miss Fortune, what did you think of my brother?'

Caroline, accustomed to her tongue being quick even when her mind was not, was surprised to find herself struck into silence for a few moments. 'I found I wanted to quarrel with him,' she said finally.

'Oh, I do know what you mean,' Miss Milner said, which was more than Caroline did. 'He will not take anything seriously. And for all I love him, I am afraid that is a grave failing, is it not?'

Caroline, in truth, could think of many that were graver, and was some distance from thinking it a failing at all. So, avoiding a reply, she said: 'He is not opposed to your marriage, I hope?'

'No—that is, no more than to marriage in general, which he calls a fool's game. But he says I am too precipitate, and should wait a while. When I would gladly be married next week—tomorrow.'

'You are very eager!' Caroline said, with a smile.

'I am,' Miss Milner said, without one: which left Caroline with the problem of what to do with hers, as it felt so inappropriate: so she plumped for a quick diversion, crying out: 'Ah, now, I wonder, can you tell me the name of that flower? It is so very pretty.'

'That is a daisy,' Miss Milner said, after a moment in which politeness overcame disbelief.

Even town-bred as she was, Caroline had that much botany: this, she thought, was not one of my better diversions; and then at that thought she was lost, and began laughing like an idiot. It was a moment at which a friendship is either formed, or becomes an impossibility. A frozen stare would have signalled the latter. But Miss Milner began laughing too, quite as helplessly.

'I can see I shall have to instruct you in these rural matters, for your own safety,' Miss Milner said. 'I would not have you walking into a pasture not knowing a cow from a bull.'

'That, you may rest assured, I *do* know.'

'Oh, you—there goes my wretched blush again!'

'Truly, though, I do wish I knew the names of flowers and things like that. You are already well up in all that sort of thing, I'll wager.'

'Yes,' Miss Milner said simply, 'I am: at the Manor we have a quantity of gardens, and they have always been my delight—oh, especially my herb garden: I hope I can show it to you some day.' She darted a look at Caroline. 'Though that may not be a very thrilling prospect for you.'

'I should greatly like it—and I do wonder what conception people must have of me. Am I popularly supposed to have spent my life amongst fleshpots? Whatever they are.'

'Of course it is presumptuous to draw conclusions about a person from what one has heard,' Miss Milner said earnestly, 'and I am very wrong to do it.'

'It is the most natural thing in the world, and I do it all the time. Only I am afraid I shall disappoint people's expectations dreadfully, as I'm really not at all scandalous, or stylish, or wicked.'

'Oh, but you are,' cried Miss Milner, adding hastily, 'stylish, I mean. You have a look—well, I'm sure that's what they are all wearing in Town.'

'If they are, they are very secretive about it.' Caroline laughed. 'But I'm flattered—and I can return the compliment, and more truthfully, by telling you that what *you* are wearing is quite the elegant thing. Lord, such mutual cordiality! We must surely begin savaging each other soon.'

'Oh, but we won't do that,' Miss Milner said, her face seeming all luminous blue eyes. 'I know you are funning, but still . . . I beg your pardon, I'm very serious, an't I? I know it, Stephen is always reproving me for it. In truth, I did have this gown from London—my last visit there. When my father was alive we would spend a month in Town every year. Stephen, though, prefers ruins and those hillocks with bones in.'

'He is sick of London? Then he has had his share of it?'

'Oh, he was there a good deal, after Cambridge: he was quite the town-buck for a time. But,' Miss Milner said, with a shy look, 'not all men are like Stephen.'

'Ah—you mean your future husband? I approve him already. But wait, do you mean he will be taking you off to live in Town? Am I going to lose my first friend here so soon?'

'Oh, no, we shall live at Hethersett—his place, you know. Well, of course, you don't know. It is only six miles off. But we shall spend a part of each season in Town, I think. That is—we have agreed so. If you will look, Miss Fortune, there is the Seven Stars Inn, on the corner of Splash Lane, and that's Mrs Vine who keeps it. And Splash Lane is so-called because right at the bottom there is a ford.'

'And when you go through it, you splash!'

'Just so. And down there at the turning is the Old Grange, lately occupied by a new-married couple named Hampson. He is a lawyer, and she is a Bristol heiress with more money than'—Miss Milner caught herself up with an abashed look—'than many people. They are very fond of entertaining—you are sure to be at a Hampson carpet-dance before long. That is—I do beg your pardon, Miss Fortune, I don't know whether you are accepting invitations yet—under the circumstances.'

'Well, I know my father would want me to, that's all I can say: just as he always loathed mourning weeds, and would hate to see me in them. And while we are about the business of flouting convention, let me entreat you to call me Caroline. We can go back to Miss-ing each other when we are in company, if you like. And now, if you *don't* wish to call me Caroline, I shall be in rather an awkward position, and I shall have to go and throw myself in the splash.'

'That I could not allow—Caroline.'

Isabella, as Caroline was to call her companion, proceeded to be her guide about the village. It had an appearance of quietly thriving, and Caroline's eye fell with appreciation on the cottage gardens, still bright even at this late season with their flowers. Her chief satisfaction, however, on returning to the Rectory, was the friendship she had discovered with Isabella. And it was with the tender perception of friendship that she noticed how comparatively little Isabella spoke of Wythorpe's chief landmark—her own home, the Manor, which was visible as a cluster of chimneys on the high ground to the west, at the end of an avenue of oaks—and how little eager she seemed to go back there.

That the regard was mutual was evinced over the next few days as the two young women spent much time together. There did remain patches of reticence about Isabella, and these included her feelings about her home life; but quiet hints there were, and Caroline was soon acquainted with the facts relating to the Milners of Wythorpe Manor.

The family had long been prosperously settled in Huntingdonshire. If they were notable at all, it was for a habit of not distinguishing themselves. But Isabella's late father had sought to be a public man: he had made no less than two speeches in Parliament, and had further benefited his country by raising and equipping a force of Volunteers to repel Bonaparte if the Frenchie should ever reach Huntingdon, as a result of which he was duly rewarded with a knighthood.

In his private capacity Sir Henry had met with no less success. He was married early to a lady of firm principle—the sister of the Rector, Dr Langland; and she had borne him three children. The loss of this lady to a consumption, some five years since, was universally mourned. Yet as time passed, Sir Henry contracted a violent affection for a woman thirty years his junior—none other than the governess appointed to the instruction of his younger daughter, Fanny—and, to the consternation of his friends, would settle for nothing less than marrying her.

To the usual awkwardness of a young stepmother—actually younger than the eldest offspring and heir, and not much senior to the others—was added that of the employee transformed into mistress of house and family. Nor could she escape censure for the promptness with which she had accepted a proposal so materially advantageous; for even the most charitable observer could not have supposed that Sir Henry's suit would have been successful if he had not had a knightly name, a mansion and park, and nine hundred acres to lay at her feet. Not that there was much belief in a suit on the gentleman's part: it being generally assumed that the young lady had gone all out to land him.

However, Sir Henry seemed happy with his new bride: but this felicity was fated soon to end. A twelvemonth after his marriage, he was felled by a heart-stroke, and followed his first wife to the churchyard, leaving the former governess mistress of Wythorpe Manor, and all manner of complications in the bereft family.

It was not that Sir Henry had encumbered the next generation with legal difficulties. He had settled a comfortable jointure on his widow, whilst the estate passed naturally to his son: nor were his daughters dowerless. But he had insufficiently considered that much more unstable currency, the feelings. Lady Milner must continue to live at the Manor, but in a very singular relation to her stepchildren, one of whom was the master of the house, whilst over the two girls she bore a sort of authority, surely very awkward for all parties in its ill-definition. Had there been friendship, or even cordiality, between the young stepmother and her late husband's family, all such difficulties might have been swept aside; but this was emphatically not the case, and one hardly needed further evidence than the continual absences of Mr Stephen Milner, who seemed unable to bear being in the house.

Such at least was the general impression of what went on at Wythorpe Manor—but Caroline was eager to see for herself. That she might learn something to the disadvantage of clever-stick Stephen Milner was, perhaps, a further incentive, and quickened her pulses when at last the Langlands readied themselves to call at the Manor and introduce her.

Isabella was the first to welcome them at the Manor. Indeed she came running down the oak avenue to meet them, explaining a little bashfully that she had seen their approach from her window.

'And I thought I should tell you, before you come in, that Captain Brunton is here again.'

'Who? Who? Oh, to be sure, Brunton. He is a captain,' Dr Langland explained. 'But, my dear Bella, why must you warn us?'

'I think Isabella meant to spare us the awkwardness of surprise,' Aunt Selina said, 'especially as—well, it seems he has only just gone away.'

'Well, and who is this Captain Brunton?' Caroline asked, slipping her arm through Isabella's.

'A kinsman of my stepmother—Lady Milner.'

'I believe he is a second cousin,' Aunt Selina added.

Wythorpe Manor revealed itself as a substantial Dutch-gabled house built of mellow limestone, not more than two hundred years old, with two projecting wings either side of a central porch. Within, Caroline was enfolded at once by a smell of old varnish, woodsmoke and beeswax.

A comfortable morning room, steeped in autumn sun, was where they were received by their hostess. Such at least they must call her: but there was not much that was hospitable about the young lady who stiffly dabbed her fingers into Caroline's palm and then swiftly reclaimed her seat by the fire. She was remarkably handsome, in a tall, high-chinned, black-browed style. She asked how Caroline did, and how she liked the country, and how she was settling in at the Rectory, in such an absent and mechanical way as suggested she was mentally ticking off a list of the requisite civilities. She was richly dressed, and seemed to have a finicking consciousness of it, suddenly turning her attention, when Caroline or her aunt was speaking, to rearranging the embroidered shawl over her shoulder.

With her was a muscular, light-eyed man of thirty whose weathered complexion would have proclaimed the naval officer, even without the blue tail-coat and white waistcoat. Lady Milner introduced him with the words, 'My cousin, Captain Brunton, late of the *Northam*.'

'Well, well, Captain Brunton, had you no luck with their lordships at the Admiralty, hey?' Dr Langland accosted him. 'I recall, when you were last here, you were going to wait upon them in hopes of a commission.'

'No luck—as you say, sir,' the Captain answered. 'But I am still—as you say—in hopes.'

'What about the merchant service? That's the other side of the peace, you know—there'll be more trade upon the seas now. Well, at any rate, Captain, you have a comfortable safe harbour here, hey?'

'That reminds me,' said Aunt Selina. 'When can we expect Stephen back at Wythorpe?'

'I hear nothing,' Lady Milner said. 'I should be glad to, indeed.'

'Ah, yes, I think Isabella would be glad of his return likewise,' Aunt Selina said, 'so she can proceed with her marriage plans, isn't it so, my dear? You must both take this sad fellow to task when he comes home.'

It was a game attempt, Caroline thought—trying to make step-mother and stepdaughter feel they were in the same boat; but it would surely take a lot more than Aunt Selina's gentle persuasion to heal the disaffection in this room. She was just wondering how the visit was to be got through when a newcomer burst into the room, pursued by a yipping spaniel, and bringing with her a new atmosphere.

'Uncle John—Aunt Selina, how long have you been here? Only I didn't know—I was rambling round the garden and I quite forgot—'

'And without your shawl, I think,' Lady Milner said reprovingly to the young girl, who had gone over to kiss Dr Langland's cheek.

'Oh, pooh, Augusta, it's absolutely mild out, as you would know if you came away from that fire for a change. Ain't it, Bella?'

'I don't know about *absolutely* mild,' Isabella said, with a smile.

'Old Grave-Airs, how you talk!' the girl cried, planting a boisterous kiss on Isabella's cheek also. 'And now *you* must be Caroline!'

'I have told you before, Fanny,' Lady Milner droned, 'it is not proper to address me in that way.'

'Why, I can't call you Miss Howell any more, because you ain't,' said Fanny robustly. 'And to say Stepmother or Stepmama would be just too fantastical, when you're hardly older than Bella. Now then, how do you do'—Caroline's hand was seized—'I'm Fanny, and I don't mind *what* you call me, only I must say I was never so glad to meet anyone.'

Fanny Milner, who had plumped herself down beside Caroline on the sofa, was all in a glow from her exercise, her chestnut hair coming down in wild spirals: white-skinned, buxom, with a short nose and a determined chin, and a charmingly evident belief that her seventeen years had taught her all she would ever need to know.

'The way Aunt Selina found you, and brought you here—I vow it is the most romantic thing. And then your father was actually in the Peninsula, and wounded! How surpassingly glorious! And now is it true he was absolutely an actor on the stage once as well? How perfect!'

'Well, opinions might differ as to the perfection of that,' Caroline said. 'In the eyes of some people it was not at all respectable.'

'I wouldn't care for that,' Fanny said decidedly. 'I have an absolute scorn for stuffy conventions—we are imprisoned by them in *this* place. And I suppose you have been behind the scenes at theatres too,' she went on, her eyes shining at Caroline. 'What are the actresses like? Were they, well, you know . . .'

'You should not badger Miss Fortune so, Fanny,' her stepmother said.

'No, no, Lady Milner, I am not badgered—only a little perplexed how to answer without disappointing. Most of the actresses I saw were married ladies, who went home to exemplary domesticity.'

'What a pity! Oh, but I'll wager they *weren't*,' Fanny said, with a poke in Caroline's ribs, 'only you can't say. Well, what about the Peninsula? Did your mother not follow the drum? I would have.'

'It is a hard life, for an army wife,' said Aunt Selina, giving a momentary impression of being about to break into poetry.

'Oh, la, I can bear any sort of discomfort,' Fanny said, jumping up. 'You see how dreadfully dull we are here—really you must enliven us, Caroline. I count on you—oh! and you have been lately at Brighton, I know—tell me, is it as fast as they say?'

'There are some—fast characters to be met with there, certainly,' Caroline said, thinking of Mr Leabrook. 'But for my part I prefer slow and honest.'

'Oh, you have to say that,' Fanny said, giving her an expressive wink. 'And what about the Prince's Pavilion—is it as fantastical as they say?'

'It looks rather like a grand birdcage crowned with onions.'

'The Pavilion is built in the Oriental style. That is why it looks odd to you, Miss Fortune,' Lady Milner informed her.

As there was no reply more civil than 'I know' to be made to this paralysing remark, Caroline contented herself with a polite nod. It was Isabella who came to her defence, saying: 'Of course Caroline knows that, ma'am, she was trying to give us a picture of it.'

'Quite a vivid one indeed,' said Captain Brunton, 'though to be sure, Oriental is the correct term, Miss Milner.'

'I thank you for the instruction, sir,' Isabella said, very coldly; and Caroline saw, with mingled sympathy and amusement, that the neck-blush was called forth by anger as well as modesty.

The amusement was possible to her, of course, because she could come away from that house: as the Rectory party very soon did, with Dr Langland blissfully remarking on what a pleasant chat they had had. But for poor Isabella there was no such escape—except by the early marriage for which Caroline could now see some persuasive reasons.

'Not an easy woman by any means,' Caroline said later, when Aunt Selina tentatively asked her opinion of Lady Milner. 'But I dare say that, like everyone, she improves upon acquaintance.'

Aunt Selina replied, 'Ye-es,' in such a dubious tone as suggested that in this regard Lady Milner was the exception that proved the rule. 'But it is so very awkward for Fanny, who was used to her as a governess.'

Privately Caroline thought the irrepressible Fanny much more at ease with the situation then her quieter sister, and was only concerned at the young girl's propensity to make a heroine of herself.

When Isabella made her usual call at the Rectory next morning, it was with Fanny alongside her; and during their usual walk, it was Fanny who plied Caroline with numerous questions about London, about Bath and Brighton, about actresses and dandies, ladies' boarding-schools and nocturnal elopements from the same (which she seemed to think so frequent they were virtually part of the curriculum), and other worldly excitements, whilst Isabella remained relatively quiet. Fortunately for Caroline's peace, Fanny was devoted to her dogs, and would suffer no one but herself to feed and exercise them, and accordingly she had to hurry back to the Manor for that purpose.

Caroline slipped her arm through her friend's, and was rewarded with a sigh that came from a full heart.

'It is very stupid. I feel very ashamed,' Isabella said.

'My dear girl, what have you done? I see no constables in pursuit.'

'You are quite right, it is trivial, and you have probably guessed it. There was another quarrel this morning—no, I should not put it so. I had the quarrel, with my stepmother. Isn't that dreadful?'

'For you it is, I can tell. Though there are some people who like nothing better than a good, regular quarrel, like a dose of rhubarb.'

'I'm sure it must be my fault, but we just cannot get along. Stephen said we would eventually settle down like two cats in a basket,' Isabella said, shaking her head. 'Oh, I wish I could be like Fanny: she either ignores Augusta, or laughs her off. But then she hasn't got Captain Brunton to deal with as well.'

'Dear, dear, you quarrel with the Captain too?'

'It isn't that. He is constantly intervening. I fancy he has taken it on himself to convert me to my stepmother's side. Well, I am being perfectly horrible today, so I may as well go on and say I do not trust his association with my stepmother.'

'Lord! Do you mean you suspect them . . . ?'

Isabella shrugged. 'I should say no more. But they are so very thick together: and when I walk into the room, and they are deep in one of their talks, and break it off so that we can all be uncomfortable together—well, I feel rather like an intruder in my own home.'

'I can only come up with that most unsatisfying of counsels; patience. This is very disagreeable for you, but it will end.'

'You are right, of course. I must keep that in mind—once I am married, there will be an end to all this.'

It occurred to Caroline that a very great burden was placed on a marriage that represented an escape from misery, as well as an admittance to happiness. But she was distracted by Isabella's bursting out: 'And—and how lucky I am to have someone like you to unburden myself to! There, I dread to think what colour my neck is now.'

'Between pink and lobster. And when you are a bride, you know, you may leave Lady Milner and her salty suitor to do what they will. Unless you do not like the thought of leaving Fanny in their company?'

'I would not, if Fanny were not so very well able to take care of herself. Besides, you know, she will have her heroine near at hand. You are her model of all that is daring, dashing, and unconventional. You will have gathered she is of a romantic spirit, and to know someone who has lived in the world as you have has quite put her into transports.'

'Well, I fear she will suffer a great disappointment, when she comes to realise that my favourite excitement is a little plain-sewing in the evening, followed by a quiet hand of penny whist.'

Isabella took this last no more seriously than Caroline meant it: yet it had some relation to the truth, in that Caroline greatly valued the harmony, peace, and mutual consideration that prevailed at the Rectory. Still, she was gratified when they were invited to dine at the Manor a few days later, and all the more so because the invitation proceeded from the master of the house, who had given no hint of his imminent return to Wythorpe.

Caroline discovered in herself a strong wish to encounter Mr Milner again. She had a cause with which to tax him—her friend and his sister, Isabella, who was unhappy and surely might be made less so, if he would only exert himself. And there was a certain remark about cats and baskets, which made her feel so satirical she could hardly wait for the appointed evening to arrive.

Caroline dressed with care for the occasion—an evening gown of dove-grey poplin with pearl buttons gathering the sleeves: it had been finished by Aunt Selina's Bath dressmaker, just before their departure, and now came out of its tissue-paper to her mingled admiration and dubiety. It was very handsome: but was it too handsome for her? However, once inside it, and with her hair dressed and curled by Aunt Selina's maid, Caroline recovered her confidence. 'And besides,' she considered, 'I need to be dressed to advantage tonight, for *he* will soon find something to remark on if not.'

He was Mr Stephen Milner; and his disobliging words about her, overheard at Bath, were much in Caroline's mind as they rode up to the Manor. The representation of her as *trouble* struck Caroline as more and more unjust; and she was determined to demonstrate to her host that she had not set the neighbourhood by the ears.

On arrival they were greeted by Mr Milner himself on the steps. 'Uncle John, how d'you do, sir? Aunt, give me a kiss, you look well—ah, and Miss Fortune.'

'Mr Milner.'

He shook her hand, scrutinised her very briefly, and then turned aside to give some directions to the coachman on the stabling of the horses. He is no more civil than before, thought Caroline.

In the drawing room, though it was a mild evening, Lady Milner clung close again to the fire; but if this was with some notion of thawing herself out, it was not working, judging by the bare, stiff courtesies she extended to the guests: nor was there any more ease in the manner of Captain Brunton, who stood over her like a benign warder, not knowing what to do with his hands. Joining them, besides the family, were the youngish couple by the name of Hampson, whom Isabella had described to her: he very handsome in a fat way, she very plain likewise, and both unremitting in their attention to one another, with an armoury of secret smiles, nods, and glances.

The real surprise for Caroline, however, was the change in the feeling of the house. Isabella was in cheerful looks, Fanny's animation was more genial and less noisy: the servants were more amenable: even the spaniel's yap seemed mellower in tone. Caroline was forced to conclude that Mr Milner had wrought this change, simply by his return.

This was the subject of Dr Langland's first remarks: the Rector, smiling upon the company, pronounced: 'Now this, my dear Stephen, is what I joy to see. The master of the house in residence, and all as it should be. You were missed, Nephew, greatly missed.'

'I thank you, Uncle,' Mr Milner said, 'and I'm glad to be back. I always am, right up to the moment when I go away again.'

'Dear, dear—what will settle you, I wonder?' cried Dr Langland. 'Perhaps a pretty young wife, like our friend here?'

There being no pretty young wives in the room, attention fastened, after a momentary bewilderment, on Mrs Hampson, who coloured appropriately. 'Ah,' said her husband, with a rapt gaze into his consort's eyes, 'how true, sir, how true. I can honestly say, that I never knew felicity till I knew Felicity!'

This compliment to Mr Hampson's bride, with its pun on her name, was loudly admired by the Rector. 'Ha, I see Caroline smiles,' Dr Langland went on, 'which means, I think, that she approves my prescription.'

'I doubt whether Miss Fortune approves matrimony any more than I do,' Stephen Milner said, with a foxy smile, and a decided air.

'I'm flattered, sir,' was Caroline's calm rejoinder.

'*Are* you? Good God. Why?'

'Oh, wait, this is revealing, Mr Milner—that you are surprised at having said something nice to a woman.'

'You are wrong, Miss Fortune,' he said collectedly. 'I am not surprised, I am astonished.'

'No more astonished than I at hearing anything like a compliment from *your* lips: but so I have: and the highest compliment of all, perhaps. You have suggested that I think as you do.' Caroline made a bow of mock reverence. 'Surely no greater praise could be bestowed.'

'Absolutely so,' said Mr Milner, with a look of keen enjoyment. 'For is this not how we all proceed? "I met a very pleasant woman at the coach-stand this morning." In what way was she a pleasant woman? "Why, she agreed with everything I said.'"

'Oh, Stephen, for shame,' Aunt Selina put in, smiling, but serious. 'People may be friends without agreeing on every subject.'

'So they may, Aunt: and secretly each will be hoping to convert the other to their belief. But that is only the common run of friendship. I cannot conceive true friends who are not absolutely candid with one another, including where they differ.'

As this was Caroline's own view, and a fair description of her relation with Isabella, she let it pass, observing only: 'And what about your despised matrimony—should the same prescription not apply?'

'Oh, I don't actually despise it. I only know it would not do for me.'

'True friends may be married also,' Aunt Selina said. 'Your uncle John has been my best friend for nearly thirty years.'

'Lord! Thirty years!' cried Mrs Hampson, appealing to her spouse. 'Only think of it, my love!'

'Oh! Caroline—you will never guess what Stephen has brought me,' burst out Fanny. 'It is *Glenarvon* and, you know, I do not find it dull. Glenarvon himself is so darkly fascinating, really I would be quite ready to throw away my reputation for him.'

'Tut, Fanny, this is not proper in a girl your age,' Lady Milner said.

'Isn't it? Oh, Augusta, do tell me at what age it *will* become proper to throw away my reputation,' Fanny responded, with a wicked smile. She turned, still glinting with mischief, to Caroline. 'What do you say? Isn't it possible for a woman to *fall*, and still keep cheerful?'

Caroline was careful. 'I dare say it is, though society is so severe upon such a woman that she may not find cheerfulness easy to come by.'

'Oh, society—it can only hurt you if you care for its opinion,' Fanny said airily, stretching herself out on the sofa, 'which I do not.'

'Dear, dear, I begin to repent of bringing you that book, Fanny,' her brother said. 'To think of such sensational stuff sullying Father's library.'

'Well, it isn't—I don't go in there to read any more. There's no fire lit in the mornings now. Apparently it's mistress's orders,' yawned Fanny.

'I decided to discontinue the practice, at least until it is true winter, since it seems rather wasteful,' said Lady Milner, drawing herself up. 'I have not told you of this, Stephen, as I understood that these domestic matters were to be my province: though if that is no longer the case, please inform me, and I will observe the alteration accordingly.'

I must try to be charitable, Caroline thought: probably she doesn't mean to sound as if she is continually translating from Latin.

'No, no,' Stephen Milner said, 'of course not: only I hope if my sister wants something in her own home, she may have it.'

'Certainly: I have only to be asked.' Lady Milner's glance fell on Isabella, who had risen and moved away with an unsettled look. 'Such other innovations as I have made,' she went on purposefully, 'are not, I think, numerous or considerable. There is one which I believe Isabella disapproves, and that is the servants' bedchamber candles. I consider wax a needless extravagance, and have ordered tallow instead.'

'Yes,' said Isabella, her eyes shadowy. 'I don't think it is fair on them.'

'But it is what I use in my own bedchamber,' her stepmother said. 'I do not ask them to make any sacrifice that I am not making likewise.'

'Sacrifice, forsooth,' groaned Mr Milner, pacing, 'what is this business about sacrifices? Are we poor all of a sudden, Augusta, that you must go burning tallow in your boudoir? No more of it, I say. I hereby reinstate wax. It is like me, bright and sweet-smelling.'

'Your late father never had occasion, I think, to find fault with my domestic economy,' Lady Milner said dourly.

Scrubbing violently at his hair, and seeming, as an amused Caroline saw it, to close his eyes in momentary exasperation, Mr Milner paced harder. 'Augusta, you take everything much too seriously,' he said with decision. 'And to show I am quite even-handed, I may say that you do too, Bella. So does the whole world, come to that. Now, one of the few things that is worth taking seriously is a good dinner, and my nose tells me ours is ready, and so I think we should go in.'

Lady Milner sprang up with surprising alacrity, and so glided her stiff-backed way to the dining-parlour before everyone else. Stephen Milner in his restless prowlings had fetched up closest to Caroline, and so he offered her his arm: Dr Langland, with many compliments and jests to Mr Hampson about stealing the lady away, took Mrs Hampson's, while Mr Hampson, with many jests likewise, escorted Aunt Selina. Only now did it occur to Lady Milner that she was unaccompanied: she stopped, and turned to look for Captain Brunton. He was at that moment offering his arm to Isabella, but at his cousin's significant look he paused, and appeared as if he might have remained helplessly fixed to that spot for ever more, had not Isabella settled the matter for him.

'Sir, you are wanted, I think: please escort Lady Milner,' she said coolly. 'My sister will be glad to walk in with me—won't you, Fanny?'

'To be sure!' cried Fanny, seizing her arm. 'I have never understood why a woman must have a man to take her into dinner.'

'Probably because of our barbaric ancestors,' her brother opined, 'all hacking away at one roast boar, and devil take the hindmost. A man's assistance would at least assure you of a decent thighbone to gnaw on.'

'And yet, you know, women can be quite as grasping and overbearing as men,' Isabella gently suggested.

'Well, now,' said Uncle John, all smiles, 'isn't this pleasant?'

Probably no one but the blissfully obtuse Dr Langland could have found it so, but it was certainly, Caroline thought, mightily interesting. She felt the moment had come for a direct attack on her partner's defences; and so, as he was seating her at table, she quietly observed to Mr Milner: 'Your cats are not settling in the basket.'

'Eh?' She had him off-guard: but he quickly recovered. 'Oh, that.' He chuckled reminiscently, then shrugged. 'Hey, well, devil knows what's to be done with them.'

'Does it not occur to you that perhaps grown women are beings of a good deal more complexity than cats?'

Mr Milner gave this a deal of perplexed attention. 'Well,' he said at last, 'cats can be very temperamental creatures too, you know. Will you take some wine, Miss Fortune?' He presented to her a face of infuriating bland puzzlement. 'What? Have you turned Methodist, perhaps, and take only water? I confess I find it hard to believe—'

'I will have some wine, thank you, Mr Milner,' she rapped at him, fighting down a smile, 'and you will not divert me from my question.'

'Does it not occur to *you*, Miss Fortune, that questioning a man you hardly know at his own table makes you a forward little piece?'

'Does it? Well, I'm progressing anyhow. At Bath you called me a bold little piece: "forward" is just slightly less insulting. And I did get to know you tolerably well there, sir.'

'I see: and now you have added to your knowledge by talking about me with my family.'

'Oh, there are many other more interesting things to talk about, believe me—but you do come up, Mr Milner, from time to time.'

'You come up *all* the time. Fanny has made you her touchstone in her perpetual war against the conventions; and I know what a favourite you are with Isabella already.'

'She is a great favourite with me: I never knew anyone more amiable, more truly gentle-hearted, than your sister.'

'Which you find surprising, having met me first.'

'To adopt your own figure, sir, I am not surprised, I am astonished. But come: considering I am bold, forward, and—what was your other elegant expression? ah, yes—*trouble*—'

'You remember everything I say!' Mr Milner said, in a tone that mixed wonderment with approval. 'Do you write it all down?'

'Considering I am all these things,' she went on, ignoring this, 'you must confess I have not yet had the baleful influence on Wythorpe you predicted. For you see, here are no earthquakes or revolutions.'

'I am willing to concur with all you say, Miss Fortune, because of that one significant word: not *yet*. You have not been here long, after all.'

'Long enough,' she said, refusing to be provoked even by his satisfied smile of triumph, 'to have grown attached to Isabella, and to wish— well, to wish to help her: except that that does not lie in *my* power.'

'Oh, I understand you,' he said nodding, 'indeed I do: but I fancy you overestimate the ability of a mere male to settle the inevitable differences of two women under one roof.'

'From what I see, they are eased, if not settled, simply by your presence under that roof. There, that is the first compliment I have paid you.'

'No, it isn't, it is a reproach,' he said collectedly, helping her to soup, 'and a just one as far as it goes. I certainly am disinclined to botheration, and follow the natural impulse to fly from it whenever I can. But the fact is'—he took care to lower his voice, though Lady Milner was at the other end of the long rosewood table—'Father did leave us rather awkwardly placed by that unexpected decision of his autumn years. I'll only add that it has confirmed my opinion of marriage as a fool's game.'

Fortunately Lady Milner's economies had not extended to the table. Plentifully came the haddock, the ham and tongue, the boiled fowls and batter-pudding and roasted saddle of mutton. Taken together with this lofty dining-parlour, with its capacious fireplace and monumental buffet, it afforded Caroline a glimpse of an old country style of entertaining, very different from what she was used to.

As if divining her thoughts, Mr Milner said: 'Plain roast-and-boiled, you see, Miss Fortune. For my part I hanker after ragouts and fricassees sometimes, but our cook does not enjoy them, nor, as a rule, our guests. A suspicion hovers that sauces will turn you into a Frenchie.'

'I own I am fond of a little spice, sir—though this is very fine fare, to be sure. Perhaps you could venture to serve macaroni: that at least has not the reproach of being French.'

'With Bologna sausage, Parmesan-cheese, and garlic,' he said dreamily. 'Ah! And then my neighbours would have me taken away in a strait-waistcoat. So, how *are* you settling in?' As she hesitated he went on: 'I realise that is a fiendishly difficult question. Take time to think it out.'

'It is because it is a simple question, and it comes from *you*, that I mistrust it. You must mean something teasy and ironical.'

'Must I? Probably I do, deep down: but let us pretend me capable of sincerity, and of recognising that, troublesome as you surely are, you have lost a parent, been transplanted to a new world, and had to make a deal of adjustments, none of which can have been easy.'

Now she was at a loss: it was delicately said, it seemed truly meant. So all she could do was reply honestly: 'I'm settling in very well, I thank you. Indeed it feels as if I have known you all for years.'

He gave a shout of laughter. 'Why, that, Miss Fortune, is because you have already plumbed our country dullness to the depths—and have experienced a true Wythorpe evening, in which the hands of the clock do not seem to move at all.'

'I would call this unfair, if I thought you meant it, which surely shows that I am a loyal Wythorpe native already. As for dullness—well, you are not dull, Mr Milner, I will say that for you.'

'Pray,' came Lady Milner's carrying voice, 'tell us what the jest is, Stephen, Miss Fortune—do not leave us out.'

'Oh, I was shamefully abusing our quiet old neighbourhood, and Miss Fortune was defending it.'

'Ah—I see. The joke is, it is Miss Fortune who is the outsider.'

'Oh, newcomer, surely, rather than outsider,' cried Isabella warmly.

'That is what I meant, Isabella. Of course that is what I meant.'

'But what *can* you find to say in favour of this deadly place?' demanded Fanny. 'To be sure, there are the winter assemblies and balls, which would be some consolation if there were more of them—but one miserable mustering a month is about all our dismal district affords. Oh, but I make an exception for you, my dear hospitable sir,' she said, turning to Mr Hampson, '*you* and Mrs Hampson have made a very appreciable difference to our entertainments, and I thank you for it.'

'I am glad to hear it, Miss Fanny—do you hear, my love? And on the subject of entertainments, Miss Fanny, I may add that we intend a supper and carpet-dance at the Grange on Friday next, to which we would be very glad to welcome you, and all the present company.'

'Do you suppose, my love'—Mrs Hampson made some girlish mouthings at her husband— 'that our picture will be ready by then?'

'My sweet girl, it is hardly begun! We are having a bridal portrait painted,' he pursued, smiling on Aunt Selina. 'And no doubt, ma'am, you are ready to call us monstrous vain for it!'

'Not at all—a charming notion, Mr Hampson. You have been sitting to the artist already?'

'Aye, aye—a remarkable young fellow, comes to us for the sittings. He has been engaged upon some views at Hinchingbrooke, but is turning his hand to domestic portraiture also, for select clients. I am anxious that he should do *justice* to my Felicity.'

As it was difficult to conceive of an artist being actually unflattering to Mrs Hampson, not even Aunt Selina's politeness could find to reply to this beyond a smile and a murmured agreement. Fanny, however, had not done with her own subject.

'You must promise, Bella, that when you are married you will be regularly giving parties. Is there not at Hethersett a room quite large enough to accommodate a creditable private ball? Indeed, Stephen, when is this wedding to be? Here have we been waiting for you to come home and get matters settled with Isabella.'

'What matters?'

Caroline could not keep silent. 'A woman going to be married likes to have such things as the date of the wedding fixed, Mr Milner—and so, accordingly, orders made for trousseaus and lace and such.'

Mr Milner raised his eyebrows and looked over at Isabella. 'Well, what say you, Bella? Are you all for getting these matters settled?'

'As I have mentioned to you, Stephen,' she answered, her voice quiet, 'I would like to be married before Christmas, and you know Richard is on his way home, and writes me that he is in perfect agreement.'

'Well, it doesn't leave a great deal of time for the arrangements,' Mr Milner said. 'And I really don't see the need for haste. Consider: you have not been properly acquainted above eight months, nor engaged above four. And if it is a true, sound attachment, as I am assured it is, then it must be a hardy plant, and will not wither for a little delay.'

'But if it is a true, sound attachment, then it needs no delay,' Caroline said to him. 'And besides, Mr Milner, how can you, who are so avowed an enemy of matrimony, presume to this expertise on the subject?'

'Oh, very easily,' he replied with energy. 'A man who stands aloof on a high hill looking down on a landscape, sees it much more clearly than one grubbing about down there in the boggy lowlands.'

'The elegance of your language is overpowering.'

'I've always thought so,' he said, with a comfortable smile, then, turning: 'But be it as you will, Bella. As soon as Richard is back at Hethersett, let us meet and make our plans. You might at least credit me, you know, with a generous motive, that I don't want to lose my dear sister.'

'I might, but I won't,' said Isabella, cheerfully. 'You'll hardly notice I'm gone, knowing you, Stephen; and besides, I am not moving far.'

'Ah, Hethersett is not far as the crow flies,' he said, shaking his head, 'but it is, after all, over the border—over into Northamptonshire: where folk are queer, so I hear. They butter their bread before slicing it, and no good can come of *that*, Miss Fortune, you'll be the first to agree.'

'I didn't know we were so close to Northamptonshire,' Caroline said, again tempted to smile, yet troubled also by some fugitive memory.

'Very close,' he said solemnly, patting her hand, 'but don't fear: if they try to invade us, we shall hurl them back across the Ouse.'

'Mr Milner—I make one simple remark, and you turn madman!'

'Yes, Stephen,' Lady Milner said precisely, cutting across Caroline's laughter. 'Miss Fortune meant only that she is unacquainted with the local geography. Here we are at the meeting of the eastern and midland counties, Miss Fortune,' she went on instructively, 'and when Isabella becomes Mrs Richard Leabrook of Hethersett, she will become a resident of Northamptonshire, though only six miles away.'

'Yes,' Caroline said, faintly and mechanically. 'Yes, I see.'

Now, while Lady Milner continued with some dusty remarks about county boundaries, she must somehow contain her shock and dismay. Isabella's intended husband could be none other than the same Mr Leabrook whom Caroline had met at Brighton. The same Mr Leabrook who—while engaged to that gentle, trusting young woman at the other end of the table—had coolly attempted Caroline's seduction. Isabella was deceived in her estimate of Mr Leabrook's character.

'Now tell us, Caroline, what do you think of long engagements?' came Fanny's voice—not, just then, a welcome sound.

'I think there is something to be said for them,' she answered after a moment, 'because in an engagement, at least, one has a choice of duration: whereas all marriages are long—life-long.'

'Life-long—ah, thank the stars for it!' sighed Mr Hampson, gazing on his bride. 'Miss Milner, I wish you the same joy as I have found!'

So do I, thought Caroline. So do I, and yet I fear, I do fear, that with Richard Leabrook you won't find it.

Chapter Seven

AFTER A NIGHT of dragging torment, interrupted only by a doze in which the same harrying thoughts visited her as dreams, Caroline is sitting at her window, solaced only by the novelty of watching the sun rise. She has forced herself to go over every moment of her association with Richard Leabrook in order to make sure—to make doubly sure—that her own conduct was not at fault in that dismal episode.

What troubles Caroline the most is what angered her that night in Brighton: the fact that Mr Leabrook so little valued her as to treat her like a piece of disposable goods. That cold and calculating unconcern was detestable. And that, she realises, is why she cannot rest with the idea of Isabella marrying a man so insensible to the feelings of others.

Of course, not all her uneasiness is for Isabella. She is not saint enough to disregard her own plight—the awkwardness and unpleasantness of meeting Mr Leabrook again, the difficulties in which it may place her, and indeed the not knowing just how *he* will react in turn.

But then this is begging the question—the one unavoidable question that has kept her from sleep. Should I tell Isabella?

Imagination shrinks from the consequences, but they must surely be profound. Isabella's view of her fiancé must be transformed—Isabella, in all the joy and pride of her approaching nuptials, to be so knocked down! And what must be the effect on their friendship?

However, I must not let that be my first consideration. I must think what's best for Isabella. Yet even now, with the sun almost above the trees and the first stirrings audible in the kitchen downstairs, she is no nearer to deciding what that is. She only knows she cannot bear being imprisoned with her thoughts any longer. Snatching up her bonnet and pelisse, Caroline runs out of the house, and is soon striking out across the field-paths with the dew still spangling the turf.

Aunt Selina was surprised to see her niece coming in from a walk at such an early hour; and she had further occasion for surprise after breakfast, as Caroline actively sought all the dullest housekeeping tasks. Later in the day, when she had done all that could be done with storerooms, preserves, hemming and silver-polishing, Caroline was actually to be discovered in the parlour busily quilting: a sight so surprising that even Dr Langland was startled out of obtuseness, and asked if she was quite well.

What she sought in industry, of course, was distraction from the ceaseless turning of her mind. Fortunately there was no visit from Isabella today, which spared her the difficulty of keeping her countenance through the inevitable talk of Mr Leabrook. On the other hand, her absence must mean she was busy with wedding plans . . . Relief came at last with oblivion: the disturbed night and the busy day sending her drooping to an early bed.

Of course, there must be a waking, and so a return to her dilemma. But she found that, like a fever, this burden of indecision could be

414 | Jude Morgan

borne, simply because it had to be. She was even able to go on her usual walk with Isabella, and endure the discussion of the wedding. Still, the most difficult day of all was coming towards her: the day of Richard Leabrook's return.

First, however, there came a welcome distraction in the shape of the Hampsons' evening-party. Aunt Selina and Uncle John, feeling that the dinner at the Manor made them sufficient gadabouts for this month, chose not to go, but only on the assurance that this would not prevent Caroline, who was already invited, to accompany the Manor party. The Milners' carriage stopped accordingly at the Rectory gate.

The Old Grange was, as its name suggested, a venerable building of grey stone, in which it was possible to imagine a substantial farmer feasting his work-folk at a long oak table: until you got inside, when it became impossible to imagine anything of the kind. Mrs Hampson's fortune had gone towards a thorough refurbishing in the most modern style, and the eye was assaulted by a profusion of Chinese wallpapers, silk screens, Turkey rugs, chaise-longues and cheval-glasses. But neither was there any stinting in the welcome extended by their smiling hosts. There was a great fire, there was choice wine, there was a new pianoforte and an angular female relation to play it; and once the carpet was rolled back and the occasional tables shifted, there was room for six couples to dance as many country-dances as they liked, while a generous supper awaited in an adjoining parlour.

Caroline, being civilly handed by Mr Hampson to a sofa, enquired how the bridal portrait was coming on; and was rewarded not only with a full account of its progress, but with an introduction to the artist. This was a slightly built young man whose long crop of dark curling hair and large, brown, intense eyes gave him a little of a gypsy look. Mr Hampson, like a resourceful host, managed to recollect something about Caroline—that she came from London—and announcing the happy coincidence that Mr Charles Carraway had trained in London, left them to converse on the strength of it.

'For as long as I could,' Mr Carraway answered, when Caroline asked him if he had studied at the Royal Academy schools. 'I was brought up by an uncle—the kindest of guardians, but of limited means, who could sponsor me only so long. Then I spent some time in a sort of apprenticeship: painting foliage in the background of vast canvases. In truth none of this quite suited me, for I longed to paint from nature. So, I have struck out alone.'

'Have you returned to native ground in Huntingdonshire, sir?'

'I have connections here,' he said, with the vaguely smiling, dreaming look that seemed to descend periodically over him. 'And a commission for topographical views at Hinchingbrooke was offered which, in my position, I could scarcely refuse. But what I have found so entrancing in this part of the world is the skies. They are incomparable.'

'Skies, sir?' put in Fanny Milner, who now came briskly up with her usual lack of ceremony. 'We have *those* in this country, to be sure: but the pity is, that there is so little beneath them that is worth noticing.'

'Do you really find it so?' Mr Carraway answered. 'Tell me how.'

'Well.' Fanny for once was a little taken aback. 'Well, there is nothing very grand or exciting to be met: it is all narrow provincial dullness.'

Mr Carraway, with his dreamy smile, waved a hand. 'Dullness it is that perverts and corrupts the spirit—but it is always possible to look past the dullness, and see the bright, shining heart of things.'

'It may be so for you, sir,' Fanny said, 'but how I—'

'Please,' Mr Carraway said, leaping up from the sofa, and gracefully whisking Fanny down on to it. 'I'm not sure how to explain. I express myself poorly in words—poorly enough with the brush in truth, but—'

'Oh, you are the painter!' exclaimed Fanny. 'The one who is doing the Hampsons' portrait. Well, I am glad, very glad to see you here.'

'Are you?' he said quizzically.

'Yes, because it is very liberal of the Hampsons, for at most of the parties one goes to there is no one of an artistic sort to be found, because they are not drearily respectable enough—is that offensive? I assure you it isn't meant to be—quite the reverse!'

'Oh, the respectable world and I are on easy terms. I ignore it when I choose, and it does likewise with me. Life is shockingly short to trouble about such things. I don't know if there is such a word as unrespectability,' he said, with an engaging laugh. 'If not, I hereby create it.'

'I like the word. I like the thing, at any rate,' Fanny said, her eyes shining. 'There, but you have the artist's eye—'

'Everyone does. At least, everyone has something of the spirit that animates the artist.'

There was an uncommon vivacity in Mr Carraway's tone and expression, and, as he continued on, Fanny's glowing looks showed that she was much enthused by his ideas. It occurred to Caroline that she ought to make it known to Mr Carraway who his eager listener was. 'Well, Mr Carraway, this is Miss Fanny Milner, by the by,' she put in. 'Mr Charles Carraway. There. Now you have been *introduced*, you may begin talking.'

This was just the sort of jest to appeal to Fanny—not indeed that she saw it entirely as a jest. 'Exactly!' she cried. 'And there is that absurdity of dullness: that two human creatures cannot talk together without society first putting them on ceremony together, and making them uncomfortable. Oh, I mean no disrespect to you, Caroline—or the Hampsons' party—I have the greatest regard for the Hampsons. Tell me, Mr Carraway, do you need to *know* your subjects before you paint their portrait? That is, are you trying to capture their characters?'

Caroline felt free to leave her with an interlocutor so much to her taste, and go in search of claret-cup. Finding it, she found also Isabella.

'Now, my dear Caro,' she said, slipping her arm through Caroline's. 'I ought to be in a good temper today of all days, because—well, a note came from Hethersett this afternoon. Richard was just arrived home. Yes! I shall see him tomorrow.'

'Oh, you must be very happy.' Somehow Caroline's lips had spoken the words, and with a fair degree of conviction, while her heart drummed and her mind thrashed. She wondered if now was the time to say she had met him. She wondered if Isabella would talk to him of her new friend. If so, then he would be placed in a similar position to herself.

'I am very happy. And very warm—do you suppose there will be ice at the supper-table? Oh, look, they are beginning the dancing. My dear, are *you* feeling the heat? You look a little flushed. I have some aromatic vinegar, if that would help.'

'No, no. A drop more claret-cup will set me right. And now you, I think, are to be dancing.'

It was Captain Brunton who had come up and, with a civil if ungainly bow, invited Isabella to the dance. Unwelcome as the invitation might be, Caroline saw that Isabella was determined now not to be churlish, and so with equal civility her friend accepted, and walked on to the floor with the Captain. But there was another party present, Caroline noticed, who evinced no satisfaction at this development. Lady Milner watched with her most pale and peevish look. But Caroline had troubles of her own to dwell on just now; and seeing a stout, smiling beau preparing to walk over to her, she withdrew to an adjoining room, where a couple of card-tables were set out. Here she became aware of Stephen Milner, prowling with a book in his hand.

'Ah,' he said. 'You don't happen to have a knife about you, by any chance?' He held up the book: the pages were uncut.

'You can't come to Mr Hampson's party, and then settle down to reading his books.'

'No, I can't, because they are all like this.' He sighed. 'Which leaves me quite at a loss.'

'You do not dance, Mr Milner?'

'I do—once in an evening. When I dance, though, I must talk all the time. Otherwise I begin thinking about how absurd dancing is. Well: do you want to go through the ghastly motions with me, Miss Fortune?'

'How can I refuse such a charming invitation?'

Caroline found that Stephen Milner danced quite creditably for a man who hated dancing. She, on the other hand, loved it: but her spirits were still damped by Isabella's news, which she could not help alluding to.

'So the famous Mr Leabrook is home, I hear.'

'Aye, for a mercy: we may as well get the precious pair spliced, and then perhaps I can take off again. A correspondent in Chichester writes me of some delicious Roman remains, and I'm sorely tempted. But perhaps I won't go just yet. I want to be here to see my prophecy fulfilled.'

'Prophecy?'

'About you, Miss Fortune—about you being trouble. Oh, by the by, who is that young fellow arguing with Fanny?'

'That is Mr Carraway, the artist, and I doubt they are arguing: she seemed very much struck with him.'

'Ah, that explains it: Fanny always seems to be arguing when she's excited. Dear, dear, and he does look as if he finds the world endlessly fascinating: what a bore. I shall have to play the stern elder brother and be introduced to him later. And what is the matter with Augusta?'

Lady Milner was not dancing; she was seated, as ever, by the fire, and Captain Brunton was standing by her chair: he high-shouldered and discomfited, she grimly silent. If there really was a lover-like relation between them, Caroline thought, then she was an exacting mistress.

'What a damned plaguey set we are,' Stephen continued. 'You know, Miss Fortune, you needn't fear that Isabella will drop you now that her beau is back.'

'What makes you say that?'

'Why, it's the way girls are, isn't it? They swear eternal friendship, and then as soon as a man's in the case it's all forgotten. But Isabella is different: she is very loyal and steadfast in her feelings.'

All too convincing as this was as a portrait of Isabella, it did not make Caroline feel any better. 'Every time I am deluded into thinking you human, Mr Milner,' she told him sweetly, 'you come out and say something to confirm my earlier opinion. "The way girls are", indeed: I never heard anything so arrogant and conceited.'

His enjoyment of this exchange was so great that it seemed to last him till the end of the dance, at which he made his bow, and took himself off, as he had suggested, to meet Mr Carraway. It was like him to ignore the convention of handing his partner back to her seat; but she was surprised to find Captain Brunton suddenly at her elbow, and performing the office. She thanked him, and hinted that she must not detain him: her glance straying to Lady Milner; but he, after a polite request for permission, sat down by her as if disposed to conversation. However, as he seemed more ready to frown than talk, she made a beginning, asking him if he saw any prospect of going to sea again.

'As a Navy man, Miss Fortune, no—candidly, no, though it goes hard with me to say it. I think to apply to the East Coast Revenue Service, as soon as I—well, as soon as may be,' All at once he squared his shoulders, and addressed her in his gruffest manner. 'You must suppose me a dilatory fellow.'

'I do not hold you to be a dilatory fellow, sir. And if I did, I should like to know what right I had to make such a judgement.'

'You are very good. It's—it's odd: I can talk with you.'

Privately Caroline thought that if this was Captain Brunton's articulacy, she would hate to see him tongue-tied.

'The thing is this. When I say I mean to apply to the Revenue Service, I do mean it. I would willingly be gone in a moment. But one hesitates to open a new chapter, as it were—'

'When the old one is not resolved?'

'Exactly so.' He smiled again. 'Curious creatures we mortals are—how we do not know what we want, or how to get it if we do.'

'There is probably some wonderful folk wisdom on that subject.'

'To be sure. Never—never tread upon a weasel on a Thursday, or something like that.'

Caroline laughed. Her opinion of Captain Brunton was altered: she detected sincerity and warmth; and she was satisfied also that she understood his cryptic confidences about what kept him at Wythorpe.

'But I have wearied you, talking about myself. What do you think of the Grange—a handsome old building, is it not?'

Caroline agreed that it was, in some surprise: for in the first place, she had asked him about himself, and in the second, most men could talk about themselves for several hours before it occurred to them that the subject might lack variety. Besides, she thought, he had not really been talking about himself: he had been talking about Lady Milner.

Well, there could only be two results. Either Lady Milner sought only the consolation of a tame suitor forever dancing attendance, or else Captain Brunton would win her. Neither would be greatly appealing to Isabella—but then that, Caroline reminded herself ruefully as she stepped into the Milners' carriage that night and looked at her friend's profile, did not matter now: because Richard Leabrook was returned, to make everything right. She was not to be spared further reflections on the dreaded event, for Fanny was full of Mr Charles Carraway and his art, and was soon urging her sister to do something to advance them.

'What you have not considered, Fanny, is that you have not seen any of Mr Carraway's work,' Lady Milner said, with her customary severity.

'I can tell Mr Carraway's art, from his character,' said Fanny, loftily, 'and that is spirited, natural, forceful, and earnest. And before, Augusta, you fall into any suppositions about my having a *taking* for him, I will say we find much to talk about. I hope two rational creatures may do that, even in Wythorpe, without petty minds fancying an engagement.'

'Then that is very well,' returned Lady Milner, 'for an engagement to a travelling painter, without family or prospects, is not something that could be seriously considered for the daughter of Sir Henry Milner.'

Caroline's first thought on waking the next morning was that Mr Richard Leabrook would be at the Manor today: her second, that she would not go anywhere near it. But she had reckoned without Aunt Selina, who declared after breakfast that she would walk over to the Manor, to give Lady Milner the recipe for orange wine she had been asking about, and who anticipated that Caroline would go with her.

Turning out of Rectory Lane into the High Street, Caroline did experience a moment of pure curiosity—about what it would be like to see Mr Leabrook again, and how he would react. However, a moment later her every thought and feeling was thrown into disarray by the sound of a horse's hoofs, and by her turning to behold Mr Richard Leabrook, coming up behind them, mounted on a fine bay.

Aunt Selina, turning too, called out a cordial greeting. Mr Leabrook reined in, doffed his hat—and saw Caroline's face.

'Mr Leabrook. We heard you were returned to us. Will you allow me to introduce my niece, Miss Caroline Fortune? She has come to live with us at the Rectory. My dear, Mr Leabrook, of whom you have heard tell.'

For an instant, as he gazed upon Caroline, Mr Leabrook's handsome face wore a fleeting expression that might have been fear; and then, with the self-command that she remembered, he gathered himself.

'How do you do?' he said, and then: 'I trust, ma'am, I find you and Dr Langland well.'

So, he was not to acknowledge her. While Aunt Selina replied, all Caroline's anxieties and misgivings were swept aside by a sudden wave of anger. She had a vivid memory of the last time he had come to Mrs Catling's house, when he had coolly contrived to treat Caroline as if she did not exist. Now here he was, aloof and sleek as his thoroughbred mount, doing the same again.

'In fact, Aunt, Mr Leabrook and I have met before. At Brighton,' Caroline pursued. 'Do you recall, sir?'

'Ah. I believe so, yes.' As Aunt Selina looked at her in surprise, Mr Leabrook inclined his head a little: then, responding to a very slight shake of the bridle, he said in a regretful tone: 'This horse of mine never will wait. You are going on to the Manor, I take it? I shall have the honour of seeing you there anon. Mrs Langland: Miss Fortune.'

Horse and rider went elegantly on their way; and Aunt Selina remarked, with a slight smile of approbation: 'He is in a hurry to see Isabella, no doubt. But, my dear, fancy you knowing Mr Leabrook!'

'Knowing only slightly. Mrs Catling kept so much company there— one met everybody.'

Her aunt appeared satisfied with this; but Caroline could find no equivalent satisfaction in their meeting. Seeing him again had reminded her of how much reason she had to dislike and mistrust him. She could not even feel the relief of having got the meeting over with, as it must in a sense be gone through once more when they arrived at the house.

There they found all the family gathered in the drawing room: Mr Leabrook attentively seated next to Isabella, who was pink with plea- sure. She put out her hand warmly to Caroline, crying: 'Oh, Caro, I have looked forward to this moment—now I can introduce you—'

'Ah, I was going to say, my dear,' Mr Leabrook put in smiling, 'Miss Fortune and I were reacquainted in the lane just now. Reacquainted, yes: we happened to meet when I was at Brighton in the summer.'

'Really? My dear, fancy not saying you already knew Mr Leabrook.'

'Oh, I have absolutely no memory for names,' Caroline said, with a wave of her hand, 'that was why. But when I saw Mr Leabrook's face— why, *then* I remembered.'

A short bow was all the response he gave to this; soon he was being loaded with enquiries about the relations he had been visiting, about his mother's health, about the state of the harvest at Hethersett, and so on. Fanny also was not slow in telling him of Mr Carraway, and press- ing the painter's talents on his attention.

At length, however, the claims of engagement were acknowledged, and Mr Leabrook and Isabella went out to walk in the gardens. Caroline, feeling unequal to conversation, was grateful for the talkative Fanny.

'There—I knew there was something else—I was going to scold Richard about giving a ball at Hethersett. We *must* have one soon, else I shall perish. Besides, Hethersett is very much a place worth seeing, and Caroline has not seen it yet. Caroline, you must back me up,' Fanny insisted. 'He cannot resist us both.'

'Miss Fortune does not seem to share your eagerness, Fanny,' said Stephen Milner, infuriatingly, as Caroline hesitated. 'You needn't fear, I shall be quite happy to favour you again with my one dance, Miss Fortune. I'm generous like that.'

'I'm overpowered by your liberality, Mr Milner, but I must insist that you grant the favour to some other fortunate girl next time. The unforgettable experience of performing a cotillion with a dancing bear is not one I would wish to arrogate entirely to myself.'

She had meant only to answer him in kind, but it came out, to her own ears at least, quite acid; Lady Milner forgot to primp long enough to look surprised, and Stephen's eye fell on her more ironically than ever. I am betraying myself, she thought: I must be natural; but it was hard, especially when she had just caught a glimpse, through the window, of Isabella and Mr Leabrook walking arm-in-arm across the sunlit lawn. And though she was soon granted the relief of the visit coming to an end, worse was to follow, for Stephen himself invited the Rectory family to come back and dine with them later.

Again there was no possibility of escape without drawing to herself exactly the kind of attention she sought to evade. Indeed, Caroline found herself that evening seated only two places away from Mr Leabrook, so that he was able to turn to her and say: 'Miss Fortune, I am informed you have suffered a signal loss: pray accept my commiserations: and my sincere hope that you find yourself happily settled with your aunt.'

It was said with perfect correctness: obviously Isabella had talked to him, freely and innocently, of her friend's history, and he was making the appropriate response; and only the blankness of his eyes, while his lips pronounced these words, revealed his true feeling. Caroline thanked him in the same mechanical way. Here was the summit of awkwardness and unreality; she felt it acutely, and was sure he must too.

Fanny soon returned to the attack about a ball at Hethersett, in spite of her stepmother's reproofs; but Mr Leabrook was quite amenable. 'An excellent notion,' he said. 'I have some company coming up from London at the end of next week, and I was a little concerned for their entertainment. I wonder when the moon will be at the full—'

'Thursday sennight, sir,' put in Captain Brunton.

'Ah? I'm obliged to you—then Thursday sennight it shall be. Does that meet with your approval, Miss Fanny?'

'That is just the sort of decisiveness I like,' Fanny said, 'and now all that remains is for me to badger you about Mr Carraway once again.'

'No need: Mr Carraway may certainly come to the ball: I shall be happy to meet him. Beyond that, Miss Fanny, I make no promises.'

'Hey, well, at least you have no qualms about inviting a mere painter to a reception. Augusta thinks he must be quite below the salt, you know.'

'Fanny, you misrepresent me,' her stepmother intoned. 'I remarked only that, without independent means, the young man's place in society must be an insecure one.'

'Tell me now, Mr Leabrook, how is your sister—Georgiana, isn't it? Is she still at school?' asked Aunt Selina.

'She does very well, Mrs Langland, I thank you—knows her own mind wonderfully. She continues at school for another year.'

'The school is at Brighton, is it not?' Aunt Selina went on. 'Where you and Caroline met, of course.'

'At Brighton,' Mr Leabrook said. 'Just so.'

'And then she came to us,' Aunt Selina said brightly and fondly. 'It's almost like fate, is it not? If one believed in such pagan notions.'

Stephen, who had been gazing into his wine-glass, suddenly stirred and said: 'Talking of pagan notions, and matrimonial choices, there are many places in the world now, just as in antiquity, where bride and groom never set eyes on each other before the wedding day. And yet they go along famously.'

'I do not see how they can,' cried Fanny. 'It is monstrous.'

'Oh, it is because, since they bring no expectations to the match, there is no risk of disappointment.'

'Come, Milner, ' Mr Leabrook said, laughing. 'If you would have us adopt barbarian customs, there's a prime one for you: what say you to polygamous practices—multiple wives, like your Turk with his harem?'

'A deplorable custom,' Dr Langland said heatedly.

'But a custom, Uncle John, that would be eagerly embraced by the average Englishman,' Caroline said, to a general murmur. 'Oh, I think it would, you know—for there are so many who do not appreciate what they have and, like greedy little boys, would grab another sweetmeat even while they clutch one in their hands.'

Isabella, laughing, appealed to her fiancé: 'Oh, this is shocking—come, Richard, you must defend your sex.'

Mr Leabrook shook his head. 'To do so would be to contradict a lady,' he said, in his softest accents, 'who must, I presume, have grounds for this peculiar knowledge.'

'Ask Stephen,' Fanny said. 'He could find a defence for the devil.'

'Thank you, Fanny, but this time I must disappoint you, because I happen to believe that what Miss Fortune says is entirely true.'

'About men with many wives?' cried Isabella. 'But, Stephen, you don't even want one!'

'True: but that is because I admit that what I *would* want from a wife is an impossibility. This fantastical creature would not mind any of my follies and inconsistencies—she would be my warmest friend—she would drink too much wine with me—laugh at society instead of courting it—never talk in the morning until at least half past ten—happily stay indoors for days, and then on a whim go a journey of twenty miles—and all this time remain naturally elegant, clever, and good-tempered.'

'My dear nephew,' Aunt Selina said, smiling, 'I think you would as soon find a mermaid.'

'Well, Milner, having found my own mermaid, I can only wish you the same luck in your fishing as I have had,' Mr Leabrook said.

'Thank you, Leabrook—that is, if I ever should decide to *go* fishing.'

'What is this?' cried Dr Langland, in bewilderment. 'Never go fishing? But I have seen you do so, Stephen, down at the Staunch . . .'

Aunt Selina having patiently explained that the fishing was metaphorical, a proceeding that lasted through the taking away of the first course and the laying of the second, Dr Langland at last gave a hoot of understanding. 'Ah. The subject of the metaphor is courtship. But come! This determination against matrimony will never do. We must throw temptation in your way. Now if some creditable person were to hold a ball, with a good deal of company—I beg your pardon? You are, Mr Leabrook? Lord, I had no idea. Well, then there is our opportunity.'

'Uncle John, if you absolutely insist on matchmaking for me, then I cannot prevent you,' Stephen pronounced firmly, 'but I would urge you to take up some easier pursuit, such as catching moonbeams in a net.'

Chapter Eight

INVITATIONS TO THE BALL at Mr Leabrook's house were quickly accepted in a neighbourhood not over-supplied with such entertainments at this season; and now there was nothing to do but prepare in happy anticipation—or, in Caroline's case, to dread.

Mr Leabrook, in the flush of hospitality, talked of the whole Wythorpe party sleeping overnight at Hethersett as his guests, so they need not leave the ball so early to ride home; and the whole Wythorpe party must mean both Manor and Rectory families. But fortunately Lady Milner expressed doubt about the propriety of Isabella staying under the same roof as her fiancé before the marriage; and Isabella herself raised the more practical question of how so many people were to be accommodated at Hethersett, when Mr Leabrook already had company staying for that week. So Caroline was thankful to find that idea dropped—though it did raise another idea that had been plucking at her, and which at last she had confirmed by Isabella: just who were these people from London that Mr Leabrook had to stay?

'A young couple named Downey. He invited them to come and see him a good while ago, when he was at Brighton, I believe. Oh, Caro, perhaps you know them too, then, from that time?'

Caroline struggled a moment, then said: 'Yes—certainly, they are agreeable people from what I know of them. They are not a couple, by the by, but brother and sister—relatives of my late employer.'

So, the company from London was none other than Matthew and Maria! Only now did she remember that invitation Mr Leabrook had urged upon them at Brighton. It was another jolt of surprise in the placid surface of her new life. The Downeys, when they met her again, were likely to reminisce, and such talk must reveal that Caroline had known Mr Leabrook much better than her casual references to their acquaintance would suggest.

In the meantime preparations for the wedding went on apace. It was now fixed for Christmas, and everyone agreed there could not be a nicer season for it. 'Aye, nothing could be more apt,' Stephen commented, 'as Christmas is really a pagan midwinter festival, when you always sacrificed a maiden or two.'

The evening of the ball was fine and dry, and the carriage drive to Mr Leabrook's house took them into an appreciably different sort of country, rolling and well wooded. Hethersett itself came splendidly into view on a ridge of high ground above a negligible village—a proper turreted Tudor mansion, much improved, but retaining such satisfactorily picturesque elements as a crenellated roof, mullioned windows, and a lodge-gate giving admittance to the park.

Menservants were at once on hand at the house to see to the stabling, maidservants whisked away their wraps in the galleried hall, and a hundred candles welcomed them to the ballroom, where a score of people were already gathered. The Manor party had followed directly after their own carriage—this as a further insurance for Aunt Selina, who could console herself that if they went into the ditch, their friends behind might effect a rescue—and it was with looks divided between bashfulness and pride that Isabella took the arm of their host, whose fine figure showed at its most elegant in a narrow-waisted coat.

'This has been all new fitted-out, I believe,' Aunt Selina said, whispering in admiration. 'Just look at that ornamented ceiling!'

There was no music yet from the quartet of musicians tuning up at the far end of the long, panelled room: the evening was at the standing-about stage, in which dresses were scrutinised, introductions offered, insincerities exchanged, and alliances and enmities silently plotted. Caroline, looking about at the spaciousness, the card room with tables ready, the company swiftly growing in number and noise, began to feel that the evening might not be so difficult after all: it was on such a large scale that one might easily melt unnoticed into the background.

'Caroline Fortune! It really is you!' a voice cried across the length of the ballroom. 'I thought Mr Leabrook was funning when he said you were here. Lord!'

Maria Downey's tone was unusually animated, though it was with the old feline languor that she made her way across the room.

'Miss Downey. I heard you were coming to stay. It—it is all a great surprise, is it not?'

'Great? My dear, I'm positively overpowered with it, and you know it takes a great deal to rouse me to any emotion. But pray tell, what is the story? Mr Leabrook says you have family hereabouts.'

'So I do: my mother's family. I am living with my aunt, who is the kindest and best—but first I had better hear what story your aunt has told, about how we came to part.'

'Oh, an absolutely unfair one, no doubt, knowing Aunt Sophia. She informed us that her companion, having lost her father, had become quite ungovernable in temper, and so there was no choice but to dispense with her services.'

'I see,' said Caroline, unmoved, and pleased to find herself so. 'Well, Miss Downey, with no disrespect to you, I must tell you I do not at all care what Mrs Catling thinks or says about me. I feel able to say this, because I understood that was your position also.'

'So it was,' Maria said, with a pretty yawn and a distant look; and then, shaking herself, 'So it is, my dear. Though I must tell you, or at least I don't have to but I may as well, that my own independence of Aunt Sophia now stands upon shakier ground. You remember I told you of my rich overseas gentleman? Alas, a letter has reached me across those unthinkable seas, which gives me to understand that he must linger longer under the tropic sun, and I am not to look for his return. In short, my dear, I am jilted! Is it not inconvenient?'

'Something worse than that, I would say,' Caroline answered. 'Though I do not know how deeply your feelings—'

'They were not deeply anything, my dear, thank heaven, but it is a great nuisance nonetheless. But what you say about Aunt Sophia is absolutely right, of course. Truth to tell, when we came away from Brighton I remember thinking, I doubt that poor girl will last a month—not because you didn't handle her well, my dear, but simply because there is no pleasing her. Well, I'm glad it has all turned out for the best anyhow. That angelic being on Mr Leabrook's arm must be his future bride, I think?'

'Isabella. Yes, she—he is a very lucky man.'

'And they smile at each other, and seem fond of each other, and everything! I must look about me. Let's see, who is that long-legged man who took himself off—the one with the provokingly sleepy eyes?'

'Oh! That's Stephen—Mr Stephen Milner, that is. Isabella's brother. You would have to work very hard to captivate that gentleman.'

'Better and better—I enjoy a challenge. My dear, I must go and get my introduction to the future Mrs Leabrook, and then perhaps I can secure one with her brother.' A lazy laugh followed the end of the sentence as Maria's elegant form rippled away.

Left alone, Caroline took the opportunity of bracing herself with wine before Isabella came upon her, and bore her off to make an introduction. This was to a lady seated in throne-like state on a sofa before the fire, who seemed to be receiving a file of visitors. She was Mr Leabrook's mother, as might have been surmised from the aquiline good looks; and she was not at all intimidating, Isabella confided in Caroline's ear. This Caroline found, in the course of a short interview, to be true: for to intimidate, one must be aware of the victim, and Mrs Leabrook would have talked on about her dovecotes if you had fallen at her feet in a faint.

Caroline was able to step away at last, knowing that, as Isabella had said, there would be nothing for her to fear from Mrs Leabrook. Indeed, everything appeared set fair for this marriage—with the single exception of Caroline's dark knowledge; and that began to seem more like some deceptive dream as the rooms filled with guests and Mr Richard Leabrook, welcoming and welcomed, moving genially among them.

'I know,' said Fanny, appearing beside Caroline, and nodding towards the figure of their host, 'I often look at him too, and think how splendid that Bella is going to be married to him. I have already introduced him to Mr Carraway—and he is most interested, as I thought, in patronising an artist of such promise—and in short he could hardly be better, considering he is getting towards the age of thirty, when really not much is to be expected from people. At least, not in this dismal country—London I dare say is different, people are surely not so staid and fudgy there. Charles has lived in London—Mr Carraway, I should say—oh, but I needn't trouble about that with *you*, need I?'

'Well, I am not about to reprimand you for calling a young man by his first name. I have never quite seen why it is considered so shocking.'

'Exactly! If only everyone thought like you. Just as the world makes a great fuss if a woman and a man who are not engaged or married write each other letters. Is this not the most absurdly repressive convention?'

'I confess I do not see the harm in it,' Caroline answered honestly: though with a faint suspicion that what she was agreeing to was not a general proposition, but something rather more specific—a suspicion that deepened as she saw the burning look Fanny bestowed on the figure of Charles Carraway, who was paying his respects to his hostess.

'Do you know? I have sometimes felt I would go *mad* for the lack of someone to confide in,' Fanny said. 'Bella is dear, and sympathetic, but rather conventional. Whereas you—I feel I could say anything to you, and you would understand and not judge!'

'My dear Fanny, there are limits.' Caroline spoke lightly, but with purpose also—for she was burdened with quite enough secrets.

And here came the donor of one of them now: Matthew Downey.

'Miss Fortune, is this not remarkable? How do you do—really there was never anything so remarkable . . .' Matthew went on remarking on the remarkableness for so long that Fanny, who was in any case itching to rejoin Mr Carraway, made an escape.

'And so you have actually discovered a long-lost family—quite a delightful and romantic notion: and I who have known what it is to have a family's love, Miss Fortune, can certainly rejoice for you in that.'

'Thank you,' Caroline said peaceably. 'I'm very happily situated now. But how do things fare with you, Mr Downey? There was a lady whose name begins with P whom you used to tell me of: she is well, I hope?'

'Of course, you must often have thought of that,' he said, beaming. 'She is well—yes, I thank you, and even bears up under the strain of this intolerable secrecy. I regret to tell you, Miss Fortune, that greatly as I esteem her, there is no denying that Aunt Sophia's temper is more exacting. I do wish, you know, that she had not been forced to dismiss you, Miss Fortune—it was a thousand pities for everyone!'

'Mr Downey, it might be truer to say that I was *forced* to leave,' Caroline said. 'My father had died, I wished to go to his funeral, and she would have prevented me.'

Matthew shook his head. 'Well, I think it a great shame—and yes, I must say it, you have made matters more difficult for *me*.'

'Mr Downey, this is doing it a little too brown,' she said, with warmth, remembering the effort she had put into pleading his cause with his aunt. 'I had and have nothing but cordial feelings towards you, but I insist that you at least consider the novel notion that not everyone thinks exclusively about you all the time.'

Matthew shook his head again, more sadly: she remembered that he had, to put it lightly, never been one for irony. 'I think you are still feeling your loss, Miss Fortune, and that is why you are not yourself. After all, it was a position from which you might have had hopes—hopes that, if I could not approve, I could certainly understand.'

'Mr Downey,' Caroline said, finding her breath, 'Mrs Catling occupies, quite naturally, such a central place in your life that you assume it is the same with others. I assure you it is not. And if you and I are to meet without arguing—which I would much prefer—then she is a subject probably best avoided between us.'

'Very well.' Matthew gave her a hurt, wistful, nobly forbearing, look. 'And yet, you know, I had thought you friendly to me, Miss Fortune. I would never have entrusted you with my secret otherwise. And the way you speak of my aunt, an estimable lady for all her foibles, and who was so good to you—really I am baffled.'

Caroline gave a laugh—a short and vexed laugh, but the best she could manage. 'Clearly, Mr Downey, we are *not* avoiding the subject. Now the dancing is beginning, so let us exit severally and perhaps when we meet again we shall rub along better.'

Couples were forming up. Caroline knew well that Stephen Milner had only been joking when he talked of having his one dance with her again, but someone who did appear to ask her to dance was Captain Brunton. As they joined the set, she began to wonder, was he, in fact, if not out of love with Lady Milner, then a little in love with herself?

It was not a happy thought, for her regard for him, increased though it was, did not extend to reciprocation: but no sooner had she entertained it than she began to doubt it. He was more abstracted than attentive, and where his grey glance did fall was on Mr Leabrook and Isabella. At last Caroline made a remark about Mr Leabrook's having laid on a splendid entertainment, and Captain Brunton burst out: 'So he might—he is secure in a felicity such as I can never aspire to.' Then he subsided into such a stiff-jawed silence that Caroline received a pitying look from Fanny, who was dancing with Mr Carraway.

Caroline did not lack for partners in the succeeding dances, but then, in order to escape the attentions of one drunk gentleman, she withdrew to the card room. It turned out to be a mortifying mistake, for Richard Leabrook, unengaged, had just stepped in there likewise; and Dr Langland, who was seating Aunt Selina at her customary game of piquet, bore down on them with all his blundering benevolence.

'This will never do—my dear Caroline, my dear Mr Leabrook, you are neither of you an old ruin like me, to be lurking about in card rooms when the sound of a country-dance calls—that is a Boulanger if I am not mistaken, and just the thing for two such elegant dancers as I know you to be. Let us see you tread the measure . . .'

There was no help for it. Soon they were being thrust onto the floor, where with the coldest of bows, and the briefest of curtseys, Caroline and Mr Leabrook faced each other.

'You have seen our mutual acquaintances, the Downeys, I think,' Mr Leabrook said at last, with colourless correctness.

'Yes. They are well, I believe.'

'You know, Miss Fortune, as we have been thrown together in this unexpected way, with no help for it, I think we ought to try at least to be civil with one another,' he said, all honeyed reason. 'You have formed a friendship with Isabella, I find. Surely for her sake at least you would not wish to cause unpleasantness.'

'Certainly I would not. But you chiefly want me to behave myself, Mr Leabrook, for your *own* sake, not for Isabella's. You want me to save your skin, which is a different matter.'

'If that is in the nature of a threat, Miss Fortune, I may as well say that Isabella trusts me implicitly.'

'I do not mean any threat, Mr Leabrook: if I were to speak, don't you think I would have done so before? I care only about Isabella.'

'I must say you make very free with my fiancée's name, when you have only a few weeks' acquaintance. I would remind you that she and I have known each other much longer.'

'I query whether she has *known* you at all, sir. I wish to do nothing, Mr Leabrook, except to warn you that I will not see Isabella's happiness threatened. And now, lest people think we are being too serious, we had better talk about the weather till the end of the set.'

It had been an agitating exchange, and as they parted she withdrew from the ballroom and looked about for some retreat other than the card room, which had proved so disastrous. Or had it? She had at least told him plainly enough where they stood.

Caroline opened a door at random, and found herself in a handsome library—but not, alas, alone.

'Now this is a real library,' Stephen said, stepping from behind a bookcase. 'The books have plainly been read. Though I think it was Leabrook's father who was the collector. This is an original Urquhart Rabelais, marvellous thing. You are unhappy, Miss Fortune.'

Caroline turned hastily away. 'Indeed I am not,' she said, in a voice so full of tears she might as well have howled it.

'Is it to do with the general unsatisfactoriness of life,' he asked, balancing the book on his nose, 'which it is best, by the by, to ignore?'

'Why? I mean, supposing it were—if it were in your power, Mr Milner, would you help me?'

'I might at that,' Stephen said, replacing the book on the shelf, 'because when you're low like this, there's no fun in arguing.'

Caroline was silent as she considered a whole clutch of paradoxes. Stephen Milner, with his independence of mind, his disinclination to rush to moral judgement, would surely be the one to help her. And yet the absurd thing was, she did shrink from confiding in him. I do not wish to be sunk in his estimation, she admitted to herself. And I know it makes no sense when I did nothing wrong, but I cannot help it.

'I'm a little hot and tired, that's all,' she told him.

'Well! that's a relief, at any rate,' he said, after studying her—she had her back to him, but she could feel it. 'It means you have been dancing. I was rather afraid *my* absence might desolate you so much you would remain a tragic wallflower all evening. Oh, look, Byron—and Scott and Moore—these must be Leabrook's additions. As is that chimney-piece, I fancy. Fanny has been plaguing me to do the same to the Manor. Stucco and a Chinese room and a grotto, you know.' He peered gloomily into a folio of maps. 'I always think Brazil is too big.'

'Oh, Mr Milner, don't,' she cried. He looked up in surprise. Again she didn't know why, but the thought of the Manor being remodelled in the grand Hethersett fashion distressed her. 'I mean—your house has a good deal of character as it is.'

'Do you think so?' He smiled. 'I confess I'm fond of the old place, though when I was a young pup I thought it the dullest box in creation and could hardly wait to leave it. We always think we know what we want: when in truth there is nothing we are less likely to know. There, I make you a present of that piece of wisdom, Miss Fortune.'

'Well, I certainly wouldn't pay for it.'

He grinned. 'Ah, you are looking better already. I shall vex you back into good humour before I'm done. Would you say we are related?'

'No—or only in the loosest sense—but I'm trying to think what this question is going to lead to.'

'Well, you are my aunt Selina's niece, on her side, and I am your uncle John's nephew, on his side, so I suppose we are not really relatives. A true relation would allow us to be Stephen and Caroline to one another, instead of Mr Milner and Miss Fortune. Think how much more naturally and freely we could quarrel if we were on those terms.'

'Oh, do be serious!'

Quite gently he said: 'I am trying to be.'

But whether this were so, she was not to know—as at that moment Mr Leabrook himself came in.

'Ah!' he said, his gaze just skimming over Caroline, his smile unfaltering. 'Dwellers in the abode of peace. I'm afraid I come as a destroyer, though: Isabella has commissioned me to find her scapegrace brother—sorry, Milner, her words—and make him join the dancing.'

'Oh Lord, must I? In a minute then. Only when there are no damnable fiddling quadrilles.'

Caroline, meanwhile, was already on her way to the door: she had had enough of Richard Leabrook's proximity for one night; and so quick was she that she hardly noticed the look, alert, hard and speculative, with which Stephen observed her rapid exit.

'**N**ow, my dear girl, are you content?' Isabella said, taking Caroline's arm as the bell was rung for supper. 'You know I simply can't be happy unless everyone else is. Oh well. The person I am concerned for is Captain Brunton. I don't like to see him looking so mumpish. What can it be, do you suppose? Has he quarrelled with my stepmother?'

'I think it may be a love-trouble,' Caroline answered carefully, 'but I'm not sure of what sort. And I dare say the sight of Mr Leabrook's house has put him in mind of his own situation, which is so different.'

'I never thought of that,' Isabella said. 'But then he has been a naval captain in the war; he can surely hold his head up in any company.'

'Perhaps you should tell him so—in a subtle way.'

'Perhaps so. You are a thoughtful creature, Caroline Fortune.'

'Oh Lord, not I.' Caroline laughed, feeling uncomfortable—and then feeling more so when Matthew Downey appeared, and offered her his arm to go in to supper.

'You'll forgive me, Miss Milner,' he said, 'but I know my friend Leabrook will claim his exclusive right to *your* arm—and as for me, I claim the rights of old acquaintance. Now then,' he went on cheerfully as Caroline, seeing no way of refusal, took his arm, 'is this not wonderfully reminiscent of the old days in Brighton, Miss Fortune?'

'Uncannily like.'

Caroline saw Stephen and Mr Leabrook approaching, and wished they had been a little quicker.

'You see, I have been thinking,' Matthew confided, 'and as you no doubt perceive, I have decided to disregard our earlier conversation. I find I can always forgive where I understand: and I understand, Miss Fortune, that you were *hurt* by my aunt's dismissal of you. But I think it not impossible that Aunt Sophia might be brought to acknowledge you again; at least as an acquaintance. What do you think of that?'

As it was not possible to tell Matthew what she thought without resorting to the vocabulary of the barrack-room, Caroline only said: 'I do not look for such an honour, Mr Downey.'

'Well, I might put in a word . . . Ah, Leabrook, I was just saying to Miss Fortune how like old times this is. Do you remember when we all danced at the Castle? Maria, do you remember?'

Miss Downey, who had positioned herself at Stephen's elbow, yawned and said: 'I make it a rule never to remember anything before last week. It makes life more interesting, wouldn't you say, Mr Milner?'

'Now I am supposed to ask you how,' he said, yawning back, 'so consider it done, Miss Downey.'

'You cross creature! Because, sir, you can greet even the dullest acquaintance with pleasure, if you have forgotten the dreary story they told you last Monday.'

'You must remember, Leabrook,' Matthew pursued, 'because it was the very next day you took yourself off. I never did understand why you were in such a peculiar hurry.'

'Lord, what a memory you have, Downey,' Mr Leabrook said, laughing. 'I fear mine is a sieve like your sister's. Well, shall we go in?'

'Do you know Brighton, Mr Milner?' Maria enquired, insinuating herself onto his arm.

'It's a town in Sussex, Miss Downey,' Stephen said. Caroline suppressed a smile: Maria certainly had her work cut out.

At their supper-table they were joined by Lady Milner and Captain Brunton and then, breathless and flushed, Fanny and Mr Carraway.

'Outside!' Fanny cried in answer to her stepmother's wishing to know where she had been. 'To look at the stars! We were not alone, heaven forfend, we went to the stables to consult with your groom, Richard—old Mr Blades. He has a true countryman's knowledge, you see. We were wondering how the weather would be tomorrow, when Mr Leabrook has promised us a *fête* out of doors, and I said we must consult a man of nature. Mr Blades took a view of the stars and declared that tomorrow will be fine and bright.'

'Well, if Blades is right, a picnic it shall be,' Mr Leabrook said.

'Oh, Richard, surely it will still be too cold for sitting down outdoors,' Isabella reproached him. 'We haven't all your constitution.'

'Perhaps you're right,' Mr Leabrook said equably. 'Well, we may certainly take a turn about the park, even if we do not eat outdoors. Mr Carraway, I shall be interested to learn what you think of the improvements. It was an associate of Repton's who did the designing. Lady Milner, you have an eye for such things, I judge—you will join our party tomorrow, will you not? And you, of course, Captain Brunton—'

'I beg your pardon, sir,' Captain Brunton said, in a bristling manner, sitting bolt upright, 'why do you say "of course"? It happens, sir, that I have other business tomorrow.'

'Edward! What can you mean?' Lady Milner cried in surprise.

'It's a small matter,' Captain Brunton said, 'not worth the mentioning.'

'Then it can surely be put aside, to take up Mr Leabrook's invitation,' said Lady Milner, with a look half beseeching, half peevish.

'Of course, if you wish me to come, Augusta, then—'

'Oh, please, sir, don't inconvenience yourself,' Mr Leabrook said.

'Welcome to the country, Miss Downey,' Stephen said to Maria, 'where people actually argue themselves out of their pleasures. Puritan strain, you know. Cromwell was from hereabouts.'

'Was he really?' Miss Downey said. 'How very curious!'

'The country is where I always feel most reflective,' Matthew said. 'But that would not do all the time—not for me. Now Brighton, Mr Milner, you would like it greatly—it is the liveliest of watering-places.'

'Brighton, no thank you,' Stephen said. 'I have been there—all bright and smart and sticky like new gingerbread.'

'You droll creature,' Maria said, tapping his arm, 'yet it is plain you know London pretty well.'

'To be sure he does, but he won't take *me* there,' burst out Fanny.

'Certainly not. Your head would be turned in a second,' Stephen rapped out.

'Oh, Caroline, wasn't it in London that your mother met your father, and ran away with him?' Fanny cried. 'The most romantic story.'

'Well! Brighton, you know,' put in Matthew, 'I am surprised at you, Mr Milner, for not liking it—for I like it extremely—and you, Miss Fortune, liked Brighton too. Is it not strange Mr Milner not liking it?'

'You must all have known each other pretty well at Brighton—isn't that curious?' Isabella said.

'Not really curious,' Mr Leabrook said, 'for that's the way Brighton is—continual society. Now, about tomorrow . . .'

He did not like talk of Brighton, Caroline thought: there was something they had in common, at any rate.

Supper over, the music struck up from the ballroom again, and Maria Downey, rising effortfully from her seat, stretched her long limbs at Stephen and drowsily asked: 'Are you as averse to dancing as you are to watering-places, Mr Milner?'

'Yes—but as I *have* been to Brighton, but have *not* danced this evening, I may as well even it out, Miss Downey.'

Well, Caroline thought, with a certain nibbling vexation as she watched them take the floor, if Maria thought she could induce him to seriousness, then it showed how little she knew him. Now Isabella was being led out by her fiancé, and Mr Carraway stood ready again at Fanny's elbow. But then Lady Milner looked up and intervened.

'Fanny, recollect yourself, please. No young woman of good breeding should show exclusive partiality to one partner all night.'

'Oh! well, I don't care,' Fanny said, springing up.

But then Captain Brunton stirred and said: 'Miss Fanny, your step-mother speaks wisely, and I do wish you would heed her.'

'Do you, sir? But as you are not even my stepfather, I can hardly consider it any of your business.'

'Really, Fanny, this is shocking,' lamented Lady Milner.

'No, Augusta, it isn't,' Fanny said cheerfully, 'but I know you mean well, and so I shall have this dance with Mr Downey, if he will be so good, and redeem myself as a young woman of breeding—on condition, Mr Carraway, that you dance with Caroline. Because she at least knows there is more to life than these deadly conventions.'

As no one could object to this, Caroline took the floor with Charles Carraway: who was full of praises for his late partner.

'She has the most irrepressible spirit, has she not? Ah, spirit. Beautiful word. It is so important to think for yourself, is it not? But Fanny has told me you agree on that.'

'I suppose I do: though sometimes Fanny seems to attribute ideas to me before I am even aware I have them.'

Mr Carraway laughed pleasantly. 'Ah, but I'll wager she is always right. Such is the delicacy of her perception, you know, I have more than once found her putting into words my own inmost thoughts!'

'Tut, dancing with a lady while singing the praises of another—is this your gallantry, Mr Carraway?'

'I know you don't mind it, Miss Fortune,' he said, whispery and warm, 'because you are on our side.'

Well, if it were a matter of sides, Caroline would always incline to

Fanny's view of things, rather than the chill proprieties invoked by Lady Milner; but she was rather alarmed at the idea of sides being taken at all, and she might have addressed herself more seriously to this question, if her mind had not been still taken up with Richard Leabrook.

The next day was, as Mr Leabrook's groom had predicted, fine and bright, though with the full sharpness of autumn in the air. The party Mr Leabrook had gathered, comprising the Downeys, the Milners, Mr Carraway, Captain Brunton, and Caroline; and the plan was to take a tour of the grounds and park, return to the house for a collation, and amuse themselves with cards and billiards and books as they liked, or go out again, just as their fancy and the weather dictated.

A good plan; and as there was nothing missing for their enjoyment, it was all the more curious to find how heavily the day went. There was a strained quality about their host's repeated professions of hospitality, that was plain at least to Caroline, and she guessed also to Isabella, judging by her friend's troubled looks. Captain Brunton had not wanted to attend, and was as gruff as was consonant with politeness. Matthew Downey had been expecting a letter from his aunt Sophia in Brighton, and could not refrain from wondering aloud why it had not come, in spite of his sister's enumerating several plausible reasons.

Only Fanny and Mr Carraway were really happy.

'Mr Carraway, you must run a race with me. To that summer-house. And you are not to let me win.'

'Oh, I shall not do that, Miss Fanny, never fear. But I cannot run in these . . .' his hessian boots. He sat down on the grass and began tugging at them. 'I wonder if one of you gentlemen . . . ?'

'I'll do it.' Fanny grasped and heaved, nearly went over backwards. Caroline, on edge though she was, found their young laughter infectious: a pity that Lady Milner would surely nip it with withering disapproval.

But no. There was even a look in Lady Milner's eyes, as she watched them haring off, that reflected Caroline's own feeling—that there was a beauty about the two of them which sent a wistful pang to the heart.

Stranger still, when the party followed them, at a sedater pace, it was Lady Milner who attached herself to Caroline, and deliberately slowed her steps so that they walked apart from the others.

'Miss Fortune, I wonder if I might ask you a question about personal matters. You cannot fail to have observed the intimacy that has grown between Fanny and this Mr Carraway. What do you think of it?' Caroline's surprise at her opinion being sought must have shown, for Lady Milner went on: 'You are young, yes, but older than Fanny, and I think you have had a good deal more experience of the world.'

'Well, I think—I think it is very natural. Fanny has a romantic temper, and so it seems has Mr Carraway: they both love to talk; and they have been thrown much together lately.'

Lady Milner gave her a pained, unsatisfied look. 'Miss Fortune, I should tell you that I feel a great responsibility for Fanny. I promised Sir Henry faithfully that I would do my best for my stepchildren. It is not always easy, for a woman alone. But that is how it must be. Certainly I shall not marry again. That is what I mean by faithfulness.'

It was difficult to take in such a strong dose of confidence. Caroline's mind made swift reappraisals while she tried, and failed, not to look over in the direction of Captain Brunton.

'It must be a great responsibility, indeed,' Caroline said. 'And Fanny is a very—lively creature.'

'She is headstrong and wilful, and she *needs* direction. Isabella is soon to be respectably settled: I have no anxieties there. But with Fanny—I fear that she may be led into indiscretion by her—her liveliness, as you term it.' Lady Milner grimaced. 'This Mr Carraway seems to be respectable—as artists go—and Mr Leabrook has a high regard for him, which must be in his favour. Still, I feel that Fanny should be aware that this over-familiarity with the young man may compromise her reputation.' She sighed and waved a hand. 'But I have said all this to her, and not been heeded. That is why I wanted to ask you, Miss Fortune, if you will speak to Fanny. She listens to you.'

Caroline, about to deny it, stopped. For it was true. She was, heaven help her, Fanny's oracle. She tried to sweep her thoughts together.

'Fanny will not like to listen to that, I'm afraid,' she answered at last. 'That is, if I am to caution her about her behaviour with Mr Carraway— and really, Lady Milner, I'm not sure that I see anything reprehensible in it. I'm flattered that you think my influence so great, but—'

'I don't mean to flatter, Miss Fortune. I would rather Fanny heeded me, but I must perforce turn to someone to whom she does listen.'

'I will do what I can,' Caroline said.

And suddenly there was warmth. 'Thank you—a thousand thank-yous,' Lady Milner said, turning a brilliant, anxious smile on her.

More reappraisals. She is young after all, Caroline thought—the *gravitas* made one forget. And now the thought occurred to her for the first time: was Lady Milner the person to speak to about her secret knowledge? She was concerned about Fanny flirting, what must she think of her other stepdaughter's prospects, if she knew about Brighton? It was a thought—but still, no more than a thought. If you were going to speak out, Caroline nagged herself, the time to do it was right at the beginning. Lady Milner would think—why now?

Isabella would think it.

Dear God, look—we are chess-pieces, Caroline thought, as she cast her eye over the party. The fitful autumn sunlight made chequered patterns on the grass, across which the scattered figures moved in purposive clusters. In this game, Caroline reflected gloomily, there is no doubt that I am only a pawn, whilst Richard Leabrook of course is a king—king of all this lush domain. Yet a pawn could checkmate a king; and she felt he knew this. Even the back of his dark, elegant head—which was all he tended to present to her—seemed to say it.

'**O**h, Caro! You too?' Fanny said. 'But I have already had the lecture from old Jack Tar within, and you may be sure I took it very amiss.'

It had not been easy to contrive this meeting alone with Fanny: Caroline had been forced to the expedient of calling at the Manor, waiting for Fanny to take her dogs to exercise, and then jumping up to go with her—which Isabella, settled in for a confidential chat, plainly found most odd. Now, with Fanny firing up as soon as she had tentatively mentioned the subject of Mr Carraway, Caroline inwardly cursed Lady Milner for this commission she had laid upon her.

'Well, I wonder who will address me on the subject next,' Fanny said, with asperity. 'I shall have to start making an appointments book.'

'My dear Fanny, I don't intend a lecture. I care for your welfare.'

'Oh, Caro, I don't mean anything against *you*, and I know Augusta has put you up to it, hasn't she?' Fanny squeezed her arm. 'I wouldn't mind if you did give me the lecture, because I'd know you wouldn't mean a word of it. Now with Captain Brunton it's a different matter. He came to me last night after dinner and began to talk about Mr Carraway—about Charles. Heavy hints about the danger of too great an intimacy after too short an acquaintance and so on. At last he grumbled that I should think about what he said, not merely for my stepmother's sake but for my own. Now, were *your* instructions much the same?'

'I am, I know, all too easily persuaded, but the last time I took *instructions* was when I was at school,' Caroline said.

'I have offended you,' cried Fanny, almost with excitement, 'and you tell me so, instead of going all stiff and brooding! That is what I like about you, Caro. Oh, I don't mind what you say to me. I will even admit that one *must* be careful in these matters, yes. But the fact is I'm not a silly young girl and my head is not easily turned.'

'I suppose we none of us like to think we are silly. But all must acknowledge that they are capable of silliness, from time to time.'

'And what a dreary world, if it were not so! But you do not subscribe, I'm sure, to the belief that grown people with rational minds somehow do not know what is best for them.'

'No, I don't believe that,' Caroline answered honestly. 'But . . .'

'But me no buts,' Fanny laughed.

Caroline sighed. Well, Lady Milner, I tried, she thought, as she walked home through the village pursued by her thoughts. She turned in at the Rectory gate, and found loosely tethered there a horse she did not recognise; a horse steaming as from a hard ride.

'Mr Downey!'

Matthew it was who stood beneath the porch, the riding-crop raised in his hand to rap. Arrested, he swung round upon her staring.

'Mr Downey, this is an unexpected pleasure. Please, won't you bring your horse round to the stable, where—'

'The horse will do very well where it is. I do not intend a long stay. What I do require'—Matthew mopped his brow with his gloves—'is a private interview with you, Miss Fortune.'

'With me? How odd—I cannot conceive what . . .' She waited, nervously smiling; but though she had no notion of what it could mean, she feared it was not good. Short of vaulting over the hedge and running away, however, she could see no help for it. Matthew looked dramatically determined.

Uncle John was in his study, steeped in the Early Fathers, and Aunt Selina was on a sick visit: it was simple enough to take Matthew into the winter parlour, close the door, and brace herself.

'Miss Fortune, I must speak first, and ask you only to hear me. It is far from my habit to dictate the conversation in this way, but the circumstances . . .' Giving her a long, bleak look, he drew a paper from his pocket. 'This,' he intoned, 'is a letter from my aunt's lawyer in London. At Symond's Inn. He is a Mr Coker. "Dear Sir"—'

'Mr Downey, please, I must ask you to desist. I do not want to hear a letter from your aunt's lawyer. These are private matters with which I have nothing to do.'

Matthew laughed shrilly. 'Oh, excellent! Oh, you surpass yourself, Miss Fortune—this is your famous joking, I take it.'

'If you do not begin behaving like a man in his senses, Mr Downey, I shall be obliged to ring.'

'Very well.' He straightened, glanced over the letter with glazed eyes. 'I will play your charade, Miss Fortune, and tell you what this letter is about. Mr Coker informs me—on Aunt Sophia's behalf, as she does not choose to have any further communication with me directly . . .' He gathered himself. 'Informs me that I am forever excluded from Aunt Sophia's favour. There you have it, Miss Fortune. Are you satisfied?'

'Why? Why should this be a satisfaction to me, Mr Downey? I don't understand any of it. Why would Mrs Catling do such a thing?'

'Oh, you keep it up finely, Miss Fortune. Thus, you will make me rehearse my humiliation before you, as well as having caused it.'

'Caused it?' Caroline shook her head and went to the sideboard. 'All I can think, Mr Downey, is that you have been given the run of Mr Leabrook's wine-cellar; and all I can suggest is that you take a glass of canary. One that brings you full circle back to sobriety. As for this letter—well, is it not perhaps merely a threat?'

'I hardly think Aunt Sophia would employ her solicitor to make an empty threat. Besides, I have a communication from my banker also. No, Miss Fortune, it is all real, I assure you: if this was your ultimate aim, it is all achieved.' He ignored the glass of canary she offered him and paced. 'One need look no further than motives of interest—but to betray a sacred confidence; and worst of all to betray Perdita—'

'Perdita? Your—the lady in London? I know nothing of Perdita, Mr Downey, but what you chose to tell me.'

'Precisely! And that is precisely what Aunt Sophia now knows!' He brandished the letter aloft. 'Listen. "It has come to my client's knowledge that a clandestine engagement of a most disreputable character has long subsisted between yourself and a Miss Perdita Lockwood, of Snow Hill, London. The wilful deceit practised upon my client, who supplied the above-mentioned funds on the express understanding that nothing of this kind would be entertained, is such as to render it impossible there should be any further communication between my client and yourself. The funds already advanced, my client is inclined to regard as money gained under false pretences." You have the flavour now, I'm sure, Miss Fortune. Is it piquant enough for you?'

Caroline sat down, moving through the slow mist of realisation.

'You think—Mr Downey, you think I told Mrs Catling about your secret engagement.'

'I beg your pardon, it is not a *secret* any more. It was a *secret* that I entrusted to only one person, Miss Fortune: yourself.'

'Mr Downey, you are mistaken,' Caroline said, meeting his wild glare. 'I am sorry indeed for what has happened, but this shock has made you jump to an entirely wrong conclusion, sir. You must think in what other ways this information could have come to Mrs Catling's ears—'

'There are none! Upon my soul, Miss Fortune, you have a curious notion of what a man means when he says he is entrusting you with an exclusive confidence. To be sure, I do not *want* to believe you could have done this. And yet I have been putting two and two together, and they most assuredly make four! I was only remarking to you the other day, was I not, that it might be possible for you to be reinstated among my aunt's acquaintance? And meanwhile you already had your little plan in hand, to reinstate yourself *much* more fully!'

'Good God. If I have you right, sir, I hardly know which to marvel at most—your impudence or your absurdity. Mr Downey, I am most happily reconciled with a kind and loving family. And you actually suppose that I spend my time in making mischief between you and your aunt, in hopes that the old crocodile might leave me something after all? I say again there must be some other explanation. I suggest you ignore those threats and apply to Mrs Catling herself, to discover where she heard this intelligence.' She rose. 'And if you have nothing else to say to me beyond baseless accusation—'

'I came,' he said, 'hoping—hoping at least that you would acknowledge the truth. I am no faint-heart when it comes to unpleasant truth. Indeed I have always taken a bracing sort of pleasure in facing it.' For a moment, being interested in himself again made Matthew almost cheerful; but then his brow puckered, and he snatched up his hat and riding-crop. 'I shall apply to my aunt—but I know there is no recovering from such a position. So, what do you intend doing to Maria, Miss Fortune? She will surely come before you in the will.'

'I have a plan to push her off a cliff, of course, though I must overcome the trifling obstacle of our being fifty miles inland. Really, Mr Downey, you are ridiculous.'

'Still brazening it out, eh? I suppose you have to. The mask must not slip. And to think I welcomed you!' Emotion made him alliterative: 'It was a black day that brought you to Brighton!'

'No, it was not, it was a sunny day, I recall it perfectly,' Caroline snapped, feeling tears of vexation and hysterical laughter pulling her both ways. She turned from him, drank off the canary wine herself, and was presently informed by the sound of stamping boots and slamming doors that Mr Downey had left.

After a while, and a little more canary, Caroline sat down to consider how it was that Mrs Catling had found out about the engagement, but soon dismissed the question as no great mystery. For all his denials, she thought, a man who liked talking about himself as much as Matthew did was bound to let it slip in any number of places. No, the more pressing question was what he would do now. Fly to Brighton, of course: but before he did, would he keep his suppositions to himself?

Knowing Matthew, she rather doubted it. Confirmation of a sort arrived little more than an hour later, when the maid announced the arrival of Stephen Milner.

'Miss Fortune, how d'you do?' he asked, sauntering in with his hands in his pockets. 'Would you like me to stir that sulky fire for you? And, more importantly, what the devil have you done to Mr Downey?'

Caroline groaned. 'Not very well, yes, please, and nothing at all, are the answers to those questions, Mr Milner.'

'You do look rather dreadful,' Stephen observed sympathetically, wielding the poker. 'Well, I hope it is something deliciously wicked: it will make such a refreshing contrast with damnable wedding-clothes and bride-cake. Oh, I forgot.' He reached into the breast of his coat and drew out an indiscriminate ball of fluff, which resolved itself into a tortoiseshell kitten that yawned a display of needle teeth. 'I've found homes for all of Sukey's litter: this is the last. Will you have her?'

'Oh, Mr Milner, thank you—she's beautiful—I must ring for a saucer of milk . . .' Caroline hugged the mewling weightlessness to her breast. She did not need to feign delight: just now it was wonderful to embrace a creature that was entirely without opinions about her. 'What shall I call her? I seem to see Matilda in that face, but I'm not sure. Oh, d'you know, Mr Milner? I never had a dog or cat before.'

'I do know, or guessed. The effect should be to domesticate you, though we'll have to see about *that*. Also, having a cat is good preparation in case you end up an old maid.'

'I always wonder, Matilda, whether Mr Milner's charm comes naturally, or whether he works at it.'

'A little of both. Now pray tell what Mr Downey meant by his extraordinary descent on the Manor this morning. He strode about with a lot of dramatic breathing through his nose, and at last announced that this was a sort of farewell call, as he had to leave. I'm not sure, but I do believe he said he was forced to go and confront his unlucky and undeserved fate. Does that sound like something Mr Downey would say?'

'You have made him live,' confirmed Caroline, glumly.

'Well. Isabella asked, in that innocent way of hers, whether he had had bad news. Yes, says he, if bad news be the wilful destruction of his credit with the one person in the world upon whose goodwill he depended—I quote again, by the way. He cannot talk about it, he goes on, except to say he has been monstrously used, and if we would know more, ask *her*. With a gesture hither. So.' Stephen sat down, stretching and crossing his long, booted legs. 'I insist upon hearing *everything*.'

'Mr Milner, I can't tell you, because—oh, dear.' She gave the kitten her forefinger to bite, studying the cunning patterns of its coat. 'You have heard that I met the Downeys when I was living at Brighton. They are the only relatives of Mrs Catling, who was my employer—'

'And an old dragon.'

'Well—certainly Mrs Catling is a difficult and capricious woman.'

'Prune-faced, flint-hearted old dragon, in fact.' He shrugged. 'I'm sorry, do go on.'

'The Downeys came on a visit—'

'Ah, this was when you met Leabrook. Sorry again.'

'We were a good deal together,' Caroline resumed, giving him a glare, 'and got along very well. And presently Mr Downey favoured me with his confidence. He was almost entirely dependent for his present comfort and future prospects on Mrs Catling, and was accordingly anxious not to forfeit her favour. And one crucial element in this was that he should not marry, or undertake to marry, at least before he was thirty. Well, Mr Downey confided to me that he had contracted a secret engagement. He knew that Mrs Catling would fiercely disapprove, indeed that she might cut him out of her will if she knew. But he was, it seemed, very much in love. She—the lady was, is, certainly not eligible. She is poor. Her father lives at Snow Hill and is an apothecary. I promised to keep Mr Downey's secret, as it was certainly likely to do him a great deal of harm with Mrs Catling if it were known.'

'Well, I can guess the rest,' Stephen said, with his boots up on the fender. 'The dragon has now found out about the engagement.'

'Yes—and disinherited him for it.'

Stephen whistled. 'Decisive in her. So, did you do it?'

'Mr Downey thinks so. He marched in here and accused me of betraying him, and now *you* don't believe me—'

'Oh, but I didn't say that,' Stephen said, grinning. 'I merely posed the question, as it's sure to be in the air with Mr Downey storming about in that way of his.' He grinned again, yawned, relented. 'No, I don't believe it. It rather goes against the grain to say so, because as I remarked when we first met, you look like trouble. But no . . . If you were going to make mischief, I imagine it on a much grander scale.'

'Thank you—I think. What did Isabella say?'

'Oh, Bella adores you,' he said, 'and you know she'll go to any lengths rather than think the worst of someone.' He unfolded himself and stood. 'Well, no doubt we shall hear more. Ah, look, Matilda has made you her first offering. Come and dine with us tomorrow.' He was gone: somehow, unseen and in passing, briefly pressing her hand.

Chapter Nine

FROST CHALKED THE RECTORY roofs and crisped the lawns the next morning. It was as if winter, like an invading army breaking through defences, had stolen nearer overnight. Caroline took a cheek-tingling walk that turned into a call on the Hampsons and then, although she was to dine there later, a call at the Manor too. In spite of Stephen's assurances, she wanted to know if she still had Isabella's good opinion.

The door was answered by a maid, but it was Fanny who appeared breathlessly in the doorway a moment later and hustled her aside. 'Go, go, Jane, I'll see to this. Caro! Oh, my dear Caro.'

To her surprise Caroline found herself being embraced by Fanny, who then glanced over her shoulder at the empty hall and whispered: 'Now, I want you to know: I do not believe a word of it.'

'Oh! Oh, you mean what Mr Downey said. Well, I thank you, Fanny.'

'Oh, not that! Though that too—but you know there is more, much more. Of course you wouldn't know—'

'Fanny, you alarm me—what more? What has happened?'

Fanny fixed her with a solemn look. 'Mr Downey was here again early this morning with Mr Leabrook. Mr Leabrook was driving Mr Downey in his gig to the coach-office at Huntingdon—but they stopped off here. Oh Lord, such uproar!—but we had better go in.'

In the drawing room there was peculiar confusion rather than uproar. Isabella was rapidly and strenuously walking up and down, whilst Lady Milner, who had plainly been in tears, was making a perspiring Captain Brunton search her reticule for sal-volatile.

Then they all saw Caroline, and everything stopped.

'Yes, she is here, you see,' said Fanny, at her side, 'and I have told her that I do not believe a word of it.'

'Whatever is the matter? Bella?' All at once Caroline felt as if she were breathing gauze. 'Won't someone please tell me what's going on?'

'Miss Fortune, it is all very shocking, and I am not sure—I am not at all sure we should be receiving you here,' Lady Milner said. 'It is all so very unprecedented. Probably you had better go away—'

'Nonsense, Augusta,' said—to general surprise—Captain Brunton.

'Miss Fortune is the very person who should be here, to settle this matter. But as it concerns Miss Milner, I think we should leave her and Miss Fortune to talk alone.' He put his hand firmly under Lady Milner's elbow. 'And you, Miss Fanny, I'm sure are wholly in agreement.'

'Oh! yes—to be sure,' said a staring Fanny, allowing herself to be piloted out.

'But, Edward—what about Stephen?' Lady Milner protested. 'He really should be consulted.'

'And will be, as soon as he can be found, and as he must be somewhere about the estate, I'm sure your man will bring him back soon.'

Presently the door was closed, and Caroline faced Isabella, who was still pacing.

'My dear Isabella, please stop walking up and down. Here, sit down.' Caroline drew up a chair. The sight of her friend's stricken white face turned her sick. 'I think I must sit down too. What *is* this about? Is it what Mr Downey said? I wanted to come and see you about that. It—'

'Mr Downey,' Isabella repeated blankly, as if trying to place the name. She sat down and looked at her hands. 'Yes, I suppose it begins with Mr Downey. Began. We had heard about Mr Downey's aunt disinheriting him. And how he blamed you. Surely not true, we all thought. But Richard—Richard confessed to Mr Downey that he was not at all surprised—that he was sorry to say that he *could* believe it of you. Mr Downey wanted to know why—and so Richard came out with it. And once it was out, he thought I had better know. He stopped here this morning to talk to me about what happened when you were at Brighton.'

'Good God,' breathed Caroline, 'he *told* you?'

With great effort Isabella met her eyes. 'He said he was sorry that he had not spoken before—but he knew I was fond of you, and thought it best to leave it—but now with what had happened to his poor friend Mr Downey, he could not keep silent.' Isabella's eyes went to her hands again. 'He said you threw yourself at him most shamelessly, even though he made it clear he was engaged to be married. That one night you actually offered yourself to him, which was why he felt he ought to leave Brighton at once. He said he could understand it,' Isabella hurried on, as Caroline launched herself from her chair, 'for you were unhappy with your situation and longed to escape it—at any cost. When he learned that you had lost your position, he suspected some such behaviour had driven Mrs Catling to your dismissal, though again he did not like to say so, because of our friendship.'

'And, oh, Bella,' Caroline cried, unable to contain herself any longer, 'do you believe that what Mr Leabrook has just told you is the truth?'

'Richard is the man I love and am to marry,' Isabella said slowly, 'and so in that sense I must believe him. But, Caro, there is nothing I would rather not believe than this.'

Caroline stood looking down at her friend, and all at once the anger cooled down to a leaden, ashy sorrow. 'You do believe him,' she said. He has done this because he fears me, she thought lucidly. Richard Leabrook is a worse man even than I supposed, and he will surely make Isabella miserable. And there is nothing I can do, unless . . . 'Unless you choose to believe my account, Bella, I don't see how we can go on. It's what I have most feared, and why I haven't spoken. Will you hear it?'

Isabella trembled, but she nodded. 'Yes, Caro. Of course.'

Plainly, and as unemotionally as she could manage, Caroline told her. Isabella listened, motionless, and Caroline suspected that no more important moment had ever occurred in her friend's life—and even perhaps in her own.

'I'm not going to wake up,' Isabella said dully, when Caroline had finished. 'This is real. This is not a dream.' She got up and began walking again.

'Bella, that is the truth of what happened at Brighton. I wish, I so wish it were not. But I cannot defend myself against—against what is being said about me, without telling it. Ever since I first heard your fiancé's name, and realised who he was, I have thought over and over again what was best to do. I could see no happy resolution.'

'If this is true,' Isabella said, pausing with her back to her, 'then he cannot love me. But why—why would he do that? We had had no quarrel when he went to Brighton—everything was as it should be—'

'All I can say is with me it was not a matter of love at all. I was to be—an adventure. A conquest. Bella, I was to be his doxy.'

Isabella turned: there was an emergent look of sympathy; then she shook it off. 'I cannot believe this, not of Richard. His character is quite otherwise. Oh, I'm sorry, Caro—only—only if it is possible that I have been deceived in Richard, then is it not equally possible that I have been deceived in you? That you invent this—account, merely out of your own jealous designs, in order to destroy what Richard and I have?'

Caroline could say nothing except: 'Oh, Isabella.' It issued from her as a pure extract of sorrow. 'Mr Leabrook was no novice in Brighton. He knew very well what he was about. I only wish I could convince you that my one concern, all the time, has been for you not to be hurt. And yet now—now the hurt has come.'

'True,' Isabella said, gasping back tears. 'I am hurt—and confused.' She covered her eyes. 'I must see Richard. Look into his face, yes,' she added to herself. 'And I must think.' Now she looked up at Caroline. 'And for now, Caro, I must—I must think alone.'

Blindly, somehow, Caroline got out of the room. It could hardly have gone worse, she thought, standing in the hall. It could hardly have gone worse—and then she looked up to see Stephen enter.

The look he gave her was rueful, speculative. 'Well, well,' he said softly, 'the curse of being always right! Trouble I said, and trouble it is!'

And, not unkindly, but seeming to leave a scrupulous distance between them, he found the door for her.

'**M**y dear, you have told me it is the truth, and I believe it is the truth,' concluded Aunt Selina staunchly that night, after Caroline had poured out the whole story to her. 'And now what I want you to do is get a good night's sleep, and let it all rest until the morrow. My one concern is that your health should not suffer from all this upset.'

Thus her dependable aunt, with one of her neat, dry kisses. And yet if anyone was pale, it was Aunt Selina. Plainly the whole thing shocked her: the very ideas of seduction, duplicity, and intrigue seemed to taint the air of the Rectory. And Caroline, for all her aunt's assurances, could not help wondering whether now, at last, those regretful thoughts of cuckoos and nests were passing through Aunt Selina's mind.

For Caroline the next day, two short letters.

> *Ma chère Caroline,*
>
> *I write you from Hethersett and thus with a certain degree of delicious secrecy—maid's brother entrusted with smuggling out missive for a bribe of sixpence. Of course you will know that Matthew has gone post-haste to Brighton to beat at Aunt Sophia's closed door and equally closed heart. Yes—yes, I heard all about it, and whom he blames for the catastrophe—and my dear, I may as well say I cannot believe it of you. Not that I would blame you if you had told our aunt—dear, dear—Perdita from Snow Hill forsooth—what was he thinking? Anyhow I told Matthew I would stay here and enjoy the bountiful hospitality of the Leabrooks till the end of the week as we first agreed— thus I hope I may be able to call and see you BUT now one hears even more scandalous tales about you!—you wicked creature! I don't know what to believe but also, my dear, do not greatly care. I am the least moral creature in existence, and all I would like is the pleasure of your company again, if it can be managed. In the meantime, love and whatever you like—and oh! you wicked creature—*
>
> *Yrs ever,*
> *Maria Downey*

My dear Caro,

I told you I did not believe a word of it. And now I have heard from Bella what you said—and I am vindicated. Yours, my dear Caro, must be the true account: and what a deceitful devil is Richard! I am shocked and disgusted at him. Isabella continues in a much confused state— wretchedly torn and distressed; and in the meantime Stephen has summoned Richard (O! I should not write his treacherous name thus) to come for a thorough talk with him and Isabella—and he (Leabrook let me call him) is expected here any moment. My dear Caro, rest assured I shall do everything in my power on your behalf—even if that can only be to let you know what happens. Courage, my dear friend!

Yours most affectionately,

Fanny

Caroline took what heart she could from these messages; still she could not be easy for a moment with the thought of what must be going on beneath the Manor roof today. Her aunt, observing her restlessness, at last found a task for her. She was to go and call upon a young woman who lived in Splash Lane, and ask her if she would come and do needlework at the Rectory two days a week.

Having fulfilled her errand, Caroline stepped out for home, thinking some hard thoughts, just as the woody flutter of a ring-dove startled from a tree above alerted her to the approach of rapid hoofbeats.

For a moment, turning, she thought Richard Leabrook was actually going to ride her down, but he reined in and touched his hat. There was an angry jut to his cheekbones as he said: 'Miss Fortune. You are to be congratulated on your success. Yes: all our plans are destroyed, Isabella is in tears, and there is to be no Christmas wedding as she had hoped: instead, an indefinite postponement. Well, are you glad?'

'Yes—assuming such a rudely posed question requires an answer, yes, sir, I am glad. But I am glad as I would be at a spell of sunshine— because it is simply a good thing, not something I brought about.'

'Very pretty. Very tedious. Well, you were on your way to the Manor to find out the results of your efforts, I'm sure, so I've spared you the trouble. It was Milner who insisted the wedding be put off.'

There was a sharp contempt in his voice that pricked her beyond self-possession. 'If you were a better man, Mr Leabrook, I would call that unworthy. Mr Milner cares for his sister's well-being. It's lucky she has such people about her.'

'You would count yourself amongst this angelic host, of course. Despite what your jealousy has done to her. Oh, come, don't give me that look: is it regret for saying no in Brighton? I may as well say I have long repented that moment's folly: I must have been bored indeed.'

'Mr Leabrook, you cannot insult me any more than you did that night. Since you maintain that you sincerely love Isabella, I ask you to consider how you would feel if she were so treated by a man.'

'But, my dear Miss Fortune,' he said, with a small laugh, 'you must see the difference. Isabella is a well-bred young woman of fortune: you are a mere soldier's get, brought up one jump ahead of the streets, and accustomed to hiring yourself out one way or another.' He touched his hat again. 'I'm sorry to be the bearer of unpleasant truths.'

It was of no use crying after him, as she wanted to do; his opinion of her—if you could call outright hatred an opinion—was confirmed. What she really needed to know, and dreaded to find out, was the opinion of her prevailing at the Manor. It was with a heavy tread that she entered the oak avenue that used to be her favourite walk.

Not Fanny but Lady Milner came hurrying out to the hall. 'Miss Fortune, how do you do? You find us a little disturbed domestically again, I am afraid, and so your welcome may not be all that civility should dictate. I hope you are quite well? I realise,' she added, with a rare tinge of humour, 'that these formalities may seem rather absurd at such a time—but really I don't know how to explain to you—'

'Well, I have just seen Mr Leabrook. He was . . . informative.'

'I see.' Lady Milner's eyes searched her face. 'I may as well say, Miss Fortune, that I think this postponement a good idea. Mr Leabrook emerged from his private interview with Isabella looking furious. He said if there were any shadow of suspicion attaching to him, then he did not see how they could go on. I do not think he expected Stephen to say so promptly that, in that case, the wedding should be put off.'

'This,' cried Stephen, flinging open the drawing-room door, 'is exactly what I loathe about the whole business. All this whispering together in corners. Come in, Miss Fortune, and let us all talk openly and frankly, for this concerns you quite as much as anyone.'

'Oh, yes, Caro, you must come in, and you must know you are vindicated!' cried Fanny. 'Bella, tell her she is absolved and shriven!'

'Fanny, stop being sensibilitous for one minute,' snapped Stephen, who was in his shirt sleeves. 'And, Bella, leave off that writing.'

'My dear Stephen,' Lady Milner said hesitatingly, 'your coat—'

'My coat? It is on the floor, ma'am, where I threw it, because I am excessively hot and bothered and in a mood to throw something.'

'I must get these letters written,' said Isabella, who was seated at the writing-desk. 'There are people to be informed—things to be cancelled.' Her unhappy eyes met Caroline's for a moment, then veered away.

'Oh, Bella, I don't know what to say,' Caroline said, drawing tentatively closer to the writing-desk. 'Is that what you want?'

'I want,' Isabella said, examining her pen, 'I want none of this to have happened. I want it all as before—but of course that's impossible. And so, while I cannot believe what you have told me about Richard, I cannot believe you are . . . what he said you are.'

'Well,' Caroline said, her throat tight, 'thank you for that—but I wish it had come to no such choice, Bella, truly—'

'I'm sure, my dear,' Isabella said, with a sunken smile. 'Forgive me, I can't be very welcoming just now, because when I look at you I think of *him*, and so—we are perhaps not the best company for one another.'

'Yes,' Caroline said, miserably. 'Yes, I see.'

'Bella! You should be thanking Caro. You would *never* wish to be reconciled with a man who behaved so monstrously,' said Fanny hotly.

'Not your business, Fanny,' Stephen said, irritably tugging at his loosened cravat as if he longed to shed it. 'That is Bella's business only. And I say again, Isabella, there will also be time enough later to write those damned letters.'

'I will help you, Isabella,' Lady Milner said, and then: 'If you will allow me, we shall make sure that everything is done correctly.'

'Thank you,' Isabella said, with a dazed look.

'Correctness!' snorted Fanny. 'Caro, do you hear them?'

'You think it mere empty convention, Fanny,' Lady Milner reproved her, 'but it is really another word for doing what is right.'

'I think,' Isabella said, gathering up her papers, 'if you will excuse me, I shall carry on with this upstairs.'

As she got to the door, Captain Brunton appeared—or rather, he had been there all the time. Now, he seized the handle. 'Miss Milner—I—I—if there is anything at all I can do that may be of service to you, then I hope you know you have only to name it.'

Isabella looked at him, smiled as best she could and said: 'Thank you, Captain Brunton. You are very kind.'

She passed by; and Caroline saw her go, and saw him bow, in a dazzling tableau of realisation. No, no, she thought, it is not kindness: no, no, it is much more than that.

Fanny, a little irritatingly, was at her side. 'Don't pay any heed to Bella, Caro. She will see that you have actually done her a service.'

'I would rather not have done any such service,' Caroline said bleakly. 'What will happen now?'

'We must wait and see,' Stephen said. 'But they had better keep apart just now. And I'm afraid she seems to feel the same about your presence, Miss Fortune: thoroughly irrational, but then of course she is a woman.'

'Yes,' Caroline said rising, 'I was forgetting what an expert you are on our sex, Mr Milner. Well, I shall go—'

'Oh, but this is unfair,' Fanny cried. 'Stephen, she cannot consider herself banished!'

'I don't,' Caroline said, with a constrained laugh, 'but it's best, just now, if I leave, especially as Isabella is not comfortable with me.'

'Spoken with excellent and surprising sense,' Stephen said. 'I shall see you home.'

So she found herself returning down the oak avenue with Stephen striding at her side, in a baffling silence that at last she broke by asking: 'Mr Milner, *do* you think me guilty?'

'Do I think you guilty? It depends what you mean. The curious point, Miss Fortune, is why you should care for my opinion.'

'It is curious, but let us put it aside while you give me an answer.'

'Oh, you know that is beyond me, Miss Fortune. All I can say is, I do wish you had spoken sooner.'

'Well, that is all very well for you to say: you have not been through my difficulties. Indeed, I would urge you to put yourself in my position for a moment, and then consider what you would have done.'

'In your position? Well, let's see. I am asked by Leabrook to run off with him to London and abandon myself to dissipation . . .' He shook his head doubtfully. 'I don't know: he is undoubtedly a handsome fellow, but really there are laws, you know.'

'You are incorrigible,' she said, aiming a mock swipe with her bonnet, 'and really we should not be laughing. It is a sad time.'

'So it is, but it will get better. Isabella is no Lent-lily; and as soon as she shows some little sign of being herself again, I shall take myself off, far away from all this infernal muddle.'

The anger that rose in her was so complete, so white-hot, that she might have wondered whether it was really not against him but the whole cumulative situation.

'Yes, that's right, run away,' she cried. 'Whenever there's trouble, whenever life becomes complicated, then you must take to your heels.'

'I was thinking of going by post-chaise,' he said imperturbably.

'It hardly matters how you go—or even *if* you go—because even when you are not running away, Mr Milner, you are running away. Some might say that it was the root of all the trouble in the first place.'

'It would be very presumptuous of them, if so,' he said softly; and the hard glitter in his eyes showed her that now, at last, he was truly vexed.

'They might as plausibly point to the beginning of the *trouble* as your arrival in Wythorpe, Miss Fortune.'

'Oh, that has always been your belief, and there is nothing I can do to alter it. But at least when you are off poking about in tombs, Mr Milner, you will be spared having to observe the effects of my delinquencies here.'

He frowned down at her: but a part of him appeared to wish to step back to good humour; awkwardly he said: 'This is not one of our best quarrels. It seems rather too meant.'

'I meant all of it,' she said, crushingly, untruly; and walked away with her head held as high as only utter misery could make it.

Fanny Milner descended on her as usual the next afternoon with many embraces, gazes, hand-squeezings, and urgent avowals of solidarity against the blinkered and narrow-hearted world.

It was kind in her, it was touching, and it was very slightly irritating: Caroline did not have the crusader's spirit. Still she was not so over-supplied with friendship just now as to undervalue that which Fanny offered her. She even accompanied Fanny, the next week, to one of the Hampsons' evening-parties: but the experience was not pleasant. Mr Charles Carraway was, naturally, of the party; and Fanny, naturally, was much with him, but Caroline could not help but sadly turn in her mind the memory of a previous occasion here, when Isabella and Stephen had been present—as they were now so glaringly absent. Stephen Milner had left for Dorset earlier in the week, intent on seeing Maumbury Rings, according to Fanny.

'Oh! by the by, there is another change at the Manor. Would you believe we are to be free of Captain Brunton at last? He leaves for London tomorrow. Really it is not a moment too soon. Indeed, he was actually quite rude to you the other day, Charles, was he not?'

The painter shrugged and blinked his beautiful eyes. 'He is an unhappy man, I think.'

Ah, yes, thought Caroline: and he is making himself go away from the source of his unhappiness.

'Well, *I* fancy he is jealous because Augusta is not so thick with him any more. And *that*, most curiously, is because she devotes so much time to Isabella. Yes, she has shown herself rather sensitive and thoughtful! You simply never know, do you?' Fanny concluded.

The departure of Captain Brunton, whom Caroline had come to respect, seemed of a piece with this wintry and denuded time. Everybody is going, she thought, as she took a solitary walk later, like those leaves: she gazed up at the horse-chestnuts, almost bare now, one especially solitary leaf clinging like a rag to the end of a skeletal bough and offering her a gloomy image of herself. Leaflike she drifted home, and found Captain Brunton in the parlour with her uncle.

'Ah, my dear—here is our friend Captain Brunton. He is off to London tomorrow! Is it not the greatest of pities? My dear girl, what *have* you done to people hereabouts? They are all taking to their heels!' Dr Langland was so innocently oblivious that only he laughed at this joke. 'So, my dear sir, have you hopes of a commission at last?'

'I mean to try again at the Admiralty, sir, yes. But I have other business besides, and I felt I should step over and say my goodbyes, and present my compliments.' Captain Brunton inclined his head towards Caroline, his eyes seeking hers.

'Well, I wish you good fortune, my dear sir!' Dr Langland cried, with a great clap of his huge hands. 'But I'll tell you what you should do besides, Captain Brunton—besides looking about you for a berth, you should look about you for a wife. It *grounds* a man most securely.'

'That I do not doubt,' Captain Brunton said, with a tight, shadowed smile. 'And I believe the married state to be—all you say, sir; but I do not anticipate entering it myself, at least not—not soon.' He turned to Caroline. 'Miss Fortune, you have had a pleasant walk, I trust.'

'Oh, that's what all you young fellows say,' Dr Langland boomed over him, 'until the moment when a pair of pretty eyes smites you, and then—bang! Your goose is cooked! Ah—yes, Nancy? Am I wanted?'

'Yes, sir. Old Mr Powlett,' said the maid, who stood in the doorway. 'About getting his wife churched after her last 'un.'

'Ah, indeed, I'll be there directly. Pray excuse me, Captain Brunton.'

'Miss Fortune, I had hoped for a private word with you,' the Captain said, easing his tight cravat, when Dr Langland had gone. 'This is opportune. I . . . I wish I was one of those fellows with ready tongues!'

'There is such a thing as a too ready tongue,' she said, smiling. 'Captain Brunton, I am very sorry you are leaving.'

'So am I. Well, in some ways. Not in all. In other circumstances . . . Miss Fortune, I wish I might go knowing you were still a welcome visitor at the Manor: it would reassure me to think of you there.'

'Oh, Captain Brunton, it is what I would like myself above all things: but while matters stand so awkwardly . . . Unless you feel—do you?— that I might make the attempt?'

He winced. 'Just now—I think not. If I had to choose a word to describe Miss Milner, it would be *raw*. My cousin tries, with some success, to keep her mind fixed on other things. But as for Miss Milner—I believe that she still cannot quite let go of . . .' He peered into his hat, colouring. 'I should not speak of her so. It is not my place.'

'I know you do so out of kindness, sir. And I would like to think of *you* still at the Manor too. I hope, Captain Brunton, you will find it possible to come back,' she said, holding his gaze.

'I hope so too,' he said, after a moment. He stood up as abruptly as if someone had told him his chair was on fire. 'Miss Fortune, if I should need to write to you, may I do so care of your aunt?'

'I'm sure that would be quite proper. Not that you need concern yourself about propriety, you know, when it comes to a person like *me*,' she said, with a wry laugh.

December came in rimey and rheumy. Freezing fog stealthily stalked the hollows about Wythorpe: the sheep breathed wet plumes in and out, chimney-smoke made smudgier columns in the misty air, in the church Dr Langland preached above a condensing cloud of rasps and wheezes. In this church, a couple of times, Caroline met an Isabella still hollow-eyed and noticeably thin, and they exchanged tentative words. A couple of times, also, she went with Aunt Selina to call at the Manor, yet to Caroline it all seemed still stiff and empty.

Stephen was on his wanderings down in the southwest, and favoured them, Fanny told her, with the occasional scrawl. The idea of his writing letters awoke in Caroline an absurd wish that she might get one. She kept thinking of their last meeting, and thought that even to receive a page of nonsense, which was how she imagined Stephen's letters, would at least efface that impression of a last, bitter word.

Fanny still clove loyally to her, and confided one morning, after a little wide-eyed hesitation, that there had been a civil exchange of notes between Isabella and Mr Leabrook.

'No more than that,' Fanny said, 'yet I really believe Isabella simply cannot let go of love—and who can blame that? Is it not the hardest thing in the world to relinquish, once you have it?'

'I think it is,' Caroline heard herself say. 'And the hardest to grasp also. You have to seize it at once, else it may be too late.'

'I knew you'd agree,' Fanny said.

It was two days after this that the maid, bringing the letters in to the breakfast-parlour, caused Caroline's heart to do a peculiar and unaccountable leap when she said: 'Here's an odd one for you, miss.'

But no, not actually a letter: sealed, but not posted: only the direction 'Caroline', in what she recognised as Fanny's handwriting. And then a sharp misgiving turned her heart gymnastic again.

'It is my second Advent sermon this Sunday,' Dr Langland was saying, 'and I think to keep to tradition, and preach on Judgement—'

'Hell and buggery,' Caroline cried out, jumping to her feet with the opened letter in her hand. 'Oh—forgive me—it's just that this news is so . . . Oh, dear. I'm afraid Fanny has run away with Mr Carraway.' And while her uncle and aunt gasped she stared again at the ensuing words: *just as you, my dear Caroline, advised me!*

Chapter Ten

CAROLINE, HER UNCLE AND AUNT were at the Manor before the breakfast things had cooled. They found Lady Milner and Isabella in a state of agitation bordering on the frantic. A similar note had been left on the chimney-piece for them and the servants had confirmed that Miss Fanny's clothes were gone. The housekeeper announced with a certain veiled satisfaction that Miss Fanny's dogs were howling for their exercise, and there was nobody free to do it. And none of this was helped by their having to explain to Dr Langland exactly what had happened.

'No, no,' he kept saying, 'there is a mistake here. The fact is she cannot have gone off alone with that gentleman, for you know Fanny is a young girl—that is, a maiden, you know: and they are not married.'

In a kind of tight-jawed wail, Aunt Selina said: 'That is precisely the point, and that is precisely why we are so dreadfully concerned.'

Dr Langland's mouth fell open. 'Lord, bless my soul.' Blinking at his wife, he sat down heavily.

'Oh, Fanny,' Isabella said, drooping, 'what have you done?'

Perhaps, probably, she did not intend it: but Isabella's moist eyes did alight on Caroline as she said these words, and Caroline felt the cold touch of accusation. Colder still when Uncle John, saying they must examine the evidence, proceeded to read out the farewell notes in his strongest pulpit voice.

'"You must know that Charles and I are united by a love of the truest, profoundest and holiest kind. Such a sensitive plant cannot flourish in the stony soil of a provincial backwater. The place for us is London. There are the most promising chances for one of Charles's avocation:

there we shall be together and happy. Life is here to be lived—it is a crime to let convention and caution stifle it—so we are off tonight—seizing the moment, just as you, my dear Caroline, advised me!"' Dr Langland gaped mournfully. 'Oh, Caroline! Oh, my dear girl, this really was not responsible in you! Did you *know* of this scheme?'

'We must remember,' Aunt Selina put in, touching Caroline's arm, 'that Fanny always does tend to put her own complexion on things. And *I* cannot believe that Caro would have encouraged this.'

'Indeed I did not know about it,' Caroline said. 'That is, she did not tell me about any plan to elope with Mr Carraway, though, to be sure, she was often talking of him and her—her feelings generally.'

Suddenly she realised she was talking about Fanny in the past tense: as if she were dead. And of course it was not that bad . . . but . . .

Charles Carraway did not *appear* a heartless seducer who would take what he wanted and then abandon a girl: he seemed too romantic, unworldly. But the mere fact that he had taken off with an innocent girl of seventeen showed him either blind or criminally careless.

'I wish they had not gone to London,' Isabella said. 'It's so big—a person can just disappear there.'

So it is, as your fiancé well knew, Caroline thought: it was where I was to go and be his mistress, and when he had tired of me, no doubt I was to disappear—into that deep, deep pool of lost women, their reputations gone. God forbid that should happen to Fanny.

Lady Milner said: 'Well, I have written Stephen at his last address. I can only hope it reaches him. He must come home. He is needed.'

'Yes,' Caroline said aloud, before she even knew she was going to speak. 'Oh, yes, certainly—that is the best idea.'

The following two days brought no news of Fanny. Lady Milner said that she shuddered to think, without specifying what it was that she shuddered to think.

The third day brought Stephen.

He had travelled post, setting out as soon as he received Lady Milner's letter, hardly pausing to eat or drink. 'Nor, I fear, shave—he looked quite a Robinson Crusoe,' related Aunt Selina, who had been at the Manor when he arrived.

'And how is he?' demanded Caroline. 'Annoyed at having to leave his precious ruins to come back and take charge of his own household?'

Aunt Selina looked as surprised as Caroline felt at this tartness.

'Well, he is, I think, most seriously concerned for Fanny,' Aunt Selina said. 'Though, characteristically, he calls her a little fool and says she deserves whatever she gets. But I'm sure he doesn't mean that.'

'Oh, who can tell, with Stephen?' Caroline said airily, and, arming herself with stout gloves and secateurs, she went out to the front garden and began cutting holly-boughs to dress the Rectory windows.

'Miss Fortune, I wish to pick your brains.'

Stephen Milner had stolen upon her so quietly, and broken into her thoughts so abruptly, that she bit her tongue, nearly dropped the secateurs and turned round on him with a yelp. 'Mr Milner! Really, you could have made me cut off my finger!'

'Oh, the gloves look very strong. A minor incision perhaps, no more. I *am* sorry to interrupt you, because you looked so splendidly pagan.' He picked up a cut sprig of holly. 'Roman feast started this custom. Saturnalia. Guzzle, gobble, and grope. Not so very different from Christmas.' He looked weary, his face all bony angles. 'Now about those brains. Ow, I've pricked myself.'

'Curious consequence of handling sharp objects. I'd say how d'you do, but I gather we are missing out the usual exchange of greetings.'

'Well, time is pressing,' he said, sucking his long finger. 'What with Fanny's reputation imperilled, if it ain't gone already. I don't know why I'm being flippant, I don't feel it. I would love her still whatever happened, and so would you, but the rest of the world won't. God! Why did she have to be such a fool?' he burst out. 'Why couldn't she just come to me and say she wanted to marry Carraway?'

'You weren't here to ask,' Caroline said, as gently as she could. 'And what would you have said?'

'I'd have said, "No, you're too young, and besides he gazes through his curls too much." But it would have been a start.'

'And then, I rather fear, she would have proceeded to run off with him. You said marry—do you think that's what she hopes? Or he intends? Or is she not thinking at all?'

'The last sounds more like Fanny. But these are precisely the questions I wanted to put to you. You were the one she was so thick with just lately—or so I hear.'

'Well, you cannot believe everything you hear,' Caroline said. 'I will say, for the last time, that I did not know of Fanny's plan or encourage her towards it. And a gentleman should beware, Mr Milner, of vexing a lady when she has an instrument like this in her hand.'

He did smile then, but she still thought she saw a sparkle of distrust as he bowed and offered her his arm.

'Where are we going?' she said, just before taking it.

'Around the garden. I am still brain-picking, you see. Because if anyone knows something, it must be you. I mean,' he said, holding up a shielding hand, 'because Fanny talked to you more than anyone. What about family? Has Carraway any that you know of?'

'I remember him saying he was brought up by an uncle.'

'Hm, that doesn't sound promising. There's nothing like a stern father with an unsigned will to make a young man behave respectably. Well, they must live on something. I hear the Hampsons paid him well for the wedding-portrait, and Bella tells me Fanny's jewels are gone with her; but none of this is a fortune. So, if they are in London, they will be residing modestly at least, and not in the west-end squares. Therefore, that is one place I need not look.'

'You're going to search for them?'

'Yes. I'm only here to garner what information I can, and then I'll be off after them. Carraway may *be* the one for her, and if so good luck to them: but I'll have to be convinced of it first. If they are truly in love, then he should marry her.'

'I thought you didn't believe in marriage.'

'A man who never contradicts himself must become horribly bored with his own conversation. Oh, on the whole I don't believe in it, except when there is genuine love, which is such a compound of affection, warmth, ease, esteem, and various other spices and condiments, that one hardly expects to come across it once in a lifetime.'

She studied him. 'You know, in your way you are quite as romantic as Fanny.'

He conceded a smile. 'That's what my father said . . . However, fascinating subject though I am, we are not here to discuss me but Fanny. I was in the not very productive process of picking your brains.'

'I'm afraid I cannot think of anything that may help you, Mr Milner. There is only—well, Fanny did have an absurd veneration for my past. My life with my father—it all seemed wonderfully exciting to her, the regiment and the theatre and the gaming-clubs. If she is in London, I fancy that is the world she will be drawn to. Covent Garden, Haymarket—and then all the places along the Strand towards St Paul's, which is also where cheap lodgings are to be had, of course.'

'Well, I thank you, Miss Fortune, that may help indeed. If I do have any news, I shall write at once to Augusta and Bella—'

'Will you write to me?' Her cheeks were stinging: the afternoon had turned so cold. 'There, you knew I was a bold-faced hussy, so that shocking request can be no surprise to you. But as you are so elusive, Mr Milner, I could at least then pin you down to a postal address.'

'Certainly I shall write, Miss Fortune, at your request,' he said, with a smothered wry look, and a short bow. 'But surely you are able to call at the Manor now without tearing of hair and gnashing of teeth?'

'In a way . . . Tell me, how is Bella? Yes, I've seen her—but it hasn't been the same. Even you must understand that.'

'Even I?'

'Even you as a blinkered insensible obtuse dunderheaded male.'

'Well,' he said, suppressing a smile, 'she is still in the dismals, because she is Isabella and she takes things seriously; but she is not in a decline, and she has, I must confess, a good solid friend in Augusta; and I have hopes she will come to the realisation that she is after all pretty well placed. Now, I must go. Will you present my compliments to my uncle and aunt?' His hand on the gate, he wore an arrested, thoughtful look. 'I have been wrong about Fanny. I thought she would come to no harm, left to her own devices. I thought there was no need for fuss.' He followed the flight of a rook overhead as he spoke, though his eyes were not seeing. 'I thought I didn't have to be my father.'

A new world of Stephen was opened up to her then, but some instinct told her that she should respond to it only in the old style.

'Well, I'm pleased to know you have joined the rest of the fallible human race at last, Mr Milner,' she said. 'And I hope you will live to be wrong many, many times again.'

'Including about you?' he said, with a feline look.

'Fascinating subject as I am, we are not here to discuss me,' she said—lightly, yet with an inner feeling of lifting some heavy weight.

'True. I must say goodbye. I suppose I should wish you a merry Christmas also, as I don't know whether I shall be back for it.'

'Goodbye, Mr Milner.' She put out her hand. 'Please—please scold Fanny for me if you find her.'

ATTEMPTS TO KEEP the matter of Fanny secret had met with all the success that might be expected in the neighbourhood; and as Mr Hampson said, at an evening-party the Hampsons were hosting, for their part both he and Mrs Hampson had never found Mr Carraway to be anything but a gentleman, and Felicity was so very fond of the portrait . . .

'There is, I suppose, Miss Fortune, no—how shall I put it?—no word?' enquired Mr Hampson. 'No word about the young lady from the Manor whom we, to our great regret, do not see any more?'

'No.' No: though Caroline had received a letter from Stephen Milner in London, to tell her that he was staying at Batt's Hotel in Jermyn Street, that London was foggy, murky, smoky, and muddy, but that he was not without hopes of success.

'I do hear,' said Mr Hampson, abandoning an unpromising subject, 'that there are visitors again at Hethersett for Christmas. Mr and Miss Downey—charming people—Mr Leabrook introduced them last time.' And then, realising that this was also an unpromising subject with Caroline, Mr Hampson smiled and perspired himself into silence, before escaping across the room.

Well: she wondered if she was to expect another visitation, from Matthew Downey, accusing her of fresh enormities, or whether there had been a peace treaty with his aunt. Not much caring, she only mildly wondered; and then, two days before Christmas, she greatly wondered at seeing a carriage pull up at the Rectory gate, which she recognised as Mr Richard Leabrook's carriage. Maria Downey got out; though she was, as Caroline could see from the two dark male heads within, not the only occupant of the carriage, which then drove on.

'There, my dear, you see I keep my promises.' Maria pressed a cold cheek against hers with a dry kiss, floated over to the parlour fireplace to warm her hands. She was in travelling dress: fur-trimmed pelisse, bonnet and muff. 'I promised I would try to come and see you next time I was at Hethersett—didn't I? And so how do you do, my dear, and now are you ready for the most astounding piece of news?' Maria sat on the sofa. 'Would you believe, my dear, Aunt Sophia is no more?'

'No,' Caroline answered, truthfully. She sat down too, then reminded herself of what was appropriate. 'Oh, Miss Downey, I am sorry.'

'My dear, you *sound* it!' Maria said, with a chuckle. 'Come, I'm sure we may be frank. Even I am only a little sorry, for after all she was not exactly a woman to inspire affection. Well! Matthew and I had only just settled ourselves at Hethersett for a proper traditional Christmas season of gluttony and sloth, and then comes this letter from a solicitor in London—Mr Coker of Symond's Inn—acquainting us with the news that she died at Brighton last Friday—suddenly, of a heart-stroke. You may imagine how Matthew is feeling.'

'I can indeed.' Not, though, with any lively sympathy. 'I gather there was no reconciliation before . . . ?'

Maria shook her head. 'Not for want of trying on Matthew's part. But Aunt Sophia remained—oh, that word that's like obstinate.'

'Obdurate. Was that Matthew I saw in the carriage?'

'Yes. Matthew—and Mr Leabrook.' Maria's smile was a little diffident. 'The fact is, Mr Leabrook is taking us to London directly in his carriage, which is excessively civil of him. On our way we thought to say some goodbyes. That is—Matthew and Mr Leabrook have gone on to call at the Manor, whereas I—well, I elected to call on *you*, my dear. I do gather the unpleasantness still lingers. All I can do is apologise for my brother's rudeness, but he still has those peculiar ideas about you—'

'And Mr Leabrook, I'm sure, is always happy to back them up.'

'Now you mustn't be provoking, my dear,' Maria said, lips twitching. 'He may well have his wicked side, as which of us does not, but he has been excessively obliging to us.'

Dr Langland came in at that moment, full of hearty enquiries, and so was soon acquainted with Miss Downey's news. 'I hope your late aunt was offered spiritual comfort before the end, Miss Downey.'

'It's enchanting of you to hope so, sir, but I'm rather afraid the only comforts Aunt Sophia cared for were a glass of wine and a hand of cards.'

'Sad, sad!' cried Dr Langland, with a shake of his head.

'Isn't it?' yawned Maria. 'Ah, I think I hear the carriage. We are always parting! It's supposed to be sweet sorrow or something, isn't it?'

Aunt Selina had been at the Manor that morning, and on her return she confirmed that Mr Downey and Mr Leabrook had called there.

'Isabella did not exactly look happy—but rather as if she wanted to be happy if she could manage it,' Aunt Selina said, with a thoughtful look. 'Not that it was a long visit. Mr Downey was anxious to be off— what a high-strung young man he is!—and besides Lady Milner could not be *very* welcoming, for it seems Stephen left strict instructions that there was to be no sort of *rapprochement* between Isabella and Mr Leabrook without his presence and consent.'

'Oh, high and mighty!' remarked Caroline: with an inward cry of *Good for you, Stephen.*

If Isabella was yearning back towards Leabrook, there was nothing Caroline could do about it—except feel this nagging dread and trouble, which she did her best to conceal through the festivities of Christmas. Here, the Yule log borne in and heaved to the back of the parlour fire, here the carollers from the village singing while the spiced ale steamed, here the ivy round the fire, the plum-cake, the wassail-bowl; and somewhere, unknown, far from home and friends, Fanny; and likewise, in a hotel at least, but alone, Stephen. When they dined at the Manor on Christmas Day, no amount of goose and chestnut-stuffing could divert the mind from the empty chairs.

One welcome addition, though. Captain Brunton had arrived after a punishing journey by public coach and carrier. That, perhaps, accounted for his appearance—pale, heavy-eyed, close-mouthed, and seemingly wrapped in gloom.

His flush, after dinner, however, when the men rejoined the ladies,

Indiscretion | 461

showed that he had made free with the port. But he drank his tea in separate silence. Caroline intercepted a few curiously baleful looks before he sauntered over to her: 'Miss Fortune. I trust I find you well.'

'Thank you, Captain Brunton; but I'm afraid you are not in spirits?'

'Not at all. That is, I have had good news. An opening for a command in the packet service out of Falmouth. Cornwall.'

'I *am* pleased. Though to be sure Falmouth is a long way away.'

'It is,' Captain Brunton said, 'a long way from *here*. At any rate, I will not be called upon until the new year—'

And that was the end of it, for just then the squeaking of a fiddle and a fugue of coughs announced the arrival of the village carollers.

Was Captain Brunton gloomy, Caroline wondered when she went to bed at the Rectory that night, because he had heard of signs of a reconciliation between Isabella and Mr Leabrook? If so, she thought, then Falmouth, or indeed any other place, would be better. She resolved to tell him so; but sleet and ice kept her in the house for nearly a week.

The first meltings and drippings, however, saw Caroline making the walk to the Manor through a world of steely sun-dazzle and crystalline puddles. She found all well there, and Isabella, with something of her former warmth, jumping up and urging her to the fire. But Lady Milner was subdued, severe, and shook her head bleakly when Caroline asked her if she had heard anything of Fanny.

'Nothing. Nothing. And I assume the same with you.'

'Don't be downcast, Stepmama,' Isabella said, squeezing her arm. 'I know this sounds odd, but I have a feeling—a presentiment that all will be well in the end. Captain Brunton, what is that you see out there?'

The Captain was standing at the window, his hands tucked under his coat-tails. 'I'm not sure, Miss Milner. Well, it is a gig; but it has come half down the avenue, and stopped. I do believe . . .'

Isabella came and stood by him. It was the glass, perhaps, that made her voice hollow as she said: 'Mrs Leabrook.'

'We are very glad to see you, Mrs Leabrook,' Lady Milner put in, as Mrs Leabrook set up camp on the sofa. 'But you must see that we are also a little puzzled—anxious even—to know what this matter is that you must talk to us about.'

With hen-like fluffings and croonings, Mrs Leabrook turned herself towards Isabella. 'Miss Milner. The news I have to tell you is news that you—yes, I acknowledge it, you have a claim to know—'

'Good God,' Isabella cried, white-lipped, 'is it—it must be Richard—'

'He is married.' Mrs Leabrook closed her eyes for a moment. 'Yes. My son writes me today'—she made a pantomime of extracting the letter from her pocket—'Yes. He was married yesterday, in London, by special licence. He bids me be happy. I *am* happy. No woman, I venture to say, who has known the goodness of a son such as Richard, could refuse to bestow her blessing.'

'I would be obliged, ma'am,' Lady Milner said, moving close to Isabella and laying a hand on her rigid arm, 'if you would tell us who Mr Leabrook has married; and how this has come about; and how he explains himself, when he was publicly engaged to my stepdaughter—'

'Ah, now, my dear Lady Milner, there was a certain degree of dubiety about how precisely matters stood between my son and Miss Milner—'

'Indeed there was not, ma'am. That engagement was not broken off. There was an indefinite postponement of marriage, pending the resolution of a difficulty.' Lady Milner's glare seemed to pin the fluttering matron to her seat.

Mrs Leabrook, resentfully humbled, made a pantomime of searching for a handkerchief. 'Dear me. The lady—the lady is Miss Downey. That is to say, she *was*, for of course now her title is Mrs Richard Leabrook. Quite a favourite of mine she has been, and—pardon me, Miss Milner, but speaking *objectively*, as it were—I really cannot reprove his choice, even so sudden as it is: in all other respects it is a most eligible match—'

'Wait, ma'am,' Caroline interjected, 'are we speaking of the same Miss Downey? I hardly think you would call that an eligible match, unless . . .' Cold, sure knowledge came like a cloud across the sun. 'What was the result of the will, ma'am? They were going to London for the reading of the late Mrs Catling's will.'

Mrs Leabrook's dim pretty eyes roamed all around the room: then she seemed to make a decision, and with a hoist of her chins adopted a proud look. 'Miss Downey, as my son informs me, inherits her aunt's entire fortune. This I consider, as does he I'm sure, a tribute to her character. Mrs Catling obviously saw her niece's worth, her beauty, elegance, taste, and accomplishment, and chose to reward it accordingly. As my son also perceived those qualities, and—and saw fit to pay them the tribute of his hand.'

So Maria got everything! thought Caroline. Poor Matthew. Poor indeed. Her thoughts skipped speedily and surely. Those expensive improvements at Hethersett. Maria's peculiar liking for country living. No, no, they have been intriguing for some time. And now Leabrook has made a very astute matrimonial choice: beauty and wealth. As for Maria—well, he is handsome, sophisticated, and also landed: in place of her unstable, peripheral life, she will be chatelaine of a mansion. And as for how they have behaved, there will be some talk, some censure, —but nothing they cannot weather, with riches and power.

Caroline made herself look at Isabella. She was still, stiff, and pale. Now she rose to her feet. 'Mrs Leabrook, I am obliged to you,' she said, in a steady voice. 'Thank you for coming to tell us, and I hope the journey has not inconvenienced you.'

'Oh, not in the slightest, my dear Miss Milner, and even if it had I was determined to do it, rather than that you should hear the news in some other way. I like to do things properly, it's how I am and . . .'

But Isabella could not be interested in how Mrs Leabrook was or where she had got it from, and with the help of a renewed firmness from Lady Milner, the visitor was very soon got rid of.

And then Isabella looked blindly around. Caroline was never sure who instigated it, but it ceased to matter, anyhow, as she held her sobbing friend in her arms.

The short grey candle of winter afternoon was nearly spent when Caroline left the Manor. There had been talk—of course—though not too much, and not too deeply.

Some things, though, needed to be said, and were, between Caroline and Captain Brunton, who accompanied her to the front door.

'I do want, just once, to kick him,' Caroline remarked. 'And not from the rear.'

'I fear he would have to be standing up for that, Miss Fortune, and in my mind I have already thrashed him to the floor,' Captain Brunton said. 'But this is monstrous violent language.'

'Yes, thank heaven for it. Will you escort me home, Captain Brunton?'

'Of course.' Eyes front, the Captain took her arm as if it were a stick or umbrella. Along the oak avenue a rising wind licked at the black slush-puddles and tugged at the leafless branches like malicious fingers in hair. 'I'm afraid I can't speak, Miss Fortune. Because if I do I must use the unconscionable word "bastard".'

'It is a very good word in the circumstances . . .' This was a day, she thought decisively, for truth. 'Captain Brunton, I'm so sorry.'

'So am I, Lord, so am I . . .' He glanced down at her with a jerk. 'D'you mean—sorry for me?'

'Yes. Because it is painful to see someone suffering what you must be suffering. That is, watching someone you love be so cruelly hurt.'

Captain Brunton looked at her as if she were a witch. 'How—how could you tell? I have never—I have striven never to betray myself.'

'Oh, I know. But one can sense these things. I'm sorry if this is—

intrusive. I speak only from sympathy; and you may be sure I have breathed no word of it to anyone, nor will.'

'Oh, I trust you, Miss Fortune. I'm just astonished. Oh great God,' he burst out, 'what I have heard today—to think of the deceit and insolence of that man . . . But, of course, you did your best to warn us of his real character. For my part, I could not be sure how far my feelings against him were the mere result of jealousy. And when should one speak, and when keep silence? Here—with my cousin's family—I have always been conscious of seeming to interfere. Miss Fanny used to tell me that very plainly . . .' He slowed his pace. 'There too, in that regard, I wonder whether I should have spoken.'

'About Fanny?' Caroline said in surprise.

'Not exactly . . . But I will tell you now, and let you judge. When Miss Fanny began to be intimate with Mr Carraway, something about his name revived a memory. Two years ago, my ship was refitting, I shared a set of rooms at Deal with a brother officer, name of Harvey. He was the sole support of his sister, a gentle little creature, at a boarding-school in Chelsea. Well, there was a young visiting drawing-master at this school who—well, I regret to say he seduced Harvey's sister, and prevailed upon her to run away with him. Harvey was much distressed, and took off for London at once to try to trace them. He did find his sister at last: in lodgings alone. The drawing-master had deserted her, having—well, having enjoyed her.' Captain Brunton's cheeks reddened. 'Well, I think you may guess her condition. Saddest of all, Harvey went to this lodging one day to find she had gone. There was rent owing, and she had simply taken herself off, in Lord knows what mixture of despair and shame. Poor Harvey, I remember he was shockingly cut up. And I remember—well, I would have said the drawing-master's name was Garraway or perhaps Garrity . . . well, you may see the trend of my thought. But I had no *certainty*, none. Though the possibility has nagged at me in a way you cannot conceive, Miss Fortune!'

'I can conceive it very well, Captain Brunton. And I can imagine your feelings also, on finding that Fanny had eloped with Mr Carraway.'

'I doubt you can,' he said, with ferocious gloom. 'If this *is* the same man, then I fear it is a poor outlook for Miss Fanny. I wish with all my heart I had spoken before—yet even then I wonder if I might not have been reproached for mere scurrilous hearsay.'

'By Fanny, I think you would indeed: it would have taken a great deal to alter her resolution, and I fear opposition, or warning, would be the one thing that could strengthen it,' Caroline said: a little more lightly indeed than she felt. 'All I can take hold of is this lodging that your friend found his poor sister in—do you recall where it was?'

'I never went there. But I know it was in the Borough, hard by Guy's Hospital. Rooms above a tallow-chandler's, if you please.'

The tallow-chandler's in the Borough, hard by Guy's Hospital: Caroline concentrated her imagination so intensely upon it that she could almost smell the tallow. And at the end of the second night, yawning but wakeful in the foredawn hush, Caroline was packing a bag.

The Borough was not a part of London she knew well, but she could find her way around: nor did the prospect of going to London alone trouble her in the least, as it might many young ladies. She sat composedly waiting for first light, when she could slip out of the house and walk to meet the early carrier who passed on the Alconbury road.

Aunt Selina, Uncle John: I love you more than I can express, or can ever hope to express in what I hope will be our long, long association; and certainly more than I could get into that craven little note I left you before slipping out this morning. But I had to do it this way, because if I had announced my intention of going to London to find Fanny, you would surely have tried to prevent me. And you must understand (*pursued Caroline in thought, as the coach struggled muddily up Highgate Hill*) that I am very well used to going about alone and will be perfectly safe until my return.

And also—my dear aunt, I think after all you will understand this— while I feel that contrary to general opinion I have done absolutely nothing wrong at Wythorpe, I do have a great wish, an unconquerable wish, to do something right.

Chapter Eleven

THE WHITE HART in the Borough, south of London Bridge, was a huge and ancient inn, galleried around its great central yard. As a young woman taking a lodging alone, Caroline was given her share of sidelong glances, but having taken the precaution of wearing her soberest clothes, along with a ring on her left hand—a brass ring from her bed-hangings at home—and of calling herself Mrs Milner (the first name that came to mind), she was able to retire to her gallery bedroom free of the suspicion that she was there to entertain gentlemen.

She woke to the rumble of wagons and the smell of coffee, and a protracted shiver of misgiving: just what *was* she doing? Tucked into her mind was the thought of Stephen: why not just call on him at Batt's Hotel, give him her information, and simply hand the business over . . .

To his superior male brain? she concluded. No, no.

Fortified by pride and breakfast, she went out into the Borough. The little winding streets around Guy's Hospital were represented by every noisome trade, it seemed, from tanneries to dung-farmers, but not a tallow-chandler was to be found. It was only when she emerged in Borough High Street again, baffled and back to her starting point, that she saw what had been there all the time. Directly in front of her, on the west side, was a row of tall square-bayed houses with latticed shop-fronts, and in the middle hung a signboard—peeling and faded, which was perhaps why she had missed it: *Gerrard & Son, Tallow-Chandlers.*

She was so excited that she did not stop to think how she might best approach this. She hurried across the road, burst into the dingy ill-lit shop, and waited for the cracked bell to summon someone from the glassed-in counting-house at the back.

'May I be of service to you, madam?'

It was a pale pretty watercolour of a woman in her worn thirties, wiping her hands on her apron and presenting a smile.

'Oh, good morning. You must be Mrs Gerrard.' Caroline took what she hoped would be an inspired plunge. 'Charles has told me so much about you. I was wondering if this was a convenient time to call on him.' She reinforced her own smile as that of Mrs Gerrard faded. 'Charles Carraway, you know.'

'I'm sorry, madam,' the woman said at last. 'I fancy you've got the wrong house.' She began to retreat. 'There's no one here of that name.'

'Not Milner then? Miss Fanny Milner?'

'I don't know who you mean,' Mrs Gerrard said, shaking her head, avoiding Caroline's eyes. 'It's like I said—' She stopped, tight-lipped. 'Now I must be getting to my work, madam, and I'll bid you good-day.'

'Like you said? Pray, what do you mean? To whom?' But already the chandler's wife had shut herself up in the counting-house.

Going out into the street, with an acrid feeling of triumph and dismay, Caroline was certain that Mrs Gerrard *did* know something.

Coming out of abstraction, she saw a lounger in greatcoat and pulled-down hat lean out of a doorway ahead, and readied herself for evasion. This district was full of seedy fellows—

'Oh my God!' she cried, as Stephen Milner lifted the hat and smiled his lopsided smile.

'It would appear we've followed the same trail,' he said, offering her his arm. 'Will you? I know I look rather disreputable, but it is a necessary disguise, because I've been watching the house, you see. And my guess is that Fanny and friend have the rooms at the second pair back.'

'Then they *are* there! I thought—'

'Oh, yes. That little downtrodden woman said she'd never heard of 'em, no doubt? Same with me yesterday, when I tracked them to this charming spot. But I definitely glimpsed *him* this morning, slipping through an alley near Guy's. My guess is there's some tortuous back way behind those rambling old places, and they use that, but I can't find it.'

'You saw Mr Carraway? Oh, thank goodness.'

'Why? Never tell me *you* have a taking for him as well.'

'Oh, Stephen, stop it. I'm relieved because—well, it means he is still here, that he hasn't abandoned her.'

'Ah, I see.' He looked into her face. 'I see more. You are serious, Miss Fortune. A bad sign. What more have you to tell?—and incidentally, how *did* you end up here, and are you all alone?'

'I am alone, Mr Milner, and quite comfortably so, and I will tell you—but I long to know how *you* found this place?'

'It was rather brilliant of me, wasn't it?' he said, with satisfaction. 'Oh, it has been a long, frustrating business. The key at last was thinking of Fanny's character, and putting that together with what Augusta told me, that she had taken her jewels with her. She scorns such artificial frippery, which suggests that she had a purpose to sell them to help finance the clandestine liaison. So, it was then a simple matter of seeking out such jewellers as are unscrupulous enough to buy family jewels from an obviously deluded schoolgirl. The rogue who had bought them was canny enough to require an address from the vendors in case of trouble—and so, here we are. Now where are you staying? Somewhere, I presume: and can one get a good meal there?'

So: the White Hart, where she ate luncheon with Stephen in a private dining room. Much to tell. Captain Brunton's story first, because it was germane, and because she still hesitated over the other.

'That was why I was so relieved to hear you'd seen Mr Carraway— because I was afraid of Fanny being deserted, as he did with this poor Miss Harvey.'

'I see, I see.' Stephen was thoughtful. 'There *may* be some other side to this story. The problem I anticipate is Fanny's stubbornness. I still doubt we will wean her from him, even if she were to know this discreditable tale. If there has not been a marriage ceremony, as I presume there has not, then we must remind the forgetful Mr Carraway of this little omission. Will you take a little more of this veal-and-ham pie? And will you tell me what else is troubling you?'

'How can you tell something's troubling me?' she said, rather sharply.

'Because you're drinking a lot of wine.'

'That's not a sign of trouble, Mr Milner: that is me: I like drinking a lot of wine,' she said loftily, drinking.

'I'm glad to hear it. We topers must stick together. Still—'

'Oh, Stephen, it's Isabella. No, no, don't be alarmed, she is quite well—but plainly you have not heard the news?'

'The last letter I had was from Augusta, last Thursday I think.' His eyes were flinty. 'Tell, tell.'

She told. At the end of the telling, he called for another bottle of wine, and they silently drank while the fire popped.

'If you wish to use a bad word,' she said at last, 'about Leabrook, I mean, then don't be shy of it. Captain Brunton used a very good one. He called him a—'

'Yes, to be sure. I am thinking of—well, I am thinking of many things. I am wishing Leabrook all the ill-luck in the world, of course, but also I am—well, I am thanking heaven for Isabella's escape. Indeed, this may be the most amazing stroke of luck, because even with what *I've* learned about Leabrook, I wasn't confident of being able to cure Bella of him.'

'You mean you know more—worse about him?'

'Oh, yes: and that's why I left instructions that there was to be no reconciling while I was away. Yes, I found out about our friend Leabrook, when I went away from Wythorpe the first time in November. It was when he said that you had thrown yourself at him at Brighton, and you said that he had sought to seduce you in same.'

'Yes—and you skipped off somewhere to see your wretched ruins.'

'Quite right, and quite apposite, as one of the ruins I went to see was a lady well known to you. I refer to your former employer and, I would guess, tormentor, Mrs Sophia Catling of Brighton.'

'The devil you did!' Caroline sat back, open-mouthed. 'You—going to see Mrs Catling! I'm just trying to imagine it.'

'All my grace and elegance contrasting with that crabbed monstrosity, I know. She was not in health when I saw her. That was partly why she did not grant me a long interview—the other reason being that I was, let's see if I can remember her honeyed words, an insolent puppy to come quizzing her about that underbred chit of whom she could recall only so much as to confirm in her mind that she was well rid.'

'Now I know you have seen Mrs Catling. Oh, Stephen, I am sorry.'

'Don't be, it's no fault of yours. Take another glass of this. Well, the said Mr Leabrook, she asserted, was a man of impeccable taste and manners, and would not so demean himself; and as for you, Mrs Catling said she was too careful an employer to allow any kind of amorous goings-on. The reason she dismissed you was that you were wilful and impertinent and set upon going absent without leave—yes, that was her military phrase. And so be off with you—to me, I mean.

'Well, off with me I went, more suspicious of Leabrook on account of it. And then I had an idea, which—well, let's just call it genius and leave it at that. I bethought me of Leabrook's sister—the one at the Brighton boarding-school. It did seem odd to me that she so seldom came home, and I wondered what she could tell me about her brother. So I procured a Brighton trade directory, and I found the place at last. As she had heard of me, being brother to Leabrook's fiancé, I got permission to take Miss Leabrook to tea at Dutton's. It seems they are estranged, because last year Leabrook "interested" himself in a friend of hers—a pretty girl lacking family and protection—in quite an inappropriate way: denied all, when it came out. By which time the girl, much distressed, had got herself moved to another school—and of course Leabrook's sister had lost her friend.'

'Dear God!' exploded Caroline. 'I had a feeling that I was not the first he had approached in that way—but a schoolfriend of his sister's!'

'Unsavoury, isn't it? Well, that settled it for me. I knew this man must not marry Bella, but the question was how to accomplish that. Then, before I could come to a decision, there arrives Augusta's letter telling me of Fanny's mad escapade, and so I had to rush home, pick your brains, as you remember, and then rush here. So in a way I'm glad that Leabrook has decided matters by showing his hand.'

'Well, Bella is very thankful for her escape.'

'And you are too magnanimous to say that everyone should have listened to you in the first place, so I'll say it for you.'

'Thank you. But I would rather never have been right.'

Stephen looked down. 'Look, we've finished the bottle. Shall we take a turn in the yard? I need to clear my head before we go on.'

Yes, she needed some air: a little time too, while she took in all he had told her. He let her think while they strolled about the inn-yard. An old carrier in smock and gaiters was unloading his parcels, and a small boy was rolling on the ground in noisy ecstasies with an excited puppy.

'What did you mean about going on?' she asked him at last.

'Oh, I suppose go on to survey the chandler's house again. I must confess that I am now somewhat at a stand. My hope is that Fanny must come out, at some point, and then—then I pounce.'

Caroline was gazing fixedly at the little boy with the puppy. 'Stephen, I have an idea.'

A very young and dispirited costermonger, on the corner of Borough High Street, supplied them with what they needed. The half-grown mongrel appeared to think it was all a great game at first, when his master tied him to a bridle-post just outside the tallow-chandler's shop and then retreated, with Caroline and Stephen, to a passageway down the street. The pup yapped excitedly for a while: then, sensing something amiss in his master's continued absence, began to howl.

The shop-door of Gerrard & Son had opened, and Fanny Milner stepped out. With a glance up and down the street she hurried over, as Caroline had guessed she surely must, to comfort the puppy.

She was still rubbing his ears and crooning that his master was a brute, when she became aware of the three figures surrounding her.

'Hello, Fanny,' Stephen said amiably.

Fanny, rising and red-faced, looked from one to the other in gathering outrage. 'Oh! Oh, I am entrapped! Stephen, how could you—and, Caroline, you, above all how could *you*?' And to the coster: 'I'm afraid I don't know you—'

'No, that's so, and I ain't the brute you said I am,' the coster said, with dignity, gathering his squirming dog into his arms and walking away.

'A ruse, to be sure,' Stephen said, very tenderly and deftly securing Fanny's arm, 'but really, my dear Fanny, you are so deuced elusive you left us no choice. Why you are so determined not to have your dear brother and your dear friend call upon you I can't imagine—'

'You know very well,' Fanny said grandly. 'It is because you wish to drag me back to my dreary imprisonment.' She glared at her brother. 'Stephen, I am free, and I am happy. Can you not understand that? Caro—surely *you* can?'

'I would be very glad to be absolutely sure of it, Fanny,' Caroline said, with a feeling of crossing stepping-stones.

'Well, you *can* be sure,' Fanny said. 'Indeed, step in, by all means, as you now know where we reside. You will be supposing, of course, an illicit liaison. I may as well say we maintain separate establishments within our set of rooms.' She looked so crimson as she said this that it was impossible to say whether it was a lie or the surprising truth.

'Devil take it, Fanny,' said Stephen. 'As we said, we've come to see you, that's all. Now lead the way, do.'

Partly mollified, yet with several suspicious glances, Fanny led the way. Presently they were passing through the shop, where Mrs Gerrard peeped out at them like a wondering rabbit, and climbing some narrow stairs. Here Stephen paused for a moment, and whispered urgently to Caroline: 'Whatever I say, no matter how absurd, agree with me.'

He had been right: the second floor, at the back, was where Fanny and Mr Carraway had their lodging; and it was not so very bad. There was a large sitting room, and opening out of it a smaller room with a good window, which was obviously Charles Carraway's painting room, as he was to be seen there, staring at the visitors. As for sleeping arrangements, Caroline couldn't tell.

'My dear Charles, you see we are pursued,' said Fanny, in an excessive voice, 'pursued and actually caught, but apparently we needn't fear, as my brother *says* he has simply come on a visit, and is not going to drag me away.' She went and set a kettle over the fire. 'If he does, you know I shall fight—but I don't want you to, do you hear me?'

Judging by Mr Carraway's perspiring pallor, this advice was superfluous. But he cheered up a little when Stephen, advancing on him, thrust out a hand with a breezy 'Mr Carraway, glad to see you again,' and then flung himself into a creaking chair. 'Well, you are snug here, I must say. Not the prettiest of situations, though, which is a pity.'

'Charles and I care nothing for fashion, Stephen, as you well know,' Fanny said airily. 'It is far more important that we live within our means, as we intend showing this is not a mere adventure; and as we have these rooms on easy terms, on account of Mrs Gerrard being Charles's cousin, they suit us very well for the time being.'

'Oh, a cousin!' said Stephen, still amiable.

'Well, do tell me how everyone is at Wythorpe,' Fanny said. 'I have been meaning to write—but to get a reply, you know, I must give an address, and that—well . . . And they are looking after the dogs?' she put in, with a brimming look. 'They haven't—taken it out on them?'

'My dear Fanny,' laughed Stephen, 'do you suppose we whip your dogs daily, to punish you for your elopement? They are as spoiled as ever. I call it an elopement, by the by, for want of a better term.'

'Words are only words, you know, Mr Milner,' said Mr Carraway, finding his voice. 'It is our feelings that have guided us, and they, I believe'—he gave his misty sideways look—'can never lead us wrong.'

Caroline could contain herself no longer. 'It would be interesting,' she said, 'to know if Miss Harvey still agrees with those sentiments.' She turned to Fanny. 'Miss Harvey was the sister of a naval officer, a friend of Captain Brunton's. She ran away to London from Deal with—

well, I believe with this gentleman.' Who had gone very pale again.

'Yes,' Mr Carraway said, nodding earnestly, 'yes, that is correct, that was the case, indeed.'

Fanny set to making some tea with vigour. 'You never told me this, Charles.'

'Not strictly,' Mr Carraway said, with a judicious frown, 'not strictly perhaps—but you know, Fanny, I did tell you I had loved before.'

'Yes, Charles . . . Though I did not know it was that sort of love.'

'Oh, my dear girl, what other sort is there? You know my nature: I cannot tack to the winds of convention: I am all or nothing.' Mr Carraway did some wistful blinking. 'If you would know about Miss Harvey, I can tell you. I do not know what story you have heard, Miss Fortune,' he sighed, with a limpid look. 'If it represents me in a bad light, I cannot help that. We were both young and absurd, and we fell to quarrelling over trifles. Then there was a lasting quarrel, and I took myself off, and when I returned to—to where we lodged, she had taken herself off likewise, and that was the end of it. It sounds a sad tale, but there can be nothing worse than two souls yoked inharmoniously.'

'Aye, aye, there's something in what he says,' grunted Stephen, who under lowered lids had been watching the painter carefully. 'What do you think, Fanny?'

Fanny poured the tea, then glanced from Stephen to Caroline to her lover. 'I think,' she said, 'it is a great pity, Charles, that you could not tell me about this—did you think I wouldn't understand?'

'I would have to be an even greater fool than I know myself to be to think *that*,' he said meltingly, 'for you always do understand—always! But come,' he added more briskly, 'you do right, indeed, Mr Milner, to appeal to Fanny: for that is what the whole matter is about, is it not? Fanny's choice: Fanny's decision: that is, thank heaven, to be with me.'

'Quite so,' Fanny said, rallying, 'and I tell you, Stephen, you will not fence me about with your spirit-soiling prohibitions.'

'No intention of any such thing,' Stephen said, standing up and roaming about as he drank his tea. 'Just wonder whether you wouldn't like to seal it—your decision, I mean—by getting married. It would be so much better in all ways, you know.'

'How?' said Fanny, scornfully.

'Well, you love each other, don't you?'

'Absolutely! How can you doubt it?'

'My dear sister, I don't. That's why I'd suppose you'd like to show that love to the world. Proclaim it.' Stephen finished his tea and beamed.

'Pooh, you don't understand me very well, Stephen, if you think I care for that,' Fanny said, with tense gaiety; and stole a look at Caroline. 'You understand, Caro—don't you?'

'Oh, yes,' she answered easily, 'though I do tend to agree with Stephen—about showing your love to the world, I mean.'

'And then there's your money,' Stephen went on. 'Dear conscientious Father made sure you and Bella had your fifteen thousand apiece as a marriage portion, and it seems a pity that it should lie there a-rusting.'

'Money,' Fanny pronounced, 'is sordid stuff, and we don't care for it.'

'Not a whit,' Mr Carraway said, with—to do him justice—what seemed like complete sincerity.

'Don't you? Hey, well, it does seem a shame,' Stephen said, shrugging indifferently, 'as when two such people as you are in love, it's nice to see them properly set up. A good painting-studio, for example, and plenty of room for dogs, and—well, anyhow, it was just a thought. Really that's not why we're here. Aha, you are about to say, then why are you here? I'll tell you: to give you our news. Our own most happy, most delightful news.' He came over and took Caroline's arm. 'Caroline and I are getting married. Yes!' he cried loudly, covering her yelp of surprise. 'Yes, is it not the most delightful thing? We've come to Town to get a licence, so we can be married as soon as may be. Oh, we did think about going through the whole business of calling the banns, but it takes so long— and why delay? When you're in love everything is romantic—even getting a marriage licence from Doctors' Commons. Isn't that so, Caro?'

'Yes, Stephen,' she managed.

'Well, aren't you going to congratulate us?' Stephen pursued. 'I had thought, Fanny, that you would be pleased for us. I know how fond you are of Caro—and now you are going to be her sister-in-law!'

Staggered as Caroline was, she did register a small pleasure in seeing the rather too self-assured Fanny reduced to such silent astonishment.

'Yes, Fanny,' she said, 'I hope you are as pleased as I am, my dear.'

'I—yes, I am,' stammered Fanny, 'only it is so—so very unexpected!'

'Love is always unexpected, I believe,' Caroline said. 'As for me, I can think of nothing better than being united with the man I love for the rest of my days—openly and in the eyes of the world.' She found this both very easy and intensely difficult to say.

'Quite so,' Stephen said, with hearty approval. 'Well, that's our news. And now, what say you dine with us on the strength of it? The four of us, tomorrow evening, at Grillon's—what d'you say? Call it a settled thing. I'm at Batt's in Jermyn Street if you need to say nay for any reason. But do come. It would give us great pleasure.'

'Then—yes, thank you, we shall be happy to join you,' said Mr

Carraway, who had the dawning look of a man woken from a bad dream. 'And—many congratulations to you. Eh, Fanny?'

'Yes,' Fanny said, in a small voice.

'When you said agree with you on everything, no matter how absurd,' Caroline said, as they turned into the yard of the White Hart, 'I didn't know you would—'

'Say something so *very* absurd? Yes, apologies for that, it must have quite shocked you. But you see my reasoning. Fanny has always taken you as her model, inexplicable as it is; and so my hope is that if she supposes you reconciled to marriage, then . . .'

'Oh, yes, I do see. But do you want your sister to marry Carraway?'

'Yes, because if she doesn't, she will ruin herself for his sake; and because she does, God help her, love the man, and I think he loves her. And besides, I do believe she can manage him. What do you think?'

'I think . . . yes, I would go along with that.'

'You're not under obligation to agree with me now, you know.'

'I know, idiot. Stephen, this pretence'—she glanced at the ring on her finger—'it will surely have to be revealed at some point.'

'Oh, we'll cross that bridge when we come to it. And with luck it will have done its work by then. You're tired, I think. I prescribe an early supper and bed. And in the morning I'll call for you. We should go shopping: find something nice for Aunt Selina, who is no doubt sick with worry. And for Bella.'

'That's a good thought . . . And, Stephen, might I pay a call tomorrow? Being in London puts me in mind of Matthew Downey. I'm sorry for him. He was so dreadfully disappointed in his expectations from Mrs Catling, and he did so try to please her.'

'Hm, and was not half so obliging to you, as I recall.'

'Well, yes, and as I said I don't know why I should care.'

'I know why,' Stephen said, in his cryptic way, leaving her.

Caroline, lingering in the coffee room of the White Hart next morning, looked at the Dutch clock on the wall, saw the morning was half gone and called down curses on the head of Stephen Milner, who had said he would come for her and had forgotten.

She sprang up, resolved to find a hackney, and found Stephen's waistcoat in front of her nose.

'Trifle late, sorry. The fact is I had a visitor at my hotel.'

Drawing in breath to say she didn't give a damn about that, she found herself saying: 'Oh, who?'

'Carraway. Come come, I've a hackney waiting for us. That gown's pretty, is it new? Yes, it was Carraway, with his curls combed and his coat brushed, and actually, I suspect, absent from Fanny without leave. He had come to return the favour of my call, he said, and he had been thinking over—they had both been thinking over—what was said about marriage yesterday, and the end of it was that he was very ready to obtain a marriage licence, if I would be so good as to show him how it was done.' Stephen handed her into the hackney waiting at the mouth of the yard. 'So I took him straight down to Doctors' Commons to apply for a licence, and now he has gone home to tell Fanny.' Stephen rapped on the carriage roof. 'Oh, by the by, we're going to Golden Square now—I don't think the Lent law term is sitting yet, so I dare say you'll find Mr Downey at home.'

The Downey house in not-very-fashionable Golden Square stood tall, shadowy, sooty, behind an ornate railing. Their names, Mr Milner and Miss Fortune, produced a peculiar flurry at the top of the stairs in the roomy, tomby hall, the maid peering uncertainly up. Presently, with an audible hiss of 'Oh, *Mother*,' Matthew Downey himself descended.

'Mr Milner—Miss Fortune—this is so very unexpected, you must excuse . . .' He did not say what they must excuse, but stood irritably rubbing his neck. 'Hannah, is there a fire lit in the drawing room?'

'Not as I know on,' said the maid, stumping away.

'Perhaps you'll be so good as to step into the study, if my papers won't incommode you. I was studying late last night.' Matthew, unshaven and unbrushed, looked a little seedy. There was a brandy-bottle amongst the tumble of books and papers on the desk.

'We came, Mr Downey,' Stephen said, 'because we were in Town, and we wished to pay our compliments, and above all to say that we are sorry about your aunt's death—and sorry also for the sequel.'

'Exactly,' Matthew said heavily. 'And the sequel includes what my sister has done. Believe me, Maria has shocked us all. The fact remains she has married the man who was to have married Miss Milner—that is why, sir, my mother is so embarrassed—'

'Oh! Lord, she needn't be,' said Stephen, soothingly. 'Believe me, sir, for my part, I wish the new Mrs Leabrook well, as I'm sure you do.'

'Wish her well?' cried Matthew. 'I wish her ill, Mr Milner!'

'Come, I'm sure you don't mean that,' Caroline said. 'It must have been a great blow when Mrs Catling—did what she did with her for-tune; for you had indeed been a devoted nephew. But that was her caprice, and Maria really can't be blamed for that.'

'I see you do not know the half of it,' Matthew intoned, slumping into a seat. 'Miss Fortune: I am glad of this opportunity. I owe you—an apology.' This cost him a visible effort. 'That time at Wythorpe . . . I fear I jumped to entirely erroneous conclusions about who had betrayed the secret of my engagement to Aunt Sophia.' A thick sigh escaped his chest, and lowering his eyes he said: 'It was Maria. She was the one who told Aunt Sophia about my—about Perdita. It turns out—as I discovered only by accident, from a chance remark by the servant who takes in the post—that she has long been opening my letters. And one of them—a very tender, very private missive from Perdita—was even found among my aunt's effects. So. Pray accept my apology, Miss Fortune, and consider me punished enough.'

'Oh, Mr Downey, I am so very sorry. That was a dreadful thing for Maria to do—I am quite disgusted with her.'

'It is no matter, Miss Fortune. There is a last irony. My Perdita—is not my Perdita any more. She has severed our connection, and is already affianced to another. He is a grocer and tea-merchant in the City. Perdita informs me he has fifty yards of frontage.'

'A man stands no chance,' murmured Stephen, shaking his head.

'I hardly know what to say,' Caroline said, discreetly treading on his toe, 'except again that I'm sorry, and—well, Mr Downey, it seems to me that almost everyone has acted in a deceitful and shabby and disgraceful way, except yourself. It may be difficult to see that as a satisfaction just now, but I hope that in time it may come to be so.'

'Thank you, Miss Fortune,' Matthew said, with rich despair, 'but I do not see how!' Yet there seemed to be a newly thoughtful look in his eyes as they left him amongst the folios and tobacco-fug.

'Well, I think you were right,' Caroline said, as they took their places in the hackney once more. 'Leabrook and Maria Downey are very well matched, and I dare say will soon begin making each other as unhappy as they have made others.'

'Amen to that; and I have some moderate good news on that score. A letter from Isabella this morning, telling me the Leabrook story in her own honest fashion, assuring me she is in good spirits, and seeming— well, it's hard to be sure in a letter, but seeming quite strong and sensible. Augusta, she says, has been a great help to her—and also Captain Brunton, which is a surprise. Are they rubbing along better now?'

'They are rubbing along very much better: and besides, Captain Brunton is in love with Isabella, and has been for a long time.'

'The devil he is! Why—why did he never say?'

'Discretion, Stephen—have you no notion of discretion?'

'I suppose not. Hm. Well, she does ask in this letter, as I have been everywhere in the kingdom, what Falmouth is like.'

'That's where Captain Brunton has a post in the packet service.'

'Well, well. I wonder . . .'

'So do I: but let us just have quiet hopes. One wouldn't wish to tempt Fate, when everything has turned out so well.'

'Turned out well? I don't know about that: I don't know that I can quite echo your satisfaction, Miss Fortune. Turned upside-down is the phrase I would use to describe my world since you arrived in it: truly there has never been a moment's peace. There is only one thing for it. You will have to marry me directly, as you are surely as much in love with me as I am with you: and I am the only one who can restrain you, my darling Caroline, from creating disaster wherever you go.'

'This is . . .' She looked at him. 'This is . . .' She looked everywhere but at him. 'This is Covent Garden.'

'Yes, I know a good jeweller's here, and really we must do something about that ring. May I take it off?'

Trembling, she gave him her hand. 'I don't understand,' she said.

'Insanely soft skin. What don't you understand?'

Everything: nothing: her mind was somewhere off circling in space. 'When I said I didn't know why I cared about Matthew, you said you knew why. And I didn't understand.'

'Oh, yes, I knew: I knew why you cared: because that's you: because in spite of your manifest faults and weaknesses, which I have always been kind enough to point out to you, you are still, Caroline Fortune, the dearest, warmest, most generous, and good-natured, amusing, entrancing, and bewitchingly beautiful woman in creation.'

'Oh . . .' Abruptly she seized his hands in wild, absurd excitement. 'Oh, Stephen, what are we going to do?'

'After the ring, you mean? I suggest follow the prevailing fashion, and go to Doctors' Commons for a marriage licence. After that, we shall live, love, and be happy as mortals can be: we shall drink and make merry, we shall be silent and watch the herons, we shall go to the races and go to blazes, and we shall talk as only you and I can talk. But now, Miss Fortune, I must ask you for a formal answer, for as this is the only proposal I ever intend making I don't want it wasted.'

'Oh, Stephen,' she cried, laughing. 'Yes.'

Jude Morgan

Having devoured the novels of Jane Austen and Georgette Heyer when I was growing up, I was delighted to discover Jude Morgan's glorious Regency historical *Indiscretion*. My second discovery was that the author was a man. But why was this so surprising? Perhaps because most historical novels tend to be written by women but also because his portrayal of heroine, Caroline Fortune, is just so believable.

To find out more about Jude Morgan, I travelled to Peterborough, where he lives on the edge of the Fens, to meet him. I asked him why he had chosen to write in this particular genre? 'I have been writing books since 1986,' he told me, 'and have appeared in print under a variety of pen names. My first historical sagas were set in the Fens, which was unusual at the time because most historicals seemed to be set in the North or in Cornwall. After that I wrote historical crime. I have always loved Regency England and it seemed a natural progression, eventually, to write about it.' I wondered if his readers are surprised to learn that Jude Morgan is a man? 'Yes, I do get a reaction from readers when they discover Jude Morgan is a man,' he answered, with a smile. 'Perhaps it's because I write from a woman's point of view, because historicals tend to be female centred. For me, as a writer, the most interesting part is trying to imagine other people's experiences. The ultimate is putting yourself in another gender—and then putting her in a period of history that you love.'

Although Jude is obsessive about historical research, he claims not to be a historian. 'My background is literature with a degree in English Literature from the University of East Anglia and an MA in Creative Writing.' In addition, he was once a contestant on the BBC's *Mastermind*, his chosen subject 'English Literature of the Romantic Period'. He made it through to the semifinals, where his next subject was 'The Life and Works of Charles Dickens'.

For pleasure, and research, Jude immerses himself in writings on Regency England; when we met he had just finished reading a biography of Beau Brummell. 'He was the arbiter of taste and fashion in Georgian society. He led the trend for men to wear understated but beautifully cut clothes, adorned with elaborate neckties. He claimed to take five hours to dress and recommended boots be cleaned with champagne! People would come to watch him dress in the morning—fascinating detail . . . I've also discovered that some of the most interesting historical nuggets are revealed in contemporary writings, letters and memoirs, which record the mundane details of everyday life: how much things cost; what it was like to wear a powdered wig; how, after you had a child, you threw a party for all your friends and drank a special drink for childbirth.'

Talk of alcohol prompted me to ask him what the 'canary wine' was that he mentions in *Indiscretion*? 'Literally, it's wine from the Canaries, a Spanish sweet wine not unlike a sweet sherry. Britain was constantly at war with France at the time so French wine was not always easy to come by. Oh God, I'm so glad I knew the answer to that,' he laughed.

'I do get a reaction from readers when they discover Jude Morgan is a man. Perhaps it's because I write from a woman's point of view because historicals tend to be female centred.'

Does Jude Morgan have a favourite character in *Indiscretion*? 'I like Caroline very much. But my favourite is Stephen, definitely Stephen. I felt that he had truly come alive. I was desperate not to make him a clichéd Regency hero—they were often rather wimpish— and so I made him a little eccentric, which was seen as a flaw at the time. I also enjoyed creating the relationship between Caroline and Stephen. When they first meet in the novel, there is a flash of wit and understanding and the reader is immediately aware that they are made for each other, even though they cannot see it. This verbal sparring is very much a Jane Austen influence—Emma Woodhouse and Mr Knightley, Elizabeth Bennet and Mr Darcy.'

So would Jude like to have lived in Regency England? 'In some ways, yes. As long as I was wealthy! It was a period of great style, intelligence and wit. I just wouldn't have wanted to die at the age of forty, which was the average life expectancy for a man at the time!'

Jane Eastgate